BEST BET

"If it turns out I'm right, you owe me a forfeit," Rupert said, a devilish gleam coming into his eyes. "A kiss will do, I think."

Immediately, the air between them changed. Their easy banter was replaced by something far more electric. Something, Mallory's instinct instantly told her, that had never happened to her before, and something she had to handle very, very carefully.

"Is that the only circumstance under which you'd consider kissing me?" she said lightly, subtly flirting, yet promising nothing unseemly.

"I believe it's the other way around. *You* kiss *me*."

All I have to do is turn my head, she thought, and then caution stopped her. Why should I make it easy for him? a voice inside her warned. As far as women are concerned, he's had it so easy . . . a man of thirty would envy him . . . don't be his first New York conquest . . .

Mallory did move her head—pulling back until she was able to look directly at Rupert. Her heart was pounding in a combination of excitement and anticipation, but her logical mind was ruling her potentially ardent heart.

"I believe we've struck a bargain otherwise," she purred softly, putting her fingers over his mouth, marveling at the feel of his warm, firm flesh. "Two months from now," she went on, "and then *only* if you're winning."

KEEPSAKE

BY
ELEANORA BROWNLEIGH

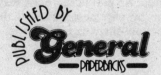

A Division of General Publishing Co. Limited
Toronto, Canada

A General Paperback Edition
Published under license from Panda Books, Inc.
475 Park Avenue South
New York, NY 10016

ISBN 0-7737-8284-2

First printing: August 1984

Printed in the United States of America

For Dary Derchin, who always has time to listen

A special thanks to the following kind people:

Mr. Edward W. Moles, Area Director of Public Relations, The Sheraton Corporation—for providing me with information about the St. Regis Hotel.

Miss Elizabeth A. Naum, Director of Sales and Public Relations for the Alexandria Hotel in Los Angeles—for the data she sent me regarding the Alexandria's early days.

And finally, an extra word of appreciation to Cynthia Cathcart and the staff of the Condé Nast Library—who helped make my research even more fun than it usually is.

. . . New Yorkers are nice about giving you street directions. In fact, they seem quite proud of knowing where they are themselves . . .

Katharine Brush

. . . Commuters give the city its tidal restlessness; nature gives it solidity and continuity; but the settlers give it passion . . .

E. B. White

Elegance is refusal.

Diana Vreeland

If one's rich and one's a woman, one can be quite misunderstood.

—Katharine Graham

Belgrave Square

The Rolls Royce Silver Ghost traveled at a stately pace past Wellington Arch and along Grosvenor Crescent to Belgrave Square and pulled up in front of a handsome Georgian-style house with its front door painted a startling shade of Chinese lacquer red. There was almost no discernible break between the motor car's engine being turned off and the chauffeur coming around to open the door of the tonneau to help the passenger out.

"Thank you, Hadley," Mallory Kirk told the man who was the driver for the Earl and Countess of Saltlon, and walked gracefully across the sidewalk, drawing appreciative glances from passersby. Back home in New York, Mallory always attracted looks of surprise and appreciation from people on the street, and it wasn't any different on the other side of the Atlantic. Well-dressed women weren't a rarity in London, and neither were attractive ones, but a young woman who measured nearly six feet tall without her handmade shoes and before she put on her hat was *always* going to get second looks from complete strangers.

Mallory took all of this with a grain of salt. At twenty-five, she was well-adjusted to both her height, which meant she could wear almost anything Lucile or Poiret

9

came up with, and her looks, which she didn't consider to be in any way extraordinary. Although her expression might have been happier for a woman who had spent the afternoon at Lucile's on Hanover Square, being fitted with beautiful clothes that she would wear during the coming winter in New York, she moved easily, and greeted the butler who opened the door for her.

"Good afternoon, Moss. Is everyone else here already?"

"Yes, miss," the middle-aged man replied. "Lady Saltlon, Lady Thorpe, and Mrs. Phipps are all upstairs with Lady Emma in her sitting room."

"I imagine they've given me up for lost," Mallory remarked, amused. Gently refusing the butler's offer to show her upstairs, she left the black and white marble-floorèd entrance hall. This handsome house with its coolly elegant interior was the home of Sir Nathaniel Goodman, the brilliant young financier, and his wife, Lady Emma Benjamin, the daughter of the Earl and Countess of Saltlon. During the London Season it was a popular gathering spot for the members of the young married set, but in this July of 1910, the always-looked-forward-to season of receptions and parties and grand balls was almost non-existent. Less than two months earlier, King Edward VII, who had been coronated only eight summers before, had died, plunging the nation into mourning, and leaving behind a feeling of disbelief that this greatly loved monarch was gone. Ascot had gone on as usual, with everyone wearing black, but, except for small private dinners and theatre parties, all the galas associated with summer in London had been cancelled.

Mallory had to admit that, despite the fact that there were no parties and gala balls to dance 'til dawn at, she rather liked the quieter social pace. Without a doubt, this summer, filled with visiting galleries and museums during the day, and theatre or dinner parties at night, and weekends that were spent either in the country or—taking a few extra days on either end—in Paris, was, considering her present mood, a very pleasant way of life.

Beginning to feel somewhat happier, she walked along the carpeted corridor, pausing every so often to admire the simply framed watercolors that decorated the walls, and smell the white summer flowers that were arranged in generous bouquets and placed on marble-topped tables, her Lucile dress of blue silk with very pale blue insets and a twisted girdle of blue and orchid silk rustling as she approached the door that led to Emma Goodman's private sitting room.

"Here I am at last," she announced a moment later to the four women all seated near each other in the pleasant room. "I really didn't think that my fittings were going to take so long. Am I too late to admire your baby, Emma?"

"Not at all. I've been keeping Nanny at bay until you got here. After all, I can't send Arthur back to his nursery before he has been properly admired," Emma laughed, and patted the place next to her on the sofa. "Come here and sit with me."

Placed in front of the sofa was a modern white wicker movable cradle where eight-week-old Arthur Goodman slept, oblivious to the women cooing over him.

"I think he gets heavier each time," Mallory said laughingly as she held the baby and gently kissed his carefully brushed reddish-brown hair.

"Oh, I agree," Emma said. "He's positively thriving. Of course, back in January, everyone was telling me how lucky I was to be having my baby in early May—that I'd have my figure back in time for the Season."

"At the time, it was an appropriate comment," her mother, the Countess of Saltlon, pointed out. "And, in a manner of speaking, it still is."

"Oh, yes, and with everything so quiet because of the mourning, it's nice to have more time with my baby than

11

I would have had otherwise. Naturally, Nanny's complaining that there isn't enough for her to do!"

"Oh, just remind her that in a few years the nursery will be filled to her heart's content," Alix Thorpe advised teasingly, and they all laughed.

"*Please!*" Emma exclaimed, taking her son back, her titian-red hair, so much like her mother's, providing a perfect foil for her Lucile tea gown of white linen embroidered in white and trimmed with insets of Valenciennes lace. Just over two years ago, Emma's had been one of *the* weddings of the 1908 London Season. As befitted the daughter of Isaac and Cecily Benjamin, the Earl and Countess of Saltlon, she had been married from the Central Synagogue, and among the guests both there and at the reception at Saltlon House, had been King Edward and Queen Alexandra, whose present to the bride had been a diamond and turquoise bracelet. "You were lucky, Alix, being able to hire your nanny cold. Ours was Nathaniel's when he was a boy, and from the day he went off to Harrow, she's been counting the years until he got married. When Nathaniel took me to meet her for the first time, just after we got engaged, and I passed Nanny's 'inspection,' it took both our combined efforts to persuade her not to give notice on her current position just at that moment."

"But what about *your* nanny, Emma? What if she'd wanted to have the position?" Mallory asked, fascinated by the keeper-of-the-nursery's determined and dogged loyalty.

"Oh, we were quite safe from *that* conflict. At this moment, my old Nanny Carson is employed by a nice family in Sevenoaks, marking the time until Simon gets married," Emma replied airily, referring to her nineteen-year-old brother. "In fact, when she came to tea last week, after she'd seen Arthur and conferred with Nanny

12

Douglas, I was informed that she's keeping a list of 'possibles' for Simon, and can't wait to see which he picks when the time comes!" she added as they all began to laugh.

Unlike the formal rooms downstairs which were decorated in fine French furniture covered in soft colored silks and striped satins, this upstairs sitting room was very English. There were soft chintzes, filmy white curtains that fluttered in the faint summer breeze, and end tables that held family mementos, photographs in silver frames, and vases filled with flowers in full bloom. In this calming atmosphere, Mallory felt herself finally relax, the faint cloud of unhappiness that had been hanging over her slowly lift, making her feel more like her normal self.

"Well now you look better," Alix remarked from her armchair, looking elegant in a Lucile afternoon dress of pale mauve silk edged in darker mauve.

"Have I really been that noticeable?" Mallory smiled as she took off her gloves and Reboux hat of beige Leghorn straw trimmed with blue and orchid satin ribbons. She and Alix were second cousins, and they not only resembled each other, but their minds frequently ran the same way.

"A little . . . on and off. You hide things as well as I do, cousin, but I was there first." She crossed her legs, exposing several inches of superb ankles and legs encased in flesh-colored silk stockings. "In fact, Esme and I are beginning to wonder if London is the best place for you this summer."

"We might send you over to Paris for a few weeks," Esme Phipps, Mallory's godmother, a very attractive woman in her mid-forties, offered. "Solange would love to have you."

"What, and have to give up being part of our

wonderful entourage? If Cecily wants us out of Saltlon House, we have to go as a group!" Mallory shot back teasingly.

"What nonsense," Cecily laughed. "We love having all of you at once. Isaac says your menagerie helps fill up the house."

It would take a regiment to fill up Saltlon House on London's fashionable Park Lane, but for the past five weeks it had been the very elegant, very welcome headquarters for the visitors from New York. Including everyone—Henry and Alix, their four children, three servants, Esme Phipps, Mallory, and their maid—they had made an even dozen. Quite a sight on board the *Mauretania*, on debarkation at Liverpool, and upon arrival at London's Victoria Station. It was only when they all stepped through the double lacquer-green doors of the limestone edifice that was Saltlon House, did their group take on more normal proportions.

They were discussing Lucile's latest collection when Nanny Douglas arrived to take Arthur back to the nursery, and deciding to take advantage of this pause, Mallory stood up.

"Will you all excuse me for a few minutes?" she said with a smile. "After two hours of having clothes fitted, I'm rather sticky."

Cecily, cool and chic in a Doucet afternoon dress of pale violet silk, waited until Mallory was well out of earshot before turning to Alix, a concerned expression in her green-gold eyes.

"Mallory isn't very happy, is she, Alix? I don't want to pry, of course, but this isn't quite the same girl I saw in New York last winter."

"What Mummy is discreetly doing is trying to find out if Mallory has been through a bad love affair," Emma interjected with a sparkling glance.

"Not unless something went on that I don't know

14

about," Alix said, looking over at Esme.

"Nothing," Esme said in a troubled voice, smoothing a fold of her Drecoll afternoon dress of blue and black silk. "Not that she doesn't have dozens of interested young men. Newton says you can populate the floor of the Stock Exchange with Mallory's young men," she went on, referring to her husband, a prominent investment advisor. "But there's no one special for her. I *was* hoping this summer in London might turn up someone to catch her fancy, but—"

"But it's the same old faces over and over," Cecily finished, laughing. "It's not like it was for Alix—no Henry Thorpe conveniently standing on my staircase!"

"Considering I was about to go falling backward down your Palladian marble masterpiece, I was *very* lucky—in more ways than one," Alix agreed, her own laughter bubbling over as she remembered that it had been only eight summers earlier that she had come to London—as discontented as her cousin was now—and on her first full day in the city, at the home of Cecily Saltlon, she had met the man who was the love of her life. "But it's different for Mallory. Or then, it might just be that working for Thea is getting her down," Alix added.

"Oh, Alix, really," Cecily scoffed. "You can't tell me that Thea makes Mallory's life difficult."

"Not in the usual sense of the word. Thea is wonderful and sweet and intelligent and loving—as long as you don't mention Elsie de Wolfe to her."

Cecily raised her eyebrows. "That fifth-rate former actress?"

"Among other things." Alix looked amused. "And that's the nicest reference Thea ever makes to her competition."

"So she tends to rant about her lady competitor," Cecily offered, placing a slight stress on the next to the last word.

"Rather. Thea's always been very successful, but that de Wolfe woman with her connections and inferences—! Thea was in business two years before Elsie de Wolfe decided to stop prancing around the stage in plays people went to only to see the Paris clothes she wore, and besides," Alix added with a wicked-looking glint in her hazel eyes, "Charles is much nicer to show off than Bessie Marbury ever will be!"

They all laughed for a minute, gossiped about the "bachelor-girl" establishment that the rather middle-aged Misses de Wolfe and Marbury kept on Irving Place, and were swapping nasty *bon mots* until Esme brought them back to the matter at hand.

"When Thea married Charles, she made her own decision not to take on any out-of-town clients and to operate her business on a smaller level. Six years is a long time, and I'm sure she knew there was going to be competition somewhere along the line. The fact that she can't tolerate Elsie de Wolfe is *her* problem, not Mallory's, and it's her we have to help."

"Shall I have a word with Mallory?" Emma volunteered. "We can go to lunch and a matinee and have a nice, long heart-to-heart afterwards. She may talk more readily to me since I'm not directly involved in her life. I could be her sounding board the way Mummy was yours, Alix, back before you and Henry were married."

For a minute, Alix thought back to the summer of 1902, and how she'd depended on Cecily's good sense during those awful first weeks when the possibility that Henry Thorpe didn't care was very real indeed. Cecily had counseled her, commiserated with her and, in general, had put up with her various flights of fancy, but as good-hearted as Emma's offer was, Alix was well aware that this was not quite the same thing.

"Oh, Emma, that's so sweet of you to offer," she said at last. For years Emma had called her Aunt Alix, but when she turned eighteen three years before, the honorary title had been dropped and they addressed each other as equals. "But I don't know if that would really do any good—"

"Because I'm younger than Mallory?" Emma suggested. "I can see where that might be a bit galling to her. But really, if you don't mind my saying so, why don't you leave her alone? She knows all of you care, and when and if she's ready to talk it all out, Mallory will."

Mallory slowly turned off the gold faucets mounted on the marble sink and reached for a towel made of the finest Irish linen. Instinctively she knew that back in Emma's sitting room she was the major topic of conversation and, in spite of the free-floating feeling of unhappiness that drifted around her, Mallory smiled in amusement.

I wonder what they'd all say if I told them everything that was on my mind? It certainly wouldn't be anything they expected to hear, I bet. Or maybe they *have* guessed—or Alix has. She told me once that, after a while, you don't keep secrets, they keep you. Well, Mallory, face it, four years is quite long enough for your secret, she thought, drying her hands.

The marble length of the vanity shelf was decorated with silver-topped crystal bottles that held all the powders and perfumes and cremes female visitors might need in order to help them freshen up. Mallory opened the clasp of her purse, took out the things she'd need, helped herself from the selection offered and, looking squarely at herself in the excellent mirror that hung above the vanity, began to repair the effects of having spent an afternoon in a small warm fitting room at the best fashion salon in London.

As she opened her gold compact and began to powder her face, Mallory reflected that her godmother had hoped

17

she'd go back to New York with more than simply new clothes. In other words, a major romance.

Dear Aunt Esme, she had all the fantasies of my meeting the man of my dreams. Poor darling, how can I tell her that I already have, but he didn't—doesn't—want me? Mallory thought as she carefully applied her gold-mounted tortoiseshell comb to her dark brown hair which was swept back in the latest fashion; a style which owed its inception to the Gibson Girl look of a decade before but which was now simpler and closer to the head.

I wonder if I'll ever have anyone special again? she mused silently, adjusting a hairpin. After all, what am I but an almost six-foot, almost twenty-five-year-old Barnard graduate with a degree in chemistry who decided to be an interior decorator instead of a doctor? Oh, Mallory, what a funny life you've woven for yourself!

She swirled a few loose tendrils of hair around her face and touched up her lip color. Like Alix and all of her other friends, Mallory painted her face, using tinted powders and rouge and kohl and mascara, each carefully blended to look as natural as possible. Until a few years ago, there had been only Rimmel for mascara and Leichners for foundation creme and powders, but like the motor car and the airplane, advances had been made in what women had to put on their faces.

But now, in London, there were delicate cremes and lotions available from Helena Rubenstein, tinted make-ups from Frances Hemmings' Cyclax salon, and in New York, all the smart young women were busy patronizing the fledgling salon of Elizabeth Arden.

All this frosting, Mallory thought wryly, regarding the results of her handiwork. It doesn't solve any of my problems or answer any of my questions, but it certainly makes me look a whole lot better while I try to come up with the answers, and that just may be the half of it. Now put on a smile, that's a bright girl, and go back to the sitting room for tea. Remember, nothing can be as awful as you think it is!

Tea was appropriately lavish. Emma, raised on the excellent way her mother ran both the Park Lane house and Tantley Hall, the family estate in Buckinghamshire, knew exactly how to care for her guests. Steaming hot Earl Grey tea was poured from its silver pot into delicate Minton cups; hot, fresh-baked scones with sweet butter and strawberry preserves were passed; there was a plate of delicate, crustless cucumber sandwiches; another plate of éclairs stuffed with coffee creme; and a silver, three-tiered cake stand held gaily decorated *petit fours*.

"Now, Alix, we all want to hear the latest news," Lady Joanna Garland, the wife of a Foreign Office official, was saying as Mallory returned to the sitting room to find that their group had increased in number and the tea was set out. "You haven't uttered a word about him since you and Henry got to London. Come now, tell us how Romney is getting on in New York."

"Romney *Sedgewick*?" Alix's voice was tinged with suspicion.

"Of course, my dear. Do we know another?"

Mallory watched with amusement as her dearly loved, very self-possessed cousin looked—for one of the few times in her life—utterly nonplussed.

With great care, Alix returned her tea cup to its saucer and placed it on the table closest to her in an obvious attempt to gain time to gather her thoughts.

"Romney's in New York?" she questioned. "This is the first *I've* heard about it. Joanna, are you *sure*?"

"Oh, if only I weren't!" The elegantly dressed older woman brushed an imaginary speck of dust from the shoulder of her blue and white foulard dress from Redfern. "Ernest was *dreadfully* upset when Romney handed in his resignation. I do think Basil could have been of more help than he was in this situation, Anne," she added somewhat indignantly to an attractive younger woman seated alongside Esme.

"Basil felt that if Romney wanted to resign his post, he should be quite free to do so," Lady Anne Summerfield said calmly as she helped herself to a paper-thin cucumber sandwich. Both her husband and Romney Sedgewick were considered to be shining lights by the heirarchy of the Foreign Office, and although Romney's departure *had* upset Basil, Anne was not about to confide that fact to the wife of her husband's superior.

"When did Romney do this?" Alix inquired, mystified. Henry and Romney were good friends, and her husband—assuming he knew about this matter—hadn't divulged any of the details.

"In April," Joanna supplied. "As Ernest tells it, Romney walked into his office and handed in his resignation. Packed in his whole career just like that!"

"Well, it is his right," Alix said gently. Joanna and her mother had been friends when they were girls, and she was therefore rather reluctant to strenuously disagree with the older woman.

"That's what I don't understand about Americans," Joanna sighed. "You feel that it's perfectly all right to walk away from a position merely because you've become bored."

"Romney joined the Foreign Office when he was twenty-two, and he's forty now. That's quite old enough to know one's own mind," Cecily put in, and drew from Joanna a considering look.

"I suppose he talked this all out with you?"

"He did, but I certainly didn't make his mind up for him," Cecily countered. "Romney had already reached his own decision."

"But why New York?" Alix wanted to know.

20

"I gather because it's there." Joanna helped herself to an éclair. "Have you *truly* not heard anything from him?"

"Not a word. Of course you have to remember that in New York, people who want to can literally lose themselves. For all I know, Romney can be living in the Dakota, but if he wants to stay hidden we'll never know about it."

"Do you suppose Henry has been in contact with Romney?" Esme hazarded.

"It's possible—and that's also his business." Alix was a strong believer in marital privacy. "Romney will come to the surface eventually."

"He might not even be in New York," Laura Fitzwilliam pointed out. The same age as Emma, Laura's late father had been a noted naturalist, and her stepfather was the Earl of Rossford, an Irish peer. Like her best friend, she too had made a brilliant match at almost the same time as Emma, marrying a young Canadian millionaire Hugh Fitzwilliam, and they divided their time between London and Ottawa. "The only thing we're certain about is that Romney sailed on the *Lusitania*. He might very well be anywhere—including sailing back and forth!"

Laura's off-handed remark served to diffuse the slight tension that was forming over their tea party, and their gossip about the secretive actions undertaken by Romney Sedgewick began to branch out to other topics.

"As long as we're speaking of people who live in New York," Emma said as she refilled their cups, "what is Rupert Randall doing?"

"Oh, the Seligmans are managing to keep him very busy," Alix replied, amused.

"That's much better than leaving him to his own devices," Emma remarked. "Do you remember, Alix, eight years ago when you took me to a matinee of *Ben*

Hur, and Henry was there with Rupert?"

"I remember your pointing out Henry to me as the man I should marry!"

"Yes, but you'd already reached that conclusion on your own. I also remember telling you what a beastly temper Rupert had, and how horridly spoilt he was," she went on. "Is he still the same?"

"Well, he's not spoilt any longer, at least not in the way you meant eight years ago—you were a precocious thing, Emma—and he keeps his temper pretty well under control."

"Surprising that he hasn't married yet, though," Anne put in. "All that money."

"When he came back here three years ago for those few weeks just after his mother died, Emma and I were positively frantic that he might become interested in one of us," Laura laughed.

"I think we both knew Rupert far too long to view him objectively," Emma agreed. "But what about you, Mallory? Weren't you and Rupert practically engaged?"

Mallory, who had been listening to this turn in their conversation with a heart that seemed to alternately pound sickeningly or else plunge to the pit of her stomach, felt as if she'd stopped breathing. Could they read her mind? she wondered, gazing with sudden distaste at her half-eaten éclair. She forced herself to take a sip of tea.

"You can't get engaged unless a man asks you first," Mallory replied in a voice she barely managed to keep even, "and Rupert didn't."

She made a gesture of disinterest and dismissal, but Emma, like her mother, wasn't easily put off, and she turned to regard Mallory who sat beside her with some surprise.

"He didn't even *hint?*"

Quickly, Mallory sorted through her jumbled

thoughts. From the moment Emma had mentioned Rupert's name, she knew that their past relationship was going to come up for present speculation.

Were you really hoping to get off without having to answer any questions? she asked herself. Suppose I say the wrong thing and Aunt Esme guesses? Or Alix? *Damn.* Oh, well, nothing stays hidden forever, and Uncle Newton can hardly push a shotgun marriage at this late date, but I'm not going to let anyone here feel sorry for me—

"No, he didn't," she said at last, not really lying. "And I could hardly *make* Rupert propose to me."

Oh, yes, you could have, her memory reminded her.

"Well, there are *always* ways," Emma drawled, and they all laughed.

"Yes, but can you ever be truly happy after you've used them?" Mallory countered, and to her immense relief, her statement moved the topic onto the subject of female wiles.

"It's all a question of proportion," Alix remarked. "Every so often Henry says that in the weeks between when we met and he proposed, I made his life hell. Of course I always tell him it was just what he needed, and that he loved every second of it!"

"And here I thought you were always so proper with Henry," Joanna said, her good humor restored.

"And I didn't think you were proper at all," Cecily added.

"Which proves love is in the eye of the beholder," Esme offered, and Mallory knew she was no longer the center of attention.

Gradually, as their conversation moved on to far more general subjects than matters of the heart, Mallory began to relax. Well, you're safe this time, but for how much longer? she thought, leaning back against the sofa's chintz cushions. Funny how when you're thinking about someone, that person's name always turns up in conversation. I wonder what he's doing now in Chicago? Probably devastating some other girl . . . No, Mallory, you weren't devastated, so don't pretend otherwise. It's only these past weeks that you've realized that the relationship that ended four years ago isn't over yet . . .

Alix Thorpe was obliquely regarding her cousin, a small core of certainty forming in her middle. All her suspicions and unanswered questions suddenly seemed to be resolving themselves.

So, it's Rupert, she thought. Oh, well, Mallory isn't the first woman to have had her heart dented by a cad, and she won't be the last. The first one is always the worst . . . I wonder how far they went . . .

Alix had never been deeply fond of Rupert Randall, nor had she ever truly trusted him. In her mind, she had never been able to totally disassociate the brilliant young man he now was from the sulky-mouthed university student of eight years earlier. With far too much money and nothing to challenge his excellent mind, he had cut a wide swath of self-indulgence, and he seemed to take a special delight in annoying the man whose ward he was: Henry Thorpe.

A lot had happened in those intervening years, but that first impression stuck, and Alix had never envied Bill and Adele Seligman their task of keeping Rupert on the straight and narrow when he arrived in New York in 1903.

I won't ask her, Alix decided. After all, I don't treat people in a way that I wouldn't have to be treated in return. God knows, her secret can't be any worse than the ones I kept, but you can't hide them forever. I had six years of lies, secrets and half-truths behind me in 1902, Mallory's got about four years of evasion on her record. Well, I won't ask, and if Esme questions me, I won't tell her anything either, but somehow I have to let Mallory know that her secret is safe with me. . . .

Alix knows, Mallory thought suddenly as she caught sight of her cousin's face. It's that through-the-lashes look; it must drive Henry crazy. What do I do now? I don't know . . . Yes, I do, but I have to think it out first . . .

The tea party began to break up and, as they all began to discuss appointments for fittings, and luncheon plans, and various other social obligations, Mallory knew that at some point, probably after they left England, she would have a coherent plan of action, and then she'd be ready to confide in Alix.

Next time I cross the ocean, I'll take the train.

—Groucho Marx in *Home Again*

The Mauretania

Mauretania. Arriving Aug. 4th: Lord and Lady Thorpe, Mr. and Mrs. Morgan Browne, Mr. and Mrs. James Seligman, Mrs. Newton Phipps and Miss Mallory Kirk

Almost from the moment of its maiden voyage just over three years earlier, the *Mauretania*, pride and joy of the Cunard Line, the largest liner afloat, was a natural—almost as if the transatlantic passage had been waiting for this liner to be built.

She was the ship that was the representative of the new century with all its technological advances. Along with her sister ship, the equally impressive *Lusitania*, the *Mauretania* had transformed ocean-going travel. Holding the Blue Riband of the Atlantic as the fastest ship afloat, she was known affectionately as the Greyhound of the Atlantic, her time of passage covering a remarkably swift four days, twenty hours, and fifteen minutes, assuring those who sailed on her—particularly the first-class passengers—that this floating city-hotel was the very last word in fashion.

From the utilitarian quarters that housed the steerage passengers to the boiserie paneling that enveloped first-

27

class, every inch of the *Mauretania* gave off a feeling of security—something that people crossing the often dangerous Atlantic needed in large doses. Nothing, everyone agreed, would *ever* go wrong on this ship. It was more than her 31,938 tons and imposing superstructure topped by four vermillion, black-topped funnels; in every vibration the *Mauretania* seemed to be saying that it was all going to be all right.

On every major transatlantic liner, no matter what the parent company, first-class passengers follow certain fixed rules when it comes to dressing for dinner. One didn't dress on the first night, the last night, or on Sunday night, but this Tuesday night was the night of the Captain's Dinner, the gala of a multi-course dinner followed by dancing and harmless fun and games and helped out by endless bottles of champagne. Men and women dressed as they would for a night on the town in London or Paris or New York.

Earlier in the evening, the center of gaiety had been the Francis I-inspired dining room where each intricately hand-carved wall panel of finely weathered oak was different from the one next to it and the three-deck tall ceiling was topped with a cream and gold dome. But now, at nearly midnight, with the musicians alternating seate waltzes with the far more popular ragtime two-steps, the grand salon with its paneling of superbly grained mahogany, each panel topped by delicate gold mouldings, separated by pilasters of the palest lilac marble, and finished with fine ormolu mounts, was the merrymaking center for the *Mauretania*'s contingent of first-class travelers. The library was all but deserted, as was the ladies' writing room, only a few disgruntled, disapproving male passengers could be found in the walnut-walled smoking room—that safe, clublike enclave which no woman could enter. Although there were couples taking a refreshing walk on deck or enjoying a late bite to eat in

28

the popular new Veranda Cafe where rush matting covered the floor and the wicker furniture was accented by strategically placed potted palms and trellises, the grand salon remained very crowded.

Seated on a Louis XV sofa, her green-flecked hazel eyes surveying the vast room, Alix Thorpe, at least to the casual observer, looked rather like a wallflower. A very elegant wallflower to be sure, her Poiret evening gown of Nile-green crepe de chine with a tunic of embroidered white crepe contrasting perfectly with the sofa's green and white striped silk upholstery, her necklace of diamonds and peridots sparkling in the room's soft lighting. She was enjoying this temporary time alone in the well-placed alcove that gave her a perfect view of the entire salon, her companions of the evening, at least for the moment, scattered to other parts of the ship.

Henry had gone back to their suite to make sure all was well with their children, Angela Dalton Browne was also checking to be sure that her son and stepdaughter were settled for the night, Morgan Browne had been waylaid by a fellow Texan, Esme Phipps had been persuaded by a Pasadena couple to join them for a midnight snack in the Veranda Cafe, and James and Katharine Seligman were happily occupied on the dance floor, as was Mallory, who was undoubtedly proving herself to be one of this crossing's most popular young women.

Relentlessly, the detached, clinical part of her trained doctor's mind was reviewing their last weeks in London. Alix was certain now that Mallory had made some sort of decision as to what she intended to do with the problem that was shadowing her life.

Now, Alix noted that the unhappy, faintly distracted air that had hung around her cousin like a thin cloud had vanished, and for the remainder of their stay in London, whether Mallory was searching through that city's myriad of antique shops for objects suitable to offer to clients of Thea Harper's firm, or having supper in a fashionable restaurant after taking in a popular play, or at a dinner party where one was obligated to hold up one's end of the conversation, she was cheerful and open and ready to have a good time.

Like the one she's having tonight, Alix thought as she caught a brief glimpse of her cousin among the couples two-stepping to the music of "The Ragtime Dance." Maybe she's decided that after four years it's time to find Rupert and punch him in the nose. Or, better yet, tell Bill Seligman that his protégé is still a rat—the sort that stamps all over a woman's heart, she finished.

"You have the most positively *malicious* gleam in your eyes," Angela Dalton Browne remarked, sitting down beside Alix on the sofa, her Poiret gown of green chiffon over saffron satin swishing expensively. "Just whom are you planning to do in?"

"No one, Nela," Alix replied, smiling at one of her oldest and best friends. "I just came to the conclusion that Mallory has reached a new threshold in her life, made a great decision of some sort."

"Well, isn't that one of the options of being young and independent? Remember some of the conclusions you and Regina and Thea made about eight years ago?"

"All of them." Alix tucked a diamond-studded hairpin back into her brown hair. "We were a rather determined group—then *and* now!"

Both women laughed, recalling the summer of 1902, the last summer when they were all unmarried and domiciled in New York City. By the end of that summer, Alix had married Henry Thorpe, and Nela had gone to San Francisco, to work for I. Magnin while she waited for her parents, Admiral and Mrs. Dalton, went to Peking on a government assignment that lasted for sixteen months. By the end of another summer, Regina Bolt, the daughter of a wealthy Wyoming rancher, Nela's roommate at

Vassar, a reporter for the *New York World*, had married Ian MacIverson and gone to Santa Barbara to live. And by the autumn of 1904, Thea had married Charles de Renille, and Nela was married to Morgan Browne of San Antonio, Texas. Now, only Alix and Thea remained in New York, but their four-way friendship remained as strong as ever.

With a wave of her hand, Alix signaled to a passing white-jacketed steward. "A bottle of champagne, please, and six glasses. The rest of our group will be along shortly."

"Very good, my lady," the steward replied with the correct politeness that the Cunard Line was justly famous for, and once the man had left to fill Alix's request, both women resumed their conversation.

"Christy was just adorable tonight," Alix said, referring to Nela's stepdaughter Christine. At fourteen going on fifteen she was considered old enough to join her parents' and their friends in the dining salon and enjoy part of the evening's festivities. Becomingly dressed in a Paquin *jeune fille* gown of soft white chiffon printed with dainty lavender flowers over China silk with a sash of lavender chiffon, she had proved herself an intelligent and poised dinner companion, and when the ship's clock read eleven, she had uncomplainingly gone off to bed. "I'm sure quite a few people here tonight thought she was at least sixteen."

"Christy's the same as we were at her age. No awkwardness, not childish or immature-looking, and too tall not to have more grown-up looking dresses."

"She's going to be thrilling to dress in another three years when she's ready for college. I suppose she already has definite ideas about clothes, the same as we did?"

"Oh, very much so!" Nela exclaimed, delighted. "What else would you expect from Morgan's daughter? She and Michael think that their father founded

31

Browne's of San Antonio so that they could have this marvelous playroom away from home filled with beautiful things!" she went on, speaking about the superb women's specialty store that her husband was founder and sole proprietor of. "But just the same, I have this feeling Christy's going to end up a newspaper gal like her mother was," Nela finished, referring to her husband's first wife who had been a journalist.

"Good for her, whatever she wants," Alix remarked as Morgan Browne joined them, the champagne-bearing steward following close at his heels, depositing his heavy silver tray with its burden of ice bucket and champagne bottle and crystal stemware on the inlaid table around which the large sofa and three comfortable chairs were grouped, retreating deftly to the background at Alix's instruction not to pour their refreshment just yet.

If Morgan Browne had changed at all in the eight years since she'd met him in one of the lifts of the Savoy Hotel when the then six-year-old Christy had mistaken her for the recently deceased Ellen Browne, it was only for the better. Just like Henry, Alix reflected as Morgan, after kissing both women on the cheek, sat down beside his wife. Morgan Browne wasn't handsome, his nose was a shake too prominent and his mouth too large and his high cheekbones unbalanced his face somewhat, but his eyes were a deep, perfect blue, and his tawny hair was thick and straight and perfectly barbered.

"How was your one quick drink with that old friend of your father's from Austin?" Nela inquired with an amused smile. "I think that was about four dances ago!"

"Joe McClintock told me that the happiest moment of his voyage on the *Mauretania* was when he discovered that they stock bourbon in the bar," Morgan told them, amused. "He says that from now on, whenever he has to go to Europe, it's Cunard for him."

"I'm sure the line will be thrilled," Alix put in drily.

Morgan smiled and eyed the bottle of Moet et Chandon nestled in the silver ice bucket. "Are we waiting for the others?" he asked. "Joe insisted that I join him in the down-home mint julep. I can't believe that rational people actually drink that concoction. The idea of ruining good bonded bourbon is a crime, a scandal, a—"

Laughing, Nela motioned toward the steward. "Now have a glass of champagne and relax. You can always write an indignant letter to Cunard and tell them that you think teaching the barmen to make mint juleps is carrying the concept of pleasing the American traveler a bit too far!"

At Nela's signal, their ever-attentive steward attended to his proper duty of opening the bottle with a minimum of fuss and transferring the liquid to three of the tulip-shaped glasses.

"Fill all but one of the glasses, please, Diggs," Alix advised as the music ended and she saw James and Katharine Seligman coming toward them. "You can trust us to remember to save a few drops for Lord Thorpe."

The proper middle-aged man, an employee of Cunard since the days when their vessels sported sails and crossing the Atlantic was a test of hardiness and personal bravery rather than several days of extreme comfort if not outright luxury augmented with champagne and caviar and the latest dance music, smiled with the proper degree of correctness at Alix's small joke and finished pouring out the bubbly, golden liquid.

"We have expert timing, I see," Jimmy Seligman said, flashing a bright smile as he and Kate arrived. "There's no better refreshment for thirsty dancers than champagne."

"And no better drink to get the taste of a mint julep out of your mouth with," Morgan put in.

Except for the still-absent Henry, their group was complete, and they eagerly claimed their champagne glasses.

"What does the *Mauretania* remind you of tonight, Jimmy?" Morgan asked, the gleam in his eyes a combination of amusement and bittersweet remembrance.

"The Tampa Bay Hotel," Jimmy replied without hesitation, brushing his dark, thick hair out of sapphire blue eyes that immediately mirrored his friend's expression. "That five-hundred room Moorish fantasy that—for a very short time—was the place to see and be seen." He looked around him. "I think the *Mauretania* will last a great deal longer."

Throughout history there is an unspoken bond formed between men who have trained together for an armed conflict that the passage of the years never reduce. In the spring of 1898 both Morgan Browne and James Seligman had proffered their services to the First U.S. Volunteer Cavalry—Theodore Roosevelt's Rough Riders. They had been among the several hundred men, ranging from New York aristocrats to Texas ranch hands, who had responded to the charismatic former Assistant Secretary of the Navy who'd resigned from that position in order to form his fighting group.

In an egalitarian spirit, Colonel Roosevelt decreed that officer rank would be awarded only on merit and bravery, and on May 29, 1898, when the Rough Riders had broken camp in San Antonio and loaded their supply train, Morgan Browne, who had been recruited by T.R. in the bar of the Menger Hotel to serve as supply officer, was a newly made captain, and James Seligman wore lieutenant's bars.

On the broiling hot four-day trip across the Deep South to Tampa, Florida, Morgan and Jimmy and another friend, Richard North, who had resigned from his editorial position at Harper Brothers when that firm had been less than enthusiastic about his joining up, along with Woodbury Kane, a Harvard classmate of Theodore Roosevelt's, who, even in khaki, managed to look totally distinguished, had played endless rubbers of bridge, drunk hot coffee, picked at cold, rather unappetizing food, speculated about Cuba and, in Dick's case, smoked Turkish cigarettes one after the other.

None of them who had been on that train ride would ever forget that trip. At every stop along the route, through the part of the country where the Confederacy was revered and the Lost Cause mourned, they were greeted by cheering crowds who supplied them with cold beer and watermelons and demanded a look at Colonel Roosevelt and the Social Register members of his troop—and waved the Stars and Stripes at them. The wound of the Civil War might never fully heal, but after thirty-three years the stitches had finally come out.

Waiting in Tampa had been worse than waiting in San Antonio. They all had the feeling something was wrong, and on June sixth, following a formal regimental drill that stirred all who saw it, Theodore Roosevelt and Leonard Wood learned that there were not enough transport ships to take all the Rough Riders to Cuba. The decision as to which men would come and which would remain behind became an almost agonizing chore.

Sergeant Dick North, who had developed a chest cold and was confined to the infirmary, was one of the first cut, and Jimmy Seligman, who in the weeks in San Antonio had shown off his conciliatory abilities when it came to smoothing over the ruffled feathers of various saloon keepers who didn't like having overly rambunctious troopers use their mirrors for target practice, was the last.

He was needed here in Tampa, T.R. told him gently, to work with other officers in keeping order, and to go on to

35

the mustering-out camp—wherever that would be—to help prepare things there. He could take Sergeant North with him to help, but he was sorry, Jimmy wasn't going to Cuba.

For a day and a half, Theodore Roosevelt had had to give variations on this speech and then watch helpless as officers and troopers alike burst into tears of frustration and disappointment, but Jimmy Seligman's reaction wasn't exactly the same as his compatriots. The eyes of the young lieutenant whose twenty-third birthday that day was, did fill with tears, but the reply he gave to Colonel Roosevelt gave that weary man his only laugh of the day.

"Remember—'stuck in the middle of nowhere with only a lousy restricted hotel,'" Morgan said with a brilliant smile twelve years later as the *Mauretania*'s band played *Tales Of The Vienna Woods*.

"I wasn't trying to be funny," Jimmy pointed out, a slight smile nonetheless tugging at his mouth.

"The main thing is that T.R. was so touched—or amused—by what you said that he promised to come to our wedding," Kate smiled, smoothing a fold of her Paquin gown of rose chiffon trimmed with loops of ribbon.

"Now that was a red letter day for Cos Cob, Connecticut," Jimmy smiled, but out of affection and tact for Nela, neither he nor Kate ever reminisced about their wedding day in any great detail when she was in their presence.

On that beautiful late September day, just five days after the final mustering-out of the Rough Riders at Camp Wickoff, among the wedding guests who had come to the estate of the Gilbert Flowers', one of the oldest Jewish families in Connecticut, to celebrate the marriage of their youngest daughter Katharine to James Seligman of the equally old New York investment family, were

36

Theodore and Edith Roosevelt, the colonel having only the previous day decided to accept the nomination of Governor of New York, assorted members of the First U.S. Volunteer Cavalry, and Morgan and Ellen Browne. Indeed, there were so many guests on that happy, perfect day, filling the Georgian-style house and the garden and lawn, that it wasn't until nearly six years later, in April of 1904, in San Francisco, when Morgan—by then a widower for nearly three years—was preparing to marry Angela Dalton, that he and Alix discovered they'd both been at the wedding and had never met.

To have been a Rough Rider carried a certain cachet, and when he was introduced as having been one, Jimmy frequently felt like a fraud. Not as bad as Dick North felt, of course—there was, after all, a certain inglory in being the first one of their group cut—but a bit of a cheat nonetheless. And Morgan Browne's comments that the bloodiness of those days in Cuba were nothing to be envied was a relative thing. But in any case, one didn't swap those tales in front of one's wife, the visual signal between the two men went, and their conversation moved on to safer—if somewhat more commonplace— topics of interest.

They were talking about the Royal Aero Club and the flying school at Hendon and refilling their champagne glasses when Henry Thorpe sank into the chair closest to Alix, and reached for his wife's hand.

"I'm sorry, darling, but you wouldn't believe the gamut I just had to run in the name of old acquaintance."

"Is that what's left you looking so pale around the edges?" Alix asked, immediately noting that her husband's hooded lids had drooped down over his deep brown eyes—a sure sign that something was bothering him.

"It's nothing that a glass of champagne won't fix," he replied, his expression lightening. "I trust that you did

37

save me a few drops?"

"We made a concerted effort, but in this crowd it wasn't easy."

At just forty-seven, Henry Thorpe looked and felt better than he had at thirty-seven. At the turn of the century he had resigned himself to a permanent state of confirmed bachelorhood. A noted art historian, he kept a splendid bachelor flat at Albany, the famous London building where apartments were referred to as chambers, furnished in fine antiques, and whenever he doubted this life, he would remind himself of his collection of paintings and rare books that he had to look at and read, the vintage wines he had to drink, and how the best hostesses in London were ever appreciative of him as the much-sought-after wealthy, available, presentable extra man. He used those excuses to himself over and over again until the May afternoon eight years before when Alix Turner blazed into his life like a comet—a comet that had absolutely no intention of burning out.

Eight years, a complicated courtship, a move to New York City, two apartments and four children later, Henry often felt he was looking at his life through a wonderfully satisfying rose-colored haze.

Now he settled his slender, almost six-foot-one frame more comfortably in his chair, sipped his champagne, and chatted with their friends—all the while holding Alix's hand in his.

"Are you ready to tell us whom it is you met?" Alix asked a few minutes later, judging him to be ready to talk.

"And what happens if I say no?" he countered, eyes dancing with fun.

"I'll take my hand back."

"A threat well taken." Henry regarded their little group out of worldly eyes. "Do all of you want to hear this?"

"Whatever else are friends for?" Nela smiled.

"You do manage to meet very interesting people," Kate put in.

"There's nothing like hearing an Englishman—even a transplanted one—tell his tale of adventure," Morgan added.

"I think you'd better tell your story, Henry, before you collect any more compliments like these," Jimmy advised.

Henry looked directly at Alix. "I ran into Evelyn Weldon."

"Oh, *God*. What is *she* doing *here*?"

"Being seasick, apparently. I was coming from our suite—where our children are peaceably sleeping, I might add—when we bumped into each other in the passageway."

"Naturally she was delighted to see you," Alix said, raising her eyebrows expressively.

"Without a doubt." Henry's expression was deadpan, and at that moment it was difficult to judge if he were going to laugh or be angry. "Evelyn told me that her *mal de mer* was so severe that tonight was the first time she felt up to joining in on the festivities."

"And of course tonight's being the Captain's Dinner had nothing whatsoever to do with it," Nela said in her best sweet-nasty voice.

"Well, wouldn't you make it your business to get better just in time for the night when everyone shows off their best clothes?" Alix asked knowingly.

"Not to mention the next-to-the-last opportunity to catch up on eating all that delicious caviar," Kate interjected.

"I wish Cunard would consider offering their seasick passengers their allotment of caviar as a present when they disembark," Alix observed sharply. "It would keep people like Evelyn Weldon out of the public rooms and in her cabin where she belongs!"

"Now, darling, you didn't have to make conversation with her. I did."

"I'm sorry, darling, but that woman simply infuriates me. I suppose she's on her way to Canada to see Sybil?"

"You're partially correct." Henry drained his glass and then unceremoniously leaned forward, grasped the bottle by its gold-foil covered neck, and refilled his glass. "She is on her way to see Sybil—in New York, that is. It appears that Sybil is expecting another addition to her family, and apparently the doctors in Toronto are rather old-fashioned, so—"

"I gathered Evelyn didn't spare you any details," Alix remarked, holding out her own glass for Henry to refill, her eyes scanning the huge salon. "Where is she now?"

"I don't know, and to tell the truth, I don't particularly care."

"There's my darling husband. Look at it this way, if it hadn't been for me, Evelyn Weldon would have done her best to make you her son-in-law."

"So she's one of *those* women," Morgan said just as their steward—thoroughly shocked that Lord Thorpe had poured his own champagne—returned to their group to tend to pouring out the sparkling refreshment.

"That isn't even *half* of it," Nela advised, brushing back a tendril of her champagne-colored hair.

"It's women like that who give mothers a bad name," Kate observed.

Alix sipped her drink. "It's so easy for you, Nela. In two weeks you and Morgan go back to San Antonio, but Henry and I will have to consider including Evelyn Weldon in on at least one dinner party."

"The problem is, you don't give *those* sort of parties," Nela said knowingly. "No bores at your table."

"And no people you don't like, either," Jimmy added. "Are you going to have to grin and bear this one?"

"Probably," Alix admitted as the musicians stopped,

took a brief rest, and then struck up again. "But right at this moment I have a much better idea. They're playing the 'Maple Leaf Rag,' and I'm not in the mood to discuss courtesy invitations to people I don't care for. Let's all dance!"

As she turned in her partner's arms, her Lucile gown of pale pink silk tulle and ecru lace embroidered with opalescent sequins and crystal beads shimmering under the soft lighting, Mallory had a clear view of her friends at their comfortable alcove spot, but felt absolutely no urge to join them or to show off her dancing partner, Edward MacDonald, to them.

As it happens on ocean voyages, most of the younger married first-class passengers had formed their own group. During the day they met to play deck tennis, and at night, after dinner, they gathered together to dance. In some cases they knew each other beforehand, in others it was acquaintance based on school or business, or, in a few instances, they were strangers, invited to join in on the fun because of the general air of conviviality that surrounded the crossing, particularly when one was young, independent, and well-off.

There was no real pairing off in the romantic sense, but since they were always viewed by the older passengers with great interest toward that end, certain precautions had to be taken. Therefore, on the first night out, Mallory Kirk and Edward MacDonald had, in an informal and agreeable way, attached themselves to each other. Edward, a Chicago stockbroker, was going to be engaged when he got home, and was therefore not interested in running the risk of attracting a young woman whom he couldn't—and didn't want to—see after the ship docked. For her part, Mallory, taking into consideration the decision she had reached for herself, practiced a small

41

deception and told Edward her situation was something like his, and they became social protection for each other.

"I think we've done rather well for ourselves," Edward said as they twirled around the highly polished floor, "although I did notice your godmother looking at us earlier with an interested glint in her eyes."

"That's Aunt Esme," Mallory laughed. "But don't worry, she isn't going to press the matter. She's a firm believer in respecting one's privacy."

"An admirable woman." They two-stepped to the music. "Your friends are joining us."

"Good. I was beginning to wonder when they were going to get tired of swilling champagne. I'm only joking," she added quickly. Edward was a stockbroker, and one never knew how seriously they took things. "Alix, for one, can stay on the dance floor all night."

"Your cousin is a terrific dancer," Edward said, his gray eyes amused. "However, I thought it diplomatic to keep our partnering down to one turn around the floor. Her husband doesn't look to be the unobservant or compliant sort."

"Henry's not—but then he's not foaming-at-the-mouth jealous either."

"Still, there are times when it's better to make a mistake on the side of restraint."

Mallory laughed. "Your fiancée is a very lucky girl, Edward. Tell her that for me. Most men generally muck up one way or another when it comes to potentially sticky situations," she said, a long-buried memory coming back with a sharp pang.

"Thank you. And what about the fellow you're interested in—is he equally as deft?"

"Oh, he knows all the right moves."

Mallory looked obliquely at Edward's dark, handsome face. There was no way he could know, but still. . . .

42

They danced past Jimmy and Kate, and the two couples exchanged brief, friendly greetings.

"I had a strange conversation with Jimmy the other day," Edward remarked. Like most of the athletically inclined men on the *Mauretania*, he keenly felt the lack of a swimming pool or a proper gymnasium, Cunard preferring to leave those showy innovations to the German liners, and trodding the dance floor at night was far more enjoyable than circling the deck at a brisk walk. "We were having a pre-lunch drink in the bar, talking about the Chicago Board of Trade, when he asked me if I'd seen his brother this past winter."

The music picked up its tempo, and Mallory felt something deep inside her lurch, but she forced an interested look on her face, and looked at Edward, waiting for him to continue.

"I said no, I hadn't," he went on, "and was sorry to have missed either Cliff or Gareth—whichever was in Chicago. Jimmy gave me this funny look and said he meant his younger brother, Rupert."

"It's a private joke," Mallory offered, feeling she had to say something or give it all away by her silence. "Rupert's not a relative of any stripe."

Edward smiled. "I was beginning to wonder. I've known Mr. Seligman for years—he and my father did some business together—and he never struck me as the sort of man who. . . ." He left the sentence hanging, his unspoken implication obvious.

In that brief pause, Mallory gathered all her acting ability together. She was going to carry this off, she hadn't come this far to disclose her feelings on a dance floor, of all places.

"Oh, it's nothing of that sort," she assured him. "But it's a very tangled web nonetheless. Seven years ago, Rupert Randall came to New York to see Henry Thorpe, who was his guardian. Henry and Alix had just had their first baby and there wasn't room for Rupert in their apartment, so William and Adele Seligman offered to put him up in their guest room. I think he came for a visit and simply never went home," Mallory finished with what she hoped was a casual shrug.

"Then why did Jimmy say that Rupert was his brother?"

"A private family joke—so to speak."

For a moment, Edward looked at her in nonplussed silence, instinctively sensing something behind his partner's words.

"Did you know him rather well?" he ventured at last.

"Of course I did." She forced a twinkle into her eyes. "After all, I'm nearly six-foot tall, and Rupert's six-foot-two, just like you—a perfect dancing partner! I'm not about to do any complaining."

"Neither am I."

"I'm curious, though. *Did* you meet Rupert in Chicago?"

"Sure. He's not a bad fellow. Smart as a whip about the market, too. I used to run into him at parties, and we had a business dinner together one night at the University Club. He was very popular with everyone, invited to all the best parties."

"He always is," Mallory said, stifling the remembrance of one party almost exactly four years before. "Always a good guest, but never the sort of man where you're ever sure of what's going on behind his party facade . . ."

Edward blinked at Mallory's purposely oblique, obscuring words. Suddenly he realized whereas he had told Mallory everything about the girl he was about to become engaged to, she had told him nothing about the fellow who was supposed to be so important to her. She didn't appear to be the type to become involved with a married man, so who could—? He longed to ask, but there was something about Mallory's cool self-possession

44

that made even the most carefully phrased inquiry impossible.

"The last dance," Mallory said as the musicians began the first notes of "After The Ball," the traditional closing number. "Tonight just flew by, didn't it? I think I could dance for another hour or two at least. . . ."

Mallory was lying. Well, not really, since she loved to dance, she rationalized to herself as she and Edward returned to their group of friends, but in truth the last half-hour had crawled by.

Just let someone mention Rupert and you turn inside out, she thought. I wonder if Edward thinks. . . . Of course he does, dummy. You tell him that you have a man you're very interested in, then you never utter another word about him, but as soon as his name comes up, you begin asking terribly clever questions. Lucky you that there's only one night left to this voyage.

With a slight smile, Mallory looked across the length of the salon.

Well, the moment is at hand, she thought, feeling butterflies form in her stomach. I had to wait until the time was right. These past few weeks I've kept telling myself I'd know when everything fell into place for me, and tonight is right.

With a final good-night to her shipboard friends, made up of both those she knew on land and those who were new-found to her, Mallory began to make her way across the highly polished floor, through the crowd of chattering, laughing men and women.

She had thought everything out and now she had a cohesive plan of action, but now, before she set the wheels in motion, there was one big step left to take: she had to talk to Alix and tell her everything.

In another hour, the *Mauretania* would be quiet. The

45

lights would be dimmed, merry-making passengers would be resting and recovering from their night of fun, and a cleaning crew would be hard at work, washing and wiping and dusting and polishing, making sure the liner would be in pristine condition by the first light of dawn. But now, at shortly after one in the morning, the crowd moving from the grand salon to the rest of the Main Deck Forward was taking its time, obviously reluctant to put an end to this happy night.

As Mallory approached her cousin, she and Alix made eye contact and exchanged a silent signal.

Henry, standing beside his wife, saw their look, and knew instantly what was about to take place.

"Would you like me to go back to our suite?" he asked quietly. Alix had confided in him a few weeks before, and he had agreed with her that the best tactic was to stay on the sidelines until asked to do otherwise. Interfering would be of no help at all, although personally, had Rupert been handy, he would like to have thrown a well-directed punch at his former ward.

Alix nodded. "I think so. Mallory may want to have a long talk, and we'll have more privacy in her room than if I asked her to come back to our suite," she said, just as Mallory came up to them.

She greeted the Thorpes, and wasn't a bit surprised when Henry, after a brief exchange of pleasantries, wished her a good-night and left them alone.

"Henry's a very perceptive man, isn't he?" Mallory inquired, her smile knowing.

"I like to think so," Alix replied, her smile a shade more special.

"I take it then we can have a private talk."

"For as long as you want. Your cabin?"

It was a rhetorical question, but one that Mallory deeply appreciated. Unlike some women, Alix took nothing for granted and certainly never presumed.

"That would be the best place," she agreed. "I don't know if Aunt Esme is back or not, so we'd better avoid the sitting room. Not that she wouldn't be very understanding about what I'm going to tell you, but right now I'd prefer to keep my story very private and just between the two of us."

At that moment, the grand staircase, designed to follow the 15th century Italian mode, was so crowded with first class passengers that the soft green carpet laid over it was all but obscured.

After one look at the slow-moving crowd, Mallory and Alix, by mutual agreement, headed for the bank of elevators suspended in the well of the grand staircase. During their brief trip inside the decorative car where the faux 15th century grillwork was made out of that new material, wrought aluminum, both women kept up a casual conversation, mainly centering around the captain's dinner.

"Esme's rather pleased about your attracting Edward MacDonald," Alix remarked casually as they left the elevator and walked along the broad, paneled passageway to the section where the best suites were located.

"She won't be for much longer," Mallory replied, and she and Alix exchanged amused looks. "Edward's about to become formally engaged."

"Is that why you've let him be your escort while we're on board?"

"It seemed to be the best strategy available," Mallory said.

"You take after me," Alix said with admiration. "But, darling, you can't stage that act more than once."

"I don't intend to." They reached their destination, and Mallory opened the door to the suite she and her godmother were sharing. "That's why I want to talk to

47

you now."

All of the *Mauretania*'s first class accommodations were decorated in either Adam or Sheraton or Chippendale furnishings, all excellent reproductions. The two-bedroom suite that Mallory Kirk and Esme Phipps had taken was done in the classic, restrained Adam style furniture upholstered in jewel-colored silk, enhanced by personal ornaments and vases of fresh, expertly arranged flowers, and the well-proportioned bedrooms boasted the innovative shipboard luxury of a telephone.

In Mallory's bedroom, the stewardess had already turned down the bed, placed a Lucile nightgown of cream-colored silk trimmed in cream satin ribbon on the chaise lounge, and turned on the white silk-shaded lamps so that the women did not have to grope around for a light switch.

With a soft swish of expensive fabric, Alix sat down in the oval-backed armchair covered in yellow and white silk and surveyed the room. A Wedgwood vase placed on the dresser held yellow and white tea roses and statice, her perfumes and cosmetics were set out on the tulipwood dressing table, and books and magazines were arranged in neat piles. Alix glanced quickly through the magazines—the most recent issues of the *Illustrated London News*, *Tatler*, *Queen*, *Gentlewoman*, *Vanity Fair*, *Sketch*, and *Bystander*, all purchased during their time in London—set out on the table closest to her.

"I didn't invite you here to have you look through my reading material," Mallory said in an amused voice. "Don't you have the same magazines back in your suite?"

"Of course I do. Reading any good whodunits?"

"Two of them, in fact." Mallory looked at the books on her decorative bedside table. "*The Hemlock Avenue Mystery* and *The Carleton Case*."

"They're not precisely Edith Wharton."

48

"No, but then I don't believe that Mrs. Wharton writes her novels with her readers' relaxation in mind."

The cousins smiled at each other.

"As you said, that's not what you invited me here for." Alix's amused look softened into something else. "Do you still want to talk?"

"More than ever." Mallory kicked off her pale pink satin evening shoes and sat down on the edge of the bed. "I've thought this out so carefully but now I'm not sure where to begin. Would you mind if I start at the end?"

"My favorite place to begin a story or book."

Mallory stretched out against the pillows and regarded Alix evenly.

"I want to see Rupert again."

Alix leaned back and returned the look. "You're a grown woman, Mallie. You can see—or not see—anyone you choose. But why now, after four years, if I may ask?"

"Because I'm still in love with him."

"The best reason of all."

Alix's tone was honest and logical, free of any sarcasm, but Mallory was beginning to feel a bit strange. Wasn't this supposed to be happening differently? Why did she feel so calm? Why was it that situations never turned out the way you imagined they would?

"Oh, Alix, let's stop talking like characters out of *The New York Idea*! I need your help."

"You're right. But what you want isn't all that hard to arrange. A dinner party, something large so it doesn't look too obvious. How does that sound? We'll find out when Bill is going to bring Rupert back from exile in Chicago, and work out our plan from there."

"Alix, that sounds good—and not so good. The idea of having to wait in your drawing room until Rupert walks in . . . No matter how casual you make it seem, he'll take one look at me and see through it all." She shuddered slightly. "There has to be another, better way. How did you maneuver to see Henry alone? When you first met him, I mean?"

Alix looked pleased. "Didn't I ever tell you? Shortly after we met, he developed a bad throat and a fever, and as soon as I found out about it, I paid a house call on him!"

"You look positively delighted with yourself! Did it work?"

"It very nearly didn't. Henry was *outraged*. But when I went back to see him a week later, he was in a very different mood. We didn't settle anything that day, but we did get started."

"Not bad, cousin."

"Well, Henry was the man for me, and I knew it the minute I looked at him. But back to you . . . Now that you've told me that you want to see Rupert again, are you ready to tell me why you stopped seeing him? Emma was right a few weeks ago, you know. Most of us were thinking of the two of you as practically engaged, and we figured that once you got your graduations from Barnard and Columbia over with. . . ."

The rest of what Alix was saying was lost on Mallory. Well, you started this, and now you have to go all the way and finish the whole mess of a story, she told herself, feeling her eyes begin to burn with tears.

"Do you remember the week President and Mrs. Roosevelt came to visit at Cove House?" she asked finally.

The Roosevelts had been guests at Cove House, the North Shore Long Island estate of the William Seligmans on numerous occasions, but instinctively Alix knew exactly to which time Mallory was referring. Early August of 1906. That was it, it had to be.

"Yes," she said. "I remember."

"They had the state suite . . . it's so isolated from the rest of the house . . . most guests don't even want it . . ."

"Remember how T.R. asked Bill if being given the state suite meant he didn't like him any more?"

Mallory smiled, forcing herself to relax. Alix would understand, she reminded herself.

"This happened after they left . . ."

"I should hope so."

"Oh, we observed *some* of the proprieties."

"It's strange how couples *always* manage to cling to some vestige of how they were raised—even in the first flush of passion."

At Alix's last word, Mallory swung her long legs over the side of the bed and stood up. Silently, she walked over to the dressing table, selected a bottle from among those arranged on the surface, and began to dab on perfume. The scent of Guerlain's *Aprés L'Ondée* which both women were already wearing, drifted over the room, and Mallory turned to face Alix, sitting down on the little padded bench in front of the dressing table.

"The day after they left," she repeated, "we went up to that suite and we spent the afternoon as lovers—making love together for the first time."

Mallory felt her heart pounding as she waited for Alix to reply.

"Did you plan it that way in advance?"

The question was softly put, totally unjudgmental as only Alix could be, but Mallory felt a deep need to reassure her.

"No! It—it just happened. We didn't even go up there together. There was nothing premeditated about it, we just wanted each other. I guess we had for a long time, but until that day it was never right." She gave Alix a searching look. "It doesn't sound terribly romantic, does it?"

"It's not supposed to," Alix said comfortingly. "When you're alone with the man you love it's private and personal and very, very special—not a thing that

51

translates well into a confidence."

Even if the man you're with is a rat, Alix added to herself.

"I know you don't like Rupert, Alix," Mallory said quietly.

"That has nothing to do with your situation, and besides, that goes back to before you two ever met, and had more to do with how he used to act toward Henry," Alix avowed. "Darling, if you and Rupert love each other it's wonderful, and if you've had some sort of disagreement—"

"Not a disagreement, an out and out fight." Mallory felt her heart begin to pound with a sickening pace, but no matter how she felt she had gone too far to back off now. "That night at the party," she said, picking her words carefully, "Rupert danced me out to the terrace, and then—then he told me that he had no intention of marrying me."

"That bastard." Alix spat out the words.

Mallory moved to sit down at the foot of the bed. "I know he's that, but I still love him."

Alix gave her a sweeping glance. "As long as you don't make excuses for Rupert, how you feel about him in your heart and how you think about him are entirely separate matters."

"For a few years I didn't think about Rupert. I decided that if he didn't love me enough to contemplate our spending the rest of our lives together, I wasn't going to think about him at all."

"It didn't work very well, did it?" Alix said with an understanding smile, recalling all the times during their courtship when she had tried with no great success to put Henry out of her thoughts.

"Well, I never sat at home by the fire, as you very well know," Mallory retorted. "But over the past year. . . ."

"He seeped back in."

"Exactly. It began the night we heard Rachmaninoff play his Piano Concerto Number 3 for the very first time. All that beautiful music, composed especially for his first American tour, and there I was in Carnegie Hall when I began to think about Rupert, about how nice it would be if he were sitting beside me. And that was the beginning of it. From then on, I began to wonder where he was and what he was doing—sometimes at very inopportune moments. At balls, at dinner parties, at opening nights, the night Pavlova danced for the first time at the Metropolitan Opera House. . . ."

"And generally while you were thinking about—or were with—some other eligible young man," Alix suggested. "I used to do that all the time with Henry."

Mallory smiled slightly. "Did you ever notice how some of these men are eligible only to other people? Remember Peter Beardsley?" Mallory knew she was diverging, but now that she was talking about the feelings she'd spent four years hiding, other incidents that she'd either dismissed or glossed over came bubbling to the surface. "I thought he was terribly nice and that he might turn out to be someone special for me, and then he took me to the theatre. . . . Oh, Alix, how could I be expected to fall in love with a man who takes me to the opening night of a play called *The Girl with the Whooping Cough*?"

"With a title like that I'm surprised it managed to eke out twenty-four performances," Alix remarked. "Give the poor fellow the benefit of the doubt, Mallory. The past six or seven months will not go down in Broadway history as having produced shows everyone will always remember. Peter probably didn't have much of a choice."

"True, but we could have gone to see *Madame X* or *Mid-channel* again."

"Is that what you think Rupert would have done?"

"I don't know, Alix. Chances are we would have gone

to that same awful comedy, but I've reached the point where every time something like that happens, I start to wonder how different it might be if I were with Rupert."

"That's dangerous. Very, *very* dangerous."

"I know, and that's why I want to see him again. To get rid of all the old memories. We never did end properly, and I think that if we can talk together again I can heal the breech between us. I'm afraid that if I don't, every time I meet a new man I'll start the same routine of compare and contrast. Since Rupert, I can't keep track of the nice men I've discouraged. I might have found something special with any one of them, except—except—"

Mallory stopped to take several deep breaths and blink back tears.

"I don't want an obsession running—or ruining—my life," she went on, her voice growing stronger. "Rupert and I could have had everything together, but if he didn't want to go the rest of the way with me, that's *his* loss. I won't let it become mine. I may never stop loving him, but once and for all I want this situation behind me."

Alix sat back in her chair, silently admiring her cousin's sense of purpose. She's as resolved as I've ever been, she thought proudly. Know what you have to do and follow it through. Make things right no matter how difficult it is. But all the time I was doing just that, I liked to indulge in emotional cul-de-sacs and what-ifs, and I used to find most of my situations to be amusing, one way or another. Does Mallory?

"What are you thinking, cousin?"

"Doing a bit of compare and contrast myself."

"You and me?"

"Hmm. We're something alike, you and I. We want to face out our problems, and when we have to go into subterfuge we're experts at half-truths and outright lies. But there's one thing—and you don't have to tell me if

54

you don't want to—do you want to see Rupert again *only* to finally put him out of your life?"

A surprising smile formed on Mallory's face. "You mean do I think Rupert is going to say he's sorry and I'll fall into his arms, or else I'll take one look at him, forget my good intentions, and do something to force his hand?"

"You'd never trick a man, or back him into a corner no matter how tempting the idea."

"What I'd really like to happen is a fantasy," Mallory said miserably.

"Don't decide anything in advance," Alix warned. "This has to be taken moment by moment."

"I know that," she said, standing up. "Four years ago, I could have gotten Rupert to marry me. Just the slightest hint to anyone about what happened would have been enough. But I didn't want him like that."

"No real woman would."

"I made love with Rupert out of my own free will. He certainly didn't force me, and if he didn't want anything after that, well, I have to take the consequences."

Alix stood up and came over to Mallory, kissing her on the cheek.

"I think you've been very brave and that you're doing the right thing now, but one question; Mallory, when Rupert said he wasn't . . . that is, he didn't want to have anything further to do with you, did you just *stand there* and take it?"

"Oh, Alix." Mallory began to laugh, remembering the one amusing moment in the whole debacle. "I'm not your cousin for nothing. Of course I didn't just stand there on the terrace like an idiot. I told Rupert what I thought of him—and then I pushed him off the terrace and into a rose bush!"

* * *

Alix and Henry Thorpe were occupying the *Mauretania*'s largest suite. Here the sitting room and each of the four bedrooms were done in the style of the last great eighteenth-century furniture designer, Thomas Sheraton, with highly lacquered, beautifully inlaid pieces made of mahogany and satinwood, the chairs and sofas upholstered in pastel satins and striped silks. Like the suite she'd just come from, these rooms also carried the personal stamp of its occupants with vases holding arrangements of vari-colored tulips, a few well-chosen photographs in sterling silver frames, a plethora of books and magazines and, in a corner of one of the sofas, accidentally left behind by her owner, an exquisite French Jumeau doll with delicate bisque features, long golden curls and a sweet expression, wearing a blue satin dress.

Laughing softly at the sight of the doll sitting on the sofa as if to say this was rightfully where she belonged, Alix picked up the doll that was the favorite of her seven-year-old daughter Isabel, and went first to the room that her girls were sharing.

In the almost dark cabin with only a soft night-light glowing, Alix carefully placed the doll on the chair closest to Isabel's bed so her little girl could see it when she woke up in the morning.

She stood quietly between the beds. In one slept her first child, and in the other her last, eighteen month-old Gweneth. Both girls slept on peacefully, oblivious to their mother who bent over first one and then the other, adjusting blankets, smoothing pillows, and kissed them both.

The next bedroom, the smallest of the four, was occupied by Miss Darty, the children's nurse, and the bedroom after that was the shipboard province of five-year-old Robert, and three-and-a-half-year-old Stuart. Here Alix repeated her love-filled motions of a few moments before. If the girls took after her, she recognized, the boys, even at their young age, bore the imprint of Henry Thorpe's fine features.

With a final, very proud look she softly closed the door and crossed the sitting room, eager to rejoin Henry. He would be reading, she decided, or else making notes for the upcoming semester at Columbia University where he held seminars for those Columbia and Barnard seniors interested in the technique of museum acquisitions.

After eight years of marriage, Alix felt she knew her husband pretty well, but when she opened the door and stepped into their room she had to remind herself that one of the things she loved about Henry was the fact that he didn't necessarily behave the way others expected him to.

Alix leaned back against the door, regarding her husband who was stretched out across their bed, his arms folded behind his head, wearing the white silk pajamas piped in dark blue silk that she'd had made for him at Sulka's, an expression of amused concentration on his face as if he were thinking up some grand manner of revenge on one who'd wronged him.

"Ah, what do we have here? A rare portrait of Lord Henry Thorpe at leisure," she announced in a deliberately provocative tone.

Henry turned his attention to her. "You mean at leisure in any bed that we share, don't you?" he said, his expression changing.

"That's the general idea, and I've just come from looking in on the proof of that activity," Alix said, moving toward the center of the room.

Women's clothes had changed dramatically in the eight years since Henry Thorpe had prevented Alix Turner from falling backwards down the Palladian marble staircase of Saltlon House. Ladies' ankles might still not have made a formal public appearance, but gone forever were the long sweeping skirts and full sleeves that had been the mode of the summer of 1902 and a few years after. Now the silhouette was long and straight, brushing the top of the instep, and designed to make the wearer appear smaller at the feet than at the shoulders. Some men might mourn the loss of the fabric-swathed, tightly laced female figure, but for women like Alix and her friends—tall and slender and bosomy—these clothes which seemed designed specifically to flatter and accentuate their good points were exactly how they liked to look.

Alix took off all her jewelry except for her wedding ring and eight-carat oval-cut canary diamond engagement ring and placed it on the dressing table. There was a wall safe in the room, but Alix made no move to use it. Traveling on an ocean liner was safer than being at home. Whether on Cunard or on one of the ships of the Compagnie Generale Transatlantique, she had never found a single item missing at any time during the voyage. As far as she was concerned, the stewards and stewardesses who served these lines were absolutely honest, and if there were professional thieves on board they generally had the good sense not to become interested in one's jewelry until after the ship had docked. It was far simpler—and safer—to ply the trade of cat burglary in the great Continental hotels which were large enough to allow for blending into the crowd.

"When I came in, you had an expression on your face worthy of Professor Moriarty," Alix said teasingly, placing a bracelet between two bottles of perfume. "Would you care to let me in on what you were thinking?"

Henry smiled. "I was plotting the appropriate revenge I'd like to take on a certain former failed Jesuit seminarian turned translator turned temporary secret agent for Theodore Roosevelt turned teacher and writer of magazine articles turned literary agent for talking me into trying my hand at writing a book! *Patterns Of Collecting and Acquisition*—what a laugh!" he exclaimed, motioning toward a small, decorative desk that was covered with sheets of paper. "While you were with Mallory, I decided to look through some of my notes, and what a useless muddle *they* are!"

"Poor Henry. But look at it this way—there's no publisher, no signed contract, and when we get home you can always tell Charles that you're not interested after all. Not that you're going to do that," she added, as Henry swung himself out of bed and went over to the desk to begin to stuff his papers back into his dark green leather portfolio.

"Right now, all I want to do is unhook your dress," he said softly a moment later, coming over to kiss the back of her neck, his hands touching gently at the gown's delicate fastenings.

"Oh," Alix moved close against Henry, feeling her tiredness melt away at his touch. "That feels so nice."

"Was it a difficult time with Mallory?"

"Not really. She knows exactly where she's going."

Her dress unhooked, Alix stepped out of her gown and draped it carefully over the closest chair and then moved on to the marble-heavy bathroom.

"You're not going to tell me what went on, are you?" Henry inquired, amused, as he watched Alix dab cold cream around her eyes to melt off the kohl and mascara she used to accent them, carefully wipe it off, and then wash her face thoroughly with cucumber soap.

"Not a single word," she said, patting her face dry with a thick, fluffy towel.

"Is it because it's not my business, or because I wouldn't like what you tell me?"

"Both."

Together they returned to the bedroom and Alix

finished undressing. Her green satin shoes came off first, and then her silk stockings. Like the rest of the clothes women wore, undergarments had also changed in the past eight years, and the elaborate, unyielding satin and whalebone stays were now banished by all elegant and fashionable women and replaced by a supple corset that was made of either silk elastic or silk tricot with a minimum of bones, all designed to leave the body free and supple.

There was a faint undercurrent of strain between the Thorpes, and Alix moved to dispel it, stepping close against Henry to slip an arm around her husband's waist and rest her head against his shoulder.

"I thought we'd never be alone together."

"I know. I felt the same way." Henry's fingers moved deftly along the front of the cream silk tricot corset, releasing the clasps so that a moment later all she wore was her lacy Lucile lingerie.

Alix wove her fingers through Henry's dark brown hair and then moved down to caress the back of his neck, pressing against him for love and comfort, feeling the warm surge of his body. Then Henry's hands were at her hair, taking out the jeweled pins, and finally traveling down to her shoulders to lower the satin straps of her camisole.

Freeing them from their soft lace covering, his hands circled her full breasts, and at the same time their lips met, and at that kiss desire burned between them, demanding immediate fulfillment.

Alix felt herself melt against Henry, her hands pressed against his shoulders, her newly bared body separated from his only by the fine silk of his sleepware.

Her senses were swirling, but before they could totally engulf her, she pulled back enough to unbutton his pajama jacket and loosen the drawstring at his waist. It was her turn now, and she let her fingers drift sensuously over him, alternately touching, massaging, and teasing as they traveled his fine flesh from neck to thigh, ending at his hard velvet length.

Throbbing with desire, they were across the bed, their bodies joining in one motion. They moved together, weaving their own private world of pleasure and love and satisfaction. It was like this every time, and as they reached their peak and then began to spiral slowly downwards, Alix could only think that no matter how frequently they made love there was always something new to be discovered; it was never the same, and different always meant better.

It seemed that it was an endless time later that Alix felt Henry stir beside her and lean over to kiss her hair.

"I know you won't betray the confidences Mallory shared with you, and I won't ask, but will you answer one question that has been bothering me?" Henry asked in a quiet voice.

Alix turned to face him. "Of course."

"Did all of this—what you discussed—have something to do with Rupert?"

Alix laughed softly. "Are you telling me you had any doubts on that point? It's not funny—particularly for Mallory—but it's everything I suspected all along. More than that, she wants to see him again, to smooth over their rift."

Henry propped himself up on one elbow. "Odd, Mallory never struck me as the sort of young woman who likes to be hurt."

"Oh, she isn't. But she has the idea—and not a totally wrong one, I might add—that unless she sees and talks to Rupert again, she'll never be able to forget what happened between them."

"I'm afraid to ask what 'it' is." Henry's voice held a tinge of amusement, but there was an undertone of carefully controlled anger that Alix caught at once.

61

"Lucky you're not the sort of woman who hears a secret and then tells all," he went on, "because I have a feeling what Mallory told you would leave me wanting to have my fist make contact with Rupert's jaw."

"Your feelings, as usual, are rather accurate," Alix remarked, reaching up to smooth back his rumpled hair. "But . . ."

"But right now all that is none of our business," Henry finished.

"Exactly. Mallory needed someone to share her secret with, and now that she has, the rest is up to her."

"Do you suppose she wants Rupert back?"

"Again is more like it. And yes, I think she does. But Mallory's a lot like me—strong-minded all the way. She wants Rupert, but only if he also wants her—and says so first!"

"Smart girl. And as long as you've mentioned sharing—"

Alix drew Henry down to her. "You always know the key words."

"Only because I was lucky enough to meet the woman who taught me all about sharing," Henry replied softly, and a minute later neither of them was thinking about either Rupert or Mallory.

In her cabin, Mallory found herself rereading page forty-five of *The Hemlock Avenue Mystery* for the fifth time, and no more able to make sense of the page than if it had been written in Swedish. With a sigh of regret, she closed the book, placed it back on the bedside table, and switched off the light.

See what happens when you spill all your deep dark secrets, Mallory, she told herself. You lose all your powers of concentration.

With a feeling of dejection, she made herself

comfortable in bed, fixing the pillows and adjusting the silken covers so that she was supremely ready to pass the next seven or eight hours in luxurious solitude.

All things considered, she decided, she should have drifted off to a dreamless sleep, lulled by the *Mauretania*'s gentle motion and the fact that she had finally shared her secret with Alix.

Thank God for Alix, she thought. Alix who had divined her situation before a word was said between them. Alix who had listened intently to her. Alix who had questioned and commented but never, ever presumed to judge either her actions or her subsequent behavior.

But why aren't I relaxed and sleepy instead of keyed-up? I'm thinking in five directions at once, and if this keeps up I'll be of no help to myself at all. One look at Rupert and I'll start crying, throw myself in his arms, and ruin it all. I have to keep my dignity if nothing else. Once we finish talking, settling all we left unfinished, I can find a quiet spot somewhere and stop being so strong and above it all.

Then why am I crying now? she wondered as her eyes filled and burned and overflowed. Resolutely, she brushed away her tears. Oh, I know why. I've lost the man I love, and no matter how many times I go over it, I know there was nothing I could have done to change the outcome—either then or now . . .

Did every woman remember what she was wearing at every important incident in her life? Mallory speculated as she began to relax and feel sleepy. I can remember exactly what I had on the day I met Rupert. I even remember how he looked, coming out onto the loggia at Cove House, holding those two martini glasses . . .

She had been hearing about Rupert Randall for days before the actual moment when she looked up from the issue of *Connoisseur* she was leafing through and saw him holding two long-stemmed glasses.

Alix and Kate had been the first bearers of the news, coming to lunch the day after Newton and Esme Phipps and Mallory had returned to New York following a summer spent in Switzerland and Paris and London.

At first the talk on that hot late August day had centered around Alix's daughter, born a short month before, then had moved on to the topic of Lausanne and Geneva and Paris and London in the summer, and then finally touching on what interesting things had been happening in New York.

"I suppose Henry's awfully relieved to have Rupert settled and more or less off his hands," Kate remarked as they ate orange ice and nibbled at Napoleons.

"I think Henry was positively thrilled when Bill said he thought that Rupert would be better off living with him and Adele," Alix said, licking her fork clean of the pastry's cream filling.

"What is all this about?" Esme inquired, her curiosity sparked. "We leave town for a few months and come back to find all sorts of changes. And who is Rupert?"

"Rupert Randall, if you please. Lady Allison Randall's son."

"Oh, *her.*" Esme was disdainful. "Five minutes around her would make any man crazy. Frankly, I'm not surprised that boy of hers is so wild."

"What exactly has he done?" Mallory added with interest. She had been taking in the slightly cryptic conversation, her own natural sense of curiosity growing.

"Oh, about a year ago he decided that Oxford was a pretty dull place and he smuggled two very high-priced ladies of the evening into his rooms—for his amusement alone," Alix supplied informatively. Like herself, Mallory had not been brought up ignorant of the facts of life and the world around her, and she therefore had no compunctions about mentioning any subject in front of her.

"What a greedy boy he must be."

"Among other things," Alix smiled.

"Then what has he been doing since then?" Esme asked, and both Alix and Kate began to giggle.

"He's been scrubbing floors in a monastery in Gloucestershire," Alix said, drawing a deep breath. "A year of punishment after he was discovered in his compromising situation."

"Well, I hope he paid his women beforehand. I wouldn't think that there was too much time after he was discovered," Mallory said, joining in the amusement.

"How did he come to New York?" asked Esme, ever aware of certain practicalities.

"To see Henry about his cigarette case," Alix shrugged. "Henry took the case from him on the day he delivered him to the custody of the monks. It's no secret that Rupert can't get on with his mother—not that I blame him there—and once his time of confinement was up and he came home and saw he wasn't particularly welcome at Berkeley Square, he decided to come to New York. His timing in the matter was not the best," she added.

"I can imagine, particularly with Isabel just born," Esme murmured sympathetically. "Not much room in the castle, so to speak."

"It's amazing how small a ten-room apartment can become," Alix agreed.

"That's where my esteemed mother-in-law and father-in-law come in," Kate added, still amused. "As you know, they have that nice, empty guest room, and since Rupert couldn't be left to his own devices during the day, Father began taking him down to Wall Street."

"Such is the stuff of which new interests are born,"

Alix said, raising her eyebrows expressively. "Events after that become rather complicated, but to make a long story short, today, probably right at this moment, Rupert is taking his qualifying exams for Columbia."

"Poor Nicholas Murray Butler," Mallory said, referring to the president of Columbia University. "Like it or not, I expect he's going to have to take on the malcontent as—what?—a junior."

"Sorry, sweet cousin," Alix gave Mallory a look of amusement. "Rupert, provided Bill, even with his influence as a trustee and Regent, can get him accepted—will be a sophomore, just like you." She considered her cousin for a moment. "You might find him amusing."

"That could be the understatement of the century," Mallory retorted. "But since I'm going to have to meet this Rupert sooner or later, I have the usual important questions to ask you: is he good-looking, does he dance, and is he tall?"

"If you like the sort, I expect so, and about six foot one or two," Alix shot back, sending her friends into gales of laughter. "You'll find out soon enough."

That had been Monday afternoon, and now it was Thursday, and Mallory was sitting on the loggia at Cove House. Here the white wicker sofas and deep, comfortable chairs had cushions covered in bright chintzes, and the view stretched out to encompass the terrace, the long expanse of rose garden, and the Long Island Sound. Dressed for the evening ahead in a Lucile gown of pale pink chiffon trimmed with pink ribbon and Valenciennes lace, Mallory turned the pages of the magazine and wondered just what sort of supercilious brat Rupert Randall was.

She wasn't sure which might be worse; that he was either champing at the bit for his first taste of freedom after a year of confinement, or else that he was now so reformed that he was going to turn out to be the worst sort of bore. So far, though, no one had made any comments about whether she was to seek him out or avoid him and she was happy to let the matter rest until etiquette demanded she do otherwise.

Mallory was reflecting that there was nothing better than being eighteen and having the income of her inheritance and a year of college successfully behind her with three more demanding, intellectual years ahead of her, and the prospect of attracting admirers who were not at all fazed by the prospect of a young woman who was nearly six feet tall when she heard someone step out onto the loggia.

"A cold, dry martini from the good offices of our host," a British-accented voice said, and she looked up to see a black-haired young man wearing faultless, obviously brand new, dinner clothes and holding a frosted, long-stemmed glass in each hand, standing beside her. "I'm Rupert Randall."

"I'm Mallory Kirk," she smiled, liking at first glance what she saw. "Are you going to sit down or just toss the glass at me and hope I catch it?" she asked smartly.

"Mind your manners," he warned, sitting down beside her on the sofa and handing her one of the glasses, "or I won't ask you to tell me all about university life on Morningside Heights."

"You've been accepted then. How wonderful for you!" Mallory found herself truly happy for Rupert. Obviously, from the talk she'd been hearing, he couldn't go back to a British university, and it was also quite clear that he wasn't yet considered trustworthy enough to be off on his own at Harvard or Yale or Amherst.

"Columbia University will do well enough, I expect," Rupert replied, a slight sneer forming around his words. "All things considered, they're probably quite delighted to enroll Sir Rupert Randall." He raised his glass so the late afternoon sunlight glinted off the Tiffany crystal glass.

Mallory took a small, somewhat experimental sip of

67

her drink—she was getting used to drinking cocktails—
and smiled. "Admittedly at this moment you look like the
lord of all you survey, but unless I'm terribly wrong,
about a month ago you were busy scrubbing floors and
washing windows, *Sir* Rupert!"

She looked directly at him, taking in his thick-lashed
silver-gray eyes, strong nose and good bone structure
accented by an even suntan. Slowly, Mallory began to
feel herself grow warm in an entirely new way. She had
been having beaux since she was sixteen, but as much as
she liked the young men she saw at parties and danced
and talked with and whose company she generally
enjoyed, none of them, so far, were particularly special to
her.

Not that Rupert Randall is, either, she reminded
herself. But on the other hand, she had to admit that in
these few minutes she felt more aware of him than she
ever had with any other male contemporary.

It was only his high-handed attitude toward Columbia
University that annoyed her, but as she continued to
look at Rupert, his facade of disdainful disinterest
crumpled like a plaster mask hit with a hammer as he
began to laugh.

"You *do* care!" Mallory exclaimed, vastly relieved that
he had only been pretending.

"Yes, I do, rather," he admitted. "I couldn't imagine
what I'd have done if Columbia hadn't accepted me."

"Oh, the Seligmans would have kept you on—as an
office boy or something."

"You sting," he said, breaking into a wide smile.

"I've been told about you."

"I'm sure you have been. Particularly since Alix
doesn't care for me to any great extent."

"Alix is my cousin."

"So I've heard. But," he went on, a soft look coming into his eyes, "I think that even without the resemblance—well—" Uncharacteristically, he hesitated for a moment. "I wasn't expecting you."

Mallory caught on immediately, but decided to hedge. "Oh, then you just like to wander out onto loggias carrying two martini glasses?"

"No, I was instructed to come out here and meet you. You're supposed to be giving me tips on American university life."

Again, Mallory caught the implication behind his words, and deftly decided to pass over it. "Fortunately, nearly everyone is still upstairs dressing," she said humorously. "This could take a while."

"Really?" Rupert looked doubtful. "At Oxford I was told American universities were a snap—nothing to them."

Mallory smiled down at the surface of her cocktail. "Do you actually think so? Are you sure you wouldn't like to talk about that?"

"I'd rather talk about you." Silver-gray eyes moved to take her in from the top of her carefully arranged Gibson Girl coiffure to the tips of her pink silk shoes, a look that sent a warm shiver down the length of her spine. "I met your godfather last week."

"He's remarkable, isn't he? Just eighteen months ago we weren't sure Uncle Newton would live. That's why we had to sell the 70th Street house and move to an apartment at 667 Madison Avenue. With all those stairs at the house, he needed the elevator," she explained, and Rupert nodded in understanding even though the large impersonal apartment buildings of New York were still a phenomenon to him. "Aunt Esme and I think the move saved his life. He still has to be careful about his heart and not get too tired, but otherwise he's just fine."

"Have you lived with the Phipps a long time?"

"Just about half my life. I went to live with them when my parents died."

"But since you're Alix's cousin, wouldn't it have been more logical for you to go to the Leslies?"

"Possibly it would have been. But I'm not a Leslie." Mallory smiled at Rupert despite the pang of pain and loss she felt whenever she mentioned or thought about her mother and father. "My mother and Alix's father were first cousins, so I'm connected to the Leslie family by *very* tenuous ties."

"I see."

For some reason, the tone of Rupert's reply put Mallory off from mentioning anything further about either Newton or Esme Phipps or her own parents. Her father had died of pneumonia when she was five, and her mother had followed two years after, mainly, most people said, from a broken heart. Before either of those eventualities, however, they had had the foresight to name their closest friends, the Phipps, who were unable to have a child of their own, as the godparents and guardian of their small daughter.

She would have liked to tell him some of this, but as she regarded his profile, Mallory decided that this was not the time to tell such stories. First, because she really didn't know him, and second, because if all she'd been hearing was true, her telling about growing up with loving parents—first natural and then surrogate—might not be his cup of tea.

I don't envy the Seligmans at all, Mallory thought.

"I suppose you'll be taking history courses at Columbia," she said at last, wisely concluding that this at least was a safe topic of conversation.

"That and economics," he replied easily. "I'm also registered with a Professor Albright for something called Calculus One."

"You poor thing," Mallory said, smiling. "Professor

70

Albright's reputation is *very* widespread—he'll put you through the wringer."

"Not too likely," he shot back with a wide smile that was a shade *too* sure of itself. "With your university being so easy, I daresay I'll survive all my classes rather well."

"Come and tell me that two months from now," she challenged. "Uncle Newton and Aunt Esme are giving me a dance at Sherry's for my eighteenth birthday, and you're invited—provided you can spare a night away from your studies, that is!"

"Fair enough. But if it turns out I'm right, you owe me a forfeit," Rupert said, a devilish gleam coming into his eyes. "A kiss will do, I think."

Immediately, the air between them changed. Their easy banter was replaced by something far more electric. Something, Mallory's instinct instantly told her, that had never happened to her before, and something she had to handle very, very carefully.

"Is that the only circumstance under which you'd consider kissing me?" she said lightly, subtly flirting, yet promising nothing unseemly.

"I believe it's the other way around. *You* kiss *me.*"

"Ah." Mallory paused for a moment. "But isn't the concept of a proper kiss for the two people involved to come halfway?"

"Generally so." Ahead of them, they could see the sky over Long Island Sound begin to turn pink and gold, blending in with the bright summer blue to form the beginnings of a perfect August twilight. As they watched this beautiful act of nature, Rupert moved his head closer to Mallory's, his mouth brushing against her hair and stopping a tantalizing inch from her right ear.

"Shall we try coming halfway with each other now?" he whispered, and Mallory thought that at that moment there was nothing she'd like better than finding out how Rupert Randall kissed.

All I have to do is turn my head, she thought, and then

71

caution stopped her. Why should I make it easy for him? a voice inside her brain warned. As far as women are concerned, he's had it so easy . . . a man of thirty would envy him . . . don't be his first New York conquest . . .

Mallory did move her head—pulling back until she was able to look directly at Rupert. Her heart was pounding in a combination of excitement and anticipation, but her logical mind was ruling her potentially ardent heart.

"I believe we've struck a bargain otherwise," she purred softly, putting her fingers over his mouth, marveling at the feel of his warm, firm flesh. "Two months from now," she went on, "and then *only* if you're breezing through your classes."

Before she could draw her fingers away, he quickly kissed them, sending another wave of new feelings through her. "It'll be worth the wait. Difficult, though."

"That's chemistry."

"I take it you know about such things?"

"Chemistry and biology are my majors at Barnard."

Rupert's eyes sparkled. "What propitious subjects."

"Oh, they'll come in handy—sooner or later."

Late afternoon was turning into early evening, and from their spot on the loggia they could hear the sounds of servants moving from room to room and guests coming down the stairs. Any moment now they could be joined by family or friends, and in a very short time they would have to go in to the yellow and cream main drawing room where all the guests gathered before dinner.

With a graceful gesture, Rupert saluted Mallory with his glass. "My dear Miss Kirk, this is one agreement I'll be very happy to drink to."

True to his word, Rupert did not try to kiss her before the two-month period preceding her eighteenth birthday, or even on the night itself, since the private room at

Sherry's that Newton Phipps took, spacious as it was, was not set up for trysting couples. But the Dakota, with its secret corners and extra rooms and areas of waste space, was.

Despite the fact that Barnard College ran adjacent to Columbia University along Broadway from 116th to 120th Streets, once the new academic year began in September, Mallory and Rupert saw relatively little of each other on Morningside Heights. Except for the rule that allowed seniors from both institutions to share library and lab privileges, the two campuses were independent entities, and at Barnard, among the more straightlaced and hidebound members of the faculty, debates were ongoing as to whether the young lady students, should they happen to meet along the walkways young gentlemen students that they knew socially or were related to, would be best advised to either stop and greet them and be considered bold and fast by strangers, or else to avert their eyes, ignore any greetings, and run the risk of being thought rude.

As far as Mallory and her friends were concerned, it was far more fun to be considered bold and fast, and they always stopped to say hello to those Columbia students they knew. Not to look at them, they decided, was worse than rude—it was boring, and that, as every right-thinking woman knew, was a sin.

Nonetheless, except for the occasional brief encounter along the paths, Mallory often reflected that she and Rupert could be attending schools separated by several state lines instead of by one street. Sometimes, seeing him at parties on Friday and Saturday nights, or at informal Sunday night gatherings, was her reminder that they were in the same city.

Fortunately, it was a situation that caused her more

amusement than annoyance, and as for Rupert's opinion— Well, Mallory supposed he was far too busy to think that much about it. In the entire sophomore class at both institutions, she didn't know of one student with a heavier load of classes.

Not that I'm precisely playing here, Mallory reminded herself as she walked through Barnard's gates on a bright Fall afternoon, the first Friday in November, six days after her birthday dance. No ladylike courses and easy C-average for you. Let's see, there's General Chemistry II with two classes and one lab a week and General Physics with two classes and one recitation period a week and . . .

She had finished reviewing her classes and was halfway to the Ninth Avenue Elevated station at 116th Street when she saw Rupert on the other side of Broadway, obviously heading for the same place she was.

Unlike Rupert, Mallory rarely rode on the city's mass public transportation system. It was not out of any sort of snobbery, but rather out of location. Living on Madison Avenue and Sixty-first Street meant that the nice, straight, rather quick five-stop trip that Rupert had wasn't possible for her. But today was different. On Fridays her last class was over at one, leaving her free until ten the following Monday morning, but this afternoon she had stopped to speak with one of her professors, and now she was on her way downtown to see Alix. The last person she'd expected to see was Rupert, and she couldn't help but wonder if he were cutting his last class of the day.

On the other side of the street, Rupert was somewhat ahead of her, but since he had to wait for the traffic to halt so that he could cross Broadway, they reached the foot of the massive iron and steel staircase that led up to the elevated platform at almost the same moment, his face breaking into a bright smile when he saw her.

"Isn't this rather late on a Friday for you?" he

questioned teasingly. It was nearly one-thirty.

"And aren't you a tad early?" Mallory returned as they began to climb the stairs. "Have you acquired the American university trick of class cutting?"

"I wouldn't dare. No, my calculus class was cancelled this afternoon. Professor Albright has a family emergency and had to go out of town. With any luck, Monday's class will go by the wayside as well."

Mallory suppressed a smile. Through the grapevine she knew that Rupert was near the top of every one of his classes—except for calculus, where Professor Albright was living up to his reputation as a stern taskmaster. Of course, if he wanted to tell her the absolute honest truth, she reflected as they reached the top of the stairs, entered the station house, deposited their nickels in the turnstiles and proceeded out to the platform, he'd tell her that despite the fact he was doing well, it was by an awful lot of hard work, and he wasn't "breezing through" at all.

Oh, good, Mallory, she told herself wryly. What other wonderful fantasies are you going to come up with? How Rupert's doing is *his* business.

"Is this how you usually travel back and forth?" Rupert inquired as they waited for the train.

"Not at all, usually. When I started at Barnard last year, Cooper—that's our coachman—drove me up in the brougham, but right now he's busy taking driving lessons so he can operate the new Model K Packard Uncle Newton just bought, so every morning I take a hansom cab up to college and then back down again in the afternoon."

"But today? Dare I hope we're both standing on this somewhat windy platform because you wanted to see me alone?"

Mallory put her hand on her hat brim as a brisk early November breeze blew along the length of the platform. "Please, I don't want to be held responsible for your

75

flattering yourself to such an extent," she said, inwardly admitting that if she hadn't seen him when she did she'd have probably taken a cab. "I'm on my way to see Alix."

As she finished speaking, the floorboards under their feet began to vibrate, then rumble, and a few moments later the loud rushing sound of the train entering the station filled their ears.

"Did you have a good time last Saturday night?" Mallory asked as they entered one of the cars and sat down on wicker seats that ran along both sides of the car, making sure that they were a safe distance from their fellow passengers. Morningside Heights was a center for education, medicine, and religion, and they didn't need an acquaintance from any of those institutions listening in on their conversation.

"It was a wonderful party," he told her sincerely. "And I was very pleased when the invitation read Saturday evening."

"Oh, you're not the only one who has to watch the clock Monday through Thursday nights," Mallory said. She was well aware that Rupert's curfew, unlike hers, was not voluntary, but she had no wish to embarrass him or injure his pride, so she tread as tactfully as she could around the matter. "Since my birthday fell on a Monday this year, I thought postponing the party until Saturday was a grand idea. That way, everyone could dance all night and not have to look at the clock—"

"No one did," Rupert chuckled.

"But when I told Uncle Newton and Aunt Esme I wanted my birthday dance six days after the actual date, I somehow forgot that that meant it would be Halloween! Do you know how many guests rang me up and wanted to know if I meant for them to wear costume?"

"That would have been a different sort of coming-out."

"*Please.* I *did not* have a coming-out, and I refuse to

76

think of myself as a debutante: some silly creature who doesn't do anything but live from one invitation to the next, and who spends her days having one fitting after another, and hardly ever reads a book and almost never opens a newspaper!" she told him fiercely. "When I graduated from Brearley last year, Aunt Esme and Uncle Newton said that I was ready to go to parties and all the rest provided I worked as hard as I could at Barnard. You see, in New York, once a girl is finished with school—and I skipped a couple of grades along the way—even if she's not quite seventeen, for all intents and purposes she's out."

"And ready for the mad social whirl with its ultimate goal for the newly fledged young lady?" he questioned with raised eyebrows.

"Don't patronize me," she warned him softly. "This isn't England, and I'm not some innocent, ignorant miss six months out of the schoolroom with a fourth-rate education and an eye on the main matrimonial chance."

Her eyes seemed to be shooting angry bits of green glass at him, and Rupert quickly backed away from his blasé pose. In England his experience had been gained with older, very sophisticated women whose jaded opinions he'd absorbed, while contemptuously dismissing seventeen- and eighteen-year-old girls as holding no interest whatsoever for him. But Mallory was a revelation to him. He thought she was sweet and intelligent and chic and definitely had a mind of her own, and at that moment, as the train roared into the 86th Street Station, he was very sorry he'd tried to mock her.

"Please forgive me," he said sincerely. "As you know, I'm famous—or is it notorious?—for saying and doing things without thinking. And if I did think, I generally went ahead and did it anyway."

"In other words, you're still learning that your new life has to be different," Mallory said, smiling at him, feeling her anger melt away, replaced by the same attraction that had passed between them on the loggia.

"Just about," he agreed, returning her smile, and they passed the remainder of the trip chatting companionably about the music from Victor Herbert's new show, *Babes In Toyland*; how funny the new Weber and Fields offering, *Whoop-De-Do* was; the anticipation surrounding the upcoming American debut of the magnificent Italian tenor, Enrico Caruso, who would sing the role of Il Duca in *Rigoletto* at the Metropolitan Opera on November 23rd; and the New York visit of the Earl and Countess of Saltlon, who had arrived six weeks before and would stay until the first week in December.

"Are you planning to go on to medical school?" Rupert asked unexpectedly a few minutes later as they descended the stairs from the station platform to the street.

"Right now, all I'm planning on is graduation in two-and-a-half years," Mallory said as they reached the last steps. "That decision can wait until then."

Together they walked along Columbus Avenue—the new name for Ninth Avenue—toward the 72nd Street corner. They were both well over average height, and Mallory—perfectly turned out for the warm autumn day in a navy serge suit trimmed in narrow black corded silk braid and a white silk blouse set off by a strand of good pearls and two gold bangle bracelets encircling her right wrist—and Rupert—in a dark gray Brooks Brothers suit that was a shade *too* new, with a blue crew-necked Shetland wool sweater over his shirt and tie—caught more than their share of attention as they crossed Columbus Avenue and started down the long block that would take them to the Dakota at the corner of Central Park West. As they covered the distance from the tenement-lined avenue to the luxury apartment building, every so often a passer-by would stop and look after them.

"We seem to be attracting a bit of attention," Rupert remarked, amused. "Does it bother you?"

"Of course not. I've been this tall since I was fifteen. By now I'm all adjusted." She gave Rupert a sidelong glance. "Funny how people never look twice at a tall man, or think he's anything too extraordinary. Naturally, though, they consider me an Amazon."

"Oh, you're not an Amazon to me. You're my Minerva—goddess of learning and healing," Rupert said as they reached the high-arched, lamp-flanked entrance of the Dakota.

Built in 1884 when Central Park still had farms and Central Park West—still known then as Eighth Avenue —was mostly empty lots and small buildings of no particular importance, the Upper West Side of Manhattan was so remote that taking an apartment in the newly completed building was tantamount to moving to the Dakota Territory. Even now, nearly twenty years later, with Central Park West an ever-increasing handsome expanse of townhouses, apartment buildings, and houses of worship, the Dakota, built on one of the highest points of land in New York, was still a clearly visible building. In fact, the yellowish-brown mass of stone which could not be laid to any particular style of architecture, was one of the city's most easily recognizable buildings.

For the next minute, Mallory was grateful for the short, tunnel-like length of passage that blocked out direct light. The last thing she wanted Rupert to see was the warm color flooding her face at his flirtatious compliment. There was no way she could blame the extra pink in her face on rouge!

The Dakota was built around a good-sized—although not particularly impressive-looking—courtyard dominated by a bronze fountain at its center, and each of the building's four corners held the entrance to the elevator lobbies; well-designed areas with wainscotted walls and handsome wrought iron staircases that wound their way up nine stories.

"You are coming to dinner at Alix and Henry's tonight, aren't you?" Mallory asked as they stepped into the carved wood cage of the Otis elevator, greeting the lift's female operator.

"Of course I am. How could I possibly refuse?"

"And I suppose you gave up some other intriguing adventure in order to accept?" Mallory inquired archly.

"Just the usual unmentionable undergraduate distractions. How could that measure up to being your partner tonight?"

"Well, I want you to know I'm very flattered. Of course there'll be other women at the table tonight who'll also be interested in sharing your company."

"Not all of them," Rupert replied with a wry smile. "Your cousin, for one. But to leave that aside . . . Twenty-four for dinner, if I heard correctly?"

"Yes . . . and Alix told me we're having quail with wild rice and something incredibly chocolate for dessert. She won't tell me what, though."

"Gateau Marjolaine, perhaps, or gateau de Nancy, or possibly even a chocolate velvet," Rupert mused aloud as the operator stopped the car on the fourth floor.

Here, the semi-private hallway—there were never more than two or three apartments to each section of the building—shared by the Thorpes and the Seligmans was paneled in a superbly grained mahogany rubbed to a fine finish, and the large, heavy wood doors boasted elaborately formed brass doorknobs. Set between the doors was a beautiful seventeenth-century console table of gilded limewood with a marble top, and a red and gold Portuguese needlepoint rug was laid over the marble floor.

"Oh, you're an absolute beast to mention desserts like

that when I haven't had lunch!" Mallory threw over her shoulder, laughing, as she walked ahead of him.

Quickly, she put her books and purse down on the table beside a highly polished copper bowl holding an arrangement of yellow asters and orange chrysanthemums and took off her hat so that she could check her appearance in the carved and gilded wood-framed mirror. "This has been *such* a day. I want Alix to help me with some chemistry problems, and since there's the dinner party tonight I had to have Rosie come over with the things I'll wear later. My darling cousin is going to give me a late lunch, and I'm famished!"

As she looked into the mirror, tucking pins back into her hair, she could see Rupert come to stand behind her and place his own books on the table, a new emotion revealed on his face.

"I'm famished, too," he said, placing his hands on her shoulders and turning her around, "and not for food. My dear Miss Kirk, I believe you owe me a kiss."

"Breezing through, are you?" Mallory challenged even as her heart seemed to turn over and then begin to beat in a very different way.

"You know the answer to that," he replied in an amused voice, and the next moment he pulled her close, his warm, sensual mouth brushing over hers in the lightest of kisses.

For a small moment they clung together, parted, and then looked at each other, amazed at what had just passed between them. There was a subtle change in the air around them, an inescapable crackle of electricity, and with one swift motion Rupert moved to back Mallory against the wall, his mouth pressing against hers in a very different way from before.

Mallory had been kissed before, but never like this. The others had been mere pecks on the cheek by comparison. Instantly she knew what it would have been like had she allowed Rupert to kiss her two months before. His firm, warm mouth closed over hers, gently at first, then with increasing pressure as he demanded that she give as well as receive. Her mouth opened under his pressure, and when she felt his tongue gently exploring the tender inside of her mouth it was as if the invisible electricity around them had finally touched her.

At their first touch, Mallory melted against Rupert, her arms around his shoulders while his arms closed possessively around her, his mouth by turns gentle and demanding, obviously savoring the experience.

From that moment on, all Mallory wanted to do was melt against Rupert's lean, muscular frame. Now he was kissing her forehead, her hair, her eyelids with a passionate gentleness, murmuring endearments she couldn't quite catch, and as she ran her hands over his thick black hair and caressed his neck, slipping her fingers under his shirt collar, she could feel the heat rising from his body and his desire mounting.

This, she knew instinctively as the hallway seemed to melt and spin around her, that this was the moment that every woman waits for and longs for and sometimes tragically never finds: to discover intellectual and emotional and physical communion with one special man.

This is where it all begins, she thought, joyfully pressing against him.

I want to be alone with Rupert. I want to hold him close and kiss him and touch him. I want for him to make love to me, and then, afterwards, I want to show him how very much I love him. I want to see Rupert without his clothes.

Each of these thoughts flashed through her mind as her senses reeled under his tender assault. Then Rupert's voice whispered in her ear and whether or not she wanted it, everything changed.

"Do you know what I want to do to you?" he whispered huskily, and Mallory's heart stood still for a moment.

Held close in his arms, her body molded against his, she would have been happy to dissolve against him in the first mindless joy she had ever known—until he spoke. She was on the very edge of ecstasy, but his voice brought her back to reality.

The cold facts invaded her mind. She'd been eighteen for less than two weeks, and there was so much ahead of her. To begin with, there was college to finish, and so much more besides that. The fact that in every society in the civilized world she was of a ripe age for matrimony had no bearing on the subject, she realized. This was *her* situation, her *life*, and that she and Rupert wanted each other was an indisputable fact—but love?

They had stopped kissing and caressing each other, but they continued to stand tight against each other, the right side of her face pressed against his, their ragged breathing matching. With belated clarity, Mallory recognized that they could be discovered at any moment, and if Rupert truly did want to make physical love to her, he would have to take her somewhere else. Up to the ninth floor, probably, that depressing rabbit warren of rooms where the maids employed by the Dakota had their dreary quarters, or, better yet, up to the empty twenty-room apartment on the sixth floor that Alix and Henry Thorpe had just leased.

But what if they did?

The consequences of a few hours of pleasure weighed against what others were expecting of them. If they were discovered here, now, like this, the worst that would happen to them would probably be an understanding lecture on the imprudence of their actions, but if they went ahead to some secret spot and made love—

Even if they weren't discovered, the emotional toll

that a secret tryst would take on her was too painful to contemplate. In a flash of comprehension, Mallory realized she was too young for this. Her sophistication was clothes and maquillage and conversation and a first-class intellect, but it didn't extend far enough to encompass this new experience—yet . . .

It wasn't fair, she thought rebelliously. Rupert's frustration might be more direct than hers, but he would be able to deal with it in a way acceptable to all men, and all he would have to part with was some cash.

I wonder if he'll pick a girl who looks like me, or a direct opposite? she speculated with a vicious dart of jealousy. She had no reason to expect physical fidelity from Rupert—and unless she gave in to her newly awakened desires she had no right to that sort of loyalty.

"I want you so much."

Rupert's voice sent warm shivers along Mallory's spine, but the conflict inside her still raged. Her heart and her body wanted one thing while her mind restrained her, reminding her not only of her responsibilities, but of his.

"I want you, too," Mallory said at last, and moved to kiss his cheek. Rupert smelled pleasantly of Guerlain's sandalwood soap and shirt starch and fresh air and an unmistakable masculine scent that kept her pulses racing and her newly awakened desire clamoring for satisfaction and made her decision all the harder. Taking a deep breath, she pulled back from his embrace. "But the answer is no."

He let her go instantly, his silver-gray eyes now darkened to resemble a storm at sea. Impulses suppressed for over a year were at the surface again, this time blending with a new tenderness and meaning. With unerring sensual instinct he had measured up Mallory's capacity for response that afternoon on the loggia and had wisely bided his time, waiting for the most appropriate moment. Now she was refusing him. Not with fear or distrust, but with a sort of reluctant calmness, her voice making it painfully obvious she could not be persuaded otherwise.

"It's just too soon," Mallory explained, her heart still pounding. "I've never had a man kiss me like this, and I don't think I'll ever want any man to kiss me the same way again except you—but not for a long time, Rupert, because the next time I won't be able to resist you. But right now we're just too young and the consequences are too great."

Half a dozen responses—all of them pure male logic—formed on his lips and died there. In all truth he had never meant for this to go so far. His plan had been for a brief interlude, but the intensity of their kisses and the feel of Mallory's soft body against his had led him to the next logical step. At that moment, as he stood looking at her, Rupert belatedly realized that Mallory had the ability to think for both of them, and that he had made a promise to William Seligman—a promise he'd made with all his heart. Breaking it now would be an open insult to the hospitality being given him.

"I'd never force you, Mallory," he said seriously, "and you're right, it is too soon. But you're better than champagne—"

Rupert took a step toward her, but Mallory was quicker, grabbing her books and purse and hat from the table and holding them in front of her like a shield.

"I know, I go to your head," she said, and laughed.

"I used to be rather original," he said, also smiling, "but now I seem to be rather out of practice."

"In case you missed it, I haven't been complaining," Mallory said, and then began to move backwards toward the Thorpes' door. "But you'd better go in now and we'll see each other again in a few hours at dinner."

Mallory waited while Rupert fished his key out of his

85

jacket pocket, inserted it in the lock, turned it, and opened the heavy wood door.

What would have happened if I said yes? she wondered, leaning back against the wall. Where would we be now? And what would it be like?

The questions paraded through her head, frustration burned through her body, and the knowledge that she had done the right thing was no comfort at all. The only small ray of hope that she could focus on was all that she had ahead of her. Not only school, but travel and parties and new plays to go to and new restaurants to eat in and lots of nice young men who would want to dance and talk and flirt with her. In the end it might still be Rupert, but she had plenty of time in which to make that decision.

Resolutely, Mallory pushed the buzzer and a moment later, Hodges, the Thorpes' butler, opened the door for her.

"Good afternoon, Miss Mallory," he intoned politely. "Her ladyship is waiting for you in the library."

"Thank you, Hodges. I hope I haven't kept my cousin waiting."

"Well, her ladyship was beginning to become a bit concerned."

"Friday afternoon traffic," she smiled, mentally noting how easy the implication that she had taken a hansom cab was when it was nothing more than an evasion, an excuse, and an outright lie.

Well, better this lie than the ones she'd have had to tell if she let her heart rule her head, Mallory temporized. She had been wise enough to know she needed time, and she mustn't ever speculate on what could have happened this afternoon and just take the experience as it came and wait for the proper moment.

For Mallory, as she walked from the entry hall dominated by a mahogany bombe chest with a Thomas Cole view of the Hudson River Valley hanging above it, to the library where Alix, writing out the placecards for that night's dinner, was waiting for her, the time to pass would be two years and nine months before she and Rupert would once again have to deal with the full force of the feelings in each other that they had awakened.

New York City, between the autumn of 1903 and the summer of 1906, made its first major claims on its quest to be the world's greatest city.

With the entire island of Manhattan coming under the realtor developers' savvy, the only direction to take was up—taller and taller office buildings, particularly in the financial district, earning them the sobriquet of sky-scraper—and out—in the fashion of more and bigger and increasingly luxurious apartment houses, opulent mansions to line the upper reaches of Fifth Avenue, and finely designed townhouses to fill the streets between Fifth and Madison and Park Avenues in the increasingly popular East Sixties and Seventies.

The most natural extension to this growth was the expansion of the city's restaurant and hotel industry. By the Christmas season of 1904, the St. Regis, Gotham, and Astor Hotels joined the ever-popular Waldorf-Astoria and Hoffman House, and a few years later by the Knickerbocker, the Savoy, and the Netherland, all well-thought-of holsteries—and finally, in 1907, by the glorious French-chateau influenced Plaza, the grandest of them all.

Restaurants seemed to bloom almost overnight in the city, the theatre seasons offered more and more variety, artists of international repute appeared on the stages of the Metropolitan Opera House and Carnegie Hall, and as the city gleamed like a brightly polished jewel, an entirely new social life grew up around those new diversions.

To be sure, the older and more status-conscious

members of New York society preferred to pretend that these new alternatives to entertainment didn't exist. But others, heartily bored with a steady diet of grand balls, stiff receptions, dull and overly large dinners, and stifling musicales, made their own fun and their own rules.

Mallory Kirk and Rupert Randall were part of this new social form, and unlike young people of previous generations who were rigidly chaperoned everywhere except on the dance floor during approved-of balls, they had an almost unheard-of amount of freedom with no sharp-eyed dragons looking at their every move, looking for the first sign of improper behavior.

In any case, Newton and Esme Phipps didn't believe in unnecessary social restraints, trusting Mallory's good judgment to be her own best supervision, and they fully approved of the way young people now went to the theatre or ballet or concerts and to a restaurant afterwards in a "gang"—a group of like-minded young couples which always included at least one couple from the "young married set."

This was the best way of all, Mallory frequently thought over the next two and a half years as she and Rupert alternately took their schoolwork very seriously and treated their fun in a very carefree manner. In the friendly groups they traveled in, she had all the advantage of being with Rupert, of having the all-important opportunities to get to know him, without having to find themselves in the precarious situation where their feelings threatened to overwhelm them.

Of course she saw him alone. New York City was made for courting couples. By quiet prearrangement they met on Saturday mornings on one of Central Park's many bridle paths, and if the weather was inclement, the vast Metropolitan Museum of Art was a grand place to walk and talk. And the summers at Cove House provided equal advantages for them. No matter how large the house party was, they could always find some time to be together with no one else around.

As she'd decided on that November afternoon, Mallory did not limit herself to Rupert, but no matter how attractive or well-spoken or intelligent or well-off her admirers were she always—in an emotional sense—came back to Rupert.

Instinctively she knew that Rupert—who was equally sought after by any number of girls—was reaching the same conclusion she was and no matter how blasé she tried to be about it, there was no way to suppress the delight that he still wanted *her* and not anyone else.

Despite the natural feminine regret she'd felt at having to halt their tryst before it ever really began, Mallory had no interest in an early marriage. The three women she admired most had all taken their time, she reminded herself in the early spring of 1906, with her Barnard graduation fast approaching. Alix had married at twenty-seven, Thea less than two months before her twenty-sixth birthday, and Esme had taken the plunge when she was twenty-one—a rather advanced age for an eligible young woman in the New York of the 1880s.

As her college graduation approached, Mallory had scrapbooks filled with theatre programs and dance cards and menu cards—all proof of the popularity she enjoyed and the fun she had, and all of which wouldn't have been possible had their actions on that afternoon forced a hasty marriage.

True, she probably would have gone to after-theatre suppers at the Café des Beaux Arts and twirled spaghetti at Roversi's and eaten steak in the warm and clubby atmosphere of Browne's Shop House and gone to parties in the opulent private dining rooms at the Café Martin as well as dined in the sumptuous French decor of the restaurant's public dining room, but this way it was all lagniappe. She didn't have to worry about pleasing a particular man. She hadn't given up her freedom to learn and grow on her own for the dubious honor of being a young man's child bride. Whatever else happened to her after graduation, Mallory felt, she was on the road to being her own woman.

Located in the corner of one wing on the third floor of Cove House was the rarely occupied state suite. Designed by the house's architect as a self-enclosed apartment comprising a large formal sitting room, small study, and five bedrooms each with its own dressing room and bathroom, as well as conveniently situated servants' rooms, it nonetheless wasn't particularly popular. Despite the opulent furnishings, despite the sweeping view finishing in an endless view of the Long Island Sound, and despite the well-placed dumbwaiter so that breakfast arrived still warm from the kitchen, it was simply too far removed from the pulse of Cove House which, like it or not, was centered on the first and second floors. True, the nursery was on the third floor, but it was on the other side of the house, so its occupants were not to be heard by those important personages, and the remainder of the single bedrooms were likely to be assigned to the bachelor guests who regarded their rooms as places to sleep and change clothes.

So the architect's dream of a state apartment remained—much to the amusement of the Seligmans and their friends—something of a white elephant, but the visit of the President of the United States made certain demands on a host and the mostly unused rooms became a center of activity.

Like the great English country houses whose owners are always prepared for a visit from their monarch, Cove House numbered among the impressive houses along the length and breadth of the United States who were eager to welcome the popular Chief Executive and his family as their guests.

Thus, in the last week of July 1906, en route from Washington to Sagamore Hill, Theodore and Edith Roosevelt, their daughter Ethel, and their next-to-youngest son Archie, stayed for nine days, suffusing the apartment's somewhat isolated splendor with a new life and energy.

The secret service men who accompanied the First Family politely blended into the woodwork, the members of the press who converged on the house for a conference with the President followed by a buffet lunch set up in a special tent on the lawn were amazingly well behaved, and all in all the visit was a rousing success.

But, inevitably, when they left, a hole seemed to be created. The Roosevelt personality was such a pronounced one that even the normally carefree household seemed quiet by comparison, Mallory decided as she lounged in the oak paneled library reading *The Marathon Mystery*, a whodunit she'd been too busy to read when it had been published two years before.

And now I have all the time I want, she thought, stretching luxuriously on the leather chesterfield and looking up at the elaborate carved plaster ceiling. No more classes or labs or term papers or any of the rest of it—unless I decide to go on to medical school, of course.

Sighing, Mallory closed her book, put it aside, and stood up. It was the middle of August, and although she'd been accepted to Bellevue Hospital's Medical School for the new term beginning the next month, she hadn't indicated to anyone as to whether or not she'd be attending.

Restlessly, she wandered over to one of the broad windows that faced out over part of the wide, sweeping, perfectly manicured green lawn. There were at least thirty adults in residence, and numerous servants, yet

Mallory had the distinct feeling she was all but alone in the eighty-five room house. On a perfect summer day like this everyone was either down at the beach or riding the bridle paths or getting up a baseball game or playing tennis or squash or else had motored over to the Garden City Golf Club for an afternoon on the links.

But, of course, you're snug indoors. Smart girl, Mallory, she chided herself, thoroughly aware that her unresolved predicament was the reason she was avoiding those she knew. Right now, all of her friends seemed like an ambush party, coming at her with questions she didn't want to answer—and not all of them were about her acceptance at medical school.

Well, now, what to do, she thought, sitting on the window seat. Medical school or not? And if not that, then what else? Marriage? Well, remember you have to be asked for that.

Mallory ran a list of pros and cons through her mind. She could do medical school easily enough. Her college grades were a clear indication of that, and the prejudice against women as physicians was nowhere near as strong as it had been ten years before when Alix literally had to buy her way into Physicians and Surgeons.

Alix. In a way, it all came down to her cousin. She admired Alix so tremendously that when she'd registered for classes at Barnard there wasn't any question that her studies would center on the sciences. But Alix had been driven by very personal demons: the horrific, tragic deaths of her parents. She had gone to medical school to keep occupied and in doing so discovered her scientific abilities and clinical turn of mind.

But that wasn't her own case, Mallory acknowledged. And becoming a doctor out of admiration for another was no reason at all, as Alix could have told her. But she hadn't, trusting her cousin's common sense to eventually set things right.

Still, she wouldn't eliminate medical school altogether, Mallory decided. Her degree in chemistry, even without any further advance study, might be good for something—a research position, possibly.

It was inconceivable to Mallory that she might do nothing and just live, as she had said to Rupert, "from fitting to luncheon to new invitation." How revolting not to contribute something, even if it was only a volunteer committee.

Turning over all the possibilities open to her, Mallory left the library and returned to the long marble entry hall that ran the length of the house, and began to mount the massive marble staircase that swept up to the second floor and was the first sight visitors saw as they entered. She was halfway along the corridor leading to her room when she stopped, a delightful thought forming.

The Roosevelts had left, and what better time was there than now to go up to the state suite? She would sit down at the writing table in the study and make a list of her choices. It was possible that the air of decision-making that so marked the President had left a faint trace behind that would be of help to her.

In the south corridor the Lalique glass French doors that led to the entrance of the state suite could be closed, effectively separating the apartment from the rest of the third floor—a fact that had pleased the security-conscious secret service men even if they failed to admire the beauty of the glass and didn't properly appreciate the Gustave Courbet oil of a riverbank near Charente that hung on the wall outside the doors.

With great care Mallory closed the French doors behind her and paused for a moment in the minute-sized alcove decorated with a Louis XV loveseat upholstered in dove gray velvet, and a small mirror framed in blue and gold enamel hanging above a miniature console table of inlaid bois de rose. With a flash of amusement at her vanity, she ran her hands over her hair, and smoothed down a few folds of her short-sleeved, low-necked white handkerchief linen summer dress. After all, she reasoned, she had to look worthy of the suite she was about to enter.

Every room in Cove House was a tribute to fine furniture making and fabric and rug weaving, but in the summer it was without a doubt a house that was *lived* in, a residence where people ate and talked and danced and generally enjoyed themselves, but stepping into the state suite was like paying a visit to a museum dedicated to the art of Fine French Furniture.

All was silent in the sitting room, and Mallory's footsteps were muffled by the cream and rose and gold Aubusson rug laid over the parquet floor. Here the walls with their delicate plaster moldings were painted a soft, creamy white. White brocade curtains lined the windows, a small Baccarat chandelier hung from the center of the finely molded ceiling, and the furniture was a fine mingling of Empire bergeres upholstered in ivory and blue satin and Louis XV sofas covered in pastel and white brocades, and the small decorative tables of tulipwood and giltwood, some of them signed.

Being in this suite gave Mallory a delicious sense of privacy. Here was a wonderful place that—at least right now—no one was going to come in to. Everything here was momentarily hers. A secret palace within a palace, and she twirled around the formal sitting room, investigating each piece of furniture as if she'd never seen them before.

Next she went into the study, big enough only for an inlaid ebony writing table and a pair of Louis XV-style wing chairs upholstered in a floral brocade, stopping only long enough to run her hands over the fine calf-bound volumes that filled the shelves lining the walls before going on to the bedrooms.

She visited the smallest first, the one that boasted a Recamier bed painted old blue and lined with green and gold and covered in yellow satin and filet lace and whose soft cream lacquered walls gave the impression of being in a jewel box. Next was the master chamber, a large, square room with finely molded plaster walls and ceiling and Louis XVI furniture, the magnificent bed covered in a lace spread intricately patterned in point applique, and the fauteuils upholstered in fine tapestries.

This was a room that could have been lifted from a fine Parisian *hotel particulier* on the Avenue Dubois, and Mallory felt she could imagine anything here, and her active mind was spinning out fantasies when she turned the ornate handle on one side of the double door and walked straight into reality in the person of Rupert Randall.

"If this door opened out instead of in, I'd have a nice black eye right now," he said teasingly, and the next moment they were in each other's arms.

"I'd almost forgotten how nice it is, kissing you like this, not having to take into account that someone else might be nearby," Mallory said an endless minute later, her voice more than a little breathless, her heart beating very differently as they drew apart.

Rupert reluctantly removed his hands from her waist. "I agree, we haven't had too much time alone together lately."

"Oh, I seem to recall a few interludes here and there over the past few months." Mallory's voice was amused. "Wasn't it just a few weeks ago that we just 'happened' to run into each other in Macy's and you took me to tea at Maillard's? Lucky for us that it was filled with tourists who didn't have the least idea of who we are."

"There are times I'm ever grateful for long, hot summer days where nearly everyone we know is out of town. But I didn't get to kiss you then."

"Is that why you followed me up here?"

"I most certainly did not follow you." Rupert sounded injured. "The President just rang up, and he seems to think that he left a pair of eyeglasses behind. I promised him I'd have a look around," Rupert said, gracefully stepping around her into the room. Mallory watched as he went over to one of the little painted wood Louis XVI bedside table, checked the drawers, came up empty-handed, and went around the bed to check the other table. A moment later he triumphantly held up a black leather spectacle case.

From her place by the door, Mallory applauded. "A first-class effort," she told him, laughing. "What do you do now?"

"Ring back Sagamore Hill. I expect the President will send a messenger over for it tomorrow."

Rupert put the case in the pocket of his white duck trousers and recrossed the room. With only one half of the double doors open and Mallory standing on the threshold it was almost too narrow for him to pass through. With a skillful step he turned sideways so they were facing each other, once again only inches apart, their gazes locking into each other's.

For over two years Mallory had made sure that there was enough space—both physical and emotional—between them so that, while she couldn't and didn't control the way her imagination ran, there was no chance of what had occurred in the hallway of the Dakota happening again. Even the kisses that they shared since that afternoon were marked with a sort of caution on her part and remarkable restraint on his, but now, as they stood facing each other, they both knew without saying a word that the last safeguard had been removed and the moment they had so carefully postponed had finally arrived.

Rupert was wearing an old, soft white shirt that was

open at his neck and the sleeves were rolled up above his elbows, white duck trousers, and tennis shoes, and as she took in his attire, Mallory thought that even in those casual summer clothes Rupert managed to carry off the same sort of elegance he projected in his more formal clothes. An air of inexhaustible energy seemed to crackle around him, and as she reached up to brush back the thick black hair that had tumbled over his tanned forehead, Mallory knew that more than anything else she wanted to keep on touching Rupert, to kiss him and love him—

"Whenever I'm around you I feel like dry straw waiting for the inevitable carelessly tossed match," Rupert said in a hushed, emotional voice. "Thank you, Mallie, for not being a careless girl."

Never before had Mallory known so many different feelings sweep over her at once. Her eyes misted over at the sound of Rupert's voice and the compliment he was paying her, but her body was growing warm with the desire that for too long she'd pushed aside.

"Suddenly I feel very reckless," Mallory said, letting her fingers wander from his forehead to his cheekbones, tracing the planes of his face. "There's a time every woman has to know to take care, not to rush, but eventually—" She paused for a moment, watching his eyes darken and feeling her knees go weak in a very special way. "Eventually everything has to be different or else we really don't live."

"I love you," Rupert said, and Mallory felt her whole world change. "I've wanted to tell you for so long, but I couldn't find the right time or place—"

His well-bred voice, far less British in its intonation than it had been when they met, sent shivers down her spine, and as if by some silent signal only lovers could understand they melted into each other's arms, sharing a kiss that Mallory wanted never to end.

In that moment they crossed over some invisible border together, breaking through the last barrier, and from now on the course to chart, the pattern to live by, was theirs alone to create.

"I want to make love to you," Rupert said against her hair.

Every bit of good, sound, logical sense that Mallory had always depended on disappeared under the pressure of Rupert's mouth, the touch of his hands, and the feel of his body. Only one thought surfaced in her mind.

"*Je suis une vierge*," she said, realizing that French seemed to be a very appropriate language at the moment.

"*Je comprends*. If this wasn't the right moment for us—"

"Is that why you've been side-stepping me for the past few days?" Mallory rested her head against his shoulder.

"It's dangerous to be around you, and worse to try and face going on without you."

"I wanted us both to be sure," Mallory said, her heart beating rapidly, looking at Rupert to catch his every reaction.

"I was—two-and-a-half years ago."

"Plus a few months." She moved her hands up to the back of his neck to gently stroke the firm, cool flesh under his collar.

"Here?" His voice was husky.

Mallory thought quickly. "No—we can't. It wouldn't be right. It would be like making love in the Lincoln Bedroom at the White House—"

Her words triggered the sense of the absurd that they both shared, and in a moment they were laughing, thoroughly delighted with themselves, and with a single sweeping motion Rupert lifted Mallory into his arms.

"You're right," he said. "We need a room made for lovers, not one for a head of state."

As Rupert carried her across the sitting room Mallory

98

began to flutter her lashes in butterfly kisses on his face, and when he put her down and she saw the room he had selected her heart overflowed with love.

"My favorite room of all," she said as she saw the chamber that was just the right size, with paneled walls that were painted French gray and inset with decorative flower paintings. The windows were framed by curtains of flesh pink taffeta, and the furniture was highly polished fruitwood. The room itself carried a hushed, expectant air—a room for a man and a woman to be alone together in. "How did you know?"

"There must be something to mental telepathy after all. I knew this was the perfect place for you—for us."

His hands were at her shoulders, making gentle, caressing gestures, as if she were a delicate creature he did not want to startle, slowly bringing her closer and closer against him.

Just as Mallory began to dissolve against Rupert, wanting to melt into him and stay that way forever, a sliver of doubt raced through her mind. Was this right? Was this what she wanted? To go recklessly wherever he was leading her with no assurance whatsoever that this was for all time?

Yes, she thought as Rupert's mouth nibbled gently along the sensitive side of her neck. This would have been right the first time, but you were right to wait. But now you have the only man you want and he wants you. Act like the grown woman you are and not a silly girl—a girl who poses and teases but doesn't mean a word of what she says—

"I love you," she said at last, knowing instinctively that he had had to speak those words first, and then if there had been any chance of going back, of waiting, of taking another look at their relationship, their future, it evaporated in the super-charged atmosphere around them.

Swiftly, Rupert stepped away from her and moved to the bed to strip back the fragile-looking spread of Valenciennes lace over flesh-colored taffeta that covered the delicately carved bed which had a headboard of flesh-pink satin striped taffeta, to reveal flawless white sheets with finely scalloped edges.

He turned back to Mallory, and together they undressed each other, trading kisses and touches and whispered comments as new areas of their flesh were revealed. Everyone assumed they were someplace else, and they had all the time in the world in which to discover each other.

Finally, their clothes were scattered over the cream and pink and gold Aubusson carpet, and they faced each other in their nudity for the first time. Rupert had no modesty to speak of, and Mallory's pang of intense modesty faded the moment she saw the adoring look that came into her lover's eyes.

Mallory was innocent of nothing except the act of love itself, and as Rupert's hands went to her hair, taking out the pins, running his fingers through it, and burying his face in the shining mass that fell around her shoulders, she felt herself begin to tremble.

She was entering a new world of emotions and feelings and response, but it was all so natural, all exactly the way she dreamed it would be, and Rupert was so unself-conscious, so intent on pleasing her, on learning what she liked and wanted, that the deeper aspect of what they were to embark on failed to register with her.

As they discovered each other, any wide-reaching effect that their actions might have didn't matter to them. They were made to be each other's lover, and the fact that they were now irreparably changing their lives, that they could never be truly sundered from each other again never crossed their minds.

Mallory thought that no bed had ever been so

welcoming, and no sheets as soft as the ones she was lying on, and certainly no male body as perfect as Rupert's. With new appreciation she ran her fingertips up and down the long length of his spine and heard him groan in delight and press his mouth against hers in a kiss that left her gasping.

She arched against him as his hands made their journey from neck to hips, cupping her breasts with gentle hands, moving down over her curves, his fingers exploring her gently, intimately, until Mallory thought she would expire from the aching need growing inside her.

"Do you want me, Mallie?" he whispered thickly, his long, lean body pressing hers into the mattress. "Do you?"

Mallory felt herself absorbed into a swirling black vortex. Each new touch brought another wave of delicious sensation, each kiss was deeper than the one before and more possessive.

"I want you," Mallory heard herself say, her voice sounding as if it were coming from a long way off. "I— want you—so much."

He moved then, gently parting her thighs, and pressed his hard, throbbing maleness against her, entering her soft body slowly, gently, not wanting to frighten her at this last moment.

Mallory felt a flash of pain, and in the time it took her to sharply draw in her breath they were merged together. As she felt the building pressure inside her, Mallory pulled Rupert even closer to her, her arms tight around his shoulders, and as he moved against her for the first time, her body answered, moving beneath him, with him, not wanting to lose one precious moment of this experience.

On sheer female instinct alone, she knew they were going too quickly, but Rupert's urgency propelled him like a flash flood, and Mallory, her own body responding even beyond what she dreamed her capacity would be for this first time, followed his lead, giving herself to him utterly, and they cried out their shared joy at the same moment.

For a seemingly endless time they lay side by side, holding each other close, waiting for their ragged breathing to return to normal, and when Rupert broke the silence between them his voice was infinitely tender.

"If I still had my title, you would be my lady," he said, smoothing back her hair as her head rested on his chest. Somewhere in the past thirty-three months he had become an American citizen, thereby renouncing the rank of baronet that carried the title of Sir which he had inherited at his father's death. "Would you have liked to be my lady?"

Mallory's heart leapt into her throat. Was Rupert making a proposal of marriage or merely complimenting her? And what was the proper conversation after you'd made love for the first time?

"It isn't titles I care about, it's *you*," Mallory said with more than a touch of indignation, sitting up and tucking the sheet around her. "If you were still Sir Rupert Randall, well, that would simply be part of the territory, but it's never affected how I think about you. Is that what you've been thinking about me?"

"Never, not for a single moment," Rupert said tenderly, sitting up beside her, his portion of the sheet falling to his narrow hips as he took Mallory into his arms. "I've never loved any woman the way I have you."

"Even now?" Mallory questioned. The love and comfort offered by his embrace made her want to forget everything except them, but the need to have an answer pressed at her. "Even after the last hour? I know most men prefer virgins, but I have an idea that that exists mostly in theory, while the actual fact is quite, quite different," she finished in a voice more bitter than she intended.

"What a clod you must think I am," Rupert said instantly, contritely. "You're a beautiful, wonderful girl and I probably don't deserve you, and if I had any brains, any consideration, at all I would have waited, but—"

"But it all just happened, and I wouldn't have wanted it any other way. We made this decision together," Mallory told him, her heart lifting with joy as his arms tightened around her.

They slid back down under the covers, their seriousness not lasting any longer than it took for their limbs to entwine. They were still getting used to the sight and feel of each other, and at that moment any responsible, adult discussion didn't seem terribly important and could certainly wait until after they finished finding out what a wonderful tangle two tall people made and how delightful it was not to have anything between them and the concentration it took to discover each other's most sensitive spots.

"Whatever are we going to do about this bed?" Mallory inquired in mock consternation as Rupert ran his fingertips along her collarbone.

"I was just assuming we'd stay here for a while."

"That isn't what I mean, and you know it," Mallory laughed, inwardly wondering if there was some way they could persuade the Seligmans to give them this bed for a wedding present. "We can't leave it behind looking like this. One of the maids will come in and—"

"I see what you mean. But I have an idea that we're not the first—and won't be the last—couple who've made use of this suite for romantic purposes."

"Well, if that's the case, you should have thought to lock the door," she said tartly, pressing her lips against Rupert's shoulder. "We don't want our privacy invaded by another enraptured duo."

"That might be rather off-putting," Rupert admitted with a considering smile. "But, of course, it would be the other couple's loss since we wouldn't be going anywhere."

"This conversation still isn't solving our problem, though."

"Well, there are men and women who smoke cigarettes after they make love, and others who sip champagne, but we're going to remake our bed. There's a linen closet in the suite, and I'll put the sheets we . . . made use of into the laundry chute afterwards."

Mallory managed to look delighted and skeptical at the same time. "Rupert, do you know how to make a bed?"

"During my year of residence I was taught what's generally called household skills. I can manage if you can," he replied easily, suddenly very intent on tracing a rather baroque pattern across Mallory's breasts.

"If you keep on doing that we won't get to the fresh linens for a very long time," she warned in a dreamy voice, closing her eyes as she drew Rupert's head down to hers. "But we have time, don't we?"

"Ages," he said, gathering Mallory closer to him. "And now that we've taken care of certain future necessities, we can concentrate solely on each other."

Hours later, with all of Cove House ablaze with light, and that night's summer ball in its last hour of festivities, Rupert Randall, thoroughly dashing in his flawless full-dress suit, grandly waltzed Mallory Kirk through a set of French doors, and across the loggia, her Lucile ball gown of white mousseline de soie and white lace embroidered in gold and silver swirling around them as though it were made of fairy stuff, before coming to a stop at the low stone balustrade that separated the terrace from the rose garden.

From their secluded spot they could faintly hear the music coming from the crystal and gold ballroom that they'd just left. A cool breeze from Long Island Sound wafted over them, and Mallory leaned against Rupert, slipping her arms around his waist and resting her head against his shoulder.

At that moment she felt as bright and blazingly happy as the lights that shone through the mansion. It was only after midnight and yet the events of the afternoon seemed to have taken place ages ago. Only the new tenderness within her body and the memory of their lovemaking reminded Mallory that she hadn't dreamed up the ecstasy they'd shared.

They had made love twice more, both times slower, wanting to prolong every moment as long as possible, until time had made its undeniable demand on them and they had reluctantly left their secret bower. With considerable regret it had been decided that there was no opportunity to bathe together in the bathroom's pink marble tub, and once they were dressed again they found fresh linens in the closet, stripped the bed, and remade it to the best of their ability.

Exercising great care, Rupert had made her leave the suite first, and now, hours later, she smiled, remembering the final act of their stolen hours.

"Somehow I don't think either of us will ever qualify for domestic service," she said softly. "Why doesn't someone invent a sheet that doesn't require all that folding and tucking? Speaking of which, did you make it to the laundry chute without any trouble?"

Rupert's hands were resting lightly on her shoulders. "No one saw me, and since the sheets provided for the state suite are the same as those for the rest of the house, we're not likely to be found out."

With those quiet, matter-of-fact words, the bright burning flame inside Mallory seemed to flicker down a bit, and an automatic warning signal rippled through her.

Naturally she hadn't been expecting Rupert to sweep her into his arms in front of the assembled guests and announce to one and all that she was the woman he loved and was going to marry. That was fine for fantasies, but when it came to reality Mallory knew that Rupert, like most men, could be oddly sensitive about the strangest things, things that wouldn't upset a woman at all—such as publicly displaying their newly found love!

Again an instinctive warning sent a faint chill through her. This afternoon, when she and Rupert had parted, he had been tender and ardent, but since they had come downstairs for the evening he had been polite, but distant—not the manner of a lover at all.

"You must be so tired," Mallory said in a soothing voice, a part of her mind wondering if she were beginning to grasp at straws. "We can always talk in the morning and make our plans then."

Rupert took a step backward and regarded her out of half-closed lids. "Do we have any plans to make?" he asked with deliberate blandness. "I thought our little . . . episode this afternoon was like the suite we were in— self-enclosed."

In the five seconds following his words, Mallory felt her heart plunge down to her stomach, and when it rose up again it had turned to ice. The idea of mentioning the word *marriage* to Rupert was repugnant to her, he knew that, and Mallory realized she was right and proper caught in her own trap made of good manners. Anger and confusion dropped over her like a suffocating cloak.

"You might have told me that in the beginning," she said, amazed at the calmness in her voice, but determined to be as cool as he was.

"True, I might have. I probably should have. But in the end the result might not have been the same—or as pleasurable." He gave her a narrow smile. "I've wanted you in my bed for a long time, Mallory."

She refused to flinch before his words. "I wonder why men think that that line is such a great compliment. Are you inferring that if I hadn't been just as willing as you were, you might have used, shall we say, *other means* on me this afternoon?"

Mallory was operating on her nerves, and she was pleased to see that her blind shot hit home. At least he still has the grace to be embarrassed, she thought, seeing the look on Rupert's face.

"Would you have?" she pressed, wanting to hurt him as he was hurting her, but when he answered his voice was as satisfied—and as detached—as before.

"No, I knew my charms were sufficient enough so that I didn't even have to consider anything as ugly as force."

Well, that's one for your side, Mallory thought, wishing she could just turn around and walk back into the house, but she couldn't get her legs to move. A small kernel of hurt had formed inside of her and was growing with each passing second.

"Was I really that easy?" she said, looking Rupert full in the face, forcing herself not to recoil at the sneer she saw form around his mouth and the contemptuous look grow in his eyes.

"In every way."

"I love you—and you said you loved me," she said, hating how the words came out, hating herself for saying them.

"Very old words used with great effect by men through the ages, so I can't claim any great invention on my part. Only the phrasing is changed to fit the situation," he said in a mocking tone.

"So this is what you used to be like before," she said scathingly. "Or is it just for me that you stripped off your polite, pleasant veneer?"

"Consider yourself fortunate, my dear Mallory.

Imagine what your life could have been like if I'd had any intention of marrying you." He raised one eyebrow. "That is what you thought I was going to do when I waltzed you out here, wasn't it? Tenderly put the question to you, then speak to your Uncle Newton, followed by an announcement which would have thrilled absolutely everyone. Dear, sweet Mallory and her reformed Rupert. Well, my darling, despite this afternoon—and you did live up to my every expectation— that pleasant scenario is simply not to be."

He reached out to touch her cheek, and Mallory recoiled as if he held a poisonous snake. Her own bright, shining world was laying in a shattered mass at her feet. As warm as the night was, Mallory felt ice cold, beyond tears, beyond pain, beyond any feeling at all except the awareness that she had been used by the man she loved and he was gloating over it.

Rupert lounged casually against the low stone ledge, his arms crossed on his chest.

"I won't tell, of course," he said, and suddenly Mallory's dormant temper flared.

"Well, I don't care if you do!" she shouted, and with both hands shoved strongly at his shoulders, pushing him backwards.

Had Rupert been standing normally, Mallory, as tall as she was, wouldn't have had too much of an effect. But his casual, mocking stance had him off balance. With both surprise and satisfaction, Mallory watched as Rupert, an amazed expression on his face, pitched backwards and tumbled head over heels over the stone ledge and landed squarely into one of the bramble rose bushes below.

Mallory's first reaction the next morning was that she had to leave Cove House at once. There was absolutely no way she could remain under the same roof with a man who had taken her love and then repudiated every word he had told her. Staying under the same roof with Rupert would be a clear-cut case of adding insult to injury.

This morning, following a night where sleep was intermittent and hardly refreshing, she had dressed for bravery in a Paquin model of white French muslin ornamented with a printed floral border piped in pale pink. Even though she'd left him deposited in the rose bush, she expected that Rupert was all right, and the only delight she felt now was malicious. If she was now in a precarious position, it was only fair that Rupert share in it by having to explain how he fell off the terrace. No doubt he was all right. Rupert would always end up on his feet, but if she wanted to keep face she had to make a temporary exit from Cove House.

She was mulling over her options as she descended the stairs, trying to determine which one was best for her, when she saw Sackett, the Seligmans' English butler, approaching the foot of the stairs, his normally reserved features relaxing when he saw her.

"Good morning, Miss Mallory. I was about to ask one of the maids to see if you were awake. There's a telephone call for you from Miss Nevins at Sea Crest. The library is not in use at the moment. You may take the call there if you wish."

Don't get too excited, Mallory warned herself as she thanked Sackett and turned in the direction of the library. Melinda's probably only calling to confirm your visit at the end of the month.

Melinda Nevins was Mallory's closest friend. Together they had gone through Brearley and Barnard, forming a pact based as much on their mutual height—Melinda was five feet seven-and-a-half inches—as much on the fact they really liked each other. Melinda's parents had a house further out on Long Island, at Southampton, but since Sea Crest was a mere thirty-five rooms, the guest list had to be carefully arranged so that everyone had enough room. Mallory had promised to come for the end of August, but as she picked up the receiver she held out little hope of Melinda's being of help. The Nevinses were extremely sociable, but unlike Cove House they couldn't absorb new guests at a moment's notice.

"Hello, Mellie, how are you?"

"Just fine, but I wish I could say the same for my cousin Cara—the one from Baltimore who was supposed to come up this week. She's had a bad fall—no, nothing serious, just a badly sprained ankle—but we're left with this hole in our guest list. Could you possibly come out today—"

Mallory only half-caught the rest of her friend's words. If she ever wanted proof positive that Heaven did indeed look out for fools, drunks, and women who gave their love to men who ended up by doing them wrong, she had it now.

"Please say you can come." Melinda's voice brought Mallory out of her reverie. "Or has something else happened. Has Rupert—"

A pain formed around Mallory's heart and her eyes stung. Here was where the explaining began.

"No, Mellie, I'm not engaged, if that's what you're asking."

"Well, then, what better reason to come and visit a bit early? We can see if there's anything to that old saw about absence making the heart grow fonder."

"Somehow I doubt that," Mallory replied, a small ray of hope nonetheless filtering through her gloom. "But I'll come early anyway. As soon as I speak with Aunt Esme and Adele, I'll ring you back and let you know which train . . . talk to you again in a little while . . ."

Mallory, who admittedly wasn't given to much prayer, nonetheless sent up a small word of thanks, not only as she hung up the phone, but a minute later when she entered the sun-filled breakfast room whose only occupants were Esme Phipps and Adele Seligman lingering over a second cup of café au lait.

Both women were sympathetic to Mallory, and insistent that she go ahead with her new plans.

"We'll have Sackett make your train reservation—I think there's one at noon—and as soon as you've finished breakfast I'll give you Moira and Jane to do your packing." She paused for a moment. "Will you be coming back here for Labor Day weekend?"

"I—I'm not sure, Adele," Mallory said uneasily, sipping at her coffee, and seeing her hostess and her godmother exchange significant looks.

"That was just a logistical question, dear," Adele said soothingly.

"It's perfectly all right if you want to go back to New York from Southampton," Esme added. "But if you're going to medical school—"

Mallory felt as if a heavy weight were pushing against her chest, and she eyed her café au lait and croissant with distaste. In the past twenty-four hours so many things that she'd taken for granted had been smashed, and the man who did the destroying—as men always seemed to be able to do—was going to walk off and leave her holding the bag.

Suppose Rupert tells everyone what happened between us yesterday afternoon? Mallory wondered. Normally, she knew, he wouldn't, but if his pride was injured—not to mention a few other things from his visit to the rose bush—he might just get some malicious joy out of telling about his conquest, and by the time he calmed down and thought about his actions it would all be too late. Her reputation would be ruined, and far from being regarded as a fellow who could charm any woman into his arms and bed, Rupert would end up being tarred with the same brush he smeared her with.

"I might as well tell you this right now," she said finally, decided there was one thing she had to settle. "I've decided against going to medical school."

"Are you certain, darling?" Esme questioned. "Is there a . . . particular reason?"

"Only that I'm tired of school. I don't want to sit in a lecture hall or do any more lab work. Don't worry, I'll do *something*, but medical school just isn't it. Are you very disappointed, Auntie, or is it very relieved?"

"Neither. I'm just proud and happy that you know your own mind and aren't about to go charging off without really having thought this decision through."

"Mallory, if you don't mind my asking, does Rupert fit into any of your future plans?" Adele asked quietly, and Mallory felt as if her heart were breaking. This breakfast, which could have been one of plans, was now one of evasions.

"I think that right now Rupert and I have agreed to disagree, but before we reached that conclusion we decided not to see each other again."

She watched as a look flashed over Adele's aristocratic features, but before she could try and read it, her usual gentle expression returned.

"I understand, dear," Adele said in a tone that implied young people had to be allowed to decide such things for themselves even if it was a shock and surprise to those who had been expecting to hear other much more pleasant news. "But this is a bit startling, not to mention rather sudden."

"But didn't—didn't Rupert tell you that it was finished between us?" Mallory inquired, genuinely surprised. She had been imagining Rupert rushing downstairs this morning all bright-eyed—and she hoped good and sore—to tell anyone who cared to listen that he wanted nothing more to do with her.

"He was gone before I got up this morning."

112

It was as if a bombshell had landed in the room and only she could see it, Mallory thought, not even trying to cover herself.

"Gone?"

"Yes. Bill told me that Rupert took rather a nasty spill last night, but apparently it hasn't stopped him. He said he'd had enough of Long Island for the time being and wanted a head start on his first project for the firm. There's always something hanging fire, so Bill said he was happy to oblige. Rupert left for New York over an hour ago."

The fact that Rupert had also left Cove House made no difference whatsoever to Mallory, and two hours later, changed into a Poiret princess gown of hydrangea-blue Chinese silk with a neckpiece of yellow guipure lace and trimmed with gold embroidered taffeta buttons, she kissed her godparents and her hosts good-bye and left for Woodbury Station and the train to Southampton.

The trip wasn't a long one, but Mallory knew she had to put as much distance as possible between herself and Rupert.

So he, too, had fled at the first opportunity, she thought over and over as the train covered the miles between the two stations. Not out of feelings of guilt or pain at his actions, she'd bet. Probably just fear of being found out, called on the carpet, and made to do "the right thing."

I'll never say a word about this, Mallory swore to herself over the next weeks as she was easily absorbed into the summer activities at Sea Crest. Like Cove House, Sea Crest was full of guests and fun and good food, and unlike the great establishments at Newport, no one worried overmuch about the face they were presenting to the social world.

It was inevitable that Rupert's name came up, but Mallory handled it as she had that first time at the breakfast table, reiterating that they had decided not to see each other again. No, not forever, just for a nice long time.

Several years earlier, before she was truly old enough to understand the meaning behind her cousin's words, Alix had told her that if you were going to tell a lie to cover your actions the trick was to make up one story and stick to it no matter what.

Now, some seven years later, Mallory knew exactly what her cousin—who was a prime example that not being particularly pure had nothing at all to do with one's future eligibility in marriage—had meant, and she followed this golden rule exactly.

And it worked.

"Oh, I'm *so* sorry," Melinda said sympathetically when Mallory finished her "agree to disagree" tale. "But there *are* plenty of other fish to catch," she said determinedly, running a hand through her chestnut hair. "Did you see Evan Prescott downstairs? He's terribly cute, and is coming to Brown Brothers next month after three years at First Philadelphia. I think he's getting interested in me, but if you want—"

"You'll be generous enough to toss him my way?" Mallory laughed for the first time in almost twenty-four hours. Both girls were enjoying a late tea in Melinda's small upstairs sitting room, all white wicker and pink and blue cushions, that separated their bedrooms. "No, thank you. If it's all the same, I'd rather toss my own line in the ocean and see what I can come up with."

"Don't worry, there'll be dozens of eligibles coming here for the next few weeks."

"And when we get back to New York—"

"Absolute heaven!"

"We'll have to go shopping," Mallory decided. "Lots

of new hats from Henri Bendel and Maison Bernard, and piles of shoes from Slater's and Carcion and Manfre and Cammeyer's—"

"And fur boas from Revillon."

"And the latest imports from Redfern and Thurn's and Giddings—"

The two friends passed the rest of the afternoon like that, and Mallory's healing began. She needed a new perspective, and her time at Sea Crest gave it to her. Her real pain at Rupert's betrayal of her might never totally fade, she accepted that, but there was no reason to remain like a motor car stuck on a muddy road. She had a life to get on with, fun to have and things to do, and the sooner she learned to cope the better.

Mallory kept to this philosophy, and little by little it worked. By the time she returned to New York with the Nevins family in the week following the long Labor Day weekend, she felt almost like her old self.

Almost.

It was silly and superstitious and she knew it, but not once in the remaining weeks of summer did Mallory wear again the extravagantly beautiful Lucile gown she'd put on for the first time the night she expected Rupert to propose. And the day before they returned to New York, she took the dress up to the attic, folded it in an old sheet, and buried it under a pile of ancient clothes no one ever wore in the most inaccessible trunk she could find.

In the next two months after she was once again at home at 667 Madison Avenue, Mallory found frequent occasion to reflect on how easy it was for her and Rupert to avoid each other. Word of their rift—although, naturally, not the reason behind it—spread quickly through their set, and friends planning out their theatre parties and opera nights and dinner dances made sure they were not on the same list. Outwardly at least there was very little gossip or speculation. True, everyone had been expecting an engagement to be announced, but it certainly wasn't the first time that a young man and woman had decided that the time had come to drift apart in a thoroughly civilized way, so the inevitable whispers soon died down as other meatier bits of gossip with longer-lasting potential came to light.

In fact, Mallory frequently thought, for all she heard about Rupert, he might not even be in New York. It was almost as if they were back at Barnard and Columbia, being in the same area yet not seeing each other except by accident. But this time if they ran into each other by accident, Mallory was sure the results wouldn't be the same as that November afternoon that now seemed so long ago.

Although the official New York social season began with the first night of the Horse Show at Madison Square Garden, iconoclastic New Yorkers began entertaining as soon as they knew enough of their friends had returned from their summer outings and a good-sized party could be put together.

As each day passed, Mallory found more and more invitations in her mail, but despite the endless round of activities she embarked on she was aware of the need to *do* something.

At first she luxuriated in the freedom from years of schooling. No more lecture halls to sit in and no more ten-pound textbooks to study and no more term papers to write. She had always enjoyed breakfast in bed, but now she could sleep late as well, and except for the two days each week she went with Alix down to the Henry Street Settlement to do volunteer work in the dispensary, she could spend her days exactly as she pleased.

For the first weeks it was fun, but now, at nearly the middle of November, it was all beginning to pall. Not that she wanted to go to medical school, *that* would have been a major mistake, almost on the par of the one she'd made on a beautiful summer afternoon with a man she thought loved her . . .

Enough of that, she told herself harshly. You've been doing so well, Mallory, don't ruin it now.

At first, a small part of her had hoped that Rupert would come back to her and say he hadn't meant any of the things he'd said, but as the days became weeks and the weeks had now become almost three months, and as she healed emotionally from Rupert's verbal assault, she gradually let go of that fantasy. In fact, at this very moment, she hadn't the slightest idea as to what Rupert was doing beyond the common knowledge—because it was announced in *The Wall Street Journal*—that he'd formally joined the Seligman investment firm.

It could have been bliss for us, she thought, but if he didn't want me I refuse to make it my fault. Let some other woman think she's getting a grand prize in him. Now I know better.

She leaned back against the dark green leather upholstery of Newton Phipps' newest Packard. Today had been another day spent in pleasant aimlessness. She had met Melinda at the Astor Library and had spent the morning viewing the major exhibition that was on, showing the plates of architectural designs by the brothers Robert and James Adam, some recent Japanese lithographs, and color plates of Russian ecclesiastical architecture. Then they proceeded to L.P. Hollander to view that store's latest Paris imports, and finally ended up with a late, long lunch at the Colony Club where Melinda's mother was a member.

And how much longer do I keep this up? she asked silently. It would be different if I were getting married, but I'm not. And just where am I? No medical school, no one all-important man, and nothing to keep me

117

really busy . . .

She was still turning her problem over in her mind when Cooper, the Phipps' driver, turned the Packard into the *porte cochère* entrance of 667 Madison Avenue, and it wasn't until she stepped out of the tonneau that she noticed a familiar Oldsmobile Touring Car parked just ahead.

The doorman saw her pleased look. "Mr. and Mrs. de Renille came home on this afternoon's *La Savoie*, Miss Kirk," the middle-aged man offered helpfully. "I can't ever recall seeing so much luggage at one time—thought we'd never get it all unloaded and sent upstairs."

"I can just imagine," Mallory said, feeling her spirits take an instinctive lift upwards. "That's what they get for leaving New York for all these months and making us miss them so—a ton of baggage that'll take ages to unpack!"

She was smiling happily when she went inside a few moments later, and after exchanging similar comments with the elevator operator, requested that he take her up to the seventh floor. Thea and Charles were home and she wanted to be among the first to see them again.

The moment she stepped out of the car and into the semi-private hallway, Mallory saw exactly what the building's employees meant. Mallory was used to a lot of luggage, but what she saw spread ahead of her could have done for a family of at least six, not a young couple traveling with their year-old child.

The de Renilles' front door, painted a shiny, bright lacquer black, was open, and as she stepped carefully over the threshold, sidestepping two solid-looking packing cases, she saw that a trail of Louis Vuitton trunks and suitcases, hatboxes and dressboxes bearing labels from the finest European salons, and additional packing cases marked with return addresses from noted antique dealers extended from the semi-private hallway, past the

118

door, into the small square hallway beyond, and then the reception room that opened off to the right.

There she found the de Renilles—Charles on his knees in front of an open trunk, searching through its contents, and Thea in front of the mirror framed in black and gold enamel, taking off her Talbot hat, a striking-looking creation of champagne-colored felt bound in pale tan velvet and set off by aigrettes.

"Welcome home!" she exclaimed, hugging them both. "We weren't expecting you until Christmas, or even after the first of the year. Why didn't you all write and let us know? We would have met you at the pier."

"With a brass band, probably," Thea laughed. "We felt that we made so much fuss getting off that it was only fair we come back quietly."

The de Renilles had left for Europe in mid-May with manifold reasons behind their trip. Most important of all, they wanted to show off their baby daughter Tatiana to Charles' family in France, then Thea was looking to buy antiques for her decorating firm, while Charles was searching for authors interested in having their works translated and published in the United States. They planned to stay until the hunting began in Normandy, and possibly through the Christmas holidays as well, returning to New York in January. Their friends had been bombarded by letters and picture postcards bearing postmarks from London and Normandy and Paris and Brussels and Vienna and Budapest and Florence, all exclaiming what a wonderful time they were having but giving no indication of when they expected to return.

"Well, this just goes to show that we can't stay away from New York for too long," Charles said, his topaz-colored eyes sparkling. "We saw all the sights we wanted, took care of our businesses, showed off our daughter, and decided that we really didn't want to be nomads any longer."

"A very wise decision," Mallory smiled. "And speaking of your daughter, where is Tatiana?"

Thea tossed her hat on the two-drawer beechwood bombe chest set beneath the mirror. "She's in the nursery, fast asleep. The quickest way to get through customs is to have an absolutely adorable baby that the inspectors fall in love with," Thea said proudly. "We hardly had to open a trunk."

"Not one of which Thea would subsequently allow to be brought up through the service entrance," Charles said, brushing back his thick, shiny black hair. Born to one of the oldest, most aristocratic horse-breeding families of France, and educated at Stonyhurst and All Souls College, Oxford, his English bore a British inflection somewhat refined after two years in New York, but still noticeable.

"That's how you lose luggage," Thea put in informatively. "Do you have any idea how often trunks and suitcases vanish between being taken off the break and brought up the service elevator?"

"If anyone from the building complains to me about how we monopolized the passenger elevator this afternoon, I'll tell them that," Charles said wryly, retrieving a brown paper-wrapped parcel from the open trunk he'd been searching through. "A manuscript I think has a great deal of promise. Mallory, if you and Thea will excuse me, I have to make a telephone call. I'll also put a bottle of champagne on ice, and call Sherry's and have them send dinner over to us. Care to join us, Mallie?"

"Oh, no, your first night back belongs to the both of you," she said definitely, taking off her Reboux hat of white moire bound with taupe-colored velvet with natural large quill feathers gracing the left side of the crown. She put it down on the reproduction Hepplewhite sofa covered in a striking black chintz splashed with pink peonies. "But I trust that the mention of champagne includes me?"

"We wouldn't have it any other way," Charles said, and as he went off in the direction of the bedrooms, Thea put an arm around Mallory's waist and both young women navigated around the endless pieces of black and white striped Louis Vuitton luggage and went into the forty-eight foot long drawing room/library.

While Mallory made herself comfortable on one of the deep-pillowed sofas that were covered in ice-blue silk, Thea moved expertly around the room, pulling open the blue silk curtains, opening a window, patting the Louis XV carved giltwood and marquetry gaming table as she passed it, and otherwise assuring her that she was home again, her Paquin dress of Delft-blue shadow velvet with a bolero border of Venetian point lace contrasting perfectly with the room's predominantly blue and cream tones.

A minute later, her tour completed, Thea sat down beside Mallory, and over the next half-hour filled her friend in on her European visit. She told Mallory about their stay in Normandy, both at the de Renille *haras* and at the Hostellerie de Guillaume le Conquerant, the justly famous country hotel with sublime cuisine, located between the resort cities of Trouville and Cabourg, where they had stayed for four days in early June. She sought out antiques and he visited a reclusive former Sorbonne professor and came away with a scholarly manuscript about Henri of Navarre which he planned to translate and hopefully find a New York publisher for.

Thea told Mallory about London where they had danced until dawn at lavish balls in great houses; about shopping in Paris with her mother-in-law and two sisters-in-law; about Brussels where Charles had taken her first to Le College Saint Michel where, for a few months at the end of 1901 and the beginning of 1902, he had taught English, then to the Compagnie des Indes where he bought her lace, and finally to the Art Nouveau designed masterpiece of the Baron Victor Horter, Wolfers Jewelry Store on the Rue d'Arenberg where he bought her jewelry—emeralds, he said, to match her eyes.

Vienna had been all charm and correctness, Thea related. They had eaten their way through the vast pastry selection at Demels, enjoyed the perfect luxury of the ornate Imperial Hotel, and had had several sittings with Fraulein d'Ora, that city's most fashionable photographer.

"Wait until you see them," Thea laughed. "In one, Charles and I look positively decadent. I'm threatening him to have it made into a Christmas card!"

"No one will be able to show it off, but you'll have some couples green with envy," Mallory smiled, her spirits rising higher than they'd been in weeks.

"Good." Thea patted her glossy brown hair. "Now, what have you been up to? No—don't explain, I heard all about you and Rupert. Alix and Adele and Esme have been keeping me posted."

For a moment Mallory played with the Valenciennes lace frills on the collar and cuffs of the deep ivory French batiste chemisette that set off her Lucile dress of parchment-colored broadcloth piped in taupe velvet before finally saying, "I didn't know that—that you've been getting regular reports on me."

"Oh, honey, not reports at all," Thea protested, "just information so that I didn't put my foot in it when I saw you again. Now, do you want to hear about the fabrics I bought in Budapest, or about the galleries of Florence, or would you rather tell me what you've been doing to keep busy?"

"Today, or since I came back to New York in September?"

"Let's start at the beginning. Do you like being free of Barnard?"

"I'm thrilled. I loved college, but those four years were a long time. Not as bad as if I'd been at Smith or Vassar or any of the others, but still— It's fun to do just what I want now, only . . ."

"Only it gets a little boring around the edges. Like today."

"Just like today," Mallory agreed, and related her morning's activities. "We also had lunch at the Colony Club," she added with a touch of trepidation, well aware that since the women's club had been decorated by Thea's arch rival, Elsie de Wolfe, she resolutely refused not only to join but to set foot inside 120 Madison Avenue.

"Oh?" Thea raised her eyebrows. "How was the food?"

"I've eaten worse. Do you mind my being there?"

"Why should I? Of course I'd like to have a full report on Elsie de Wolfe's decor—or should I say handiwork?— since I have no intention of ever going inside."

"On principle, of course." Mallory couldn't resist the jest.

"Of course," Thea replied, playing along. "I've reached the conclusion that clubwomen are rather like Germans—perfectly charming as long as they're alone, but don't let them get into a crowd unless you're looking for trouble!"

They were still laughing when one of Thea's maids came in carrying a silver tray with three tulip-shaped glasses and a bottle of Moet et Chandon 1902 resting in an ice bucket.

"Mr. de Renille said to tell you he's delayed on the telephone, madam," she said, placing the tray on the low inlaid table in front of the sofa. "He wants you and Miss Kirk to go ahead, and he'll join you for the second glass."

"Thank you, Janet," Thea said, and as the young maid left she spent a few silent seconds concentrating on

123

pouring out the champagne.

"What shall we drink to?" Mallory asked, accepting a glass.

For a moment Thea looked quietly pleased.

"What about the new baby Charles and I are going to have next year?"

"Oh, Thea!" Mallory hugged her friend. "It looks like you did more in Europe than just buy antiques!"

"Oh, I'm just blaming it on Demel's pastry!"

"I just bet. When?"

"The beginning of June, which is really the best timing on our part—delivering before the hot weather starts."

"So that's why you came home early."

"We could have stayed over as long as we'd originally planned. I'm as healthy as a horse, which, when you consider Charles' background, is quite a compliment. But we talked it over and decided that we'd done everything we wanted including getting some hunting in and attending the special Mass that's given on November third, St. Hubert's Day, in the Cathedral in Lisieux, and we knew it was time to come home."

They touched glasses and sipped their champagne.

"Since I'm never sick, I won't have much of a figure by February, and will really have to 'retire' by April," Thea continued a moment later, "and that means I'm going to have to find and train an assistant. It didn't matter the last time, but I have more business now—and more competition."

Mallory studied the contents of her glass, forcing herself not to think. This was a turning point, but there were no bells, no trumpets, no raising of voices, only her own intuitiveness telling her this could be turned to her advantage, be her answer, but she had to play it by ear.

"What would your assistant have to do?"

"First of all, work with me and watch what I do, then learn my clients; while I'm waiting for the baby to come

124

she has to follow through on any jobs that are pending. Later on, if all goes well, she'll be on the lookout for antiques and can attend all the auctions she likes," Thea added brightly. It was a well-known fact that Thea couldn't stand auctions and attended as few as possible.

"I can do all of that," Mallory said, looking directly at Thea, taking a deep breath so her rapidly pounding heart wouldn't choke her voice and give her away. "Would you trust me with your business?"

Thea gave her a secret smile. "I was only waiting for you to ask. But it's only a trial offer," she warned, holding up a hand. "We'll give it 'til the first of the year."

Mallory felt her heartbeat slow down to normal, and a feeling of *rightness* flooded her. "When shall we begin?"

"Right here, tomorrow morning about eleven. We can go over my purchases and I'll show you my client book and how to handle invoices." Thea studied her friend's face. "Mallory, are you *sure*?"

"As sure as I can be right now. Thea, I have to try something. Going to galleries, shopping, and having lunch at the Colony Club is fine once a week, but not every day."

"Well, you have taste and style, and I have an idea we can work well together, so interior decorating may be it for you."

"From earning a degee in chemistry and almost attending medical school to trying my hand at learning to be a decorator—that's hardly usual," Mallory mused in a bittersweet voice.

"It's probably better this way. Your mind isn't cluttered up by endless art history classes. There's nothing like science to keep you thinking straight."

"I guess we'll find out soon enough," Mallory said, flashing a bright smile. "I wish Charles would hurry up and finish his call so he can join us and help us toast our new—" She hesitated for a moment. "Enterprise?"

125

"Sounds fine to me. There's nothing like a brand new enterprise to make a woman forget an old love affair and make her ready for a new one. And since Rupert's left town—"

"Left New York?" Mallory interrupted. She silently cursed the ice-cold feeling that swept over her. Just when everything was looking so bright. But she had to know. "When?"

"Oh, I *knew* I'd put my foot in it!" Thea groaned. "Both Adele and Alix wrote us, so I was sure you knew. It seems that after the earthquake and fire last April, some of the Seligman people out there panicked and had to be transferred. The office is in shambles, clients aren't being dealt with, and something had to be done. No matter how you feel about Rupert personally, you should be rather proud of him in this. He's very young to be given such a great responsibility."

"He'll pull it off," Mallory said, wanting to be fair. "But what exactly is he doing?"

"You really *don't* have the slighest idea." Thea looked amazed. "Oh, well, I may as well be the first to tell you. William Seligman appointed Rupert acting head of the California office. He was sent to San Francisco—or what's left of it—six weeks ago."

Mallory's eyes fluttered open and she looked up at the ceiling of her shipboard bedroom, aware that at this moment she was happier than she'd been all summer. It was more than a good night's sleep, it was the certainty that she'd reached a decision and intended to follow through on it.

She stretched like a cat and luxuriated in the feel of the bed. Today was the last full day at sea, a day best spent in doing some preliminary packing and making sure her business receipts were in order to the customs inspectors.

Nearly four years of working for and with Thea had refined and deepened her own innate good taste and released a flow of creativity that complimented that of her friend and mentor and associate. Mallory threw herself into a world of furniture and fabrics, and by the time Thea took a rest from her business to wait out her pregnancy, she was familiar with clients and suppliers and billing, and was mastering the myriad of details involved in running a decorating firm. And by the middle of 1909, when Thea announced she and Charles were expecting their third child, Thea Harper: Antiques and Interiors was Thea Harper Associates.

As Thea had informed her, Mallory's busy days merged into very social evenings with no shortage of eligible men, and now, as she rested dreamily in bed with nothing more than the quiet pitch of the *Mauretania* to disturb her, she mentally ran down a list of all the men she knew, ranging from casual beaux to her seven proposals of marriage.

It's just like making a list of lovers, she thought, except that the only man who was my lover in the real meaning of the word was Rupert. I've never wanted another man in the same way, but once I've seen him again and set my life straight, I'll see what I can do about remedying that.

Mallory took her time getting out of bed and going into the bathroom to wash her face and brush her teeth and comb out her hair. That done, she rang for the stewardess.

"I'm ready for breakfast, Bess," she told the forty-ish Scottish-born woman in the neat Cunard uniform a short time later. "Strawberries and cream, please, and two croissants with butter and strawberry preserves."

"Right away, miss," she replied smiling. "I expect you

127

want to start some of your packing today?"

"That's right. No need to feel rushed tomorrow morning."

"That's a good way of thinking, miss. Get all the important things out of the way first."

Mallory leaned back against the pillows and smiled. "True, Bess, but I have the feeling that all the very important things I have to do will take place *after* I leave the *Mauretania*!"

You must make your own blunders, must cheerfully accept your own mistakes as part of the scheme of things. You must not allow yourself to be advised, cautioned, influenced, persuaded this way and that.

—Minnie Maddern Fiske

131 East 66th Street

Whenever Theodosia Harper de Renille was interviewed for articles in the popular women's magazines—which was often, considering her looks, her talent, and her natural conversational abilities—she always explained the reason she used her maiden name by saying, "Theodosia de Renille is the most romantic sounding name in the world, but Thea doesn't sound good with anything but Harper."

That sort of question always amused her, but on this sunny Friday morning, the first one in August, her current telephone conversation was anything but pleasurable.

"I understand completely, Mrs. Greer," she said in a voice that was coldly sweet. "You so love the beautiful job Elsie de Wolfe did with your friend Mrs. White's house that you want to know if I can do the exact same thing—excuse me, decor—for you."

Thea paused for a crucial half-second.

"My dear Mrs. Greer, since you're so enamored of Elsie de Wolfe, I suggest you call Irving House and hire *her!*"

She slammed the receiver back into the cradle. "Ooh,

that *infuriating* woman!" she shouted. "Of all the *nerve!*"

"Thea, is everything all right?"

"Fine, Amy," she told her secretary who appeared at the door. "It's a lucky thing for Mrs. Greer that she telephoned instead of coming here in person."

"Well, before you throw any other clients out the door, remember this building is a cooperative and they frown on that sort of thing," Amy Collier Banning remarked, smiling. She was a pretty young woman with light brown hair and sky blue eyes, wearing a smart summer dress of beige and black figured foulard. About the same age as Thea, she had been her secretary since late 1902. "But to move on to a happier topic . . . Mallory's coming in today, isn't she?"

"She should be here in a little while," Thea replied, her own smile deepening. "Nice to think that she had this lovely long summer in London. But until she comes, it's back to work for me."

"I'll tell anyone who calls that you're otherwise engaged," Amy said wisely, leaving.

But in spite of her good intentions, once she was alone again, Thea found it difficult to concentrate on her work, and with disdain, looked at the papers arranged neatly on the fifty-four-inch length of her Louis XV bureau plat of kingwood and marquetry with ormolu mounts.

"I think that you're just going to have to wait a while longer," she said softly, and stood up and walked across the off-white and powder blue and taupe Chinese carpet that covered the parquet floor to lean against the wall between the room's two windows that looked out on East 66th Street.

Just about three years earlier when she and Charles had purchased this cooperative duplex apartment in the brand-new eleven-story building, they reached the decision that they could manage very nicely without a music room and a billiard room, and had transformed those two connecting rooms into the offices of Thea Harper Associates.

She surveyed the room with a deep sense of satisfaction. The walls, like the walls of nearly every other room in the apartment, were lacquered a perfect shade of ivory-white, making a fine backdrop for the careful mix of furniture, some of it from her former office, some of it new, that she had put together.

The connecting door between her office and the one Mallory and Amy shared had been removed and replaced by an eight-panel Chinese screen of blue flowers on a yellow background, divided to form folding doors, and although the closets of both rooms were filled with bolts of cloth and carefully packed boxes of antique accessories, in her own office Thea confined herself to a single glass-fronted cabinet in which to show off her favorite pieces of blue and white Chinese porcelain. Over the small marble fireplace, Thea hung a mirror narrowly framed in red lacquer, and in front of the fireplace she arranged a black and gold stenciled Sheraton settee upholstered in taupe silk, a cane back Louis XV reproduction fauteuil with taupe silk seat and arms, and a pair of black and red lacquer trays set on black wrought iron legs, bought six years before in Mexico City on their honeymoon, making a nice setting for her to talk with clients over lunch or tea. One delicate, inlaid Sheraton table held a Limoges cache-pot filled with a lush arrangement of pale pink peonies, columbine, tulips, and statice, all made of silk and satin and velvet by Fromentin in Paris, another table was graced by a silver bowl filled with hybrid lilacs and tulips, real ones this time, and a bookcase built into one wall panel held books by famous collectors and catalogs from famous auction houses.

On the wall behind her desk, Thea displayed an India ink drawing of a Hungarian Vizula—the hunting dog of

Hungary's aristocracy—holding a basket of flowers in its mouth.

This was the symbol that appeared on her business card, and Thea never failed to smile when she looked at it. The trademark on Elsie de Wolfe's business card was a wolfhound with a flower in its paw, and there had been some catty whispers that Thea had stolen her rival's idea. But when anyone had the nerve to ask Thea, all she did was point to the lower right-hand corner of the drawing where the artist she had found in Budapest had not only signed his name but the date in June 1902 when he'd drawn it—a time when Elsie de Wolfe was on the last leg of her theatrical career.

Feeling somewhat calmer, Thea returned to her desk and began to look through her mail. For the time being, she put the newest catalogs from various dealers and auction houses aside in favor of her letters and spent the next fifteen minutes engrossed in a long letter written her by Mrs. Frank Mason, the wife of the American consul general to France, and President of the English-speaking "Cercle" of the Lyceum Club of Paris.

True to her word, Thea had still not darkened the doorway of Stanford White's edifice and Elsie de Wolfe's interior on Madison Avenue and Thirtieth Street, but the Lyceum Clubs were different. Located in London, Paris, Berlin, Florence, and Rome, each women's club was situated in a handsome building and offered members and visitors a pleasant spot for lunch or tea, a library and lounge to rest in between gallery visits and fittings at the dressmaker, well-appointed sleeping quarters, and a good restaurant. In Paris, Thea's mother-in-law Solange, the dowager Comtesse de Renille, was one of the club's titled patrons, and Janine, one of her two sisters-in-law, was an active member.

Since Paris has never been known for the warmth of its greeting to the woman traveler not on the arm of a man, the Lyceum Club was a welcome spot but, like so many other enterprises, their charming headquarters at 28 Rue de la Bienfaisance, which had been set up only two years before in 1908, was now too small.

In the fall they would be relocating to a fine *hotel* on the Rue de Penthievre, Mrs. Mason wrote, and she was contacting Thea on the advice of Solange, Comtesse de Renille. There were *so* many details involved in this move, and the comtesse had been generous enough to suggest that her American daughter-in-law, who was a noted New York decorator, might have some suggestions to make about the new decor—

Unlike many decorators, Thea had no compunction against giving a bit of free advice. First, because her fees ran so high many women hesitated asking her for fear of a bill arriving in the next day's mail that there were very few such requests, and because those who did pluck up their nerve and ask had a way of eventually becoming clients.

It wouldn't take long, Thea knew, to answer Mrs. Mason. She would make some suggestions, recommend several dealers whom she knew would enjoy dealing with the ladies of the Lyceum Club, and advise that she interview a painter who lived, literally, in a Left Bank garret, but who painted the most delightful flower panels, but at this moment she wasn't in the mood to draft a letter.

Thea kept a few photographs in simple silver frames on the wide expanse of her desk. Her children, five-year-old Tatiana, three-year-old Stephanie, and six-month-old Raymond were each lovingly studied in turn, and then she moved on to the fourth frame, a photograph of herself and Charles taken four years before.

It was a delightful remembrance, recalling that this picture was only one of a series of sittings they'd had in Vienna with Fraulein d'Ora. Nearly all of the photographs of Thea and Charles had been made in the photographer's studio, but this one had been taken in their hotel suite. The Imperial's furniture had been shifted around for the best effect, the Fraulein had set up her equipment, and she had then posed the de Renilles on an Empire sofa covered in white brocade that had been placed under one of the sitting room's broad windows.

At the last moment, just before the camera clicked, Thea had leaned back across Charles, his arms around her, their gazes deeply locked, and when the picture was developed, their smoldering sensuality seemed to burn off the print.

Thea had never gone through with her original plan to make the photograph into their Christmas card for 1906, and any magazine writer she offered it to as a possible illustration for an interview tended to ooh and aah and then reluctantly ask for something a little less, well, *provocative*. But Thea kept a print framed on her desk for all to see, and made sure Charles had one on his.

Feeling restless again, Thea rose and went over to one of the windows. How she loved this apartment, she thought. She had grown up at 36 Gramercy Park South, spent the first years of her married life in equal happiness at 667 Madison Avenue, but when she and Charles, like all good New Yorkers, discovered that they needed more space they had come to 131 East 66th Street as one of the building's first tenants.

At almost the same time the purchase papers were being drawn up, the management at 371 Fifth Avenue had changed, and not, to Thea's way of thinking, for the better. After a great deal of careful consideration she had broken the lease in the building that had been the center of her professional life since 1902, and moved her decorating firm into the new apartment.

She loved the apartment, and loved the two-room office suite she had carved out of it, but there was the indisputable fact that if something was bothering her, there was really no way to avoid difficulties.

Not that you have any pressing personal problems that need escaping from, she reminded herself. So far, this year is going to be very successful for you, one of your best, even if you haven't taken an out-of-town offer in over six years.

For several moments she dwelled on the lucrative decorating jobs that had come her way so far this year. There was the town-house on East Seventy-second Street, two apartments, a master suite, a drawing room of almost ballroom proportions, a doctor's office, and a photographer's studio numbered among her successes. And now there were two more jobs hanging over her, making her more uneasy than she'd been in eight years. One assignment was just hanging, and would, Thea guessed, remain that way for the next few months, and she was forcing herself not to think about it, but the other. . . . That would be decided one way or another this afternoon, and since it had gotten off to such a rocky start, Thea, who was superstitious about such things, was almost convinced that it would end with all concerned being very polite but no firm contract.

From her place by the window, Thea could see the green, peaceful garden of the Church of St. Vincent Ferrer, and in spite of her anxiety she began to laugh.

No matter what happens, Thea, you always seem to find yourself in the middle of the most delicious ironies, and this is certainly one of them, she told herself silently, her amusement momentarily calming her nerves. Here you are, practically living in the backyard of one of New York's most fashionable Catholic churches, and Charles decides that now is the time to become an Anglican!

Recognizing the fact that until Mallory arrived she was

too distracted to get any work done, Thea left her office and began to wander through the apartment's first floor, taking pride in all she surveyed.

There was something so right-feeling about seeing the home she and Charles created to live in, love in, raise their children in, and entertain in, and every room, every square inch of the large apartment was organized for the way they lived.

The small entry foyer was, by and large, a recreation of the reception room she had first designed at 667 Madison Avenue, and the very wide forty-five foot long hall, the doorway flanked by a pair of graceful porcelain-glazed whippets, off which the other rooms opened, had one wall mirrored, the other papered in heavy ecru parchment, and was sparsely but handsomely decorated with a Louis XV-style fauteuil and a French eighteenth-century bench. Both had cane backs and were upholstered in peach silk and set on the gleaming inlaid floor.

Her next step was the library where the walls were set with a fine bleached English oak paneling, their shelves filled with books, deep leather sofas and armchairs, and tables holding all the latest magazines.

In the dining room she smiled at the room's large French Directorie table that she and Charles had purchased during their honeymoon in Mexico City in 1904, and was perfectly set off by the white boiserie walls and French tole chandelier.

By the time she reached the double height drawing room, her distracted thoughts were falling into place. Here, fresh flowers were arranged in lush bouquets, the deep-pillowed sofas and chairs were upholstered in cool silks, and the paintings on the walls were part of the collection of American Impressionist art that she and Charles had been collecting since their marriage when Alix and Henry had given them a Childe Hassam landscape as a wedding present.

Thea made a quick visit to the kitchen where Mrs. MacKay was preparing lunch, and after a brief word with the cook, she stepped into the butler's pantry where one full-length cupboard was fitted with sliding shelves holding trays completely set with linen and china and silver, ready to be used for breakfast in bed or tea in her office. But not even checking the glass-fronted wood cabinets and smoothly sliding drawers filled with china and crystal and silver had a soothing effect on her this morning. Nothing would do until she could talk with Charles.

Now was the perfect time. Tatiana and Stephanie had been taken by their nanny to Central Park, Raymond was asleep in the nursery, Amy was busy typing letters, Mallory wasn't due for at least a half-hour, and as Thea mounted the steps, her mind began to recall all the changes she and Charles had been through together in the past six months.

It had all begun before that, of course. Thea had seen that Charles was going through some sort of inner conflict that had taken hold shortly after their return from Europe in 1906, and never really sure if what was troubling him simply came and went or was a carefully hidden ongoing problem, she had sidestepped the matter, knowing in advance that her husband would talk to her and tell her everything when he was ready and not one moment before. In the meantime, he ran a thriving literary agency, was the perfect host at the parties they gave, was an active and adoring father, and was the husband who never for one second forgot that he loved her with all his heart.

None of those utterly normal things, Thea believed, was the sign of a man having a crisis of faith. A problem like that simply wasn't one that would attack Charles. As complicated as he was, he would rise above any questions or doubts when it came to religious beliefs.

Or so you thought, Thea reminded herself. You thought it was something very different, and even if you'd known all along what it was, you'd never have thought for one second that Charles would have taken the solution he did.

It had been their first night out since the final two months of her pregnancy that ended with Raymond's birth just over two weeks earlier, and they were celebrating with dinner at Sherry's, followed by the opening night of *Madame X* at the New Amsterdam Theatre.

Since she was nursing the new baby, they had decided in advance against going on to the Café Martin or any of the other popular after-theatre restaurants, and as soon as the final curtain came down they returned to East 66th Street.

There were no signs of portents for Thea to know that this night was the night her husband had chosen. No inner suspicions whispered at her that the moment when he would reveal all was at hand, and even his first question sounded like nothing more than the concern of a loving husband.

"Are you very tired, darling?" he asked as they stood in the entry hall and he helped her off with her Poiret evening cloak of embroidered tobacco-brown velvet.

"No, but it's still a bit too soon for what we're both thinking of," Thea replied teasingly, turning to look at Charles, and her smile froze in place when she saw the look in his topaz-colored eyes.

This is it, she thought with sudden clarity, almost as if a veil that she hadn't even known was there had been swept away. He's resolved his problem, and now he's going to tell me what it was. It could only be one thing . . . I thought we were too happy to have it happen

138

to us, but I suppose every wife thinks that. I only hope it's no one I know. I could stand a stranger but not a friend. I can't let him see that I suspect. . . .

"I want to have a talk with you," he said, and fresh fear clutched at Thea's heart. "It's important that we have this out together."

"Raymond's waiting," she said, her voice sounding amazingly normal as she heard it. "Shall I keep our son waiting for his late-night meal?"

"No," he said quietly, "first things first. I'll wait for you in the drawing room."

The next half-hour was agony for Thea. She returned to their room, removed her Poiret gown of pale green silk trimmed with fur bands and metal embroidery, fed Raymond, settled him back in his crib for the night, checked on the girls, and finally changed into a finely pleated Fortuny caftan of pink silk gauze with a stenciled border. Every action, no matter how quickly completed, felt as if it took a century to complete, and when she entered the drawing room and found Charles seated on the sofa in front of the fireplace, his arms folded across his chest, his face reflective as he looked into the flames, only one thought filled her mind and set her heart thudding in a sickening pattern.

"I've discovered that no matter how effective and necessary steam heat is, there's nothing quite so welcoming on a cold winter night as a fire," Charles said as Thea sat down beside him, and he moved to put his arms around her.

"I think it also helps if there's something to discuss," Thea said urgingly, placing cool hands at the base of his neck, and in spite of her fears a very familiar warmth spread in her as Charles rested his head on her shoulder.

"There's really no room for discussion on what I have to tell you," Charles said, gently kissing her neck before raising his solemn face to hers. "My decision is made, and

139

my only regret is that I kept you in the dark about it for so long. I want to tell you that by the end of the month I expect to be received as a communicant at the Church of the Transfiguration—"

His words washed over Thea like the cool sea on a hot day, and her relief was so strong that their meaning failed to register.

"You haven't had an affair, and you're not leaving me for another woman!" she exclaimed, and Charles' expression turned to horror.

"Is that what you thought? There's never been another woman for me but you, not since the day we met."

"I know that. But I also know that something's been eating at you for a long time, and after a while I decided that you must have met someone and no matter how hard you fought against it, you eventually gave in and you were only waiting until after I had the baby to tell me that you want some sort of separation . . ."

"I never heard of such a story!" Charles was honestly shocked, and he silently cursed his secretiveness. Never for one moment had he thought this was the way Thea was thinking. "And as for meeting another woman— Where would I ever find the time to do that? You do manage to keep me very busy," he said with a faint smile. "Or is that an ulterior motive in itself?"

"Of course it is. But any man who wants to stray, no matter how busy he is, will find the ways and the means, and considering that up until eighteen days ago I hadn't had a figure worth mentioning for months it would have been easy for you to look somewhere else. It'll be another month before we can make love again, and added on to the last seven weeks . . ."

"I can wait for you. No matter how difficult, I'd never sully that reunion for one night of self-serving pleasure.

140

That's for a bachelor, not a married man with a beautiful wife—"

Together they fell back against the silk cushions, their arms around each other, and it was several minutes before the meaning of Charles' decision came back to her.

"Charles." Thea's voice was like crystal. "Were you trying to tell me that you're converting—"

"I hate that word," he said against her neck, and then, as if by some prearranged signal, they both sat up.

"Why?" Thea questioned softly. Now that her worst fear had been dispelled the unbelievability of this situation was crowding in on her. To think that Charles, whose Catholicism was such an ingrained part of his life and heritage that he'd spent five years as a Jesuit seminarian, was planning to turn away from the faith that had been his since the cradle was incredible. Catholics tried to convert Protestants, they never looked the other way—or so she'd assumed until now. "You've been thinking about this a long time, haven't you?"

"Almost from the moment we came back from Europe four years ago. No, not all the time, but something went very wrong with my sense of always needing the Church while we were abroad. We were in some of the most Catholic cities on the Continent, and no matter how many services I went to telling myself this one would make the difference, I had a greater and greater feeling of isolation."

"Could it have been from the fact that you weren't living in France any longer and weren't a part of the Continental Catholic community but a resident of New York—a tourist instead of a visitor?" Thea asked, understanding the enormity of Charles' dilemma and all he must have gone through to get to the point where he now was.

"That's what I tried to tell myself, and I managed to

141

submerge my feelings, but—" Charles shook his head. "Actually, I've dwelled on this on and off for years—an idea that really wouldn't go away," he went on, taking her hands in his. "It's funny the way an idea planted years before can come back again. . . . We'll blame it on my British education. My father sent his three sons to school in England. All those years at Stonyhurst and Oxford—it was bound to take effect on one of us sooner or later."

"But Stonyhurst is a Jesuit school, not a stronghold of the Church of England the way Harrow and Eton are."

"But I was still in England, the land of Shakespeare and Milton and John Donne. Did I ever really think I could study their words and their works and their lives and not have it influence me?"

"There's more to it than just literary admiration, though."

"A great deal more, but every concept has to have a base, and that one is mine. In fact, to me, what I'm doing is as much a moral move as it is a religious one. I couldn't stand being a fallen-away Catholic, or a lapsed one, always waiting around to be brought back into the fold. Over the past year I've been drifting toward the Anglican church in a way that frightened me at times, but also answered questions for me that my own church either couldn't or wouldn't."

As they sat together holding hands, Thea cast her mind back over the past twelve months—and further— belatedly seeing the signs that signalled her husband's religious conflicts. Charles had been a faithful communicant at St. Jean Baptiste since his arrival in New York in February 1904, but now Thea recalled the skipped Sundays when he'd told her that he wasn't going to Mass because the weather was inclement, or that they'd been out too late the night before, or that he had a manuscript to check or a contract to read or . . . or . . .

She hadn't cared, it wasn't her business, that was the tacit agreement of their "mixed" marriage, and she'd accepted the excuses—whether flimsy or logical—at face value, until now when she saw them for what they'd been.

Signals, she thought, all clear signals, and I never asked him a single question. What conflicts Charles had been going through and I never probed below the surface, tried to find out what was troubling him. I just made up my own answer.

"I'm sorry," she said aloud, kissing him.

"Whatever for?" Charles was surprised.

"For not paying closer attention. For not asking you what the matter was. For not helping you through your crisis of faith—"

Charles winced. "Not that expression, please. I'm convinced that one of the reasons our marriage has been so happy—besides the fact we love each other passionately—is that you're agnostic enough for both of us. If you were Catholic, either from the cradle or converted, at this moment our marriage would be in a fairly rough state, and if you were a practicing Protestant—well, that would also cause complications. This way, it's been my quest, my solution, and my decision. As much as we share everything else, Thea, this situation was of my making alone."

His arms went around her shoulders and she rested her head against him.

"You still haven't given me a reason. There has to be more to it than just your education or literary admiration." Thea felt as if she were walking on glass, but if Charles had decided to make this drastic a change, she had a right to know the reason—*all* the reasons.

"I started doing what a good Catholic—a good French Catholic—is never supposed to do, I began asking questions and I wasn't at all satisfied with the answers."

"Such as the topic of birth control?" Thea couldn't resist asking. "You've had to listen to me on the subject since we've been married—as well as being my silent partner-in-practice."

"It started with that, and then it seemed that there was one thing after another, primarily having every Catholic convert whose path I crossed barrage me with questions on church philosophy and laws and rules. I'm not a theologian, and little by little it dawned on me that I was a very discontented Catholic. "That's when I began—" he hesitated painfully "—to look around for answers to my questions."

"Was there a lot of that?"

"No, I sorted out my options first. I'm no more interested in being a 'fashionable Episcopalian' any more than in being a lapsed Catholic, so that eliminated St. James, St. Thomas', St. Bartholomew's, and the Heavenly Rest. After I did that, the Church of the Transfiguration seemed to be the logical choice for me."

The Church of the Transfiguration, better known by its sobriquets The Little Church Around The Corner and The Actors Church, *was* the best choice Charles could have made, Thea knew. Considered to be a somewhat bohemian congregation by the rest of New York's fashionable Episcopalian community, its, well, off-handedness must have been a welcome refuge for him.

As she considered Charles' decision with love and understanding for the silent ordeal he had subjected himself to, another thought surfaced in Thea's mind.

"Charles, are you doing this because you're considering the Protestant—the Episcopalian—ministry?"

Her husband began to smile very slowly, setting her fear to rest. "At this late day and age? No, my darling, that isn't even in my most remote plans, so I'm afraid you'll have to continue to be content to live with a literary agent."

144

"I think I'll manage," Thea replied, smiling, her good nature restored. "And I want you to know that you have my full love and support. But have you considered what's going to happen when the news gets out?"

"I've taken precautions. People don't pay much attention to what goes on at Transfiguration, and since I'm going to be received just before Lent—"

Thea began to laugh. "Oh, Charles, people *always* care what someone else is doing with their lives, particularly when it's somewhat unexpected. That's part and parcel of life in New York. Just you wait and see," she warned him with a knowing smile. "When word gets out, none of your religious friends will think poorly of you, they're just going to lay all the blame on me!"

Their talk had taken place in the late hours of February second and the early hours of February third. Now it was August fifth and, as Thea mounted the stairs to the second floor of their apartment, she smiled, recalling just how uncannily correct she'd been when she'd told Charles what the reaction to his conversion would be when word got out.

By the end of February, just before the beginning of the Lenten season, Charles de Renille quietly left the Catholic Church for what, with his British education, he continued to call either the Anglican Church or the Church of England.

At first he'd kept his change of faith secret, and Thea privately suspected that Charles, with his intensely ingrained sense of privacy, had no intention of mentioning the matter. It was a situation that might have hung fire indefinitely until the week in mid-March when *Town Topics*, the society weekly that devoted itself to the chronicling of New York high life, and whose publisher, Colonel William Mann, actually had a nice sideline going

145

in blackmail for the gossip he *didn't* print, felt it was his duty to inform his readers that:

> It has come to our attention that a prominent young Frenchman who has made our city his home has recently abandoned his cradle Catholic upbringing for the less dramatic ritual of the Church of the Transfiguration. When more than a few of our finer citizens have turned toward Rome, it is perhaps only proper that, in exchange as it were, this aristocrat with his beautiful American wife and three splendid children, find his way to Canterbury. ... .

There had been no mistaking the person implied in that blind item, and now that the matter was out of his hands, Charles de Renille handled the ensuing upheaval with such tact and grace that the matter faded within a reasonable amount of time.

Close friends, regardless of religion, overlooked his dereliction in not telling them and closed ranks around him, but there were professional contacts who were less than kind, and Thea burned with anger and indignation every time she thought about it.

Two of the most prolific authors Charles represented, both highly strung young men with fine writing careers ahead of them and books that sold into the hundreds of thousands of copies, departed from his agency within days of the appearance of *Town Topics* on the newsstands. Both were Catholic converts, conversions that had more show than substance, more dramatic impulse than deep faith, and to their way of thinking, the action Charles had taken in his personal life became an outrage and an insult.

If they had meant to wound Charles in the pocketbook, their move was an utter and complete failure since he had a substantial private income that usually outdistanced the five percent fee he charged the authors he represented. He could live without clients whom he had discovered and found publishers for and continued to encourage and nourish, but business was business and he knew that it was only the law of averages taking over and determining that he would both lose and gain clients as the years went on. But what Charles couldn't abide was the fact that what he considered to be an essentially private act became a topic for malicious gossip.

It's surprising how much harm two put-out authors can try and do when they set their minds to it, Thea reflected wryly. The tales they told made me the Scarlet Woman with Charles as my hapless dupe. The only good thing that came out of this whole mess is that eventually slimy people ruin only themselves, and that Charles is happy and content and did the right thing for him.

Smiling now, Thea leaned against the open doorframe of the smallest bedroom which Charles took as his office-away-from-the-office, and which Thea had decorated for him, and listened in as he concluded his telephone call in a combination of English and French.

"The trick in biography, Georges, is not to be either too much in love or in hate with your subject. I think your *idée* for a full-length study on the life of Eleanor of Acquitane is perfect, and so do Dick North and Frank Doubleday, but not from your opening chapters. *Pas de tout*. You are too *reverentiel*. Take another look, show her good points *and* her bad. She was a fascinating woman in a time that created great men. Yes. *Ça va . . . alors . . .* okay . . ."

Charles hung up the phone and looked up at Thea, taking in every detail of her carefully arranged glossy brown hair, skillfully applied maquillage, and Drecoll

147

dress of French blue silk banded in black satin with elbow-length sleeves and a cream lace collar.

"Difficult morning?" he asked sympathetically.

"You always know," she smiled. "One of the worst, if you want the truth. But just now you didn't sound as if all were going swimmingly with you. Are you sure you want to listen to my difficulties?"

"I can't think of another person I'd rather talk to right now."

Thea regarded her husband carefully. "Was Georges being truculent?"

"Not at all. Surprisingly, he's just having a spot of trouble starting his new book," Charles said, pushing away the papers he was working on. "I warned him in advance that biography is far more difficult than fiction, but he insisted that he was ready to try his hand at something new."

Georges Bergery, like Charles de Renille, was the youngest son of a wealthy and noble French family who had made a new home and a new life in New York, although, unlike Charles, Georges had been a rake, a playboy, notoriously fond of *la vie bohème*. But late in 1902, after one escapade too many, his family reached the conclusion that their twenty-eight-year-old son could find his amusements in another city than Paris, in another country than France.

With a substantial monthly remittance assured him, Georges arrived in New York only to discover that while life could indeed be good in the New World, people didn't accept men of his status as easily as they did in Europe. Using his native intelligence, Georges wisely told all his new friends that he was writing a novel—a suitable occupation for a gentleman—until one night at the Whist Club when a man of his own age seated at the next table leaned over and handed him a business card, said he was Richard North, an editor at Doubleday, Page, and he'd be happy to look at the completed manuscript.

Georges had few ambitions beyond living well from day to day, but that night he went home and began work on a novel, putting his study of French history to work for the first time since he'd left the Sorbonne, and four months later, with the help of a hired typist, sent Dick North a nicely turned out, slightly melodramatic novel set in Paris after the downfall of Napoleon. To his immense astonishment, Richard North bought the book, and when Doubleday, Page published it, the reviewers and buying public alike called it a fine tale rendered by a promising new talent.

Naturally, there had to be another historical novel to follow, and by December 1904 when Dick introduced Georges to Charles at the de Renilles housewarming party, his second book was well under way. When the time came that the new novel was on the bestseller lists and the third book in outline, it just happened to coincide with the moment when Charles decided to branch out from writing and translating and teaching. Although Georges wasn't Charles' first client, he was his first New York-based one, and it was a partnership both men cherished, and one that wasn't about to be undermined by discontented babble. When the inevitable gossip reached his ears, Georges—who considered himself a good Catholic since he went to Mass at Christmas and Easter—merely treated the matter in a manner typically French: he shrugged, said a man's private decisions were not his concern, and treated the whole matter as if it had never taken place.

"I had lunch with Bettina yesterday, and she said that Georges with his new book is like a miner who has struck gold," Thea remarked from the door.

"Well, the vein is going to run out very soon unless he gets more objective than he is now."

"He doesn't have to be," Thea pointed out. "There's a

149

point where objectivity turns into dullness, and if there's one thing that's unreadable it's a dull biography of an otherwise intriguing person."

"So is one dripping adoration and too much reverence," Charles said, leaning back in his chair. "Georges is going to have to find a happy medium. Tell his wife that for me."

"Tell Georges that yourself, lover," Thea drawled. "He's your client."

"That's a fighting word."

Thea saw the look in his eyes. "Which one?"

"Come here, lover," he said, holding out his arms, and Thea came over and sat in his lap, winding her arms around his neck and concentrated on kissing him under an ear.

Charles had a handsome office at Madison Avenue and Thirty-second Street that was all polished wood and walls of books and softly covered carpets and fine English furniture that Thea had found for him, but he had closed it for the summer, giving his assistant and secretary a fully paid vacation while he worked at home. Since he didn't like the idea of leaving manuscripts in the library where a guest, looking for a moment's distraction at a party, might take the liberty of leafing through it, or one of their daughters, both of whom had a healthy curiosity about the world around them, might decide that a collection of papers would make a better plaything than their expensive toys, and since their bedroom, large as it was, was also impractical—"I don't bring fabric swatches and paint chips into our bedroom," Thea had informed him, "and I think the same should apply to your book contracts and manuscripts"—Thea had taken the smallest of the apartment's bedrooms and, for Charles' thirty-fifth birthday present the previous November, turned it into an office for him. From the least important of the numerous rooms which comprised the duplex's sleeping quarters, Thea had transformed it into a perfect workroom with the most important pieces being a modern Swedish carpet made of pale yellow, soft brown and quiet tan fine wool woven into a striking geometric pattern that had been given them as a wedding present by a friend of her father's from the University of Stockholm, and a black lacquer desk inlaid with mother-of-pearl that was designed by Charles Rennie Mackintosh, the innovative, sometimes controversial, Scottish architect and designer who headed the Glasgow School of Art.

After a few minutes of cuddling, Thea kissed him on the temple and asked, "Now that you've set Georges back on the right path, what other magic are you up to today?"

"Is that what you think being a literary agent is— pulling white rabbits out of black silk top hats?" he teased her.

"Of course it is—just like being an interior decorator. What we do didn't exist ten years ago, so we simply have to make up the rules as we go along!"

"Come to think of it, that is how we work," Charles said. "And as to my latest trick, I think I've found someone to assist Henry with his book."

"Assuming, that is, if he wants to write it," Thea reminded him. "When you suggested that he might want to write a book about great collectors and their art, Henry was amiable but not that enthusiastic."

"You're being charitable. When I first brought the matter up, Henry looked at me the same way he used to when I first came to New York and would make some awful gaffe. By the time he sailed, I'd talked him around a bit and—"

"And you think that the combination of sea air and a pleasant sojourn in Europe had a salutory effect on him."

"That and Alix's gentle persuasion," Charles grinned. "And if he has come around, I now have a secretary

151

for him."

"How triumphant you sound." She tugged playfully at his thick black hair. "What exactly does this secretary look like?"

"I really haven't the slightest idea—except that over the phone he sounded like a typical middle-aged Englishman," Charles said with deliberate slowness, very well aware of what his wife wanted to know. "It seems that he's just arrived from London and had my name from Peter Hawkins," he went on, referring to an Oxford don, the author of a sprightly book about the men who'd surrounded Elizabeth I at her court that Charles had sold to Scribner's with fine results. "Mr. Gresham is seeking a proper sort of employment—"

"I hope that's a direct quote." Thea's voice was tinged with amusement.

"Straight from the horse's mouth, as they say. He assured me that his references are impeccable—personal private secretary to several authors as well as one or two peers—and if Henry decides to go ahead with the book, this man can probably be a great help to him without getting in the way too much."

Finishing his explanation, Charles buried his face against Thea's soft neck, breathing in the expensive Guerlain perfume, *Rue de la Paix*, that she wore with such pleasant olfactory results. Six years before she had worn only the equally costly and intoxicating *Jicky*, and he used to say that even when they were separated he was always aware of her because of the scent that clung to his clothes.

"I think that we've spent more than enough time talking about me," he said, his lips brushing against her glossy brown hair. "Tell me, what are you more apprehensive about today, seeing Romney or having to continue to wait and see if the Ritz-Carlton people are going to hire you?"

"Oh, don't even mention the words Ritz-Carlton!" Thea groaned. "I've been talking with the committee for months, the hotel itself is almost half-built, and they *still* won't let me know one way or another. If they don't want me to decorate some of their rooms and suites, fine. I'll be disappointed, but there'll be new clients and other jobs; it's this *game* they're playing with me that's making me so angry. One week it looks good, the next week they can't stand me, and the week after that it's all back before the board where they decide they aren't ready to reach a formal decision."

"And Romney?"

"To tell you the truth, he's the first prospective client that I ever insulted and then had come back and want to talk about hiring me."

Charles chuckled. "Remember, Romney's spent all his adult life in the Foreign Office. He's grown so used to double talk and platitudes that you were like a breath of fresh air to him."

"Or maybe he just didn't like Elsie de Wolfe. I heard via the grapevine that he was talking with her," Thea offered glumly, cringing slightly as she recalled the night exactly two months and one day ago.

It was the opening night of Lew Fields' production of *The Summer Widowers*, starring the producer himself, the comic actor Eugene O'Rourke, the debonair Vernon Castle, the charming Irene Franklin, and the delightful child actress Helen Hayes, whose New York debut had been made in *Old Dutch* at the Herald Square Theatre the previous November. It was a muggy, sluggish early June night that seems designed solely to warn New Yorkers of what the coming summer will be like, and the enjoyment and laughter Thea had found in the musical faded quickly when she left the theatre and found that the late hour did nothing whatsoever to decrease the day's heat. She and Charles were waiting in the line that snaked back from the edge of the sidewalk, under the marquee of the Broadway Theatre, back into the lobby as the audience waited for the doorman to hail them cabs or open the doors of their motor cars and carriages as they drove up.

The de Renilles weren't talking much as they waited. It wasn't a major disagreement, just a sort of mutual uneasiness that all couples experience at various intervals and must simply wait out, and when someone behind them called their names they turned, curious at the English-accented voice, and found Romney Sedgewick standing behind them.

"I thought it was the two of you," he said cheerfully as they exchanged greeting. "It's been far too long since we've seen each other."

"I agree. Are you visiting New York?" Charles asked.

"No, I'm happy to tell you that I'll be taking up residence here. I've done a bit of traveling over the last few months and New York seems to be the best spot for me," Romney informed them just as a chic-looking new model Renault town car with a neatly uniformed driver behind the wheel drove up.

"That's our motor car," Charles said. "Can we give you a lift?"

"Thanks, but I'm going downtown . . . out of your way, I expect."

"Then ring us up tomorrow. We're in the directory."

"I'll do that, but one quick question. Thea, are you still in the interior decorating business?"

It was a friendly question, a totally innocent one, and one Romney Sedgewick—with his years of diplomatic training—should have known better than to ask as Thea's eyes flashed fire.

"Are you still in the business of breathing?" she snapped, and swinging around disappeared into the tonneau of the Renault in a swish of pale blue charmeuse, effectively ending their conversation. Romney didn't call

them as he'd promised, and since she was infuriated
enough not to try and locate him, Thea simply pushed the
matter aside, only occasionally wondering if she'd lost
both a prospective client and an old friend, and his call on
Monday was a complete surprise to her.

"I never thought I'd ever see someone from the
Foreign Office standing on the street with his mouth
open," Charles observed two months later.

"There's a first time for everything," Thea said, and
with a bittersweet laugh she reluctantly eased herself out
of Charles' embrace, stood up, and gracefully navigated
around the desk to sit down in a reproduction of a late
19th century bamboo Chippendale arm chair. "I know
it's a little late for apologies, but I'm sorry if I
embarrassed you that night."

"But not sorry for what you said."

"No. To me, a remark like that is like waving a red flag
in front of a bull."

"Taken in that context it *was* an insulting thing to
say," Charles agreed, "even though Romney didn't mean
it. He told me that he thought he was being rather
witty—"

"A few more witty remarks like that and I could be out
of business. You know how fast gossip travels in this
town."

"But you won't be." Charles' voice was confident.
"And you know Romney's coming here to do more than
talk—he's going to hire you."

"For what? Or do you know more than you're telling
me?"

"Possibly," he said, smiling in secret amusement.
"And if you come back here where you belong I might
just be inclined—or persuaded—to let a few secrets
slip."

"Mallory will be here soon," Thea pointed out, her
voice nonetheless delighted as she stood up, "but that

shouldn't stop us. It's been a long time since I've been a secret agent, and I've always wanted to capture someone and worm secrets out of them in some particularly wonderful way!"

While Thea and Charles were busy sharing secrets, Mallory was steering her Baker Electric Motor Car up Madison Avenue. This upright, shiny black four-passenger coupe which was controlled completely from within and ran at a low speed was the perfect urban vehicle since its closed body was ideal in bad weather. These electric motor cars were popularly known as the "lady's vehicle," and on any given day, up and down Manhattan's fashionable thoroughfares, well-dressed women—the majority of them well under fifty—could be seen driving their electrics to go shopping or pay calls or attend a matinée.

Mallory did all of those things, but she considered her Baker to be first and foremost an integral part of Thea Harper Associates, since she used it when visiting dealers and clients, or attending auctions, and, best of all, for transporting such diverse objects as rolls of wallpaper and bolts of fabric discovered in out-of-the-way shops and various bibelots bought at auction—items for which she didn't have to make the firm dependent on a freight service for.

Just like you're doing this morning, Mallory told herself as she stopped the coupe for a red light, her hands resting lightly on the steering tiller. Both on the seat next to her and on the back seat and placed on the floor, a variety of packages, some of them gift-wrapped, all the results of her summer trip, adorned the auto's pink-beige velvet interior.

I must look like the Mallory Kirk delivery service, she thought, but I don't care, it's so good to be back in New

York. I think the only thing more exciting than sailing out of New York is coming home again!

The *Mauretania* had arrived back in New York harbor right on schedule early Thursday afternoon, and when the complicated procedure of docking was completed and their group of travelers came down the first-class gangplank onto the well-trod boards of Pier 52, Newton Phipps had been waiting for them with open arms, a ready group of eager customs inspectors and, outside their pier on West Twelfth Street, behind his new Cadillac limousine, was the Packard truck he'd hired to transport their luggage.

Let other people rest up for a day or two from the rigors of traveling. For us New Yorkers it's right back to work—and play, Mallory thought with satisfaction. Today she would check in with Thea, show off some of her purchases, and find out what was new on their schedule; tonight she'd be part of a theatre party, going to the Jardin de Paris to see the *Ziegfeld Follies of 1910*, followed by a late supper at the Astor's Roof Garden; and on Monday or Tuesday, after the contents of their luggage had been unpacked, sorted, freshened up and made ready to be repacked, they'd be going out to Cove House.

At the thought of Long Island, Mallory felt something deep inside her constrict while the palms of her hands grew damp inside their gloves, but with a new determination she took a deep breath and lifted her chin.

Now is *not* the time to get nervous. Save that for when you have to confront Rupert . . . if he's even coming to Cove House, that is. For all you know, he may be spending the rest of the summer in Chicago—which is proper punishment, considering, she thought as the traffic began to move again and she made a neat right-hand turn, forcing herself to think about other topics.

I wonder what Thea's attracted in the way of new

clients, or if she's heard one way or the other from the Ritz-Carlton people. Now *that* would be exciting. It was such fun doing that suite at the Gotham last year . . . no clients changing their minds in the middle of a job.

She was still dwelling pleasantly on what she considered to be the preferability of decorating hotel suites and offices and other public spaces where everything regarding decor was decided beforehand, rather than dealing with individual clients who sometimes went into a state of panic at the idea of new furniture and had to be handled *very* carefully, when she pulled the coupe up in front of the canopied entrance of 131 East 66th Street, and the doorman came forward to open the door, a broad smile lighting up his face when he saw her.

"I thought that was you, Miss Kirk. Welcome back."

"Good morning, Cavanaugh, and thank you," Mallory said as she stepped out of the car and noticed that the doorman nodded approvingly at her Jeanne Hallee dress of pink and beige figured foulard with elbow-length sleeves and a straight, shirred skirt, and her Hattie Carnegie hat of champagne-colored toga straw trimmed with champagne-colored plumes. "How has Mrs. R. been getting on without me?"

"Oh, she's been busy as a bee, near as I can figure out, but I suspect Mrs. de Renille will be very glad to have your help again."

Mallory suspected that the doorman, as friendly and cheery as he unfailingly was, didn't really understand what it was she and Thea did beyond the fact that they "arranged furniture," and his good nature toward them was based on their being attractive, well-dressed women who never treated him like a flunky. Mallory was proud of the work she did, and proud of Thea for being one of the profession's trailblazers, but as long as the doorman summoned the building's call boys to carry her packages up to Thea's apartment and took care of her car and had it in front when she was ready to leave and always had a smile that let her know if her dress enhanced the tone of the building, she could pass over Cavanaugh's not quite grasping the importance of being an interior decorator. There were, after all, drawbacks to every position, Mallory reminded herself as she crossed the quiet lobby toward the bank of elevators, and this was probably the most minor one of all.

Unlike some New York City households, the de Renille home was not overburdened with live-in servants. Only Purcell, their ever-correct English butler, his wife, Violet, who was the downstairs maid, and Miss Grayson who looked after the children, actually lived on the premises, while Mrs. MacKay, their cook, and Aggie and Cora, who took care of the upstairs and did the heavy cleaning, came on a daily basis. Of those seven, only Miss Grayson was missing as Mallory entered the apartment, and they all dropped their tasks to crowd around her in welcome. Each and every one of them was very fond of Mallory. They admired her talent which they considered to be only somewhat less than that of their mistress, and while their master and mistress did provide them with a romantic atmosphere, Mallory's being unmarried and in great social demand allowed them a great deal of room in which to speculate both about various romances that she might be involved in and to play matchmaking games, deciding which of New York's most eligible bachelors was worthy of her.

As she always did when she came back from a trip, Mallory had bought presents for everyone, and as she found them from among the pile of packages the call boys were carrying, she answered all their questions and told them brief, funny stories about shipboard life.

"I'd say it took you a good fifteen minutes to get here from the reception room," Amy declared, getting up from behind her Adam-style mahogany inlaid writing table to hug Mallory.

"It sure beats customs, though," Mallory replied as they embraced. "Those boys pawed their way through *everything*. Next year, *Thea* can go to Europe! Incidentally, where is she?" she went on, glancing toward the Chinese screen.

"Upstairs visiting a certain literary agent."

Mallory raised her eyebrows in amusement. "When I get married, if I ever do, I hope I'm not strong enough to let my husband work at home at the same time I'm there."

"To each his own," Amy said with equal amusement. She was married to a doctor currently completing the complicated surgical residency, and the salary she earned from Thea helped pay for a handsome apartment on West Eleventh Street and such necessary luxuries as theatre and opera tickets. "I don't see all that much of my husband, so I can see where Thea's method of operation has its points."

For the next few minutes both women were kept busy showing the call boys into the office, tipping them, and then arranging the boxes around the office that they shared.

The room where they worked was somewhat larger than Thea's, with Amy's desk placed near the door that opened off the hallway, while Mallory's Sheraton mahogany writing table with inlay decorations was placed closer to the Chinese screen. An antique Chinese rug in shades of blue on yellow with cream and rust accents covered the floor, an Empire-style table ornamented with ormolu was placed in the center of the room with the past year's issues of *Connoisseur*, a selection of auction house catalogs and several art books arranged on

160

its smooth surface, and finely framed floral watercolors were hung on the walls.

"The market for porcelain gets better every day," Mallory remarked, making a brief inspection of the solid cherry display vitrines with glass tops and beige velvet pads that held small porcelain objects and were placed at strategic spots around the room. "Nothing that was here in June seems to be here now."

"They've practically been walking out on their own," Amy agreed.

"And I've been worried that I bought too many things in London and Paris. You wouldn't believe what was available." Mallory took off her hat and tossed it on a nearby caneback fauteuil that was cushioned in rose cotton damask. "Thea's going to be thrilled."

"I certainly hope so."

"What's that supposed to mean? You sound as if things aren't going too well."

"Oh, we're splendidly in the black, but—" Amy's pause was significant.

"The Ritz-Carlton job—we've lost it?" Mallory asked with a sinking feeling of disappointment that was far more for Thea than for herself.

"Worse. They won't make up their minds one way or another."

"What a mess."

"Exactly, and if you don't mind a word of advice, don't mention this subject to Thea."

"I won't. I'm sure she'll tell me on her own accord soon enough." Mallory turned to the nearest pile of packages and a minute later she held out to Amy a box wrapped in gilded paper, tied with a profusion of rainbow-hued satin ribbons, and decorated with artificial flowers. "And now that you've warned me about the trouble spots, why don't you open your present?"

The next few minutes were very pleasantly spent as a

delighted Amy slowly, carefully, undid the wrapping and opened a white paste-board box to disclose a fitted vanity case of black lacquer resting on a bed of shredded ivory and pink silk paper.

Mallory was describing Paul Poiret's latest couture collection when the hallway door opened and Thea walked in.

"Well," she announced, her eyes sweeping the room, great amusement evident in her voice, "do I get a present?"

"It took you so long to get here I'm not sure you still deserve it," Mallory retorted with a laugh. "Oh, Thea—"

"Oh, I think you've been away long enough," Thea said as they embraced. "But let me see you—I'd say a summer spent mainly in dull old London did you good. You look positively marvelous."

"So do you," Mallory said, but as she looked at Thea's glowing face something clicked inside her. *She and Charles have been making love,* she thought with a flash of envy at the de Renilles self-evident happiness. Ashamed at her emotions, Mallory lifted up another gift-wrapped box. "Here it is."

"Thank you, darling. Oh, it's heavy! Let's see . . ."

Thea set the box down on the Empire table, undid the complicated wrapping to reveal the familiar dark red leather Cartier presentation case, and slowly lifted the lid, issuing an exclamation of excitement and surprise when she saw the contents.

"A mystery clock! Charles and I were going to order one. Oh, Mallie, you shouldn't have!"

"Well, I wanted to. Just consider it an early sixth anniversary present."

Together the three women stood back to silently admire the latest work of art to come out of the Cartier workrooms. Like all Cartier clocks that had come before it it was an artistic masterpiece that no other clockmaker

162

could seem to quite equal. But the mystery clocks—so named because the diamond-studded hands seemed to move freely around perfectly faceted faces that were made out of such materials as rock crystal, jade, citrine and topaz—put on sale in the Paris salon only a few months before, had already achieved success as the object that every forward-thinking person with the wherewithal to purchase it had to own.

"Louis Cartier gave us a tour of the workrooms and told us how the clock works," Mallory said as they continued to exclaim over her selection which had a base of black onyx, a case of clear crystal outlined in gold and a face of diamond-studded rock-crystal. "The face isn't one solid piece, it's made up of layers," she offered. "The hands are set in the center layer and then are attached to crystal disks that rotate."

"But where are the mechanisms that make this beautiful thing keep time?" Amy asked.

"It's all hidden in the base," Mallory smiled.

"What does Alix's clock look like?" Thea wanted to know.

"It's a black onyx base with topaz and diamonds. If you don't want this one, Thea, I'm sure Cartier's here will do an exchange."

"Not like it?" Thea echoed. "Oh, Mallie, you know I love my mystery clock. But you know me, I have to know what everyone else has."

"Well, as long as you're not going to offer it to a client!"

"Horrid girl! I'm probably going to carry it around with me from room to room as you very well know. Now let's get Charles down here so he can admire it, and then we can look at all the other things you've bought."

Charles de Renille was as thrilled as his wife with the mystery clock. He looked at it from every angle, giving it such careful inspection that Thea and Mallory teased him about being able to get a job as an inspector in Cartier's workrooms should the steady stream of manuscripts he continually received dry up. Finally he opened his own present: a simply framed print of a dandy of the Second Restoration wearing a coat *à l'Anglaise* and a tall beaver hat.

"It's just what my office upstairs needs," he said, holding up the 1826 color fashion plate to the light. "As soon as I get back from my meeting I'll find the best spot for it."

"Would you care to add that your meeting is lunch at the Waldorf with one of your authors and an editor from Harper's?" Thea said archly.

"It's just another summer day's work," Charles replied with smiling good humor as he glanced at his Cartier wristwatch. "I'm sorry I can't wait any longer to see Romney. Say hello to him for me."

"Romney?" Mallory asked when Charles left. "Not Romney Sedgewick by some chance?"

"By every chance," Thea said with satisfaction. "He'll be here within the hour."

"Do you know that everyone we know in London is wondering where he is?" Mallory said, and told her about Joanna Garland's indignant views at Emma's tea party. "They knew he sailed for New York, but after that, nothing at all."

"Well, I'm no expert on where or how Romney spent his time—except for one night, that is," Thea said, and told Mallory and Amy about their meeting two months before under the marquee of the Broadway Theatre.

"And tell us, Mrs. Lincoln, how did you like the play?" Mallory quipped when Thea finished.

"Under the circumstances, I thought I was rather witty."

"That's a good way to witty yourself right out of a nice,

164

fat commission," Amy pointed out, "despite the fact it was absolutely the right thing to say."

"Then I have no apologies to make," Thea said airily.

"But then how—?" Mallory left her question unfinished, but its implication was clear.

"I have Charles to thank for that. He likes to go to the early morning service at the Little Church Around The Corner, and apparently Romney does too. No, Charles didn't apologize—he wouldn't be able to look me in the face if he had—they just had a nice little talk. Oh, look, he'll be here soon, and over lunch we'll get him to tell us everything. Right now it's time to see some of the results of Mallory's summer expedition."

"Then you'll have to count me out," Amy said, "I have two more letters to finish before I can leave. Thea, I'll bring in everything I've been working on before I go. Ted and I are going to the theatre tonight. It's the last performance of *Tillie's Nightmare*."

As Amy finished talking, Thea looked at her assistant and her secretary, then let her gaze travel over the office the two women shared, and the variety of boxes that Mallory had brought in with her.

I'm so lucky, she thought, feeling some of the strain she'd lived with for the past months lessen. Why do I want to continually pick at matters I can't do a thing about? The Ritz-Carlton will either hire me or they won't—and the same for Romney. But right now I have other things to do and I can't spend the morning lost in fantasy.

"Mallory, let's start with the fabrics you wrote me about. I have an idea we're going to be needing bolts and bolts. Amy, take care of those letters and you're a free woman until we get back from Long Island. Have a good time tonight—Charles and I have seen *Tillie's Nightmare* twice and it's wonderful—and when you're at the Herald

165

Square Theatre tonight, be sure to give Marie Dressler a hand for the both of us!''

For Romney Sedgewick, Thea had decided to serve lunch in the dining room, the first time she'd ever done that for a client, but she knew better than to serve a tray lunch to a six-foot-tall man, even in a setting as perfect as the one in front of the fireplace in her office.

Instead, hand-embroidered Madeira linen placemats were put on the dining room table's gleaming surface, the china was the traditional red and blue and white Imari, there were simple crystal goblets from Baccarat, the silver was the restrained elegance of Tiffany's Shell and Thread pattern, and the centerpiece was a crystal bowl filled with red and white carnations and baby's breath. It was a perfect summer table, and Romney Sedgewick was properly impressed.

He'd arrived right on time, a tall, well set-up man just nudging forty, with reddish hair and fine, deep gray eyes; and as far as Thea was concerned he was the very picture of the ready-to-be-impressed prospective client.

"Tell me, Romney," Thea couldn't resist asking as Violet removed their plates of fresh asparagus with sauce vinaigrette, "how did you find Elsie de Wolfe?"

"She's an interesting woman. Are the two of you friends?" he asked, and heard Mallory's stifled laughter.

"Surely you jest."

The implication behind Thea's words was so clear that Romney silently thanked his years of Foreign Office training which always made him proceed on unfamiliar ground with great caution. He most certainly did not want a repeat of the incident of two months before—even if he had deserved every word she'd said to him.

"Well, we did have an interesting discussion," he said at last, smiling. "But I think she was rather put out about

166

two things: first, that my establishment is not going to be terribly large, and second, that I'm not a tame tabby cat." He paused for a second. "Does that disturb you?"

"To answer both questions at once—not at all," Thea replied definitely, and they all laughed, the last threads of tension easing.

"If you do my new flat one-half as nice as this, I'll be perfectly content," he went on as Violet put plates of cold crabmeat salad in front of them. "The last time I was in New York, though, you had your office and showroom on Fifth Avenue. Do you mind, well, living with the store?"

"It *does* have its disadvantages, but then so do most things," Thea smiled. "No, seriously, I like the way things are arranged right now. And with an assistant like Mallory, and a secretary like Amy, things work out rather well." Thea took a sip of her iced tea. "All the work is portioned out. I supervise all the work, buy from the dealers, and handle all the decorating assignments; Mallory buys at auctions, handles the smaller decorating assignments, and works with me on the larger ones; while Amy handles all the invoices and charts, keeps the books, and writes the letters."

"That's admirable organization. I'm truly impressed."

"Take your bow, Thea," Mallory said with a bright smile. "That's the Foreign Office paying you compliments."

"Former Foreign Office," Romney corrected, smiling.

"Well, former or not, thank you very much."

Thea is in her element, Mallory thought as she listened to her friend tell anecdotes about various jobs. I know she was upset about seeing Romney again after what happened, but you'd never know it to listen to her. That's just how I'm going to behave when—

Mallory heard Thea ask Romney where it was he intended to live, and his answer cut short her reverie.

"I was hoping you could help me with that."

"I don't find houses or apartments for my clients, and I don't install furniture or supervise workmen," Thea said serenely, signalling for Violet to serve their dessert of pineapple sherbet accompanied by chocolate leaves. "Now, Romney, you know New York from past visits, and you know what you like. Surely you can put the two together and come up with what you want. Besides, I take all the responsibility for what's *in* your home, so—"

"So I'm responsible for where it is," he finished. "In other words, a delineation of responsibility."

"Exactly. But you have been looking?"

"And looking and looking," Romney laughed.

"In another month you'll be ready to transport the Albany brick by brick across the Atlantic and reassemble it in some appropriate spot," Mallory suggested, referring to the justly famous block of flats in London where Romney had lived until April.

"Please," he smiled. "I've discovered that real estate agents can be terribly aggressive about the least proposing properties."

"Welcome to New York," Thea said with wry amusement. "But even without your having a new home we can get quite a few things settled today. Shall we all go back to my office?"

"Thea, can you and Mallory keep an important secret?" Romney asked a few minutes later as they settled themselves comfortably in front of the fireplace, Thea in the caneback fauteuil, Mallory and Romney on the settee.

"Of course we can."

"There's nothing we'd like better."

"Well, in that case . . ." A pleased smile played around the corners of Romney's mouth. "My new home won't be for me alone. I'm engaged, and will probably be married by the end of this year," he told them, and happily accepted their chorus of congratulations and good wishes.

"Is that why you're here in New York?" Mallory asked. "In London, no one can quite decide what you're doing on the other side of the Atlantic."

"Can't they really?" Romney looked amused. "I really didn't think too many people would care one way or the other."

"Take my word for it, you're a favorite topic over the teacups."

"And I thought I was making my life so simple by quietly slipping away. Ah, well. This is a rather long story, in fact, there are two parts to it, but you both have the right to know it all.

"Back in the eighties, my father was Leo Sackville-West's *chargé d'affaires* when the latter was the British Minister to Washington. I was with him during that time, going to school first at Phillips Exeter, and then to Princeton for two years before we went back to England. This past winter, I received a letter from our ambassador in Washington telling me that they had been doing some general house-cleaning at the embassy and they found an old trunk that had my father's name on it. At just about the same time I became engaged.

"My fiancée is an actress," he went on. "An American who specializes in musical comedy, and she'll be with her show at the Drury Lane until November. The theatre keeps her very busy, and this show is very important to her since she'll be retiring when we get married. We discussed the matter and decided that it would be easier on both of us if we kept our engagement a secret and if I went to Washington to see about this trunk of my father's."

"That was a very admirable move," Thea offered. "I know that if it were me and Charles, I might not be able to stand being separated from him for that length of time."

"I never said it was easy, only that it was the best of all possible options."

"I see where your story has two parts," Mallory said.

"Did you know in advance what was in your father's trunk?"

"No, and it might have been old clothes. In any case, I decided that the time had come for me and the Foreign Office to part company. I handed in my resignation and came directly to New York."

"According to Joanna Garland, you positively vanished the moment you stepped off the *Lusitania*," Mallory told him.

"That's a fairly easy trick, I'm afraid. I went down to Washington right away, which probably accounts for it. Our ambassador's a good sort, and he understood my not wanting to be caught up with the embassy crowd. The trunk was waiting for me when I got to the Shoreham, and when the locksmith opened it, I found it contained a complete record of my father's years in Washington—his journals, his appointment books, and every letter I or anyone else wrote him. For a long time I simply sat there alone in the sitting room looking at all of those papers," Romney went on in a hushed, emotional voice. "The contents of my father's trunk are as much a record of eight years of my life as they were of his, and I knew I had to take every single scrap, read it thoroughly, and put it all in some sort of order for possible publication," he finished quietly, proudly.

"Of course you didn't need any old friends gathering in droves around you just then," Thea said understandingly. "You had to keep what you were undertaking as private and personal as possible."

"That's exactly how I felt," Romney said with a smile that showed how grateful he was at her immediate comprehension. "Not that I turned into a hermit by any means. I gave myself plenty of diversions. Washington in April is beautiful, and in May I went down to Virginia to visit an old Princeton classmate."

"Still working on the side?" Mallory asked.

"More like trying to put everything in order according

170

to year, and that is a major task in itself. I came back to New York in June—dragging my trunk behind me," he added with a smile.

"Which is when we all met."

"Please, Thea." Romney looked embarrassed. "What I said that night . . . It was stupid and inconsiderate of me and I hope you'll accept my heartfelt apology."

"You'll find that out when you get my bill," Thea teased, flashing a smile that let him know that the incident was now all water under the bridge.

"In that case, possibly I should retrace my steps to Irving House—"

"Don't you dare!" Romney was only teasing, and Thea knew it, but all the same she couldn't help playing up to him. "And, for the record, I accept your apology."

"Charles told me I was on rather shaky ground with you."

"It sounds like that must have been an interesting after-church conversation."

"It's amazing the things two men can discuss after early morning service with the rest of the day spread out before them. When I came back to New York from New Hampshire a few weeks ago, I decided to find a nice church that was more than just another fashionable parish, and an actor friend suggested I try visiting Transfiguration." Romney paused for a moment as if he were not quite certain how to proceed, and both Thea and Mallory knew what was coming. "I hadn't heard that Charles—"

"Then you must be the only person who didn't."

"It must have been a difficult time for you."

"Not really. There have been a few sticky moments, but by and large our friends have been wonderful, and Charles is very secure and happy in the step he took."

Romney nodded in understanding. "We've discussed it a few times."

"But eventually your conversation moved on to topics

other than theology." Thea's voice was practical. "Is Charles your literary agent?"

"Not yet. Not until I've completed what I'm doing. No one will see a single page until then. But are you interested in being my decorator?"

"I'd never forgive you if you hired anyone else," she said, and held out her hand.

"I promise to put finding a proper flat at the top of my list."

"Good, but don't sign a lease until I've seen it. When a man has lived alone for a long time it's sometimes difficult to think in terms of two—or more," she said, proceeding carefully since Romney was a widower of long standing who had been deeply in love with his young wife.

"You're absolutely right," he told her. "As soon as I have some interesting prospects, I'll let you know."

"Charles and I are going out to Long Island on Monday, to Cove House."

"That's the Seligman house, isn't it?"

"You know it, then?"

"Very well."

"I'm glad to hear it. You can ring me up out there, or, better yet, you can pack a bag and come out. There's always room for another guest."

"It's a very tempting invitation, but I still think I'm best off seeing as few people as possible for the time being."

"Then I guess that means I can't persuade you to join us at the *Ziegfeld Follies* tonight. Henry and Alix would love to see you."

"And I them. But not right now. And I've already seen the *Follies*."

Thea and Mallory exchanged amused looks.

"Then I guess trying to tempt you with seeing Lillian Lorraine and Fannie Brice and Bert Williams is not going to do any good."

"No, but thank you all the same for asking, and I promise to start making my presence known after this month."

"That's a good idea," Mallory put in. "After all, when your fiancée arrives, you don't want her to find that you've become a recluse. Incidentally, can you tell us her name?"

"I did leave that out, didn't I? It's Tildy—short for Matilda—Barnett."

"I've seen her on Broadway. She's very pretty."

"And very popular, too," Thea added. "Romney, are you going to write your fiancée and let her know we're fans?"

"As soon as I get back to my hotel," he assured them as they all stood up. "And if you have to get in touch with me, I'm at the Knickerbocker."

"A good choice."

"I'm glad you approve, but Thea and Mallory, one thing—my engagement is a secret, both here and in London. Can I impose on both of you not to tell anyone that we know? I realize I'm being rather silly about this, but for the next few months, considering the way newspapers behave about proper Englishmen marrying actresses, I'd rather have as few people as possible privy to my private life."

"What a complicated man," Mallory remarked a few minutes later when Romney had gone and she and Thea were looking at samples of chintz.

"The best ones always are."

"Until he said what he did, I'd actually forgotten that he's *Sir* Romney Sedgewick, and a nephew of the Duke of Alchester."

"I guess he takes it all for granted—which, all things

173

considered, is a very good sign," Thea laughed as she put the fabric swatches in order. Chintzes with white backgrounds first, then pastel, then the ones with backgrounds of gray, blue, mauve, maroon and black, and finally the classic black and white *toile de Jouy*. "He's a very lucky man, the way things have fallen together in his life just at the right moment."

"And he's probably very wise to keep himself tucked away like this. He is a *very* eligible man."

"Oh, yes. And as for eligible men—how are you doing on that score?"

"Peter Beardsley is going to be my escort tonight," Mallory said, knowing this was not what Thea wanted to know.

As Mallory expected, Thea wrinkled her nose. "He's not your sort *at all*, and if you don't discourage him right off, you'll *never* be rid of him!"

"Well, he was the best of the sorry lot that's in town right now."

"You don't have to explain. I remember times like that. But all it takes is one good man to sweep them all away."

Mallory forced herself to laugh. "But I haven't met him yet."

Thea looked obliquely at her. "Haven't you?"

"You mean Rupert?" Mallory felt her face grow warm. She couldn't tell Thea what she'd told Alix, but evading the issue and saying nothing wasn't the answer either. Thea was the one who'd taken her on when she was drifting from day to day and made her a part of a new profession.

"Why not?" Thea pressed as Mallory gathered her thoughts. "Both of you had something that was very real and very right, and that doesn't disappear because of a disagreement or a separation."

"What about pushing him into a rose bush?" Mallory

asked lightly, beginning to smile.

"Did you really? Good—he probably deserved it," Thea stated, laughing. "And yes, it can outlast even one of those amusing little incidents."

"Well, a girl has to defend herself."

"Of course you did, and four years is quite long enough to keep avoiding each other."

"I'll find that out when I get to Cove House. That is, if Rupert's back from Chicago."

"He will be. When I rang Adele to tell her we'd be coming out on Monday, she told me that today's Rupert's last day at the Chicago office, and he'll be leaving on Sunday's Twentieth Century."

Sixteen hours from Chicago to New York, Mallory thought, her heart plunging downward. He'll be back in New York on Monday and come out to Long Island on Tuesday. I have to be there first. Not that I want to make things all *that* easy for him, but—

"Have you thought about what you'll say?" Thea inquired, interrupting Mallory's thoughts.

"All I can think about is seeing him again, not the words I'll use," Mallory said truthfully.

"That's a good point. You can always know in advance the exact thing to say when it's someone you don't care about, but when you do care . . ."

"All you want is to be with that person again," Mallory finished.

"Take the moment as it comes, Mallie," Thea advised in a wise voice. "You'll know what to say when the time comes."

"Suppose I just call him names?"

"I did that to Charles once in the beginning," Thea said with a smile of remembrance. "You'd be amazed at how it helps to clear the air."

The two women shared a secret smile.

"I have an idea that I might just be finding that out

175

myself very soon."

"I generally don't hand out blanket advice, but a couple of well-chosen words can sometimes have a far better effect on a man than all the trickery and cajoling—provided you follow it up with lots of kisses afterwards, of course!"

As Thea finished talking, Mallory finally began to laugh, her world once again sliding back into perspective.

I can handle whatever is going to come down the pike, she thought, her spirits lifting. And not only that, but I'll come away knowing I did the right thing.

"Thank you, Thea. Thank you very much," Mallory said at last. "You're right, it's useless to try and imagine a situation beforehand. On Tuesday night, I'm going to wear a dress from Lucile with a neckline down to *there*, drench myself in perfume, and not say a single word to a certain man. I'm going to set the stage, but I think I'm going to leave the first words up to Rupert Randall!"

A half-hour later, Thea, wearing only a sheer white batiste negligee, lay stretched out on the pink brocade upholstered beechwood chaise lounge in her mirrored dressing room. Her dress for this evening, a Cheruit theatre frock of pink messaline trimmed with bugle embroidery, was draped over a nearby chair, her pink satin opera slippers were set beneath it, and the afternoon's mail was arranged on the robin's egg blue leather-covered drop panel of her petite English inlaid satinwood *secretaire*.

Thea stretched easily, feeling far too lazy to do anything as constructive as opening her mail or taking the first steps toward getting ready for the evening's festivities.

It's only half-past four, she thought. I have plenty of time. I wonder what kind of apartment Romney will

176

choose? Should I have made an exception and offered to help? No—that's taking on what I don't do. Oh, I hope he doesn't take a liking to the Dorilton—awful rooms. I should have asked him if he shipped any of his old furniture over.

Thea was busily spinning plans for her next meeting with Romney when Charles appeared at her dressing room door.

"I didn't know you were home," she said, holding out her arms to him. "How was your meeting?"

"Too long for a hot day like today. I got home a few minutes ago, changed, and decided to come in to see you before I shower," Charles said. "How did your meeting with Romney go?"

"Very well. I was silly to be so nervous."

"You're too good a decorator for that."

For a long minute, Thea looked at her husband standing in the doorway wearing only an ankle-length robe made of toweling material. She knew that Charles, born and raised in the Norman countryside, sometimes found the unrelenting heat of New York City summers difficult to take.

"Come here," she offered. "You look all worn out, and I can have you purring like a cat with a bowl of cream in a half-hour."

"How can I possibly resist a suggestion like that?" he said, coming over to stretch out beside Thea on the chaise.

"Then why do you want to take a solitary shower when we can share a bath together?" Thea inquired as Charles rested his head on her shoulder and she began to massage the back of his neck.

"I think you decided this was the apartment for us the moment you saw that your bathroom had a sunken tub," Charles said, a soft groan of relaxation escaping from his throat as Thea's fingers did their work, moving downward from his neck to his shoulders. "And I think I'll stay with my shower—after all, we do want to get to the theatre tonight!"

"Ah, yes. Social obligations do make certain demands."

Charles propped himself up on one elbow, and with a free hand gently separated the sides of her negligee, gazing reverently at her full bosom.

"Did you say a half-hour?" he whispered as she tugged at the belt of his robe.

"I think that's just about right for us—when we're watching the clock, that is," she purred, pulling him down to her.

Their passion flowed between them like a strong, steady stream, and the morning encounter they'd shared, which had been more play than passion, left them eager and ready for each other instead of satiated.

"Is this more like it?" Thea questioned a long time later, her fingers stroking the length of his spine.

"Very much so." Charles' mouth moved gently along her hairline. "I'll be glad when we get out to Long Island where we won't have to worry about such things as appointments in the middle of the day interrupting us when we'd rather be doing something together."

"That's true," Thea said teasingly, deliberately misunderstanding. "Beginning Monday we'll have long days where we can swim and play tennis and ride and go sailing and—"

"And also do none of those things and only what we're doing right now," Charles finished, gathering Thea closer to him. "Are you happier now?"

"I'm always happy when I'm with you."

"I feel the same way, but I was referring to your meeting with Romney."

"Oh, that."

"I must say that you're remarkably casual about an

assignment that's going to bring in your usual substantial fee."

"That's the only kind of fee to charge!" Thea said emphatically, rumpling Charles' black hair. "And you forgot to add that Romney will be absolutely thrilled with the apartment I'm going to do for him and his bride."

"Bride?" Charles echoed, raising his head. "Romney's not married."

"Tildy's his fiancée right now, but as soon as she gets here from London—" Thea began, and then looked intently at her husband. "Charles, you *do* know that Romney's secretly engaged?"

"No, I do not—he never said a word! Apparently a man will confide things to his interior decorator that he won't tell to his potential literary agent," Charles remarked with growing merriment.

"Romney probably wanted to test the news out on two understanding women like Mallory and me," Thea temporized. "Since she's an actress, he may have been a little bit apprehensive about our reaction."

"That's ridiculous. No one we know cares about something like that. An actress is as respectable as—as an—"

"As an interior decorator?" Thea suggested archly, and then she saw a look of puzzled amazement slide across Charles' face. "What is it, darling? Is something wrong?"

"Romney's fiancée—what's her name?"

"Matilda Barnett, but he calls her Tildy."

"So does everyone else," Charles remarked, his color mounting. "It's my past transgressions coming back to haunt me—"

"What *are* you talking about?" Thea asked, and then she remembered. She and Charles, passionately in love and about to make love for the first time, and he had taken that moment to tell her about his one fling in America. A fling with a musical comedy actress in

179

Boston's Touraine Hotel. Charles had told her about the experience, but not the actress' name, and now, six years later, she looked at her husband, choking back her laughter. "Charles, are you trying to tell me that— that—" she got out before laughter took over.

"Yes! And why are you laughing? This isn't funny. Not at all."

"But it is."

"Really? And how do I tell Romney that six years ago I spent several intimate hours with the woman he intends to marry?"

"Considering how some couples are carrying on with each other, *you* really don't have anything to worry about. *And* you know perfectly well you'd never say a word to Romney on pain of the worst torture," she rushed on forestalling Charles' objections. "*And* you also know perfectly well that if Romney wanted an untouched, innocent female he wouldn't have gotten all that serious about Tildy in the first place."

"It's just that it's all so bloody embarrassing," Charles said, sitting up and swinging his legs over the side of the chaise. "What do I say when I see her again?"

"Oh, little things like hello and best wishes. I'm sure Tildy's going to find it all terribly amusing."

"What bothers me is that you do, too," he remarked, looking down at Thea as she stretched in a particularly luxurious manner. "Why do you think this situation is so funny? I'd expect you to be jealous."

"Why, do you want to make love to her again?"

"If you remember correctly, it was really the other way around."

"Whatever," Thea smiled and, reluctantly, so did Charles. "As far as I'm concerned, it doesn't matter at all. When I write to Tildy I'll tell her that. Now go take your shower and let me have my bath," she said as she sat up and put her arms around Charles. "I love you very much, and I'm sorry if this bit of news has been unsettling for you."

"It was for about fifteen minutes. I'm finally beginning to see the humor of the situation. Be sure to give Tildy my best regards when you write her, and mention that I remember her very warmly."

Thea tugged playfully at Charles' hair. "I'll deliver the first part of your message, but I think the second half is going a bit too far, even when it concerns pleasant memories like yours." She glanced at the decorative little clock on the *secretaire*. "I don't believe where the time has gone! We'd better start getting ready, and later, when we get home again, maybe we'll play out our own version of your Touraine Hotel seduction!"

Well, time wounds all heels.

—Jane Ace

The Dakota

"Welcome home, Mr. Rupert. And if you'll permit my saying so, it's very good to have you back again."

Rupert Randall smiled wearily at Sackett's welcome, and he gladly surrendered his raincoat, overstuffed briefcase and armload of newspapers to the Seligmans' butler who had flung the door open for him even before he pressed the bell.

"Thank you, Sackett. I never thought I'd be as happy as I was a few minutes ago when my cab turned into the Dakota's courtyard," he remarked as he stepped into the anteroom of the fourth floor apartment.

The butler nodded in understanding. "I know the feeling well, Mr. Rupert. Those long train trips can be very wearing in this hot weather, particularly when there's a delay."

"A washout near Albany, in my case," Rupert offered when Sackett paused discreetly. "Did the trunks I sent ahead last week get here?"

"Oh, yes. They got here safely," he assured the younger man. "I've seen to your clothes, and they're all ready to be repacked first thing tomorrow morning. Ah, here is the boy with your suitcases. Just let me show him where to place them, and you'll be settled in your room again."

"Even though it'll only be for one night, there's nothing I'd like better," Rupert said truthfully, glancing at his watch. "But first I'm going to ring up the office and then call Cove House and let them know I got here safely and tell them what train to expect us on tomorrow," he went on, silently hoping that Sackett wouldn't notice that in between the pages of Sunday's *Chicago Tribune* was a copy of the previous Friday's *Chicago Journal of Commerce.* The strongest unwritten law in the Seligman household was that no financial newspaper was to be brought into the apartment despite the fact that in the library one of the two telephones was a direct line to the Wall Street office. The head of a family-controlled financial firm founded when the New York Stock Exchange formed its first chapter, William Seligman left the world of high finance—except in the case of emergencies or illness or bad weather in winter—behind him when he came home at the end of the day.

But now, late on Monday afternoon, Rupert wanted nothing more than to take a long shower, have something to eat, go to sleep and forget his train trip. The Twentieth Century might very well be the last word in American train travel, but that in no way made up for the unrelenting heat and the hours-long delay outside of Albany.

The heat. Even safe inside the confines of the Dakota whose thick walls provided a warm, snug interior in the winter and relatively cool comfort in the summer, Rupert flinched when he thought about Chicago. He'd arrived in the sprawling, wide-open city in early February when the meanest winds blew off Lake Michigan, but by the first week in May the weather had changed, and over the weeks that followed, as the temperature inched its way relentlessly upward, Rupert, growing more and more exhausted, lost interest in the entertainments offered by Chicago's theatres and music halls as well as in its finest and most exclusive diversion of all, 2131 South Dearborn Street's Everleigh Club where the sister-owners, Minna and Aida, made sure their clientele of wealthy and well-connected gentlemen received a warm and proper welcome.

But he had other things to tend to besides reliving his adventures, and it was more than an hour before Rupert could leave the confines of the library. His conversation with his colleagues on Wall Street had been professionally satisfying, and his longer talk with William Seligman had met a deeper, more personal need. Talking with the man he considered to be his foster father provided much-needed balm for some of the problems that were plaguing him.

After he left the library, Rupert paused for a moment at the double doors that led into the drawing room where the fine furniture and paintings were safely under their Holland covers for the remainder of the summer, looked across the central hall that ran the length of the apartment and was papered in hand-blocked Chinese wallpaper at the closed doors of the dining room, which, like all the other dining rooms in every other apartment, looked out onto the less than pleasing sight of the courtyard, and then went into his bedroom, loosening his tie as he entered the room.

"Sackett!"

"Yes, Mr. Rupert," the butler said as he came out of the bathroom. "Is something the matter?"

"Sorry," Rupert said instantly. "I didn't mean to shout. I thought you were in the kitchen."

"No," the older man replied, turning skillfully from butler to valet as he took off Rupert's suit jacket, "I've been getting everything ready for you here, making sure there were enough towels and that you had a new bar of sandalwood soap and laying out your night clothes. I assume you'll be wanting dinner on a tray in bed, but if you'd rather not—"

"There's nothing I'd like better than dinner in bed, and probably breakfast as well. I'm worn out from the trip, and as pleasant as the University Club was, it's nothing like home."

"One would certainly hope not," Sackett murmured, and then left, promising to return in forty minutes with the tray.

Smiling at Sackett's somewhat stuffy comment, Rupert stripped off his clothes, and for one of the few times in the past seven years, left them where they fell, too tired and too much in need of a shower to drape everything over the back of the nearest chair.

As Sackett promised, the marble-heavy bathroom was completely ready for him. Moving quickly, Rupert turned on the shower attachment, adjusted it, and stepped into the steady stream of warm water, closing his eyes as the water ran over his body, easing out the strain and tension. He didn't want to think right now, Rupert decided, pushing his wet hair out of his eyes and reaching for the fat bar of Guerlain's sandalwood soap. There was no need to start dredging up old memories this early in the evening—not when he had the rest of the night to do just that.

Twenty minutes later, toweling his hair dry, another towel wrapped around his lean hips, Rupert stepped back into the bathroom, dripping slightly on the thick cream, green, rose and buff rug.

No matter how long or how often I'm away, this is my room, he thought with a surge of belonging, his gaze taking in the cream-colored walls, the fine four-poster double bed hung in jade and cream chintz with matching curtains at the windows, and the night tables whose bedside lamps were dull green jars with mauve silk shades. He looked at the mahogany writing table with its sage green leather surface, now adorned only with a dark green shaded student lamp, but which during his years at Columbia had held a typewriter while the bookcase, now filled with bestsellers and whodunits, had been the repository for his textbooks.

He looked at the room the way one might look at an old and very cherished friend.

A fine Chinese print hung over the small marble fireplace and the wing chair drawn up next to it was upholstered in a soft, buff-colored silk. Technically, it was the guest room, but for just over three years, from August 1903 to October 1906, he had been its sole occupant, and to Rupert's way of thinking that made this *his* bedroom, even if in the past four years he hadn't spent much time here.

With a flash of amusement, Rupert noted that while he was in the shower, Sackett had not only come back to collect the clothes he'd carelessly left on the floor, but had thoughtfully placed two new books on one of the night tables, and ten minutes later, when the estimable butler returned, Rupert, wearing the fresh pajamas that had been set out beside his pillow, was relaxing in bed, reading the opening chapter of *The Trail Of The Lonesome Pine*.

"Thank you for the books, Sackett," he said, putting the volume aside as the butler settled the white wicker tray across his lap. "I read everything I had with me at least twice through between the LaSalle Street Station and Grand Central."

"I thought as much." Sackett took a step backwards, a knowing look in his blue eyes. "The newspapers you brought home with you, Mr. Rupert—will you be needing them?" he asked in a way that let Rupert know that he had indeed seen the secreted copy of the *Chicago Journal of Commerce*. "Since we're leaving for Long Island tomorrow and the apartment will be closed for the next month, I really don't care to leave old newspapers

187

about. That is, unless there's something of interest that you wish to point out to Mr. Seligman," he amended.

"Put it all out with the trash, Sackett," Rupert said with a grin, "and if you don't mention my little oversight, I promise not to violate the house rule again—even accidentally."

"I understand completely, Mr. Rupert," he intoned politely, the closest he'd ever come to telling Rupert that all was forgiven.

For a moment, Rupert looked at his handsomely set tray and at his meal—cold jellied consommé, chicken salad on a bed of Bibb lettuce, cloverleaf rolls, a small pitcher of iced tea, and a serving of lemon mousse with whipped cream—before speaking again. He was hesitant about asking Sackett a question that might be taken as his stepping over the unseen boundary separating them, but the information he wanted might serve to put some of his troubled thoughts in order.

"Sackett, before you go, there's something I'd like to ask you. But you don't have to answer if you feel I haven't been here long enough to make certain inquiries—"

"Not here long enough? If you'll allow me to say so, Mr. Rupert, there are times I think you've been with us right from the beginning, just like Mr. Clifford and Mr. Gareth and Mr. James. Mrs. Sackett has said so herself," he continued, pretending not to notice that Rupert's right hand had begun to shake so badly that he had to put his soup spoon down. "It's almost as if you were in the nursery at the house on Fifty-first Street."

"It's the Fifty-first Street house I want to ask you about," Rupert said somewhat unevenly. "Twelve years ago, when the Seligmans decided to move from Fifth Avenue to smaller quarters, did you ever think about not coming with them to Central Park West, about finding another large house to be butler in?"

Martin Sackett looked nonplussed at the younger man. He didn't like how Mr. Rupert looked, not at all. He was far too pale, strange to see in a young man who was usually so tanned in the summer, and as for those purple smudges under his eyes—they were almost as distressing as the question he'd just asked.

"Finding other employment wouldn't have been for Mrs. Sackett and myself, Mr. Rupert," he explained carefully. "We thought of it, of course, Mr. Seligman was quite open on the subject, but we decided to remain."

"But you've never looked back, never wondered what might have happened if you'd gone to work for someone else?" Rupert pressed.

"I can't say I have, Mr. Rupert," Sackett murmured. "And if I did, what possible good could it do me? What is, is."

"I expect you're right, Sackett. We can never go back and wish we'd done something else or behaved differently." He looked down at his temptingly set tray. "This is all until I ring tomorrow morning. When I'm finished eating I'll leave the tray outside."

"Very good, Mr. Rupert, and have a pleasant evening."

Rupert ate his dinner methodically, not really tasting any of the food set before him, but this was the first meal in more weeks than he cared to count that he wasn't so exhausted by the sweltering Chicago weather and his day's work at Seligman's financial district office that he was responsible for re-organizing that the sight of a multi-course dinner didn't leave him on the edge of nausea.

His meal over, Rupert left the tray outside his door and then returned to bed, spending the next hour alternating between *The Trail Of The Lonesome Pine* and Mary Roberts Rinehart's *The Man In Lower Ten* until his eyelids began to grow heavy and his temples began to

189

pound with a dull ache.

This is enough, he thought. I'll finish these on the train tomorrow. Where are the bookmarks? Oh, Sackett, no matter how estimable you are it's good to find there's a chink in your perfection somewhere!

Getting out of bed again, Rupert went over to the writing table, searching through the drawers for something suitable to use as a bookmark. An old envelope would do—

No . . . of all things why did I have to find this now after all these years? he thought, groaning inwardly as he looked at the white Bristol board card engraved in black script that he'd pulled from the back of the center drawer:

Mr. and Mrs. Newton Phipps
request the pleasure of
Mr. Rupert Randall's
company at a dance in honour of their god-daughter
Miss Mallory Kirk
on Saturday evening the thirty-first of October
at nine o'clock
At Sherry's

Kindly send response to
667 Madison Avenue
New York

Just what I need, he thought painfully, putting the invitation face down on the writing table, a feeling of intense weariness washing over him. Another reminder—as if I needed one to tell me in no uncertain terms that I'm a cad and a bounder, plus a few other things . . .

Still berating himself, Rupert switched off the lamps and got into bed, pulling the covers over his head in a fruitless attempt to smother his old memories in the darkness.

One by one they rose through the layers of his mind, breaking through the restraints he kept on the greatest cruelty he'd ever committed. All of the memories that had begun to come back to him during the long, hot Chicago nights when he'd lain awake in his room at the University Club now swirled around in his head.

Not only thoughts of Mallory Kirk assaulted him, but the recollection of how he'd come to this room, first as a guest and then staying on to make it his, and ended up— except for the one incident he'd done his best to put behind him but now wouldn't let him rest—by changing and enriching his own life as he'd once tried his best to destroy it.

When he first arrived in New York in the worst heat of the summer of 1903, Rupert liked to tell people he'd only come to collect his cigarette case from Henry Thorpe and then stayed on because it was either a case of going on to Columbia University or getting a job as a day laborer. That glib answer, which was rather characteristic of the personality he projected, actually had more than a grain of truth in it, Henry having confiscated the heavy sterling silver case from him on the train ride from London to Gloucestershire a year previously.

A year of punishment to be passed in a monastery, a farming community best described as Spartan. A year of washing windows and scrubbing floors and helping in the kitchen and tending the garden and looking after the farm animals—all considered to be proper punishment for a young man who had managed to smuggle two very expensive ladies of the evening into his rooms at

Magdalen College, Oxford. And for a young man who'd never done a bit of manual labor or thought about anything beyond his own pleasure, Rupert had come through the experience far wiser and far more ready for change than he'd ever care to admit to anyone.

When the monks had told him his time with them was over and he'd returned to London, going to New York had been the last thing on his list of things he was now free to do. However, the reaction he'd received upon arriving at his mother's Berkeley Square house had left no doubt that he was not welcome back in her household. After their brief and very outspoken reunion, Rupert had stopped only long enough to collect his checkbook and then he was gone, leaving the handsomely furnished house without a backward glance. Almost without thinking, as if propelled by an inner force, he arrived at Cunard's ticket office minutes before they closed for the day and booked passage on the next day's sailing of the *Lucania*.

All he knew was that he had to leave London, get out of England, and if indeed there were any answers in his life, he might find them in New York. He didn't even wait for the morning's boat train. Instead he ate a solitary dinner in the restaurant at King's Cross Station and then took the night train to Liverpool, arriving in that port city in the early morning hours. He had breakfast, purchased several last-minute necessities, and was the first person to mount the first-class gangplank.

He spent the one week from Liverpool to New York sleeping as late as he wanted after nearly a year of rising every morning at half-past five, reading voraciously from books his steward brought him from the ship's library, and ordering complicated meals which he consumed in solitary splendor in his stateroom since he had no clothes with him other than the suit he boarded the *Lucania* in.

It was his first transatlantic crossing and he thought it would go on forever, just days of endless sunshine and blue water and nights like black velvet, and then, abruptly, they were in New York Harbor with its fascinating skyline, and faster than he would have believed possible, he was on the Cunard pier—hot and crowded and reeking of the flotsam that floated in the North River.

With no lengthy, inquisitive customs inspection to detain him, he was the first passenger off the ship, down the length of the pier, and out the doors and onto the foot of Twelfth Street where hansom cabs were lined up, eager for the lucrative fares and tips that awaited the drivers whenever a major ocean liner arrived.

"Do you know of the Dakota?" he asked the first driver, dredging up the name of the block of oddly named flats where his mother had said Henry Thorpe was living.

"There's not a driver in New York worth his hack who doesn't know where the Dakota is. It's a regular landmark," the cab driver replied, a trace of Irish brogue in his speech, his black eyes taking Rupert in, seeing a tanned young man with the voice of an English gentleman, the hands of a laborer, an excellent suit that could have fit a bit better, and a Burberry tossed over one arm. "I'll be pleased to take you to your destination, provided your money's the right color," he added cautiously, since, like all New York's drivers-for-hire, he was a monumentally careful man where payment of his fares were concerned.

With a laugh, Rupert pulled out his billfold to show the driver its contents: a nice collection of crisp, new American banknotes that he'd wisely exchanged for his British pounds in the office of the *Lucania*'s purser.

"Will these do?"

The driver nodded. "Better than most. Now get in and I'll have you up on Seventy-second Street before you

193

know it."

The driver was as good as his word since New York City traffic in early August was traditionally light—about the only time of year it was—and he provided Rupert with the scenic route. He went east across Fourteenth Street to Fifth Avenue and then north up the magnificent thoroughfare to Fifty-ninth Street. By the time the briskly moving hansome turned west again and passed the statue of Christopher Columbus before turning up Central Park West, Rupert's head was swimming with the sights he'd seen—a sensation that increased when the driver stopped the hansom and he stepped out and saw the Dakota looming up in front of him.

"A right and proper haunted house," he muttered half-aloud, reaching for his billfold and handing the driver a five-dollar bill. "Will this cover my trip and your tip?"

"Very good, sir," he said with a wide grin and a tip of his hat. "You'll be all right now, won't you? Your people are expecting you?"

People, I have no people, Rupert thought.

"Yes, I'll be just fine," he said aloud, skillfully passing over the rest of the inquiry. "And thank you for the fine trip up here."

Feeling somewhat more apprehensive than he'd ever care to admit to anyone, Rupert presented himself to the doorman, was guided to the building's office, and after a dint of persuasion where he convinced the switchboard girls and Mr. Knott, the Dakota's manager, that he *didn't* want to be announced, was directed to the proper elevator lobby and told to tell the operator to take him to the fourth floor.

The nice woman who ran the Otis lift pointed out the proper apartment door to him, and for a moment he stood in the silent, cool, semi-private hallway, his heart pounding. For the past eight days he'd been running;

194

running away from a mother he didn't love, running away from a past filled with too much indulgence and money, running without thinking, and now he had made direct contact with a wall. Or was it his own conscience?

What's wrong with you? he challenged himself, approaching the elaborately carved wood door. Did your year with the monks take away all your nerve? If I'm not wanted here—which wouldn't be so unusual since no one else wants me—I'll just set myself up in the best hotel in New York, and do exactly as I please . . .

He pressed the buzzer with a short, determined jab, and stepped back to wait for the results, all of his old defences rising to the surface.

"Hello, Hodges," he said a moment later, ironic amusement heavy in his voice. "Is his lordship at home?"

"Yes, he is, Sir, and her ladyship, too," Henry Thorpe's butler replied calmly, opening the door the rest of the way and taking the younger man's Burberry. "If you'll wait here for a moment—" he began politely. Hodges had been in service for too long and had seen too much to be caught off-guard by a young man deliberately looking to shock and surprise.

"Don't announce me," he instructed, stepping across the threshold, his silver eyes taking in the entry hall. He saw the bombe chest that looked English but wasn't, the excellent painting whose subject matter—a vast, green river valley—he couldn't place, and his own reflection in the mirror that lined the opposite wall.

Without waiting for Hodges to direct him, Rupert forged ahead, swinging to the right, into the central hall off which all the rooms opened. He saw Alix first, tall and slender in a white batiste summer dress, standing by the double doors that led to the drawing room, and for a moment their gazes met and locked.

Alix Turner Thorpe hid her surprise well, and a bubble

of amusement rose up in her.

Well, we certainly weren't expecting *this*, she thought, taking a step backward to better view the encounter that was going to take place in a moment. But Rupert is Henry's responsibility, let him take the first step.

Somehow Rupert seemed to sense Alix's thoughts, and he knew that although in the past he'd always been able to charm women into helping him he'd get no help from Lady Henry Thorpe. But better that than another elegant lady who couldn't resist the idea of taking Allison Randall's son into her bed, he admitted reluctantly to himself, and out of the corner of his eye he saw Henry Thorpe.

Together, separated by nothing more than the width of the corridor, the two men faced each other down. It was obvious neither was going to give an inch, and for a moment their strong wills were so evident Alix would later swear that she could see them hanging in the air, and then it was Rupert who moved first.

Somewhere deep inside him a voice he didn't often hear or pay attention to reminded him that he hadn't come three-thousand miles to start his old game of matching wits with the man who was more or less his guardian, and in two steps he crossed the space separating them and flung his arms around Henry Thorpe.

"A year ago I hated you," he said shakily. "But I think now I have to thank you for saving me."

Henry placed both hands on the younger man's shoulders and regarded him solemnly. "So you've come full circle with no hard feelings?"

"None—and I didn't have to be beaten into realizing it either," he said in an oblique reference to Henry's parting words to the monks when he'd left Rupert in their care, giving them full permission to beat Rupert as frequently as he needed it.

"I never really thought they would have to," Henry replied, beginning to smile. "Have you met Alix?"

"Not really. Does that entitle me to kiss the bride, even though it's a year later?"

"Oh, why not?" Alix said, joining the conversation, not quite believing the tableaus that had just unfolded in front of her. One never knew . . . She turned an elegant cheek for Rupert, and after his lips brushed her at a point midway between cheekbone and mouth, she gestured toward the drawing room. "Would you be interested in tea?"

"More than interested—I'm famished!"

"Well, we can remedy that," Alix offered, slipping an arm through Rupert's. Last summer, Rupert Randall had been a sulky-mouthed young man whose taste for wine, women and song far out-distanced what was proper for his almost nineteen years and which was beginning to show on his face and body, but now Alix saw that the faint signs of dissipation were off his face and his frame was as lean and hard as a young tree. She might never truly like him, but he certainly deserved a second chance to prove himself. "And until our tea is served, you can meet the newest member of the Thorpe family," Alix went on, wanting to make him feel welcome despite her natural hesitation about him.

For a moment, Rupert was almost dizzy from the beauty of the drawing room. Underfoot was a cream, blue, apricot and gray Bessarabian rug contrasting off the soft white walls and the profusion of fragrant summer flowers arranged in great bouquets. As if in a blur, he saw the elegant side tables, the framed mirror over the fireplace and the two portraits flanking it. Then, as it all began to slide into place, he saw the fine Impressionist paintings, the silk-covered chairs and deep-pillowed sofas and, finally, between the marble fireplace and the twin sofas in front of it, he noticed the pink-ribboned, white lace bassinet.

"There's a baby?" he questioned as they approached.

"When I took you out of the way of the world for a year, I didn't think your isolation would be that total," Henry remarked as he reached the bassinet. "I assume your mother heard our news. Didn't she tell you?" he asked, skillfully transferring the small, sleeping baby from his arms to Rupert's, and instructed, "Say hello to Isabel. She's just two weeks old."

In any case, Rupert would have been glad of any excuse to put off talking about his mother, but as he looked down at the slumbering infant who was all pale pink and porcelain white, a warm wave of affection swept over him, and when Isabel opened her long-lashed lids to look up at him, he was utterly lost. He held her until Doris and Carrie, Alix's maids, brought in tea, and even as his cup and plate were filled he kept stealing glances into the bassinet.

"Do you know this is the first baby that I've ever held?" he said, eating a cucumber sandwich.

"Well, you did very well," Alix assured him, adding small sandwiches of shrimp salad and chicken salad and rolled bread spread with cream cheese and caviar to his plate. "You may hold her any time you wish."

"Thank you," he replied, took a sip of tea, and eyed Henry. "Do you want to ask me all those necessary questions now? I can assure you that for almost a year I was a model of hard work and repentence."

"You didn't have much choice," Henry shot back with a knowing smile. "Did you hate it very much?"

"Loathed it—and you and Isaac and Patrick for thinking it up in the first place," he admitted cheerfully, referring to the Earls of Saltlon and Rossford, co-executors of Leonard Randall's will along with Henry, who had come up with the plan to remove the recalcitrant Rupert Randall from his less than respectable amusements if he stepped out of line again.

"You *were* warned in advance," Henry pointed out in an equally cheerful voice. "As far as I can determine, no one threatened you into pulling your last escapade. I hope you were left with some pleasant memories of it."

"Considering where I was, it was all I had. I was up every day at half-past five to bake bread and scrub floors and wash windows and take care of the animals and the garden and—" He continued on in the same vein for a few more moments and then viewed the three-tiered silver cake stand with great interest. "May I have an eclair, Alix? Or do I call you Aunt Alix?" he asked in a teasing voice.

"Not unless you're interested in a very fast and expensive trip to the dentist," she retorted, reaching for the silver tongs. "And as for the pastry, have two, one chocolate and one mocha," she smiled. "Would you also like a piece of angel food cake? Mrs. Wiley, that's our cook, does a superb one. Just look at that pink frosting."

He took all of her suggestions, and as he ate Alix began to slowly relax. The Rupert Randall she disliked wasn't seated across from them; it was only a good-looking boy who needed a better haircut and had obviously been working with his hands and was hungry for his tea. Well, let him eat all he wanted and then some, she thought, but what they were going to do with him when afternoon tea was consumed was another matter entirely.

"Where's your luggage?" Henry inquired, enjoying his own eclair.

"I haven't got any. Except for my Burberry which Hodges took possession of, I'm just as you see me, which, if you recall, is the same suit I was wearing when you took me off to expiate my sins and—"

"That's enough, Rupert." Henry's voice was devoid of humor. "Let's have the whole story. Now."

Rupert put his cake plate down on the oriental

rosewood coffee table. "The monks of St. Desmond's—who aren't a bad lot by the way, they just worked me like a slavey and wouldn't let me near the chapel which was all right by me—had a visitor coming, a high-up Anglo-Catholic mugwump whom they couldn't let see me, and since I had what they euphemistically call the visitor's bedroom, I exchanged my work clothes for the best of Saville Row and—and—" Rupert's voice ended on a ragged note and Henry pressed his advantage.

"So you came back to London, and ended up by having it out with your mother." It was a statement, not a question.

"You already know the answer to that!" Rupert snapped. "You've certainly known my mother long enough. She had it all fixed in her mind that I was going to have some great religious conversion, a miracle that she could describe over the teacups to all the churchmen and tame tabby cats who come to rub their fur against her ankles. Naturally, I wasn't in the least welcome when I did show my face again at Berkeley Square."

"So you ran away from home," Henry stated without embellishment.

"I'm of age. I won't go back and you can't send me!"

"If you don't calm down I'm going to send you to stand in a corner!" Henry warned. "If you want to stay in New York, fine. But since you don't want to go back to England, what *do* you want?"

The hostility faded out of Rupert's eyes and was replaced by a faint uncertainty. "I'm not sure."

"That's all right," Henry soothed. "I don't expect you to have some sort of life plan already established. I just thought that you might have thought up something special during your trip over."

"If you stay with us, you'll have to sleep in the library," Alix put in, deciding to get over this hurdle right now.

"I don't suppose I could set myself up at the Waldorf-Astoria?" Rupert parried.

"Not if you still want to be welcome here. After all, we're a good source of free meals," Henry pointed out as the butler entered the drawing room. "Yes, Hodges?"

"Excuse me, my lord, but Mr. Seligman is here. He said to tell you it's about champagne."

"Champagne? Well, why not? What's a few bottles between good neighbors?"

"Now this isn't what I was expecting," Henry added a moment later as William Seligman came into the room carrying four bottles of champagne.

"It's my own fault if you thought I'd come to borrow, but I asked Hodges to be a bit cryptic," he said, setting the bottles down on the coffee tables next to the tea things. "Our Paris wine dealer just sent us a case of new champagne, and Adele and I thought you would like to put these away for Isabel, since by 1921, 1903 is going to be considered a very good year."

"Oh, Bill, thank you. This is just perfect," Alix said, kissing the tall, distinguished man whose thick black hair was heavily silvered at the temples. "We're going to mark them, 'For Isabel Leslie Thorpe on her eighteenth birthday,' and we'll expect you and Adele to be there to help drink and toast from the first bottle!"

"We may be a bit long in the tooth by then—and *don't* tell Adele I just said that—but we'll be there."

"In the meantime, can we persuade you to have a cup of tea and a slice of angel food cake?" Henry offered. "After all, this is about the only time of the day when champagne isn't quite right. Bill, this is my ward, Rupert Randall. Rupert, I'd like you to meet Mr. William Seligman who has the apartment next to ours and who, during the day, runs Wall Street."

"There are some who might think that is somewhat of an overstatement," William Seligman said lightly as

Rupert stood up and they shook hands. "Are you visiting Henry and Alix?"

"It seems like a good thing to do for the time being."

"I see," Bill said simply, and sat down on Alix's other side. He knew exactly who Rupert Randall was, but there was no need to bring up the troublesome incident Henry had told him about. He graciously accepted a cup of tea and a plate of cake. "Are you interested in Wall Street?"

"I'm always interested in money, and I'd like to see the seats on your Exchange."

"Really? There's no place to sit down on the floor of the Stock Exchange—but that's another story," Bill said, amused, as Alix and Henry stifled their laughter. "It's a slow time right now, and I'll take you on a tour tomorrow if you like."

"I think I'd like that. It'll help make up for my upcoming night on the library's sofa," Rupert said with a flash of fun.

"The sofa?" Bill repeated, looking at Henry. "Why consign him to that particular penance?"

"A shortage of bedrooms," Alix pointed out. "We're spread rather thin at the moment. It's amazing how one small baby can take up so much room."

"Oh, I remember! But as for Rupert here, there's an extra bedroom in our apartment."

"We couldn't allow it," Henry began in protest, deliberately not meeting Alix's eyes, well aware of what his wife's reaction to Bill's offer would be.

"Why ever not?" Bill turned to Rupert. "Would you be interested in moving next door? My wife and I would be happy to have you as a guest."

"Yes, thank you. I'd very much enjoy having a bed to sleep in tonight," Rupert said without missing a beat.

"Then that's all settled," Bill said definitively, and Henry was too honest to make false protests. "We'll just have Hodges turn your luggage over to my butler,

Sackett, and—"

"And I'm afraid I haven't any luggage," Rupert interrupted, his face flushing under his tan, sounding embarrassed for the first time that afternoon and for the first time ever that Henry could recall. "I expect you know all about me . . ." His voice trailed off for a moment. "You see, I left London with the clothes on my back and got off the *Lucania* this afternoon the same way. The night clothes and razor I bought in Liverpool I left on the ship," he finished in a rush and waited for the reaction from the man who sat across from him.

It was not the philosophical reply he was expecting.

"That's a perfectly plausible thing to do," Bill said with a slight shrug. "No doubt you'd like to get rid of your suit as well. You look about the same size as my youngest son, Jimmy, and we have his old dinner clothes and some other odds and ends in the guest room closet. They'll get you through tonight, and tomorrow I'll take you to Brooks Brothers."

"Fine," Rupert said, having no idea to what he'd just agreed to, except that, for the first time, an older person was extending an offer to him that didn't have strings attached or was somehow tied into his behavior.

A few minutes later, after some pleasant summer conversation, William Seligman stood up. "I'm afraid it's time to go back next door or else Adele will begin to think I've disappeared. Rupert, are you ready to see your room?"

Hastily consuming a last forkful of cake, Rupert rose, an old gleam of fun in his eyes. "Alix, tea was delicious. My compliments to your cook. And Uncle Henry, thank you for the offer of your library sofa, but since America is the land of opportunity, I'm moving on to greener pastures."

Henry's only reply to Rupert was a somewhat withering look, but his question to his friend and neighbor was born out of his long experience with the younger man.

"Bill, are you sure you don't want to rescind your offer?"

"Of course not, Henry," Bill replied in a genial and very amused voice. "Adele and I have raised three sons, and despite any interesting detours this young man thinks he discovered, by this time there isn't too much wool left to pull over my eyes!"

Alix and Henry spent the next fifteen minutes sharing the last eclairs.

"I suppose that if Adele was going to put her foot down and order Rupert removed from her apartment he'd be back here by now."

Henry applied his fork to the final chocolate eclair, neatly dividing it. "I guess that for the time being—as the saying goes—we're off the hook."

"Then you were as delighted as I was when Bill offered to put Rupert up!"

He savored the rich chocolate. "Of course I was, but, my dear doctor, one of us had to maintain the proprieties, and since I'm the executor of Leonard Randall's will, it was up to me to offer his son lodging."

"It might all work out," Alix offered, taking her own half of the eclair. "Rupert seemed fairly honest about the past year. And since I'm no fan of Allison's, I can see where her son might be happier away from her. Last year, you and Isaac and Patrick kept insisting that Rupert had a good mind and fine potential and had to be shown the error of his ways. Well, maybe it's worked and he's ready to try and live his life in a different way."

"There's nothing I'd like better, but for the next few days he's Bill's responsibility and I'll let him have it with my blessing," Henry said, slipping an arm around Alix and pulling her close for a kiss. "In fact, I'm so pleased at this turn of events that I'll offer Bill a whip and a chair in case Rupert resumes his old ways!"

William Seligman firmly believed that a young man's attendance at his first baseball game was an important rite of passage. Not as important or life-changing as some other events, of course, but still important in the scheme of things. So on this hot, sunny Friday afternoon, three days after he'd invited Rupert Randall into his home, he had an ulterior motive in mind when at breakfast he announced that instead of going downtown today they'd be taking in America's pastime. His own grandchildren were still too young for this special treat, he explained, and he would be interested in seeing Rupert's reaction.

For his part, Rupert approached his afternoon at Washington Heights' Polo Grounds with his mask of slightly amused detachment firmly in place. He loathed cricket and didn't expect baseball to be any better. He held on to that belief through their arrival at the stadium, while they were settling into the private box with its unobstructed view of home plate, and as Bill and his middle son, Gareth, explained the program and pointed out the players, a few of whom came over to say hello and shake hands. But as the game began, as he saw Christy Matthewson, star pitcher for the New York Giants, who would win over ninety games in the 1903-1905 seasons, pitch his famous fade-away curve to lead his team to a 7-5 victory against the Boston Red Sox, Rupert's carefully cultivated cover of indifference cracked and fell away, and by the time the last base was being rounded, he was on his feet and cheering as wildly as everyone else in the house on Coogan's Bluff.

The three men left the Polo Grounds together; Gareth to where his driver was waiting with his Packard Model

K, and Bill and Rupert to the black, shiny family brougham, the elder Seligman promising his son yes, come November and the Fourth Annual Automobile Show, he would seriously consider ordering a motor car.

"I suppose I'll have to," Bill said to Rupert as they settled across from each other in the brougham's taupe velvet interior. "The age of the automobile, at least in the city, is upon us and I may as well learn to enjoy it. After all, it doesn't look very good for me to go around recommending automobile shares for investment purposes while I stay with a matched pair. I wonder how MacBride is going to take to his driving lessons?" he mused as his young companion leaned back against the soft upholstery and closed his eyes.

Full of Harry Stevens hot dogs and cold beer, his heart still pounding from the excitement generated by the game, his throat raw from cheering on the Giants, and finally feeling the effect of the past days where he had been escorted from Brooks Brothers for new clothes to the barbershop at the Waldorf-Astoria for a haircut and then at last to the canyons of Wall Street, Rupert was too pleasantly exhausted to give his full attention to his host.

This was just the moment William Seligman had been looking for. He'd been observing Rupert Randall very carefully, and his financier's mind had already judged him to be very intelligent, very polite because he had to be, and entirely in control of his emotions out of a sense of fierce self-protection. With the exception of this afternoon's game, the only other time he had seen a grin of pure enjoyment and astonishment on the younger man's face was when he'd first seen the frenzied action that took place every weekday on the floor of the New York Stock Exchange. He could have asked him then, as the plan occurred to him, but caution and consultation ruled. He and Adele had been in complete agreement from the first, and Gareth and Jimmy and their wives had been encouraging. Clifford's explosive reaction made William Seligman smile. His eldest son still had to learn that in certain instances he was not responsible for his father's life.

"Rupert," he asked quietly, waiting for the younger man to open his eyes, "did you have a good time today?"

"Wonderful—the best—I wish it didn't have to end," he replied, and his appreciation was genuine.

Bill smiled. "Sometimes the next day can be both different and better." He paused for a crucial half-minute, letting the questioning look come into Rupert's eyes, letting him wonder about what was coming while he was still too sleepy to second-guess. "Rupert, would you like to stay on in New York?"

Instantly, the boy's lassitude vanished. "More than anything!"

"And since you have to do something, would you like to go to Columbia next month?"

"The university?" Rupert couldn't quite believe his host's words. The morning hours had been devoted to a trip up to Morningside Heights for a tour of the Columbia University campus followed by lunch at the Faculty Club. And among the reading material placed on his bedside table last night, included with books like Alexander Dana Noyes' *Forty Years of American Finance* and Francis Eames' *The New York Stock Exchange*, was the Columbia University course catalog for the academic year 1903-1904. Intrigued, since no such companion volume existed at either Oxford or Cambridge, he'd read it thoroughly. "Can it be arranged?"

"Probably." William Seligman wasn't one to make rash promises. "Of course you'll have to agree to certain things first. Otherwise, I won't speak to Nicholas

207

Murray Butler."

"Such as?" The catch, Rupert thought, it's always there.

"Such as living with us, living according to the rules we lay down for you." Bill's voice was quiet, friendly, and totally uncompromising. "Adele and I want to have you with us, but not at the price of your having *carte blanche* to tear off and do exactly as you please with consideration for no one except your own temporary gratification. I realize that right now I'm asking you to buy a pig in a poke, but are you willing to take the chance?"

It occurred to Rupert that he could very well be trading one set of unyielding strictures for another, but another impulse urged him on. He wanted to try another university.

"What rules?"

"You'll find out later—if I can arrange everything. Your reputation precedes you . . . but enough of that. Now, yes or no?"

"Yes," he said, and grinned.

"I'll speak to Henry tonight. This concerns him as your guardian, and I want his approval. But in the meantime," he went on with the smile of a man who has engaged in a very tricky negotiation and won, "do we have a deal?"

"We have a deal," Rupert agreed with a pirate's grin. "After all, I'm very well known for trying anything once, and Columbia University is next on my list!"

The dinner had been perfect for the warm summer night. Mrs. Waterly, the Seligmans' cook, as much a jewel to them as Alix's Mrs. Wiley was to the Thorpes, had prepared iced cucumber soup, a green salad accompanied by a fine runny Camembert, a tenderly perfect filet of sole with mushrooms and rice, and finished off the meal with a superb chocolate mousse cake that the five people at the table greeted with exclamations of delight.

When their second servings of dessert were placed in front of them, William Seligman looked down the table at his house guest.

"Rupert, right now Adele and I have some things to discuss with Alix and Henry which, at this point, don't include you. I think you should take your cake and pour yourself another glass of champagne and go to your room."

To Henry Thorpe's barely concealed surprise, Rupert drained his cup of *café filtré*, refilled his glass from the bottle of champagne resting in the ice bucket and, with glass and plate in hand, politely said good-night to the Seligmans and the Thorpes.

"Well, I've always said that there's nothing to top off an excellent meal like a very unexpected surprise," Henry remarked when Rupert left. "However did you manage Rupert's graceful exit?"

"Oh, put it down to his wanting to be a good guest and don't rake up old stories about him," Bill said easily. "Now, there is something we want to discuss with the both of you. Shall we finish our dessert in the drawing room? What we want to take up with you and Alix will go down better there."

The two couples rose from the English Regency table, left the cream and blue dining room, and crossed the hallway to the large drawing room that overlooked Central Park. By a silent signal that passed among them, their conversation was kept in a light vein until the Sacketts, who had followed with their dessert and champagne and coffee, withdrew closing the double doors behind them.

"I expect you know that I want to talk to you about Rupert," Bill said as both couples sat opposite each other on twin deep-pillowed sofas upholstered in sea green silk.

"I was wondering what would take you so long," Henry said in all seriousness. "Bill, I have to congratulate you and Adele for having the patience to put up with Rupert for the past three days."

"Henry, I'm afraid you're misreading the situation. We're not withdrawing our hospitality." He paused for a moment. "We want you to give Rupert to us."

For a moment the elegant room with its light wood furniture covered in pale silks with Impressionist paintings on the walls and flower-filled oriental vases ornamenting the side tables was bathed in silence—stunned on Henry's part, considering on Alix's, and patient on Bill and Adele's.

"Bill, are you and Adele *sure* about this?" Henry said, finding his voice at last.

"Yes, we are," Adele said in a definite and patrician tone, answering for her husband. "Believe us, Henry, Bill and I aren't given to flights of fancy."

"But *why*?" Henry's voice was perplexed. "Your sons are married, and you have a pleasant and well-ordered life. There's no need to drag Rupert into it."

"That's all true," Bill allowed. "But you don't want Rupert—and what's more, you shouldn't," he went on, forestalling Henry's comments. "Just hear me out, please. You have Alix and you have your baby, and at this point in your life that's all you should have: a brand new family, not a menagerie because you've tacked a nineteen-year-old boy onto it. On the other hand, it's not too much for us; we've been through it three times before."

"I wouldn't compare any of your sons to Rupert."

"In the sense that people can't be duplicated, I agree with you. Besides, we've always wanted a fourth child and we'd be getting one at exactly the right age. No need to worry over prep school grades or dentist appointments or birthday parties or piano lessons or any of the other things you have to take into consideration until a child is eighteen. It's really a basic situation now, all we have to do is nurture him through the next few years."

"Still, he's my responsibility."

"Which is the worst reason for anyone doing anything," Alix put in, and was rewarded with a warm smile from Bill.

"Thank you, my dear. To tell you the truth, I think Rupert is at a crossroad right now. He won't go back to England, and he doesn't want to live with you and Alix. He has too many old memories in both places. This afternoon I asked him if he wanted to live with us and go to Columbia and both answers were very positive. I want your approval on this matter, of course, it wouldn't be right otherwise. But if this doesn't pan out—either by your not agreeing or by Columbia's not accepting him—Rupert may very well go back to the way he was a year ago. He certainly has the money to do as he pleases, and neither of us has any jurisdiction over him."

"That isn't an eventuality I care to contemplate."

"Then you have an option open to you."

Henry and Alix exchanged looks. He was well aware of what his wife's opinion in this situation was, but he had known Rupert for far too long to think that his polite, well-behaved manner was anything more than veneer, or that the Seligmans, both of whose families had arrived in New York in the late 1600s, would be in for an easy time.

"Rupert isn't the nicest person in the world," Henry felt he had to point out. "He could end up turning on you."

"That's pretty much what Cliff said," Bill smiled. "And I'll give you the same answer he got: I've spent the past thirty-odd years involved in high finance, and since I'm neither easily deluded, diverted or senile, I'm not likely to be fooled by one young man."

"Besides," Adele added in a practical tone, "we're not Catholics, which seems to be a rather prime consideration with Rupert. I really hate to say this, and it's not as if the Couderts and the Noels and the Ryans haven't been family friends for years, but considering his mother and what she thinks, I'm not surprised how that boy is starved for affection."

"Affection? Rupert?" Henry choked on his laughter.

"Adele has her own theory about Rupert," Bill put in. "She thinks he has never really had any sort of permanence or stability in his life. His father was a womanizing wastrel, and his mother—well, for delicacy's sake I won't say religious zealot, just a woman who has found too much comfort and attraction in her faith. Also, your highly valued British system of upbringing and education, beginning with nanny in the nursery and preparatory school at eight followed by Eton or Harrow and ending up at Oxford or Cambridge backfired with him. He's probably felt that the only time anyone cared about him was when he was acting outrageous—if they were interested even then."

"And you think you can help him?" Henry questioned, silently agreeing with everything Bill just said.

"Don't sound so skeptical, Henry. We think Rupert needs the same place to come home to every night, someone to pat him on the head when he's doing well and swat him on the rear when he steps out of line. It's not that you and Alix can't do that; it's that you shouldn't have to."

"He'll disappoint you, Bill."

"And maybe I'll disappoint him. It's an unfortunate fact of life that at some point parents and children always let each other down over something."

"Well, you've probably never done that to your children," Henry said, and was surprised when Bill and Adele and Alix began to laugh.

212

"Excuse us, Henry, but this is an old story with us. About ten years ago I disappointed Cliff when I turned down Grover Cleveland's offer to become Secretary of the Treasury."

Henry looked suitably impressed. "That's quite an honor."

"Only if you've been asked to be Chancellor of the Exchequer. In our government, the Treasury post is more ceremonial."

"So you refused it."

"Not for that reason, but because the country was entering into one of its interesting financial crises," he explained quietly. "What started as a simple bankers' panic in early 1893 was a full-scale gold crisis two months later, and it went on until February 1895. In twenty-three months, six hundred banks closed and there were fifteen thousand commercial failures. By July 1893, the price of silver dropped to sixty-five cents, and I saw half a dozen railroad stocks go from one hundred and fifty to fifteen dollars a share. How could I go waltzing off to Washington to sit comfortably in the Treasury Building and leave the clients and companies we represented? Cliff was too young then—just two years out of Columbia—to have it all left in his hands, even though he thought he wasn't. He wanted me to have the honor and the prestige, but I knew something else was more important at the moment than a Cabinet post. At any rate, what I'm trying to point out is that you can disappoint children but you must never fail them. I've never done that to any of my sons, I wouldn't do that to Rupert, and I think with that foundation he won't turn on me or fail any of us again."

"Optimist," Alix smiled, and looked at her husband.

Henry Thorpe knew that it was now all up to him. It was like playing tennis, and the ball was in his court. Only this was not a game. Quite possibly a young man's future was at stake. Well, possibly he shouldn't go quite so far, but still . . . The moment Bill had broached the subject he'd known what his answer would be, and his procrastination now was unforgivable.

"I don't know why, but you may actually be good for Rupert. In any case, I'm more than willing to see if being with people he hasn't known all his life will do more for him than all of us who knew him when," Henry said, and raised his glass in a toast. "To you, Bill and Adele, with mine and Alix's best wishes on your new and difficult undertaking!"

Seligman Mr and Mrs Clifford (Julia Newstadt)-Cl. At. Au. Ar. Mid. Ny. Rv. Gg. Cl'91 . . . Phone No 224-81 . . . 923 Fifth Av

Seligman Mr and Mrs Gareth (Susannah Prince)-Cl. Au. Ct. Mid. Lt. W. Cl'95 . . . Phone No 64-79 . . . 22 E 64

Seligman Mr and Mrs James (Katharine Flowers)-Cl. Au. Gg. Mid. Lt. Pl. Cl'97 . . . Phone No 4091 . . . 667 Mad Av

Seligman Mr and Mrs William (Adele Franks)-Cl. Lt. At. Gg. Ct. Au. M. Mid. Ny. Rv. Ar. Cl'68 . . . Phone No 767 Plaza . . . 1 W 72

Thorpe Mr and Mrs Henry (Alicia L Turner Bd'96)-At. Au. Lt. . . . Phone No 1259 . . . 1 W 72

Phipps Mr and Mrs Newton (Esme Schuyler)-Cl.

At. Au. Rv. Ar. C. M. Ul. Ct. Mid. Lt. W.
Cl'68 . . . Phone No 4074 . . . 667 Mad Av . . .
Miss Mallory Kirk

Neal Mrs Lewis (Kathryn Maitland) . . . Phone No
631 Plaza . . . 150 W 59

North Mr and Mrs Richard (Megan Copeland)-Cl.
At. Au. Lt. Pl. W. Gg. Cl'94 . . . Phone No 991
Plaza . . . 205 W 57

Leslie Mr and Mrs Philip (Kezia Jay)-Cl. C. At. Au.
Ar. Rv. Ct. M. W. Lt. Cl'84 . . . Phone No 224-
41 . . . 160 W 59

Rupert was reading the *Social Register*. He'd found this
small blue book in the writing table, and when he asked
his hostess if this were the American version of *DeBretts*,
Adele had laughed and told him, "Don't give it airs it
doesn't deserve. When you get right down to it, it's more
like a fancy telephone directory. But if you read it with a
grain of salt, you'll find it rather amusing."

Now he sat flipping through it, looking for the names
of people he'd met over the past days, ignoring for the
moment such light reading as *The Riddle Of The Sands*,
Brewster's Millions and *Beyond The Law*.

He checked the Seligmans' listings, dividing the family
from others with the same name, noted with abstract
delight that Henry and Alix were listed as Mr. and Mrs.
instead of Lord and Lady, and found Richard North,
who'd come to dinner last night, bringing with him
several of the latest offerings from the presses of
Doubleday, Page where he was a senior editor. He saw

that Kathryn Neal, a very elegant *grande dame* who'd also been a dinner guest last night, had the shortest listing; that Philip Leslie, who was Alix's cousin, and his wife, Kezia, had one of the longest; and was surpassed only by Newton Phipps, a rather grand, semi-retired investment banker, just returned from a summer in Europe a week ahead of his wife and god-daughter, who appeared to have the most club memberships to his name.

Over the next half-hour, Rupert ate his cake, drank his champagne, and with the aid of the key printed on the opening page, he deciphered the National Arts from the Automobile of America, the Sons of Revolution from the Sons American Revolution, Manhattan from City Midday, Lotus from Players, Whist from Garden City Golf, and Union League from Century.

And never for one moment, as he relaxed in the wing chair, laughing at his form of diversion, did he doubt that at the same time William Seligman was talking Henry Thorpe around.

Finally, putting aside the *Social Register*, he lifted his tulip glass and held it up in a silent toast to the room he was in, a toast to a new beginning.

Whatever else his faults—and he had many—Rupert had a strong streak of loyalty in him, a trait that until three days ago no one had bothered to try and discover if he had. Now someone had actually decided to take a chance on him, and was challenging him to prove himself.

Rupert's gaze moved on to the bed, already perfectly turned down for the night, his nightshirt neatly laid out on the topsheet. It was quite different from the narrow bed with the hard, serviceable mattress that he'd slept on for nearly a year, but its wide, inviting expanse brought back other memories. Deprived of sensual gratification, his rebellious biology first burned, then simmered, and finally abated into an adjustment of sorts—but for how long now that he was no longer a slavey in a Gloucestershire monastery but an about-to-be university student in New York?

Not that he'd ever contemplate recommitting the scenario that had gotten him first sent down from Oxford and then delivered into the strict arms of the monks. No, thank you, he decided quickly. One way or another he'd adjust to sleeping alone in this bed, but as for other amusements . . .

Well, they'd never include two women at the same time, not ever again. Rupert's great enjoyment of women had no grounding whatsoever in exhibitionism. He considered lovemaking—even when the encounter was based on a cash transaction—to be a private act between a man and a woman, and his first threesome, undertaken in the spirit of experimentation (not to mention the thrill of the absolutely forbidden), was undeniably his last.

"And here I am," he said aloud. "Uncle Henry once accused me of having the luck of a cat to always end up on my feet. Well, I've done it again. But what next?"

Columbia, I hope, he wished silently, too superstitious at that very moment to say the words out loud. And to live here as well, he added as he stood up to answer the polite rapping on the door.

"Lord and Lady Thorpe are ready to return to their own apartment, and the master would like you to come into the drawing room to say good-night," Sackett said without preamble when Rupert opened the door.

"Tell them I'll be right there," Rupert replied, and grabbed his new dinner jacket from the chair he'd draped it across.

His heart was pounding with a new excitement, and when he had his jacket on again and was at the door, Rupert paused to survey the chamber again, certain that

217

when he came back across the threshold again it would no longer be the guest room but his room.

If there was any greater surprise waiting for Rupert than the toughness of Columbia University's qualifying exams, it was his first sight of Cove House late on Tuesday afternoon.

Monday had been spent in a small room at East Hall, Columbia's administrative building, under the watchful eye of a proctor, taking the written examination that would determine if he were suitable material for this leading American university. As far as he was concerned, this was a natural part of the procedure, and he had no way of knowing that when William Seligman had first broached the matter of Rupert's attending Columbia to Nicholas Murray Butler, the school's president had generously offered to waive the entrance exam and mark the young man in as a member of the sophomore class without further ado. William Seligman had carefully considered the offer and then politely rejected it. There was no reason to make things *that* easy for Rupert, he informed Dr. Butler. Let him want to work for this a little more—and while they were at it, there wasn't any reason for him not to make up the freshman requirement in mathematics under the watchful eye of Professor Albright, the department's undisputed dragon.

But despite the unexpected toughness of the exams, Rupert felt he passed them with flying colors. It was only the waiting that was difficult, and two mornings later at breakfast he was eagerly looking forward to another day spent on Wall Street to take his mind off the matter.

The financial district was a new and fascinating world to him. Besides having been given the tour of the Exchange the week before, Rupert had been taken by Gareth Seligman to the offices of *The Wall Street Journal*, and had been introduced to C. W. Barron, the paper's corpulent, colorful owner who'd autographed a copy of his book, *The Boston Stock Exchange*, for him, and yesterday morning he'd actually met the king of Wall Street, J. P. Morgan.

It had taken place in the ornate, mosaic-tiled lobby of the modern office building where for the past few years the Seligman firm had occupied two well-decorated floors. Morgan and his entourage had been on their way out while William Seligman and his entourage— consisting of his youngest son, Jimmy, the office manager, Mr. Gibbs, and Rupert—were making their way toward the elevators. The two groups met almost head-on, and now, twenty-four hours later, Rupert savored the moment, reliving it as he ate breakfast.

The two millionaires exchanged cordial if somewhat restrained greetings. Even at the end of summer, with Wall Street operating with skeleton staffs, eight-forty in the morning was a busy time, and since they were in a public place a certain form had to be adhered to.

When Rupert had been introduced, he was suddenly aware of the magnate's piercing gaze that seemed to catalog every inch of him. It was as if he were looking for something, a possible secret that could be used at a later date as some sort of leverage—

"Rupert, I'm sending you out to Long Island this morning."

Bill's words jerked Rupert out of his reverie with a start.

"What?"

"I'm sending you out to Long Island," Bill repeated patiently. "Sackett is packing your clothes right now. He'll go with you to the station and make sure you get on the right train, and Dugan, our country coachman, will meet you at Woodbury station."

"I'd rather go to Wall Street this morning."

"I thought you were looking forward to Cove House?"

"I am. I just thought that on Friday . . ." His voice

trailed off as a certain suspicion surfaced in his mind, and he took a deep breath. "Is there a reason you want me off ahead of time? Yesterday, when Jimmy took me to lunch at the Players Club, he said that the reason that J. P. Morgan was studying me so closely was because he was trying to see if I'm your bastard son."

"Is a ten-second scrutiny the new way to tell?" Bill said lightly. "Now that's a new one, but to give Jack credit he wouldn't spread such a story unless there was proof—not that he isn't going to do his best to find some. You see, Wall Street—and New York—loves rumors like that, so that bit of gossip may end up being bandied about. I think Jimmy was trying to prepare you. Are you going to mind if it happens?" he asked as they finished their waffles.

"No," Rupert said emphatically, then hesitated. "Will you?"

"That would be the least of my worries." He gave Rupert an amused look. "Come to think of it, you do look rather like the rest of us. I should have thought about that. Ah, well."

"Still, all anyone has to do is think of my mother and realize that that possibility never could have happened."

"That and the fact that at the time you would have been conceived I wasn't in England, and your mother certainly wasn't over here."

Rupert sopped his last bit of waffle in the Vermont maple syrup sloshing around on his plate. "Have you heard anything about Columbia?" he asked in a voice that was a shade too casual.

"No, it'll be a few days more until your test scores are added up and evaluated. In the meantime, the best place for you is Cove House. The rest of the family is there, and some very nice guests. The food is good, my grandchildren seem to adore you, and you can have your fill of swimming and sailing. I envy you. Sackett and I will have to keep bachelors' hall here until Friday when we join the rest of you."

It was not in Rupert's makeup to beg. Far better, he decided wisely, to appear acquiescent than to engage in a conversation that would only end with his dignity in shreds.

It wasn't that he didn't get on with the other members of the family—far from it. Gareth and Jimmy had accepted him with calm equanimity, their wives seemed rather amused by his presence, and Adele treated him with the greatest of warmth and consideration and concern. The only fly in the ointment was Clifford. While his wife, Julie, was hospitality itself, and his children, Paul, Jonathan, and Virginia, adored him as a newly discovered uncle, William Seligman's eldest son was quietly and calmly letting Rupert know that he was not only well aware that the younger man was an interloper who would probably break his father's heart at the first opportunity, and it was therefore up to him to make sure he didn't feel too welcome.

All through the train ride, Rupert had Cove House pictured in his mind. It would be a large, rambling, heavily shingled house set at the edge of Long Island Sound, and filled with furniture that had undoubtedly come from a good place but was now aged by the sea air.

It was a concept born of his lively imagination and lasted until Dugan drove the open landau onto a private road and through a pair of massive wrought iron gates.

By the time they reached the end of the mile long avenue of beech trees and the vista opened up to show wide sweeping lawns and an all-dominating four-story rose brick Georgian-style house, a very taken aback Rupert was more than willing to admit that the joke was on him.

Adele, cool and elegant in a soft green silk afternoon dress, was waiting for him at the front door.

221

"Are you very surprised?" she asked, kissing his cheek and then leading him into the marble entry hall.

"It's very different from the Dakota," was all he could say, his eyes taking in the magnificent marble staircase that swept up to the second floor. "I feel rather foolish," he went on as Adele tucked her arm through his and led him into the small Chinese sitting room where tea—since the weather had turned inclement—was being set out. "Cliff and Julie's house on Fifth Avenue should have tipped me off that Cove House wasn't about to be an informal seaside retreat."

Set on seventy-eight acres of land, with its own dairy filled with placid cows, a greenhouse where fine and rare flowers were tended, tennis and squash courts, a brick carriage house finished with circular turrets, and a wood-framed bath house at the edge of the beach, Cove House, built in 1895, was the largest private home on Long Island's North Shore.

Over what remained of Wednesday, and for several hours on Thursday, Rupert explored this new world. Acutely aware that while he was more than a guest he could not be considered a member of the family, he nonetheless turned on all his charm in order to be a good guest. He rode along bridle paths bordered by cherry and linden trees, saw the masculine preserves of the Turkish bath and the billiard room, as well as admiring the mosaic-tiled indoor swimming pool that was used instead of the beach in bad weather. But now, late on Thursday afternoon, he was alone, stretched out face down on a steamer blanket placed over a patch of soft white sand with the blue water of Long Island Sound softly lapping less than three feet away.

Rupert was luxuriating in the heat of the sun when he turned his head just in time to see a pair of well-polished black calf shoes sinking somewhat into the sand as they halted an inch from the edge of the blanket. His gaze moved upward to take in Sackett, thoroughly unruffled despite the informal surroundings.

"You're here early," he said, blinking from the bright sun. "Or are you here alone?"

"No, the master is here and would like to see you," Sackett replied, and Rupert could recognize a command when he heard one, no matter how politely spoken.

"What time is it?" he asked, getting to his feet and reaching for the neat pile of clothes at the edge of the blanket.

"It was nearly half-past four when I left the house and it should be a few minutes past that now, Mr. Rupert," the butler said, and Rupert, pulling on a pair of white duck trousers over his jersey tank suit, gave the servant a sidelong glance. From the day he'd arrived, Sackett had been calling him Sir, the perfect form of address for a house guest who also happened to be a baronet. But now, suddenly, unexpectedly, he was Mr. Rupert. Still absolutely correct, but a form reserved for a close family friend—or a member of the family.

With deliberate calmness, Rupert began buttoning his shirt. "Is there something I should be aware of, Sackett?"

"Only that the master wishes you to join him in the library—when you're properly bathed and dressed, that is," he added, as Rupert grinned and put on his tennis shoes.

"Am I expected to use the back stairs as well?"

"I believe that choice is up to you, Mr. Rupert. But please remember that removing sand from the rugs *is* a chore."

Thus advised, Rupert gathered up the blanket, Sackett having made no move to touch it, and the two men started back to the house, along the beach path, through the large rose garden, and skirting the loggia they went through the kitchen garden where Sackett relieved him of the blanket before they reached the Dutch door.

"As you know, the dressing bell isn't for another forty-five minutes," he said, "but the master wants you downstairs for a private talk in the library before any of the family or guests are ready."

As Sackett finished speaking, Rupert felt an uncharacteristic pang of apprehension. Something had happened, he was sure of it, but whether it was in his favor or if once again he'd be left to his own devices only one man knew.

Refreshed by his long, hot shower, and resplendently turned out in his new Brooks Brothers dinner clothes, Rupert slid open the doors to the library just as the dressing bell sounded. Closing the carved wood doors behind him, he paused for a moment to take a red carnation from a silver bowl that rested on a nearby table and put it in his buttonhole before crossing the length of the room to the corner sofa where William Seligman, also dressed for dinner, was waiting for him.

"You look as if you've been having a good time," Bill remarked with a smile as Rupert sat down. "Sackett said you were taking the sun like a cat."

"I'd probably still be there if he hadn't come to say you wanted to talk with me. Incidentally, thank you for insisting I come out to Cove House."

"I'm glad that you've been enjoying yourself. My grandchildren seem to think of you as some sort of magical new uncle who can take care of broken toys and find lost puppies and tell them tales about King Arthur. You're something of a success with them."

"Much to the delight of their three nannies," Rupert said, not bothering to cover his feelings. "They love their charges but don't mind turning them over to me for an hour or so."

"Well, now that you're settled in, and as long as we're discussing you, shall we have a drink?"

On the low, inlaid wood table in front of them was a silver tray holding a cocktail shaker, a dish of salted almonds, and several long-stemmed glasses imbedded in a bowl of crushed ice. With the greatest of ease, Bill poured out two icy martinis and handed one glass to Rupert.

"I think that it's very appropriate that we drink to your acceptance at Columbia University for the Class of 1906."

For a moment, Rupert couldn't speak. There had never been the slightest doubt in his mind that he would be accepted, but from the moment he began to fill out the application forms, he became aware that life, which had always held everything out to him on a silver platter, was now holding that tray a little closer to its chest.

"I'm very happy it's worked out this way," he said truthfully as they touched glasses. "What happens now?"

"Well, first of all, you have more papers to fill out," Bill said, handing him a good-sized envelope that he'd hidden behind the sofa's decorative pillows. "There are more forms for you to fill out. The Bursar wants more information, and so does the Registrar. You also need a pass for the library stacks. When I went to Columbia, we didn't have to worry about filling out these things," he observed, amused. The year the seventeen-year-old William Seligman had entered Columbia University, then located at Madison Avenue and Forty-ninth Street, Sherman was marching through Georgia.

"I can't tell you how much I appreciate your speaking to Dr. Butler about me," Rupert said, fingering the thick envelope.

"Yes, but what I'm really interested in from now on is your actions, not your words," Bill said. "Last week you agreed to what amounts to a blind offer. Now you're going to find out what you bought."

"Do I need another drink to prepare myself?"

"I think not. Do you really assume I'm going to give you rules that are that difficult to live by?"

"I couldn't be sure. But I thought it was worth taking a chance on." He studied the surface of his drink. "You may as well let me have it."

"First of all, you're going to have a nice vacation here at Cove House. Swim, ride, play tennis—whatever you like. I want you to enjoy yourself, not only because you're young and this is a paradise for young people, but come the middle of September and the start of classes, your nose is going to the grindstone and is staying there."

"I suppose it's too late to say I'd prefer to do some traveling?" Rupert inquired, amused. Columbia was bound to be easy. Everyone at Oxford and Cambridge alike knew that American universities were pale copies of their British counterparts. No doubt he'd gallop straight to the top of the second-year class. But why then did he feel a sudden prickling of apprehension?

"You've already made your choice, and I'd hate to find out you're the sort of young man who doesn't know his own mind," Bill said mildly, leaving Rupert with a pang of conscience.

"You're expecting a great deal from me, aren't you?"

"Nothing that you can't deliver, Rupert. You have a first-class intellect, an inquiring mind, natural curiosity, and you love to read. Unfortunately, you also seem to have a predisposition for wanting to see how far you can push people, and that is something I won't stand for."

As he heard the older man out, Rupert felt his amusement and carefully cultivated air of superiority seep relentlessly away, leaving him far more vulnerable than he'd ever remembered being.

"I've really put myself in it this time, haven't I?" he questioned quietly, taking a sip from his glass before returning it to the tray.

"Oh, come now, it's not as bad as all that. Besides,

what I'm really pointing out is that for the next three years you're a university student, not a fledgling financier, and certainly not a boulevardier."

"So it's back to the cold showers?"

"If that's what it takes." Bill's voice was easy and equitable, but there was a definite no-nonsense inference that Rupert not only caught but actually respected. "For someone who isn't quite twenty, you have a history of escapes, escapades, and conquests some men never achieve. Not that I find anything wrong with that, but a man's life has to have a certain order and pattern, neither of which you've formulated. It's time you moved back a few steps. Right now, I don't think there's too much wrong with you that a full day of classes, a good dinner, and several hours preparing for the next day's classes for five nights out of seven won't cure."

"Are you going to be a rather stern taskmaster about it?" he asked, keeping his mask of bravado in place.

Bill smiled. "It's my home and my rules and you passed the point of pick and choose a week ago."

"Well, then, you may as well give me the rest of the rules so I can figure out how to get around them."

"That'll be interesting to see, considering the load of classes you're going to be carrying," Bill smiled. "Up by seven every morning to make your nine o'clock class, I believe you'll be quite happy to fall into bed at eleven."

"I'm on curfew?"

"In a word, yes. From Sunday night through Thursday night, when you come home you don't leave the Dakota. You can have dinner with us, or with Alix and Henry, or eat in the restaurant, or accept a dinner invitation from someone in the building, but by eleven or shortly thereafter you're to be back in your room. There'll be exceptions, of course. When Caruso makes his debut at the Met in November, for instance. That's not a night to miss. And a few other opening nights and parties, too. As far as Friday and Saturday nights and vacation time is concerned, you can stay out 'til dawn. Also," he continued, not letting Rupert get a word in, "I suggest that you forget all about being Sir Rupert. A title isn't going to make your way any easier. If you truly want a fresh start you don't go dragging old battle flags with you."

For a long time, Rupert was silent. He reclaimed his martini glass and sipped the cold, fortifying liquid. Why was he so calm? he wondered. Why wasn't he outraged at rules better suited for a schoolboy? One of the advantages of life in New York was that he could come and go at will, answerable to no one—or so he had thought. Instead he'd just cheerfully consigned himself to—to what?

To what you need, a voice in his head said. This is what you want, admit it. You want to go back to university. You want to see if there is such a thing as a happy family. You never had a father except in the biological sense, and now is your chance to see if someone saying *you go this far and no further* means something.

"What about my money?" he asked at last, aware he was grasping at straws.

"Your money?" The older man shrugged. "Do as you please with it. As soon as your checking account is established you can try and buy the Brooklyn Bridge. And now, Rupert, there is one more thing—I like to think I'm a flexible man, and an understanding one. You have a home with my wife and me. Our family is now yours. Any questions you have, any problems, I'm here for you to talk to, and I'll help you any way I can, but—" A tight look came over William Seligman's aristocratic features. "But if you ever pull the trick that got you tossed out of Oxford, or any variation on it, I'll make any reaction you got from Henry Thorpe look like water off a duck's back. Am I making myself clear?"

"Perfectly. I'll do my best not to disappoint you or disgrace you," Rupert said, and meant every word of his promise.

"And that's all I'm asking," Bill said, smiling again, and picking up the cocktail shaker and one of the additional glasses, he filled it and then refilled Rupert's glass.

"Is someone joining us?"

"No, you're joining someone. In fact, she should be out on the loggia right now. Her name is Mallory Kirk, and she's not only Newton Phipps' god-daughter but Alix's cousin."

"Which means she knows the time of day."

"You could put it like that. But what Mallory does know first-hand is university life. Next month, she'll be a sophomore at Barnard, and I think you should take yourself and these two martinis out to the loggia and say hello to a nice young lady who I'm sure will be very happy to fill you in on the intricacies of American university life. And when you see Mallory, you'll—" He smiled at Rupert. "Well, I think I've given you quite enough advance warning for one day and I'm going to let you find out all the rest for yourself."

Whether he liked it or not, over the years Rupert had become a confirmed early riser, and when he opened his eyes on Tuesday morning, sunlight was just beginning to filter into the room.

I think I could sleep for a week and not feel rested, he thought, slowly turning and piling the pillows up behind him so that he could lay on his back and drift half-asleep, half-awake until his body adjusted one way or another. I can't remember the last time I was so tired. Oh, yes, I can, he reminded himself, it was when I started Columbia—

Nothing in the year that Rupert Randall had spent at Magdalen College, Oxford, prepared him for Columbia University in September 1903. The hour or so a week he'd spent with his tutor bore no possible relationship to the daily round of classes, seminars, quizzes, home assignments, library work, and term papers he was plunged into.

For the first month he'd lived with a cold knot of fear in his stomach at the thought of failing out. Even now, nearly seven years later, he could recall exactly how he felt three times a week when he walked into Professor Albright's classroom to master the intricate world of calculus: a world made up of functions, derivatives, examples, limits, integrals and variables, all taught by the very precise, totally demanding professor who wrung the best out of his students. And it was because of this mathematics class that the last barriers of self-protection that he'd erected around his life had fallen away.

It was worth being put through the wringer for what came out of it, he thought, and then the feelings he'd been pushing out of his way for months rushed over him as he recalled exactly who it had been who first used that expression to him.

Like most acts of great cruelty committed in a moment of panic, the enormity of what he'd done to Mallory didn't really dawn on Rupert until months later in San Francisco. Even on the night that should have ended so very differently for them, as he picked himself up out of the rosebush, sore and scratched and bleeding, Rupert's only emotion had been total relief—relief that he wasn't going to have to marry Mallory, and that she would definitely never want to see him again.

He still had the grace to be ashamed of himself, however, and it was this feeling that made him even more

230

eager for San Francisco than he would have been had the assignment been offered him under more normal circumstances. He wanted to put three thousand miles between himself and his actions, to lose himself in someplace utterly different than New York, and no place seemed better suited to his needs than the city at the end of America's rainbow.

Five months after the earthquake and fire that had destroyed over a third of the city's developed area, San Francisco was still the city that wouldn't give up. Despite the fact that four-hundred blocks of real estate, over twenty-eight thousand buildings covering four point seven miles and two thousand acres that included Chinatown, the financial district, the retail district, and the slopes of Telegraph, Russian and Nob Hills had been decimated between the early morning hours of April 18, 1906, when the first tremors ran through the city, to seventy-four hours later, at seven-fifteen on Saturday morning, when the fire was put out, San Francisco had once again turned into as much of a boomtown as it had been during the days of the Gold Rush.

In the beginning there was far too much for Rupert to do to think about Mallory. True, he wasn't like the city's homeless, many of whom were still living in tents in Golden Gate Park, eating in community kitchens where the bread and beans inevitably became mixed with sand, but he was working at a pace that made even the frantic world of Wall Street and the Stock Exchange seem somewhat slow by comparison. With half the staff of the Seligmans' West Coast office gone, either having panicked and demanded transfers or else still recovering from injuries suffered in April, he was not only the acting director but covering several other positions as well. Instead of gradually growing into a senior position, he was pushed head first into responsibilities that shouldn't have been his for years, and he thrived on it.

He dealt with businesses looking to rebuild and clients wanting to preserve their portfolios, and without a doubt Rupert's favorite client was Elinor Tierney, a tall, slender, exquisitely dressed woman in her early thirties—who until New Year's Day, 1906, had been the city's youngest, richest, and most beautiful madam.

"I got out of the business just in time," she told him in her compelling voice. "Of course my profit margin would be tremendous right now, but my Kearny Street house . . . It's just not worth the effort," Nell went on languidly. "Fortunately, I was in the southern part of the state in April, but I've been back since July, buying real estate."

"Time to move on to other things, then," Rupert said, feeling somewhat mesmerized by this woman whose dark red hair and green eyes and royal manner made him think of Elizabeth the First, all modernized and brought up to date. "You have a very good portfolio with us, a bit on the conservative side—"

"One has to be with some things."

"But an excellent base," he went on, enjoying the subtle flirtation between them. "I take it that now you want to concentrate on purchasing real estate?"

"That's the best route for me—at least to begin with. I came back here the day the streetcars began to run again, but there was still enough confusion for me to make several good deals with people who just wanted to sell up and get out. That panic is about over now, and since I'm fairly recognizable . . ."

Nell rose from the comfortable leather chair on the other side of Rupert's desk and crossed the Persian carpet to look out the window at the scene on Van Ness Avenue, watching lorry trucks and dray wagons loaded with brick and lumber and other building supplies pass by.

The fire line had stopped at Van Ness Avenue, leaving

the broad street largely untouched by the destruction that had run rampant elsewhere, and it was now the city's business and retail center, the place to see and be seen in San Francisco's pecking order. Among the firms that had temporarily (and it was easily admitted that "temporary" could mean years) relocated themselves into the avenue's private houses and apartments was the Seligman office since the suite of offices that had once been theirs in a leading financial district office building was now a pile of brick and cinders. Thanks to the foresight and bravery of several of the firm's employees, the records had been saved, taken to the relative safety of Presido Terrace, a new real estate project on Arguello Boulevard where the recently retired office director lived. Mr. Thaler had the files put in his basement, and as soon as he could safely venture into the burned city he'd made his way to Van Ness Avenue and rented the best house he could find. The standing joke around the office was that kindly, sixty-year-old Mr. Thaler had acted as much out of self-interest as out of concern for the firm he had so loyally served—he had no intention of setting up an office in his brand-new house which was built in the style of a Japanese bungalow.

"Will you work with me?" she asked a long minute later in an utterly businesslike voice, turning to regard Rupert as he sat back in his large brown leather chair, properly dressed for the business day and yet managing to look both elegant and dangerous—something no woman could resist. "Your interests are primarily commercial, and so are mine. I realize how busy you must be, but—"

"But you've entrusted your financial portfolio to this firm for nearly ten years. Whatever investments you want to make now will benefit everyone concerned, and my father wouldn't accept my not giving you and your interests every consideration. Mrs. Tierney," he began, standing up and crossing the room toward her.

"It's Nell," she corrected warmly, taking the hand he offered her and looking directly into his eyes.

"I'm honored to advise you on any investments you care to make, or to make them in your name," he said, and the look that passed between them promised far more than simply business.

Without saying a word, at that very moment it was taken for granted between them that they would become lovers. Not that first afternoon, or even that first business week when they saw each other nearly every day, but on the weekend, when the staff was gone and Rupert had the house to himself with only a Filipino houseboy to look after him, was the perfect time for them to get to know each other on more intimate terms.

"So you have the library for your office and the master bedroom to live in," Nell remarked as they lay together in the highly polished satinwood four-poster, her red hair and Rupert's black hair standing out in sharp relief from the pristine white sheets with their scalloped and embroidered edges, now pleasantly rumpled from their afternoon's activity. "Not quite roughing it, are you?"

Over Nell's shoulder, Rupert studied the vast chamber where the blue and cream oriental rug was soft on the parquet floor and quiet silks covered the chairs and sofas and the windows were curtained in heavy silk damask to keep out the noise from the street and the writing table and beside tables were resting places for his personal objects.

"Compared to some people in this town, I'm very lucky. But until this afternoon, it's been all work and no play."

Nell laughed and pressed her hands down on his shoulders, bending over to press her lips against his forehead. "Well, we can't have that," she said between the tiny kisses she deposited on his face. "Your family

234

would never forgive me if I let you turn into a grind."

"I was one at Columbia."

"Funny, you don't look the sort. But when it comes down to it, you were better off being kept to your studies than skylarking about."

"Have you been talking to my father?" Rupert demanded, and then, unlike the previous week, he caught his mistake. "Forget what I just said, please."

"Why? I think that your considering William Seligman to be your father is very sweet."

"And very accurate in every way except the biological sense of the word. The past three years—" he began, and hesitated.

"Go on," Nell urged him. "When a man and woman are all naked and snug in bed on a rainy San Francisco Saturday, there's no better time to talk—until they're ready to make love again, that is. And from now on, we don't talk business in bed, and we don't bring personal topics into the conversation when I see you about investments. But now . . . tell me anything you want."

Over the weeks that followed, Rupert found that he could indeed tell Nell anything at all. As they viewed parcels of land that ranged from the new landfill area around the Bay or at Presidio Terrace or down in the financial district they either discussed the business at hand or else pleasant and impersonal topics, saving their more intimate talks for when they were alone together in the Van Ness Avenue house.

But even as he told his secrets to Nell, Rupert was aware that his client, his lover, was a woman of mystery. Her financial life might be an open book, but her private world was as secure as an ancient castle with its drawbridge firmly up. In all the time they were together, he never learned where she was living, although the rumor mill had it that she was staying with Mary Anne Magnin.

They talked about mutual friends, Nell freely telling him that when she'd been "in business"—her cheerful euphemism—all the clothes she and her girls wore came from I. Magnin, and from October 1902 to April 1904, her personal salesperson had been Angela Dalton.

"I even introduced Nela to her husband," she told him gaily. "Morgan is an old friend of mine from before . . . well, let's just say the old days when we were children together in . . . no, back east will do. Morgan was in San Francisco for a vacation and was paying a call the same day Nela came to show me the latest spring clothes. These things do happen," she drawled, and Rupert began to laugh at both her descriptions and her evasions.

He knew very well that this was the closest he was going to come to hearing about Nell's life prior to her soujourn as a member of the world's oldest profession. This woman guarded her secrets well, but he didn't mind. After three years of being around women who wore their intelligence like a superbly designed diamond brooch, he found that he was now constitutionally unable to bear being in the company of a stupid woman—and that not only included women who were naturally unbright, but those ladies who felt that pretending dumbness was the best way to attract a man.

"Do you know that there are only two things I regret right now?" Nell said as they reclined together in his bed on the Saturday after Thanksgiving.

"Only two?" Rupert asked tenderly, pulling the covers closer around them.

"When you consider my life, that's really not bad. The first is that you didn't come to San Francisco while I still had my house. My girls would have loved you."

"I'm flattered. And the second?"

"That my daughter isn't here with me. You'd probably be magic with her."

"That comes from having more children than I can

236

count at the moment calling me Uncle Rupert," he said blithely, hiding his surprise at her having mentioned her child.

Not that it was a secret. Nearly everyone knew that Elinor Tierney had a ten-year-old daughter named Lucey that she kept with her nearly all the time, and that she was now safely with friends down south—San Diego, people were saying—until her mother concluded her business.

"In case you're wondering, Lucey's quite legitimate. I was married, but now I'm divorced," Nell said, and Rupert recognized that her two sentences were a self-contained statement and no further questions would be permitted.

"I'm glad," he said, closing his eyes.

"Are you going to sleep on me?" Nell demanded with a laugh. "You're too young for that!"

"Sorry, darling. I had a dinner meeting with A. P. Giannini and his brothers last night, and between the food and the conversation I didn't get back here until three in the morning. Still, it was worth it," he went on. "I don't think San Francisco would be rebuilding at the rate it is if it weren't for A. P. seeing to it that loans were made at sensible interest rates to businessmen who wanted to rebuild."

"Whether or not it works in the long run, at least people have stopped laughing at the Bank of Italy," Nell observed. "You should bring the Gianninis and Dr. Devine together."

"How do you know I'm dining with Dr. Devine tonight?" Rupert demanded, laughing, pressing Nell into the bed's softness. Dr. Edward Thomas Devine was a professor of social economy at Columbia, and President Roosevelt had appointed him to represent the Red Cross relief operation. "Are you a witch?"

"Oh, I have my sources! And even if I didn't, it

wouldn't take magical powers for me to figure out that of course a recent Columbia graduate, who's both in a responsible position and a bit homesick, would seek out a former professor," Nell said as she smoothed back his hair. "You are a bit homesick, aren't you?"

"Now that you mention it." Rupert's voice was bittersweet. "I haven't had too much time to think about missing everyone back in New York. Besides, an experience like San Francisco isn't going to come around again."

"I certainly hope not—if you catch my drift. And think of all the stories you'll have to tell. Of course you know what you should do when you go back to New York?"

The corners of Rupert's mouth twitched. "No, what?"

"Find a nice girl—a nice, beautiful, well-dressed, intelligent girl who isn't going to be afraid of going to bed with you, and marry her. Go back east and get a move on it."

"I've already found her—and gotten rid of her," he said slowly, hating the words as they came out of his mouth. He had never mentioned Mallory to Nell, but now he did, telling her everything that had happened three months before, and as he finished and watched her facial expression change, he wished he'd never opened his mouth.

"You did what?"

"I told you. I made love to her and then changed my mind about our relationship," he said crossly, irritated by her tone of voice. "Right now, you sound just like Alix would have if I'd told her, except that she would have punched me in the mouth. I thought you'd understand."

"Oh, really! Do you think that because I was a madam I'm supposed to find your actions amusing?"

"I never thought anything like that! I just expected

238

you would see my side of the situation—no one else would."

"Oh, spare me spoiled little rich boys!" Nell snapped. "All right, you wanted a little love in the afternoon without having to march down the aisle afterwards." Her eyes narrowed. "Were you too cheap to pay for it or too lazy to go casting after one of those promiscuous married ladies?"

"I was in love with Mallory!"

"Gosh, but you had a funny way of showing it! And I always thought I ran a fairly respectable sporting club for gentlemen, and any client with a taste for whips or handcuffs was told to take his business elsewhere; now I realize I let a whole subcategory slip by me. The heartless cad who'll do and say anything to the woman he says he loves in order not to take up his share of the responsibility!"

"All right, it was the wrong tack to take, I admit it now. But I panicked. It was the only way I could think of."

"So much for junior Phi Betta Kappas," Nell said, and got out of bed, putting on her satin and ribbon teddy. "Tell me, is your Mallory intelligent and understanding and sympathetic?"

"You know she is."

"Know? I *know* Alix. We met at an intimate little dinner the Daltons gave before Nela and Morgan were married. I do not know Mallory—only what you've told me about her. What I asked you . . . yes or no?"

Rupert leaned back in bed, his heart pounding against his ribs. This was not turning out the way he imagined. And worst of all, he was beginning to fathom the pain and distress and shame he'd brought Mallory.

"Yes," he said at last.

"And you couldn't get a rein on your emotions long enough to tell her how you felt. You didn't trust her

239

enough to think she'd understand," Nell stated.

For the next few minutes, the only sound in the room was the rustle of expensive fabrics as Nell dressed. Arrayed in a suit that was a Doucet model of royal blue serge with a cream silk blouse, she turned back to Rupert.

"I want to go to Hillsborough day after tomorrow," she said, referring to an exclusive suburb. "A real estate agent who owes me a favor had put me on to something that sounds promising. Italian Renaissance, I think he said, and not too much damage. Will you take me out there? After all, how many times are you going to watch while property values go down?"

Rupert smiled slowly and with effort. A cold edge of ice was forming around his heart.

"Is that all you're going to say to me?"

Nell's silver laugh rang out. "My poor darling. I think that if there's anything else, you're bright enough to figure the rest out yourself. Dear Rupert," she went on, stepping into her shoes and reaching for her hat. "You're just not as amoral as you like to think you are."

With something of a start, Rupert looked at the bedside clock, noting with some surprise that it was nearly eight o'clock. Time to get up and shower and shave and dress and go out to Long Island.

And see Mallory again.

Rupert had remained in San Francisco until February 1907 when the telegram that his mother was dying sent him back across the length of the United States, from the Overland Limited to the Twentieth Century, and then straight from Grand Central Station to the French Line pier where the *La Savoie* was sailing that afternoon, with almost no time at all to see and talk to William Seligman except for the conversation they were able to have as the chauffeur drove them from Forty-second Street to the foot of Morton Street, reaching the dock a scant ten minutes before the gangplank was lifted away.

He reached London just in time, and in the final forty-eight hours before Allison Randall died of heart failure, mother and son finally had the chance to put their past resentments and misconceptions behind them.

The endless details involved in settling the estate kept Rupert in London for months afterwards, and when he returned to New York in the summer, Bill kept him at the home office until January 1908, with only brief soujourns to Boston and Philadelphia where he had the opportunity to both put his organizational abilities to work as well as learn the workings of two other major Exchanges. May 1908 until September 1909 was spent in Washington, living in the splendor of a bachelor apartment on fashionable Sixteenth and L Streets, then it was back to New York for a brief time and, finally, Chicago.

I wonder where Dad is going to send me next? he wondered, running the razor across his face. God, please not St. Louis. Of course, if I'm in New York, there's the question of seeing Mallory . . .

As he washed the remainder of the shaving soap off his face, Rupert wondered how he'd managed to avoid seeing Mallory again, or even running into her by accident. Careful hostesses, he supposed. Unpleasant scenes at dinners and balls were fine for other people's parties.

He thought about Nell. Their affair had been drawing to its natural end at the time he was summoned to London, but it had never been right again after that November afternoon. Nell had touched some deep, well-hidden nerve in him, and each time he saw her he thought about Mallory.

The other women he'd seen since then—actresses, the

occasional young widow, and very high-priced ladies of the evening—hadn't stirred old, unwelcome memories, and they were transitory affairs. It wasn't as if he were avoiding "respectable" young ladies, but he wasn't seeking them out, either. Besides, when compared to Mallory, they failed in all areas and requirements.

For four years he'd been expecting to hear of Mallory's engagement to some worthy fellow or other, but so far it hadn't happened, and now, as he rang for Sackett to bring in his breakfast, Rupert wasn't sure if he were glad or sorry.

A long time ago he'd come to terms with what had happened between them. It was all his fault, but all they had meant to each other was undoubtedly past history.

Except that during the past weeks, ever since Chicago went on its never-ending heat wave making sleep next to impossible, he was no longer quite so sure.

On those long nights in his room at the University Club, she'd invaded his thoughts to such an extent that he swore he could reach out and touch her and hold her in his arms and make the apology he should have made the moment those ugly words left his mouth.

Well, now he was going to have the chance to set it all to rights. He would see Mallory, tell her all the reasons behind his stupid actions, his hastily planned act of cruelty, tell her the reasons he'd given Nell, and hope for the best, which, in this case, meant a return of some sort of civility between them.

Sackett brought him his breakfast, and Rupert ate blueberry muffins and drank café au lait, still dwelling on Mallory.

For four years he'd escaped from the memory—and the responsibility—of what he'd done, but now all the pretense he'd fooled himself with had fallen away, and he was left with the pain and the overwhelming sensation of belated disgrace.

You're like the proverbial dog with that damned bone, Rupert told himself. You thought that because you'd never physically hurt Mallory, anything else you did or said was justifiable. Well, I was good and wrong, and I only wish I'd had the intelligence to learn a long time ago that it's different when you're in love.

Courts and camps are the places to learn about the world in . . . Take your tone from the company you are in.

—The Earl of Chesterfield
Letters To His Son
Volume Three

Cove House

Le Caviar
Le consommé Madrilène
Le pompano Bercy
Le filet de boeuf Richelieu
La sauce Madère
Les pommes souffles
Les haricots verts au beurre
La salade de romaines
La glace vanille Nesselrode
Les friandises

10 Aout 1910

Mallory looked up from the menu card that was set in a shell-shaped silver holder in front of her place setting and looked across the width of the oblong Sheraton table, over the centerpiece that was a sterling silver soup tureen filled with a great summer bouquet of white and yellow tulips and tiger lilies and freesia, to really look at Rupert for the first time in four years.

It was half-past eight on Tuesday evening, and twenty-six men and women were seated around the seemingly endless length of table in the dining room with the beige silk chinoiserie wallpaper, a pair of twelve-light Georgian crystal chandeliers overhead and, underfoot, an oriental rug woven in shades of beige, rose and blue.

Mallory had dressed for tonight's occasion in a Lucile gown of pale blue chiffon over rose-colored satin with the tunic and bertha cut in one-piece of *point d'alençon* lace and a girdle of twisted rose-colored silk. Her hair was bound with a bit of rose-colored satin studded with pearls, a bracelet of rose-cut diamonds encircled one wrist, and her generous application of *Quand Vient L'Été*, Guerlain's latest perfume, wafted around her.

Does he resent me that much, or is it something else? Can Rupert be as nervous about seeing me again as I am about seeing him? Mallory wondered, taking advantage of the flurry of activity caused by the footmen replacing cups of jellied consommé with plates of pompano prepared with fish stock, white wine and shallots, to finally look across the table, something she'd avoided doing while the caviar had been in front of her. Then, with Peter Beardsley on her left and Evan Prescott on her right, discussing the merits of beluga versus malossol, she'd been too suitably occupied to think about or look at the man across from her. But no longer.

Oh, he looks so tired. The sympathetic thought rose impulsively in Mallory, and now she looked straight at Rupert, not bothering to gaze at him through the shield of her lashes, or to pretend to be looking at something or someone else. And I've never seen circles like that under his eyes, her thoughts ran on. Has he been getting any sleep at all?

Looking at him, studying Rupert's face feature by feature, Mallory had to admit that despite his slightly worn look augmented by the purple smudges under his eyes, he looked wonderfully handsome. To be sure, the carefree look of a university student was gone, but the aura of responsibility, plus a certain amount of power, suited him even more.

By this time Saturday night, when the house is full, he's going to have every available woman—and a few who aren't—after him, and I won't have a chance, Mallory thought, glad that for tonight he was seated between Susannah Seligman and Marie-France de Laulan, both safely and happily married. She thought: What am I doing now? I have to make up my mind one way or another. Funny, a few weeks ago all I wanted was to settle matters between the two of us, and now, before we even say a word, I'm getting all possessive, as if I want us to go back to the way we were that afternoon. I know that can't be, but just the same. . . .

With a great deal of effort, Mallory turned her attention back to her fish course, and then, as the conversation of the other people at the table swirled around her, unable to resist the temptation, she looked up and across the table again just as Rupert finished talking to Marie-France and was about to turn to Susannah, and their gazes met and locked.

Her reaction was instantaneous, and Mallory felt as if she'd been hit. Her breath came sharply inward, her heart seemed to halt for a fraction of a second before racing helplessly on, and a strange warmth began to radiate through her.

No, she thought, not after all this time. I can't act like a schoolgirl with a crush on a matinée idol. It's just asking for his contempt, and I've had enough of that already.

But as annoyed as she was with herself, Mallory noted that Rupert's reaction didn't seem to be so very different from hers. His eyes seemed to be slightly glazed, a red stain was spreading over his untanned cheeks, and to her utter amazement, after an endless moment, he actually

247

focused his gaze downward to his plate as if he were unable to bear her scrutiny for another second.

"In case you've forgotten, conversation goes from left to right, not across the centerpiece," a waspish voice said softly, and Mallory turned her head to speak to Peter Beardsley.

"I wasn't conversing, I was looking," she couldn't resist saying. "That's quite a different thing."

"Well, what would you say if I told you that everyone at this table has noticed your behavior?" the young stockbroker pressed on in a disgruntled voice, and Mallory began to question what she'd ever seen in this man to begin with. He was perfectly charming as long as everything went his way, but let one wrinkle develop—a new play turn out to be a bore, a book unavailable in Brentano's, Sherry's out of his favorite dessert—and he turned short-tempered and petulant, unable to laugh off a situation. His fine features and wheat-colored hair were set off to perfection by his dark dinner clothes, but as she finished her mental evaluation, Mallory remembered that she never really liked fair-haired men.

"I think the food is too good for anyone to be paying much attention to me," she replied, managing to keep the acid out of her voice. "And if someone has noticed, exactly what is it they're supposed to be saying about me?"

"That you're fast."

"Which is rather old news. Oh, Peter, surely you can come up with something better than that!" she exclaimed haughtily, and turned to her right, to Evan Prescott.

A tall, rather elegant man who sometimes looked more British than American, Evan had been married to Melinda Nevins since May of 1907. Mallory was the godmother to their daughter, and he met Mallory's eyes with a smile.

"And what do you think?" she asked, but this time her

voice was truly amused.

"That Rupert doesn't recognize how lucky he is."

"Since he's seated between Susannah and Marie-France, I'd say he's a very fortunate person."

"Don't obscure the situation," Evan said with a smile.

"I wouldn't dream of it," Mallory assured him. "But there's nothing to discuss, either."

"As you wish," Evan said as they finished their fish course.

For the next few minutes footmen once again moved around the table, removing fish plates, replacing them with dinner plates, both of the elegantly gold-embellished Imperial pattern from Ceralene, and refilling Baccarat glasses with a steady stream of vintage champagne. While this was going on, Mallory tried once again to catch Rupert's eye, but this time he successfully evaded her—a reluctant *pas de deux* which was finally catching attention up and down the length of the table.

At one end, Adele Seligman, elegant in a Paquin gown of silk net embroidered with gold, silver, pale pink and copper sequins over lavender satin, reached over and quietly touched the hand of the man seated at her left.

"Have you seen what's going on down at the center of the table?" she asked the silver-haired Newton Phipps.

"If you mean my goddaughter making your and Bill's protégé rather hot under the collar, certainly," he replied, amused. "Such encounters seem made-to-order for young people. Do you remember when you and Bill were courting?"

"1869." Adele laughed merrily. "No electric lights, no telephone, no motor cars, and construction had just begun on the Brooklyn Bridge. It seems like a century ago—and our clothes! We were going from hoops to bustles that year. Thinking back, it's a wonder couples ever got together!"

"It appears that they have trouble even now," Newton

249

said, his smile fading. "Neither Esme or I have ever been able to find out what really happened between Mallory and Rupert. That business about deciding not to see each other again. . . . We've had our suspicions, of course—"

"So have we—"

"But we decided to take it all at face value."

"And that's the best strategy of all. Particularly when two people have the same story and stick to it." She shrugged expressively. "Well, let them have their fun, and if something comes of it this time—" She turned to the guest to her right. "Adolph, you will save space on the Sunday social announcements page, won't you?"

"Of course I will, Adele, and the fact that some of my favorite stockholders are at this table has no bearing on the subject," replied Adolph Ochs, the courtly publisher of *The New York Times*, ever the southern gentleman. "It was about this time eight years ago when I saw to it space was made so everyone could know that this young lady had had a Paris wedding."

Seated at the publisher's right, Alix, in a Poiret gown of ivory satin with a black net tunic, put down her fork and leaned forward, her double strand of white pearls swinging forward for a moment. "Thank you, Adolph, and I think all these preliminary plans are fine, except—" she paused and arched her neck like a swan "—except that I think we should let Mallory make Rupert's life uncomfortable for a little while longer!"

At that moment, if a poll could be taken of all those at the table—excluding the two principals, of course—the vote would be overwhelmingly on Mallory's side. Not that Rupert was disliked or unpopular, but the majority of men would have felt it was now his turn to be raked over the coals by a woman, and the women, married or not, would have determined that he'd cut a wide enough swath and now deserved whatever Mallory dished out.

But as the meal progressed, going from main course to

salad to dessert, Mallory felt neither amused nor triumphant, merely rather confused.

In a manner of speaking, she now had what she wanted. She could practically reach across and touch Rupert, but in actuality they were as isolated from each other as they had been for the past four years.

What did I expect? she asked herself. Rupert won't say a word to me, won't look at me, won't do anything unless he wants to, and by this time it's perfectly clear he doesn't want to have anything to do with me. Whatever affection Rupert had for me disappeared the minute we got out of bed.

An unstoppable despair was rising in Mallory, and she was struggling to keep her composure when she looked across the table again to find Rupert's eyes upon her. The electricity was there again, but now there was something else as well. Biting back her first heart-pounding inclination to turn away, she forced herself to look directly at his face, to study his reaction to her, and found her seemingly bottomless unhappiness suddenly mixed with equal parts of amazement and delight.

Why he's just as nervous as I am, she thought, an understanding warmth spreading over the mean coldness inside her, and then, with the grace of an opponent who knows another chance is coming, she smiled at Rupert and moved her gaze away.

"Now, Mallie, you all come right over here. Marie-France and I want a word with you."

Susannah's Maryland drawl was friendly, but there was a particular glint in her thick-lashed blue eyes.

"Oh, why not," Mallory replied lightly, tucking an arm through Susannah's. "But I have to warn you in advance that I may not tell you what you want to know."

"We'll take our chances."

251

Dinner over, the women had left the men to their cigars and brandy and port, and were now milling around the yellow and cream main drawing room in groups of two and threes, sipping icy glasses of champagne, and in a few cases puffing on ivory-tipped cigarettes, talking and laughing until the men rejoined them.

Together, the two women crossed the cream and yellow and apricot and blue oriental carpet to the marble-manteled fireplace where Marie-France, in a Drecoll gown of pale mauve chiffon with scalloped edges of the palest pink, was waiting for them.

In spite of her name, Marie-France Pinguary de Laulan was not French but American, born in New York twenty-three years before, and was married to Jean-Christophe de Laulan, the son of the Belgian Minister to Washington. Jean-Christophe worked for the Seligmans, where he directed foreign investments, and his wife and Gareth Seligman's wife had formed a friendship based on the fact that they were rather outsiders.

Susannah was Baltimore born and bred, kept her Sixty-fourth Street house staffed with black servants from home, saying that she'd never trust an English or Irish servant as far as she could see one, served southern specialties at her table, and bore with general good grace what she considered to be the perplexities of her Yankee in-laws. Marie-France, on the other hand, had far greater difficulties to contend with since her in-laws considered their son's marriage to her to be a definite misalliance. It wasn't her being an American that the elder de Laulans minded; it was the hideous fact that the Pinguarys, although undeniably a very good family, were, horror of horrors, French Protestants.

If Jean-Christophe *had* to marry a Protestant, the minister and his wife had asked two years earlier when he'd made his plans known, couldn't he find a nice, *real* American girl? According to the conservative, continental couple, Marie-France's parents, who had come to New York on their honeymoon and simply never returned to Paris, were not true Americans.

"Am I going to get a lot of advice?" Mallory asked, suddenly feeling very lighthearted.

"A reasonable amount," Marie-France said in her throaty voice. "Susannah and I have been making some observations."

"Not that we think you all need any help, understand, but still—" Susannah raised her expressive eyebrows and fluffed a fold of her Cheriut dinner dress of yellow gauze over yellow satin, embroidered in silk floss. "Rupert is absolutely ripe."

"Mallory already knows that, Susannah, or why else would she be bothering?"

"Why, for the fun of it, of course!"

How did I let myself get into a situation like this? Mallory speculated in amusement as she focused her attention on the white onyx French clock that adorned the mantel. Are Susannah and Marie-France serious? Of course they are. Am I serious about Rupert? Damn serious, but there's no reason at all to act that way.

"Somehow I don't imagine Rupert hanging from a tree, waiting to be shaken off and tumble into the right hands."

"Don't you?"

I do, she thought, but only smiled at Susannah. Everyone knew how southern girls loved to endlessly play upon the theme of flirtation.

"I think Rupert is feeling quite wretched," Marie-France stated.

"Well, that's hardly my fault."

"But you can take the credit," Susannah shot back. "Marie-France asked him if he didn't think you were looking beautiful, and Rupert turned at least five different colors."

"He's quite a talented man."

"Mallory, why are you pretending you don't care?"

"Oh, Marie-France, I do care. Rupert is the one who doesn't," Mallory said, and the instant the words were out of her mouth she realized far too late that she had just revealed far more than she ever intended to.

Both women exchanged looks that Mallory couldn't begin to read. Were they pitying her or amused by her or, worst of all, bored by her self-containment? she speculated as a dull ache began in her temples. What an idiot she was to think that this was either going to be easy or that no one else would be interested.

"We can talk about other things," she pointed out finally, a slight touch of acidity in her voice.

"Such as when you're going to stop acting as though Peter Beardsley is of some interest to you," Susannah said pointedly.

"*Acting* is the key word here. What Peter needs is a girl who's just out and not too sure of herself and will be very happy to do nothing but please him. That's not me, and it never was," Mallory said, "and it's a fact for which I'm very grateful."

"As are the rest of us," Susannah replied. "Which is why we'd like to help you with Rupert."

"Oh, no." Mallory shook her head and her eyes flashed a warning.

"But why not? We'll sit you together at small dinners, at theatre parties, at—"

"Marie-France, do you think I want to see Rupert discomfitted?"

"But the occasions I have in mind are very pleasant. Sometimes courtship—or the road to it—has to be a bit public." Marie-France's voice had an unmistakable ring of practicality. "And men like Rupert— Well, let's be honest, they've never had too many problems, and this is our only chance to make them a tiny bit less superior."

But it's not exactly the same for Rupert, Mallory silently protested. Gareth and Jean-Christophe had been raised in warm and loving families, and as young bachelors their vices had been those of amusement untainted by spite. Rupert was different. He'd had a father he'd hardly known, a mother he couldn't get on with, and he'd left England with a history of activities that even now, years later, were best left unexamined. His years with Bill and Adele *had* changed him for the better, rubbing off the worst of his ego, smashing forever the mask of superciliousness he'd so cultivated; he'd been made to crave responsibility and give back loyalty, but even after these years of tempering, his moods could be mercurial, and the last thing Mallory wanted to do was expose his intense pride to being the butt of their friends' romantic attempts at matchmaking.

"No," she said firmly, looking directly, evenly, at both women.

"Don't be so standoffish," Susannah advised. "We all need help every now and then."

"I'm not saying that, and I certainly don't mean to sound ungrateful, because I'm not, but—"

"But—"

"But Rupert and I both need a chance to get reacquainted," she said. This was an evasion, but suddenly it was also the truth. "Suppose we've both changed so much that the idea of seeing each other again in a romantic way is ridiculous *and* embarrassing?"

Even as she spoke, even as she saw with relief the dawn of understanding and agreement in Susannah's and Marie-France's eyes, Mallory was acutely aware that her secret plan was becoming more public by the day. A short week ago only Alix had known, then Thea, and now Marie-France and Susannah. Probably Aunt Esme was beginning to suspect her motives, and she would confide to Adele, and on and on and on . . .

I have to move quickly, she thought. A house party like this is worse than a small village full of gossiping old busybodies. Or is it the same thing in a different wrapping? Never mind. Alix knows my secret, the one I'll never tell anyone else, but as for my plan. . . . There's no way to keep that a secret. But if I wait much longer the whole house will be talking about how I'm trying to patch things over with Rupert, and I'll never have a chance to settle it all between us.

Or is what I really want is for us to start all over again?

That disturbing thought floated through her mind, sending a series of tiny shocks through her. The far-fetched hope, the dream, the fantasy that she'd first confided to Alix that night on the *Mauretania* became a possible reality to Mallory, but before her lively imagination could take over, spinning tales of what she would like to happen, she faced Marie-France and Susannah, aware that before anything else she had to deal with the situation at hand.

"Thank you, though," she went on at last, acutely aware that these women were her friends and she didn't want to hurt them because of her sense of pride and self-protection. "I don't need your help right now, but if I do, I'll let you know."

"As you wish," Marie-France said, smiling quietly. "You know best of all what you have to do."

"And we'll be here if you need us," Susannah added just as the drawing room door opened.

Almost immediately there was a preceptible change in the atmosphere. Conversations dropped off to be continued at another time as the women shifted their attention to the doors to see which of the men would come in first.

This was the accepted procedure at all dinner parties, and Mallory prepared herself emotionally for the rest of the evening. No doubt Rupert would stay as far away

256

from her as he possibly could, and she understood. For now.

Funny how all her nerves seemed to settle, and with all the natural elan of a woman who knows exactly what she's doing, Mallory began to look forward to what the next day would bring.

"Dad—" Rupert came into the library to find William Seligman seated behind his massive desk, a substantial amount of paperwork—reports and charts and pages covered with figures—covering its fine surface. "I came in to see if you were ready for lunch, but it seems as if you're otherwise occupied—not to mention breaking the house rule about not bringing in work from the office."

"I'm only bending it, since all of this arrived a couple of hours ago by special messenger," Bill replied genially as Rupert dropped into the large leather wing chair opposite him. "Are you familiar with Horton Steel and its owner?"

"Let's see . . . Last of the independents. A self-made Pittsburgh millionaire with three daughters that he's married off to, respectively, an Italian count, a Swedish baron, and, most amazingly in this the time of the dollar princess, a Louisville horse breeder," Rupert said, finishing up the amusing details before dealing with the harder statistics of profit and loss and the steel industry. He was also well aware that the question had been a rhetorical one, and if he hadn't been able to give back the pertinent details about George Horton, he might as well go out to the stables and start on his new career of mucking out the stalls. "Why the quiz, if I may ask?"

"Because George has decided that at sixty-three he wants to truly enjoy the fruits of his labor, and since he hasn't any sons he has decided to sell."

Instantly, Rupert felt his skin prickle with anticipa-

257

tion. "To whom?" he asked, already half-knowing the answer.

"U.S. Steel. The board at Horton approved the sale yesterday. That's why all of this . . ." Bill gestured at the papers.

Rupert's smile went from ear to ear, his well-trained financial mind working out what would come next: the announcement, the transfer of stock and all the rest that was involved when a sale of this size took place. Steel magnates, by the very nature of their business, were not nice men, Bill had explained to him years before. That would have to wait for later generations, and frankly, most of the old men loved being robber barons. Nonetheless, George Horton was better than most, and his association with William Seligman went back to the early 1880s.

"I want to work with you on this," Rupert said earnestly, leaning forward in his chair. "There are stockholders to consider, the transfer of stock issues from Horton to U.S. Steel, an in-depth study of the annual reports so that—"

"All in good time," Bill laughed. "And I may have other plans for you."

"If by that you mean you're going to ask me to go to St. Louis, I'm afraid I'm going to decline the honor."

"How did you pick that particular city?" Bill inquired, more amused than offended. "Oh, never mind. If you've had enough of the Midwest after Chicago, all you have to do is say so. I've never had to strong-arm you before, and I'm not about to start now. Besides, if I did, you might decide to decamp."

"Hmm." Rupert pretended to look considering. "I can always take my talents to the House of Morgan."

"And they'd be happy to have you," Bill said, more than happy to be truthful about that particular fact since both knew that would never be an eventuality. "But let's put business aside for the moment. Don't you have better things to do on a beautiful day like today than sit here and discuss steel mills? You're hardly back from Chicago, and now you're asking to take on more work," Bill went on, his light tone growing serious. "This should be a time for you to rest and recoup. And in case you don't look in the mirror when you shave, the circles under your eyes make you look like the loser in a prize fight, not to pass over the fact that your color makes me think you've been living in a wine cellar."

"Have you finished cataloging me?"

"I'm not cataloging—this is just a nice father-son discussion."

The last barriers between them had fallen away years before and there was no subject from the most complicated of business matters to the deepest of personal problems that they couldn't and hadn't discussed, but for the first time in longer than he cared to remember, Bill saw a defensive look form in Rupert's eyes, a look that had vanished about six months after he came to live with them.

"Why don't we have lunch here, on trays, and that way we can talk about Horton Steel plus a few other things," Bill asked cheerfully, deciding to sidestep the next issue he wanted to bring up for the moment. "Have you been doing anything else besides thinking about business? You've only been here twenty-four hours, and I'd hate to think that all the diversions we have here have no more interest for you."

"Oh, I gave up being a full-time grind the day I graduated from Columbia," Rupert said, his guard coming down. Like most of the younger men at Cove House, he was wearing an old white shirt with the collar open and the sleeves rolled up, white duck trousers and tennis shoes. It was the accepted male costume unless one planned to take part in formal sports or set foot in the dining room. "I had a long ride this morning, and I have a plan or two for this afternoon."

"And do any of them include seeing Mallory?"

"Of course I'll see her. How can I avoid it?" Rupert said flippantly. "At dinner tonight, we'll both be at the table gazing covertly at each other to the delight of everyone else!"

"First of all, don't use that tone of voice, and second, you know that isn't what I meant. Hasn't enough time passed to heal whatever happened between you and Mallory?"

"Nothing took place!" Rupert said more hotly than he intended. "We reached an impasse—nothing could be done—we decided that our university romance couldn't go any further," he went on, hating every lie that came out of his mouth. "It isn't as if we haven't been able to live without each other. I think I've done well in whatever came my way, and as for Mallory— Well, for a girl who talked about becoming a doctor, she seems to have done awfully well as an interior decorator . . . and last night she never looked more beautiful," he added, finally glad to be able to tell the truth.

"Then why don't you just tell Mallory that, or write it in a note and send it with some flowers?"

"I don't need help managing my love life!" Rupert snapped, and as soon as the words were out of his mouth he felt a curtain of shame drop over him. For a minute he hid his face in his hands. "Dad—I'm sorry—I didn't mean any of what I just said. It's just that it's all so difficult, much harder than I thought it would be."

"If you'd just go ahead and get it over with, it's only the first ten minutes or so that are bad, then it's all downhill—and much more pleasant," Bill said musingly. "I'm surprised that with all your experience you've never picked up the art of kiss and make up."

"I have an idea that's not my forte."

"Well, why don't you give it a try anyway?"

Rupert rubbed the back of his neck, suddenly aching and stiff from all the tension he was under. "If I agree to try and make amends to Mallory, do I get the chance to stay in New York and work on the Horton Steel transfer?"

"That's a fair enough bargain," Bill said. "Of course, I'd have kept you in New York *and* given you the Horton Steel portfolio to direct without your making that offer. But since you have—"

Rupert groaned as he heard the unmistakable sound of the trap of his own making close firmly over him.

"Oh, don't worry, I'll live up to my offer," he said at last, "but I'm not going to find it very easy or pleasant or—"

"It's all right, son, you don't have to explain," Bill said gently. "I trust that you'll handle it the best way possible. And now," he went on cheerfully, "why don't I ring for our lunch and you can tell me all about Chicago? Considering all those changes of weather you went through out there, I wouldn't blame you if you demanded hazard pay!"

If there was one place in Cove House where Rupert felt his welcome was absolutely unqualified, it was in the large, sunny, third-floor nursery playroom with its gaily painted furniture and Kate Greenaway prints on the walls and an over-abundance of toys.

On the day before he left Chicago, Rupert paid a visit to Marshall Field's children's department, and now, later on Wednesday afternoon, he was surrounded by the playroom's occupants as he handed out dolls and books and chess and checker sets and magic and chemistry kits and toy models of the latest in French aeroplanes and British motor cars. As far as he was concerned, it was a blessed relief to spend an hour and a half in a place where his attention was demanded by a variety of young people who thought he was wonderful and weren't at all concerned with whom he was or wasn't seeing.

"Uncle Rupert, aren't you going to stay and have ice cream and cake with us?" Virginia, Cliff and Julie's fourteen-year-old daughter asked, drawing him away from the other adoring children to one of the broad window seats. She was the oldest of the children and took her role as leader very seriously.

"No, honey, I can't. I'm on my way down to the boathouse to join your father and some of the other guests. We want to take *The Wanderer* out on a practice run before we all go sailing on Sunday. Do you like your doll, though?" he asked to ease her obvious disappointment. "When I was buying it, I realized it's just about the last one I'll be able to give you. Next year you'll be too grown up."

Just as he hoped, Virginia brightened at his words. "I remember when you first started coming to the nursery to visit us; the one in New York, not here. You'd come almost every Sunday, just in time for lunch," Virginia recalled, "but when it was time for dinner you almost always went over to Uncle James' and Aunt Katherine's apartment because Aunt Mallory lived in the same building and you could see her."

I can't escape, not even in the nursery, Rupert thought, finding himself for one of the few times in his life at a loss for words at what to reply to Virginia's self-evident statement.

"Why don't you and Aunt Mallory care for each other any longer?" she asked with an innocent directness that made Rupert glad he was sitting down.

"Of course we care for each other, Ginny," he got out, feeling utterly floored.

"Well, you have a funny way of showing it. Why don't

262

you give her some flowers and—"

"And you sound just like your grandfather," Rupert interrupted, amused, despite his consternation, at this pretty girl with her mother's auburn hair and her father's sapphire eyes; without a doubt she would be a beauty in just a few more years. "I know you have more to say on the subject, but right now I have to be someplace else," he went on, glancing at his wristwatch. "We'll talk again tomorrow, honey."

Virginia hugged him, and then he stood up and crossed the floor, a variety of emotions assaulting him as he pressed down the door handle, pulled it in—and found Mallory, in a beguiling Cheruit dress of apple-and-leaf figured muslin over rose satin, on the other side.

Their shock and surprise was mutual and mirrored on each other's faces and in each other's eyes. The resemblance between this unexpected meeting and the one four years before when, for one brief afternoon they were lovers, was suddenly too strong for either of them to take with any sort of equanimity, and unable to break away, they stared in fascination at one another, oblivious that both the children and the servants witnessed the interesting scene.

The only coherent thought that Rupert could put together was that Mallory looked stunning. Long trained in the art of observing without really appearing to be looking at the other person, he studied her, noting the new hairstyle, her carefully made-up face—less cosmetics than last night, he noted, but more than four years ago—and the even look in her kohl-rimmed eyes that let him know in no uncertain terms that he would have to make the first move.

"You—you look wonderful," he said in a low voice that set Mallory's heart pounding with the same sickening beat that it had taken on that day in Emma's sitting room.

"Thank you," Mallory replied, feeling her throat grow tight, and suddenly becoming aware that all the good intentions she made were useful only when Rupert wasn't around. "I—I didn't see you in the drawing room last night," she got out, taking a step over the threshold only to have Rupert immediately take two steps back to avoid coming in closer contact with her.

". . . tired," she heard him say. "I decided that since there wasn't any dancing, I'd be better off upstairs in my room," Rupert said, wondering why he couldn't break down and add that the real reason he had sought the refuge of his bedroom was that it was too dangerous to be in too close proximity to her, but that in the end it had offered him only privacy and precious little rest.

To Mallory, Rupert's voice sounded clipped and distant, almost as if he were reciting a set piece, but none of that kept her from going weak at the knees.

Almost as if she were another person watching this unfolding tableau, Mallory looked past Rupert to someone who was taking in their encounter, to Virginia, patiently sitting on the padded window seat, holding the elaborately costumed doll Rupert had given her. With an effort, Mallory forced herself to remember why she had come up to the nursery.

"Ginny darling, your mother sent me up here to get you. Have Nanny Winters help you into another dress; you're having tea with us!" she said, injecting a note of gaiety into her voice at the mention of this treat.

"Who else is going to be there, Aunt Mallory?" the girl asked, and it was obviously not a question born of truculence, but one from a silent observer not ready to leave the scene.

"Well, at last count there's me and Aunt Alix and Aunt Thea and Aunt Megan and Mrs. Bergery."

"Can Uncle Rupert come also?" Virginia inquired, looking from Mallory to Rupert.

264

"I don't know," Mallory said whimsically. Why do I suddenly think this is all so funny? she speculated. This is driving me crazy, that's why— Oh, what the hell. . . . "Are you up to joining several ladies puffing away on ivory-tipped cigarettes?"

"I don't smoke any more," Rupert said with the faintest hint of a smile.

"Then you're coming with us!" Virginia said excitedly just as Nanny Winters came bustling into the playroom with an air of such brisk efficiency that Mallory was instantly certain she'd been eavesdropping.

"Come along now, Miss Virginia," she said in her precise voice. "I have your dress all laid out—it's that nice pale green one your mother ordered from Best and Company. Let's leave Miss Mallory and Mr. Rupert to talk—"

When they were alone, Mallory made her way across the floor, sat down on the window seat, and patted the place next to her. It can't be this easy, she thought, and in the next instant she knew it wasn't going to be. At her words, the faint smile around Rupert's mouth faded.

"Can't we talk for a few minutes?"

"Is there anything for us to talk about? I thought we said it all four years ago."

You know we haven't, Mallory wanted to shout, but her vocal cords wouldn't work and the moment was gone.

"I'm going down to the boathouse now," he told her in a quiet voice. "Tell Virginia that for me, and since we've agreed that we have nothing further to discuss . . . Well, at least this house is big enough so we won't be running into each other very much."

"We haven't agreed to anything that I can recall," Mallory said finally, but again she was too late, and Rupert was already out the door.

Oh, why didn't I say something sooner? she berated herself, trying to blink back the tears filling her eyes. No,

I had to sit here like a lump of clay and ruin it all. You stupid, silly *bitch*.

It would have been of very little comfort to Mallory at that moment, but if Rupert had deliberately, with all of the cool consideration he had at his command, picked a place to exchange his first words with her in four years, he couldn't have come up with a worse spot than the nursery playroom. Nearly all of the assorted Nannys and Misses and Mam'selles had seen part of their encounter, as had several of the older children, and by the time dinner was announced several hours later, all those who had been observing with amusement Rupert's reaction to Mallory, would know via the servants' grapevine that Rupert was not only avoiding Mallory, but now he had made her cry.

"Mallory darling, what are you going to do?"

"Actually, Auntie, I was thinking about taking a nice, long gallop."

"Now that isn't what I meant at all, and you know it!"

"Are you questioning me of your own accord, Aunt Esme, or are you the appointed head of an interested committee?" Mallory said more waspishly than she intended, and a moment later she threw her arms around her godmother. "I'm so sorry, Auntie! I didn't mean that. It all just came out wrong."

"I know, darling." Esme hugged her back. "Some men—well, most men—can be very difficult at times." She cupped her goddaughter's face in her hands. "Shall we talk about it?"

It was early Thursday afternoon, just after lunch, and Mallory and Esme had separated themselves from the rest of the guests and had gone into the Chinese sitting room.

For one of the few times in her life, Esme Phipps found

266

herself not only at a loss at what to do but what to say. Mallory, in her opinion, was behaving just like Alix in her unmarried days, turning away all sympathetic inquiries and good advice and doing just as she pleased. Now, years later, she speculated on the possibility as to whether Mallory was imitating her cousin or if her behavior was some sort of Turner inheritance, strange because Alix was always more of a Leslie, and Mallory wasn't one at all. Like everyone else at Cove House, she had heard about the incident in the nursery playroom, and her heart ached to do something for Mallory, but the girl's calm self-reserve held her off.

Normally they had a close and sharing relationship, closer in fact, Esme often observed, than some women she knew who *were* mother and daughter. Distractedly, Esme fluffed out the ruffled white collar of her wine-colored linen summer dress. At fifty, she was still a tall, slender, attractive and chic woman, with expertly touched-up dark hair and sparkling brown eyes. Those eyes were now serious as she watched her goddaughter standing beside an 18th century Chinese lacquer table whose surface was decorated by photographs in sterling silver frames.

"I finally spoke with Rupert yesterday," Mallory said, "and the more I think about it, the more I'm certain that I was too nice to him." She began to laugh. "I probably would have gotten a better reaction if I'd kicked him in the shins!"

As concerned as she was, Esme nonetheless saw the humor in the situation, and joined in the laughter, easing the air of strain around them.

"I can tell you from past experience that a little anger applied in the right places does work. Try it the next time."

"I just may do that—if I get the chance," Mallory said, and for a moment she turned back to the table to study one of the photographs. It was Rupert in San Francisco, taken by Moshe Cohen, the photographer of the *San Francisco Call* who had been instrumental in taking a photographic record of the city during its crisis. Rupert was standing among the ruins of what had been the grandeur of the Fairmont Hotel; his hands were stuck in his pockets and the grin on his face plainly told her that he was enjoying his situation. "I've also decided something else, Auntie."

"What, darling? That is, if you want to tell me," she amended as Mallory turned away from the table.

"Oh, I'll tell you. I want to. Of course you'll have to promise that in between talking about the Work Horse Parade that the Women's Auxiliary of the ASPCA held on Decoration Day you won't drop little tidbits of what I'm going to tell you."

"I promise," said Esme, awash with curiosity.

"Last week, on the *Mauretania*, I decided that the time had come for me to be friends—or at least behave in a civilized manner—with Rupert again. I told myself that that was the best to hope for. But after Tuesday night . . . I want him again, Auntie. I want to see if I can make him love me the way he did. If he were involved or interested in another woman, I wouldn't do a thing, but he's not, so I'm not doing anything unfair," Mallory stated, and then waited for her godmother's reaction.

"Well, why are you standing here and talking about it? Go after the man!"

"Oh, Aunt Esme, I knew you wouldn't let me down!"

"Were you really worried I might? Sometimes a little nastiness is what does the trick. You're not vindictive, Mallory, no matter what may have passed between you," she went on, treading carefully. "You'd never harass him needlessly, you'll just deal with what's on your mind. As a rule, bachelors, particularly successful ones, never appreciate women being nice to them. They always tend

268

to think that it's some sort of trick."

"And with some women it is," Mallory said with a conspirator's smile. "At least being nasty ought to grab his attention. Thank you, Auntie," she said with a hug and a kiss. "Now I'm going to go riding and get all of this settled in my mind. I'll see you at tea."

Mallory left the sitting room swiftly, full of new resolution, but ten steps up the grand staircase she paused, her dress of Chinese blue muslin and ecru batiste swirling around her slender ankles. What was she doing? The thought of having to go upstairs and change into riding gear left her weary before she was even halfway to her room. No, she decided, the weather was warm and the sun was shining, and there was something better for her to do that required less in the way of clothes.

"Sackett!" she called out, spying the butler as he came out of the library.

"Yes, Miss Mallory. Is there something I can do for you?" he inquired as she came back down the stairs.

"A few minutes ago, I told Mrs. Phipps that I was going riding, but I've changed my mind. If you see my godmother, please tell her that I've decided the best place for me to think about what we discussed is on the beach, not on the bridle path, and I've gone swimming!"

"Why are you standing there looking so down in the mouth? Have you misplaced your autographed copy of *The Protocols Of The Elders Of Zion*?"

Rupert swung around from the wall of finely bound books whose titles he was studying, his eyes burning with unexpected tears. "Do you enjoy jabbing at me, Cliff?" he asked in an emotional voice. "Do you really hate me so much?"

"Oh, I don't hate you, Rupert. If I hated you, you'd never have any question about it," Cliff drawled, crossing the library floor so that he could sit beside Rupert who was now perched on the back of one of the library's chesterfields. "No, what I've never been able to stomach is your inveigling your way into our family and trading on other people's ignorance or discretion to let strangers assume that you're one of us. Other than that, I rather like you. It's just that I never wanted to let you have a too easy time of it."

While Rupert digested this, Cliff stood up and wandered over to the desk. "What's this?"

"Horton Steel."

"So this is it. Do you mind if I have a look?"

"Not at all. It's all in the family," he couldn't resist adding.

"So that old buzzard's finally selling out," Cliff mused. "I can remember a time when Horton swore up one side and down the other that he'd built the steel works with his own hands and he'd pull it all down before he ever sold out. In retrospect, he gives new meaning to the cliché about every man having his price. And as long as we're on the subject," he went on smoothly, "what's your price?"

"Concerning what?"

"Mallory."

"Do me a favor, Cliff; get out of here," Rupert said roughly, getting to his feet. "I've had this out once with Dad, and I'd rather forget the past two evenings."

"So you are suffering," Cliff said with obvious satisfaction in his sapphire-blue eyes. "I wasn't quite sure, you never seemed to be one for retroactive guilt—although what you did to Mallory four years ago should earn you at least that."

Rupert felt a shiver of ice pierce his heart. "What do you mean?"

"I think you know very well what I'm referring to. Or shall I refresh your memory about a certain August afternoon when you went up to the state suite to look for T.R.'s spectacles?"

The color ebbed out of Rupert's face. "What did you see?" he demanded, coming to stand at the other side of the desk.

"See? I *saw* nothing at all. I'm no voyeur. But I heard enough.

"You were taking so all-fire long to come back downstairs that I thought you were having some trouble and I came up to see if I could be of some help," Cliff explained. "Of course when I got there I realized you weren't having any problems at all, and I discreetly left the two of you to your pleasures."

Rupert closed his eyes and took a deep breath in the fruitless hope it would slow his racing heart. Through the open windows he could hear the summer breeze passing through the trees and the laughter of children and adults, all of whom had no idea that his house of cards had finally come tumbling down and he was standing among the ruins. There was no way to go back, and the path ahead was strewn with broken glass and barbed wire, leading ultimately to—to what?

"Why didn't you say something then?" he asked at last, opening his eyes. "What kept you from nailing my hide to the wall?"

Cliff sat down in his father's chair and regarded Rupert in cold amusement. "Do you really think that you're the first to use the state suite as a trysting place? It's about the only thing that white elephant is good for. Besides, I assumed that by evening you'd be engaged to be married. I even gave you the benefit of the doubt for a very long time—not all engagements run on greased wheels, after all. I even thought the story that Mallory went around telling was some sort of cover. But after you'd been in San Francisco for about a month, it finally dawned on me that you'd pulled a beauty of a fast one, and by that time I didn't see where going to Dad was going to help. You were doing a superb job out in California, and a few months after that, when it was apparent Mallory wasn't either suffering or pregnant, I decided to let the matter alone, since a shotgun marriage wouldn't have had much point. You were very lucky, weren't you?"

"Are you finished judging me, Cliff? Do you want me to cry, grovel on the carpet, tell you how miserable I've been for months because I took the wonderful love I had and smashed it?" he asked in a voice thick with emotion.

"No, I just think the time has come for you to set this matter right." Cliff's voice was oddly gentle. "Or have you tried to do that and mucked it up again?"

"Maybe I did," he answered evasively, already sure that Cliff knew the answer as well as all the details of what had gone on the previous afternoon, "but I'm not in much of a mood to discuss it. Cliff, the Horton reports are all yours. I may be a fool—and where Mallory is concerned I probably am—but I'm not a grind. This is my vacation and I intend to enjoy it. Kindly tell anyone who's interested that I've gone swimming!"

Mallory settled herself more comfortably in the wood-framed canvas backrest looking upward at the unco-operative sky. The large beach umbrella that had shielded her pale skin from the sun when she'd first arrived on the beach was hardly necessary now, two hours later, with clouds moving in and out.

Being alone on this sandy beach was beginning to lose its appeal. To be sure, the solitude had been wonderful at first, but with the sunny weather suddenly turned uncertain, it was getting lonely since she knew that those in the house who wanted to swim were now amusing themselves at the indoor pool.

Face up to it, Mallory, she told herself, reaching into

her box of Wilbur Chocolate Buds and unwrapping a silver paper-covered swirl, if you'd opted for the comfort and safety of the pool, or if there were more people here with you, you'd have to be a bit more covered up than you are now, and considering what that means, enjoy your solitary state!

Underneath her flowered cotton kimono, Mallory was wearing a man's tank suit, the sort worn in collegiate swimming competitions, which, although it covered her quite respectably, was not at all what women had designed for their beachwear. *Vogue* and *Harper's Bazaar* might write on in endlessly cooing terms about dark-hued satin bathing dresses piped in light trim with jaunty sailor collars and skirts that ended daringly at just above the knee, properly accessorized by a matching turban to protect the wearer's hair, long dark stockings, and soft, flat slippers with ribbons that criss-crossed their way up to one's knees, but Mallory and her friends, all strong swimmers with good figures and a private beach at their disposal, either wore the detested and cumbersome suits when they were in a large swimming party made up of couples, leaving off the turban, stockings and beach slippers, but when they were alone they chose the supple and more convenient garments men had for water sports.

Mallory had changed her clothes in the beach house, selected a whodunit from the supply on hand, taken the chocolates from the well-stocked kitchen, and then gone out to the beach where a steamer blanket carefully shaded by a beach umbrella was already set up and waiting—at Cove House, all preparations for what a guest might need were taken into consideration in advance.

Well, is the only thing you're going to do this afternoon is swim, dry off, read and eat chocolates? Mallory questioned herself. What do you think your options are? Oh, I have plenty of them. I can be nasty to Rupert, or I can be nice, or I can ignore him or, best of all,

273

I can find another man! Not Peter, of course, but someone else, someone just as good-looking and sophisticated and witty as Rupert . . .

Mallory was dwelling on all the available men who would be coming out for the weekend, carefully planning out just what she was looking for in a new man, when she heard the door of the beach house slam.

Company, she thought, looked over her shoulder at the approaching figure, and froze, all the butterflies she'd convinced herself she'd quelled, rising up with wildly flapping wings as she watched Rupert coming toward her.

In the one moment when they saw each other, Mallory's only consolation was that Rupert's surprise was as great as hers. A huge house, almost uncountable acres of land, hundreds of activities to keep one occupied, and they kept crashing into each other.

Well, that was one of the tricks love played, Mallory theorized as she turned back, as coolly and calmly as possible, to her book, and tried to give the impression of being very interested in the printed pages in front of her.

"May I have one of your chocolates?"

It was the old Rupert with the sweet smile and the amusing way of putting things who stood above her, and Mallory felt a flash of pure anger rush through her, and she gripped the sides of her book. This was the Rupert who knew he could do and say anything and get away with it. Well, not anymore, not with her.

"If you're so desperate for chocolates, there's a nice assortment in the kitchen. You look healthy enough to walk back," she said with a considering look upward, her eyes traveling over his long, lean frame. Her words were deliberately disinterested, but nothing could quell her silent appreciation of him as he remained standing at the edge of the blanket. The red knit jersey tank suit that ended midway down his thighs covered but in no way concealed his masculine attributes, and her view of him

274

made her acutely aware of her own body, aware that her suit, still slightly damp from her swim, clung to her curves, and that the kimono she'd tossed over it extended only as far as her knees. Worst of all—or was it best of all?—Rupert's gaze seemed to be seeing straight through the few garments she wore.

"The sand is hot," he said, his admiring gaze taking her in. No other woman he'd ever known, not even Nell, had as good legs as Mallory.

"That," Mallory responded, biting off each word, "is not *my* problem. Make your own decision, Rupert."

"Mallie—"

"Don't call me that!" she snapped, and when he knelt down beside her and she saw the faint amusement in his eyes, it took every bit of control she had not to push him in the sand.

"Can't you spare a few minutes to talk to me?"

"If you recall correctly, I tried to do that yesterday, but you had other ideas."

"And now you've decided to turn the tables on me?"

"Oh, Rupert, don't use your charm to trample through my life—again," she added after a second's pause. "Go and do something else."

"I was thinking about swimming," he drawled, a devilish light in his eyes. "Of course, I prefer to do it in the raw, but I wouldn't dream—"

"Why not?" Mallory interrupted, smothering her laughter. "There isn't anything about you I don't know—personally, emotionally *and* physically."

For a moment, as she saw her barb hit home, Mallory thought Rupert was going to take off his suit right where he was. She wouldn't have put it past him to peel off his suit in front of her, and as he slowly rose to his feet, their gazes still locked, Mallory realized that that possibility wouldn't upset her at all.

And there's more to it, she thought as Rupert turned

275

away from her. Face it, Mallory, if Rupert had shown one bit of regret for what happened yesterday, he'd be on the blanket beside you, and if there was any nude swimming we'd be doing it together.

It was too much of a temptation not to look, and she tried to view him the way she would a piece of museum sculpture. But no piece of marble or bronze, no matter how expertly carved or cast, had back muscles that moved so perfectly. Once he had been all hers, Mallory reflected as more and more of his flesh was revealed, her gaze moving downward over hard buttocks and long, muscular legs. But how many women had replaced her and how many were still to come and did he ever miss her?

At least he still likes my legs, she reminded herself with a laugh as Rupert disappeared into the blue water of Long Island Sound, his suit a heap of red jersey at the water's edge. Too bad skirts aren't about ten or twelve inches shorter. I'd have Rupert eating out of my hand!

Reluctantly, Mallory turned back to *The Diamond Master*, but her thoughts kept sliding back to Rupert with the same insistence the sun was showing as it went in and out.

Tuesday night he wouldn't look at me, yesterday afternoon he couldn't care less, and now he's trying to be his old charming self. Well, none of that is going to work with me. But was I right the other evening? Is Rupert really nervous about seeing me again? Nervous? Don't be more of an idiot than you already are! Rupert doesn't know the meaning of the word.

Oh, yes, he does, another voice inside her insisted. He gets nervous and upset and hesitant and . . .

No, it's more like flippant and agitated and randy and . . .

"I'm sorry."

Mallory was so lost in her thoughts that the voice

didn't seem real, and it took her a moment to realize that Rupert was sitting cross-legged beside her on the blanket. For a second she looked at him in disbelieving amazement. How could she have become so distracted that Rupert could finish his swim, put his suit back on, and join her on the blanket without her being aware of it?

"What?"

"I'm sorry," he repeated in the hope that those two words would cover a multitude of inadvertent sins and carelessly inflicted hurts. He was ashamed that it had taken this long to make the first move, but nothing prepared him for Mallory's reaction. He saw her eyes turn large and green with anger, saw the book in her hand as she swung it toward him—and ducked too late.

"You bastard!" she said, all the vitriol she'd bottled up for the past four years bubbling swiftly to the surface. "You cold, cruel, heartless *bastard*. What the hell took you so long?"

The book hit his upper arm with a resounding *thwack*, knocking Rupert sideways with a combination of the force of the blow and his fruitless attempt to get out of the way. Mallory hit him again, this time on the shoulder, and then abandoned the book for her fists, pummeling his back and ribs until her fury was spent and she was gasping from her exertion.

"Wasn't pushing me into the rose bush enough?" Rupert asked cautiously as he sat up, a wary look in his eyes, dragging his fingers through his wet, slicked-back hair.

"*No*! I should have gone after you then and kicked you!" she spat out, realizing that except for his first attempt to ward off her blow, he hadn't made any effort to avoid her after that. And she wasn't a petite girl with child-sized hands, either. Not that she thought Rupert would have hit her back, but on male strength alone he could have stopped her, caught her hands. Why hadn't he? Why had he accepted her blows? "Do you like being struck?"

"No," he scowled, drawing his black brows together as he rubbed his arm. "I think your book did more damage than your fists."

"Give it all a chance; you'll feel it tonight," Mallory said cheerfully.

"Earned punishment. I deserved to have someone take a swing at me, only I never thought it would be you."

"I'm not interested in having a third party defend my honor and fight my battles," she retorted, wondering where all of this was going to lead them. They were talking again, but all the important things were going unsaid. "How was Chicago?" she asked aimlessly.

"Cold, and then hot, hotter than any other city I've ever been in," he said, taking her hand, and Mallory felt her skin begin to tingle at his touch. "I couldn't sleep at night—all I could do was lie in bed and think of you and—"

"Why you conniving—" Mallory pulled her hand away and scrambled to her feet. "You're not sorry! You're just randy, and too lazy to look anywhere else so you decided to see if I were still interested! You must have figured it wasn't going to take much—a mumbled apology, a few trite expressions, and I'm supposed to be ready to melt back into your arms!"

"It's not like that—exactly—I mean—" Rupert said, stumbling over his words as he got to his feet, getting himself in deeper, becoming aware that Mallory when furious, her eyes shooting off green sparks and her full breasts flattened under the snug knit of the jersey suit, was a beautiful sight, and he could feel his body warming in a way that had nothing to do with the heat of the day. "Let me explain—"

"No, it's my turn to do the explaining. All you have to do is look at me and touch me and I'm ready to throw

278

myself in your arms and let it happen all over again," she told him, stepping close to Rupert and placing her hands on either side of his tight waist, allowing herself a moment to enjoy the luxury of touching him again. "But first—and at long last—it's my turn. It's time you learned how it feels to be slapped and tickled . . ."

Mallory supposed that it was the heady combination of the breeze off the Sound, the brevity of their swimming clothes and the acute awareness they'd always had for each other, but in any case, even if all she wanted was her moment of revenge, she was alone with Rupert, and she'd earned this time with him, paid for it with tears and hurt and confusion.

Her hands went to his shoulders, reacquainting herself with touching him again, and then to his face, her fingers gently curving over his cheekbones as her mouth pressed against his.

She moved quickly, and Rupert, still shocked by the depth of her fury, remained passive under her attack of affection, accepting it as he had her anger. He had Mallory close to him again, her lips were pressed against his as her tongue teasingly touched his and she wrapped her arms around his shoulders. It was a threat and a promise and a dare all at the same time, but Rupert closed his eyes and reveled in the moment he thought he'd only be able to dream about.

For Mallory, there was an incredible feeling of freedom in this kiss, a heady sense of power as she pressed her body against Rupert's, feeling his long-muscled body and the satin-smooth texture of his skin again. He might very well push her away when this was over, but for now, possibly only for these few moments, he was all hers. Finally, in an old gesture, she laid her cheek against his and waited for the inevitable.

Only he wasn't pushing her away, and his hands were at her waist, pulling her back and drawing her into the

279

circle of his arms so he could look at her.

She thought her pounding heart would suffocate her. "Rupert—"

"I hate being slapped," he said in a barely audible voice. "But if what you just did to me was tickling, I don't want it ever to end."

"Until you get tired and want a change, that is." Mallory forced her voice to be even. "How long will it take this time, Rupert? An afternoon again? Or a whole night this time?" she demanded. It all had to come out this time; no more subterfuge or avoidance. "Say something, damnit!"

"You're not making this easy."

"And why should I? You've made my life miserable. You took our love and tossed it aside like a soiled dinner napkin and idiot that I am, I made it easy for you! I should have made the biggest fuss anyone ever heard. I should have followed you out to San Francisco and—"

"And I wish you would have."

Mallory felt her mouth open slightly in surprise. Was this another skillful lie, or was she finally approaching the truth? Looking at Rupert, she suddenly wished that this was the moment when she'd suddenly realize that she no longer cared for Rupert. She couldn't begin to count the number of books she'd read where the heroine would simply and suddenly fall out of love with the man who wasn't at all worthy of her and turn her attention to the highly suitable and upright young man waiting patiently in the wings. Well, there was no other man, and although whether or not Rupert was worthy of her was a debatable point, as she searched his closed face for some sign of true feeling, Mallory had never felt more sure of her love.

The fear that it had disinterested into an obsession, the worry that if she made one slip everyone would find out she'd been seduced and rejected, the regret that she hadn't listened to her instincts sooner, and the sense of weariness brought on by her silent struggle to make the right decision all seemed to fade away.

"Is that all you can say to me? After four years of avoiding me to the extent of when you're in New York you check with a hostess to make sure I won't be at a party before you accept an invitation, the only thing you can tell me is that all along you secretly wanted me to turn up on your doorstep in San Francisco?" she questioned, her temper threatening to boil over again. She looked squarely at Rupert, and then her anger melted into something very different.

I wouldn't care if he made love to me right here and now, she thought, oblivious to the sudden dimness of the sun and the chill, damp breeze. He'd probably oblige me, too, but there are a few things we have to settle first.

"No, I never thought about it as precisely as you put it," Rupert said honestly. "But if you had—"

"You might have slammed the door in my face," Mallory finished flatly when he hesitated. "Rupert, let's face facts. At the time we're discussing, you didn't want me."

"I've always wanted you. I never stopped wanting you. I'd almost convinced myself otherwise, but it didn't work."

"Did you base this on the after-effects of some sleepless nights?" Mallory challenged, not quite trusting herself to believe him. She wanted him in a way that went far beyond desire. It would be so easy for them to be lovers again, but trust and honesty had to come first, and she wouldn't settle for less. "Don't use me again. I warn you—*don't*—because this time I'll scream and I won't stop until your reputation is as black as your hair!"

"Don't threaten me!" Rupert snapped, grasping her shoulders, his patience vanishing. "*No one* does that to me and gets away with it!"

"If you can show this much emotion when you're angry, why can't you show what you feel when I tell you I love you? I keep trying to reach you, to give you a chance, but it's no use!" Mallory wrenched herself free. "Oh, why do I even try?"

Any reply Rupert might have made was cut off by a sharp crack of thunder, and they both looked up at the sky that was rapidly filling up with blackish-green clouds that swiftly blocked out the last bits of sun. A moment later, a long streak of lightning cut through the darkened, heavily threatening sky and, their discussion forgotten, Rupert and Mallory began to pick up her belongings.

"The beach house," Rupert said needlessly. "Let's run for it."

"Yes . . . come on, don't worry about the blanket or the umbrella."

Together they ran through the sand and reached the safety of the porch the moment the sky opened up and the rain poured down in torrents.

"Just in time!" Mallory said triumphantly as they slammed the door of the beach house behind them. "Let's just leave everything here for the time being," she said, reaching for a towel to dust the sand from her legs. "Shall we light a fire? I hate rain at the seashore; it turns everything damp and—"

"Mallie . . ."

She heard the tender, persuasive undertone in his voice, and her heart ached with love.

"Why are you doing this to me?" she asked, and then she looked at him and his heart was in his eyes.

"It's my pride. No matter how much I want to extract myself, I only end up getting more and more tangled up. I smashed our love—"

"No, just tarnished it rather badly," she said, wanting to reassure.

"Then will you let me try and restore it? I never meant

to hurt you the way I did, but I panicked that day. I thought I wanted to be free, but I found out too late that I wanted something very different."

"Rupert," Mallory interposed, her eyes shining softly, "didn't anyone ever tell you not to talk so much? Example, not explanation," she said, and the next moment, with the rain lashing against the house, effectively cutting them off from any contact with the rest of the estate, making their privacy total and complete, they were in each other's arms.

At the first clap of thunder, Cliff looked up from his book. "Well, there goes a quiet afternoon on the loggia while you paint and I read a novel of dubious merit," he remarked to Julie who sat at her easel, cleaning off her brushes. "Did you finish your painting?"

"No, the good light was gone a half-hour ago," Julie said, standing up and taking off the white painter's coat she wore over her green and white striped lawn summer dress. She was a talented amateur water colorist, and her paintings were much in demand for charity bazaars. "This will just have to wait for tomorrow. I hope no one is caught outside. It looks like it's going to pour."

"I love these unexpected summer storms," Cliff said dryly, reluctantly closing *The Losing Game*, which its publisher, G. N. Dillingham, was promoting as a no-holds-barred inside look at the working of a bucket shop told in the form of a novel. "You never know where anyone is going to end up. Remember last year when Georges Bergery had to take refuge in the Bertolucci house?" he asked, referring to Cove House's resident gardener who handled a full-time staff of six in order to take care of the grounds, the garden and the greenhouse. "The storm was so bad he had to spend the night."

"Oh, I know he made a fuss, but Bettina told me later

that he wrote the whole experience down in his journal and is going to use it in his next novel!" Julie laughed as she went over to the house phone. "Shall I order our tea while I'm at it?"

"No, darling. Let's wait and see how bad the rain gets."

A minute later, the footman Julie had summoned arrived to remove her afternoon's work, and almost as soon as he left, Alix and Henry stepped onto the loggia.

"You haven't picked the best of moments to come out here," Cliff remarked over the latest thunderclap. "It looks like we're in for it. Does it look as if everyone else is in the house?"

"As far as we can tell," Alix said, joining Cliff on the sofa. "The rest of the party is suitably attired for afternoon tea and are at this very moment spread out among several drawing rooms."

"I think if we slide the terrace doors closed, we can stay right here, have our tea, and not have to change clothes."

"My husband is somewhat unsociable this afternoon," Julie confided, coming to sit beside Henry on the other sofa. "I think it has something to do with your former ward."

"I don't think I want to hear this," Henry remarked. "At least not without a drink a good deal stiffer than tea."

"You're right on both counts. Rupert and I had a rather complicated discussion a couple of hours ago, and he said since this was his vacation he was going swimming. I hope a dip in the pool improved his temperament."

Alix and Henry exchanged concerned looks.

"Cliff, Henry and I were part of the group down at the pool this afternoon," she said, leaning forward slightly, looking all of about twenty in her moss-green gingham summer dress with white lawn collar and black trim. "Rupert never joined us."

With more concern than he'd ever care to admit, Cliff regarded the downpour from their insulated spot on the terrace. "Then he's at the beach. Look at that lightning. It's dangerous out there."

"Considering there are times I think you'd like to drown Rupert in a thimble of water, you're acting awfully protective and big brotherish," Julie teased.

Cliff made an expressive face. "Rupert can take care of himself—as you say, Henry, he always lands on his feet. Why don't we just relax and have tea?" he asked just as a familiar figure joined them. "Oh, Sackett, we were just going to ring for you."

"Yes, Mr. Clifford, I'll see that your tea is brought out to you immediately. But I also came to see if Miss Mallory has returned from the beach yet. Mrs. Phipps is becoming concerned."

"The beach!" Alix exclaimed. "I thought she'd gone riding!"

"Those were her original plans, my lady. But before Miss Mallory left she informed me she had changed her mind and asked me to pass her new plan on to Mrs. Phipps. I believe I spoke with her shortly after you did," he explained skillfully. "And now, if there's nothing else . . ."

The four were silent until they were certain Sackett was well out of earshot.

"So Mallory and Rupert are alone together at the beach," Henry said.

"No, it would be my guess that by now they're safely in the beach house," Alix corrected.

"At least we don't have any dangerous objects made for braining difficult men in the beach house's kitchen," Julie interjected. "Cliff, aren't you going to say anything? Or are you just going to sit there like the Cheshire Cat?"

"And so this is what it all comes down to. Rupert and

Mallory—*sur la plage*." He broke into a wide grin. "*Advienne que pourra.* Whatever may happen. . . ."

"I thought I'd lost you forever," Rupert said, his voice heavy with emotion. "I was sure that by the time I got up enough nerve to tell you how I really felt, you'd have another man."

"Oh, I was thinking about it, but no such luck for you," Mallory laughed as Rupert leaned back against the wall and pulled her against him. "I've been followed by droves of men, *legions* of them, but no matter how many I talked with and dined with and danced with and went to the theatre with and kissed with varying degrees of intensity, it all came back to you." She put her hands at the back of his neck. "I love you and no one else," she said as his arms tightened demandingly and they dissolved into a kiss that was introduction and renewal and promise all in one.

Rupert's face was transfigured. "I love you, Mallory, and I never want to be without you again. This isn't the proper time or place, but the question comes with all my heart. Will you marry me?"

Her heart filled with joy. "Marry . . . ?"

"I'm a little late, and I certainly could have picked a more romantic spot, and no matter what atrocity I committed, you're the only woman I've ever wanted. I have all along."

She rested her hands on his chest. "So have I."

"And . . ."

"Yes," she said, leaning forward to kiss him again, not only on the mouth, but small, provocative, teasing kisses all over his face. Four years before they had been properly dressed, standing in a romantic spot just made for a proposal, and it had ended in ashes, now they were together in a place that was rough-hewn by comparison and were only half-dressed, but their happiness and rediscovered joy in each other radiated in the damp air around them. The terrace had offered them an unqualified romantic, but the beach house gave them absolute privacy. "I want to be your wife. I want us to spend our lives together beginning right now."

As she spoke, Mallory began caressing him, moving her hands downward over the hard chest under the knit jersey and tracing the outline of his ribs. For a moment she rested her hands on his hips, and then, with only the slightest hesitation, the fingers of her right hand came to rest over the long, hard ridge of flesh between his legs.

His eyes closed in pleasure as she touched him, and the next moment his hand closed over hers, pressing her tighter and more firmly against his pulsing maleness.

"What you do to me," he whispered heavily, his mouth moving along her cheek. "If it weren't impossible, I'd be happy to stay here just like this."

"When there's so much else for us to do?" Mallory challenged as their embrace slowly changed. The calm, logical part of her mind said that this was too soon, Rupert still had a lot of explaining to do, that for all she knew their engagement could last for only as long as it would take him to make love to her again. But Mallory was operating on another level. All the love and passion and desire she'd held in check for so long was clamoring to be released. "This time is for us," she said, her kimono falling to her feet.

"From now on," Rupert said, slipping an arm under her knees, "the world belongs to us."

The first floor of the beach house was divided up between a well-equipped kitchen and a living room filled with sofas and chairs covered in faded chintz and wicker tables. There was a victrola with all the latest records, several bookcases, and an old Persian rug, its colors faded to watercolor softness. It was comfort without luxury, the best of everything without ostentation, and like all reconciled lovers caught in the first flush of their renewed passion, they couldn't have cared less. There was a roof over their heads, a fire waiting to be lit in the fireplace, food in the cupboards and icebox and, thanks to the storm, absolute and utter privacy. Not another thing mattered.

Rupert set Mallory down in front of the large stone fireplace, letting her go only long enough to light the fire. It caught immediately, banishing the dampness, making the beach house even more conducive as a trysting spot.

"Now," Rupert said, his face serious but his eyes alight with love, "it can't be very healthy for us to stand around in these damp suits."

"I wasn't aware that our activity was going to require standing," Mallory returned, her heart pounding as his hands went to the shoulder straps of her suit, gently tugging the damp material down, revealing her high, full breasts.

Her suit first, followed by his, and then it was like the last time, only different and better.

"You look like the Apollo Belvedere—minus the figleaf," Mallory said as they came close together again and she could press herself against his fully aroused frame.

"But you're much more interesting than I am," Rupert said, his hands going to her hair, taking out the pins and running his fingers through her shoulder-length hair that had waved from the weather. "I love you, and right now I'm wondering why I ever thought I could want someone else."

She wrapped her arms around his neck. "Later—we have all the time we need to talk—this is all for us—I want the present not the past."

They sank down as one on the nearest sofa, its soft cushions absorbing their bodies as they stretched out full length, their arms around each other and their bodies pressed tightly together.

Somewhere deep inside her, Mallory had always known this moment would come again, and she pressed her lips against Rupert's face while her fingers caressed every inch of skin that she could reach. He was working his own magic now with the fingers and mouth of a sorcerer, bringing their moment of sweet reunion closer and closer, and Mallory felt herself begin to tremble. She wanted to laugh and cry at the same time, to soar and never touch the ground, to belong to Rupert completely and to have his passion in return.

Rupert was loving her thoroughly, prolonging every moment, waiting until they were both blazing before completing their embrace, entering her slowly, inch by inch, his body taut with supreme control until they were merged fully into one another like a broken sculpture miraculously mended and surpassing its original beauty.

Mallory felt him deep inside her and she gasped once and then gave herself up to his demands, each thrust sending wave after wave of pleasure rippling through her, extending through every nerve ending. They were pulsing together now, straining for the ultimate release, and reaching the paradise they both sought at the same moment.

They lay together for an endless time afterwards, each of them reluctant to break the spell they had woven. Mallory ran her fingertips across Rupert's damp shoulders, certain that he was asleep until he slowly raised his head from her breast and looked at her, joy and pain mingling in his silver eyes.

"All the time we've lost . . . Can you forgive me for everything I did four years ago? It was fright, plain and simple. I was afraid of being caught in an early marriage. It was evil what I said to you. Blame it on that streak in me that I've never gotten out of my system, but if it's any consolation, I've never been very proud of my actions."

Everything that Mallory wanted to throw back at Rupert suddenly seemed unimportant. Four years was a long time and when she thought about it Mallory was well aware that far from destroying her in any way, the experience had made her stronger. In time the pain had faded, but her love had sustained itself, and that was the only thing she had to consider.

"That's over and finished with, Rupert," she said tenderly, her fingertips tracing the bold lines of his eyebrows. "Whatever we said to each other four years ago is lost in time. It can't come back but we can't go forward unless we let it go."

"You don't have to make it easy for me," Rupert said in a bitter voice. "I pushed you out of my life because I was frightened of my own emotions, my own happiness, and that . . . that I'd be laughed at, patronized because I couldn't hide my love for you."

"In a way there probably would have been some patronization—for you and me both. We were young and just out of school and as much as everyone loved us we wouldn't really have been allowed to make our own plans. We would have been guided—"

"For our own good, of course."

"And supervised."

"Since we couldn't be trusted too far." Rupert was beginning to smile. "Which, in our case, would have been locking the barn door after the horse is stolen!"

"Oh, not that old chestnut!" Mallory protested, pulling Rupert closer to her. "Keep me warm, lover, we forgot about a blanket."

Rupert kissed the side of her neck. "We had something more important on our minds. Where's that afghan . . . ?" Feeling around on the floor, Rupert found the multi-colored covering and expertly flipped it over them. "And now," he said, taking Mallory into his arms,

290

"when shall we make ourselves all proper and re-spectable?"

Mallory's heart leapt in joy. "Does that mean what I think it does?"

"Exactly."

Mallory considered their situation. "The sensible thing would be for us to elope. We could slip out early Monday morning, take the train to New York, go directly to the license bureau and then dig up a cooperative judge."

"Of course that means we'll have to spend the rest of the weekend pretending to avoid each other. There's no point in eloping unless you surprise everyone," Rupert observed as they cuddled together, the sofa just long enough for the both of them. "And I have to admit that the concept is rather amusing. We'll be talked about for the next six months. But—" suddenly his voice was serious, "—is this what you really want to do?"

Mallory turned her head to him. "Rupert, do you mean this?" she asked, surprised. "This is what scared you off the first time—the idea of an engagement and big wedding." She began to laugh. "I'm not going to let you get away again, and if that means a quick trip to City Hall, I'll forgo all the frills!"

"I don't want you to. I want you to have all the glory that comes with being a bride," Rupert told her tenderly. "I cheated you out of that, and now I want everyone to know how lucky I am to have you. I was afraid of my own emotions for so long that I threw our love away."

"Lucky for us it kept coming back—or never went away."

"I prefer the latter. I tried to bury my love for you, but it finally came up to the surface. I haven't thought about another woman but you in months."

"And I haven't been able to pay attention to another man all summer," Mallory said in amazement. "I would think about where you were, what you were doing, whom you were with."

"It's terrifying to think that our minds ran in the same direction at the same time. And as for whom I was with—female variety—there hasn't been anyone for me since May."

Mallory suppressed her laughter. "Then I'd better marry you as quickly as possible, before you begin to cast around for a bit of passing amusement and—"

"And there's no one for me but you, not from this moment on," Rupert interrupted, cutting off Mallory's words with a long kiss, not releasing her until they were both breathless. His embrace tightened. "I want you again."

Her arms slipped around his neck. "Yes . . . oh, yes . . ."

"My Mallory." His voice was muffled against her neck. "My one and only love . . ."

For the rest of the afternoon, as the summer thunderstorm raged on, they made love, rediscovering each other both physically and emotionally, their passion transcending desire to reach true communion.

"It's more incredible every time," Mallory said an endless time later. "I think this is why I didn't want another lover. I knew you were the love of my life and no other man would be right."

"Remember, I flatter easily," Rupert said with a rich laugh. "And if it's magical on this old sofa, imagine when we finally get into a bed again. Your room tonight?"

"No, Rupert, not my room *or* your room," she said significantly, and Rupert's face registered instant comprehension.

"Suddenly eloping sounds like a fine idea," he said whimsically.

"Oh no, you've made your ideas on a big wedding perfectly clear! And since that is what we both want, you also have to agree that when we leave the beach house we won't be lovers again until our wedding night."

"You mean every word of this, don't you?"

"Yes—and it's not because I want to play some silly female game with you. It's because I want our wedding night to be special, and if we find every pretext to slip away for an hour or two so we can make love, I don't think it will be. Look at it this way," Mallory went on in a more playful tone, tugging at Rupert's hair. "You'll have at least six more weeks of bachelorhood before you have to vow your fidelity. Plenty of time for a few last flings!"

"Oh, I think I had my last fling about three months ago in a very elegant house in Chicago, on South Dearborn Street, in a swan-shaped bed that had a special fixture attached to the canopy that sprayed perfume at the most appropriate moment!"

"The Everleigh Club!" Mallory gasped out between gales of laughter. "Does it really have a solid gold piano?"

"Of course it does—I played it to great advantage during an otherwise dreary business dinner. I couldn't stand the talk about debentures and two-for-one splits another second and I enlivened the discussion by playing out my repertoire!"

"I wish I could have been there."

"You would have put all the girls there to shame," he said, tenderly depositing tiny kisses along her hairline. "And as for my having a month or two to sow my remaining wild oats—" He buried his face in the soft hollow of her throat. "How could I? You're the only woman I want."

Mallory stroked his black hair, tears of pride and joy stinging her eyes. "I'm glad you said that, because I'm not quite as generous as I made out."

"I know you're not the irrational, jealous sort of woman, but I'd hate to think you didn't care until our wedding day."

"Oh, I intend to show you how very much I do care," she explained, drawing her fingers down the long length of his spine.

"Aren't you forgetting your plan for no pre-marital lovemaking?" Rupert asked as he pulled Mallory under him, his hands possessively cupping her rounded hips.

"Oh," she said, melting at his touch, "that doesn't go into effect until *after* we leave the beach house!"

For Henry and Alix and Cliff and Julie, the knowledge that Mallory and Rupert were trapped together by the thunderstorm had long since ceased to be a source of amusement to them, and their tea party on the loggia had turned into a foursome where very little was said in case one of them accidentally said the wrong thing. They drank their tea and ate the sandwiches and cakes, but among four friends who never ran out of things to talk about, conversation was now in the short-tempered stage.

"If either or all of us go down to the beach house, it could turn everything into an unmitigated disaster," Cliff finally remarked. "Unfortunately, I can't take too much more waiting."

"Neither can I," Henry said. "But our hands are tied."

"If he hurts Mallory again," Cliff began in a threatening voice, and then stopped, a guilty flush appearing under his tan.

"Cliff, what are you talking about?" Julie demanded.

"And what do you mean about his hurting Mallory again?" Henry inquired, an edge in his voice. "When was the first time?"

Alix and Cliff looked at each other. Both knew that the

other was privy to a secret, that it was the same secret, and that neither of them would ever betray it.

"Henry, I think you and I have stumbled into a well-guarded enigma that no one is going to tell us about, and that we should let the whole situation pass."

"Normally I'd agree with you, Julie, but not where Rupert is concerned. To use the old cliché—'where there's smoke there's fire.'"

"Darling, there are things you don't have to know about," Alix put in, rescuing the moment. "Let's just wait and see what happens. We don't even know if they are together right now," she continued, not believing a word of what she was saying.

"If that's the case, we really have something to worry about. It's dangerous to be on the water when there's a storm going on. But once again we're trapped," Cliff went on. "We can't go out to the beach to make sure they're safe because it's too much like prying."

"Well, if anything happened between them, it's already taken place and we'll just have to take it as it comes," Alix shrugged. "Let's stop acting as if Mallory's helpless and Rupert's some sort of brute. They're both perfectly capable of coming up with their own answers."

"Yes," Cliff agreed, reluctantly. "I hate your logic, Alix, but I have to go along with it. And while we wait, shall we order something a bit stronger than tea to get us through this period?"

"We may as well," Julie said, and the others agreed, debating between the merits of cognac or bourbon or if they should just get a head start on the cocktail hour.

"Sackett, you're just the man we want," Julie exclaimed as the butler appeared before they could ring for him. "A nice big pitcher of dacquiris, please," she said, settling their conversation by the simple means of being the first to speak. "We're marking time out here, just getting away from the rest of the house."

"I understand, Mrs. Clifford, and I have some possible news that may make your wait easier. The master sent me out here to let all of you know that there may be some very happy news to celebrate later," Sackett said with a smile. "Miss Mallory and Mr. Rupert came back to the house about fifteen minutes ago and left word that they wanted the master and mistress and Mr. and Mrs. Phipps to meet them in the blue salon in a half-hour."

Cliff's smile was almost unholy. "Well, what do you know."

"We don't know anything yet," Henry advised cautiously. "It could turn out very differently from what we're expecting."

"Well, my lord, they did instruct Cook to stop what she was doing and put some champagne on ice."

"That's a clear enough sign for me," Alix said, laughing merrily.

"And for me," Julie agreed. "It looks as if we're going to have an engagement this summer after all."

"Well, it's about time," Henry said, a faint smile beginning at the corners of his mouth. "And if that is the case, I think we can do a bit better than dacquiris."

"That's right. Sackett, a bottle of champagne for we four unsociables."

"Of course, Mr. Clifford. I took care of that as soon as I spoke with Miss Mallory and Mr. Rupert. I'll have it brought right in to you," he said with the certainty that on such a happy occasion as the one coming up, an old family retainer could be forgiven both second-guessing their reaction as well as having the last word.

Esme Phipps and Adele Seligman had waited a long time for this moment.

Any advice that their husbands gave them that when Rupert and Mallory sent word that they wanted to see them in the blue salon the news might not be what was so easily assumed, the order of champagne nonwithstanding, went completely unheeded.

Adele gave Sackett instructions that another bottle of champagne was to be put in reserve and that caviar was definitely called for, and then she and Esme turned their attention to what they would wear.

At the appointed hour, Esme in a striking Drecoll afternoon dress of black and white striped mousseline, Adele turned out in Callot Soeurs' equally effective dress of blue flowered silk veiled with mousseline de soie, their husbands in Palm Beach suits, were all in the blue salon trying not to look as if they knew exactly what was going to happen.

It was the announcement they'd waited for, but for the Phipps and the Seligmans, raised in a more formal time, there was something disturbingly *modern* about the next several minutes.

After less than a ten-minute wait, the doors opened and Mallory and Rupert swept in, their expressions serious but their eyes alight.

"We've come to give you all some very happy news," Rupert said without preamble, his arm around Mallory's waist as they faced their families. "Earlier this afternoon Mallory and I had a long talk and we decided that we're in love and that we're going to get married!"

"All we had to do was get stranded in the beach house for a few hours to have everything come out straight!" Mallory added, possessively brushing an invisible speck of dust from the lapel of Rupert's immaculate Palm Beach suit. It was a gesture that was lost on either of the older couples. "Are you happy for us?"

It was a purely rhetorical question; the joyous looks they were given was answer enough. Naturally, the silent consensus ran, they would have preferred a more, well, *serious* approach to such a step. To their way of thinking

297

there should have been more of a consultation, not an announcement. *Fait accompli* certainly had its obvious advantages, but it wasn't as if they could stop them and, admittedly, the transformation of Mallory and Rupert from two people who, twenty-four hours before, could scarcely look at each other, to an openly affectionate couple eager for marriage took a bit of getting used to.

"We discussed it and decided that we want a wedding with all the trimmings," Mallory said after kisses and embraces had been exchanged. The champagne was poured and the caviar passed and she and Rupert sat side by side on a Louis XVI-style sofa covered in a yellow and blue moire stripe. "We talked about eloping, but we came to the conclusion that we'd been causing enough talk for the past few days."

"All of which was my fault," Rupert said with an unabashed smile. "If I'd had any nerve—or plain good sense—I would have told Mallory that the moment I saw her again. Right now, since I'm finally smart enough to recognize that I have the only woman I've ever loved, I want all the social privileges that come with it."

"Of course I'm the one who'll have all the thank-you notes to write!" Mallory pointed out, laughing. "Aren't you all going to *say* something?"

"We haven't wanted to interrupt the two of you," Esme said warmly from her seat on the sofa opposite them where she and Newton were holding hands. "You two are a wonderful sight, and we've waited so long to see you both so happy. Oh, I'm getting sentimental and I promised myself I wouldn't—"

"There, darling. Mallory and Rupert know that we're thrilled for them," Newton said consolingly, patting his wife's hand. "It goes without saying that you have our full approval."

"And ours," Adele added happily. "And now it looks like we have a wedding to plan."

"I'm glad Rupert has found another interest to occupy

298

his mind other than the Horton Steel transfer," Bill said from his blue velvet-covered wing chair.

"Oh, I'm a very versatile fellow," Rupert responded. "I can't think of a better way to spend the next weeks than by dividing my time between Wall Street and my wedding."

"Weeks?" Adele questioned, surprised. "I assumed you'd both want a December wedding."

"So did I," Esme added, equally surprised. "Why not wait until the first week in December? If you do, Mallory, you can wear white velvet."

"Oh, Auntie, don't try to tempt me, we've made our minds up!" Mallory laughed, getting to her feet and going to stand behind the sofa. She was wearing one of her favorite Paris purchases, a Jeanne Hallee afternoon dress of pink and white striped batiste with a high waist, elbow-length sleeves, a scalloped-edged white batiste scarf followed the V-shaped neckline in the front and back and was finished with a belt of pink satin. "Actually," she went on, her hands resting on Rupert's shoulders, "we were thinking about the end of September."

"September?" With great difficulty Esme hid her surprise. "Well, it can be arranged, of course, since it's what the both of you want, but it will be a rush—"

"We don't care, Auntie," Mallory assured her godmother. "And what we don't want is preparations that go on for so long that everyone is worn out long before the wedding ever takes place. We can do it in six weeks."

"Well, before we get deep into wedding plans, shall we discuss your engagement?" Bill asked, skillfully interposing his question before either Esme or Adele could make further comments. "I assume you don't want to keep it a secret."

"We could go on pretending we don't care," Rupert drawled.

"Imagine everyone's surprise when they get an

299

invitation in the mail," Mallory added, playing along.

"People will never stop talking."

"Is there something that makes you think anything is going to keep them from talking now?"

"Children," Adele warned, but Newton Phipps laughed.

"Oh, let them have their fun. That's what being engaged is all about. Now, shall I make my little speech tonight, or do you two want a little more time?"

"What I'd like is to have an engagement ring for Mallory." He looked at his watch. "There's still time to call Tiffany's and ask them to send a salesman out on the first train tomorrow."

"And don't forget to ask them to send along one of their salesmen from stationery," Esme put in, ever mindful of the practicalities. "We may as well decide on the invitations at the same time."

"That still leaves tonight to get through," Mallory pointed out, coming back to sit beside Rupert and hold his hand. "Shall we not say anything and let everyone guess, or not say anything and glare at each other to keep up the pretense?"

"What I suggest is that you leave here for tonight," Bill advised. "The Garden City Golf Club is having a dinner dance tonight. Richard and Megan North are going with the Bergerys, and I think it would be a good idea if you joined them."

"I like that idea," Mallory said. "Rupert, shall we go dancing?"

"I'd like nothing better than to twirl you around the floor a few times," Rupert smiled. "But what shall we do about Georges and Bettina and Dick and Megan?"

Mallory playfully touched her champagne glass against Rupert's. "Oh, let's leave them guessing!"

He drained his glass. "Agreed."

"Good—because it's time for us to get dressed."

"Ah, the demands of love," he said, standing up and holding out both hands for Mallory.

There was another round of kisses and embraces and then they were gone, sweeping out the door on a wave of laughter, leaving four very serious people behind them.

"This should be a happy moment for us," Adele said consideringly, "and I *am* glad, but . . . but . . ."

"But why so quickly?" Esme fretted.

"Really," Newton said with a wry smile. "Esme, do you actually think all they did at the beach house was *talk*?"

"Oh, come now!" Esme sounded injured. "I know *perfectly* well they 'took advantage' of every moment. They'd be fools if they hadn't. But I'd always looked forward to Mallory's engagement as a wonderful long time to get everything ready, and now it's all going to be pushed through like—like—" She paused to let a particularly troublesome thought pass out of her mind. "Just to get the invitations mailed in time—!"

"I wish they were going to have a holiday wedding also, but for another reason entirely," Bill said seriously. "With the Horton Steel transfer, I'm going to need Rupert in New York until the beginning of December, at least. I didn't want to say anything just before; I'll speak to him later."

"Better make it tomorrow," Newton advised. "No need to ruin a perfect night."

"I can see your point," Bill agreed, lifting the bottle of Moet out of the silver bucket. "Shall we enjoy another glass of champagne? There's just enough time before we have to dress for dinner, and I have an idea that this might be one of the last quiet moments we'll be able to enjoy for the next six weeks."

"And what do you think we should tell anyone who

301

asks questions tonight?" Adele asked.

"Well—" Bill finished refilling their glasses. "I think we should take a leaf from Mallory and Rupert's book and pretend that we really don't know what all the fuss is about!"

"Isn't it amazing the amount of conversation one can get out of discussing motor cars?" Rupert drawled elegantly as he lay stretched out on one of the library's large leather chesterfields, his head resting on Mallory's lap. Mallory was snuggled comfortably in one corner of the chesterfield, her white satin Paquin evening gown with its low square neck and diagonally hung gold embroidered tunic of duchess lace a streak of light in the room's darkness.

"You wove a magic tale." Mallory admired her left hand, now suitably adorned with a flashing six-carat emerald-cut diamond ring, resting on his starched shirtfront, while her right hand lay on his cool forehead. "But I don't think our conversation fooled our friends last night."

"I don't think it did, either, but I did manage to keep them from asking about us."

"My brilliant love, you were wonderful!" she praised extravagantly.

"As in all things!"

"Oh, don't push your luck, lover!"

It was Saturday night, and in the crystal and gold ballroom the dance band hired from New York was playing full force, alternating waltzes with ragtime numbers, but after a few dances, Mallory and Rupert had taken advantage of the activity on the floor to slip away to the peace and quiet of the library.

A few hours before at dinner, just before dessert was served, Newton Phipps had announced their engage-

302

ment, and since the toasts were drunk they had been surrounded by family and friends who had wrapped them in embraces and then wanted to know why they had been so secretive. Appreciative as they had been at the outpouring of good wishes, they definitely needed a respite.

So far, their timing had been perfect.

On Friday evening, a scant hour after they'd imparted their news, and only a few minutes before the first of the guests would begin drifting downstairs for cocktails before dinner, Mallory and Rupert, now dressed for a night of country club dinner and dancing, had dashed down the stairs and out the door and joined the Bergerys and Norths in the massive Pierce Arrow automobile.

Dugan was no sooner steering the car down the driveway toward the gate when Rupert began a conversation centering on the merits of the six-cylinder, forty-eight-horsepower car they were riding in and which the Pierce Arrow company offered as a perfect vehicle for the rougher suburban roads. They were all passionately interested in the latest motor cars and their discussion moved on to the latest additions to the garage at Cove House which included a two-seater Baker Electric Runabout with a fold-back top and bevel gear shaft drive and a sporty, fire-engine red Buick Roadster. They were debating the merits of Packard's double coupe limousine, a completely enclosed model designed to give protection to all occupants, when they reached the Garden City Golf Club, and by that time it was too late for the other couples, both consumed with curiosity but too well-bred to show it, to ask why Rupert and Mallory, who had spent the past two days avoiding each other, were now together as if the last forty-eight hours and the preceding four years had never happened.

They were the first couple on the floor when the musicians finished tuning up, and the last couple off when "After The Ball" was played. It was obvious to anyone who looked at them that they were in love, but they sidestepped and evaded and smiled away any questions, and when they once again returned to Cove House, now wrapped in the deep silence and stillness that only half-past two in the morning could bring, their special secret was still safe.

When they'd left the blue salon, Rupert had lost no time in placing a call to Tiffany's, where the store's president, John C. Moore, was completing his day's labors in the McKim, Mead and White building which the architects had adapted from the Palazzo Grimani that had graced Venice's Grand Canal in the sixteenth century. But now it was the twentieth century, and at the corner of Fifth Avenue and Thirty-seventh Street, the dignified head of one of the world's famous jewelry stores was anxious to be helpful to the newly engaged couple. He would handle everything, John Moore assured Rupert, and shortly before noon on Saturday morning two soberly dressed gentlemen, Mr. Gray from jewelry and Mr. Haverton from stationery, arrived at Cove House. They were taken first to two adjoining guest rooms on the third floor, and after they'd been served lunch in their rooms they went downstairs, Mr. Gray to the blue salon and Mr. Haverton to the Chinese sitting room, to await their clients.

Selecting the ring came first. Mallory's ring size was on file at Tiffany's, and Mr. Gray had prepared a wide selection of engagement rings on black velvet trays so that the young couple could take all the time they wanted to make their choice.

The matter of the invitation came next, a conference for which Esme and Adele joined them. Both women exclaimed over Mallory's ring and then all four turned their attention to study the samples set in front of them. Tiffany had been *the* place to order wedding and social invitations since 1837, and if the only correct form for an engraved wedding invitation was the front sheet of the finest, heaviest white note paper measuring 5-1/8th inches wide and 7-3/8th inches deep, there was a bit more leeway when it came to selecting the engraving process. The choice of script or block or shaded block or old English was presented to them, but since both the date of the wedding and the place it would be held hadn't been definitely decided, no order was placed although one would have to be before the salesmen returned to New York on Monday.

"We're going to have to make a few decisions," Mallory said at last, her fingers tracing the planes of Rupert's face. "Does September twenty-fourth suit you, darling? That's only six weeks from tonight."

"I think I'm going to drug your champagne and abduct you and when you wake up we'll be in the driveway of the nearest justice of the peace!"

"Don't even *think* about something like that!" Mallory laughed and rumpled his hair. "Why don't we put aside our wedding plans for a moment and talk about our honeymoon?"

"I'm all for that, provided that you order a wedding gown that looks like what you have on now. Over the next weeks, as I fall asleep each night in my solitary bed, I want to imagine you coming down the aisle looking very much the way you do now."

"Just be sure you remember to lift the decolletage up a few inches," Mallory said tenderly, bending over to kiss him. "And after I've taken my wedding dress off, where do you want to go? Besides to bed, I mean," she added quickly.

To her surprise, Rupert's smile faded. "I really don't know how to tell you this except straight from the shoulder. Dad spoke to me this morning, and because of the Horton Steel transfer I'm going to have to stay on in

305

New York."

Mallory's heart sank. "Does that mean that if we get married on Saturday, you'll have to go to work on Monday?"

"No, we're going to have two weeks together, and then we'll be able to go away at the end of November or the start of December. Are you very disappointed, darling?"

"I'm relieved! I thought you were trying to prepare me for no honeymoon at all, and I certainly don't mind having to wait a few months. Where shall we go?"

"You don't want to go to Europe, do you?"

"When I just got back? When there isn't much central heating? When, by December, the English country house visit is in full swing? I don't intend to have my new husband creeping down icy corridors to a bedroom that might not be mine. I want to go someplace warm, and not the South of France!"

"Well, that makes it easy. What do you say to California?"

"It would be ideal. I want you to show me everything in San Francisco—and that includes meeting Elinor Tierney!"

"How do you know about Nell?" Rupert looked startled.

"Oh, Rupert, a woman has to have some secrets! Now . . . are you going to introduce us? Nela told me that she lives in an absolutely stunning Italian Renaissance mansion in Hillsborough."

"She'll love meeting you," Rupert said truthfully. "And when we're tired of San Francisco, we'll go down to Santa Barbara. Does a Christmas with palm trees appeal to you?"

"Very much so," Mallory said, bending over to deposit a kiss on Rupert's forehead. "How long a honeymoon trip can we plan on?" Another kiss. "Six weeks, eight weeks?"

"Give me a proper kiss and I'll see about making it longer."

"Stand up, you lazy beast, we can't kiss properly like this!"

"Then why don't we stretch out here together?"

"Susannah, it looks as if we've arrived at precisely the right moment." Charles' deeply amused voice broke into Mallory and Rupert's laughter as he and Susannah entered the library. "Another minute and we would have had to beat off Mrs. Grundy and her favorite cohort Anthony Comstock!"

"As if any bluenoses ever got past the main gate here," Rupert shot back. "Come on over, Charles. Are you and Susie the chaperones of the moment?"

"No, we just came to claim our dances," Susannah said as the strains of "The Skater's Waltz" filtered into the library. She and Charles stood in front of the sixty-inch long Hepplewhite mahogany writing table with its centerpiece of a large silver bowl filled with Marchioness of Landsdowne peonies.

"Go and dance with each other," Rupert advised. "Mallory and I have wedding plans to discuss."

"Is that what it's called now?" Charles inquired dubiously.

"Well, even if they *are* making a little time, all talk is now shifted to the wedding!" Susannah announced with a flourish, looking stunning in Poiret's lobster-red chiffon over soft white satin with a decolletage of malines lace. She tapped the pointed toe of one red satin slipper in an impatient pattern on the antique Persian Sienna rug. "If you two would just decide on your wedding date, we could send Mr. Haverton back to Tiffany's tomorrow morning along with Mr. Gray, and by Monday afternoon the workrooms can be cutting your plate," she stated, not bothering with the usual soothing or amusing preamble Southern women affected. "Back in Baltimore, we get these things settled real fast, while with you Yankees, getting the details arranged for a wedding is about the only time you all dawdle!"

Mallory looked down at Rupert, and together they burst out laughing.

"As a matter of fact we have decided on a date, and Charles, Rupert and I hope you and Thea won't mind sharing your wedding anniversary with us."

"Mind? It would make us very proud. September twenty-fourth has been a very luck date for us."

"Well, that's one out of three complications solved," Rupert said.

"And what are the other two?" Charles asked.

"A place to hold our wedding in, and someone to perform the ceremony. Any suggestions?" Mallory inquired. "We want a large wedding, so that leaves out 667 Madison Avenue. There's always the Plaza or Sherry's, but that's not what we want."

Charles and Susannah exchanged an amused look.

"Well, I happen to have it on very reliable authority that Cliff and Julie would be positively overjoyed if you asked them for the use of 923 Fifth." Susannah's voice was persuasive. "I always thought their marble staircase was made for a bride to come down."

As she spoke, Rupert finally sat up, brushing back his hair with an impatient hand, his expression not really visible in the dim room. "What do you think, darling? Would you like to be married from Cliff and Julie's house?"

"It would be the perfect place for us," Mallory said, thrilled and surprised and deeply touched. "But as to who is going to make us man and wife—you have to admit that neither of us qualifies as regular church-goers."

"As it stands, we have a better chance of having Rabbi Mendes at Shearith Israel perform the ceremony than we do with any other clergyman," Rupert added.

"Well, don't you all look at *me*," Susannah drawled. "But guess which one of us here does have some very proper connections?" She threw a sidelong glance at the man standing next to her. "Charles—"

"I'll speak to the Rector of The Little Church Around The Corner," Charles offered. "He's used to marrying people who aren't parishioners. He'll probably want to have a pre-marriage conference with you—possibly more than one—but since you want a fashionable wedding—"

"We'll make it through," Mallory laughed. "I think Rupert's in a rather respectable mood lately!"

"Please, my love, you're going to shine up my tarnished reputation!"

"Oh, you'll get used to it," Mallory teased, wrinkling her nose at him. "Wait until you see how much fun it is, being all married and respectable."

"The next six weeks is going to be a *very* long week," Rupert remarked, kissing Mallory's cheek as Susannah coughed discreetly and motioned for Charles to dispel the heady atmosphere.

"Susannah, I think you and I have been forgotten," he said pointedly. "And the mood in here is getting a bit too strong. You've had your *solitude à deux* for tonight." Charles loathed playing policeman or wet blanket or spoilsport, but he sensed the electricity between Rupert and Mallory was growing too swiftly to be contained within the bounds of propriety for much longer. "It's time to go dancing."

"Charles is right," Mallory said, standing up in a whisper of expensive fabric. "We'd better get back to the ballroom."

"If you say so," Rupert agreed reluctantly as he stood up. He slipped an arm around Mallory's waist as they faced their friends. "In case it gets too hectic later, thank you both for your help."

309

"It's not really help," Charles corrected gently. "It's more our wanting to see that it all runs smoothly for the two of you."

"So speaks a man who eloped."

"Different times, Rupert, different needs," Charles responded, sidestepping the statement.

"It doesn't matter," Mallory said as they all left the library. "Now that we have our biggest problems settled, the rest of the preparations should go rather smoothly."

Susannah laughed merrily. "Oh, Mallie, the complications have only begun. If you think the only big obstacles are the ones we just got settled, it's *very* obvious you've never been a bride before!"

In the ballroom the musicians were playing the opening notes of "By The Light Of The Silvery Moon" as Alix took two tulip-shaped champagne glasses off a silver tray held by one of the footmen and crossed the highly polished floor to join Thea at one of the open French windows.

"I don't see Charles," Alix remarked, taking a sip of her champagne. "We're supposed to have this dance—not that I particularly want to dance to *this* tune—but I guess he found something more interesting to occupy him." She leaned back against the wall, surveying the room much the way she had on the *Mauretania*, her Lucile gown of white moire with an elaborately embroidered sea-green tunic drawing any number of admiring glances. "Or shall I say that he and Susannah found Mallory and Rupert doing something interesting?"

Thea raised her eyebrows in amusement. "In the *library*? With all those bedrooms upstairs? They're too smart to risk getting caught *there*."

Alix laughed. "And since when does being smart have to do with anything when all you want to do is

310

make love?"

"Absolutely nothing." Thea fluffed out a layer of her Poiret gown of scarlet silk and white voile ninon. "I can think of several times when Charles and I never made it to the bedroom, but never when a party was in progress. And besides, Mallory isn't the sort who's easily swayed."

"But Rupert can be very compelling." Alix's hazel eyes swept the ballroom again. "I think this is a night for misplaced husbands. Henry was called to the phone almost an hour ago and I haven't seen him since!"

"At this time of night! Who called?"

"None other than a Mr. Roland Gresham, recommended to my husband by your husband. Occupation: male secretary."

"Alix, you pronounce male secretary the same way you do Republican—like it's a communicable disease!"

"Oh, I do try—and so for that matter does Mr. Gresham. He's very eager for the position."

"So Henry's going to do the book after all!"

Both women exchanged knowing smiles.

"He'll kick and scream every inch of the way—and write an excellent book. And speaking of husbands and lovers—" Alix motioned with her glass. "There they are."

Sipping her champagne, Alix watched Mallory and Rupert separate themselves from Charles and Susannah and move around the ballroom. Every few feet they were stopped by well-wishers, and even from this distance she could see the happiness on their faces. Just over a week ago, Mallory had been ready to put Rupert behind her once and for all, and now she was going to marry him. She smiled, recalling the rapid culmination of her own courtship with Henry. Having events move a little too quickly definitely added a certain thrill to the entire relationship. The knowledge that all of the proper and prescribed rituals could be swept aside. All it took was a few minutes of privacy in which all true feelings could be revealed and needs met and desires answered.

"They're quite thrilling to look at, aren't they?" Thea whispered, motioning, her diamond and ruby bracelets flashing.

"Yes," Alix replied, "almost as good as Henry and me and you and Charles."

"But . . ."

"Why you think there's a but?"

"There's a particular look in your eyes. I know you don't care for Rupert very much."

"That has nothing to do with it. He and Mallory belong together, they always have, and their chemistry was strong enough to withstand misunderstanding and separation." As she spoke, Alix studied Mallory and Rupert again. Now they were in the center of an admiring group, both so tall and elegant, so deserving to be happy together from now on. Slowly, Alix became aware of a feeling she couldn't identify. Not dread or fear, she had known those well enough, but an uncertainty about something that was undefinable yet clearly there. Yet there was no way to explain how she felt. "No," she told Thea, "all I want is for them to be as happy as we all are."

Her friend looked at her in sudden alarm. "Alix, you don't think that Rupert would—"

"No, not directly," Alix said swiftly as the musicians began to play Eubie Blake's "Charleston Rag." "His days of carelessly hurting someone and then just walking away are over. He won't be afraid of that streak of love and loyalty in him any longer. But Rupert's past is pretty muddy and there's always the chance that someone out there is going to throw a handful of it at him. *That's* what I worry about: the monumental problem that's going to come out of nowhere."

Include me out.

—Samuel Goldwyn

The Plaza Hotel

From its opening day in 1907, the love affair between the Plaza Hotel and New York City had been both instantaneous and irrevocable. It was the place to see and be seen, and for all its high visibility it was a favorite meeting spot for lovers, both actual and potential.

With that much obvious, the management designed a summer restaurant called the Champagne Porch. At forty feet long and fifteen feet wide, it faced out onto Fifth Avenue, and even on the hottest nights it caught the breezes that blew off the park and down the avenue. Here, posts and pillars and carefully attended shrubbery abounded. Latticework protected diners from both the dust and the noise of the street as well as from the too-enthusiastic interest of passersby. It was a restaurant reserved only for those with advance reservations, and the crystal chandeliers and oriental rugs and the uniforms worn by waiters and captains had all been specially designed so that it resembled no furniture or decoration or livery found elsewhere in the hotel.

For those who decided to forgo the elegance of the Rose Room, the charms of the Tiffany-glass-skylighted Palm Court, the London chophouse-inspired Basement Grill Room and the masculine preserve of the Oak Bar for the romance of the Champagne Porch, one found that a

313

special tryst could indeed have a high price tag. Here, dinner ran upwards of fifty dollars per couple, excluding champagne, which began at ten dollars a bottle.

But such monetary concerns were of no interest to Mallory and Rupert as they savored Sevruga caviar, clear consommé, leg of veal roasted with rosemary, and Belgian endive. When they finished their chocolate soufflé, one waiter cleared the plates while another brought over strawberries lightly dusted in powdered sugar.

"Believe me," Mallory said as she bit off the end of one strawberry, "I am never again going to laugh when a client complains about the difficulty of finding an apartment in New York."

"But at least you had some idea that there might be a bit of difficulty," Rupert pointed out. "I'm afraid I was very naive about the whole matter. I just realized that for all intents and purposes, I've never moved. When I was out of town I lived in clubs or apartments that were already set up, and when I came home I lived in the Dakota."

"My poor innocent," Mallory teased. "I can see where I'm going to have to take you by the hand and lead you step by step down the garden path to our perfect first apartment!"

Rupert smiled. "Why is it that I get the feeling that the path you're describing is filled with obstacles?"

"Probably because you're marvelously perceptive. And also because you're plain smart enough to know that the disappointments we've had so far may only be the beginning!" Mallory laughed as she raised her champagne glass to him in a loving salute.

It was the night of August twenty-third, nineteen days since they'd been trapped together in the beach house, two weeks and five days since they'd become engaged, and four weeks and four days until their wedding, now firmly fixed for four o'clock on Saturday, September twenty-fourth, at Cliff and Julie's Fifth Avenue mansion.

Any plans they'd had for a leisurely vacation at Cove House hadn't lasted out the first week of their engagement.

The print style for the wedding invitations had been selected, the ring was glittering on Mallory's finger, and the Tiffany salesmen had returned to New York on Sunday afternoon, August fourteenth, with Mallory and Rupert's thanks for their assistance as well as their assurance that they would visit the store soon to choose a wedding ring and order their At Home cards, the cards that they would send to all their friends to let them know when they would be settled in their first home.

"But before we can order At Home cards we need an address to engrave on them," Mallory told Rupert the next day as they went into the conservatory, successfully slipping away from the ongoing garden party that was ostensibly in their honor although Adele had planned it weeks before.

"I have an idea. Why don't we just stay in the St. Regis until it's time to leave for California?" Rupert suggested as he pulled Mallory onto a wrought iron bench, her Cheruit garden party dress of white mousseline de soie trimmed with black Chantilly lace whispering softly. "That would save a lot of problems."

"It would, except that it would also mean living in a hotel for over two months until we leave on our real honeymoon. And when we get to San Francisco, that's another hotel, and in Santa Barbara we'll be house-guesting with Regina and Ian. When we get back to New York in April or May, we'll be in the same boat as we are now. And suppose I'm having a baby by then?" It was not a possibility they'd discussed with any great depth, but Mallory knew she had to bring the subject up. "It's difficult enough to decorate an apartment when you're *not* pregnant, but when you are . . .

"Oh, Rupert, we're supposed to be having a serious discussion!" she protested, dissolving into laughter and delight as Rupert bent his head to the sensitive side of her neck and began to kiss his way upward, his arms gathering her close to him. One hand curved around her waist while he moved his other hand upward to her shoulders, his fingers tracing pattern after pattern as they approached her bosom, his activity helped out by her deep decolletage.

All talk suspended, Mallory abandoned herself to Rupert's expertise, one small corner of her mind spinning out plans of the sweet revenge she'd have on him when they were married, when she would return in kind the sensations his fingers and mouth were rousing in her now.

She clung to his shoulders as they began sharing kisses that went from gentle to compelling—kisses that had to be complete in themselves until their wedding night.

"Do you really want to live in the St. Regis until we go to California?" she questioned an endless time later as they cuddled together on the bench, her legs thrown over his lap, the secluded corner and green foliage giving them all the cover they needed to keep them safe from prying eyes.

"Not when I think about it. It smacks too much of playing house. I want us to have a long honeymoon with as few responsibilities as possible," he whispered in her ear, and Mallory could swear he was grinning. "But when we do come back from California, and if by wonderful chance we've made a baby, the only thing I want you to decorate is a nursery."

"And you secretly like the idea of being able to establish ourselves in our very own home, even if it's just for a month or so, don't you?"

"I know why I'm going to marry you. You're not only

the most beautiful and desirable woman I've ever known, but you can read my mind as well!"

"Well if you can do that, then you already know that we're going to have to go up to New York as soon as possible."

Rupert groaned, more amused than upset. "I certainly know how to make a good trap for myself. I don't think we're going to be allowed to go off on our own."

"Other couples would kill for the little chaperonage we're having." She traced a finger across a cheekbone. "We have all the time together we need with no one else around and, at night, you'll be glad of your privacy so you can slip into a nice, icy bath!"

"Talk about being right on target!" Rupert grimaced. "Are you sure that six weeks is a short engagement?"

"You'll survive," Mallory assured him cheerfully. "Shall we plan on taking an early train tomorrow morning? *The Commuters* just opened at the Criterion and got very good reviews, and I was thinking that we may as well get in some entertainment while we're at it."

While the play turned out to be quite funny and the perfect summer diversion, Mallory and Rupert were in agreement that their first attempt at apartment-hunting was anything but amusing.

They would have loved to take an apartment at 45 East 66th Street, a four-year-old ten-story building with a round tower and vaguely Elizabethan look that graced a corner of Madison Avenue, but there was nothing available.

"Oh, *why* didn't you come and see me last month!" the real estate agent they'd contacted cried in his flutey voice. "I had a perfect apartment for you, six rooms, really, it just cried out for a couple like you. The less said about the people who took it the better. . . . But never mind, we'll find something. I have some *wonderful* listings . . ."

Wonderful, they later agreed, was strictly in the eye of the beholder since they'd been swept off to see a three-bedroom apartment at the Prasada at 50 Central Park West which offered closet space that wouldn't have held half of Mallory's wardrobe, followed by another three-bedroom at the Kenilworth at 151 Central Park West, an apartment of such dark rooms and long hallways that no amount of skillful interior decorating would ever brighten.

A new real estate agent wasn't a help, either, and by the time they went back to Long Island for the weekend, they'd also seen apartments at the Orienta on Seventy-ninth and Riverside, and the Chatsworth, further down Riverside Drive on Seventy-second Street. Both were excellent buildings offering spacious and sunny apartments, none of which were "right" for them.

Money was no object, and they wanted to look at everything, but now, as they sat luxuriating in the Plaza's tender loving care and totally wrapped up in each other's presence, oblivious to the free-spending tourists and expansive financiers in the company of Follies girls, Mallory and Rupert had the uncomfortable feeling that the city's better real estate agents had seen them coming a mile away.

"There's always an apartment available in the Langham," Mallory offered in a moment of levity as they held hands across the table, sharing the last of the strawberries. "Alix told me today that she's taking Sybil Fleming and her mother around looking for a furnished sublet, and they're rather taken with the building."

"We're not *that* desperate," Rupert said briefly. "We'll stay in the St. Regis until the start of the Twenty-first Century before we'll live in the same building as Evelyn Weldon!"

"A man after my own heart. But I do feel awful about the Alwyn Court."

"Please don't, darling. I was the one who said we wanted to think about it before we decided. Let's leave apartments alone for the rest of our evening and talk about something else."

"That's fine with me." She leaned forward with a provocative look in her eyes. "You haven't finished telling me about all your adventures in the Everleigh Club. Now, I know all about the gold piano and the bed that sprays perfume, but what about the rest?"

Rupert choked on his laughter. "Let's see, there's the Turkish ballroom that was the scene for a rather irregular soirée this past January, and—"

Despite the fact that their search for their first home was not going as easily as they'd anticipated, all the other necessary social details that went into planning a wedding were moving smoothly along.

Tiffany had cut the plate for the invitations, a preliminary guest list was being drawn up, the first of the wedding gifts were arriving, friends wanted to give parties for them, and within the next week musicians would be hired, music selected, flowers chosen, and Mallory had a series of fittings scheduled at Lucile's New York salon for her wedding dress.

Had this been four years ago, they probably would have drifted through the arrangements, letting the older, more experienced heads have their way, eager to get everything out of the way so they could start their new lives together. They were no less eager now, but they were older, more experienced, and unwilling to let others arrange their important day.

Their insistence on only a six-week engagement meant that they were not the only ones cutting short their vacations. Both the Seligmans and the Phipps had reopened their apartments a month ahead of schedule, as had Henry and Alix and Charles and Thea. Their long, leisurely weeks at Cove House were now truncated. They

319

spent Thursday through Sunday on Long Island, and Monday through Wednesday in New York, whimsically deciding among themselves that the title of the new comedy, *The Commuters*, had taken on a special meaning for them.

Tonight, Alix had put together a good-sized theatre party for the opening night of *Baby Mine* at Daly's Theatre. If the audience's reaction was any clue, the comedy was due for a long stay on Broadway, and as the final curtain call was taken, by prearrangement with the Thorpes and with their delighted approval, Mallory and Rupert had slipped away from the rest of the guests and taken themselves off for a late dinner at the Plaza.

"We have to go," Mallory said reluctantly as they finished the final strawberry and drank the last of the champagne. "I have a fitting at half-past nine, and then Thea and I are going to Florian Papp to look at a lacquer table and a Louis XV two-drawer commode." She laughed. "Doesn't this sound absolutely idiotic?"

"No, it doesn't, and I love hearing every detail about what you do. And after today's disappointment. . . . Why is it that we think we're the only engaged couple in New York?" he added, signaling their waiter for the bill.

"I have an idea that all couples who are about to be married feel the same way," Mallory said a few moments later as she stood up, her Callot Soeurs dinner dress of sea-green chiffon over white satin with yoke and bands embroidered in green and gold metallic threads drawing admiring glances from the occupants of several nearby tables.

The day before, Monday, they had spent a busy afternoon, crowding in visits to three apartments. The first had been 180 West 58th Street, the very popular Alwyn Court, their second choice after 45 East 66th Street, which had been designed by the same architect. The apartment had been perfect in every way—except

320

for its second-floor location. With New York's ever-increasing traffic, all of it motorized, in a year's time that spot might prove to be very noisy indeed.

Telling the rental agent that they'd have to think it over, they'd gone on to look at a vast duplex at 563 Park Avenue, and then on to an equally vast twenty-room simplex at 998 Fifth Avenue, conveniently near the Metropolitan Museum of Art.

Those two apartments had been visions of elaborately molded plaster ceilings, parquet floors polished to a dangerous sheen, large windows with pleasant views, decent servants' quarters, and the almost prerequisite marble bathrooms. But in the end, Mallory and Rupert agreed that both apartments were too much, too overpowering for what they wanted.

Second floor and all, the Alwyn Court was looking better and better, but when they reached the rental agent first thing on Tuesday morning the apartment was gone, rented to another engaged couple, who had been wise enough not to tempt Providence and look further.

"I felt rotten when he told us the apartment had been taken by someone else," Rupert admitted as they walked through the opulent lobby to the Fifty-ninth Street side. "But the more I think about it the happier I am that we did miss out on it."

"I know what you mean. We'd have had an apartment we loved on the floor we hated, and in time we'd hate the apartment itself. That's not how I want us to start our marriage. Not when we have a choice in the matter."

They were still discussing which step to take next, and were almost at the door, when Mallory heard her name being called.

"Romney Sedgewick," she said a second later, surprised, holding out her hand to him. "I didn't expect to see you again so soon. How is the apartment-hunting going?"

321

"Much better than I ever expected," Romney responded, clasping Mallory's hand as Rupert looked on in silent amusement. "In fact, I was going to ring up Thea at Cove House tomorrow. I think I may have the place."

"How wonderful. You have my congratulations for having passed with flying colors the test of finding a place to live in New York City!"

"You haven't seen the apartment yet!" Romney laughed, and then, more serious, he regarded Mallory and Rupert as a couple. "I believe that right now all the congratulations belong to the both of you. I saw the announcement in the *Times*." They moved away from the door in order to allow a foursome to pass by them, and Romney extended a hand to Rupert. "You're a very lucky man."

"I know I am, and thank you for your good wishes." There was a deep and shining pride in Rupert's eyes as he spoke, an emotion that had been evident since the night their engagement had been announced. "But seeing you is a bit of a surprise. Mallie never mentioned that you were in New York."

"Probably because I've sworn her and Thea to secrecy about my whereabouts," Romney said, obviously amused. "I'd like to buy you both a celebratory bottle of champagne. I've just come from having dinner downstairs in the Grill Room, and while it's terribly reminiscent of London, it can in no way be called lighthearted."

"And we've just come from dinner on the Champagne Porch, and that is definitely an atmosphere we'd like to prolong. Mallory, shall we?"

Five minutes later they were settled at a small marble table in the Palm Court with another solicitous waiter pouring out a bottle of champagne.

"Where is the apartment you've decided on?" Mallory asked as soon as their waiter departed. "Rupert and I have been looking, but so far it's no go."

"You have my heartfelt understanding. My own experiences nearly drove me to an alienist. Why don't you both come over and take a look at One Lexington Avenue? The building is new and there are still a number of apartments available."

For a moment, Mallory and Rupert looked at each other in delighted disbelief. A few minutes ago, their search for an apartment had seemed like a monumental task, and now they had a new avenue open to them.

"Funny, none of the real estate people we've seen have mentioned One Lexington Avenue to us. On second thought, it's not so funny," Rupert added. "They probably thought we didn't want to live that close to the Third Avenue El."

Suddenly, Rupert looked a touch undecided. "Is the El a problem, do you think?"

"Oh, no." Mallory moved quickly to reassure him. "It shuts down at midnight, and as for living too close to it . . . Thea lived at 34 Gramercy Park South until she got married and never had any problems or complaints, and that building is closer to the El than One Lexington Avenue is."

"Well, that's a comforting thought. When can I hope to show my decorators the apartment?"

"Tomorrow is out," Mallory said, grateful that she was one of those women who could carry her appointments in her head and not have to constantly refer to an appointment book. "Will they hold the apartment for you until Thursday? I have to check with Thea, of course, but I'm fairly sure it's convenient for her."

"She's here in New York?"

"As we all are. We're getting married on September twenty-fourth, and that takes quite a bit of planning on everyone's part to make sure it all runs smoothly."

"I can imagine," Romney returned, but offered

nothing about his own wedding plans, and Mallory, recalling the promise she and Thea had made to keep his secret, refrained from asking any questions. "May I have an invitation?" he asked unexpectedly. "Or is your wedding going to be private?"

"Anything but," Rupert said. "We're having the ceremony and reception at Cliff and Julie Seligman's house, and our guest list is growing in direct proportion to how many people 923 Fifth Avenue will hold."

"It's not so much a wedding as a merging of everyone who's even vaguely connected," Mallory added. "Right now, the best we're hoping for is that everyone will get on and have a good time."

"I'm sure it will be even more than that. It's my recollection that large wedding receptions are either disasters or a raving success. I can't imagine yours being in anything but the second category. Now, are you fairly certain that Thursday's convenient for you and Thea?"

"We generally go back out to Cove House on Thursday mornings for a long weekend," Mallory admitted, "but we can take a late train tomorrow afternoon. Romney," she went on, deciding the moment had come, "are you still intent on being secretive, or are you finally ready to see your old friends again?"

"I really hadn't considered the matter," he answered truthfully. "With everyone I knew out of town, there wasn't much need to think about the matter, I could simply not make myself known. What do you say, Rupert?"

"I didn't know you were supposed to be in hiding. In fact, until fifteen minutes ago, I had no idea you were in New York. If your name passed in conversation, I assumed you to be dutifully serving king and country from your post in the Foreign Office."

"Such is fame—fast and fleeting," Romney said wryly. "Up until a few weeks ago, my resignation and subsequent relocation to New York was the main topic of conversation in Mayfair's better drawing rooms. Now no one even cares."

"Oh, cheer up," Rupert advised, refilling their glasses much to the horror of their waiter. "But please don't pick our wedding day to come out of hiding, if you please! Your appearance might very well serve to detract attention from where it should be—on the bride!"

Romney looked properly sober. "I hadn't thought of it like that."

"Well, why don't you come to Alix's on Thursday afternoon? She's giving a huge tea, and you and Henry can trade notes on your respective books."

"You're writing a book also?" Rupert interjected with obvious amusement. "I guess that proves they're publishing just about anyone these days!"

"You never change, Rupert, do you?" Romney shot back with a look of reproof.

"Oh, you have no idea how much I have changed," he replied with a tender look at Mallory.

"For the sake of your fiancée, I'll give you the benefit of the doubt, but as for going to Alix and Henry's . . . Mallory, I promise to sleep on it. Becoming a social ornament or inadvertent extra man is not my aim."

"I understand, but I'll still tell Thea we can depend on your diplomatic training to do the right thing. Besides, if you do come on Thursday, everyone will be so excited about seeing you, Rupert and I can have a bit more privacy. People *do* tend to make a fuss over engaged couples. Also," she went on, raising her glass, "I think we owe you a toast, since you just may have put us in the right direction to our first apartment. To Romney Sedgewick, who may be our good luck charm!"

The world, where much is to be done, and little known . . .

—Dr. Johnson
Volume III

Wall Street

Since the days when the Medicis held sway at the Banco Mediceo and the advent of double-entry bookkeeping which could be traced back to 15th Century Milan and Genoa, there were few investment firms that did not seek to make a favorable impression on clients and visitors as well as provide suitable if not elegant quarters for their more highly placed personnel to spend their working hours in, and the Seligman firm was no exception to this rule.

Since the beginning of the century it had occupied two floors in one of the financial district's new skyscraper office buildings, and at eleven on Thursday morning when Mallory, just arrived downtown from her apartment-hunting appointment, opened the oversized double doors made of carved African red mahogany, the greeting that awaited visitors and was made to put even the most uncertain new arrival feel at ease was extended to her.

She had barely closed the doors behind her when Miss Harley, the receptionist who was a graduate of one of the new secretarial schools and was attractively dressed in a well-cut summer suit of dark blue serge with an ecru linen blouse, stood up from behind her veneered

Sheraton desk to cross the highly polished marble floor.

"Oh, good morning, Miss Kirk," she said in a bright voice, giving Mallory's Jeanne Hallee dress of scarlet and white foulard with a yoke of cream Alençon lace and elbow sleeves banded in black chiffon cuffs a very clear look of feminine appreciation. "Let me help you with your packages. It looks like Christmas in August!"

"Doesn't it," Mallory agreed, letting the receptionist take half her brightly wrapped packages. "Rupert told me his new office is rather bare and I decided to help him out with a few things."

"That's a lovely idea, and you have such marvelous taste." They set the packages down on her desk. "Mr. Randall isn't in right now," she went on informatively. "He had a meeting here with Mr. Horton, and then he left on an outside appointment."

"For very long? We're supposed to have lunch and then look at an apartment together."

"He said to tell you he'll be back before noon. You're to wait in his office, and I'll ring for Mr. Gibbs to show you up. I know he's very eager to see you but, before I do, the entire secretarial staff wants me to convey their congratulations. We're all absolutely thrilled for you and Mr. Randall."

"Thank you, and be sure to tell everyone how much I appreciate their good wishes," Mallory said. She was deeply touched by the message of good will, but not so affected that she failed to see an unmistakable look in Miss Harley's eyes. The receptionist was in her early twenties, attractive in a manner properly discreet for employment in a firm of financiers, and there was no reason she should be above interest in a certain matter. "Would you like to see my ring?" she asked, pulling off her gloves. "If you don't want to, just say so—I'm getting to the point where I'm waving my hand under everyone's nose!"

"No, I'd love to see it . . . oh, it's exquisite—I knew it would be—just perfect. Would you think I was jealous if I said I want one, too?"

"And you'll probably have one soon. I can't imagine you turning into some vinegary old maid office terror. But look, you'd better ring Mr. Gibbs and let him know I'm here. I wouldn't want him to come out here and say you aren't paying proper attention to your job."

Five minutes later, when Mr. Gibbs came into the reception room with its fine neoclassical details, carved walnut walls and elaborately molded plaster ceiling, he found Miss Harley seated properly behind her desk conversing politely on a neutral subject with Miss Kirk who sat in the visitor's chair. Noting that all was being carried on correctly (one could never be too sure with the younger staff members, he was always reminding himself), he permitted a welcoming smile to form on his serious features.

"Miss Kirk, it's an honor to have your charming presence in our office again, and allow me to add my heartiest congratulations on your engagement. It's truly wonderful news. Now, let me take these packages for you, and I'll show you up to Mr. Randall's office."

Mallory had just enough time to exchange a quick smile with Miss Harley before she followed the office manager through the next set of double doors and into the first floor of offices where the well-lit and organized mailroom was located and where the junior staff toiled.

Instantly, all activity ceased.

It isn't too often that all these people get to see their pompous office manager carrying a pile of gift-wrapped boxes, Mallory thought, biting back her laughter as she stopped to greet those she knew and accept more congratulations. Poor Mr. Gibbs, he spends years cultivating his haughty demeanor and in ten seconds he's reduced himself to an overage call boy.

329

Giving no sign that his dignity was anything but intact, Mr. Gibbs eventually managed to remind the staffers that there was still work to do, and finally he was able to lead his way up the deeply carpeted steps that led to the next floor.

Here, too, Mallory was stopped and congratulated, but since Jean-Christophe de Laulan was a member of the senior staff, Mr. Gibbs couldn't very well send him back to his desk. Instead, he excused himself, informed her that he would place the packages in Mr. Randall's office, and disappeared down the long, carpeted hallway.

"I don't think poor Mr. Gibbs is ever going to recover from my visit," Mallory laughed as she and Jean-Christophe stood beside the clicking tickertape machine. "A few more visits by me and he'll be reduced to hiding in his office, barricaded behind a stack of old *Wall Street Journals*!"

"Even if that doesn't happen, you've probably made the clericals and juniors downstairs very happy," he replied, putting down his briefcase to run an impatient hand through his dark red hair. His English was superb as befitted a university education that encompassed a year and a half at Stanford, a semester at Georgetown, and two years at Princeton. Even after well over five years of continuous residence in the United States, his voice still bore a faint British inflection on certain words, a legacy from his English instructor from his final year at Le College Saint Michel, Charles de Renille, then in his final months as a Jesuit seminarian. "Marie-France and I both want you to know that your wedding present is on the way, and I have it on good authority that Maman and Papa are sending one as well."

"That's terribly sweet of them. Even with all the friends we have, I still can't believe the outpouring of affection for us. So far there hasn't been a single person who hasn't wished us well."

"I think that's because when one sees two people who obviously belong together and are deeply in love and are preparing for marriage, it reaffirms the basic theory that love and tenderness and happiness do indeed have an important place in our lives, in our world."

"That's terribly poetic and very meaningful," Mallory replied, admiring Jean-Christophe's way of putting into words all the emotions that had been affecting her since the engagement announcement.

"Please tell that to my father," Jean-Christophe laughed. "There are times I swear he thinks I'm still a skylarking university student!"

"If you were, you wouldn't have gotten within ten feet of handling all foreign investments," Mallory advised. She was truly fond of this tall, handsome man who was slightly younger than Rupert, and who always bore with such equanimity the remarks of people who didn't comprehend that France and Belgium are separate nations, and that his wife's being French-American did not automatically make her a Catholic. Like Rupert, he was a strong and dashing man who knew his own worth. "Rupert says that you're the youngest non-family executive to have come so high in so short a time."

"Coming from your fiancé, that might be termed a case of the pot calling the kettle black," Jean-Christophe quipped, amusement obvious in his rich brown eyes. "But, unfortunately, that's a moot point I haven't time to discuss. I'm afraid I have to say good-bye for now. I'm scheduled for a meeting with Rob de Veiga at Brown Brothers."

"I've made you late—"

"I can't think of a better person to be delayed by." He kissed her cheek. "Marie-France and I want to give a dinner for the both of you; we'll speak to you later at Alix's to arrange the date."

He went down the stairs and Mallory turned toward

Rupert's office. On the eighth floor there was no rush and the only sounds came from the clicking typewriters and the sound of the telephone bell that was answered by the second ring.

The doors to the boardroom were open, indicating that no meeting was in progress, and Mallory decided to take a small detour in order to admire the newly acquired Constable landscape hung over the marble fireplace. The richly appointed chamber wasn't to her taste, but she could understand how financial fates were decided in this room with the dark-hued oriental rug on the floor, the series of outstanding oil paintings on the molded plaster walls, and the long formal table surrounded by over-stuffed, tapestry-covered chairs.

There was nothing oppressive about the boardroom, but the power was so softly implied that a person would have to be truly insensitive not to feel and react to it, Mallory decided, and she was quietly absorbing the atmosphere when Cliff walked in, a perplexed expression on his face that faded when he saw her.

"Hello, dear," he said warmly, kissing her cheek. "Admiring our latest acquisition, I see. Knoedler's hung it last week."

"It's perfect for the room," Mallory responded, kissing Cliff back. "Is a meeting about to start?"

"No, there was one here earlier this morning. Right now you're just looking at one vice-president who has misplaced his appointment book."

"That can be a near tragedy," Mallory said with a glance down the table's shining length. "And if you've misplaced it, that must have been some meeting."

"Believe me, you do not want to know the details," Cliff told her as he went over to his assigned place near the head of the table and knelt down to examine the floor. "This rug is like the Black Hole of Calcutta. Ah, here it is," he went on a moment later, standing up and displaying a slim leather volume. "We had our first strategy meeting with George Horton, his company treasurer and four fellows from U.S. Steel, and by the time it was over you'd have thought Andrew Carnegie had sent his strike-breakers in. Rupert was in such bad shape that Dad rang up John and then sent him over to his office."

Mallory looked at Cliff in shocked surprise. John Stern was the personal physician among their circle while his wife, Emily, herself a prominent gynecologist, was depended on by the women to take care of their personal medical problems and deliver their babies.

"What happened?" she demanded, advancing on him. "Did Rupert get dizzy or pass out or—"

"Not exactly," Cliff interposed soothingly, worried that he'd unintentionally upset her. "We were having a pretty heated time of it and Rupert was holding his own, shouting with the rest of us, and suddenly he just turned white and looked as if he were about to faint."

"Did he?" Mallory demanded, a cold fear passing through her.

"No, we got him into the anteroom and Rupert insisted he was fine, but you know Dad. He sent him off to see John for a thorough checkup."

"Thank God for that!"

"It's going to be all right, Mallie. Don't worry." Cliff put his hands on her shoulders. "Rupert is probably only over-tired. Men generally don't like to let on to this, but wedding preparations can be just as hard on the bridegroom as on the bride."

Mallory hugged Cliff. "Thank you, I feel a little bit better now. I thought it was going to be so easy to get married."

"Only if you elope."

"Oh, we actually considered it."

"Well, for one, I'm glad you didn't." Cliff's voice was

warm. "Julie and I are enjoying having our house used for your wedding."

"Even though one of your drawing rooms is starting to look like a gift shop thanks to all the presents that are arriving?"

"We're just considering it good practice for Ginny's wedding in about six or seven years," he said as they walked toward the doors. "I assume that now you're going to wait for Rupert in his office?"

"Yes, but before I go I'd like to tell you that having your home for our wedding has a special significance to Rupert. He takes it as confirmation that you really don't hate him."

"Well, I never really have." Cliff looked somewhat nonplussed. "Of course when he first turned up I couldn't understand why Dad or Mother wanted to take him in. And I was certain that Rupert had something up his sleeve."

"I can see where you would have thought that in the beginning," Mallory allowed. "Rupert had quite a reputation to live down, and even though he makes fun of it now, I really think it's a part of his life he'd rather forget about."

"And with good reason. But he's made a rather good effort about everything."

"How long did it take you to come to that conclusion?"

"Not that long. As a matter of record, it was right here in the boardroom, the day after his first Thanksgiving with us. We had some huge meeting here that Friday, and I guess Dad thought it would be a good experience for Rupert to help us out and see what high finance was all about," Cliff recalled as Mallory listened, enthralled.

"We were setting up in here and I discovered a set of reports that Rupert had been given responsibility for weren't set out at each place."

"I can imagine your reaction."

"Then double it. I was furious and was laying Rupert out pretty well when the door to the anteroom opened and Dad came out. Jimmy was with him, and a reporter for the *Los Angeles Times* who was doing a financial story on us. Dad gave us one look, sized up the situation, and almost without breaking stride walked past us, looked at me and said, 'Don't talk to your brother like that.'"

Mallory blinked in surprise at his revelation. "That must have been the last thing you wanted to hear."

"Well, it put me in my place. Even an eldest son needs that once in a while. Not that I realized it at that particular moment, of course. I was fuming mad, and when we were alone again I was really going to let Rupert have it . . . and then I looked at him. There was a look in his eyes of such pride and delight that I decided if a casual remark like that, a complete slip of the tongue, could mean so much to him, I didn't have the heart to make his life too miserable."

"Not according to Rupert."

"I've told him I don't hate him, he just can't have things made too easy for him, and it's my job to give him a bit of difficulty. Spoiling is for one's private life."

"Well, your philosophy is unique enough."

"And it works," Cliff said with a smile as they parted at the door. "Have fun spoiling Rupert."

Rupert's private office turned out to be a spacious room with two windows looking down on Wall Street, a modern oriental rug on the polished floor, a long dark-red leather chesterfield, and a large mahogany Regency desk with a high-backed leather chair.

Even without a painting on the wall, I like this, Mallory thought, tossing her gloves and handbag on the chesterfield and then taking off her Reboux hat, a large flat tailor-made model made of fine black straw with black satin ribbon draped around the crown and accented with a white goat hair's brush placed near the front.

The morning's activities had taken their toll, and after Mallory put down her hat and glanced at the gold mesh-banded watch that decorated her right wrist, she retrieved her handbag and went into the private, well-equipped bathroom that opened off Rupert's office. There she washed her hands with the sandalwood soap that was set out on the washstand's ledge, carefully splashed cold water on her face, made use of one of the large white towels, and proceeded to fix her maquillage by applying a fresh layer of face powder, touching up her lip and cheek color, and finished by adding several strategic dabs of *Narcisse Noir*, the slightly scandalous new fragrance from Caron.

Returning to the office, she noted with approval that Mr. Gibbs had placed the presents on the center of the desk, neatly arranging them on the dark green leather-bound blotter. Mallory paused for a moment to rearrange their sequence, and then her glance moved to survey the other items on the desk's broad surface. To the left of the blotter were that day's *Wall Street Journal*, *Philadelphia Financial Journal* and *Boston News Bureau*, and the previous day's *Chicago Journal of Commerce*, and to the right was his stack of neatly arranged mail, all the envelopes bearing the return letterheads of major corporations and merchant banks.

Are you looking for secret love letters already? she chided herself, retiring to the chesterfield to wait for Rupert. If you really want to get upset, the news about his emergency trip to the doctor should have done it. Is something really wrong with Rupert, or is it just what Cliff said happened earlier, a business meeting suddenly turned hostile? *That* probably happens all the time, she reassured herself. Rupert's as healthy as a horse.

She relaxed in a corner of the chesterfield, mentally reviewing that morning's events.

Promptly at half-past nine she and Thea had met

it together. I promised the rental agent I'd bring you around this afternoon, and he'll keep other prospective tenants away until we have a chance to make a decision."

"Do you like it?" Rupert was all seriousness. "Do you think this is the apartment for us?"

"Yes on both counts," she said emphatically, and they smiled at each other.

"Then why are we sitting here? We'll have lunch and then go up to Gramercy Park. I assume I'm going to have the honor of having my fiancée drive me there in her motor car?"

"The doorman downstairs is keeping an eye on my Baker, but when I pulled up I got the distinct feeling that he'd be much happier if I arrived in a Rolls-Royce or a Cadillac or a Packard with a properly uniformed driver," Mallory said with obvious delight. "No doubt when we drive away with me at the steering tiller, he'll begin to feel faint."

"Feel faint? He'll probably collapse on the sidewalk," Rupert said as he stood up. "Ready for lunch, darling? I'm famished."

"So am I. But wouldn't you like to open all your presents first?"

"Presents?" Rupert's face took on the delighted expression of a boy at a surprise party.

"You might look on your desk once in a while. There's more than just financial newspapers there now."

"I'm really not quite sure what to say," he said a moment later as he sat down in his chair.

"Well, you weren't exaggerating when you said your office was bare. I would have thought you'd rate a painting or two. And where's your telephone?"

"There's a nice Cezanne tagged for me in the storeroom that'll be hung next week, and a new model telephone is being installed this afternoon." He surveyed the array of gift-wrapped boxes with undisguised delight.

The other boxes contained a desk calendar set in a frame of satin-finished brass, a lethal-looking sterling silver letter opener, a large, leather-covered appointment book, and a framed colorful drawing of Montgolfier's balloon ascension.

"I'm going to have this hung in the bathroom, and I love everything else," he said, kissing Mallory again. "But why all the largesse?"

"To say thank you for all the presents and the flowers you send me every morning. I would have bought more, but I wasn't quite sure what to expect."

"Not quite a grand suite, but anything is better than working in Chicago. But enough of that. We have other things to do."

"Rupert, are you *sure* John told you everything was all right?" Mallory asked a minute later as she put on her hat. "You don't have to hide anything from me."

"As if I could. No, I'm as healthy as a horse, and *that* is a very boring topic of conversation, particularly where a man is concerned." He put his mail into his briefcase and came over to Mallory, slipping his free arm around her waist. "I could do with lunch right now, and I have an idea that a particular interior decorator who has my heart and all my love certainly deserves hers!"

Clifford Seligman waited until he was sure that his secretary had gone to lunch before picking up his phone and giving the operator John Stern's number.

He was connected without delay, and after they'd exchanged pleasantries and discussed the latest doings of the New York Giants and Columbia's prospects in that fall's annual Columbia-Yale game, he asked about Rupert's visit.

"You're not one for wasting time in aimless conversation, are you?" John asked, amused.

341

"Not today, I'm afraid. I want to talk to you before half the firm lines up outside my door, projects in hand, in need of advice." He paused for a brief second. "Is my question violating doctor-patient confidentiality?"

"In a manner of speaking, yes, it is. But since it's more or less in the family— Oh, Cliff, stop wincing. After seven years that act is getting a bit thin."

"Never mind that. Is he well?"

"More or less."

"That isn't saying much."

"Well, to elaborate, I'd be much happier if Rupert were leaving on a nice, long undemanding—in the business sense of the word, of course—honeymoon right after his wedding."

"That's not possible. Or at least not without a lot of shifting and rearranging."

"Then I advise you shift and rearrange." John's voice was even. "From the examination I conducted and the tests I took, Rupert's basically a strong and healthy man, but he's also badly run down."

"Is that dangerous?"

"With lots of rest and good food and no responsibility beyond that of a new husband, no. But after Chicago, he's worn out, and after three more months of the same here in New York, plus all the hoopla of a big wedding, he might not be on the verge of collapse, but I won't vouch for a first-class condition. And that's not a pleasant state for a newly married man to be in."

"Am I supposed to disagree? Look, John, this matter is really out of my hands. If Rupert takes this up with Dad, and he agrees to let Rupert have off I'm not going to stand in the way."

"But on the other hand, you're not going to be Rupert's friend at court, either."

"I'm not that much of an ogre."

"You're not one at all." John sighed deeply. "That's

the whole story, Cliff. Rupert knows what kind of condition he's in, and I've urged him to discuss the situation with Bill."

"Well, then . . ." Cliff let his sentence trail off, and after a bit more friendly conversation he and John rang off.

Cliff replaced the receiver and then tipped back his leather chair to gaze at the ceiling, reviewing the conversation he'd just concluded.

Rupert's physical condition—as long as it wasn't affecting his work—was not his responsibility, he told himself. Rupert had champed at the bit to handle the Horton Steel transfer and had been given it—if there were sudden personal difficulties he had to smooth them out himself.

But even as he formed those coolly professional and detached thoughts, Rupert's face at the board meeting, growing paler and paler under his newly acquired tan, kept reappearing in his mind's eye.

Well, that's one way to break up a meeting where everyone's about to go for each other's throat, Cliff thought. I'm glad Rupert's not really ill, but as for the rest of it— Let him take it up with Dad. You have no part in this, so don't get involved, he told himself sternly, all the time well aware that Rupert, who loathed to be thought of as either irresponsible or a shirker, was not going to tell the truth to anyone about that morning's doctor's appointment.

Despite the presence of an excellent French chef, Mallory and Rupert had decided against having lunch in the firm's private dining room and had taken themselves off to The Fernery. At the beginning of the century, two enterprising women, Sarah Tucker and Alice Babcock, opened their combination florist shop and ladies' luncheon and tea spot on Thirty-third Street in the shadow of the Waldorf-Astoria. Their joint venture had been so successful with both men as well as women that they had recently expanded their operation to the Financial District. Having The Fernery downtown was a very nice alternative to the area's private dining rooms and stuffy restaurants and plain lunchrooms and men-only clubs, Mallory and Rupert agreed as their eggs *à la Russe* was replaced by chicken hash with Mornay sauce and a crisp green salad in an herb dressing.

"Besides, if we'd eaten in the dining room, I'd have had to share you with the rest of the staff and any visitors," Rupert remarked. "George Horton would have loved to have a long discussion with you and gotten a few tips about antiques. He's beginning to fancy himself a patron of the arts."

"Oh, I wouldn't have minded answering a few questions, but I think you've had enough of Mr. Horton for one day."

"Yes, but we're going to have to invite him to our wedding, I'm afraid."

"As long as he doesn't expect to spend the reception discussing stock shares and whether they should be common or preferred, I don't mind putting him on the list."

"We're also going to have to include Mr. Gibbs to represent the office staff."

"That's no problem, but I'm also going to invite Miss Harley to represent the female staff," Mallory said. "Incidentally, I take it she does have a first name?"

"It's Nancy, and it would be a nice idea to invite her. I don't think she gets too many invitations since her father lost all his money."

"How awful."

"I agree, and I feel rather sorry for her."

"Oh?" Mallory looked amused and jealous at the same

time. "Sorry for her in which way? A general concern, or a stage-door Johnny sort of interest replete with orchids and Tiffany trinkets?"

"I hardly know the girl!"

"Since when has that ever stopped a man?" she shot back, amused. "You still have a few more weeks of pre-marital freedom."

"Not in that way. I feel sorry for her in the professional world. Miss Harley is smart, very smart," Rupert went on. "She had two years at Vassar before her father's bankruptcy. Dad hired her about six months ago, but she'll never get past the reception desk, and that's a shame."

"Because all the secretaries are either men or dried up old maid office terrors," Mallory finished, her feminist instincts alert. "That's hardly fair."

"I never said it was. It's simply the way it is on Wall Street."

"Yes . . . denying a firm a fine employee. Women are doctors and lawyers and college professors, so I don't see why they can't be an integral part of a financial firm. We've got to get beyond Hetty Green someday."

"And women probably will, but just not yet."

"It's too bad Henry's already hired a secretary to help him with his book. Alix told me he's just hired some newly arrived Englishman that she already can't stand. He seems to think he's some sort of unofficial policeman, hired to keep Henry at his task. If only I'd known about Nancy Harley a few weeks ago! She could have worked for Henry, and Alix would have taken her shopping and introduced her around."

"Something will turn up for her, I'm sure of it."

"As long as it's not some overage millionaire. Oh, I just had an awful thought. What if George Horton decides the time has come for him to play the merry widower and step out on the town with Miss Harley on his arm? Now that the *Follies* have opened and closed . . ."

"Perish the thought."

"All right. Shall I tell you about the interesting conversation I had in the boardroom with Cliff?" Mallory asked as they finished their chicken and waited for dessert and coffee. "He told me how much it means to him and Julie that we're having our wedding at their house." She paused for a second. "He also told me about the day after Thanksgiving 1903."

Mallory didn't have to say another word. The look in his eyes was remembrance blended with amusement and a touch of wariness. He remained silent until their waitress set down long-stemmed silver dishes filled with lemon ice, a plate of delicate French pastries and a pot of coffee.

"Did Cliff tell you what happened later? I don't mean later that day, but the next month?"

Mallory spooned up her ice. "Cliff was as silent as a clam as far as the rest of it went. I guess he knew I'd ask you about it." She put down her spoon. "I didn't think an incident like the one he told me about would just fade away."

"Never. It was the day after Christmas and we were all out on Long Island for the holiday season. I was out riding and came back just before lunch. Everyone else was in the Chinese sitting room when I walked in and before I knew what was happening, Gareth was bending me over the nearest sofa and was paddling me with a folded up newspaper. Don't laugh! Everyone was hysterical and I was mortified. Finally, Gareth let me up, said that was twenty whacks plus one to grow on, handed me the newspaper and said welcome to the family and now it was all official.

"The paper he was whacking me with turned out to be the financial section of the *Los Angeles Times* from the previous Saturday that had come in the morning's mail, and it had the story about the firm by the reporter who'd been there that day. It was all very professional, but the last paragraph carried the required personal note. It went something like 'Mr. Seligman is married to the former Adele Franks, and the couple's eldest sons, Clifford, Gareth and James are all associated with the firm in various capacities, while their youngest son, Rupert, is a sophomore at Columbia University.'"

Mallory tried to keep her laughter under control. "I'm sorry, I know it's not funny, none of it, but . . . but . . ."

"In retrospect, it's hilarious, and meant more to me than I can say, either then or now. It gave me the first feeling of belonging that I'd ever had in my life. I'll never forget Cliff's reaction, though. I thought he'd be livid, but all he said was that he was glad that no one we knew read the *Los Angeles Times*. It's a mild remark, but it still qualifies as one of his best *bon mots*."

As they ate dessert, Mallory noted with relief that Rupert's color was back to normal and that the look of strain around his eyes had faded.

"I have an idea," she said. "When we finish looking at the apartment, and if it's right for us, let's celebrate."

Rupert gave her an unmistakable look over the rim of his coffee cup. "Do you prefer the Plaza or the Gotham or the Astor?"

"That isn't the kind of celebration I had in mind, although I'm glad to see you left the St. Regis out of your list of choices."

"I believe in observing some of the proprieties."

"That does please me, but you know my answer."

"I had to ask."

"I expected you to, but as far as celebrating goes, I was thinking along the lines of us making a major purchase together. We could go to Knoedler's and look for a painting or we can order a set of china of Tiffany's or—"

"Or we can buy a piano," Rupert interjected, his eyes

bright with anticipation. "I like the idea of that. Something large and permanent and important. A symbol of our life together."

"That's just what I'd like to do also," Mallory declared, putting her napkin beside her plate. "I'm ready to start if you are."

The check settled, they left the dining area. When they reached the front of The Fernery, Mallory paused at the long marble counter where flowers and plants were sold.

"A red carnation, please," she told the salesgirl, paid for it, skillfully cut the stem with the scissors the girl handed her, and then tucked the flower into the buttonhole of Rupert's suit jacket. "There, you needed a finishing touch, and it's absolutely perfect."

Rupert, who had been observing her transaction with quiet amusement, broke into a wide smile.

"I think all of the flowers and presents you're showering on me are going to take some getting used to," he whispered in her ear, "but I think I can learn to like taking offerings from a very special lady."

Mallory wished that decorum allowed her to throw her arms around Rupert right where they stood and kiss him. But in a little while, if they could lose the rental agent. . . . Reluctantly, she pulled herself away from her straying thoughts and back to the present moment.

"I have the distinct feeling that a lot of things are going to start changing for us, beginning this afternoon. The carnation is to mark our moment," she said gaily, tucking her arm through his. "Let's go collect my car from the doorman's tender if somewhat confused care and go up to Gramercy Park and have a look at what may very well turn out to be our first home together!"

Teaism is a cult founded on the adoration of the beautiful among the sordid facts of everyday life.

—Okahura-Kakuzo
The Book of Tea, 1906

The Dakota

"Lady Thorpe, you've really been the most *outstanding* help to us. Sybil and I really can't thank you enough!"

As the three women stepped off the Otis lift into the Thorpes' private sixth-floor hallway, Alix forced her mouth into an approximation of a smile and gritted her teeth at Evelyn Weldon's flowery compliments. Normally, she would have been delighted to help Sybil settle into life in New York City while she awaited the birth of her third child, but it was her mother, with her effusive voice and fawning manner and darting, sharp blue eyes that drained all possible enjoyment out of the experience.

Now, Alix observed wearily, Evelyn's glance was taking in the private hall, and she could practically hear the overdressed woman estimating the worth of the dark blue and salmon and celadon and beige Chinese rug that covered the floor, as well as judging the authenticity of the cabrioled-legged Queen Anne table with the gilt-framed mirror above it. As she pressed the buzzer to summon Hodges, Alix fully expected the older woman to go over to the table, examine the Lalique vase for any imperfections and check the arrangement of white roses and gardenias for their freshness.

349

"Oh, don't even mention it, Mrs. Weldon," Alix said at last in as easy a voice as she could manage. "It's rather fun to see what other apartments are on the market."

Evelyn waved a languid hand. Once as blond and pretty as her daughter, she was not aging well, and her personality, formed to be pleasing and deferential to men, had no capacity for friendship with women. "Really, I don't understand the fascination you Americans seem to have with changing your residence every few years. In England, we never move."

"Well, I like to think we move every so often in order to keep our blood circulating and our interests sparked," Alix replied just as Hodges opened the door, silently congratulating herself on her restraint when she considered the variety of retorts she had in her repetoire.

"Good afternoon, my lady, Mrs. Weldon and Mrs. Fleming," Hodges said politely as he held the door open for them. If she'd been alone, Alix would have used her key and let herself in, but she supposed that if Evelyn Weldon saw her do that there would be the usual comments about Americans not knowing how to properly treat their servants. "All the preparations for tea are well under way, Janet and Polly are putting the finishing touches on the drawing room, and his lordship is working in the library with Mr. Gresham," the butler went on, giving Alix the update of what was going on in the household that she liked to receive as soon as she returned home.

"Thank you, Hodges. I hope Mr. Gresham is going to allow Lord Thorpe time off for good behavior so that he can enjoy our tea party."

"That is to be sincerely hoped for, my lady," Hodges agreed in a voice that left no doubt that Henry Thorpe's secretary was not the most popular person in the household.

"Whatever does your butler mean by that remark?"

Evelyn queried as Alix sent Hodges off to the library to tell Henry she was home. "Really, Lady Thorpe, if you'll forgive my saying so—because I have only your best interests at heart since Americans, no matter how used they are to servants, seem to allow them far too much familiarity. We don't have that problem in England, you see. It's all a matter of control. My own servants—"

"Please don't call me Lady Thorpe," Alix interjected smoothly, trying to imagine Hodges, that paragon of propriety and reserve, ever becoming familiar.

"Well, Lady Alicia, then. With servants, one must—"

Alix suppressed a nasty comment. "Just call me Alix. Everyone does," she said as they left the mirrored entry hall for the corridor that ran the length of the twenty-room apartment and served as the Thorpes' art gallery for their favorite prints and watercolors and less than major paintings.

"If you insist." Evelyn's voice was doubtful, but her ever-roving attention was captured by an attractive landscape that hung above a mahogany bombe chest. "My word, what is this?"

"It's a Thomas Cole view of the Hudson River Valley. Even today it's a rather debatable school, and a few so-called experts have told me that they don't think it's worth much more than the twenty-five dollars my grandfather originally paid for it."

"Well, no wonder I didn't recognize it," she said with a slight sniff. "I do have a rather good eye for these things."

"Mama, please, I'm sure Alix and Henry have very fine paintings," Sybil said, speaking up for the first time since they'd left the Langham twenty minutes before. "And I find this landscape to be very soothing."

Before Evelyn could deliver a proper reply to her daughter, the closed set of double doors they were standing beside opened and a middle-aged man with graying brown hair, eyes the color of pale sherry, and a high-bridged nose which was the only thing saving his face from being totally forgettable. He closed the door behind him and surveyed the three women with the thinly veiled superciliousness that certain men display toward women they consider to be little more than decorations who intrude on the male-ordered way of life whenever they open their mouths.

"Good afternoon, Lady Thorpe," he said with exquisite politeness, inclining his head with just the right degree of correctness toward Evelyn and Sybil, obviously deciding that they were not important to the scheme of things in this household. "I'm very happy to inform you that Lord Thorpe has made a great deal of progress on his book this afternoon, but his section concerning the Earl of Northbrook's collection of Holbeins is at a very crucial point, and if it is to proceed in a satisfactory manner there must be no interruptions, and certainly no conversation that might be distracting," he stated in an officious tone and then returned to the library.

"How rude," Sybil murmured. "Alix, who was that?"

"Henry's secretary. Believe it or not, he came highly recommended, but unfortunately he has the tendency to think that without him, Henry's book would be nonexistent."

"Well, Alix, you have to admit that it's nice to see someone who is serious about his position."

"Yes, seriousness does have its points," Alix said, answering in a way that didn't give one inch of approval to Mr. Roland Gresham, whose presence in their household was, Alix felt, definitely not going to turn out to be compatible. "Now, Evelyn, I'm sure you'd like to freshen up a bit before everyone begins arriving for tea," she said with an oblique look at the older woman's Worth dress of yellow and olive-green silk, an outfit Alix considered to be highly unsuitable for a day of apartment-looking at the height of summer.

At the door to the guest room, Sybil gave her mother a determined look. "You go ahead in, Mother. There's something I want to discuss with Alix."

That statement was obviously not pleasing to Evelyn Weldon. Even eight long years after her daughter had eloped with Peter Fleming and gone to Canada to live, she still found it difficult to accept that she could not rule Sybil with an iron hand. She looked from one to the other with displeasure, but well aware that she could not refuse without causing a scene in her hostess's home, she went into the guest room.

"I'm awfully sorry about that, Alix," Sybil said a minute later as they went into the master suite. "But you know how . . . difficult Mama can be. Ever since she arrived, I've felt so—so overpowered."

"Then why did you invite her to join you in New York?" Alix asked as she took off her Talbot hat of fine black straw and motioned for Sybil to sit down on the long white brocade sofa that was set in front of the marble fireplace. "As a doctor—and a woman—I can tell you that when you're pregnant you mustn't be upset."

Sybil Weldon Fleming was twenty-eight, but even in her sophisticated Cheruit walking costume of rose-pink linen, she seemed young and rather defenseless, as though her sweet personality could be bent to the demands of others at will. It was almost as though she hadn't changed from the twenty-year-old girl in 1902 who was kept both innocent and ignorant by her mother—a perfect state Evelyn believed to attract a rich husband who would solve their financial problems. Like many another social mother with more ambition and position than actual means, she had plotted and planned to offer her daughter to the highest bidder, a machination that had come crashing down the day Sybil eloped with Peter Fleming. Although in any other circumstances—or with another sort of mother—Peter, with a good family and the promise from an uncle living in Canada that he would inherit his very prosperous horse ranch, would have been acceptable. But he had only a few thousand a year; a sum not at all sufficient to the way of life Evelyn considered suitable for Sybil—or herself—and the fact that Sybil was happy and in love with her husband had no bearing on the subject. Love, in Evelyn's set, was for amusement, and it came outside of—and after—marriage.

Sybil took off her large white straw hat. "Oh, I know I shouldn't get upset, and I don't think Mama is doing any of this on purpose, but—but there have been moments in the past few weeks that I could just hit Peter—if he were here instead of back home in Ontario!"

"Welcome to marriage," Alix smiled, sitting down beside Sybil. "I take it that inviting your mother to come to New York was his idea?"

"He thought it would be a good way for us to reconcile. I mean, she's never even seen Roger and Sophie, and they *are* her grandchildren." Her heart-shaped face was troubled, and she looked up at the Monet footbridge hanging over the fireplace as if it held an answer. "Peter *meant* well—"

"Men generally do, but then they're rarely around for the consequences," Alix said, brushing a speck of lint off her Callot Soeurs tailor-made dress of bois-de-rose serge with a same-tone satin belt and four tucked bands at the bottom of the skirt, hoping she hadn't said the wrong thing. "I wasn't referring to my marriage—or yours," she added.

"I know that! I think Mama takes pride in being difficult. The first thing she told me when she saw me again was that she thought her cabin on the *Mauretania* wasn't worthy of her."

"There isn't any such thing as a bad first-class cabin on

the *Mauretania*."

"Don't try and tell Mama that! And she doesn't like the Knickerbocker Hotel either. We have a perfectly lovely suite—just acres of space—and all my mother does is complain how common the clientele is!"

"It is not! The Knickerbocker's a fine hotel."

"But it's not the Plaza, any more than the Langham is 998 Fifth Avenue, but for what Peter and I can afford, it's more than suitable."

"Then tell your mother that! Let her know in plain simple English that as far as you and Peter are concerned—and for the length of time you have to be in New York—your hotel and now the apartment you've taken suit you fine, and she can stay or leave as it suits her."

"Oh, she'll stay regardless. You saw what a good face she was putting on about Central Park West." Sybil paused and took a deep breath. "Alix, I hate to say this, but I think my mother met someone on the trip over."

"Then why do you look like that? A new beau will occupy your mother's time. You'll scarcely know she's around."

But Sybil didn't look cheered. "I know she's met a man, but it's not for social reasons. I'm almost sure of it. When I wrote asking her if she'd want to stay with me in New York, she positively *leapt* at the idea. In fact, she seemed very anxious to leave England, but by the time she got here, there was a look about her . . ."

As Sybil spoke, Alix's mind flashed back to the last Coronation summer, to her first acquaintance with Evelyn Weldon through the daughter she controlled. With crystal clarity, Alix could recall a July weekend passed at the Buckinghamshire country house of Ivor and Millicent Rowland, a Queen Anne house filled with Chinese Export furniture and bibelots, and a rose garden made for lovers to pass secret hours in. There had been

355

intrigue that weekend as well, and Alix remembered Millicent saying that there was something unsavory about Evelyn Weldon. That was a theory Alix strongly agreed with, but eight years later she wasn't about to say that—unless Sybil brought up the matter first, of course.

"We never had money, at least the kind that mattered, you know that, Alix," Sybil was saying. "When I was growing up I knew she did things . . ."

"You mean she had a lot of schemes going. She wouldn't be the first society woman with a low bank account who devised a hundred ways to keep things going."

"And most of them were fairly handsome, but a few . . ." Sybil smiled ruefully. "I was a perfect little idiot in those days, and now I really can't say what she's planning because I never knew what came before."

"Sybil, the only thing you have to worry about now is taking care of yourself. I'm talking as a doctor. If Peter didn't feel you need special care, you'd be back in Ontario right now."

"My doctor is rather old-fashioned," Sybil said, looking relieved to have another topic of conversation. "He gave me the name of a colleague of his here in New York, a Doctor Cartright."

"Cartright?" Alix's face said it all. "He thinks delivering babies hasn't changed since the Civil War! I'll take you to my specialist, and then we can go to Best and Company's Liliputian Bazaar for things for the nursery and to Lane Bryant for your maternity clothes." She looked at Sybil's slender figure. "*When* did you say you were due?"

"The second week in March. Do you think I'll have to go to a maternity home? I was in one in Toronto two years ago when Sophie was born, and I hated it."

"Well, that's up to Emily to decide, and if you can't have the baby at home, you'll be in Roosevelt Hospital's private pavilion. That's where I had Gweneth, and it was very pleasant," she said reassuringly.

"You're being terribly nice to me, Alix, particularly since I wasn't one of your favorite people eight years ago."

"That was a long time ago."

"Still, I used to have all sorts of girlish fantasies about taking Henry away from you."

Alix smiled. "You didn't have a chance. Besides you were in love with Peter."

"Who didn't have much money, and only an uncle with a horse ranch in Ontario as an inheritance. And then there was Henry, as rich as could be. Mama used to drum it into me that while I was unspoiled and innocent, you were an adventuress; too rich and too sophisticated and with lots of shadowy areas in your life which meant that in the end Henry would pick me over you—if only I tried a little harder."

"I wish I could say I'm sorry."

"I don't want you to. You were just what Henry wanted. And as for any shadows in your past—I think Mama made them up!"

"She probably didn't. In my unmarried days, I used to do only what married ladies are supposed to. Oh, Sybil, please don't be shocked at such ancient history!"

"I'm not shocked, I'm envious! You've always had such fun and been so sure of yourself. You've always done everything you wanted and gotten away with it. You even gave me the courage to run away with Peter. Thank you for that."

"You're welcome. And everything *is* going to work out. You'll see."

"I hope so." Hat in hand, she stood up. "I'd better rejoin Mama now. She's probably going to question me about our discussion. It makes me feel like a child again."

"Well, just tell her that we talked about baby things,

and if necessary, you can remind her whose name is on the lease!"

Sybil looked a bit more cheerful. "I may just have to do that." She bent over and kissed Alix on the cheek. "You've been the best help ever, and I can't tell you how much I appreciate it, so in return I'm going to tell Mama that if she makes herself unwelcome in your home, she won't be welcome in mine!"

A scant half-hour later, Alix was at her veneered-wood dressing table, applying fresh makeup, when Henry walked in, and for a long moment they regarded each other through the mirror.

"Well, I don't believe it. You've been let out of custody. Or did you slip out when Mr. Gresham wasn't looking?" Alix asked coolly, turning around on the bench so they could face each other.

"Do you stay up all night to think up these charming comments?" Henry questioned in a tight voice.

"I don't have to. Since Mr. Gresham arrived, everything just seems to bubble naturally to the surface!"

Henry gave her a weary look. "First of all, he didn't 'arrive,' as you put it. I hired him as my secretary. He isn't a part of our household in any sense of the word."

"A fact for which I'm very grateful. The idea that if we had a larger apartment or a townhouse, Mr. Gresham would be moving in makes my skin crawl!"

"Alix!"

"I wish you would fire him," she said feelingly, standing up and putting her arms around him. "He's so damn pompous, so self-important. He seems to think that he has some grand responsibility to keep you away from your own family!"

"Now you're exaggerating!"

358

"I doubt it. I've known men like him before. They move stealthily and before you know it you can't get rid of them. You weren't terribly enthusiastic about writing this book in the first place," she went on, playing her trump card, "so why do you want to undertake the project with a man I know you don't like?"

"Because I owe him," Henry said, disengaging himself from Alix for a moment to close the dressing room door. "I knew Roland Gresham years ago in England. He happens to be an excellent private secretary, his personality nonwithstanding, and when I was asked to take charge of the king's Coronation presents, I asked him to come with me. The salary wouldn't be much, but he'd been very well rewarded by his last employer and I thought the monetary side wouldn't matter too much."

"But what happened?"

"It was my own fault, I'm afraid. I told him how easy it would be and that I wouldn't need him right away, so he went off on holiday to Italy. As you know, it didn't work out like that. I needed a secretary at once and Gresham hadn't given me his itinerary."

"How careless of him."

"Very much so, to his ultimate regret, since Howard Calvert suggested his granddaughter."

"Well, I wouldn't mind if you had Harriet Calvert— or her equivalent—working for you right now!"

Henry laughed briefly and drew her close again. "Do you realize that you must be one of the few wives who wants her husband to have a female secretary?"

"I'm not the jealous sort, at least not in that way."

"But you are of Mr. Gresham. It doesn't make sense."

"To me it makes excellent sense." She pulled away from their embrace. "Henry, look at yourself. You're tenser than I've seen you in years, and every morning, just before Mr. Gresham arrives, you get a tight look around your mouth. I can't stand to see you like this!"

she burst out.

Before Henry could reply, Alix swung away from him, going over to the closet that took up one wall, opened the mirrored doors and selected a Doucet formal afternoon dress of pink chiffon embroidered in pink glass beads.

Henry watched silently as she took off her plain white batiste robe, and wearing only her lacy Lucile lingerie, slipped the frock over her head, careful not to disturb her hair. He was well aware that her silent actions masked her anger, and he came over to hook her up the back.

"I love you," Henry said, kissing the nape of her neck, "and you know I'd never do anything to make you unhappy."

"I know," Alix responded tenderly, turning as he finished fastening the last hook, putting her arms around his neck. "I don't want to be a bitch about the matter. Let's just say I had too big a dose of Evelyn Weldon today."

"That explains a lot," Henry laughed, holding her close. "And Gresham *is* a pompous ass, but he gets the work done."

"Then I'll let it all alone," Alix promised, selecting a pair of pink silk shoes and putting them on. "I know what it means for you to produce a fine book, one you can be proud of. Besides," she went on, leaning back against the mirrored door as she began to laugh, "if Mr. Gresham had been your secretary eight years ago, he would have been so intent on protecting you from all intrusions that we would have had a lot more trouble getting together than we did!"

In the formal drawing room that measured twenty-by-forty, all was in readiness for Alix's lavish afternoon tea. The pale blue, cream and apricot Bessarabian rug, fresh from its summer cleaning, had just been relaid on the elaborate parquet floor, the pillows on the sofas were fluffed as high as possible, every table was gleaming from its application of furniture polish, and summer flowers were arranged in great bouquets.

"Thank you, Janet and Polly, it all looks wonderful," Alix praised as she entered the drawing room. Quickly, she checked her reflection in the gilt-framed mirror hanging above the marble fireplace. "Wait five minutes and then bring in the tea, please. Oh, and tell Hodges not to bother to announce anyone unless he thinks they'll be insulted by the omission. I'm expecting too many people to spare him to do that."

"Yes, madam," Janet said. "But Mr. Hodges wants to know if you'd like a bottle of champagne put on ice for Miss Mallory and Mr. Rupert."

"No, this afternoon they can drink Earl Grey just like everyone else and enjoy it," she smiled, and sent the maids on their way.

As she took her place on the white silk damask sofa, Alix reflected on the changes that had taken place in her household over the past eight years of her marriage.

Doris had been her full-time maid then, with Mrs. Land to do the heavy cleaning and Mrs. Wiley to cook. Henry's estimable valet-butler, Roy Hodges, and his wife Aileen, who was a fine parlormaid, had come over from London, bringing with them Carrie Dunn, Alix's maid at the Savoy Hotel during that gala summer.

It *had* been rather a melange of personalities and types, Alix recalled as she inspected the flawless white linen teacloth embellished with delicate Madeira embroidery that was draped over the large coffee table of oriental rosewood. What with Hodges and Aileen and Doris and Carrie living in the servants' quarters, and Mrs. Land and Mrs. Wiley coming in on a daily basis, plus any supplementary help they might need provided by the Dakota's housekeeper, they might very well all have

361

ended up at each other's throats. And despite Hodges' sometimes keenly felt lack that there was no house and proper staff—meaning footmen—for him to be butler in, they all got on well together.

But over eight years there had been certain inevitable changes. And, Alix told herself, what good was building a fine life and caring about the people around you if it all stayed the same?

Hodges and Aileen and Mrs. Wiley and Mrs. Land were still loyally with them, but in January 1907, Doris married a well-to-do young farmer from her native Dutchess County, and by the end of the same year, Carrie was also married, having met and fallen in love with the youngest son of a well-established Irish-American family that owned a chain of florist shops through the Middle West, and his family had sent the young couple off to Southern California to establish branches of their successful business in the resort cities of San Diego and Santa Barbara, the society outpost of Pasadena, and the growing metropolis of Los Angeles. Polly was a friend of Doris', who was looking for a smaller household to work in than that of George Vanderbilt's who employed her for several years, and Janet had come from the de Renille household when it turned out she and Thea's new English maid Violet did not get on.

And here we are with everything running beautifully, and in waltzes Roland Gresham. Funny, a few weeks ago it was Henry railing at Charles for wanting him to do that book, and now he's writing it and I'm the one who's angry at him for inadvertently bringing that awful little man into our lives, Alix reflected, a fresh wave of annoyance coursing through her.

Oh, Alix, can't you stop being a bitch for even five minutes? she thought. Henry has a perfect right to have whomever he wants as his secretary, and if Mr. Gresham treats you like a barely tolerable fact of life and your children like an unfortunate mistake, you'll just have to put up with it. And Henry doesn't take things forever, as you well know. A good and gentle man can be pushed just so far, she reminded herself cheerfully as her servants appeared at the drawing room doors with the tea.

A minute later, Hodges and Aileen and Janet and Polly were arranging the feast to meet Alix's exacting standards.

First, the massive silver tray holding the Tiffany tea service, spoons, forks, and neat stacks of plates and cups and saucers, all in Coalport's elaborate Indian Tree design. Then there was the food. There was the always-expected small crustless sandwiches of cucumber and chicken salad, as well as buttered white bread filled with chutney and rolled white bread spread with chopped parsley and chives. Hodges himself arranged the plates holding the caviar tarts, while Aileen tended to the covered dishes keeping warm the hot brioche loaf and the orange muffins, both accompanied by curls of sweet butter and raspberry conserves ordered from Tanrade in Paris. Three-tier silver cake stands displayed a variety of fruit tarts and macaroons, and the pound cake and the angel food cake with pink frosting and the chocolate mousse cake were placed at the other end of the coffee table from the oversized teapot. Surrounding the teapot were plates holding the thinnest possible orange and lemon slices, a bowl heaped with sugar cubes, and small crystal decanters of rum and brandy in case a guest wanted a bit more kick to his cup of Earl Grey tea.

"This is all so good-looking that I'm tempted to eat it all myself. You've done a marvelous job on such short notice. Oh, and Hodges, please tell Mrs. Wiley that as soon as the last guests have gone, I'll come in to the kitchen and speak with her," Alix said in her most complimentary voice just as Sybil and her mother entered the room. "Come here and sit down." She motioned to them. "I'm sure you're both hungry and thirsty."

"I certainly am," Sybil said frankly, and Sybil was pleased to see that both the silent companion who had first been too overpowered by her mother's forceful personality to put a sentence together, and then the trouble-beset young woman of an hour before were both gone. "I'm positively melting away from hunger. I know I'm going to be a glutton, but I suppose that's far better than constantly being ill!"

"Oh, I was never sick, either," Alix offered, filling cups and offering sandwiches. "It was such fun to eat everything in sight, and there was another delightful side effect. It surprised Henry at first," she continued obliquely, "but after the first few times he loved being woken up in the middle of the night!"

"Peter always says that a horse rancher can't get up too early in the morning!" Sybil added, completely ignoring the crushing look her mother gave her, a look that would have once reduced her to tears.

"The things you girls talk about," was all she said, however.

"That's what puts the fun in being girls together before the men get here," Alix said smoothly. "Caviar tart, Evelyn?"

The older woman eyed the tea things. "It looks as though you're expecting a regiment."

"Oh, no, just a lot of friends. I'm sure you'll enjoy meeting everyone," Alix said, arching her neck in the direction of the drawing room doors. "Mallory, Rupert, how did it go? Not that I have to ask," she added swiftly. "Your faces say it all!"

"You're absolutely right—we struck gold!" Mallory exclaimed, her face alight. "Alix, wait until you see it, it's perfect. I was all but sure when I saw the apartment this morning, and when I came back with Rupert. . . . Well,

364

we both knew it was the place for us."

"It sounds somewhat ridiculous to admit, but I didn't have to get any further than the foyer to know that Mallie and I had found our apartment," Rupert said as they sat down opposite Alix. He flashed a bright smile, but as his peripheral vision finally registered Evelyn's presence, a cold feeling ran through him.

"And we now have a properly signed and dated lease," Mallory continued. She had felt instantly the change in Rupert's demeanor, and the source of the problem was perfectly obvious.

I wish we'd come later, she thought. I should have told Rupert that I wanted to change clothes. Even fifteen minutes from now would have helped, but now we're good and stuck. Oh, what is that ghastly woman going to say?

"I'm so happy for the both of you. I've misplaced my manners, but I'm sure you all remember each other, so why don't I just bring the four of you up-to-date on each other?" Alix said with the easy assurance of a born hostess. "Sybil and her mother are going to spend the winter in New York. They've just signed for a nice apartment at the Langham, so, sweet cousin, you and Rupert aren't the only ones celebrating an apartment-acquiring today. And Evelyn, in case you and Sybil haven't guessed the happy news yet, Mallory and Rupert are engaged and are going to be married next month!" Alix finished triumphantly, neatly covering all the necessities.

"Oh, we read the announcement in the *New York Times*," Evelyn said with practiced charm. "My best wishes to you, Miss Kirk, and to you, Sir Rupert."

"Thank you for your kind wishes," Rupert said quickly, displaying a great deal of admirable restraint. "But for the record, it's not Sir Rupert, and it hasn't been for over five years. It's a little thing the government of the United States insists upon when they swear in new citizens; one isn't allowed to keep old titles. Of course, people still call Henry Lord Thorpe," Rupert went on. He was drawling his words as if this were a matter of great amusement, but Mallory and Alix, both long exposed to his moods and attitudes, knew that if Evelyn was going to respond by defending the British Empire and all its peers, she was, in the plainest of all possible terms, asking for it. "But then he looked like a lord long before he was created one, so it's understandable that people can't seem to use such a plain term as mister when speaking to him. But as far as a young baronet is concerned—" He favored Evelyn with one of his most charming smiles.

"Well, no matter what choices you've made, I'm glad to see that you can still comport yourself like the true gentleman you are," Evelyn replied with what was for her admirable tact and restraint.

But then, Alix knew as she quickly surveyed the situation, as far as a man was concerned, Evelyn would always say the praise-worthy or correct or soothing thing—a benefit that no woman in a similar circumstance would ever receive.

"I think Ben Jonson said it best—'Nor stand so much on your gentility, which is an airy, and mere borrowed thing, from dead men's dust, and bones: and none of yours except you make, or hold it,'" Alix quoted, wanting to close off this discussion immediately. "Henry always says that no matter what the pleasant effects of a title are, life is simply too interesting and too varied and too much fun to spend time dwelling on it!" she finished in a flow of wifely tact. "And since we're on the subject of apartments, how are you two facing up to the prospect of several empty rooms? The first time Henry saw all of this apartment, vacant, with absolutely no furniture, he had to go back down to the fourth floor and have a stiff whisky and soda!"

"Ah, why do you think I'm marrying an interior decorator?" Rupert teased with a wicked smile. "Empty rooms are a challenge to Mallory, not a problem."

"And we've already begun making inroads," Mallory added. "After the lease was taken care of, we went up to the Steinway studio and bought a piano. We tried out about a dozen before we found the one we liked the best."

Alix was amused and intrigued. "What did you play?"

"I played Liszt's etude in D flat major, Rupert played Chopin's Polonaise in A major, then we collaborated on a Brahms piece for four hands and finished up with Scott Joplin's 'Something Doing.'"

Alix began to laugh. "By some chance, were you two offered a job by Mr. Steinway, playing his pianos in order to attract more clients?"

"Well, he tried to get us to stay the rest of the afternoon," Mallory said, "but we told him we were in demand elsewhere for tea." She eyed the food with great interest. "Speaking of which, are Rupert and I going to be offered some of Mrs. Wiley's goodies, or are we just going to be your engaged couple on display?"

"Now, would your favorite cousin do that to you?"

"No, but you might to me."

"Rupert, I'm going to disprove that to you right this moment," Alix smiled, and stood up. "Evelyn, Sybil, you'll excuse us, won't you?"

Mystified, but thoroughly obliging, Mallory and Rupert murmured polite pleasantries to Sybil and Evelyn and followed Alix out of the drawing room and into the corridor. When the doors were safely closed and they were out of anyone's hearing, she kissed them both.

"Go into the living room," Alix instructed affectionately. "I'll send your tea in to you, and I'm sure you'd much rather be together than mingling with everyone," she continued as the buzzer sounded. "Good, here's some distraction for Evelyn. She's in full form

367

today, and neither of you need that. You're both on edge and a little privacy will take care of that."

"That's what being engaged means," Rupert responded cheekily. "Eventually we turn into over-excited children!"

"Well, since you've just referred to yourself as children, I won't have to warn you to behave yourselves since I don't intend to provide my guests with entertainment more suitable for a club in the Tenderloin!" Alix shot back just as Julie came into the corridor.

Stunningly turned out in a Doucet model of two-toned green voile and surrah, beautifully embroidered in several shades of green silk, and a turban of fancy black straw with a dashing cerise feather curving over the left side, she took in the small tableau she was advancing on and wisely decided to act as if nothing were out of the ordinary.

"Hello, darlings," she said as they all exchanged kisses. "Are you feeling better, Rupert?"

To the amusement of all three women, Rupert's color heightened. "I'm fine, Julie," he said a little roughly. "John gave me a clean bill of health."

"Alix, did you know Rupert gave us all quite a scare this morning?" Julie said deftly. "Of course men always hate to discuss their medical problems, and I'm surprised that we get to know anything at all!"

"It was only a very short dizzy spell," Rupert put in. He adored Julie, but he was all too aware of her natural ability to get details and secrets without ever seeming to press or pry; her "Philadelphia lawyer's knack" Cliff liked to call it. "Everything is all right now."

"If you say so," Julie smiled. "Mallie, this is for you, dear," she went on, giving Mallory a box wrapped in heavily glazed white paper and tied with a profusion of white silk ribbons ornamented with small silver bells. "It's not your wedding present—Cliff and I are planning on something very special for that. Just a little woman-to-woman gift."

"Is it safe to open in Rupert's presence?" Mallory asked, amused, kissing Julie's cheek in thanks.

"Well, since it's for his eventual admiration, you might as well," she responded with a knowing look. "I expect that now I'm going to have to sing for my tea?"

"I'm afraid so," Alix said apologetically. "Sybil Fleming and her mother, Evelyn Weldon, are inside. Now, Sybil is very sweet and about two months pregnant, but her mother. . . ."

"Oh, I know all about her mother. I've even had the misfortune to have met her a few times."

"Good, then as the first guest to arrive, you can go in and be charming to her. I'm afraid that right now she's raking her daughter over the coals."

"So she's one of those."

"And even more so. Please, Julie."

"Oh, don't worry. I'll live up to my Rittenhouse Square upbringing." Julie linked an arm through Alix's. "Let's go face the old battleaxe. Besides, we remember what it was like to be engaged, and from the way Mallory and Rupert look right now, our resident about-to-be-married couple want to be alone with each other a lot more than taking part in any interesting discussion that we can come up with!"

"Who's the white trash in the wretchedly overdone green and gold Worth who's busy haranguing my husband?" Bettina Bergery whispered to Alix some forty minutes later as they sat side by side on the sofa. The drawing room was now filling up with men and women, more than one would imagine were available on a weekday afternoon in summer, but like her friends, the San Francisco born Bettina Olivier Bergery missed little

369

and never hesitated to make an appropriate comment.

"Trust you, B.B., to pick out everyone's best points!"

"That's why we're friends, Alix, because we think the same way. Only this time, I said it first!" Bettina toyed with a dark chestnut curl. "Georges isn't terribly fond of London, and now I see that may be a drawback. *Who* is she?"

"The mother of that nice girl who's talking to Megan," Alix hedged, glad that Sybil was, at least for the moment, out of her mother's clutches.

"Oh, that's Sybil Fleming. Georges knows her husband. He bought a horse from him a few years ago. Imagine, *that* creature is her mother!"

"Her *mama*, if you please!" Alix said, leaning back against the sofa's deep pillows. "And she *is* something of a lion-hunter, always wanting to meet the most famous person at a party. She's relatively harmless."

"You don't sound one-hundred percent definite about that."

"I can't be. But it isn't worth the effort to try and figure out what she's really up to." She paused for a moment. "But it's probably nothing good. Her sort is epidemic. When they can't arrange fortune-enriching marriages for their children, they turn to other money-making schemes!"

Bettina's pretty brown eyes narrowed slightly. "She hardly looks as if she's taking in washing. Oh, I bet I know what Mrs. Weldon is doing to help expenses along. Mother told me that the London branch of Worth makes up its less-sold models at half-price for ladies with ways but no means," she purred in self-satisfaction, secure in the certainty that her Poiret afternoon dress of dotted blue linen with a blue satin belt around her slender waist was perfect for both the season and the occasion. "Shall we make a wager on whether or not her trunks are full of haute couture bargains?"

370

"I think I'll pass on that." Alix laughed. "And since I also have the sinking feeling that I'll have to see more of Evelyn than I'd originally planned on, it means I'll be seeing her wardrobe as well."

"Is Mallory going to invite her to the wedding?"

"That's up to her. Esme tells me that each time she thinks the guest list is complete, another name goes on. With a large wedding, you can never tell who's going to accept."

"Speaking of the wedding, are the main participants here?"

"I sent them to the living room for their own private tea."

"Is that what we're calling it now?"

"Well, I didn't give them any restrictions and they didn't offer any detailed information, but as long as they remember to lock the door, I trust them not to be too terribly outrageous," Alix said, scanning the room, making sure everyone had tea and enough to eat and no one was left standing alone. Satisfied that all was in order, she was about to turn back to Bettina when three people appeared at the drawing room door.

There was Charles, tall and thrillingly handsome, the red carnation in his buttonhole a splash of bright color against his dark suit; Thea, dramatically turned out in a Doucet afternoon dress of brilliant cherry and black foulard with a tunic coat of black chiffon, her black straw Reboux hat piled high with lighter-than-air masses of tulle and ornamented on the brim with just a touch of gold embroidery, and then there was the man with them.

For a long minute, Alix just looked at her newest guest.

I don't care what they say about Singapore, it's New York that the world comes to, she reflected, and then, without appearing to be in the slightest hurry, she stood up and began to make her way across the length of her drawing room, stopping here and there to say a word to a friend, and finally reaching the doorway where she kissed Charles and Thea, and without the least hesitation, put her arms around Romney Sedgewick and welcomed her old friend to her home.

Although the apartment's floor plan designated this ten-by-twelve foot room as the music room, Alix and Henry had transformed it into something quite different. To be sure, there was a piano in one corner, a handsome Steinway spinet, and the newest model Victrola and a wide variety of recordings were set near the fireplace, but this was the Thorpes' family living room, an absolute necessity in a household with four children all under the age of eight.

The walls were painted a soft cream, making the deep red carpet glow like a bottle of the best Burgundy, and on this hot August afternoon, all the windows were open to catch the passing breeze off the park. Inviting sofas with roll arms and squishy armchairs were covered in a glazed yellow chintz splashed with red and pink and white carnations accented with a scattering of green leaves; a variety of circular mahogany side tables held framed photographs, lamps with pleated white silk shades and bases of old Chinese enamels and Imari vases filled with bunches of white summer flowers; and built-in bookcases framed the double doors.

Despite its being a room for a family to spend time in, there was a voluptuous quality to it, an aura that Alix, like Thea, was able to create, making it also seem like the perfect hideaway for two lovers.

The lavish tea that Alix had sent in to them was reduced to used cups and plates and silver and a few remaining crumbs, and Mallory and Rupert were stretched out together on the smaller of the two sofas, their shoes off and their long legs stretching over the cool, slippery chintz, as they relaxed in each other's arms.

"It seems a bit strange to think that there's a very large party going on in the drawing room while we're all alone here," Mallory said as she cuddled closer to Rupert. He had taken off his suit jacket and vest and tie, and she reveled in the lean strength she knew was just below his meticulously tailored exterior. It was dangerous for them to be here like this, terribly, wonderfully dangerous, but nothing short of a dozen people breaking through the locked door could have gotten her to move. "I wonder if anyone's asking for us?"

"No, but I imagine they're certainly speculating about what we're doing," he whispered in her ear, his tongue moving tantalizingly along the outside rim. "I'm sure Alix isn't expecting us to be sitting primly side by side, nibbling on cucumber sandwiches."

"And you think it's only fair that we live up to common expectation?" she challenged, her arm curving around his waist, the tracing motions of his tongue sending a delightful shiver down her spine.

"Just a little love in the afternoon."

"That's what we're having right now," she replied as he pulled her closer, kissing him, sighing as his right hand curved around her breast and the pressure of his mouth increased.

In one small second, Mallory felt her heartbeat quicken and her passion begin to spiral upwards. They had both been so cautious, so careful to keep their desire in control, and now it was threatening to break free of those bonds.

Mallory wasn't a tease, and she knew perfectly well that when she made Rupert promise that there would be no pre-marital lovemaking between them that she was running the risk that he would find some anonymous, expensive woman with whom he could share an afternoon of desire with no entanglements beyond payment for services rendered. How easy it would be for him, and Mallory was perfectly and completely sure that if such an event had transpired and she found out about it, the only course of action for her to take was to understand and act as if it had never happened.

But instinctively she knew that he not only hadn't sought out another woman, but he had no intention of doing so. Was it a fidelity born out of love and loyalty, or out of unfinished guilt from four years ago, or, most compelling of all, had he been willing to bide his time because he knew a moment like this was going to come along sooner or later and her resolve would melt away?

The thought ran through Mallory's mind as Rupert pulled her alongside him, his fingers undoing the first of the scarlet silk-covered buttons that fastened her dress down the back. His index finger drew a long, caressing line from the nape of her neck to the top of her lacy camisole. He repeated the motion again and again until Mallory arched against him, seeking closer contact, feeling the increased heat and hardness of his body beneath the layers of his clothes.

"Rupert—" Her voice caught in her throat.

"I want you so much," he whispered heavily. "I want to have you right here. No one will ever know . . ."

Almost as soon as the words were out of Rupert's mouth, there were footsteps in the corridor, snatches of conversation they couldn't catch, and the laughter of a group of men and women as they made their way toward the drawing room. A semblance of sanity seemed to flow through Mallory again, and she pulled herself out of Rupert's embrace until her back was against the sofa.

"You were saying?" she said with a lightness she didn't feel. "I want you also, but it would be almost like making love with an audience. I—I couldn't, Rupert, it wouldn't feel right—or be right. Besides," she went on, "there isn't very much room on this sofa, and the other one isn't much bigger, and when we make love on the floor, I'd much rather it be *our* floor!"

Caught directly in the face of her logic, Rupert felt his passion of the moment ebb away. He still wanted Mallory, but she was right; not here and not now. Reality diluted rapture, and the idea of making love in this room suddenly seemed too much like dabbling in semi-public love.

"When it comes to our present location, I agree with you," he said at last. "But are you in the mood to be persuaded to spend an afternoon with me in a very private, very comfortable spot?" He reached out and touched her cheek. "It won't be ruining our wedding night. I promise you that."

"You don't have to treat me as if I'm fresh fallen snow," Mallory told him tenderly. "And I do want to make love to you . . . with you . . . both of us alone together."

"You had your chance at lunch."

Mallory began to laugh. "Now who's being cautious? You've been trying to maneuver me for an *interlude à deux* since the night we got engaged, and now that you have me on the verge of agreeing, you're stepping backwards. It sounds to me as if you're having one or two second thoughts. Or do you have a chorine tucked away who's keeping you so entranced that you haven't gotten around to telling her it's all over?" she teased.

"And where am I supposed to find the time to set up another woman in a *pied-à-terre*, much less visit her there? I barely have enough time for you, and it's never enough."

"A month from now, we'll be married, and every night when you leave Wall Street, you'll be coming home to me."

"Is that a polite way to tell me to take my somewhat

risqué offer and—"

Mallory placed her fingers on Rupert's mouth, preventing him from finishing his comments, her heart beating as fast as her conflicting thoughts. It would be so easy, so simple to say no. True, she longed for Rupert as much as he longed for her, but the caution that had prompted her that afternoon in the beach house came back to her again.

"When I told you I didn't want us to be lovers again until we were married, it was more than just our losing the importance of our wedding night," she told him seriously. "There is another reason. It doesn't matter about our being lovers beforehand, but I didn't want to run the risk of coming down the aisle a pregnant bride. And don't tell me about precautions," she went on, smiling as she interpreted the look in his eyes. "Nothing works all the time."

"Except not making love at all," Rupert finished, shamefacedly. "I didn't think about even the most basic precaution."

"Oh, don't look like that! We were both lucky—that afternoon I was about as safe as any woman can get." With a tender motion, she reached forward to caress his face. "If there was going to be a mistake, I wanted it to be on the side of caution and restraint. I wasn't being a tease, trying to see how much I could make you sweat until I had the ring on my finger. I think that underneath it all I knew we'd slip—or is it slide delightfully?—off the straight and narrow, and the closer to our wedding date the better."

"When am I going to stop being amazed by you?" Rupert questioned softly, still absorbing her words.

"Oh, maybe about the time of our golden wedding anniversary," Mallory said brightly. "When will that be—1960?"

"That sounds about right. I hope skirts are shorter by

then," he said with a very admiring look at her legs in flesh-colored silk stockings, now visible to the knee since she'd pulled up her narrow skirt for greater ease. "Dame Fashion should really take legs like yours into greater consideration!"

"Compliments, compliments—and all very welcome and accepted," she said, kissing him, and again felt the same desire, the same need that had enveloped her a short time before.

"Do you really want to wait?" Rupert asked a long time later. "I'll stick it out if you can."

"I can wait," she said, smoothing back his hair, "but I don't think that one afternoon in some very quiet, very romantic place, with no business—either financial or decorating—and just a cool, comfortable bed and a bottle of icy champagne will hurt a thing."

Rupert fell back against the cushions, laughing in delight. "We are going to have an afternoon . . . but all for you, Mallie. Our only problem is when."

"That, my love, is what weekends are for—the perfect time to make important decisions!"

The gold Tiffany carriage clock that graced the center of the marble mantel chimed the hour, and with a sigh, Rupert lifted his left arm to look at the Cartier Santos watch—designed for and named in honor of the French aviator—fastened around his wrist to confirm the time.

"Let's go to the theatre tonight," Mallory suggested. "I haven't seen *The Summer Widowers* yet, and Thea said it's terrific. I think we've had more than enough to eat for the time being, and we can have a late dinner afterwards. What do you say?"

"I say it's better than anything I can come up with— with one exception, of course," Rupert grinned as he sat up and swung his legs to the floor. "I expect that when I call the ticket broker, you'll want me to order four tickets?"

"And four for dinner, don't forget that," Mallory said, matching his smile. She put on her shoes. "Whom can we get to join us?"

"There should be any number of willing bodies in the drawing room."

"It sounds like you're talking about a whodunit. But let's decide now, or else Evelyn will swoop down on us in a positive delight, and we'll have to take her and Sybil to the theatre."

"That," Rupert said, "is not a nice prospect. I think Evan and Melinda make much nicer company."

"I couldn't agree more," she said, making sure that her dress wasn't too creased and taking her vanity case out of her handbag to make a few quick repairs on her makeup. "We have an entire weekend to deal with everything we discussed this afternoon," she went on as Rupert took her in his arms for a kiss. "Oh, if you keep doing that, we won't get to the theatre at all."

"But we can do much more interesting things than anything done on stage." With one arm still firmly around Mallory's waist, Rupert reached for the house phone. "Wait until you see what a brilliant fiancé you have. Hodges," he said into the receiver, "this is Rupert Randall . . . yes, you can be of great help to me. Would you find the Prescotts—I'm sure they're still here—and ask them to join us in the living room? We want to ask them if they'd like to join us at the theatre tonight. Thank you very much, Hodges. Well?" he asked when he hung up.

"As you said, you're my brilliant fiancé," Mallory said, rewarding his cleverness with a kiss. "But now, before Hodges finds Melinda and Evan for us," she said, looking down, "wouldn't you like to put your shoes on?"

"I see that you still always pour your guests their first

378

cup of tea," Romney said as he sat beside Alix on the sofa.

"Oh, in this respect, Cecily taught me well. Always pour out the first cup yourself—that's the only way to get the best gossip first-hand! Caviar tart?"

"Please, they look delicious," he said, and surveyed the drawing room with obvious admiration. "Your money becomes more beautiful every time I see it," he continued. "There's something very soothing about a lily pad; they let you admire them but keep all their secrets."

Alix arched her neck like a swan. The conversation that had taken place in Emma's sitting room was still fresh in her mind, and she knew she had to proceed with great caution. Like Henry, Romney was not a man who would take being presumed upon. Abstractedly, she wondered what Thea had found out from him, well aware that if he had indeed confided in her, she would not betray him.

"Water lilies are not the only thing good at hiding," she said significantly. "But in any case, a belated welcome to New York. Is it going to be a long visit?"

Romney searched her face for some sign of duplicity. "What I like best about you and your friends is that when someone asks you to keep a secret, you don't ring each other up afterwards to pass it around."

"Oh, we talk all right," Alix corrected. "And back in London, you're a favorite topic of conversation. But we also like to keep our promises."

"So I'm finding out. And if Thea didn't tell you that she's my decorator, am I also correct in assuming that Mallory didn't tell you that I ran into her and Rupert at the Plaza the other evening. I bought them a bottle of champagne, told them I'd found a flat I liked at One Lexington Avenue, and suggested that they might find a flat of their own in the same building."

"My cousin did leave out that little bit of information, but I'm sure it was at your request."

"It was, but you'll also be glad to hear that it was Mallory who convinced me to come out of my self-imposed exile," he said genially. "She and Rupert want to invite me to their wedding, and quite justifiably they pointed out that my unheralded appearance on their special day might prove to be somewhat distracting."

"I agree absolutely."

"I thought you would." Romney looked amused. "Where's Henry? I thought he would be here beside you, or else circulating among the guests."

"Normally he would be," Alix said with more asperity than she intended. "But he's in the midst of writing a book about great collectors and their art, and he's had the misfortune to hire a secretary who not only believes in the old cliché of putting one's nose to the grindstone, but knew him when, and doesn't think that the demands of a wife and children count for much."

"That sounds just like Roland Gresham!"

"Well, it is."

"Poor Henry." Romney's expression was sympathetic. "Gresham is from the school that says art and true intellect—if not outright genius—function only when undisturbed by the facts of life. The old boy probably thinks that your and Henry's children were found under the cabbage patch!"

"That is not funny!" Alix said, laughing despite her dismay. "Please, let's talk about something else."

"Me?"

"If you insist," she said archly. "Or do you want to wait for Henry to join us? He should be out of protective custody soon."

"I'd rather talk to the both of you, although I feel it's only fair to warn you that my life since April sounds like a travelogue." He looked around the room. "Are Mallory and Rupert here?"

"They were both rather tired when they came in, and

since Evelyn Weldon was in one of her more precious moods, it was a simple precautionary measure to send them into the living room so they could enjoy their tea *solitude à deux*."

"That was very thoughtful of you, but I was looking forward to having a word with your cousin. Mallory's a very charming young woman. But does she know what she's taking on with Rupert?"

Alix blinked, feeling somewhat nonplussed. Why was Romney acting so interested in Mallory? Oh, please, no complications like *that*, she thought. There's nothing worse than a man deciding he's attracted to an engaged woman. I wonder if Romney and I hadn't kept inadvertently raising old hurts in each other when we first met he would have pursued me despite my wanting only Henry?

"Possibly Rupert isn't sure what he's taking on with Mallory," Alix said with conviction. "Mallie isn't anyone's fool. She knows what—and whom—she wants."

Romney looked at her in surprise. "Alix, you don't think that I . . . that I'm interested in Mallory in a way that might not be proper?"

"It's been known to happen. Romney, look, Mallory and Rupert have something very special between them, and they do not need someone—even if he's a good friend—playing the would-be admirer."

"Not much gets past you, does it?"

"It never has. Are you angry?"

"I couldn't be that with you if I tried. And thank you for your advice. But you know how irresistible we extra men think we are."

"Yes, that *is* a hard pose to give up," Alix agreed in amusement. "But the Romney Sedgewick I know and care about doesn't play the flirtation game simply because there's nothing else to do at the moment."

"I've never been that needlessly cruel, and since Mallory is a very intelligent woman whose head isn't going to be turned by the first extravagant compliment a man pays her, there's nothing at all to worry about." Romney gave her a reassuring smile. "And I'm not so lonely that I'd turn a friendly admiration into something different . . . or dangerous."

"Well, as for being lonely, you have to admit that if you didn't hide yourself away from your friends, we'd keep you properly occupied!"

"Touché," Romney said, a bright look in his deep gray eyes. "Will you be happy that by the end of the year I'll be a permanent friend instead of a transatlantic one?"

"I'll be very, very happy." Her slight feeling of apprehension began to fade away. You're too suspicious, Alix, she warned herself. Romney had never been anything but an upright and honest man. *Don't* go looking for special meaning behind every casual remark.

Alix ended her silent review when she saw Henry enter the drawing room. Instantly, the atmosphere changed as he went from group to group, stopping to smile and chat, managing with his usual graceful manner to make everyone forget that he hadn't been there when they arrived.

Romney watched while Alix charted her husband's progress toward her with an emotion he couldn't quite identify. It wasn't jealousy, it wasn't even envy, it was more a feeling of regret that it had taken him so long to find the woman whose eyes followed him around like that. He didn't like making comments that could be so easily misinterpreted, but it was better than either giving his secret away or pretending that he was available to play the extra man.

"You and Henry have something very special together," he said at last.

"I know." Alix's smile was a beautiful sight. "It was

eight years on July twenty-sixth, and it gets better every day. I might be tempted to make a trite remark now, but I won't. Henry will be here in a moment, and then, as soon as our guests leave, we'll give you something stronger to drink, and we can do all our catching up."

"I'm looking forward to sharing all my travel tales with my friends," Romney replied, not at all proud of himself for the evasion he considered necessary. "Tell me, Alix, what do you think Henry will say when I tell him that I'm also writing a book?"

The Thorpes' party had reached its plateau. All the invited guests had arrived, and busily occupied with excellent food and conversation in the drawing room, no one was paying the slightest bit of attention to the man and woman conferring in the library.

"Well, you certainly took your time getting here!"

"You seem to forget that unlike you, I'm an invited guest of the Thorpes."

"And offhand I'd say that your popularity with Lady Thorpe is on a par with mine."

"That miserable witch! Oh, never mind her—they're not going to be any good to us, but someone else here is. A nice young man with a past he'd just as soon let stay in the dark. And from what I've seen, you wouldn't say that his fiancée is a properly retiring young lady. Now, listen to me . . ."

Whoever named it necking was a poor judge of anatomy.

—Groucho Marx

The Knickerbocker Hotel

With her usual careful driving, Mallory steered her Baker Electric out of the heavy traffic and brought it to a halt in front of the main entrance to the Knickerbocker Hotel at the corner of Broadway and Forty-second Street, smiling at the doorman who instantly opened the door for her.

"Good afternoon," she said, stepping out onto the busy sidewalk. "I have an appointment here. Can you take care of my car until I'm through?" she asked, discreetly pressing a five-dollar bill into the man's gloved hand.

"Of course, madam, no trouble at all," he assured her, handing her the Mark Cross leather portfolio from the car's front seat. "Here, you don't want to leave this behind."

"I certainly don't," Mallory replied, keeping her voice serious as she tucked the portfolio under an arm, wondering what the doorman would think if he knew what she had inside the soft leather case. With a secret smile, she turned on her heel and with her head held high, whirled through the revolving door into the busy hotel, looking straight ahead as she crossed the expensively furnished lobby.

At six-hundred rooms, the Knickerbocker Hotel, while

not as luxurious and exclusive as the Plaza or the St. Regis, by and large attracted the same sort of well-off, well-dressed men and women—the sort that Mallory could count on blending in with perfect ease. Acting as if she did this sort of thing every day, and barely suppressing the smile that kept bubbling to the surface, she walked past the Men's Bar with its famous mural by Maxfield Parrish, past the restaurant crowded with mostly women enjoying a leisurely lunch before attending a matinée, and toward the bank of elevators, one of which would take her upstairs to the room where Rupert was waiting for her.

They had made their decision over the weekend, concluding that the Knickerbocker was the best place for them to meet, and that Rupert would make all the arrangements.

Arrangements, Mallory thought, skirting a crowd of businessmen obviously heading for the bar, drawing admiring looks for her Poiret dress of French-blue voile de soie trimmed in French-blue satin with a belt of old blue patent leather and a tiny low neck and yoke of ecru lace, one or two of them trying to get a better look at her face shaded by her large Georgette hat of white tagal straw with a bow of old blue tulle.

Did Rupert have to pay over and above the price of the room? she wondered. Of course he did. You're an idiot, Mallory. How else, except by several judiciously offered bribes, do you think we're going to avoid becoming an item in *Town Topics*?

A string of doubt wound its way around her heart. Are we doing the right thing? she thought as she passed the bell captain's desk. I could turn around right now, get my car back from the doorman and go home. Rupert would forgive me.

But I don't want to. Oh, I thought six weeks would go by so quickly I'd hardly notice. It was a great idea, but it's hardly worked with Rupert and me. It all went fast enough in the beginning, but these last weeks are dragging. And I love Rupert too much to turn around and leave now. I couldn't if I had the house detective after me.

As she approached the elevators, Mallory checked her watch. Exactly half-past one: the time they'd agreed upon as being the least likely hour of the day to be noticed. Desire and excitement and love and just a soupçon of trepidation surged through her, making her heart pound and the butterflies take command of her stomach. The room key in her afternoon bag felt as if it weighed a ton.

Mallory stepped into the carpeted, brass-ornamented elevator car, and her mind went back to that morning, to the multi-mirrored fitting room at Lucile's salon on Thirty-sixth Street just off Fifth Avenue, where the court train of her wedding gown was measured and fitted. Just when she was being fussed over the most, the directrice came in carrying a large envelope with Mallory's name scrawled across the front.

She had accepted the delivery with a smile, asked the directrice to tell the messenger that there was no reply, gave her a dollar to tip the delivery boy with, and after placing the envelope with the rest of her belongings, she turned her attention back to her fitting.

The fitting of the train was followed by the final adjustments on her going-away dress, a check on the progress of a tea gown of Nattier-blue chiffon over pale rose satin with bands of blond lace, and finishing with the first try-on of a winter-white serge frock with cerise, purple and yellow hand embroidery around the neck and cuffs and belt—the dress Mallory intended to wear on the day they'd leave for California. For an hour and a half, Mallory stood patiently while she was measured and pinned, talked with her saleswoman and the fitters on a variety of subjects, all the time acting as if the envelope contained nothing out of the ordinary. It was only when she was in the relative privacy provided by the taximeter cab taking her back to 667 Madison Avenue, that she broke the envelope's seal and withdrew a single sheet of heavy, expensive white stationery with Rupert's letterhead and found the key and their meeting time.

At home, she ate lunch quickly, barely tasting the cook's excellent lobster salad and scarcely looking at the stack of mail and wedding presents that had arrived in the latest mail delivery, before changing clothes and redoing her maquillage.

It's a good thing that I was so rushed, she thought as the operator slid the doors shut and the car began its upward ascent. If I'd had a chance to think about what I'm doing, I wouldn't come. Oh, Rupert, please be there. I don't think I could stand waiting for you!

"Fifth floor," the operator announced, and Mallory left the elevator, waiting until the doors had closed behind her before she opened her purse, removed the room key, and began to walk down the thickly carpeted hallway toward her destination.

Slowly, her feeling of trepidation faded away. I want to be here, she thought. A whole long, beautiful, perfect afternoon alone with the man I love, the man I'm going to marry and have children with and spend my life with. And more than that, it'll be fun to have this interlude to look back on—better than just fittings and parties and all the rest of the fuss that goes into making a big wedding work!

At the door to Room 544, Mallory fitted the heavy, ornate key into the lock, turned the knob and stepped into the room, remembering to lock the door behind her.

At first glance, it was obvious to her that this was one of the best double rooms available, large and sunny, furnished with reproduction Sheraton furniture. The early afternoon sun was pouring in, reflecting off the heavy silver wine cooler with the gold foil neck of the champagne bottle sticking out and the flawless crystal flutes that were arranged on the writing table. As she leaned back against the heavy wood door, Mallory had a full view of Rupert. He was just as she wanted to find him, stretched out in bed and waiting for her. Only there seemed to be one small problem—Rupert Randall was completely, absolutely and without a doubt, sound asleep.

Mallory wasn't sure how long she stayed where she was, torn between exasperation and laughter. She noticed that Rupert's clothes were hung neatly on the wooden valet that was set near the bathroom door, and that his dressing gown was laid over the seat of one of the room's armchairs, while his wristwatch was placed within easy reach on the bedside table.

No one, absolutely no one, would believe this, Mallory thought, tenderness joining her amazement as her faint sense of annoyance faded. I was prepared for just about anything but this!

Wisely deciding that waking him up was not the move to take at all, Mallory crossed the taupe-carpeted floor to the dressing table near the window and began her preparations. She took her gloves off first, then her hat, and then her wristwatch and pearls were added to the vanity's bare surface before she reached behind her to unhook her dress. A quick survey of the closet revealed only a handful of sturdy, ugly wooden hangers which were thoroughly unsuitable for her needs, and she put her dress across the other armchair before turning back to the dressing table.

You're enjoying this, aren't you? she silently questioned her reflection in the three-way mirror. Your eyes

389

are extra bright and your cheeks are pink in a way that doesn't come from rouge. All right, yes, I admit it, finding Rupert fast asleep is just as appealing as having him awake and ready. Now, get going before Rupert wakes up. You have a lot of work to do!

Mallory opened her portfolio and took out a silk brocade lingerie case. With great care she undid the broad pink satin ribbon that held it closed, and holding her breath, lifted out her newest, most fragile, and definitely most provocative Lucile nightgown—an ankle-length slide of rose-colored satin lavished with two inches of lace at the hem, the narrowest of satin straps, and the lowest possible back ever.

A minute later, free of her handmade afternoon shoes, sheer silk stockings and lacy Lucile lingerie, she slid the confection over her head, catching her breath as the column of rich fabric came down over her already sensitized skin. This creation, Mallory decided as she took the pins out of her hair, is made to be put on for and admired by the man you love, and then taken off again—which is exactly why I brought it with me!

All through her preparations, Mallory had expected Rupert to waken, but here she was, all ready for an afternoon of rapture, and he was still sound asleep.

At least he doesn't snore, she thought with amusement, approaching the bed. He didn't stir as she lifted the covers, and as soon as she sat down, Mallory instinctively reached for his right hand and slipped her fingers around his wrist.

Rupert's pulse was slow and steady and his color was good, but his slumber was so profound that it became instantly apparent to Mallory that rousing him would not only be next to impossible, but might possibly have an adverse affect on his well-being.

"Poor baby," she whispered softly. "My poor, exhausted darling. It's all right, just sleep on and I'll be here right beside you when you wake up."

Gently, so as not to disturb him, Mallory moved away the top sheet and satin comforter that he had pulled up to his shoulders, and silently gazed at the beautiful sight of Rupert's long body, admiring him as she knew he would admire her were their positions reversed. He lay on his left side, his relaxed body slightly curled up, giving her the opportunity to drink him in from all angles. Unable to resist, Mallory drew her index finger in a straight, slow, savoring line down the center of his smooth chest, from the base of his throat to his navel. There was the ultimate temptation to proceed lower, to the manhood that was as relaxed as the rest of his body, but there were unspoken limits and boundaries and she wouldn't violate them. Reluctantly, she gently concealed his body again, dropping a soft kiss on his shoulder as she made sure the covers were where they had been when she came in.

Mallory stood up again and went over to the large windows. They had an excellent view of Broadway a half-hour before the matinée curtain came up at every occupied house. From where she stood, Mallory could see up two blocks to the seven-hundred room Astor Hotel, as well as across the street to the Café de l'Opera, the opulent new restaurant where she and Rupert and Melinda and Evan had gone on Thursday night after the theatre, climbing the imposing grand staircase to dine and dance amidst the very Eastern decorative scheme replete with black marble pillars and orange hangings. They had been the last customers out of the establishment when it finally closed at an hour so late that it was actually early, and although they went home, going to bed was such an utter waste of time, all they did was nap, change clothes, and then take the eight-twenty train out to Long Island.

The adrenaline that had taken them through a long day and a festive night had to run out, but fortunately not until they were safely back at Cove House.

The house had been full of guests, and barely able to eat lunch from the delayed exhaustion, they had gone out to the garden and in a secluded spot planned their strategy for the coming week. The simplest plan would be to borrow Jimmy and Kate's apartment, since they were the only members of the family staying at Cove House and not commuting back and forth, but that would have meant bringing in other interested parties, and what mattered most was their privacy. Which meant a hotel. One that was large and centrally located so they could blend into the crowd, and yet offered the same service and luxury they would find at the Plaza or the St. Regis.

"Well, Rupert certainly arranged everything to perfection—a good room, a bottle of champagne—but nothing works properly all the time," she said softly pulling the curtains across the windows so that the room was dark. It was obvious to her that Rupert needed to sleep, and as far as she was concerned, nothing was going to disturb him.

A minute later, Mallory was slipping into bed, settling back against the plump pillows and the cool sheets, making sure she was close to Rupert, but not so close as to inadvertently wake him up.

If nothing else, she realized, this was as good a way as any to get used to another important aspect of marriage—that of simply sleeping together.

Mallory closed her eyes and smiled. This was so comfortable. The perfect spot to relax, and who knew what the rest of the afternoon might bring. . . .

"Mallie . . . Mallie, please wake up. I don't feel very well."

Mallory came awake instantly to find Rupert sitting up in bed, the covers bunched at his waist, his hands pressed

392

against his temples, an expression of pain and confusion on his face.

Alarmed, she sat up beside him. "Darling, what is it? Please tell me."

"I have a splitting headache. Why . . . why is it so dark?" He looked around him in increasing panic. "What time is it?"

Realizing that she had to calm him before she could do anything else, Mallory reached across him for his watch.

"It's only three forty-five," she assured him softly. "Don't worry, it's all going to be all right."

"Why is it so dark?"

"Because I closed the curtains." She put her hands on the back of his neck. "Tell me what's wrong."

"I feel as though there's a band around my head, and I think there's a rubber ball bouncing around in my stomach."

Mallory could recognize a tension headache when she saw one, and murmuring soothing words, she put Rupert back against the pillows and pulled the covers up. What next? she thought. Aspirin tablets, a cold compress, and a neck rub to loosen the tightness she'd felt running from the base of his skull to his shoulders. Well, none of it was going to get done unless she got out of bed.

Upright again, Mallory moved quickly, first to the dressing table where she'd left her purse so she could retrieve the silver pillbox filled with aspirins that were specially coated to avoid upsetting the stomach. Fortunately, there was a carafe of water and a glass on each of the bedside tables; this was not a time to have to go dashing back and forth between the bathroom and bedroom.

She sat down gently beside Rupert, poured out the water, and handed him the glass and two white tablets. "Take it, darling, and you'll begin to feel better in a few minutes."

"This isn't what I had planned, but when I ruin things, you can be sure I do it all in a grand manner."

"Nothing is ruined. We're together, aren't we?" she said, using the voice she'd cultivated back in the days when emulating Alix was all that mattered. "I'm going to get a cold compress for your head."

While Rupert took his aspirins, Mallory went into the bathroom, grabbed a towel and two washcloths, and as she went to turn on the cold water she had a better idea.

"*What* are you doing?" Rupert asked as Mallory dipped one of the washclothes into the wine bucket.

"This is better than running the water for ten minutes to get it cold enough," she said, cheerfully wringing out the cloth. "There's even enough ice left for an ice pack. How is your head feeling?"

"A little better," he said gingerly, and a moment later, Mallory gently pressed the washcloth against the back of his head and applied her improvised icepack on the top of his head. Rupert winced as he felt the ice make contact with his skin. He still felt awful, but at least the first fright of waking up with a pounding headache and not remembering where he was, or what time it was, had faded away under Mallory's loving care. He reached for her hand. "What's the towel for?"

"You looked so ghastly, I was afraid you were on the verge of losing your lunch."

"If it never went down, it can't come up."

"Are you telling me you didn't have lunch?"

"No time for a little thing like eating a mid-day meal when there's a stock transfer to oversee, plus a half-a-dozen other details that I'm responsible for," he said, putting an arm around Mallory, and drawing her down to him. "Oh, this is more like it," he said as she rested her head on his shoulder.

"Yes, it is," she said, cuddling closer. "But do you want to tell me what happened to you after you left Wall

Street? You never struck me as the sort of man who's fond of afternoon naps, although after the last two hours I don't think we should ignore that activity in our married life. There's a certain charm in just snuggling up to each other!"

"No objection here, but about four hours ago, my ultimate goal was somewhat more active. Unfortunately, I was also pretty nervous—something I thought would never happen to me—so when I got here a little after noon, I went into the bar and had a double bourbon while I looked at Maxfield Parrish's mural. By the time I came upstairs, I was seeing things through a haze. I ordered the champagne, made myself comfortable, and then the next thing I knew, I felt like my head was in a vise, and until I saw you I couldn't even remember where I was."

Mallory slipped out of his embrace and sat up. "You were tired when you got here, and the liquor hit your stomach like a sandbag," she diagnosed. "You need something to eat."

"Is the champagne still cold?"

"*That* is the *last* thing you need!" She stood up, and seized by an impish idea, took Rupert's dressing gown from the chair and put it on. The blue and gold heavy figured silk was no compliment to her rose satin nightgown, but the look in Rupert's eyes was anything but uncomplimentary.

"You look better in my dressing gown than I do."

Mallory ran her hands over the sleeves. "Is it new?"

"On my way uptown, I realized I needed something suitable to sip champagne in, and I stopped at Brooks Brothers. Are you sure about no champagne?"

"Positive. You need food. Now just relax and let me call room service." She paused, her hand on the telephone. "Rupert, what name did you register under?"

He laughed. "Randall. Mr. and Mrs. Clifford S."

"Cliff is just going to love you." Mallory laughed,

picked up the phone, and asked to be connected with room service. "This is Mrs. Randall in Room 544, and I'd like to place an order. Yes . . . we'd like chicken soup, a plate of chicken sandwiches, ginger ale—preferably Canada Dry—a pot of China tea, angel food cake, ice cream—vanilla and strawberry—and an ice bucket. How long? Good—yes—that's 544—thank you."

"A bucket of ice?" Rupert inquired, taking the compress off his neck and folding his arms behind his head. "Are you planning on doing something interesting?"

"I could always pack you in ice—that ought to keep you quiet!" Mallory retorted, dipping the washcloth back into the wine cooler. "You're supposed to leave this on your neck," she went on. "Or would you prefer a neck rub?"

His smile was deliberately slow. "If you can't guess the answer to that, I can't understand why we're engaged."

With a smile that matched his, Mallory came toward the bed, slipping off the dressing gown as she approached him. "Can't you?" she challenged.

"I think you've managed to jog my memory," he grinned, holding out his arms to her, and they decided to forego the benefits of a cold compress in favor of improving upon a neck rub.

"Are you *sure* you had a bad headache?" she teased, weaving her fingers into his thick hair. "For a man who couldn't remember the time of day, you're doing rather well!"

"All compliments received with pleasure," Rupert said, his fingertips tracing the line of her neck. "Is this nightgown a glimpse of what I have waiting for me?"

"You're going to have to marry me and find out!"

"If I had any doubts left at leaving behind a rather interesting bachelorhood, seeing you like this got rid of them."

"Funny. Now kiss me."

"Anything for you," he promised. "Anything at all."

At the first touch of his mouth, Mallory closed her eyes, ready to surrender everything to the moment. Rupert's nude body was intoxicating, and her hands slipped down to his shoulders, ready to go further, eager to forget the last half-hour in exchange for the delight they'd come here to share.

"Room service!"

The perfunctory knock at the door and the waiter's voice from the other side of the wood panel put an abrupt end to their lovemaking.

"Today is not my day," Rupert muttered, and Mallory, choking back her laughter, got out of bed, retrieved the robe from the floor, and tossed it on the bed.

"Put that on and answer the door," she advised. "The moment has come for me to slip into the bathroom."

"The things a man does in the name of love," he grumbled good-naturedly.

"Yes, and you love every moment of it," she responded. "Now hurry, or the soup is going to get cold!"

Forty-five minutes later, the chicken soup—along with the rest of the food Mallory ordered—was happily consumed.

"Promise me that you won't go without lunch again," Mallory said as she poured out the last of the tea. "It's not healthy for you, and I hate to see you all worn out."

"I'll be careful from now on," he promised. "And it's not because I didn't enjoy your ministrations. You would have made a wonderful doctor."

"Because of my bedside manner?"

"Because of everything you did for me. I wanted this afternoon to be special for you, and instead I turned it into some sort of bad French farce. First, I was asleep when you came in, then you had to take care of me, and now, even if we wanted to, we don't have the time left to make the reason we came here something meaningful for both of us."

"It is too late for our tryst. The matinées will all be letting out soon, and that'll be the best time for us to melt into the crowd—separately, unfortunately."

"Always discreet," he murmured, his lips brushing against the side of her neck, but he didn't press his advantage, and Mallory reluctantly broke their embrace.

Some twenty minutes later, her hair pinned up and fresh makeup applied, Mallory was almost ready to leave. She stood patiently in front of the dressing table as Rupert hooked her up the back and fastened the clasp of her pearls.

"Are you going to let me do this all the time after we're married?" he asked, kissing the nape of her neck.

"I don't see why not. I think you'll make a superb ladies' maid, and I'm a good employer!"

"I just bet. Of course, in return I expect you to valet me."

"Is this in addition to being your personal emergency physician, or in place of it?"

"I'll have to give that some thought," he said as Mallory put on her hat and gathered up the rest of her belongings. "I'll let you know which I prefer on our wedding night."

"Somehow I knew you were going to say that," she replied, turning around and putting her arms around his shoulders. Rupert was fully dressed except for his suit jacket, and Mallory was just a bit surprised and rather delighted to realize that part of being in love was finding out you were just as attracted to the man you loved whether he was clothed or not. "Darling, I'll see you later at Gareth's and Susannah's—"

"Where I'll have to pretend I haven't seen you since

last night," he said as they walked toward the door. "I never thought I'd say this, but you had the best idea when you decided that we not make love until our wedding night. If nothing else, it saves us mishaps like this afternoon."

"Then you're not going to try and persuade me to join you for another secluded afternoon?" she teased as Rupert's arms went around her waist, pulling her close to him.

"No," he said with a parting kiss. "I'm not going to do any more persuading again until the night of September twenty-fourth. In a way, though, this afternoon hasn't been *all* bad," he went on. "We've been alone together, and that's what we wanted. But until we're married, I'd rather wait to be with you like this, and I think the St. Regis will be a lot nicer place to take our next step together in."

Mallory rang for the elevator. Without a doubt, this was not the afternoon she'd been anticipating when she first stepped off the elevator. Her mouth curved in a bittersweet smile. All that apprehension, all those nerves, all those stupid, foolish, useless fears that had assailed her—and for nothing at all.

Suppose Rupert hadn't been asleep when I came in? Oh, don't even ask yourself that, Mallory. That's posing a question to which you already know the answer. Poor Rupert, his plans for a grand, passionate afternoon all gone. And while I'm at it, poor me. Shall I tell this to Alix? I remember her telling me that she and Henry would have gotten together much sooner if only London had had some huge hotels or apartment buildings where no one cared who was coming or going. Well, she thought as the elevator door slid open, I have to tell my favorite cousin that it doesn't necessarily work!

"Mallory—?"

The operator shut the doors, and Mallory found herself face-to-face with Romney Sedgewick.

Oh, how could I forget that he lives here, she groaned inwardly, her heart sinking. I knew I should have walked down. Well, it's too late now. You'd better make this good, lady.

Summoning up all her inward strength and cleverness, Mallory smiled and held out her hand as if she were used to running into friends in hotel elevators. "Romney, how nice to see you again. Thea was going to ring you up tomorrow, she thinks she's found just the rug for your drawing room. You're looking wonderful," she went on, not giving him a chance to reply. "But isn't it a bit early for dinner clothes?"

She's sharp, Romney thought with admiration. Just like Alix and Thea—and my Tildy. Able to deflect any questions I have by simply turning the whole matter around. What *is* she doing here, though? Being with Rupert, most likely. I hope he knows how lucky he is.

"I'm ready for an early start to a long evening at the Whist Club," he said at last with a downward glance at his impeccable dinner clothes.

"You're not partnering in a foursome that includes Charles and Dick, are you?"

"That would be suitable, considering my ultimate intent," he responded obliquely as the car reached the main floor. "But tonight my partners are three other unattached men, just like myself."

There were any number of smart, complimentary replies Mallory might have made, but caution held her back. Who knew what those two disinterested-looking men—clearly the better sort of traveling salesmen—who were in the back of the car might assume from an off-the-cuff remark.

"Alix was so thrilled to see you last week," she said as

they left the elevator for the crowded lobby. "Are you glad you decided to come?"

"Actually, Thea threatened to resign as my interior decorator and turn me over to the mercies of Elsie de Wolfe unless I agreed to come, and after that I didn't need another word of warning to make my appearance."

"And you don't regret one second of it."

"Not after the first caviar tart." He gave her a winning smile. "I was counting on seeing you and Rupert, though."

"First we were in the living room, and then we left early to go to the theatre. Of course considering the crowd Alix had, our presence wasn't either in demand or missed."

"A lovely lady's presence is always missed."

Mallory laughed. "How very gallant of you to say so. But you'd better be careful, Romney. Now that everyone knows you're in New York to stay, you're going to be deluged with invitations. Hostesses love a man who knows his way around a compliment!"

"In New York as in London." Instead of looking troubled by Mallory's statement, he looked vastly amused. "As you warned me, I already have my share of invitations, but I'm going back to London for a short time."

"Soon?"

"Not until after your wedding. I wouldn't miss that for the world."

"I'm glad to hear that. But you'll have to meet with Thea and me before you go. We'll have samples for you to take along."

"There's no escaping decorating decisions, is there?"

"No, and I'm glad to see you're smiling," she remarked as they reached the central exit.

"You and Thea haven't given me any reason to do anything except smile."

"Tell me that again when you see your bill!"

They went through the revolving door, Mallory catching the doorman's attention immediately.

"We'll have your automobile brought around in a minute, madam."

"I hope your driver hasn't gotten into any trouble while he's been waiting for you to finish your business appointment," Romney said as they stepped to one side of the revolving door.

"Unless I missed something, I didn't have a driver when I got here, and—" She couldn't resist a conspirator's smile. "And you have a very fine way of putting things—things that other people wouldn't be so . . . tasteful about."

"Oh, I'm in the dark," Romney returned. So she was with Rupert, after all, he thought. He probably persuaded her— Stop it, you ass. You know perfectly well that no one ever makes Mallory do one single thing she doesn't want to. You're letting all of your secrecy get to you. You need a good, stiff drink. No, you need Tildy.

"Here's my car," Mallory said as her shiny Baker Electric, with one of the doorman's assistants proudly at the steering tiller, approached them. "Walk me to it, please."

"Of course." He took her arm. "I have to say this, Mallory. I've always enjoyed your company, but now I'm glad to have talent and your expertise at my disposal. Have I offended you?"

Mallory gave him a deliberately bland look, wishing that he'd phrased his compliment somewhat differently and very glad that Rupert hadn't come out. For some reason she couldn't identify, she didn't want him to see them together.

"It would take a lot more than that," she said, reaching the car's open door. "One thing, though."

"Anything. Just name it," Romney said, suddenly

sounding very American, a trick he'd picked up at Exeter.

"Don't say any of this in Rupert's hearing."

"Is he *that* jealous?"

"No, not the way you mean it. I understand what you just said, and if for one minute I thought you were trying to mash me, I'd give you a fast and expensive trip to the dentist. But certain compliments don't translate well, and I'd rather this stay just between us."

"I agree totally," Romney replied as Mallory held out her hand.

She got into her car and drove off, quickly disappearing into the busy late afternoon traffic, and a minute later, Romney was in a taximeter cab, heading for the Whist Club, neither of them having taken the slightest notice of Evelyn Weldon standing behind them, far enough away so as not to appear eavesdropping, yet close enough to hear every word, every vital word, every word important with double meanings.

Now she stood at the head of the taxi line, not quite believing her good fortune, the wheels of her mind busy absorbing what she'd heard and spinning out everything that was necessary to aid her later on—turning dross into gold, as it were.

667 Madison Avenue

An advance copy of the September fifteenth issue of *Vogue* was waiting for Mallory when she and Esme returned from their latest round of shopping and fittings and preparations for the wedding, now only ten days away.

Exercising a great deal of restraint, Mallory had put off looking at the magazine until she was dressed for dinner, and now, the fashionable periodical in her hands, she prowled around her private sitting room, crossing and recrossing the carpet of deep cream with its artfully woven rosy-pink Malmaison carnations scattered at selected intervals. She walked back and forth, hardly paying attention to the long, low-slung Louis XVI-type sofa upholstered in red velvet set beneath the windows, the Louis XV reproduction fauteuil in rose on cream figured needlepoint, and the comfortably overstuffed Empire-style bergere covered in ivory and pink striped

405

satin—all comfortable spots to sit down and read a magazine in. She paid no attention to the gifts awaiting her attention, and she didn't even go over to the French *cabinets d'historie naturelle* that were set into one wall and look behind the glass doors where the rows of shelves were the repository for her collection of Limoges boxes, bibelots that she'd purchased on her own and would eventually be offered to clients, and her mother's collection of silver-topped cranberry glass bottles.

Finally, Mallory could do nothing more than shake her head at the page on which the de Meyer photograph—the same pose which Rupert now had on his desk—she'd given them had been reprinted, and which the editor who handled such things had seen fit to caption: *Miss Mallory Kirk*, before continuing in the copy, *whose marriage to Mr. Rupert Randall is announced for September 24. Miss Kirk is the daughter of the late Mr. and Mrs. Edward Kirk and a cousin of Lady Henry Thorpe and the goddaughter of Mr. and Mrs. Newton Phipps with whom she lives.*

"Dear, sweet *Vogue*, I do love you, but there *is* more to my life than just who my parents were, who my cousin is, and that I live with godparents," she said out loud, tossing the thick magazine onto her writing table of Karelian birch where it landed squarely on the dark red leather top. "You might mention that I graduated Barnard, and that I work for Thea, but I guess that anything but the very social facts are forbidden!"

"Darling, did I hear you say something?" Esme appeared in the open doorway, still clad in her smart Poiret afternoon costume of champagne silk meteore with sleeves, belt and skirt band of fluid black moire. "You look rather put out."

"Oh, I was just telling *Vogue* what I think of it, and if Mr. Nast rings up, I'll tell him also. This sounds like I've never been to school a day in my life, and that I've never done anything more important than pick out a new hat!"

406

"Darling, no. I'm sure Condé simply told his copywriter to emphasize your background," Esme said soothingly as she came over to look at the magazine. "You know how he is."

"I know, Auntie, but I don't think any of *Vogue*'s readers would have fainted or cancelled their subscriptions because I'm a college graduate, or because I'm an interior decorator." In a gesture of conciliation, she put her arms around her godmother. "I may be making a fuss, but it seems that little things like this are getting to me. Why does everything seem to be unbearable all of a sudden?"

"You only feel that way because it's the last two weeks before your wedding," Esme replied, biting back the urge to remind Mallory that, if only she and Rupert had been willing to listen to reason and put their marriage off until the holiday season, all of the strain she was now under could have been eased. "A week from Saturday you'll be fine, and by the time you and Rupert are in California, this *Vogue* announcement will seem funny, and all you'll notice is what a good job they did with the photograph you gave them. Besides," Esme added wisely, "the *Times* will print your wedding announcement just the way you want it. Adolph thinks you're very accomplished, and he doesn't mind letting his readers share in the knowledge," she finished, kissing Mallory's cheek. "And if you'll notice my attire, you will see that you're not the only one running from pillar to post. All we're having is a little gathering for champagne and canapes before we go out to dinner, but I've been checking things through as if I were giving a ball!"

"No, we're leaving that honor to Alix," Mallory laughed, her good humor restored. "Go and get ready, Auntie. I'm going to put on my jewelry and then see what wedding gifts came in the afternoon mail," she went on, some of her enthusiasm seeping away since her sitting room now looked more like a small and expensive gift shop instead of her own refuge.

When the Phipps moved from their house on Fifth Avenue and Seventieth Street to the top floor of 667 Madison Avenue, they had given Mallory the last two of the four bedrooms for her own use. In that summer of 1902, she'd used the furniture that had filled her room overlooking Fifth Avenue, and had made only minimal changes over the next four years, but late in 1906, fired up over her job with Thea, as well as eager to try out her fledgling skills as a professional decorator, Mallory had redone both rooms along with the bathroom that separated them, completely changing both chambers to a manner she considered to be more befitting her new status.

Strange to think that the rooms, complete less than six months after she began to work with Thea, had caught exactly the spirit of the new profession of interior decorating where elegant rooms, restrained and cool yet comfortable became the mode—rooms that one was not going to tire of in a year or two.

Pausing at the threshold of her bedroom, her satin opera slippers sinking slightly into the deep ivory-colored carpeting, Mallory had to smile when she considered the fact that only four months earlier, just before she left for Europe, she'd decided that while she was in no way displeased with her rooms, some redecoration was called for. Well, as it turned out, she was decorating all right—the apartment she and Rupert would be living in.

Shaking herself out of her reverie, Mallory crossed the room, past the mirrored set of double doors that opened to display the deep closets that contained her wardrobe, to her dressing table set in front of the windows for the best light. While she could have purchased any of the delicate, antique *poudres* that were available from the city's better antique dealers and auction houses, Mallory had instead selected a long French beechwood desk designed on Art Nouveau lines and added a triple view mirror, deciding that she needed space for her ever-growing collection of cosmetics and perfumes, rather than a too-small piece of furniture because it had the "correct" provenance.

Nestled among the silver-backed brushes and combs, large crystal bottles from Guerlain and Caron, and neatly arranged pots and tubes and jars and bottles from such firms as Elizabeth Arden and Leichner and Helena Rubinstein and Harriet Hubbard Ayer and Cyclax, was a dark red leather case from Cartier. Mallory opened it slowly, delighting in the sight of the diamond and pink topaz necklace resting on a bed of pristine white satin. It had arrived that morning, accompanying a crystal vase brimming with anemones. The flowers were now on one of the ivory wood tables that flanked her bed, their wild pinwheel colors providing a bright counterpoint against the bed's ice-blue satin covering and the pale-blue and white Chinese wallpaper that had been subtly overglazed.

Carrying the necklace, she went over to one of the full-length mirrors and slipped it around the base of her throat. Mallory couldn't understand how women could put on jewelry or buy a hat while they were sitting down. It was how one looked while standing that counted, she thought as her fingers fastened the clasp of Rupert's latest present to her, and then taking a few steps backward so she could admire the contrast of the necklace with her Cheruit dinner dress of pale strawberry voile de soie with the same color applique hand embroidery and satin belt.

Since the first day of their engagement, Mallory had never been able to finish breakfast before either Rosie in the city or Muriel in the country came into her room carrying flowers and an elaborately wrapped box. First there had been a box of handmade, cream-colored Italian

409

notepaper; then an opera bag, eight inches high, made of old gold and brown Japanese brocade lined in white corded silk and a silk cord closing; and moved on to a pair of French Art Nouveau perfume bottles with silver rose motifs; a rose-point lace fan mounted on carved mother-of-pearl sticks, as well as bottles of her favorite perfumes, kid gloves, silk scarves, brocade lingerie cases, the latest books, and boxes of candy from Maillards and Louis Sherry.

But if presents from Rupert were a welcome and loving way to start each day, the wedding presents that were still pouring in were rapidly becoming another matter entirely. Back in her sitting room, Mallory surveyed the latest series of packages, their silk ribbons tied in perfect, pristine bows that only a few weeks before she would have been rapidly undoing.

If there was a saturation point for even the most lavish of presents, she'd passed it several days ago, Mallory decided. Only the decision she'd made when the day the first presents arrived—to send a thank-you letter on the same day—kept her going now.

Silver, she thought. Who could imagine there were so many forms to that precious metal? Besides the usual trays and bowls and vases and picture frames and chafing dishes and coffee and tea services, they had been inundated with lemon dishes and sugar tongs and Bar-le-Duc holders and Café Diabolique services and Turkish coffee sets. Mallory was sure all of these items would prove necessary in time, but after nearly six weeks of parting layers of tissue paper to see something gleaming in silver blinking back at her, she felt her natural avarice ebb slowly but relentlessly away.

Now, the first of the two robin's egg blue Tiffany boxes she opened did indeed add to her collection from Tiffany's Blue Book, but she regarded the engraved sterling silver traveling clock with warmth and pleasure since it was a present from the male staff of the Seligman firm. The next box was also from the office staff, the female employees this time, and Mallory unwrapped a cobalt-blue porcelain chocolate pot with two matching cups and saucers selected, Mallory was certain, by Nancy Harley.

She wrote the two thank-you notes in such a good mood that it carried over to another chafing dish—copper, this time—a pigskin case that turned out to be a fitted picnic kit ("for wonderful honeymoon motor trips," the card read), a dozen highball glasses, gold-rimmed and monogrammed, a dozen fine pottery custard cups lined in white and set in filigree frames, and a liquor set with tiny glasses and an engraved tray.

Mallory capped her fountain pen, stamped and stacked her letters, and sat back in her chair with a sigh of relief. Tomorrow morning, the bonded messenger service they'd engaged would arrive promptly at nine as it had every weekday morning for the past five weeks, and take her latest acquisitions to Cliff and Julie's house where they were being displayed in one of the drawing rooms. On her wedding day, until the music began and she came down the aisle, she knew the gifts would be the focal point of almost all conversation among the guests. It was all part of getting married, she reminded herself. You couldn't escape it even if you eloped. But at this minute she wasn't sure which she was more worn out by, the presents or the fittings—the ceaseless, endless rounds of shopping and fittings.

At first, Mallory had been sure her trousseau needs were minimal. Her going-away dress with all the accessories; nightgowns and negligées and tea gowns, the most provocative she could find; and a few elegantly tailored suits and subtle dinner dresses. After her visits to Paris' fashion salons, she hardly had to spend her days in their New York versions.

If only it were turning out to be that simple, Mallory thought.

No matter how extensive her wardrobe, a bride always needs more—more lacy lingerie in rainbow colors, more fine accessories, more hats the size of tea trays, more dresses of every description and for every occasion.

With the exception of her shoes and hats, everything could have been made at Lucile's, but Mallory liked variety, and since the middle of August, her shopping trips had taken her from the Milgrim brothers' shop on Second Avenue and Houston Street where, in small quarters, women's suits with narrow shoulders, tightly molded sleeves and snugly fitted waistlines were created; to the far more elegant salon of Henri Bendel on Ninth Street, where the walls were fitted with bamboo from the owner's native Louisiana; and followed closely by a visit around the corner to East Tenth Street to Carnegie Ladies Hatters, where petite, blond Hattie Carnegie, who couldn't sew a stitch and left such work to her assistant Rose Roy, designed divine hats and made adaptations of the best Paris models in her tiny shop.

Over the past ten years, Fifth Avenue from Twenty-third to Fifty-seventh Streets, as well as the side streets directly to the east and west, had become home to the most fashionable women's stores, and Mallory began her northward shopping trek in the Thirties. Here, Maison Bernard on Thirty-first Street showed their wealth of imported hats, the best of the line from Reboux and Talbot and Suzanne and Georgette; while Bergdorf-Goodman's at Thirty-two West Thirty-second Street, offered exquisitely designed clothes and fittings that were painstakingly, exactingly made; and Stein and Blaine in their Gothic building on Thirty-third Street behind the Waldorf-Astoria, had an appropriately uniformed maid to open the door to clients, and a house designer, Miss E. M. A. Steinmetz, who created such original dresses and suits that there was little need for the owners to import Paris models for adaptation.

Further along the avenue there were the required visits to Madame Frances, considered by some stuffy sorts to be somewhat risqué since so many of the city's most expensively kept women dressed here; to Thurn's, the exclusive import house, where a liveried Scottish butler tended the door; to the House of Tappe, where imports from the best French houses were offered along with Herman Patrick Tappe's own creations in a setting that included two tea gardens, trellised walls, statues of Nubian slaves, and lamps in whose bases goldfish swam.

Her visits to Alice Maynard and J. A. Giddings and L. P. Hollander's and Redfern's passed through her mind. She was reviewing Madame Mogabgab's and Bonwit Teller and Lichtenstein's and Lord and Taylor (such a nice store, *when* were they going to move to Fifth Avenue?) and. . . .

"I hope it's me you're dreaming about."

Mallory's eyes flew open. "Is there anyone else?" she asked joyfully, getting swiftly to her feet to fling her arms around Rupert who stood at the edge of her writing table.

His arms closed around her, and he waited for Mallory to finish trailing a row of kisses along his cheek before capturing her mouth in a kiss that left them clinging to each other.

"Will you still marry me if I tell you that I've been reviewing my shopping trips, not dreaming about you?" she said, slipping her fingers under the starched wing collar of his dress shirt. "Of course, you were next on my list of daydreams. Number three," she couldn't resist adding. "First was the matter of our gifts. I don't know if I can face another one today."

"Can you try? Just one? For me?" Rupert's voice was teasing and cajoling as she rested her head against his shoulder. "I've brought you something very special."

"Besides yourself?"

"A bangle or two," he added, kissing her again. "Now, I'm not used to having my presents ignored." His arms tightened skillfully around her waist. "Is this what you do every morning? Put my presents aside until you've finished the *Times*?"

"And don't forget the *World*," she laughed, pressing closer against him. "No, I always open your present first."

"Then what are you waiting for?" he questioned, his silver glance going from her face to the fancifully wrapped box at the other end of the writing table and back again.

"Another kiss."

Several minutes later, Mallory removed the gift wrapping to find a long rectangular box of dark green leather.

"It's a fire-proof jewel case," Rupert offered. "It's made of steel and asbestos—the newest thing."

"And heavy."

He kissed her neck, just above the glittering circle of diamonds. "That may be because of what's inside," he said, guiding her fingers to the lock.

Arranged on the green velvet interior was a double strand of natural black pearls with a diamond clasp curled up next to a four-strand bracelet of carved chrusoprase resting next to a huge gold butterfly set with emeralds, rubies, pearls and sapphires; a modern Lalique necklace of gold, diamonds and aquamarines contrasted against the utter simplicity and perfection of a single strand of rose pearls with a pavé diamond clasp.

For a minute, Mallory found herself speechless. "How do you always know what I like? It's jewelry for California."

"I hadn't thought of it exactly like that, but since you insist—" Rupert's smile deepened. "I really decided that

414

this was the best way to show you how much I appreciate your latest gift to me—Alfred Noyes twelve-volume biography of Sir Francis Drake, delivered daily, volume by volume."

"And if you've figured out the days properly, you know that the last one will be delivered on our wedding day. A good way for you to mark the time."

"I have a better one," he said, pulling her back in his arms.

Mallory melted happily against Rupert, closing her eyes and fluttering her mascaraed lashes against his cheeks in butterfly kisses. They were laughing too hard to get in any serious kissing, and the sound of the doorbell ended their interlude.

"They're here," Mallory said, reluctantly pulling back. "How do I look?"

"Beautiful!"

"You'd say that if I were drenched in a thunder-storm!" She kissed his cheek again, quickly, glad to see that Rupert looked like himself again. It had been at the back of her mind that if he came in looking as worn and tired as he had at the Knickerbocker, she was going to talk with him, make him see that it was important for them not to postpone their wedding trip to California. She had her arguments all lined up, but now he looked so well, so relaxed, that she had hesitated and had lost her chance.

"You could use a fresh application of lipstick."

"And whose fault is that?" Mallory asked archly, and retrieved the extra vanity case she kept in the writing table.

"Oh, anything to watch while you put on your frosting," Rupert replied as he viewed with great interest Mallory applying fresh powder to her face and a new layer of her favorite Elizabeth Arden lipstick.

"I think the only doubtful thing about having a big

415

wedding is that you make up a huge guest list and there's no way of telling who's going to accept," Rupert said, amused, as they walked down the length of the foyer, all marbleized walls and Eighteenth-Century English mirrors and console tables, from Mallory's sitting room, through the reception room and into the drawing room.

"I don't think it's so strange that Regina and Ian decided to come in from California. They usually do about this time of year."

"Yes, but you have to admit that it was quite a surprise when Hugo and Edith said they were coming over."

"Well, Uncle Newton said that they had to do something between the time fishing in Scotland ends and the hunting begins!"

"That's a different way of looking at it. But personally I think that Edith and Hugo had a long talk with Cecily and Isaac and Patrick and Lizzie, and they all probably decided that it was up to the Barrys to cross the water and represent London, particularly since he has more of a reason to visit America than the rest of them," Rupert said as they reached the drawing room where Hugo Barry, the Earl of Tilmore, and his illegitimate half-brother, Ian MacIverson of Santa Barbara, California, and their wives, were waiting to greet them.

In the Phipps grand drawing room with its pale lemon-colored walls and graceful mélange of antique treasures and excellent furniture, Kathleen and Sally, both maids caught up in the vicarious thrill of the wedding preparations, were offering tall flute glasses filled with champagne and setting down plates of hot cheese puffs, more impressed than usual. Even with the vast amount of wedding gifts and the clothes and the round of parties, there was still something special about having an English earl and his countess sitting on the yellow silk sofa, exclaiming over the green and gold Venetian secretary, the eight-panel black and gold lacquer Coromandel screen, and the Chinese lacquer tables displaying silver-framed photographs and small Lalique ornaments.

Hugo Tilmore, dark and handsome and regarded as something of a wit in his social circle, was offering his congratulations to Mallory and Rupert in his usual manner—a deft combination of true affection and sophisticated weariness.

"Well, my dear, you might have dropped a hint or two about your future plans when we were all together in London," he said, kissing Mallory's cheek and shaking Rupert's hand.

"So the invitation was a surprise to you, then?"

"Oh, you could have knocked us all over with the proverbial feather."

"Good, that's just what we wanted!"

"You still could have let us in on your happy news."

"Let's just say I came back from Chicago, and was fortunate enough to sweep Mallory off her feet," Rupert put in. He liked Hugo, but there were limits, and he was well aware that this man could make one say something that one never intended to. "Of course we hope that we didn't throw a monkey wrench into any of your precious plans."

"We were planning to come over anyway, later in October," Edith said as they all sat down. A warmly attractive woman in her early thirties, she was elegantly turned out in Paquin's ivory silk embroidered with gold beads and thread and trimmed with gold filet lace. "It was simply a matter of moving our plans up by a month."

"A bit of a family reunion, actually. Don't you agree, Ian?" he questioned his half-brother who, at forty-two, was his senior by several years.

"There are worse places to have our semi-annual reunion than at a wedding," Ian retorted. He was equally

417

as handsome as Hugo, although one had to look closely to catch their resemblance. It was obvious at once that his long years in India, years that had made him a millionaire many times over, had left a maturity on him that his titled brother would never have. "It's rather appropriate, considering that we finally met and became friends at another wedding—mine," he reminded him with a smile.

"And if anyone had told me in 1902 that a year later, when I went to India for the *World*, I'd meet your half-brother and end up becoming your sister-in-law, Hugo, I would have had a good laugh," Regina Bolt MacIverson, who, along with Alix and Thea and Nela had cut a social swath through New York, added in great amusement.

"Just remember who gave you your letter of introduction," Hugo pointed out, vastly enjoying himself. "I was doing a bit of informal matchmaking back then."

"Now you tell me," Regina shot back, amused, pushing a jeweled pin back into her golden brown hair, her Poiret dress of cream silk chiffon trimmed with cream satin and pale blue silk embroidered in gold and silver beads a perfect background for her sapphire jewelry. "And all these years I've been thinking that you wrote that letter because I'd asked you who to see in India so many times, it was the easiest way not to have to answer any more questions from a reporter!"

"Haven't you heard that it's the engaged couple who's supposed to get all the attention?" Rupert said at last, all their good-natured sniping over. They settled back to enjoy the champagne and canapes. "Since you're all staying together at the Plaza, I suggest that you clear up all those amusing little problems when you get back to the hotel."

"Rupert has an excellent point," Esme agreed. Her slightly harried air of only a few hours before, Mallory was happy to observe, hadn't outlasted her changing clothes. In Drecoll's silver gray satin overlaid with gold

418

lace and rhinestone trim, she was every inch the cool, collected hostess that no guest would ever have the slightest disagreement with. "As an expert onlooker for the past five weeks, I can tell you that whenever the conversation gets too involved, or the crowd too large, Mallory and Rupert have been known to slip off."

"Yes, the Champagne Porch considers us to be their best clients," Mallory couldn't resist saying.

"The four of us were thinking that the Champagne Porch would be an ideal place for dinner since the weather is still so nice, but I've heard it's rather like Maxim's—an excellent restaurant, but not one you go to with your wife!"

"Hugo, you're absolutely horrid!" Edith gasped.

"Besides, this is New York where anything and everything is proper order," Newton added as their laughter increased. "If you plan to use French form in this city, you're in for more problems than I can tell you about."

"Which means that if you're a wise man, you'll never be seen dining intimately *à deux* in a fashionable dining spot with a lady who isn't your wife," Regina offered.

"A very wise bit of advice," Ian said, slipping an arm around his wife's shoulders. "And now, since we've both only just arrived from opposite ends as it appears, you might tell us what we should be doing while we're here."

"How long are you planning to stay this time?" Newton asked.

"Regina is planning on the next ten weeks, at least. That will give me time to take care of all my business interests, and for Reggie to see her publisher. That will give us plenty of time to do all our Christmas shopping before we go back to Santa Barbara in time to welcome Rupert and Mallory." He turned to them. "When are you planning to come south?"

Rupert looked at Mallory for confirmation. "Around

419

December twentieth—I want to show Mallie San Francisco. Will that be good for you?"

"No problem at all."

"Good, Ian, that means you and Regina can be part of the party I'm planning for December tenth," Esme said delightedly. "That's the opening night of the new Puccini opera, *The Girl of the Golden West.* I've decided that by then I'll have recovered enough from the wedding to have an opera party. I'd love to be able to include you and Regina, and of course Edith and Hugo, if you're still in town."

"Oh, we'll not only be here, but right now we're considering going to California for Christmas," Hugo said as William and Adele arrived.

For the next few minutes there was the usual exchange of greetings before the discussion turned back to *La Fanciulla del West,* to Enrico Caruso and Emmy Destinn, who would star in it; to Toscanini, who would be conducting; and the composer, Giacomo Puccini, who would be coming over for the premier.

"It's nice to have some variety in our overseas visitors," Adele remarked in a fine good humor, her Doucet dress of champagne blue and green silk voile a colorful contrast to the pale silk-upholstered chair she was sitting in. "Quite a bit of London has transported itself to Manhattan island!"

"Whom?" Hugo inquired, intrigued. "And here I thought Edie and I were pioneers of sorts."

"Well, Romney Sedgewick, for one—"

"Romney? So this is where he came."

"He seems to be quite happy," Bill said, unperturbed by Hugo's tone, but looking rather pale.

"And then there's Evelyn Weldon," Adele went on in a less than pleased voice, and then paused. "Hugo, is something the matter?"

Instantly, all eyes went to Hugo Tilmore, whose face

was rather ashen, and his mouth a hard, tight line. In the space of a minute, all the laughter, all the amusement and wit had disappeared.

Edith touched her husband's hand. "Darling—"

"There's nothing wrong." His voice was quiet and composed. "It's simply that Evelyn is not one of my favorite people," he went on, looking more like himself. "She rather vanished from London, and I never thought she was coming here."

"Well, she's hardly popular with us," Mallory offered. "You should hear what Alix has to say!"

"Knowing her, it's probably unique and interesting and totally accurate!" With a flash of his usual smile, he helped himself to a cheese puff.

The crisis, whatever it was, was over, and as if by some silent signal of agreement, they all moved on to other topics, and a few minutes later it was time to leave for dinner.

"Now that was rather unexpected," Rupert whispered to Mallory as they trailed the others out of the apartment and toward the elevator.

"Oh, I don't know. It was a chance to see another side of Hugo." She tucked an arm through his. "He's rather like you in a way—nothing, or next to nothing, gets through his facade."

"Did you see Dad?" Rupert asked, totally passing over her observation. "He doesn't look too well."

"It's been a hot summer, and none of us got the long rest we planned on. You've given me a couple of bad moments, also."

"I'm not thirty, and as healthy as a horse," he said, pushing aside his medical discussion with John Stern. There was no reason to bring that up; they'd be leaving for California before he knew it, and the next weeks were going to pass by in a flash. Well, not too much of a flash, he amended silently, thinking of their wedding night.

421

"Dad is at the stage where he should be easing off. Cliff has been taking on more and more responsibility for the firm."

"Oh, Rupert, I didn't know. But he's so strong . . ."

"He is, and it's more of a distribution of some extra responsibility, but still . . ."

"Are you getting some of that responsibility?"

"A few crumbs here and there."

"Oh, poor baby." Mallory laughed and kissed his cheek. "It's time for dinner, and I'll see to it that you're properly fed. There's no such thing as crumbs in our life!"

They went to Sherry's, to a large table in the restaurant's best room; a table rich with crisp white linen and shining silver and crystal and a special floral arrangement ordered from Thorleys.

As they ate clear consommé and mousseline of sole Newburg and saddle of milk-fed veal with cream sauce and perfectly steamed asparagus and ended with a floating heart *merveilleux*—a heart of frozen whipped cream encased in chocolate walls and covered with vanilla sauce and fresh strawberries—Mallory felt all her complaints, all her worry, and all her sense of being rushed to the breaking point, slowly leave her.

All serious topics of conversation had been banished, and if a curtain had been pulled back earlier to show the pain of one of their party, the weariness of another, and the concern of a third, it was all now concealed under good talk and laughter.

As they made yet another toast and exclaimed over the dessert, Mallory reviewed her conversation with Rupert. Should she have made a case about their going to California without delay, or would Rupert have balked because he was afraid of appearing that he didn't care about his position?

I know the answer to that, she told herself, holding Rupert's hand under the table. But I also know that Rupert is more tired than he'll ever tell me. I saw that for myself at the Knickerbocker. So much for our stolen afternoon of passion. I have to look out for Rupert, make sure that he gets enough rest and the right food and not work harder than he has to. Simple things, easy things, but maybe for once they'll work.

Mallory knew she'd made the best decision possible— the only decision possible—but as she sat at the glittering table, she found herself speculating on how long it would be before she'd regret not having insisted on what she knew was right.

It is not by chance that the phrase "happy pair" is one of the most trite in our language, for happiness above all is the inner essential that must dominate a perfect wedding. . . . The radiance of a truly happy bride is so beautifying that even a plain girl is made pretty, and a pretty one, divine. . . . They both look as though there were sunlight behind their eyes, as though their mouths irresistibly turned to smiles. No other quality of a bride's expression is so beautiful as radiance; the visible proof of perfect happiness which endears its possessor to all beholders and gives to the simplest little wedding complete beauty.

—Emily Post, *Etiquette*

923 Fifth Avenue

Mr. and Mrs. Newton Phipps
request the honour of your presence
at the marriage of their goddaughter
Mallory
to
Mr. Rupert Randall
on Saturday the twenty-fourth of September
at four o'clock
at the house of Mr. and Mrs. Seligman
Nine Twenty-Three Fifth Avenue
New York

R.s.v.p.

The invitations had gone out in plenty of time, and on the appropriate day, if an informal poll were to be taken among the large group of reporters and photographers gathered outside 923 Fifth Avenue, even the most hard-bitten, world-weary members of the Fourth Estate would agree that covering *this* wedding was a cut above their usual assignments. As a rule, society weddings were a necessary evil at worst, and at best a respectable way to fill the Sunday rotogravure section. To be sure, they sold papers, but so did train wrecks and disasters at sea—far more interesting fare than a wedding where one had to be sure to capture the most important of the guests as they arrived—both on photographic film as well as making note of the female guests' costumes. Still, the men and women of the press agreed, being assigned to the Kirk-Randall wedding was several cuts above the usual affair of this sort.

First and foremost was the manner in which they were treated.

Even the most energetic and accurate of society reporters had over the years grown used to having her inquiries about the bride's trousseau and the gifts—to say nothing of the guest list and the menu—answered in either the briefest of terms or else turned away altogether, but from the first telephone call it was obvious that this latest wedding of the autumn season that was already providing them with at least four other equally important matches, was going to be handled in quite a unique way.

There was no struggle to obtain the details of the wedding dress or the going-away dress or the brides-maids' costumes, no need to bribe underpaid vendeuses and fitters. Every minute detail so dear to the heart of the devoted reader was supplied through Mrs. Phipps' social secretary. Over the weeks since the engagement was announced and the wedding date set, they'd learned the names of the wedding party, the menu of the formal, sit-down meal that would be served following the ceremony, which musicians had been engaged and what they would play, what flowers had been selected, and just a few days before they'd been supplied with the all-important final guest list.

But best of all was the way in which they had been allowed to view the wedding presents. Yesterday morning, on the dot of half-past eleven, all the reporters who now stood waiting on the sidewalk for the great event to get under way, had arrived en masse on the doorstep of 923 Fifth Avenue, and were taken by the butler to the doorway of a drawing room where a pleasant young woman was waiting for them. She introduced herself as Miss Keyes, Mrs. Seligman's social secretary, and then ushered them into a room with ivory walls, an ivory-colored marble mantel, a Chinese rug of blue and ivory, and old-blue and silver curtains—a perfect background for displaying the presents, all accompanied by the givers' cards. All the furniture had been removed, and tables covered with plain white damask cloths had been arranged along the sides and down the center of the room, much like a very expensive, very exclusive shop, with the added touch of several easels.

Instantly they noted with approval that this cache of treasures was under the supervision of two private detectives who in turn were kept under a close eye by their boss, George Kelly, well-known to the male contingent of reporters as Big George Kelly back in the days when he had been the bouncer—and much more, so the rumor ran—at Sinclair Poole's Bowery saloon. But those days were long past, and all concerned had gone on to more respectable—if not richer—lives.

For the next hour they were allowed to wander among the fabulous, gift-laden menagerie.

Appropriate notes were made on the blue and gold

Royal Worcester tea service from the Earl and Countess of Tilmore, the Fabergé clock from the Earl and Countess of Saltlon, the Spanish silver cache-pot presented by Don Renaldo and Dona Imelda de Veiga, the rock crystal-etched French lamps from Richard and Megan North, the crystal and jade bedside clock from Georges and Bettina Bergery, the ivory and silver box from Romney Sedgewick, the Wedgewood tray from Philip and Kezia Leslie, the pair of French asparagus plates sent by Solange de Renille, the antique Imari bowl from Ian and Regina MacIverson, and the gold and enamel Cartier mystery clock with a rose-point diamond dial from Thea and Charles de Renille.

Later, as they were served coffee and sandwiches and cake, they agreed that it was the paintings—all of which could have formed the core collection for a small, progressive museum—which were the most attention-getting presents of all, and debate ranged as to which was the most impressive of all. Was it the shockingly brilliant red Matisse given by Henry and Alix Thorpe; the small, elegant Marie Laurencin sent by Kathryn Neal; or the bouquet of flowers by Odilon Redon, where the anemones were rendered so perfectly that one could practically smell them and had been selected by the Newton Phipps as their goddaughter's wedding present? Others argued that the William Seligmans' offering of a Vuillard garden was a sight that could cheer even the most dour of reporters. And there were those who were fond of the growing field of American Impressionists represented by Melinda and Evan Prescott's gift of a soothing garden landscape by John Henry Twatchman; Gareth and Susannah Seligman's gift of a William Glackens rendering of a garden overlooking Long Island Sound; and Edmund Tarbell's soft green view of Marblehead Bay selected by James and Katharine Seligman.

The vote, however, was unanimous when it came to Clifford and Julia Seligman's present. It took great wit to offer a case each of 1874 Chateau Rausan Segla, 1888 Chateau Margaux and 1902 Moet and Chandon, accompanied by a small and perfect Renoir oil.

Now, at shortly after three, a warm September afternoon, the reporters' and photographers' pleasant conversation was rapidly being replaced by a more businesslike air. Some of the more enterprising ones had been there since noon, and had already made note of the arrival of the flowers from Thorleys and the cake from Sherry's, as well as the musicians who'd made their appearance an hour before and the prerequisite sight of Western Union men delivering handfuls of congratulatory telegrams. The red and white striped awning that provided covering from the front door to the edge of the curb, and the red carpet beneath it, had been set up within the past hour and a half.

The front door opened and Hughes, the Clifford Seligmans' butler, came out and proceeded to the edge of the curb where he would open all automobile and carriage doors.

Pencils moved across pads and photographers readied their cameras as the latest model Packard limousine pulled up and Rupert Randall and his best man, Henry Thorpe, stepped out, both of them in perfect morning dress.

Finally, they all agreed. It was going to be one long afternoon, but at least it was a first-class wedding. The accessibility to all the information they needed, the hospitality of the house yesterday afternoon, and the excitement that went with the arrival of the guests all made it a bit easier.

The female reporters made their first notes, and after their first good look at Rupert Randall, there wasn't one of them who didn't think that Mallory Kirk was one very, very lucky woman. . . .

"Rupert and I should have eloped."

Mallory sat in front of the dressing table in the pink and cream guest room, working on her makeup, when the thought struck.

"Oh, I know how you feel, but it won't last," Julie advised her, checking her own reflection in the full-length mirror. Her dress, a Cheruit froth of elaborately embroidered champagne-colored bengaline silk, was perfect for her duties as hostess. "I'll tell you something guaranteed to make you feel better. Cliff and I almost eloped," she confided. "About a month before our wedding we decided we couldn't stand all the fuss and the preparations and all the going back and forth between Philadelphia and New York, so one morning we slipped away, took a commuter train and got off at Bryn Mawr. Cliff had the address of a justice of the peace."

Smiling now, Mallory put down her powder puff. "Needless to say, you didn't go through with it."

"No, but we came awful close. In the end, we found a restaurant and had lunch and a long talk. I won't bore you with the details—and in fifteen years of retrospection they were *very* boring—but we decided that from that afternoon on we were going to ignore all the bothersome questions like why I'd ordered my dress from Paquin instead of Worth and did Cliff *have* to have Sinclair Poole as his best man, and just concentrate on each other and enjoy the good parts." Julie came over to Mallory and put gentle hands on her shoulders. "You and Rupert have been having fun, haven't you?"

"Yes. Oh, yes. But lately—"

"It's been a bit too much, being on display," Julie finished. "Rather like all those presents downstairs."

"That's a little *too* accurate," Mallory smiled, and went back to her maquillage, putting the finishing touches on delicate layers of Leichner's foundation creme, Elizabeth Arden powder and lipstick; Harriet Hubbard Ayers liquid rouge tinted her cheekbones and softly colored powder and kohl and Rimmel mascara highlighted her eyes.

"Look at it this way," Julie advised as she moved around the room, checking to make sure all of the wedding ensemble was in order, "it's three now, by five you'll be married, and after that—" Her voice trailed airily off, the conclusion crystal clear to both of them, and they traded knowing smiles as Julie slipped out of the room.

And that's the only way to think about it, Mallory told herself, checking her reflection. Hour by hour, the way you've been doing it since last night. Down the hall in another bedroom, Alix, her matron of honor, and Melinda, Kate, Marie-France and Camillia, her bridesmaids, were dressing, and she could hear their laughter.

My last few minutes of solitude.

The thought flew through Mallory's mind, and automatically she transferred her engagement ring—the ring that hadn't left her finger from the moment Rupert had put it there six weeks before—to her right hand.

That one action, so simple and yet so significant, sent a wave of excitement through her. Here was where it all began. From the moment they'd announced their engagement, every detail, every decision, led up to this moment. Even all of the preparations that had gone on so far today were now mere prelude for what was to come.

With a slight sense of *déjà-vu*, Mallory regarded her reflection. Pierre, the hairdresser who had trained in Paris alongside the famous Antoine, had arrived shortly after one and had proceeded to do the women's hair, arranging Julie's first, and then the attendants, before coming in to brush her hair out until gold threads

431

appeared among the brown, and then twist it into a high coiffure to best set off her veil. It looked beautiful, but it also reminded her of how she had worn her hair a few years before.

And that was a long time ago, Mallory thought, knowing that it no longer mattered. What did matter was beginning today.

Her glance fell on the decorative little clock amid all the bottles and pots and brushes on the dressing table. Three-ten. Fourteen hours since she'd last seen Rupert, and fifty minutes away from the moment when she would begin her walk down the stairs and then down the aisle where she would see him again and become his wife.

A few weeks earlier, when Rupert had expressed no interest in a bachelor party, and the full-scale wedding rehearsal—with Thea thoughtfully acting as "bride"—was scheduled for Thursday, Alix had decided Friday was the perfect night for herself and Henry to give the bridal couple a gala party. But what had been planned as an elegant dinner-dance rapidly ballooned into an equally elegant yet full-scale private ball.

Out of a sense of what was fair and what was utterly correct, Alix had invited everyone who had accepted an invitation to the wedding. Not everyone who was coming on Saturday afternoon came on Friday night, of course, but at the height of the party it certainly seemed like it. Not that Mallory and Rupert cared.

It was well after midnight before the crowd began to thin, and nearly one before the occupants of the Thorpes' ballroom and drawing room were reduced to the main participants.

"In the true spirit of the Twentieth Century, Mallory is seeing *me* home!" Rupert announced as the Phipps prepared to leave.

"I'll meet you downstairs in a few minutes," Mallory said, choking back her laughter. "After all, I have to deliver Rupert to Sackett's safekeeping. He promised me that he'd lock Rupert in his room so he can't take advantage of his last hours of bachelorhood!"

Together they walked down the ornate wrought iron staircase, from the sixth floor down to the fourth, without exchanging a word, and Mallory felt achingly aware of the silence, made all the more deep after the noise of the party, and of Rupert's left arm, tight around her waist.

"I've just realized that we're only six weeks short of seven years," Rupert said, his glance sweeping around the semi-private fourth-floor hallway, and then coming to rest on her, first admiring her Poiret gown of milk white Liberty satin with mother-of-pearl lights and a bodice of fine white lace over violet silk. His eyes glowed like melted silver. "Do you remember?"

"It's nothing I'd ever want to forget." Mallory not only knew what he was referring to, but as they approached the hallway, her own mind had moved in the same direction, moving backwards to remember their first real kiss, their first encounter with the passion that would eventually make them lovers, then tear them apart, and finally heal their rift and bring them back together again. She traced the strong line of his jaw. "Some things that work well bear repeating—again and again."

Rupert's mouth brushed against hers, gently pressing her backwards until her back was touching the wall, and Mallory put her arms around his neck.

"I never thought you'd get cold feet now. You're a little late for that," she said provocatively. "It's Saturday . . . fifteen hours from now we'll be married, and by tomorrow at this time . . ."

Her voice trailed off as an irresistible force that needed

433

no explanation drew them together, and they met each other halfway in a kiss that was reminiscent of the very first one they'd shared together in the same exact spot. Rupert's arms tightened swiftly, and in the dim, silent hallway, Mallory pressed herself eagerly against him, triumphantly enjoying his reaction to her at the same moment her senses began to dissolve into streaks of bright colors as his mouth parted hers and his began its intimate exploration.

"Were you really planning to put me in Sackett's watchful care?" he questioned an endless time later, his voice heavy. "It might not be such a bad idea. A few more minutes like this and my brain will be cooked oatmeal."

"A few more minutes and we'll both be totally disgraced," Mallory said a little shakily, hoping her knees weren't going to give out. "Wait with me until the elevator comes, then go in and go to bed and dream about me," she went on tenderly, tracing the planes of his face with her fingertips. "I want you to know that the past six weeks have been perfect, and I'm glad that we've had this time, but now we need a demarcation point—a short, necessary separation. When the elevator door closes, I want to know that the next time we see each other it will be four in the afternoon, in the ballroom at Cliff and Julie's, when I walk down the aisle and stand beside you and know that a little while after that we'll be husband and wife."

The opening strains of Handel's Avioso in D Major drifted upward from the spot where the orchestra was seated, bringing Mallory out of her reverie.

When it came to selecting the music that would precede the ceremony, Mallory and Rupert had decided against any vocal selections, both of them having suffered through too many weddings with full choirs as

434

well as the almost-mandatory soloist to put the guests through the same selections they'd heard at any other number of fashionable weddings, and wanted to spare their guests any similar discomfort. The Handel selection would be followed by Purcell's Prelude in G and Bach's Siciliano from the Second Sonata for Flute and Clavier and Air from Suite in D for strings—perfect music to welcome the early arrivals and make the waiting easier.

Mallory was spraying on a last application of *Aprés l'Ondée* when the door opened and Julie reentered the room.

"Are you ready?" she asked with a happy smile. "Alix'll be here in a moment."

Mallory put the atomizer down, her heart pounding in a new pattern. "I thought the music was never going to start. Is Aunt Esmé here yet—and Rupert?"

"Yes to both questions. Rupert's settled down in the library with Henry and Cliff for moral support, and Esme's stopped in to see the bridesmaids."

She absorbed that information, and looked at the bed where her wedding gown was waiting for her. "Julie, I really don't believe it's finally happening. Do you know that through all those endless fittings I never once felt like a bride, not even when it was finished and Jean Parke made the pencil sketch of me for *Vogue* and Lallie Charles took the formal picture. All it meant was that I wouldn't have to spend any more afternoons at Lucile's having pins stuck in me!"

"I know, the reality of the situation hits each bride at another time. For some, it's from the very first fitting, and others not until they've actually said the magic words." Julie's expression was a mixture of amusement and symathy. "I wouldn't think that any woman who had such an extremely early realization—or such a delayed one—has much chance of a happy marriage. Your reaction sounds as if it's come at just the right moment.

435

But how do you feel—really?"

"A little nervous, somewhat excited, very happy—and I can't wait to see Rupert again!"

"That sounds just about perfect!" Julie overcame her laughter as the door opened again. "Oh, Esme, Alix, you both look stunning!"

"Thank you, dear, and you might add I'm rather nervous as well—which is particularly surprising since I thought I wasn't going to be!" Esme said, nonetheless looking very calm and collected in a charming Lucile gown that combined a long tunic of shaded lavender chiffon over a skirt of embroidered silk. "So many things can go wrong at the last moment."

"Oh, Auntie, don't worry. You know Julie has everything under control!"

"Mallory's right," Alix advised, briefly hugging Esme. "And I have to say that of all the times I've been in a wedding party, this is the first time I've actually enjoyed my dress!"

As with all bridesmaids' dresses in all weddings, Mallory had selected one model that would be complimentary to her attendants, the only difference being in the gradation of the colors. Traditionally, the bridesmaids wore the paler shades, with the matron of honor in a deeper tone, but with her innate taste for the way things should look, Mallory had chosen the slightly deeper shades for Kate and Marie-France, a paler selection for Melinda and Camillia, and for Alix, the softest tones of all.

"I've never liked the look of a matron of honor in a deep pink or rose-colored dress walking in front of the bride," she had pointed out during their first visit to Lucile's to select the models. "A palette doesn't work like that—it has to flow softly toward white," she finished emphatically, affectively ending the directrice's conception that all brides—no matter how intelligent—weren't brave enough to depart from the norm. Following that, the elegant woman was wise enough to hold her peace and bring out the samples of silk and chiffon. After all, Lady Duff-Gordon hadn't founded her business only to end up being thought of as . . . well, as stodgy and set in their ways as the House of Worth.

No one, absolutely no one, would think she'd made an error in judgment regarding her bridesmaids' dresses, Mallory thought, regarding Alix with quiet satisfaction.

Her dress was a combination of the palest pink chiffon, the thinnest and most transparent available, set over equally pale French-blue satin, with the overskirt of narrow, close plaits falling to just below her knees and bordered in a thin blue satin ribbon. The round, scooped neck was outlined with a plaited frill of chiffon, and the delicately patterned lace overlaying the bodice also formed sheer, elbow-length sleeves. In an innovative move, the hem of the skirt ended above Alix's slender ankles, showing off her pale blue silk stockings and shoes; and her hat, in place of the typical large-brimmed picture hat, was a Cossack-style turban of pastel blue chip straw on a wire foundation so that it was high and straight up from the sides of her head and was veiled in an ornamental cloud of pink tulle laid in cobweb folds.

"Are the other girls ready?" Mallory said at last with another quick look at the clock.

"Just about," Alix smiled.

"And I think it's about time for you, too," Julie put in. "You should be in your dress before they begin to play Bonnet's 'Romance sans paroles.'"

As Julie spoke, Mallory stood up and untied the belt of the plain white satin robe she wore over her cream silk and lace Lucile lingerie. Smiling, she laid the robe over the back of a chair and put on her embroidered satin slippers. Her stockings, made of the finest white thread silk with an inset of Brussels lace, were designed especially for bridal wear by Onyx, and Alix and Kate and Marie-France and Camillia had each contributed toward the hundred-dollar cost of the hosiery, and presented the pair to Mallory as their special gift to her.

Unlike some brides, Mallory had decided that she didn't want her bridesmaids—except for Alix—to watch her being hooked into her wedding dress. She would be on display in a short while, and she wanted to keep as much of her privacy as she could for as long as possible.

"When Jean Parke did her sketch of me for *Vogue*, she said it would probably be captioned: 'Miss Mallory Kirk in her wedding gown of satin draped in chiffon and duchesse lace,'" Mallory observed as Rosie, who had been Esme's maid for over twenty years, and Guiliana, who was Julie's personal maid, joined them. "And as far as it goes, she's right, but it doesn't do this beautiful thing justice."

Only a woman as tall as Mallory could carry off the glorious creation made of beautiful fabrics richly embroidered and draped and festooned with duchesse lace that she was stepping into, smoothing and adjusting before both personal maids began the intricate work of hooking up the myriad tiny hooks and eyes.

The low, square neck—duplicating as much as possible the neckline of the ball gown she'd worn exactly six weeks earlier—left her elegant throat free, and the gown itself was a shimmering length of satin that slipped over her hips into a long, sheathlike skirt and train. The chiffon tunic—embroidered in a design of graceful sprays of orange blossoms and trimmed with a deep flounce of duchesse lace—was caught low on the sides and knotted so that it seemed to lose itself toward the back of the skirt.

Mallory regarded her reflection in the mirror. "It was worth every single fitting," she told the other women as she watched her skin take on a special glow—both from the fabric and the anticipation of what was to come.

Before she could say anything else, the door opened and Camillia Leslie, almost nineteen, a sophomore at Barnard, and as tall and leggy as her cousins, hovered on the threshold.

"I've been sent as an emissary by my fellow bridesmaids to see if we're welcome," she said merrily, her dark chestnut hair and creamy coloring set off to perfection by her costume. "Marie-France and Kate and Melinda said that since I was family, it was safest to let me make the inquiry!"

"Yes—all are now welcome," Mallory said, taking a few steps in her gown, making sure she could move comfortably. "We should have our flowers brought up, also. We'd be a very odd wedding party if we start down the stairs without them!" As she spoke, all of bridal nerves, that last attack of apprehension—not over Rupert, but over what the rest of the afternoon would require of her—lost its grip and floated away.

The music wafting up to them now was the opening strains of Couperin's "Soeur Monique"—the clear signal to those in the room that they were now on a fixed schedule.

Without any hurry or fuss, Mallory's court train, sumptuously made and in perfect proportion to her tall, slender height so that it dropped easily and softly behind her, was arranged neatly and in broad folds for the two young girls who would carry it for her. Honor North and Eliza Seligman were the only children in the wedding party, and both ten-year-olds were taking their role as train-bearers very seriously indeed, but without any undue self-consciousness they were ushered into the room by Adele, and turned around for the adults, showing off their pretty frocks of white chiffon with pink sashes, pink stockings and shoes, their pretty faces smiling happily out from under bonnet-shaped leghorn hats decorated with pale pink camelias.

"You all look so adorable, no one is going to pay any attention to me!" Mallory teased as two more maids came in carrying the large florist's boxes. "Are the flowers in good condition?"

"Don't worry about them," Julie said in a brisk manner. "I personally checked it all out when they were delivered. And don't think you're going to escape anyone's notice—there isn't an eye downstairs that isn't going to be glued to you!"

"And it's quite a crush downstairs," Esme added. "You might have thought about a few more bridesmaids so there could be a complementary number of ushers. Jimmy and Jean-Christophe and Evan and Richard have their hands full!"

"Oh, I think they'll manage just fine," Alix countered. "And speaking of Richard— What do you think of Henry's cousin, Camillia?"

"He's very cute, and just loves to talk about aeroplanes and automobiles," Camillia replied deftly, referring to Richard Thorpe, the nineteen-year-old son of Henry's cousin, the Earl of Vickford. "He has a few more days before he has to go back to Baltimore, and on Monday night we're going with Jimmy and Kate to see *Get-Rich-Quick-Wallingford*."

"One bride at a time, please."

"Oh, Alix!"

"Don't worry, Cam. Today is *my* day, and any matchmaking is going to be done over champagne and forgotten by tomorrow morning," Mallory said, barely containing her laughter. After the slight unreality of earlier in the day, the last few minutes before the wedding march began were light-hearted and full of laughter and fun. "I wonder how Rupert is holding up?"

"Probably prowling around the library like a cat," Julie remarked, amused. "You'd be surprised at how men who never blink when faced with going down to the floor of the Exchange get all pale and sickly at the sight of wedding guests arriving!"

"Men have a poor capacity for wedding festivities," Adele put in. Like the other women of the bridal group, she had also ordered her dress from Lucile: a gown of soft blue charmeuse with a skirt cut with an apron-shaped front trimmed with stripes of darker blue silk. "Poor dears, they're simply not very strong when it comes to being the main participant in their own weddings."

"Is Newton outside?" Esme asked, adjusting her triple strand of pearls.

"He's down the hall and said he'll wait until Mallory is completely ready," Adele soothed.

Mallory smiled to herself. All the fuss surrounding a wedding. She had wanted the complications kept to a minimum, and for the most part she had succeeded. But now she was down to traditions, and it was important to have those who were closest to her and who meant the most to her see her before she came down the stairs on Newton Phipps' arm.

"Where's Thea?" she asked, suddenly aware that someone very special was missing.

"She won't be coming up, dear," Adele informed her gently. "Thea asked me to tell you that she felt it would be too crowded, and you didn't need another person drifting in. She said you'd understand."

"I do . . . oh, that doesn't sound right, does it?" she said, making a small joke out of her reply—the same one she would repeat in such a short time, but with such a different meaning.

"Let's just consider this a last-minute rehearsal," Esme said, reaching for the veil.

Once the tulle veil with its crowning wreath of orange blossoms was arranged well back from her brow, it was time for a final round of embraces. Julie first, because she had to go downstairs and join Cliff; then Eliza and Honor, who would be kept in the watchful care of Nanny Winters until the moment came for them to pick up her train; then each of her bridesmaids.

"We're a long way from the *Mauretania*, aren't we?" Alix asked with a secret smile.

Mallory pressed her cheek against her cousin's. "And it didn't take too long. I love you, Alix," she said, her emotions suddenly crowding up on her.

"I love you, too, Mallie. Now, don't cry."

"I know—my mascara will run!" she smiled, coming back under control again.

"And because it's a very special day for you, and if you start to cry, every other woman will join you."

"That wouldn't be a very pleasant sight."

They hugged again, and then Alix left, pausing to collect her bouquet, a great armful of pink moss rosebuds, the same flowers that the others were also carrying.

Adele and Esme were next, giving Mallory words of love and encouragement. She would be perfect once she started down the stairs, they both assured her, secure in the certainty that all she had was a little stage-fright, not a case of pre-wedding night fears.

Clerambault's Prelude in D was finished, to be followed by Mendelssohn's "Andante religioso" from Sonata No. 4.

"We're almost there, Mallie," Newton said as he came into the room a second after Esme and Adele left.

"I wonder if Rupert feels the same way I do right now. Not really all that nervous, but just wanting to get it all under way."

"When Rupert sees you, the first thing he's going to think is that all the waiting was worth it," Newton replied tenderly, kissing her cheek, careful not to crush any of the satin, lace and tulle. "You look very, beautiful, my dear."

"And you've been very patient, waiting for me."

"Oh, I didn't mind that, it was having to come up by the back stairs—Julie's banned everyone from the main stairs until after the ceremony."

"That sounds just like her—besides being a good idea." She turned to Rosie, who was regarding her with affection and pride. "My flowers, Rosie."

Holding her great bouquet of white orchids and roses and lilies of the valley tied up with white satin ribbon, Mallory carefully crossed the room toward the door, with Guiliana and Rosie holding up her train and Newton Phipps bringing up the rear.

In the hall at the top of the marble staircase with its gardenia and satin-ribbon entwined bannister, the wedding party assembled with Marie-France and Kate first, then Melinda and Camillia, followed by Alix.

"Is everything all right?" she asked as Mallory took her godfather's arm.

"It couldn't be better," Mallory responded with a bright smile that went straight to her eyes.

"*Now* you look like a happy bride!"

"If that means that I can hardly keep a serious expression on my face and that I want to laugh and I wish they'd begin to play the processional, you're damn right I'm a happy bride!"

"Such language from a bride," Newton chided in an amused voice, his eyes shining with love and pride at his goddaughter.

"I know how you hate simpering, clinging women, Uncle," Mallory teased.

The natural tension surrounding their group as they waited dissolved in smiles and soft laughter. Like well-rehearsed actors they were relaxed as they awaited their cue, but nonetheless, a minute later, when the musicians paused, there was a general intake of breath.

Mallory had girlfriends who'd told her that on their wedding days they'd been so nervous that afterwards nothing was very clear. But it's not like that with me, she decided. I'm not going to look back on today and have only a blur to remember when I think about my wedding day.

The wedding march was Mendelssohn's "A Midsummer Night's Dream," and at the opening notes, Marie-France and Kate counted to five and then took their first steps down the red-carpeted stairs.

The music swelled around them, the Caen stone hallway providing perfect acoustics, and they moved gracefully forward, a perfectly paired wedding party coming down the magnificent cantilevered staircase and toward the ballroom doors where Jean-Christophe and Jimmy and Evan and Richard were paired off and waiting to head the procession.

Mallory had worked on the guest list, had seen the invitations when they were delivered from Tiffany's, and counted the acceptances and refusals as they came in, but now, as she paused with Newton, waiting for the rest of the wedding party to start down the aisle, her first glimpse of the assembled guests was an unanticipated surprise.

All of these people are here to see us married and wish us well, she thought, not at all embarrassed by her sudden and very unfamiliar rush of sentimentality. At this moment, viewing the seemingly endless rows of men and women seated on the little gold ballroom chairs, it seemed to be the only right thought to have.

The moment Jimmy and Jean-Christophe stepped into the ballroom the entire company rose to their feet, watching the wedding party make their way along the red carpet that ran the length of the room from the doors to the dais, now banked with rich white flowers and a white

444

satin kneeling bench. The guests were determined not to miss a second of this spectacle, but as Mallory walked down the aisle, hearing the subdued gasps and the faint murmurs of appreciation, the only person she had eyes for was Rupert, waiting for her at the edge of the raised platform.

I'm almost there, she thought, a feeling of exhaltation spreading through her. Was it only two months ago that I was wondering if I could get up the nerve to see Rupert again? Funny how things work out. No, not funny—absolutely wonderful, she decided, coming closer and closer to Rupert, his face as radiant as hers, the sea of people in the ballroom and the rest of the wedding party fading into unimportance.

Their eyes met, and Mallory felt her feelings soar higher, her certainty grow stronger, and instinctively, as if on some prearranged signal, he held out his left hand to her at the same moment she slipped her arm from Newton's and reached for Rupert's right hand.

Together they took the two steps up to the dais where the Rector of the Little Church Around the Corner was waiting for them, a quiet, welcoming smile on his face. Weddings were his favorite pastoral duty, and he didn't mind showing it.

For a moment, Mallory disengaged her hand from Rupert's, and turned to hand her bouquet to Alix, before turning back to him in a whispering rustle of expensive fabric. All the weeks of preparation had come down to this, and she was eager for the moment to begin.

"Dearly beloved—" The achingly familiar words reached every person in the ballroom, and Mallory could almost feel the silence stretching out behind her, and knew with almost absolute certainty that they were all breathing as one.

"—we are gathered here today to join this man and

this woman in holy matrimony which is an honorable estate . . ."

The wedding service, as simple and direct as if Rupert and Mallory were a totally unimportant couple saying their vows in the Rector's parlor, or in a country parsonage, proceeded with perfect ease toward its conclusion.

"You may kiss the bride," the Rector concluded, and Mallory and Rupert shared a secret smile in the moment before their lips brushed lightly together. Their guests watched their first embrace as husband and wife with great interest, but it really wasn't the kiss they wanted to share.

"This will have to do until later," Rupert said in a quick, conspiratorial whisper as they walked up the wide aisle that was framed by posts supporting heavy white silk cords.

"I'm going to hold you to that," Mallory whispered back under the music of the recessional, walking at the correct pace past the smiling guests and out of the ballroom. "You were positively restrained and re-spectable!"

"A little restraint here and there never hurts," Rupert smiled as they arrived at the foot of the staircase where the receiving line would form. "After all, that's what you've been reminding me for the last six weeks."

"Then I'll say you've learned your lesson well."

"Not *too* well." They smiled at each other. "Just consider our first kiss as a deposit to be redeemed in several hours!"

"Congratulations!"
"Good luck to you always!"

"A long and happy married life!"

"Every good wish in the world!"

"You look so lovely, dear Mallory!"

"Good luck to you, Rupert, old boy!"

Standing side by side with the rest of the wedding party, they were lined up for the only event in a large wedding that's worse than waiting for the wedding march to begin: the receiving line.

Here, they would shake hands with and receive the good wishes of those who'd seen them married. Mallory, who knew the guest list practically by heart, whispered to Rupert during a brief lull that she was going to try very hard not to recall the exact number of people they were going to have to greet.

But despite Mallory's wry words, there were few, if any, guests that she didn't greet with pure happiness. She was well aware that if she regarded this necessary part of every wedding of this size as a chore, she might as well have insisted that they elope. The receiving line was really no different than her writing thank-you notes.

Of course there were people she was happier to see than others. She was happy to see Nancy Harley, elegantly turned out for the day in a pretty afternoon dress of Delft-blue crepon embroidered in heavy silk floss and finished with frills of plaited silk, looking very pretty and very excited despite the fact that Mr. Gibbs was trailing in her wake.

"What a beautiful ceremony," she told Mallory politely. "And all our best wishes," she added, referring to the female staff members whom she was representing.

"We love the chocolate pot and cups," Mallory replied, determined to try and remember which guest had sent what present. "And for the travel clock, also," she added, shaking Mr. Gibbs' hand.

The office manager wished them the usual greeting one made at a wedding when they're not close friends and have been invited out of politeness, and then moved on toward the dining room where the sit-down dinner would shortly be served.

"I certainly hope you didn't seat that sweet young thing with that dour functionary of Bill's," Kathryn Neal whispered a moment later, kissing them both. Despite her seventy-odd years, Nela's grandmother looked utterly ageless in a Drecoll gown of pure gray satin damask patterned in gold metallic thread. "I'm sure he's terribly efficient for business purposes, but today—"

"Don't worry, Mrs. Neal," Rupert assured the grande dame. "Mallie's seen to it that they'll be seated at different tables."

"I do like to hear things like that. Love and happiness to you both, my darlings!"

The line of guests went on and on. There were Charles and Thea, pleased and proud that Mallory and Rupert would be sharing their wedding anniversary with them; Edith and Hugo Tilmore, their serious comments belied by the fun in their eyes; Antoine and Ghiselle de Laulan, the Belgian Minister and his wife, offering calm and dignified and completely heartfelt good wishes; Ronald and Helena Thorpe, the Earl and Countess of Vickford whose *affaire* before their wedding had made them quit England for a pretty house in Baltimore's Mount Vernon Place; George Horton, looking thoroughly pleased to be included in on such a splendid event; and Romney Sedgewick, who looked rather secretive under his urbane exterior.

"Almost over," Rupert whispered to Mallory as Cornelius Albright, his old calculus professor, passed through the line. "Damn and blast—it's Evelyn Weldon, dragging poor Sybil behind her as usual."

"What a lovely wedding," Evelyn stated as she shook their hands. "Quite a coup, my dear."

"What Mother means is that house weddings can be

448

very awkward, and it's being so perfectly handled here," Sybil put in adroitly. "We appreciated the opportunity to look at all the lovely gifts."

"And thank you for the candlesticks. I know we're going to enjoy using them."

"You're perfectly welcome, Mallory," Evelyn said, taking all the credit as usual. She bestowed a catlike smile on them. "And I must say that I think you've pulled it off beautifully, my dear. My best wishes for your continued success."

"What*ever* did she mean by that?" Mallory said, mystified.

"I haven't the faintest idea, but I will tell you this— you put that woman's candlesticks on our dining room table and I'll find out if that counts as grounds for divorce!"

In the formal dining room the large table that could seat upwards of a hundred people at one of Julie and Cliff's more lavish dinner dances, had been removed and replaced by a series of round tables, each seating eight, draped in white moire tableskirts with lace top cloths and centerpieces of white tulips and freesia in silver bowls. Next door, the second, smaller dining room was set up for the bridal party's meal repeating the same decor but with more flowers.

Slowly, gradually, as they went through the receiving line, the guests began to arrive in the dining room, finding their placecards with the help of the footmen who had all but memorized the seating plan.

The early arrivals had to wait for those who came through the line last, but reading the engraved menu cards and light conversation made the time pass quickly, and as soon as everyone was seated they were enjoying the lavish meal of Beluga caviar, clear consommé with a thin slice of lime floating in it, a supreme of sole Marguery, followed by individual baby guinea hens that had been boned and stuffed with wild rice and accompanied by fresh new peas, and ending with a lemon sorbet—a perfect way to clear the palate in preparation for the wedding cake, the cutting of which was looked forward to almost as much as the ceremony itself.

In the meantime, the food was delicious and the champagne flowed and conversation continued to move easily along.

From table to table it was agreed that this was *definitely* one of the weddings of the season, absolutely without flaw, but *when* were they going to cut the cake?

It wasn't much longer before the wedding cake—a four-tier confection that brought forth gasps of admiration when it was carried in—was cut to the laughter and encouragement of the wedding party and the guests who delighted in the sight of Mallory and Rupert, looking thoroughly delighted with each other.

Now, in the early evening hours, the dancing was finally under way, and Alix, satisfied that she had completed all the obligatory dances, plus having had the pleasure of being partnered with her husband for two whole dances, decided that she could now satisfy her curiosity.

Without seeming to hurry, she left the ballroom, took two glasses of champagne from a smiling footman carrying a tray of refills, and went into the drawing room where the gifts were on display.

"Hello, George," she said, holding out a glass. "Are you still quoting Shakespeare?"

"'Fair ladies, you drop manna in the way of starved people,'" George Kelly quoted, first checking to make sure they were alone in the room, a smile brightening his

450

face. At well over six feet tall, and with the powerful body of the professional boxer he'd been in his youth, he didn't seem to be the sort of man who could quote the Bard of Avon easily and at will. But Alix, who had come to know him during the time she'd worked for the Women's Infirmary, knew quite another side to the man.

"Well, I'm only one lady, but that's quite close enough," she smiled, urging him to take the glass.

"But I'm on duty, Mrs. Thorpe," he protested, his eyes saying something quite different. "It might not look right—"

"No one is going to mind. Besides, it's not a ball where you've been hired to make sure a lot of silly ladies don't lose their jewelry. It's my cousin's wedding day, and I insist you share in the festivities."

"Just seeing those presents has been enough of a celebration for me," George said, nonetheless taking the glass. "Being a bodyguard and private detective, I see mostly diamonds and such, and they all look alike after a while. This is much nicer."

"As long as you don't have to write all the thank-you notes. Believe it or not, my cousin has all of hers written," Alix said as they touched glasses.

"I'm not surprised at all, she's a very thoughtful young lady, and always had a nice word and a bit of conversation when she came in."

"Mallory isn't the sort of bride who lets others do her jobs. Of course she didn't have to write thank-you letters from three different cities. You should have heard what my husband said when he saw our presents spread out over his precious library in London!"

"Well, knowing Mr. Thorpe, it was probably a very short, very accurate comment!"

"You're very, very right," Alix laughed, remembering. "Now, tell me, what do you hear from Sinclair Poole?" she continued easily.

451

George sighed and looked down at the tiny champagne bubbles in his glass. He should have guessed that this lady would have an ulterior motive. If there was one thing he hated more than reliving "the old days" it was answering questions about his one-time employer—questions that always seemed to come from the quarter that Sinclair Poole had been born to and then cast out of. It seemed to George that the people who decided who was or was not good enough to be "one of them" still retained an unhealthy interest in anyone who carried more than a slight hint of scandal. Not that Mrs. Thorpe (he could never bring himself to refer to Alix as Lady Thorpe)—or Dr. Turner as she'd been in those days—was like that, but still . . .

"Oh, Alix, here you are!" Edith's bright voice effectively ended anything George might have said. "Thea and Regina and I were looking for you."

"Well, now we've found her," Thea said, stunning in a Cheruit dress of beige Breton lace with a surplice bodice and a skirt falling to three deep flounces and a wide belt of Liberty satin the color of an American Beauty rose. "Is this a private conversation we're walking in on, Alix?" she questioned tactfully, privately thinking that Edith had had a bit too much champagne.

"Oh, no," Alix said quickly. "Regina, you remember George Kelly, don't you?"

"Hello, Miss Bolt, it's been a long time."

"But I could never forget you, George. And it's Mrs. MacIverson now, and this is my sister-in-law, Lady Tilmore." Regina made her introductions quickly, her Jeanne Hallee dress of pale blue marquisette over shirred silk in a slightly deeper blue and a side-draped tunic rustling as she came forward to shake hands. "How's the bodyguard business these days?"

"Not as exciting as when Mrs. Thorpe—Dr. Turner

452

that was—operated on Mr. Poole and removed his appendix."

"Oh, Alix. How absolutely thrilling!" Edith's eyes were wide with amazement. "Do tell *all* the details. When was this?"

"Oh, about four months or so before I went to London and met Henry." Alix smiled and threw an apologetic look to George, who nonetheless looked interested.

"Who is this Sinclair Poole?" Edith was frankly curious in a champagne-bright sort of way. "I think I know the name, but—"

"About fifteen years ago, Sinclair Poole's father was a major financier; one who should have known better than to have allowed himself to become involved in offering shares in a company that never existed."

"But isn't that illegal?" Edith asked, pressing down a fold of her Doucet afternoon dress of Mandaran-blue crepe de chine ornamented with Oriental embroidery and a satin belt.

"Very illegal, but only if you get caught—or are set up, which Stanford Poole was," said Alix, who knew the whole story.

"Caught and put on trial," Thea put in. "It was a glorious New York scandal—except that the defendant died while the jury was still out."

"Not that it made any difference as far as his son was concerned. Sinclair had made too many enemies for his young age, and when he made it clear he wasn't about to repudiate his father—" Alix looked at Edith, who was quite familiar with the ways that an exclusive social set had of casting out those who were found out.

"Why don't we let George tell the rest of the story?" Regina suggested.

Whether it was the champagne or the fact that four

very attractive ladies were hanging on his every word, George Kelly found himself telling the story of Sinclair Poole and the Rubican Club where he had run his business of importing items of fine art from the Orient.

"Were you really a bouncer? And was Sinclair Poole's business really legitimate?" Edith sounded more interested in the former than the latter.

"Oh, it was all legal and above board, Lady Tilmore," he assured her. "Except for that business about the objects stolen during the Boxer Rebellion. But if it weren't for that, Mr. Poole never would have met his wife." George allowed himself a smile of pure delight. "If it hadn't been for Caroline Worth, things might not have worked out for him at all."

"How intriguing," Edith murmured when it became clear George was not going to elaborate.

"Well, you'll probably be able to decide that for yourself," Alix couldn't resist saying. "Sinclair and Caroline Poole live in California."

"They divide their time between Montecito and Los Angeles now," Regina added. "Ian and I see rather a lot of them, and you'll meet them if you and Hugo come back with us."

"Oh, what fun!" Edith exclaimed over someone Alix was sure the Tilmores wouldn't receive in England. Well, she decided, half the fun of traveling was doing things you'd never do at home.

"Is Mallory ready to change clothes?"

"No, she and Rupert are having too much fun." Thea was vastly amused that a newly married couple could actually enjoy themselves at a wedding of this size. "They're good for at least four more dances."

"Good for them! I'll be in soon."

"Doesn't Mrs. Poole write to you?" George asked when they were alone. "I mean you were both such good friends and all—"

"Oh, Caro and I write to each other all the time. But you know how letters are. No, it's Sinclair I'm interested in. I was just wondering if it was safe to have Mallory and Rupert meet them. Rupert's very touchy, and so is Sinclair."

"I understand, Mrs. Thorpe, but from the way I see things, Mr. Poole will have more problems from Lord and Lady Tilmore than from the Randalls."

"You're probably right." Alix looked around the room so crowded with gifts, such objects of affection, and then back at George.

"When all the guests were arriving earlier, did you notice anyone who was particularly interested in all of this? Or anyone who was making comments that seemed, well, a bit out of the ordinary?"

"It was very crowded here for quite a while. I really couldn't hear what anyone was saying, except for the usual remarks. Although the red painting you and your husband gave caused quite a bit of talk."

"Matisse tends to rouse the argumentative in people."

"I can see where it would. But Mrs. Thorpe, is something wrong? You seem very concerned."

"Oh, it's just a comment a woman I've never liked made to my cousin." She smiled briefly. "Matrons of honor have an unfortunate tendency to hear things that the bride generally passes over because she's too excited."

"I see. And what does this woman look like?"

"She's in her forties, a shade too well-preserved—you know the type—wearing a dress of very pale gray marquisette over orange chiffon with a turquoise belt—ghastly combination. She does tend to have clothes that are very noticeable, and since she's the sort of person who likes a good gloat, I thought she might have made a comment or two."

George shook his head. "I'm afraid I can't help you

there, Mrs. Thorpe. Oh, I know the woman you're talking about, but she didn't say anything incriminating or suspicious."

Alix sighed. "I didn't think so."

"I'll tell you what, Mrs. Thorpe," George offered helpfully, sympathetic because he hated to see a lady he liked so much in obvious distress. "I have a lot of assignments coming up in the next few months, and if I see this lady, I'll keep an eye on her."

"Would you, George? I'd really appreciate that."

"No problem, Mrs. Thorpe. I take it she's the sort of lady who gets the same sort of invitations you do?"

Alix laughed, not quite mirthlessly, but close enough. "Oh, George, take it from me. When this lady wants a particular invitation, she'll beg, borrow or steal for it— and those are the *nice* tactics she'll use!"

In the ballroom the orchestra was playing Scott Joplin's "Ragtime Nightingale," playing the music properly, slowly, and Mallory and Rupert were dancing to it, holding each other a little too close for propriety, but on this one occasion, no one was likely to regard them with anything less than an understanding smile.

"I've just realized that this is the first time today that we've been alone together," Mallory said as they turned across the highly polished floor.

"I'm afraid that if we start reviewing everything we've been through since the ceremony—the receiving line, posing for the formal photographs, even dinner and cutting the cake—we'll both collapse from exhaustion!"

"Oh, when and if you collapse, I intend to see that it's from something quite different!" Mallory whispered, leaning forward slightly so that only he could hear, her veil brushing against his cheek. She laughed as he swung her around. "The hardest to get through were all the obligatory dances."

"Not the toasts?"

"They were short and loving and not too sentimental. I don't know how many weddings you've been to recently, but you'd be surprised how many otherwise dignified people get all overcome by the event."

"Pure treacle?"

"Worse."

"I haven't been to too many weddings, and from your description, I've been rather lucky. But then," he went on, holding her even closer, his eyes glowing softly, "this is the only wedding I've ever had any real interest in."

Mallory felt herself melting under his touch. "Shall we get ready to leave? It doesn't look too good for the bride and groom to act as though they're having as much fun at their wedding reception as we are."

"Are you worried that if all our guests only suspected we were lovers before are sure of it now?"

"Because we're too comfortable with each other, whereas if we'd never been to bed before, we'd be a lot more skittish," Mallory supplied. "One more dance, then?"

"Anything at all for the woman I love."

Henry Thorpe and Romney Sedgewick were standing in a corner of the ballroom, enjoying the excellent champagne and watching the dancing with great interest.

"Aren't you missing Alix right now?" Romney asked. "I imagined the two of you would hardly be off the floor."

"The private detective in charge of watching the presents is a friend of Alix's from the old days, and she went in to say hello and bring him a glass of champagne."

"How nice," Romney said, deciding not to ask why Thea and Regina, trailed by Edie Tilmore, had followed close on Alix's trail. "And how is your great masterpiece coming along?" he queried.

"Very well. Of course, I have a secretary who likes to push me along and remind me of my duty toward my responsibility in my great effort to enlighten the vast American public."

"And you're putting up with that idiotic claptrap?" Romney was disbelieving. "I know you feel you owe Gresham, but—"

"Has Alix been coaching you in what to say?"

"I don't need instructions in what to say. I can tell you for myself that you're being had by a lot of pretentious claptrap by a man that you have the misguided notion that you have to repay for a situation that was his own fault!" Romney said heatedly. "And this is not the time or the place to have such a discussion," he amended hastily.

"It's all right," Henry said, as eager as his old friend to smooth things over. "Weddings tend to bring out the oddest emotions and reactions. Speaking of which, it looks as if our bridal couple are about to start their going-away preparations, and the duties of the best man call."

"It's been a splendid wedding, and right now I'm envying Rupert; tell him that for me. Mallory's very beautiful and very special, and if he doesn't realize how fortunate he is, I'll be more than happy to give him a run for his money!"

Henry gave him an inscrutable look from under hooded lids. "Don't be an ass!" he snapped, and left, leaving Romney alone.

Better to be insulted, better to be thought of as a potential suitor who arrived on the scene too late, he decided, accepting a fresh glass of champagne from a footman. Much, much better than to be considered an eligible, extra man and have to suffer being the hostess's delight. He wasn't ready to tell anyone about his engagement. Thea and Mallory knew, but he had told them out of necessity, and that was something quite different. Strangely enough, his seeming to make Mallory the object of his interest didn't do more than twinge at his conscience. Too many women over too many years as a widower who'd sworn up one side and down the other that he'd never remarry made him wary now, he supposed. In any case, the friends he made these calculatedly wistful comments to knew he was far too much of a gentleman, far too cautious, to make any advances toward Mallory. Not that he was ever going to. Without her ever having to be aware of it, she was his protection until the day Tildy came back to New York from London and they could be married.

Yes, he decided, crossing the floor to ask Julie to dance, this was the best way to preserve his privacy. The absolutely safest way of all.

"It seems that just as soon as I got used to wearing my wedding dress and veil, it's time to take it off!" Mallory laughed to Alix as she regarded her intricate, expensive, one-special-day-only dress now laid across the bed, her veil draped carefully alongside it.

"Well, just remember that a wedding dress is technically a costume, and in a way it is like going to a costume ball—just as soon as you stop feeling like a figure in a Fragonard painting, it's time to go home!" Standing by the dressing table, Alix concentrated on powdering her nose. "Are you ready, Mallie?"

Mallory checked her reflection in the same mirror where only hours before she'd seen herself arrayed in full bridal regalia. But now, less than half an hour since she'd come upstairs, the satin sheath was replaced by an afternoon gown of apricot silk with a lace-frilled bodice, and her veil by a Georgette hat of champagne-colored straw with a broad satin ribbon draped around the crown and tied in a perfect bow.

"All ready," she told Alix. "Since everyone else went down, all the guests must be champing at the bit for me to come down and throw my bouquet."

"You know how wedding guests are when it comes to that particular tradition," Alix replied, hugging her cousin. "You were beautiful today, darling, you and Rupert both."

"Oh, we make quite a couple—rather like you and Henry, I hope."

"Oh, I don't see why not. I'll join the others downstairs and you come as soon as you want."

"I will, Alix. Don't worry, it's too late for me to run away now!"

"Funny!"

I'm all ready to leave with Rupert, she thought, pacing around the room to give Alix enough time to join the others. Oh, it seems so funny to think that while I was getting dressed time seemed to crawl by, and the minute I took the first step down the stairs, it all moved so quickly.

She grinned at her reflection in the dressing table mirror. And there you have it, Mallory, my dear—an excellent wedding. Just imagine if all the guests from New York and Philadelphia and Baltimore and Washington and Boston, as well as points east and west, hadn't gotten on as well as they have! You've been to weddings like that, and they're like traveling on a second-class ocean liner—not a pleasant way to spend an afternoon and the early part of the evening.

There was just enough time for another dab of perfume, another application of face powder, and then Mallory picked up her handbag, her bouquet, and the gloves she was reluctant to put on over her wedding ring, and started for the door—and for Rupert who was waiting for her.

Just as she knew he would be, Rupert was standing at the foot of the stairs, his formal wedding clothes replaced by a dark business suit. But there was nothing at all dark about the expression on his face, and for a minute they looked at each other, oblivious to the crowd of family and friends, thoroughly and completely pleased with each other.

"Here it comes!" Mallory said, and tossed her bouquet over the marble railing, aiming carefully at Camillia, who deftly captured the great mass of flowers with a very unbridesmaidlike whoop of laughter.

While the flowers were falling through the air, Mallory went down the stairs at quite a different pace than the one she'd used earlier, and then she and Rupert were making their way through the crush of well-wishers tossing rose petals at them, and out onto the street.

Outside on Fifth Avenue, the canopy was still up, and on either side, the press and onlookers were politely but firmly held back by the police.

Smiling and laughing, they ran that last gauntlet to the edge of the sidewalk, and with a policeman holding back traffic, they dashed across the street, to the downtown side of Fifth Avenue, where Thea and Charles' car and driver, loaned for the occasion and decorated with the usual "Just Married" sign and the required old shoes.

"Look at that crowd. I think I could declare for political office right now and win!" Rupert said as they waved to those seeing them off.

"Just remember that politicians have to spend a lot of time in smoke-filled rooms," Mallory laughed as they got into the car's tonneau.

"Not a fitting place for a bridegroom," Rupert agreed.

461

He signalled to the patiently waiting, broadly smiling driver. "Let's go before they storm the car."

"Yes, sir. But do you want me to stop a little further down the avenue and remove the old shoes and the sign?"

Mallory and Rupert conferred for a moment in whispers.

"The shoes, yes, but leave the sign," Rupert advised, slipping an arm around Mallory. "I want everyone to know how happy we are," he said extravagantly as the Renault town car gathered speed down Fifth Avenue toward the St. Regis Hotel.

Too much of a good thing can be wonderful.

—Mae West

The St. Regis Hotel

From its opening day in September 1904, the St. Regis Hotel brought the fine art, pure luxury and total comfort of twentieth century hotel living to New York City. Even those so enamoured of the Plaza to such an extent that no other luxury hotel quite measured up, were willing to admit that the St. Regis, under the ownership of Colonel John Jacob Astor, was the first to pamper guests with a central air-conditioning and heating system, protect them with a fire-alarm system, and amuse them with the new innovation: a mail chute on every one of the eighteen floors.

Like the Plaza, the St. Regis's architecture was inspired by France, but unlike the former's chateau-like vastness, the latter's limestone structure topped by a mansard roof, looked more like a very overgrown Parisian mansion.

Inside, no expense had been spared in creating an ambiance of pure luxury untainted by anything even faintly commercial or in bad taste. The aim of the St. Regis was to make every guest, whether occupying the smallest single room or the state suite with its own private dining room, feel as though they were in their own homes, with a staff ready to meet every request.

When Mallory and Rupert decided to make the St.

Regis their home for at least the first month of their marriage, they had met with Rudolph Haan, the hotel's proprietor. A man with complete control of his domain, Mr. Haan had checked to see which of the hotel's eighty suites would be available for the time they needed it, and then taken them on a tour of the suites so they could select the one they liked the best. He reminded them that, in addition to the main restaurant, should they wish to give a dinner party during their stay, they could reserve the private dining room with wall panels of Circassian walnut and chairs covered with illuminated Spanish leather, while the menu of their choosing would be served on Minton china.

Hiding smiles, they had thanked Mr. Haan for his reminder, well aware that although they would use the restaurant and visit the library where polished wood bookcases held volume after volume of leather-bound, gold-tooled books, and while it was possible that Rupert might have a drink in the Oak Room and Mallory have lunch or tea in the Ladies' Restaurant, the idea that they would want to throw a private dinner was as remote to them as their giving a gala gathering in the hotel's ballroom. Honeymoons were made for a great number of things, but definitely not for large-scale entertaining.

Mallory and Rupert had planned for their arrival at the St. Regis as carefully as they had for their wedding, and now, some four hours after the ceremony, they came through one of the great bronze revolving doors into the Caen-stone walled lobby and walked arm in arm across the floor, their footsteps muffled by the heavy Kurdish rug laid over the elaborately inlaid Irish marble floor. Their registration had been taken care of the day they selected their suite, and their luggage had been sent ahead the day before, eliminating any need to stop at the office or cope with bellmen. They had also asked Mr. Haan not to greet them at the entrance as he always did when important guests arrived, and as they made their progress through the lobby, past the entrance to the vast, elegant restaurant that overlooked Fifth Avenue, where the musicians were already playing dance tunes, they nonetheless attracted a sizeable amount of attention varying from quick, discreet looks, to those who actually stopped to watch them walk by. It wasn't that they looked like newlyweds, it was a shimmering just under the surface that made perfect strangers stop and take a second look.

In the ornate elevator, they remained perfectly decorous, but when they reached the eighth floor and were walking down the corridor rich with walls of Italian marble, deep carpets and tapestry covered chairs, they were holding hands.

"Is this the point where you tell me you've forgotten our room key and you have to go downstairs to the office and ask for the duplicate?" Mallory teased as they paused in front of their door.

"No chance of that," Rupert responded, brushing his lips against hers. "Cliff made me check at least four times to make sure I had it with me." He withdrew the heavy key from his jacket pocket and held it triumphantly in front of her before inserting it in the lock. "Besides, if I did forget it, I'd ask you for a hairpin and pick the lock!"

"I don't doubt that at all. Rupert—oh—" She dissolved in laughter as he swept her up in his arms and carried her over the threshold.

"Don't worry, I'll do it again when we move into our apartment," he assured Mallory, setting her down in the center of the exquisitely appointed sitting room done all in the Louis XVI-style with carved woodwork highlighting the ivory-white walls. Furniture covered in French gray and blue silk, gilt-framed French prints on the walls, and a cabinet filled with delicate Sevres china gave the room a light, uncluttered air. "Do you suppose the grand

St. Regis has anything as mundane as a 'do not disturb' sign?"

"Somehow I very much doubt it. Just as I don't think it's likely that any member of the staff will come to our door unless we request them," Mallory laughed, holding out her arms to him.

"We're here at last. Or at least halfway to where it really counts," Rupert said, his arms closing around her waist.

"Well, we're not that far away."

"I didn't want you to think I was rushing the moment."

"Never. Come on," she said slipping an arm around his waist. "It's been a long day."

Quietly, slowly, as if they'd been married, Mallory and Rupert walked into their honeymoon chamber, a room rich with blue silk panels on ivory walls, a blue and gold antique tapestry hung on one wall, a pale blue and pearl gray rug, and ormolu tulipwood furniture, dominated by the bed with its lushly carved headboard and footboard, already turned down for the night.

Through one door, Mallory could see the marble bathroom, and others were halfway open to show ample closet space now filled with enough of their individual wardrobes to last them through the next month.

"Sackett and Rosie seem to have done a very thorough job," Mallory said, suddenly nervous, seeing for the first time the silver ice bucket holding a bottle of champagne, and, laid neatly across a small loveseat, Rupert's pajamas and dressing gown—the new silk one he'd brought for their rendezvous at the Knickerbocker—and her night-gown and negligee—a wedding night ensemble of the palest possible pink crepe de chine with panels of Spanish and Oriental lace that was made to be admired and then taken off and then—

Suddenly, Mallory felt a wave of confusion sweep over

her. "Oh, Rupert, I feel like such an idiot!"

Instantly, his arms were around her. "Mallie, darling, why? Is something wrong? Did I do something?"

"No—no, you're wonderful. It's me. All of a sudden I feel as if we've never made love, never really kissed or traded secrets or told each other how we feel."

"Will it make you feel better if I tell you that right now I'm a little shaky myself?" He pulled her closer to him for reassurance. "I think it's just a natural aftereffect."

"You're right. It was too many people and too much happening too quickly—not to mention all the food we ate and the champagne we drank. I wouldn't change one second of our wedding, but it looks like we're going to have to get used to finally being alone together."

"And I know a perfect way to begin."

"I just bet you do." Mallory put her arms around Rupert's shoulders, and gradually her attack of nerves ebbed away as she began to kiss him, savoring the warmth and willingness of his well-defined mouth, pressing closer to him as his arms tightened demandingly around her. "Shall we close the bedroom door?" she questioned quietly, brushing his hair out of his eyes.

"I'll do the door—and then I'll do you," Rupert said, stepping away from her for a second that was far too long.

"Do I get reciprocal rights?" Mallory asked delightedly as he carefully took off her hat.

"What's that old saw about a good rule working both ways?"

"Well, in that case—" She unknotted his tie and began to push his suit jacket off his shoulders.

"Oh, my love . . ." Rupert looked delighted and surprised at the same time. "It looks as if our stagefright is about to become a thing of very brief duration."

"Except that I'm not acting now—and never have been."

"Neither am I," Rupert said, his breathing changing as

467

his hands went to the back of her waist.

Slowly expelling the breath she hadn't even been aware she was holding, Mallory closed her eyes as Rupert's hands began to move upwards, separating the hooks and eyes of her dress with the greatest of ease, his fingertips brushing lightly over her skin, making her tremble from his touch.

Her dress fell in a silken heap at her feet, and Mallory stepped quickly out of it and pushed it away with one foot before kicking off her shoes. Her heart hammering, she regarded Rupert through her lashes as his silver-colored eyes took in every inch of her.

Prolonging the moment, she unbuttoned his vest and took it off him, adding it to his tie and jacket already on the floor. "In the morning, before we ring for the maid, we'll have to pick up after ourselves," Mallory said, amazed that she could still speak normally when her knees felt like water and her skin seemed to have taken on a new sensitivity.

"Light housekeeping chores," Rupert replied thickly as she began to unbutton his shirt. "Oh, Mallie—"

His shirt now completely open, Mallory had lifted up his left hand, but instead of undoing his cuff-link as he expected, she had unstrapped his watch, laid it carefully on the nearest table, and then kissed the spot where his pulse was already pounding.

"We don't have to worry about the time any more," she whispered, finally undoing the plain gold links, finishing her task the second all his restraint seemed to snap.

"I want you, every inch of you," he whispered as he pulled off his shirt and gathered her close to him.

Melting against him, Mallory rested her head on Rupert's shoulder as he took the pins out of her hair and ran his fingers through the silky strands before burying his face in the perfumed mass. They already knew each other intimately, she realized, but now, tonight, was forever, and for all time.

Slowly, delighting in every moment, his fingers slid across the silk and lace and ribbons of her lingerie, and when the last piece of froth was on the floor, he removed the last of his own clothes, and then carried Mallory to the open, waiting bed, laying her down among the profusion of pillows and silk comforters.

Full of champagne and love, Mallory watched Rupert as he bent over her, his fingers tenderly resting on one breast and then the other, tracing one pattern and then repeating it. Small motions, sweeping motions, Rupert knew them all and he was making good use of his knowledge.

How could he bear waiting so long to claim her? Mallory wondered, gasping and then moaning out loud as his index finger traced a circle around each breast before his mouth closed over a taut nipple.

Her arms closed around him as he moved his head upwards, his mouth leaving a trail of tiny kisses until his lips touched hers in the kiss she was longing for.

Caught up in the passion of that kiss, her senses beginning to spin out of control, Mallory was still aware enough to feel Rupert's long, hard body, his skin hot enough to burn, press against her, and while their tongues carried on one sweet exploration, his fingers began another, and she arched her hips, urging him closer, wanting him more and more.

There is an invisible line in lovemaking, a moment when all the shared passion can become automatic, the mutual desire meaningless, and all the skill simply a well-learned lesson. Rupert had learned those facts a long time ago, and now, in a fever-bright pitch of desire, he slipped his arms under Mallory's shoulders and fused their bodies together.

"Now, darling, now," Mallory whispered in his ear,

and in return heard all the words of love pouring out of him as he entered her. She felt him fill her with one thrust, and then, using the utmost control, hold himself very still as their bodies made the ultimate adjustment. Dizzy with the pure pleasure of having him inside her, Mallory closed her eyes, the darkness becoming streaked with bright flashes of color as they began to move together, long ripples of delight spreading through her limbs.

"Perfect . . . you're so perfect," he breathed, his mouth pressing against the side of her neck.

"So are you," she managed, bands of passion tightening around her as the pace of their lovemaking quickened, and Mallory let her mind close off as they loved each other.

Mallory opened her eyes briefly to see Rupert's passion-suffused face above hers.

"Always," she told him in a voice that didn't sound anything at all like her own.

"Always," he pledged as her fingers stroked the small of his back, and then they found the sublime moment they both sought, going to the outer reaches of a passion they always knew was there for them.

"I'm glad we waited until tonight," Rupert said, his mouth brushing lightly along her hairline as they lay together in the beautifully rumpled bed. "You were right when you said it would mean more to us on our wedding night if we weren't lovers beforehand."

"I wanted us to begin fresh, not to have our past trailing along behind us," Mallory said, stroking his hair. "And I'm still marveling that we're here together, with no one else around."

"I am too," he whispered, resting his head on her shoulder. "That's probably one of the reasons for a

470

honeymoon—or at least it is for ours. It's the time to get used to the fact that we actually made it through all the parties and the presents, not to mention the ceremony and the reception, and earned our privacy."

"We certainly have," she said as an unexpectedly cool breeze blew through the open window. "Oh, it's cold."

"Not when you have me," Rupert laughed, pulling the covers over them and cuddling Mallory closer to him.

"My beautiful nightgown and negligée. According to wedding night etiquette, I was supposed to keep it on long enough for you to properly admire it!"

"Well, you can slip into it when we have breakfast— accompanied by our bottle of champagne. Or are you hungry now?"

"Only for you. This is still our wedding night, and I want only to feast on our love." She turned over and rested her hands on his chest. "Did you forget about my turn?"

He smiled at her teasing voice. "I wouldn't dare. But first, before I'm seduced into my proper husbandly place, shall we try making this time a bit slower?"

"Oh, I think I'd like that very much," Mallory said, sliding her hand down the length of his body and coming to rest between his strong thighs, delighted at his immediate response to her. "Later on, though, you have to remember that you're all mine."

"Oh, my darling—" His voice was low and rich. "I am always yours."

The next time they woke up it was to the sound of church bells ringing up and down Fifth Avenue, and the sight of the early morning sun filling the room.

"We did it," Mallory said triumphantly as she lay in Rupert's arms. "We're finally, really married. No second thoughts now!"

"I couldn't even imagine such a thing," Rupert said, slowly smiling as he brushed a strand of hair back from her forehead. "And if this is what being married feels like, I don't want it ever to change."

"It's not only feeling, it's also seeing," she said, unable to suppress her sense of humor. "This is the first time I've ever seen you before you've shaved," she went on, running a finger along his black-stubbled jaw.

"Am I that bad?"

"No, I rather like it."

"Good—that means I won't have to hurry and shave every morning so that I don't upset you first thing."

"There's not much chance of that," Mallory assured him, laughing. "Are you hungry? I'm famished."

"So am I. What shall we have?"

"Strawberries and cream to begin with, and then waffles."

"With hot maple syrup and crisp bacon, followed by croissants with sweet butter and strawberry preserves."

"We're going to be so greedy!"

"Any complaints?"

"Not so far, although I may have one or two by the time of our golden wedding anniversary," she said, pulling him down to her. "And don't forget we need more ice for the champagne and all the Sunday papers."

"That's right, we have to read all about ourselves." He folded his arms behind his head. "What do you think about a pot of hot chocolate with a big bowl of whipped cream?"

"Do we drink it before the champagne or after? Oh, why not? We need more of a celebration than a boring pot of coffee. Oh, Rupert, do you really find the side of my neck *that* interesting?" she asked as he bent over her, his mouth finding the sensitive chord at the side of her throat.

"Only the beginning," he murmured, his supple hands

sliding down from her shoulders to curve around the sides of her breasts. "Shall we put off ringing room service for a while?"

"I take it that also means putting off sharing the marble bathtub? Not that I'm complaining," Mallory added as her heartbeat increased and she reacted to the feel of Rupert's body pressing firmly against her. "Right now, I can't think of any better way to start the first full day of our married life!"

The happiness of the domestic fireside is the first boon of Heaven . . .

—Thomas Jefferson

One Lexington Avenue

Mallory Randall paused in front of the polished hardwood door leading to her apartment and simply stood there in the corridor, key in hand, drinking in the silence, enjoying the peaceful feeling that was the bridge between a busy day and the evening and night ahead that she would share with Rupert—the first full night in their new home.

Little by little, over the month since their wedding, the apartment slowly but surely took shape until—although it was nowhere near finished—it was completely habitable and ready to provide them with the comfort they were both used to. The day before, Monday, October twenty-fourth, Mallory and Rupert had checked out of the St. Regis and come downtown to One Lexington Avenue, more than ready after a month of what was really playing house in a hotel suite, to claim their own home.

There had been the usual settling-in activities: setting out treasured pictures, making sure the closets were arranged to their liking, and putting their books out on the living room's bookshelves. Normally, they would have spent the previous night at home, probably with a fire crackling in the fireplace, but having already agreed to accompany George Horton and his daughter to the theatre, there had been time for only a late tea before changing and going on to the Astor Theatre for the opening night of the new musical, *The Girl in the Taxi*.

The last thing either of us needs is another late night at Delmonico's, Mallory thought as she inserted her key in the lock, recalling how tired they'd been the night before. Not too tired for quite a bit of ardent loving when they finally had come home, she recalled with a sweet smile, but still—

"Good afternoon, madam." The moment Mallory closed the door behind her, Hugh Dovedale, their newly hired butler-houseman, seemed to materialize out of nowhere and come forward, looking rather disappointed that she had no packages for him to help her with. "Shall I bring you a pot of tea?" he inquired politely. "It looks like quite a chilly afternoon."

"It's downright nasty out there," Mallory replied with a smile. "But no tea, thank you. Has the afternoon mail come?"

"Yes, madam, and quite a bit of it, too. It's all on the hall table, arranged just the way you and Mr. Randall instructed."

"I'm sure it is," Mallory said, sending Dovedale back to the dining room where he was setting the table, asking him to bring the cocktail tray into the living room in an hour. Treading carefully on the highly polished basket-weave parquet floor, she went over to the rare Irish Regency table set halfway down the length of the foyer, unbuttoning the jacket of her jaunty Paquin suit of dark blue velveteen trimmed with touches of black and red military braid, and a shorter, straighter skirt eased by two narrow plaits below the knee.

Poor Dovedale, Mallory thought, amused, putting down her gloves and handbag and taking off her smart

Reboux street hat of deep sapphire blue silk trimmed with sapphire blue aigrettes. I knew he was going to have difficulty getting used to a modern married couple!

Taking a quick look at her reflection in the mirror hanging above the table, Mallory pushed a few pins back in her hair and checked the mail laid out in three neat stacks on the table's polished wood surface. All the mail addressed to Rupert was placed to the right of the carnation-filled Imari bowl, her mail to the left, and the letters addressed to both of them placed squarely in the center. Gathering up her mail—a mélange of letters and bills and various notices—along with her hat and handbag and gloves, Mallory went into the living room. It wasn't finished, but they definitely had a beautiful room in the making.

The fitted carpet was the richest, deepest shade of ivory they could find to compliment the soft cream walls. At one end of the twenty-eight foot long room, a gilt-framed mirror hung over the marble fireplace, and the opposite wall was lined with bookshelves. Their first purchase together, the Steinway concert grand, was placed between the fireplace and the doors that led to the dining room, and placed between the double set of windows was an almost overpowering red and gold lacquer Queen Anne secretary purchased from French and Company on a day when they'd gone in to browse. Unlike some newlyweds who couldn't enter a room without seeing anything but their wedding presents, Mallory and Rupert had decided that another focal point was called for.

Mallory made a quick survey of the room, making sure the flowers were arranged where she wanted them and that the latest order of books from Brentano's had been delivered, before returning to the foyer and climbing the stairs to the next floor.

In the hallway at the top of the stairs, she opened the doors to the wardrobe, admiring the shelves filled with sheets and pillowcases and blankets and towels, and looked into the smallest of the three bedrooms, the one that would eventually be the nursery, but was now the storage place for all the wedding presents they weren't sure what to do with. For a moment, she paused on the threshold of the second bedroom with its furniture of black and gold lacquer and jade green hangings and carpet. This was Rupert's room, although in name only, providing him with closet space and a bathroom and a place to work in the event he brought work home from the office.

But it was their own bedroom that was complete to her total satisfaction with every single item selected with the greatest of love and care.

As she came into the room, putting away her accessories and leaving her mail on the delicate writing desk, she recalled the twinge of regret she'd felt at the thought of having to place furniture on their new carpet. It was an art nouveau creation, woven in India less than two years before, but a little too startling for most people to consider, the rug buyer from Sloane's explained to them. But the white swans woven on the bone center ornamented with flowers of apricot, pale green, sea foam and midnight blue, and the deep border of vibrant garnet splashed with a graceful tulip border was just what they wanted. As she stepped out of her blue kid leather pumps, Mallory wondered when they would make love on the deep, soft pile.

Not that their bed was anything to complain about, she thought, looking at the immense Louis XVI-style bed of white and gold with four thin white columns finished in gilt swans. On the cream-colored walls, lyre-shaped fixtures were strung with pearls, and the white satin curtains had a lining of peach-pink taffeta. They'd chosen the bedroom to hang their two smallest paintings, the Renoir and the Marie Lurencin, since they would blend best into the room and not demand too much attention away from the rest of the furnishings.

All in all, Mallory decided, if they wanted, she and Rupert could simply forget about the not-quite-completed living room and dining room downstairs and live very happily in their bedroom until it was time to leave for California.

That was a lovely fantasy, but as she took off her suit and silk blouse and hung them carefully away in the huge walk-in closet, Mallory knew that the Dovedales would be rather disturbed, and one always had to maintain certain standards of reality in front of the servants.

They hadn't set out to hire a couple to look after them, but in their admittedly casual search for a cook, circumstances had taken them in another direction.

On the Monday following their wedding, they decided at the last minute to go to the opening night of the new musical, *Alma, Where Do You Live?*, and the St. Regis had obtained tickets for them, apologizing that they were in the last row of the orchestra, over on the extreme left side of the auditorium.

Not that the location of their seats bothered them. Their wedding had received wide coverage in the Sunday papers, and being a little inconspicuous was just what they wanted, and they slipped into their seats at the Weber Theatre just as the lights were dimming and stayed in them during intermission, graciously accepting the offer of the couple next to them to join them in a glass of champagne obtained from the theatre's bar. It was the most natural thing in the world that they should strike up a conversation with the middle-aged couple from St. Louis who were also staying at the St. Regis, and when

Mr. and Mrs. Brewer mentioned they were interviewing servants, hoping to attract a butler and cook to work in their new home, Mallory and Rupert in turn mentioned that they'd better begin to look for a cook for their own apartment or else they'd be living in restaurants.

"Well, we interviewed a very well qualified couple today," Mrs. Brewer enthused. "They're English, of course, but have been in Toronto for years and years, working for a widower who just passed away. We were so tempted—he seems to be a fine butler-valet, and I understand she's a superb cook—but our maids are all German girls, and I'm not sure they'd all get on. But the Dovedales—isn't that a charming name?—would be perfect for you and Mr. Randall. They're staying at the Fifth Avenue Hotel . . ."

"Mrs. Brewer, right now I'm not sure if we're going to end up thanking you or wishing we'd spent the night in our suite the way any right-minded honeymoon pair would have!" Mallory said out loud as she padded across the floor to the bathroom.

As she turned on the taps of the tub and tossed in a generous handful of bath crystals, Mallory recalled the interview she and Rupert had conducted with Hugh and Margaret Dovedale. Without a doubt, their references were impeccable, and it was almost painfully obvious that the couple were very anxious not to return to England where positions for married servants were few and far between and almost always in some remote part of the country. She and Rupert found they liked the older couple and hired them. But the end result of bringing together a proper couple used to a certain form and manner when it came to their employers and a pair of newlyweds who preferred to do things for themselves and each other was yet to reach a satisfactory conclusion.

While the tub filled, Mallory washed the makeup from

her face, patted her skin dry with a fluffy towel, and took off her remaining pieces of lingerie. In the marble tub she slid down until the bubbles came up around her throat. The perfumed water was warm and relaxing, the perfect place, Mallory decided as she rubbed a fat bar of Guerlain soap over her shoulders, to review the day and get ready for the evening ahead.

I'm still on my honeymoon, she reminded herself. But it's a very strange—or is it very modern?—honeymoon when the bride and groom go off to their respective offices when the only thing either of them cares about is coming home again and how soon they can get through the next month and leave for California.

As she soaked, Mallory tried not to think that if it weren't for the Horton Steel transfer, she and Rupert would be in San Francisco right now.

At least we're in our own home, she comforted herself. That's much better than the last two weeks when we came home every evening to the St. Regis. That was the perfect place for the first two weeks of our marriage when we had nothing else to do but concentrate on each other.

Whenever she thought about their first two weeks together, Mallory knew she would always recall the long walks they took together during the day, the plays they went to at night, as well as the day they'd hired a car and driver to take them out to the races at Belmont Park, the antique shops they visited in search of treasures for their apartment, and the nights, the long, tender, exciting nights of love that were never long enough no matter how early they went to bed.

An hour later, Mallory returned to the living room to find the ever-efficient Dovedale had left a silver tray holding the cocktail shaker, two properly chilled long-stemmed glasses and a dish of salted pecans on the satinwood coffee table. As she checked the contents of the shining new silver shaker, Mallory decided that there was a great deal to be said for a proper butler who knew how to mix a proper martini without having to be instructed in the proper disposition of vermouth and gin. Smiling, she surveyed the room again, noting that now there was a fire waiting to be lit in the fireplace, and that the curtains were closed against the unexpectedly chilly night.

Now all that I need to make everything perfect is one slightly overdue husband, she thought, touching a match to the fire.

Mallory had changed into a Callot Soeurs at-home dress of pale blue velvet with a collar and cuffs of Venetian lace and a girdle of black charmeuse with embroidered ends of dull silver, a pair of silver evening slippers, and an opera-length strand of pearls fastened with a cornflower-blue sapphire clasp.

As she sat down on the long, deep-pillowed ivory damask sofa, she reviewed her day, but in spite of today's surprise, today's success for Thea, she couldn't help wishing that they were not in New York. Not because their love needed a change of scenery to thrive or because they needed more time alone to adjust to each other, but for some undefinable instinct that continued to whisper that it would all be better if they were three thousand miles away. . . .

Looking into the mirror over the fireplace, she saw Rupert pause in the doorway, and turning to look at him she smiled and said, "The only words I have to say to you are Ritz-Carlton."

Instantly, Rupert grasped the meaning behind her words, and a smile spread over his face. "You and Thea got the commission. I knew you would!"

"I'm glad you were, because we weren't all that sure," Mallory responded as Rupert crossed the floor toward her. She put her arms around his shoulders as he dropped down beside her. "Where's your raincoat?" she asked lightly, resting her head against the fine dark worsted of his suit jacket.

"I hung it up in the closet."

"Dovedale is going to have a fit—or give notice!"

"Not yet; he hasn't collected his first month's wages." He drew her closer. "Do I see a silver shaker full of martinis?"

"Yes, but you have to get ready for dinner before you have one."

"Not fair. Is this what marriage means, refusing your loving husband the sustenance of a cocktail after a hard day's work because he isn't wearing his dinner jacket?"

"Did you have an awful day?" Mallory asked, instantly concerned.

"I'd rather talk about yours. When did the Ritz-Carlton committee finally wake up and realize that hiring Thea Harper Associates to decorate their hotel was the smartest move they could ever hope to make?"

"At approximately eleven-fifteen this morning," Mallory told him, lifting her head from his shoulder so she could see his reaction. "Of course it's not for the entire hotel, only two suites, two double rooms and a single, and, of course we had to agree to stay within the agreed-upon hotel decor, but that's not terribly important. I listened in on the extension, and Thea got them to agree to mention her in all stories about the hotel, and she can make the connection known at once. Isn't it wonderful?"

"Yes, it is, and I can't think of a firm that deserves the position more," he said wholeheartedly, bending over to kiss her. "You and Thea make a great team."

"And you and I make an even better one," Mallory said as she felt the light scrape of Rupert's cheek against hers, then his mouth covered hers and she forgot all about the questions she wanted to ask him and how she wanted to be sure he wasn't too worn out. But the minute he touched her all that mattered was the feel of his mouth against hers.

"In another minute, if I don't stop, we'll never get to dinner, and then the Dovedales will really give notice," Rupert said a moment later, reluctantly raising his head after taking one more deep breath of her perfume, Guerlain's heady *Sillage*.

"Besides, I think you've just earned your martini," Mallory said, not trusting herself to do more than deposit a quick kiss on his lean jaw.

A few minutes later they were curled up on the sofa, sipping icy martinis and feeding each other salted pecans when Dovedale appeared at the doorway.

"Oh, you are home, sir," he observed blandly. "My apologies. I didn't hear you come in, and I only just saw your briefcase in the foyer."

"That's perfectly all right, Dovedale, I'm sure you had other important things to attend to," Rupert said, hiding his amusement. "I'm quite capable of hanging up my own coat."

"If you say so, sir," Dovedale returned evenly. "Dinner should be ready in a half-hour."

"That sounds just about right," Rupert said, draining his glass. "If you'll run my bath, I'll be up in a moment."

"Certainly, sir, and your dinner clothes are already laid out," the butler responded in a much happier tone of voice.

"See, darling," Rupert said, bending over to kiss Mallory as soon as Dovedale left them. "All it takes to keep our butler happy is letting him make a fuss once in a while. By the time we leave for California, he'll be so well trained that our opening the front door ourselves and not having to be picked up after won't affect him at all!"

"I'm afraid I exaggerated a bit when I told you 'we' got the Ritz-Carlton commission," Mallory admitted some forty-five minutes later as they sat down at their ivory-colored wood dining room table set with Ceralene china, Baccarat china and Tiffany silver. "To tell you the truth, I won't have very much to contribute to this job."

Rupert looked around the dining room where Mallory had ordered the heavy paneling stripped from the walls and everything painted white, had the radiators covered with decorative enclosures and silver fixtures installed and had hung their prize Matisse over the sideboard and filled the silver cache-pot the de Veigas had given them with red and white Rubrum lilies, and wondered how she could ever say that she had nothing to contribute.

"Isn't that all in the eye of the beholder?" he asked as Dovedale served the mushroom soup; thin and strong the way it should be on a chilly autumn evening. "I think every suggestion you make to Thea is very important."

"It's nice to have a friend at court," Mallory replied as the butler poured their champagne and then discreetly retreated to the pantry. "But when I said I wouldn't be contributing to the Ritz-Carlton project, I should have elaborated further. This is really all Thea's," she explained as they ate, "and it's going to be her imprint that the committee is looking for, not mine. I'll be helping her, of course, but it's not the sort of assignment that means a fifty-fifty division of responsibilities."

"Are you upset about this?"

"I don't have any right to be. This is going to take months, and we'll be leaving for our honeymoon trip in a few weeks. Thea is going to have to hire another person, someone she can train to take my place for the months

485

we'll be away," Mallory said, pausing as Dovedale took away their soup plates, served the cheese soufflé, and refilled their glasses. "I hope this isn't going to upset anyone's apple cart, but I told Thea all about Nancy Harley, and tomorrow she's going to try and hire her away from your firm at quite an increase in salary and more of a future than she could hope for in her present position!"

They enjoyed the first roast quail of the season accompanied by wild rice, and in the French fashion ate the salad of escarole, endive and chicory prepared with Mrs. Dovedale's special dressing following the main course instead of before it. Dessert was a meltingly delicious chocolate marquise made of chocolate biscuits filled with chocolate cream, iced in chocolate and topped with coffee cream anglaise, and by the time they finished their café filtré, Rupert was quite adjusted to the idea of Thea hiring Nancy.

"I agree that she can do far better than sitting behind a reception desk until she either gets married or until someone decides that it's time to hire a younger woman," Rupert said as they reentered the living room, their arms around each other's waists. "Do you think she'll accept?"

"Is your family going to offer her a promotion that will make better use of her intelligence?"

"No."

"Then, my darling, unless Nancy has a very strong sense of duty toward the firm, you have your answer."

At the other end of the living room, another six-and-a-half foot sofa covered in an identical damask was arranged in front of the bookcases, and they settled down there to sort through their books.

"We'll put all the impressive books down here and hide the whodunits and the romances up in the bedroom," Mallory remarked as they unpacked the complete set of Andrew Lang's *Fairy Books.*

"Which is exactly where they belong," Rupert replied with a knowing smile, checking to make sure that the twelve-volume work, published in London between 1889 and 1910, all bound in tan calf with labels color-coded to the titles, were there. ". . . yellow, blue and lilac," he finished. "Our set seems to be complete."

"Good." Mallory placed the first editions of Jane Austen's *Persuasion, Northanger Abbey* and *Emma,* all bound in tan calf with gilt spines on the first shelf next to the recently published *Jane Austen And Her Country House Comedy,* which critics were hailing as the work which was serving to reacquaint the reading public with Miss Austen's work, although Mallory needed no such introduction, having been given a complete set of all the English Regency writer's work as one of her fourteenth birthday presents. "Do you want to keep the biography of Drake down here or upstairs?"

"Upstairs, for sentimental reasons."

"Already? We've only been married a month. I thought it would take about six before you decided that you felt very strongly about everything concerning us, or that you really couldn't spare the time to care so much outside of the bedroom."

"Don't you know by now that you're my one very special weakness?" Rupert asked, standing up and putting his arms around Mallory. "There isn't anything about our life together that isn't important to me."

"I still have a bit of difficulty with that," Mallory admitted. "I'd never doubt your fidelity or your loyalty, but sentiment . . . And we're both such independent people—"

"Who just happen to want the same things," Rupert interjected. "Nothing strange about that. I finally learned to stop hiding what was important to me. Men generally hate to admit this, but a bit of sentiment here and there isn't such an awful thing."

Mallory laughed mistily and stroked the back of his head. "I think we've had enough intellectual pursuits for one evening."

"Does that mean what I think it does?"

Mallory pretended to look considering. "It *is* a tad early."

"But we're still on our honeymoon," Rupert parried, silver eyes gleaming.

"Oh, yes, that we are." Laughing, she kissed his cheek and whispered in his ear, "We have a lovely, long night ahead of us, so why don't we put on the victrola and we can begin to get ready for bed by having a dance or two in the privacy of our living room!"

"I think one of the greatest inventions of the twentieth century is going to turn out to be the victrola," Rupert said as he and Mallory danced to a recording of "Ragtime Nightingale." "Thanks to that fine machine, I can hold you as close as I like and for as long as we want without having to worry about other partners."

"And if only someone would invent a device that would keep it wound up and change the records it would be perfect!" Mallory said, moving even closer to Rupert, feeling the rising warmth of his body through the thin velvet of her dinner dress.

"If we didn't have to stop every so often to reset the needle, I'd have probably ravished you right here on the carpet by now!"

"Just give me a chance to close and lock all the doors,"

Mallory whispered in his ear.

"Shall I change records, or just set this one up again?"

His quiet, provocative voice with only the faintest hint of a British accent sent an unmistakable thrill racing through her. She caught her breath and pulled back to look at him.

"If you do either of those things," she warned him, "I'll sue for divorce the first thing in the morning!"

The master bedroom was ready for the night. The curtains were closed, the bedside lamps turned on, and all telltale signs of her daytime life were put away for the next eight hours.

"I was just thinking that the only thing the bedroom was lacking is my husband, and here you are," Mallory said several minutes later as Rupert walked into the room.

For a long moment he looked at Mallory, reclining against the pale sheets, wearing a nightgown of cream-colored crepe de chine, her makeup washed off and her brown hair down around her shoulders.

"I must have heard your thoughts while I was changing," he said, joining her on the bed. "Do you know how you make my heart beat, just looking at me the way you do?"

"Very fast, I see," she said, slipping a hand beneath his dressing gown and pajama top, and then leaned forward to press her lips against the base of his throat where a strong pulse was beating with a steady pace.

"I love you so much," he whispered, kissing Mallory's hair as he gathered her into his arms. "And I'm so glad that you insisted we move into our apartment before we leave for California," he went on, switching off the lamps before he slipped the satin shoulder straps of her nightgown down until her breasts were free. "It is different, being in our own home, setting out our own lives on our own terms . . ."

Rupert's voice became a pleasant murmur to Mallory as his hands reverently cupped her breasts, making them swell to his touch while she pulled at the belt of his dressing gown, wanting to reach the eager flesh underneath.

Somehow his robe and pajamas and her nightgown were discarded on the floor, and Mallory closed her eyes in delight, her back arching as Rupert ran one hand lightly over her bared body.

"Oh . . . yes . . ." she murmured as he eased her back against the pillows, returning his kisses and drawing him closer until every inch of his nakedness was pressing against her. "Just—like—this—"

They took their time with each other, prolonging every kiss, every touch, until neither of them could bear it for another second, and then their bodies, already entwined and entangled, seemed to come together in one searing thrust, and every movement thereafter seemed to have its own accompaniment of bursting fireworks, each more colorful and consuming than the last until the final, ultimate enchantment . . .

For a long time after their shattering climax, Rupert lay awake, Mallory asleep in his arms, waiting for sleep to claim him. He waited until it was all too clear that tonight was made for insomnia; a rare enough attack, but one he nonetheless suffered from time to time.

Carefully disengaging himself from Mallory, he slipped out of bed and put on his pajamas and dressing gown.

"Rupert, is something wrong?"

Mallory's sleepy voice startled him, and he leaned back across the bed to kiss her.

"Nothing, darling. Go back to sleep."

Pushing her hair out of her eyes, she regarded him,

490

blinking at the room's darkness. "If you can't sleep *now*, there has to be something the matter. Where are you going?"

"Down to the living room for awhile. I seem to have a bit of insomnia."

"Poor baby. Do you want me to come down with you? I can make you a cup of tea."

"Which would only wake up the Dovedales, who'd insist on bringing out the silver service. No, I'm better off by myself right now. Besides," he couldn't resist adding, kissing her again, "you've done more than enough for me tonight. Go back to sleep, darling, I won't be too long."

The Cartier clock on the living room mantle showed eleven-forty when Rupert came in, carrying his as-yet unread mail. Stretching out on one of the sofas, he switched on the nearest lamp and methodically began to open and read each piece of mail.

At first it was the usual boring things: bills from Brooks Brothers and Sulka, the bill for his annual dues to the Columbia University Club, and the run of the mill charity appeals. There were so many last-minute and belated notes from acquaintances he'd made in his travels over the past four years, all telling him they'd just learned of his marriage and all wishing him well that when it came to the last letter he opened it without a second thought.

My dear Mr. Randall, (the letter ran)

My heartiest congratulations upon your recent nuptials. Without a doubt, you and your bride are among the most handsome of young couples. So well suited to each other. And so respectable.

But we know that isn't quite the entire picture, is it? You have done an admirable job for the past eight years, covering your past misdeeds until no one can quite remember what it was you actually did in your rather violent early youth.

Do you by some chance recall the Countess of Stilldort, Lady de Gifford and the Marquise Delaude, to mention only a few of the infamous—and notorious—ladies you passed time with? I do, and I understand that there are certain publications here in New York that would be quite interested in printing such interesting facts about your past.

Naturally, I will not discuss my future plans in this matter in any way except face-to-face. I will be in touch with you shortly to elaborate on a solution that I'm sure will prove acceptable to both of us. . . .

Automatically, Rupert reached for the letter's discarded envelope, and with no great surprise he saw that the pale gray envelope contained no more information than his name and address; the cancellation mark over the postage stamp was too blurred for him to make out which post office it had been mailed from.

What was he expecting? A signature, an address, some indication of the sender that obviously had not been included?

Rupert looked around the living room, mainly in shadows, but still the same as when he had first turned on the lamp. Five minutes ago he didn't know what this note contained. Five minutes ago he would have sworn that he was the happiest man in the world, that he had everything he wanted, that everything in his life was perfect. He looked at the letter as if he'd suddenly found himself holding a dead rat, and a sick, cold feeling spread through him, all the brightness, all the happiness slowly ebbing out of him.

So this is what it feels like, he thought. Why did I think all the problems I'd ever had were behind me? Look at this room, nothing's changed, and upstairs the only woman I've ever loved is waiting for me. I feel like nothing is ever going to be right again. So this is what it feels like to be blackmailed.

You must do the thing you think you cannot do.

—Eleanor Roosevelt

Wall Street

By the time Rupert reached the Seligman offices on Wednesday morning, his initial horror and revulsion at the blackmail letter had hardened into a new resolve. Whoever wrote him that letter was not going to get a penny out of him.

At some hour between midnight, when he finally slipped back into bed beside Mallory, and half-past six when he began his day, there had been more than enough time to decide that the sort of threat being waved in his face was going to leave him unmoved. He knew of far too many men who, once they came under the blackmailer's web, found themselves captured by a force from which there was no escape.

To be sure, that knowledge had done nothing to erase the chill that had gripped him or ease the relentless pounding of his heart, but it was all he had to hold on to. The certainty that he would have only one chance to free himself before he was caught forever.

But now, at shortly before nine, suffering from the aftereffects of his unpleasant surprise and too little sleep, Rupert was painfully aware that he was going to have to lay the entire matter out before William Seligman. It wasn't going to be an event to remember with any sort of fondness, but he had to let someone know about his predicament, and he certainly wasn't going to tell Mallory.

He supposed it was, on the surface, a sort of fierce masculine reaction that nothing like this should touch his wife, but he also knew that if he took the time to closely analyze his feelings, he would come up with an altogether different answer. The old sense of isolation that he'd lived with for so long and which truly never disappeared was back, and with it the feeling that the fewer people brought into this matter the safer he'd be.

Feeling slightly sick, he opened the door leading to William Seligman's suite and came face to face with Mr. Lang, his private secretary.

"Is my—is Mr. Seligman in?" he questioned, taking a step backwards from their near-collision. "I have to see him for a few minutes."

"No, Mr. Randall, I'm sorry to say Mr. Seligman isn't in yet," the older man replied blandly, but Rupert caught a look of uncertainty in his eyes.

"It's a quarter before nine, and he's always here by now unless there's a meeting scheduled elsewhere. Is there some sort of emergency?"

"I really don't know, but I was on my way to see you and the rest of the senior staff. Mr. Clifford just telephoned and asked that I tell all of you to please cancel any outside appointments and wait for him to arrive. He wants to speak with each of you individually."

It was obvious that Mr. Lang knew nothing more than what Cliff had told him, and with a quick thank-you for the information, Rupert left for his office.

If nothing else on this raw, windy morning, there was a pleasant refuge waiting for him. A place where *The Wall Street Journal* was waiting for him. So was his mail, but as he sat down behind his desk, Rupert decided that he would be quite happy if he never received another letter.

The first draft of the report that would go to

stockholders of Horton Steel was also waiting for him, and Rupert lost himself in that, somehow successfully managing to forget the time so that when Cliff did walk in, he looked at his watch and noted with some surprise that it was nearly half-past ten.

It wasn't Cliff walking straight in without having himself announced first that sent a fresh wave of apprehension through Rupert; it was the stark, set, white look on his face.

"What happened?" Rupert asked without preamble. "It's something awful, isn't it? It's all over your face."

"So much for ever playing poker again." Cliff's voice was quiet, grim. "I've just come from Gareth's office, and Jimmy's; you're third on my list. There isn't any way to tell you this except directly," he went on, coming to sit on the edge of Rupert's desk. "Dad had a heart attack this morning."

A wave of pain so strong it actually left him nauseated swept through Rupert as he absorbed Cliff's words.

"How bad is it?" was all he could ask.

"We don't know yet. Thank God, Alix lives only two floors away. Dad passed out on his way to the dining room, and Mother got her downstairs right away. Alix knew what it was straight off, and she called John and a heart specialist she knows at Roosevelt Hospital. By the time I got there everything was under control, but I rang up an old classmate of mine who's a heart specialist down at Johns Hopkins. He'll be coming up from Baltimore this afternoon, and hopefully by tonight we'll know more. But until then, we have some important points to cover."

"But how does it look?" Rupert insisted. "You must have some idea?"

"The way it is now, it was probably a very slight heart attack—more of a warning than anything else." Cliff stood up slowly, obviously reluctant to have to move on to the next person on his list. "Is this the first draft of the

Horton Steel stockholders' report?"

Over the next fifteen minutes, the two men discussed pending work, and as he prepared to leave, Cliff unexpectedly placed a hand on Rupert's shoulder. "It's going to be all right, you'll see."

"I know. It's just the shock . . ."

"We'll adjust, and let's see what all the specialists have to say. In the meantime . . . well, I just want you to know that I'm glad I was wrong seven years ago when I told Dad that taking you in would be a mistake. I thought you'd end up bringing some sort of awful mess down on us. You haven't, and today I'm glad you're here with us, working with us, and all of us together will keep things moving until Dad is at the helm again."

After Cliff left, Rupert remained at his desk, staring straight ahead, not really seeing anything at all. The last avenue of escape from blackmail had not only been closed to him, but he was literally on his own. It wasn't that Cliff—or Henry, if it came to that—wouldn't help him; it was simply that they would never let him forget about it afterwards. All sense of trust, built so carefully over such a long period of time would be destroyed before he even finished explaining.

The one man who gladly would have given him counsel was incapacitated, and as he sat at his desk, his work ignored, Rupert faced the fact that he was totally alone in this.

And as for Mallory— There was nothing he couldn't tell her and still have her love and support, nothing she didn't already know about him, but this was different.

Secrets upon secrets, he thought. An experience in infinity.

Suppose the blackmailer sold whatever information he had to *Town Topics*? It struck Rupert as the ultimate irony that he could find himself paying blackmail to whomever wrote the letter *and* Colonel Mann, the paper's publisher.

No, one extortion at a time, thank you very much. He was willing to pay the price to make certain no scandal from his past should upset William Seligman at this time, Rupert decided as his telephone rang, and he lifted the receiver at the end of the first ring before his secretary could answer, instinctively certain of who was at the other end.

"Mr. Randall, do you know who I am?"

The voice was British, very well-bred, and as he forced back the ugly reply that came to mind, he wondered why he wasn't more surprised at the caller's accent.

"Yes," he replied coldly, abruptly. "If your letter is anything to go by, I can assume you like nothing better than long and detailed conversations, but this is a business office and I don't have time for useless chatter. Just tell me what you want."

"Why, to meet with you in a civilized manner, of course." The voice at the other end of the phone actually had the audacity to sound injured. "There's nothing like a quiet drink between friends while discussing business."

"You're no friend of mine, and the business you want to discuss, in case you're unfamiliar with American law, is called extortion."

"Oh, come now, Mr. Randall, surely after your distressing news this morning you're not going to begrudge me my, let us say, *enterprise*."

"You certainly know your way around American expressions."

"I have to admit that at certain moments, a particular colloquialism does enliven one's conversation. But to get back to business . . ."

"How much?"

"Ten thousand dollars."

"A nice round figure. In cash, I assume."

"Now, now, there's no need for sarcasm."

Rupert took a deep breath and strove to keep the hate out of his voice. "Where and when?" he asked coldly, sickeningly aware that he had just taken the first step into the steel trap of extortion from which few men were ever able to walk away.

There seemed to be the promise of a fortune in every breeze which swept over the high plateau west of the Park.

—The New York Times, 1895

The Hotel Marie Antionette

William Seligman's new Packard pulled up in front of the entrance to the Marie Antionette at Broadway and Sixty-sixth Street, and before the uniformed doorman could come forward from his post just inside the door, MacBride came around to open the door of the tonneau.

"Shall I wait for you, sir?" he asked as Rupert stepped out and cast a disparaging eye upward at the overcast sky, glad that Adele had insisted he take the car and driver when he finished his afternoon visit at Bill's bedside.

"Yes, please, MacBride. It looks like rain."

"Nasty weather," the driver concurred. "More like December than the end of October."

"Isn't it," he agreed, thinking that the thick, gray Friday afternoon not only mirrored his mood, but was a fitting backdrop for his mission. "I don't think I'll be too long." *And I wish I weren't going in at all*, he added silently.

Built in the style of the Second Empire in 1896 when the vogue for Nouveau Louvre buildings was popular in New York, the Marie Antionette had never been a particularly attractive sight, and this afternoon Rupert would have happily watched the whole ugly mass crumble under a wrecker's ball.

501

As he crossed the sidewalk, the uniformed doorman, costumed in a swallow-tailed coat and gaiters, clothes more suited for a servant at an English estate than an employee at a Manhattan hotel, swung open the elaborate iron-work door and the tapestries that served as protective portieres, to allow him easy access to the dim interior furnished in the extremely elaborate, fussy style that he had always loathed.

With his heart beating in a combination of disgust, anger and annoyance, and eager to get this whole mess over with as quickly as possible, Rupert made his way to the bar. Unconsciously grinding his teeth, he stopped at the doorway, taking in the dark, almost empty room, oppressive with its heavy paneling and stiff velvet curtains. Underfoot, a Shirvan rug covered half the floor, with a Karabagh rug taking up the remainder of the floor, both carpets having come a long way from the looms of Transcaucasia to a hotel bar on the Upper West Side of Manhattan.

As he stood beside a hexagonal Chinese plant stand supporting a not-quite-full-size potted palm, a waiter approached him with the bland manner restaurant officials adopt when they're playing go-between.

"Mr. Randall? The table in the far corner, sir."

Of course it would be, he thought, taking a seat in a baluster-legged chair with a crested back, covered in the sort of mock tapestry the lesser sort of upholsterers sold by the yard. *The seat in the farthest recess of the room where I can't see his face very clearly.*

"Mr. Randall, how good of you to be so prompt," the man opposite him said in low tones. "But then of course you would be, coming from the Dakota as you are."

How does he know my movements? Rupert speculated, suspicions flaring that he *had* to know this man, but now, with his eyes adjusted to the dimness, all he could make out was a man of indeterminate middle age who seemed utterly forgettable. It was only the voice, that reminder of his own background and heritage, that had any distinction, but no matter how he searched, it was also thoroughly unfamiliar to him.

"Bourbon, please, with lots of ice," Rupert told the waiter who appeared at his side, and until the man returned with his drink he remained silent. "Shall we conclude this as quickly as possible?" he said at last, taking a sip of his drink, and as the warmth of the liquor began to spread through his chest, he reached into his suit jacket, withdrew a long white envelope, and tossed it down on the small table. "Your blood money."

At the whiplike sound of Rupert's voice, the older man flinched and took a precautionary sip of his sherry. "Now, really, Mr. Randall."

"Well, what would you call it?"

"Insurance payments. Yes, that has a nice ring to it. Insurance against certain things ever appearing in *Town Topics*, and I'm sure that you'll find that paying me a rather definite sum over the next months will, in the end, be far preferable to indefinite servitude to Colonel Mann."

"What do you know, a short term blackmailer!"

"I don't intend to remain in this city past the middle of March, and since this is the twenty-eighth of October, an additional five-thousand dollars every week from next week to the beginning of March really won't amount to all that much."

"And one-hundred thousand dollars is going to make quite a nice nest egg for you, isn't it?"

"I have to admit it will," he said after a pregnant pause. "And I can assure you that you won't have to be concerned about any future demands."

With anger flashing in his eyes, Rupert brought a hand down on the thick envelope. "I can take my money and leave right now."

"Mr. Randall, I warn you—"

"As the Duke of Wellington said—publish and be damned!"

"Possibly. But just imagine the effect on the convalescence of your benefactor. And he's doing so well, too. And isn't he fortunate that he's going to make a full recovery?" The Englishman's voice was low and insidious. "But it's strange how even the smallest item of bad or disturbing news can adversely affect a man who has had even the mildest of heart attacks."

Slowly, Rupert withdrew his hand, an indescribable rage filling him. Here he was, with a man whose name he didn't know, paying extortion money in order to keep events eight years behind him from appearing in the scandal press.

"Now this is more like it, Mr. Randall. Do try to meet your gentleman's responsibility with grace. The difficulties, the embarrassment and the humiliation I could bring to you and your wife—"

"Leave my wife out of this!"

"Oh, but she is very much a part of this, and not only as an adjunct to you. I believe she has a history quite her own, some of it quite recent. Her relationship with Sir Romney Sedgewick, for instance. Oh, how surprised you look. Ladies do like their secrets, I've found. Not that we gentlemen can claim too much credit. There's your father—"

"Do you get some special thrill in digging up the dead?"

"Your temper is just like his," he said in a reminiscent tone of voice. "Hair-trigger. Of course he was crazy. Quite insane."

The older man's final words hit him with the force of a physical blow, and for a second, Rupert thought he'd gone deaf from shock.

"Of all the gall—" he said as the buzzing in his ears

stopped. "If it weren't for William Seligman's heart attack, I'd tell you to go peddle your trash for the few pennies it's worth." He tossed off the remainder of his drink in one gulp and stood up in a swift, single motion.

Apparently undisturbed by his pantherlike grace and hostile mood, the older man handed him a familiar rectangle of paper.

"Your card?" Rupert asked sarcastically. "Ah, yes, Mr. Smyth."

"That's good enough for our purposes. And you'll note the address."

"General Post Office Box Four-twenty-two."

"Very good, Mr. Randall. And don't forget next Friday. In cash, please. Large bills will do nicely."

"I'm not likely to forget, am I?" Rupert spat out, and as he swung around and started across the floor he could hear the shadowy figure laughing softly at him.

Without love, intelligence is dangerous; without intelligence, love is not enough.

—Ashley Montagu

One Lexington Avenue

"Well, Auntie, what do you think of our decorating efforts so far?" Mallory asked gaily, tucking an arm through Esme Phipps' as they entered the living room from the dining room doors following a tour of the apartment. "I know it's a bit raw, but I think we pretty well have an idea of what we want."

"Never mind that," Esme said, kissing her goddaughter. "I can't see where a few blank spots here and there matter very much," she went on firmly, unbuttoning the jacket of her pretty Lucile tailor-made of dull gray velveteen trimmed with bands of dark gray satin, satin buttons, and little touches of soutache braiding. "No doubt you and Rupert will find lots of interesting objects in San Francisco. Of course, I do love your hanging the Redon over the piano."

"It was Rupert who picked out the spot," Mallory pointed out proudly as they sat down on the sofa in front of the fireplace. It was late Friday afternoon, November fourth, a sunny, very chilly day, the sort Mallory normally loved. She had spent the morning at the Plaza Art Auctioneers, successfully bidding on a Sheraton dining room table and chairs for a client, had lunch in the Ladies' Restaurant at the St. Regis with Melinda Nevins

507

and Constanzia de Veiga, and had spent the remainder of the early part of the afternoon in conference with a delear in antique wallpaper before coming back to the apartment to welcome her godmother. But all the activity had not been able to still the questions that plagued her about Rupert's sudden—although very subtle—shift in behavior. "He thought the Redon in one corner and the Vuillard near the bookcases make a nice contrast," Mallory went on, her Cheruit dress of biscuit-colored velveteen trimmed in oriental embroidery emitting an expensive whisper as she crossed her legs. "As an interior decorator, I'm rather pleased that I selected a man with such a good eye!"

"As long as you don't regard him as competition in your field!"

"Oh, never that," Mallory laughed, and rang for Dovedale to bring in their tea. "We're complementing each other. I can understand annual reports and make sense of stock quotations, while Rupert can identify handblocked Chinese wallpaper and Imari porcelain."

"I have some news for you, darling," Esme said a few minutes later, selecting a tiny watercress sandwich. "Would you and Rupert be terribly upset if your Uncle Newton and I weren't here to see the two of you off for California?"

Mallory hid a smile. "Yes, horribly! We'll never forgive you. Oh, of course not, Auntie! Where are you and Uncle Newton going? It's a little early for Palm Beach."

"But it is the right time for South Carolina. Bill and Adele have been invited down to Hob Caw, and we're going with them. I'm afraid we all need a rest," Esme concluded with a small sigh.

"When do you plan to leave?" Mallory asked, unexpectedly feeling a sense of loss. Don't be an idiot, she reprimanded herself. You're not being deserted, and you know very well that they're both worn out from the wedding. The knowledge that only a few years before Newton Phipps had been far more ill than William Seligman was now, came back to her. "Maybe Rupert and I will give you all a going-away party!" she offered generously.

"But I thought you and Rupert were determined not to do any entertaining, and weren't even accepting invitations!"

"Well, those *were* our original plans, but it does seem rather selfish of us not to see those we love the best socially, particularly since we haven't exactly been in seclusion. It'll be a small buffet, or a sit-down dinner, whichever you prefer. Just tell me when."

"Rather soon. Since Bill is making such a rapid recovery, Adele is worried he'll want to make a try at assuming some work again."

"But he can't do that!"

"No, and that's why we're leaving a week from this coming Monday, the fourteenth."

"That isn't going to give me much time. We'll have it next Saturday," Mallory decided firmly. "That way there's Sunday for everyone to recover."

"Are you sure it won't be too much for you?"

"No. Since Thea hired Nancy Harley, there's an even better division of work than before. While she's learning the office details, I can visit the auction houses and antique dealers and take care of one important client with a rush job, and that leaves Thea free to concentrate on the Ritz-Carlton."

"Nancy Harley—?" Esme looked puzzled for a moment. "Oh, yes, the young woman who came to your wedding. But she works for the Seligmans."

"Worked. Thea offered her a position early last week as an assistant, and she accepted. She told us that even with all that was going on, Cliff insisted that this was too good an opportunity to miss and that she start the next day."

"And Cliff told me that because he knew he'd have to answer to both Julie and his father if he insisted she give two weeks' notice, he told her to take the position straight off. And as long as I've touched on the subject of married couples," Esme continued with a sidelong glance, "how are you and Rupert?"

"Come now, Auntie. You know I won't kiss and tell!"

"I don't have to ask you *that* sort of question. One look at you gives me a very affirmative answer. But there are always other areas."

"If it were nothing but lovemaking, no one would ever get married," Mallory quipped, and then looked down at her beige kid leather opera pumps, reluctant to tell her godmother anything that might be misconstrued as the wonderings of a young bride who didn't understand why every single thing wasn't right. Besides, what did she have to go on except her own suspicion that there had been some sort of shift in Rupert's sphere of existence, and although it had nothing directly to do with her or their life together, it was eventually going to reflect on it. "He's so tired," she said at last, dealing with a reasonable wifely concern. "More tired than he'll tell anyone about. He came back from Chicago like that, I'm sure of it. Everything would have been fine if he'd had all of August to rest in, but we got engaged, and when you add up the pressures of the wedding plus his having to complete the paperwork on the Horton Steel transfer plus the shock of Bill's heart attack plus one or two other things and the result is, ultimately, exhaustion. I don't want Rupert in a state of collapse," Mallory finished passionately.

"No, darling, of course you don't," Esme soothed, casting about for some concrete advice to give her goddaughter that did not sound like meddling. "How do you explain that a strong-minded man can't be swayed

510

from doing whatever he wants to?" she mused aloud.

"Oh, Auntie, you don't have to tell me that! I think I've known it since I was sixteen." She put her arms around Esme. "I know you didn't expect me to say what I did and I know you want to give me warm words of advice and I also know that there really isn't anything you can do for me and even if there were, I probably wouldn't want you to."

Esme's look was filled with love and a new respect. "I've always known you had good judgment, Mallory, and I'm glad to see that you didn't put it aside when you got married. You'd be surprised how many brides feel that they have to abrogate that ability to make a decision the moment they get married."

"I don't think Rupert would stay with me for five minutes if I couldn't handle my own difficulties, and I don't think I'd be able to look myself in the mirror if I didn't."

Both women stood up, Esme to get ready to leave and Mallory to accompany her to the door. Their bright little tea party had unexpectedly taken on a somewhat darker and certainly disturbing tone.

"I won't worry about you because I know you can deal with any problems that arise," Esme said as she arranged her gray fox furs to her satisfaction, "but promise me that if you think a party will be too much of a strain, or if Rupert doesn't want to do any entertaining just yet, don't be too upset. Sometimes new husbands are just as jealous of their privacy as they are of their brides, and in a situation like that it's simply better to go along and not force any sort of gathering. Men," she added with a definite twinkle in her eyes, "can be very sensitive about things like that!"

"Esme said *what*?" Rupert said a few hours later as

they dressed for dinner. "I can't think why she'd assume I don't want guests in our new—if somewhat incomplete—home."

Mallory turned around on her dressing table bench. "Oh, she said something about new husbands not being strong enough to stand such strenuous social lives."

"I think I'll make it through," Rupert remarked with a flashing smile. "Now, shall we have a sit-down dinner or a buffet?"

"A sit-down dinner," she decided firmly. "When there's a buffet, extra guests always turn up; not that we'd mind, but we can't have too many people just yet." Mallory added another touch of powder to her face, sprayed on a bit more *Rue de la Paix*, and stood up, her Callot Soeurs dress of pink silk shot with gold, ornamented with cream lace and banded in brown mink falling around her slender body in clinging swirls of fabric. "We'll decide on the menu while we eat."

"Speaking of which, what's for dinner?"

"We're having cream of curry soup, a pompano done in a paper bag, steamed rice and broccoli, and a soufflé Grand Marnier for dessert. And you sound just like a very hungry man after a hard day's work," she added as they left the bedroom.

"And believe it or not, that's exactly what I am. After a day like today, I've come to the conclusion that the only difference between me and a day laborer is that when I come home at night I take off a business suit and put on a dinner jacket."

Mallory kissed Rupert under one ear, above the wing collar of his dress shirt, smelling the crisp scent of Guerlain's *Imperiale*. "And here I imagine your doing nothing more strenuous than reading the financial newspapers," she teased gently. "Is it all secret negotiations, or can you talk about it?"

"Oh, I intend to share all the gory details with you," Rupert responded too quickly, his first pangs of conscience already attacking when he thought about that afternoon at the Marie Antionette, and what, he speculated, had led Mallory to use the very appropriate expression, "secret negotiations." "Of course, I'll expect to hear a few specifics about your day," he went on with a lightness he didn't feel. "Was it very frantic?"

"To tell you the truth, it wasn't as bad as I thought it was going to be. Nancy's turning out to be a very valuable asset—just as I always said she'd be," she said as they went down the stairs. "Wall Street has lost a fine receptionist, and Thea has hired a potential decorator."

"Are you at all jealous?"

"If I had to make a choice between decorating rooms at the Ritz-Carlton or taking my honeymoon trip, I'd still much rather go to California with you. No second thoughts about that, not ever."

"That is so flattering to hear."

"Well, fine French furniture comes and goes, but it'll never replace love and romance," Mallory said as they reached the foyer and stopped to share a kiss. "I want you to tell me all about your visit with Bill this afternoon, but first I have to tell you that I now have a client all to myself, and it's not one of the usual small jobs that I do, either."

"I'm very impressed," he said as they went into the dining room. "Would you care to tell me who the lucky party is?"

"Someone we both know rather well. Since this job isn't going to take too long, Thea decided that it was made to order for me to take over and complete before we leave. Congratulate me," Mallory went on as Rupert held out her chair. "I'm now in complete charge of decorating

Romney's new apartment!"

He was being a fool. A fool with a sick and evil mind, Rupert told himself again, repeatedly, for more times than he could count in the past five days since Mallory had told him that she was now responsible for seeing that Romney had the New York City home of his dreams. Which was perfectly all right as long as none of the client's dreams were centered around Mallory.

That had been Friday night and now it was Wednesday night, and he was seated at his black lacquer writing table, ignoring the reports he'd brought home to study in favor of staring at the envelope in the center of the dark green leather writing surface. So far, all he'd written was the address—*Mr. Smyth, General Post Office Box 422, New York, New York*—and now he found himself unable to complete the task for this, the first of his weekly blackmail payments. Tomorrow morning he'd entrust the heavy envelope to a bonded Wall Street messenger who would deliver it to the General Post Office between Broadway and Park Row at City Hall Park. Once there, the messenger would hand it over to the official in charge of the private boxes who would issue a receipt and put it in the proper box. It wasn't strictly legal, of course, but it was the only safe way to send five-thousand dollars.

Resolutely, he opened the right hand drawer and took out an oblong metal strongbox, spun the combination to the lock and lifted the lid. Inside were ten neat stacks of five-hundred dollar bills, twenty bills to each pile, and Rupert counted out five-thousand dollars, wrapped the bank notes in a blank sheet of paper, slipped it into the empty envelope and sealed it.

He put the envelope in his briefcase, painfully aware that he'd never expected to find himself in this situation, but this wasn't the only new crease in his life, he reminded himself. Bringing work home from the office was another. The unwritten office rule against it had fallen by the wayside and when it would be put back into use was a matter best left undiscussed.

As was another subject, Rupert thought, trying to concentrate on the latest survey from General Electric. Without a doubt, Mr. Smyth, or whatever his blackmailer's name really was, had known what he was doing when he'd planted those first seeds of doubt in his mind when he spoke about Mallory and Romney. He couldn't, wouldn't, mention the matter to her, but despite all his intellectual reasonings that this was all supposition grafted onto pure spite, his mind was endlessly spinning out possibilities.

Romney and Mallory. Mallory and Romney. A client and decorator relationship. Or was there something more? Had Romney come to New York with the select purpose of wooing Mallory, only to find her engaged, and was now considering a relationship that from his years with King Edward's set he was far more familiar with?

He might have had the good manners to wait until Mallie had a baby before laying his groundwork, Rupert fumed in growing resentment, pushing aside the report.

Stop that, he told himself, aware that he was letting his imagination run rampant. You know it's not true, was never true, will never be true. That sick bastard did this to me. He knew how I'd react. He knew everything about me, right up to where I'd been that afternoon. I hope he chokes on his money . . .

"Rupert, it's after eleven. Are you coming to bed?" Mallory, in a nightgown and negligée of pale peach satin and cream lace, stood in the doorway. "I don't want to disturb you if you're working on something terribly important, but you look as if you're a million miles away."

"No, I'm right here, and there's no one more

515

important to me than you," he said as she came over to sit in his lap. "This is more like it."

Mallory nestled close against him, all her nagging doubts, at least for the moment, allayed by his warm and loving presence. She wanted to give him the benefit of every doubt, to believe that the emotional pain he was trying to hide was caused by his worry over William Seligman's unexpected heart attack, the problems this awful event had caused the firm—all of which were being added to Rupert's already fatigued condition. But there was more to it than that. Mallory was as sure of that as she was that Rupert wasn't going to tell her a thing unless the problem he was hiding either solved itself or else became unmanageable.

Until then, all she could do was trust him and love him. Old standbys offered no solution, but when they were together like this, she realized, discovering Rupert nude under his heavy silk dressing gown and very willing for her to reveal and explore every inch of him, she could honestly say that this was one instance where the old way was certainly the best way. . . .

Hours later, Mallory came awake in Rupert's arms, her head on his heart as they lay entwined across the black lacquer bed. Smiling, she moved quietly so as not to disturb him, and pulled the puffed silk quilt over them.

What a perfect way to inaugerate their second bed, she thought, gently running her fingers through his thick black hair. We can do anything together. There isn't anything that we can't share.

But almost as soon as the self-evident statement passed through her mind, another realization surfaced—one that was far less pleasant and conducive to dreams of marital bliss. It was something Thea had told her last winter when she thought Charles was seeing another woman. Her friend's words came back to her mind now, sweeping away the warm afterglow of love to leave her cold and more than just a little frightened.

"Men, even the very best of men, won't tell you what's in their hearts at the moment you can help them most," Thea had said in a voice that combined humor with resignation. "And there isn't a damn thing you can do about it except wait it all out. You can't convince a grown man to do anything he doesn't want to, and unfortunately there are times all you can do is hope it all comes out right in the end."

"Well, what do you have to say for all my efforts so far?" Mallory asked with a smile that said she already knew the answer. She leaned back against one of the walls of the living room, her Drecoll dress of soft beige *cachemire de soie* with a collar and cuffs of frilled lawn and a wide black satin belt, a pleasant contrast to the soft layers of newly dried ecru-colored paint. "I'd hate to think that all you can do is look around you like—"

"—like a child on Christmas morning," Romney finished, crossing the rose-colored Chinese carpet with blue and gold medallions to take Mallory's hands in his. "I know it's not finished, but I can't wait for Tildy to see this."

"Will that be soon?"

"Not soon enough," Romney said as he studied the room again. It might still be incomplete, but from the deep-cushioned sofas of rose-colored damask to the multi-paneled lacquered Chinese screen, to the Chinese Export side tables and the oval-backed Louis XV chairs upholstered in soft rose silk was perfect. "You and Thea are worth every penny that I'm going to be paying!"

"Let me hear you say that when you get the bill!" Mallory remarked as they left the living room for the

517

dining room to admire the oblong table and the lyre-back chairs with dusty-rose silk seats over heavy hand caning. "Amy is doing the final set of estimates today, then Thea and I will go over it, which means that within the month, when the final installation is done, you'll be writing a very substantial check!"

"Thea's hardly in business for her health," Romney observed, running his fingers over the Sheraton sideboard, mentally deciding what picture he wanted hanging over it.

"No, but you'd be surprised how many prospective clients think she is."

"In any case, there aren't going to be any complaints coming from me. In fact, I'm going to move in in a few days. Now that the workmen have finished and my home is so well furnished, I see no need to continue enriching another hotel!" Romney concluded with a wicked smile.

"How many have you stayed in so far?"

"Four. I was at the Plaza when I first arrived, then the Waldorf when I got back from Virginia, followed by the Knickerbocker, and since I came back from London, it's been the St. Regis for me."

"I love that hotel so much. Rupert and I spent the first month of our marriage there," Mallory said at the memory of those days such a short time ago when everything seemed perfect and there were no sudden silences on Rupert's part, silences that told her he was troubled by something he was determined to keep to himself, and the look behind his eyes that never went away. . . .

"Please, any more reminiscences may be too much for an old widower like me to handle," Romney was saying, but when he saw that Mallory wasn't paying attention, his manner became serious. "What is it, Mallie? Did I say something wrong, or are you and Rupert having difficulties?"

"No!" she snapped, and gave Romney a look that told him that if he valued his safety he'd forget he asked her that question.

"Please forgive me," he said hastily. He'd known Mallory for years, but it had taken him until this moment to realize that her temper was as sharp as her cousin's. "I think that for at least the next hour I'll confine myself to comments about my new home, if you'll be kind enough to go through the rest of the rooms with me."

Mollified by his tact, Mallory continued her guided tour of the apartment, pointing out all the improvements, all the tiny details that made an apartment special. He admired the special glaze that had been applied to the bedroom's Chinese wallpaper, told her about his collection of Chinese wallpaper, and agreed that his pair of fine hunting prints would look best in his study—all fine, impersonal topics to discuss until Mallory felt that her temper had cooled enough for them to move back to a personal matter.

"Why don't you come up to our apartment and have a drink?" she suggested when they returned to the foyer. "Rupert will be home soon, and I know he'd love to see you again."

"Can you be sure of that?"

"Oh, don't worry, he's very hospitable. The perfect host, in fact. And my invitation also extends to dinner. You owe us, Romney, since you didn't come to our dinner party Saturday night."

"And I'm sure I missed a superb meal."

"Then why didn't you come?"

"Because I felt it was more of an evening for family and very close friends."

"I don't seem to have a proper reply to that except to tell you that tonight Mrs. Dovedale is making lobster chowder and roasting a duck with oranges and steaming wild rice that we order from a place in Minnesota and fixing a sald with special dressing and topping it all off with a perfect orange mousse." Mallory took her black and white checked wool coat with the deep collar and cuffs and big pearl buttons that was one of Bergdorf Goodman's best-selling models for the year from its hanger in the foyer closet and folded it over her arm. "What do you say?"

"That suddenly the St. Regis sounds like a very boring place to have dinner. Of course it's understood that you and Rupert will have to put up with my telling you and Rupert all about my book, and if you can put up with that, I'd love to come to dinner!"

"Romney, I want to ask you a question," Mallory said a few minutes later as they sat in her living room sipping icy Manhattan cocktails. "Rupert will be home in a few minutes, and I don't want him to hear any of this."

For a moment, Romney looked nonplussed at the dark amber-colored surface of his drink. Suddenly, the conscience that hadn't been bothering him awoke, and he began to feel like a cad. An expression of self-disgust formed on his face—a change that Mallory didn't miss.

"You already know what I'm going to ask, don't you?" she said gently. "I'd like you to tell me why you've been telling people—our friends—why you would like to give Rupert a run for his money where I'm concerned. As well as all the other things that make it seem as though you have some special interest in me. We both know that's a lie, so why have you been using me?"

There was no rancor in Mallory's voice, no accusations, and that made the sense of shame Romney felt grow even stronger. Unlike some men, he had no repertoire of evasions and excuses. All he had was the truth.

"I didn't want anyone to think I was available for

social events, and I thought that if I made myself out to be somewhat . . . enamoured of you in a very private, very proper way, I'd be left alone."

"Men are so naive," Mallory murmured, feeling a surprising bubble of amusement rising in her. This wasn't funny.

"I'm afraid we are at times," Romney admitted shamefacedly. "I've been acting like an idiot, I realize that now, but how did you hear? I thought I was being rather discreet, and I never would have said anything that made it look as if I were going to make any advances to you." He took a somewhat larger than necessary swallow of his drink. "How did you find out?"

"Here and there. People always say things and make comments. I'm surprised that you thought I would be so flattered that I wouldn't mention any of this to you." Mallory put her drink down and regarded Romney with the utmost seriousness. "Romney, are you ashamed of Tildy, or sorry you got engaged to her?"

"Never. I didn't realize how empty my life had been until I met her. But you don't realize the sort of publicity Tildy received in London when her play opened. She was the darling of the press, and if anyone had found out we were engaged, that I wasn't more than another admiring, gift-giving stage-door Johnny, it would have been a circus. I wanted to spare her that."

"And what about yourself?"

"All I could think of when I came to New York was how to avoid being the hostesses' delight."

"So you decided to pretend that you were pining after me. I don't understand."

"Men are not only naive at times, they're frequently stupid. My pride reasoned it all out. If all our friends thought my romantic interests were centered on you, they'd leave me alone," Romney said miserably as he stood up and leaned against the fireplace. "And if it helps

521

matters any, I *do* think that Rupert is one very lucky fellow."

"I think that's for you to tell him."

"Unfortunately, I remember the Rupert of nine or ten years ago, and he was a little too pleased with himself that night at the Plaza."

"We're not discussing my husband," Mallory pointed out somewhat coolly. "He hasn't been going around telling people what he thinks about another man's wife!"

"Touché."

"And what do you think all our friends are going to say when you and Tildy get married? Do you think that Alix and Henry and anyone else you've been talking to are going to like being the object of some obscure joke?"

"I never thought of it like that." Romney's voice was filled with regret. "If you think it will help, tomorrow morning I'll start ringing up all my friends and tell them I'm engaged and have been all along."

"It's not your place to announce your engagement," Mallory remarked with the first hint of a smile. "But you could stop talking about me as if you just decided that after knowing me for seven years, you came to the conclusion I was the woman you wanted to court."

"Done," Romney said, and was thoroughly delighted when Mallory jumped up and came over to him.

"Thank you," she said, putting her hands on his shoulders. "I suppose I should take it as a compliment that you thought I'd make a good cover, but if it's all the same to you, I think it's something that I—not to mention Tildy—can live very well without."

She kissed his cheek, and Romney, who had been feeling the full effect of his mistake, began to cheer up. There was nothing like a beautiful woman smelling of expensive perfume unexpectedly kissing you, even if it was on the cheek and there was no promise of any further affection.

He was about to kiss Mallory's cheek when she stepped away from him. He saw the surprised look on her face, and as he turned to follow her gaze, his heart skipped a beat when he saw Rupert standing in the doorway with an expression on his face that made it clear he'd seen everything and heard nothing.

I've had a wonderful evening, but this wasn't it.

—Groucho Marx

12 East 67th Street

"*Mi casa es su casa*—my house is your house."

Don Renaldo and Dona Imelda de Veiga stood in the first-floor reception room, a spacious area with marble floors and walls and a wall fountain with a marble fluted pool holding large orange goldfish with a four-foot tall stork, handmade with individual brass plates drawn up to it. Here they greeted their guests with the ancient, traditional welcome of Mexico, a country now in the midst of violent revolution with no settlement in sight. Since the 1600s, de Veigas had lived at Hacienda de Veiga in Chihuahua, but in the past year and a half, home for the wealthy, well-traveled couple and their children was a large townhouse on fashionable Sixty-seventh Street between Fifth and Madison Avenues, decorated by Thea to a fine, high gloss.

It was obviously a comedown in terms of real estate, but there had been little if any change in their economic situation, and unlike many of their fellow exiles who were trying to carve out new lives in Rome and Paris and Rio, living for the day when they could return to Mexico, the de Veigas had a busy life in New York, and now, on Saturday evening, November nineteenth, they waited at the foot of the curving marble staircase to welcome their guests in the same manner as they would on the gallery of the Hacienda.

This was a dinner party neither Mallory nor Rupert had any original intention of attending, but after several first nights at Broadway shows that weren't any better than they had to be, an evening that promised to combine dinner with music afterwards sounded unexpectedly appealing.

"Welcome to your first visit to our home as a married couple," Dona Imelda told them warmly, her creamy, raven-haired beauty set off by a Worth gown of pale lavender satin over cream-colored chiffon embroidered in crystal beads. She took Mallory's gloved hands in her own. "Have you heard from your families yet?" she went on in a concerned voice. "I trust the weather in the Carolinas is much warmer than it is here in New York?"

"Much nicer," Mallory said. "They rang us up on Tuesday morning and said the trip down was wonderful and made even nicer because you lent them your private car."

"It was just sitting on a siding in the New York Central sheds collecting rust," Don Renaldo said with a fond smile. "We were more than happy to have it put to such good use. In fact, since we don't plan to be doing any more traveling this winter, would you care to have it for your trip to California? It can be attached to the Twentieth Century, and then in Chicago to the Overland Limited without any difficulty, and Charles and Thea can vouch for its comfort," Don Renaldo added with a twinkle in his usually serious dark eyes. "A wedding trip shouldn't be encumbered with train schedules and overcrowded Pullman cars."

"If you're certain it wouldn't cause you any inconvenience, we'd be very pleased to take you up on your offer," Rupert said, flashing one of his famous smiles, looking at Mallory for confirmation. "As it happens, we were talking about hiring a private car. I want Mallory to have every luxury for our wedding trip. She's been so patient about the delay."

"It's settled then," Dona Imelda said with satisfaction. "Just let us know the date you'll be needing it."

"Now that's what I call the benefits of having a social life," Mallory whispered to Rupert as they mounted the stairs. "Thea told me the de Veigas' railroad car is all Honduran mahogany and gold panels in the sitting room, and the master bedroom—"

"Why don't you just let me wonder what the bedroom is like," Rupert whispered back, slipping an arm around her waist. "Maybe if we say thank-you enough, they'll throw in a couple of servants!"

At the top of the stairs they separated, with a footman to the room set aside for the gentlemen, and a maid to take Mallory to the bedroom where Dona Imelda's personal maid was waiting to help all the ladies with their wraps and hair.

As Carmen fussed with her, hanging up her Poiret evening cloak of rose-colored velvet embroidered in silver with a rose satin lining and a sable collar and then insisting on adjusting a few loose pins in her hair, Mallory found herself far more concerned with Rupert than her reflection. Usually an invitation to the de Veigas meant an almost precious attention to detail so that the formal, correct couple would not feel that they had invited someone who was not up to their standards. But ever since the other evening when Rupert had walked into the living room to find her kissing Romney (and *that* sounded ghastly, even when she repeated it to herself), his response had been so surprising, so unlike what she was sure it would be, that she couldn't stop trying to analyze it.

Rupert's bad temper was well known, but the explosion she expected never came, and he accepted her explanation without question and with a bit of dark amusement. For her part, Mallory knew she had no reason to feel guilty; she and Romney hadn't been engaged in an illicit activity, but she would have expected her husband to ask more questions or have had more of a reaction. Instead, Rupert seemed to be surrounded by an air of almost feverish activity. His mind always seemed to be somewhere else now, he was eating less and less, and the only thing that hadn't changed was what happened when they closed the bedroom door, but even their lovemaking seemed to have taken on the aspect of being used to keep the demons away rather than the fulfillment of their love for each other.

Feeling rather distracted herself, Mallory took one last look at herself in the full-length mirror, her Lucile gown of rose-colored voile de soie combined with silver and rose shaded silk embroidery set off by a low neck and, for contrast, above the soft satin belt a wedge-shaped piece of black satin was inserted, providing the perfect reason for her to wear the double strand of black pearls that Rupert had given her.

Well, Don Renaldo and Dona Imelda don't have to worry that I won't meet their high standards, she thought as she started for the door, but I'd much rather be back in our apartment. . . .

"We were just talking about *The Cub*," Henry said as Mallory joined Rupert who was standing with the Thorpes and the de Renilles in front of the Lalique doors that led from the drawing room to the small conservatory that Don Renaldo had had added on to the house. "Alix and I thought we would catch the show before it closes," he went on. "Is it worth our time?"

"Not really," Rupert replied. "But Douglas Fairbanks is quite good."

"He deserves a much better play," Mallory stated

quite truthfully since she'd been very impressed by the young actor whose style and grace reminded her so much of Rupert. "And so does Broadway. It looks like another iffy season."

"Doesn't it?" Alix agreed, looking stunning in a Poiret gown of Delft-blue satin veiled in black chiffon with a low V-shaped bodice encrusted with blue crystal beads, with a diamond and sapphire necklace around her slender throat. "*Raffles* was an awful disappointment, and so was *Getting A Polish* and *The Bachelor Belles*. As for *Anti-Matrimony*—"

"Careful, Alix, you're not supposed to say those words in front of a newly married pair," Charles said, leveling his topaz gaze directly at the Randalls. "So far," he went on with a fond look at his wife, "Thea is the only one who hasn't offered her opinion."

"Go see *Get-Rich-Quick-Wallingford* again, or catch Blanche Bates in *Nobody's Widow*," Thea replied quickly, her eyes the same color as her Poiret gown of green silk overlaid with black point d'esprit edged in colored silk floss, her emerald jewelry the necklace and bracelets Charles had bought her in Brussels. "Otherwise, just go on with your conversation. I'm admiring my handiwork."

Thea had decorated the entire house, and now, some five years after completion, it still remained her largest, most complicated job, and in it she combined the de Veigas formal outlook and tradition with her own modern concept without sacrificing any qualities important to both client and decorator, and if the fountain in the reception room was her bit of whimsy, all of her sense of elegance had been brought to use in the drawing room.

The walls had been painted the softest, palest shade of yellow trimmed in white, and the inlaid parquet floors showed where the beige, celadon, yellow and salmon oriental rug ended. Although Thea had lost count of the number of times she had been in this house, in this room, tonight, as always, Thea watched the drawing room fill with guests as if it were five years ago when it was first finished.

Watching everyone arrive, she pretended that they too were seeing it all for the first time: the twelve-panel Coromandel screen, the most expensive she'd acquired before or since; the eighteenth-century English mantel, and the Chinese Export antiques among the fine eighteenth-century French and English furniture.

"You know perfectly well everybody loves this room, that it's brought you compliments *and* clients," Charles whispered to her as they excused themselves from their group and crossed the length of the room to sit down on a yellow brocade sofa.

"Is there some reason you've spirited me away? Besides the obvious one that you want me all to yourself for a little while."

"I always like that," Charles smiled. "But the real reason is the Earl of Tilmore," he went on with an edge to his voice as he watched Hugo and Edith join the Thorpes and the Randalls. "A long time ago when I was so ill, Hugo made some rather off-color comments about me."

"I know." Thea's voice was quiet. "I heard about those comments."

"I shouldn't complain too much. That's just Hugo's way of being witty, and compared to some of the things that were being said about me, his remarks really weren't all that bad. But tonight I don't want more than one reminder of those days."

Thea touched Charles' hand. "I don't quite understand."

"Rupert. Didn't you notice his very bright eyes, the manner that's too enthusiastic, the circles under his eyes?"

"Charles—"

"It's all there," he said softly, pain in his topaz-colored eyes. "I've been there, Thea, and I can see the early symptoms in someone else. There's no mistaking them, and I'm afraid Rupert is on the track to some sort of breakdown."

A dinner party at the de Veigas was like being asked to take part in a perfectly rehearsed ballet, Mallory thought as the drawing room continued to fill.

Until their last guest arrived, Don Renaldo and Dona Imelda would remain in the reception room, and in the meantime their eldest son and daughter-in-law, Roberto and Constanzia, were acting as host and hostess, circling the drawing room, making sure that all was flowing smoothly among the guests. As usual at parties given by the Mexican couple, there were no cocktails, only slender stemmed glasses filled with the finest Spanish sherry were offered, and at shortly after half-past eight, the elder de Veigas joined their guests, going from group to group, making each person feel as if they were the most important guest invited.

"It's very nearly like being among royalty," Hugo remarked after the de Veigas moved out of earshot. "Ian said that Edie and I simply had to accept this invitation, and now I see why—in a manner of speaking it's like being invited to Sandringham in the good old days."

"With a few modern additions here and there," Alix added, suddenly understanding why Charles had taken Thea and gone to the other side of the room. At times Hugo was simply too much to take for long periods of time. "It's too bad Regina and Ian couldn't be here tonight," she continued. "Reggie told me that she plans to set her next whodunit in a New York City townhouse, and this would be a fabulous place to do some

531

research in!"

"Still, there's nothing quite like having the opportunity to watch your husband buy a semi-bankrupt shipping firm," Hugo said in a jolly voice. "We thought about going up to Boston with them, but I decided—oh, never mind," he continued, turning his attention to Mallory and Rupert. "You two are awfully quiet."

"Oh, Hugo, don't be a pest," Edith offered, her Cheruit gown of king's blue chiffon veiled with black chiffon inset with gold lace rustling as she moved to place a restraining hand on her husband's arm. "They're probably tired."

"Well, if you're not going to be tired on your honeymoon—" Hugo began wickedly, but was fortunately saved from continuing by the appearance of the de Veigas' butler announcing dinner.

If Mallory had been hoping to avoid Hugo Tilmore for the rest of the evening, she was out of luck when it turned out he had the place to her right in the dining room where the candles in the eighteenth-century Russian chandelier threw the room into glittering relief.

"I wasn't going to say anything too terribly awful," he assured her as they took their seats at the elaborately laid table.

"Well, I guess neither of us will know that now," Mallory couldn't resist saying.

"Do you honestly think I'm so awful a person?"

"Not on purpose," she said as the footmen began to serve the Beluga caviar. "I think it's just a way to amuse yourself—even if you do unintentionally hurt someone now and again. I'm amazed that you've never gotten into trouble with some of your bright and witty remarks!"

"Oh, but I have," he countered with an unexpectedly bitter look, and then moved their topic of conversation to a subject other than himself.

They were forty at the table, and in a rare thing for a

dinner party, their conversation centered around the same matter—the theatre versus the silent films that were being made with better and better story lines and more sophisticated techniques. All of them had seen Georges Melies' 1902 *A Trip To The Moon* with its hand-colored plates, as well as Edwin S. Porter's 1903 eleven-minute film made in New Jersey, *The Great Train Robbery*.

"I think that at last count there are approximately eight-thousand nickelodeons across the country," Rupert said as their hot consommé accented with a thin slice of lime was replaced by cold salmon with cucumber aspic. "It's hardly fair to say they're still a passing fad."

"Possibly not if you live in Nebraska or some such place where the residents are dependent on a touring theatrical company to come to town," Henry said wisely. "But as long as they can't talk—"

"I know, you'll take the stage," Mallory said. "That's not progress, Henry."

"Particularly not when you consider *From The Eagle's Nest*—"

"And those one-reelers from Biograph—"

"*Her First Biscuits*—"

"*The Violin Maker Of Cremora*—"

"And the Italians are doing a film version of Dante's *Inferno* that's going to be *five* reels—"

Their conversation continued on through the crown roast of rare lamb with perfectly steamed rice and baby peas and carrots, and Mallory listened and took part with full enjoyment, not only because the topic was one she was enthusiastic about, but for the pleasure of watching Rupert holding forth on this topic. With no effort at all, he was the star of the dinner party because he discussed films with the same delight he took in seeing them and the financial gold mine he was sure they were going to turn out to be if only investors were willing to wait a few years.

For a few minutes, her sense of unease began to lessen. No man who had a crushing problem could carry on a discussion with such verve, she decided. In a way, his manner reminded her of how he behaved when they were alone together in the privacy of their bedroom, and then Mallory's heart began to sink again. Whatever his problem was, Rupert had simply used his strength to put it away for a set amount of time and would resume it when his moment of glory was past.

The soufflé flavored with rum and studded with candied fruit had been enthusiastically consumed, and now that the café filtré had been drunk, the dinner party had undergone its usual separation, the women following Dona Imelda to her private sitting room, and the men accompanying Don Renaldo downstairs to his study, a remarkable room with walls covered in deep red Cordova leather, and chairs and sofas that were more than worthy of the best of London's men's clubs.

Once the brandy was poured and the fine Havana cigars offered, the men broke off into groups so they could discuss their favorite topics without either boring or offending anyone else.

"Charles has been acting as if I'm carrying something contagious," Hugo muttered to Rupert. "Besides, I can use some financial advice. Can you spare a few minutes?"

"Why not?" Rupert felt a marked improvement in his mood since dinner began. The pain and anger brought on by the knowledge that for yet another week his blackmailer had collected—and was no doubt enjoying— five-thousand dollars, plus the additional memory of seeing Mallory kissing Romney, had receded for the first time to a manageable size.

Together, the two men went to the farthest end of the

study, well out of the hearing of any of their friends.

"I need to make some money, quickly," Hugo said without preamble, all theatrical amusement off his face. "I'm not down to my last pound, you understand, but some of my English investments have gone sour, the rest are pretty well tied up, and I had a very large, very unexpected cash outlay about six months ago and haven't been able to make it up. And America is rather expensive," he added, almost as an afterthought. "I can't wait for your nickelodeons to boom and make me a millionaire."

For the next half-hour, Rupert gave him the best possible advice. True, some of it was partially confidential—news about mergers and Army contracts about to be awarded—but he had always rather liked Hugo, and he didn't want to see him in a financial fix.

"I really can't thank you enough," Hugo said, closing his notebook.

"Look, there is a risk, some of them are strictly in-and-out deals. But you'll turn a profit."

"And that's just what I want." Hugo looked at him and then laughed at his own private amusement. "Funny, though, you're the last person I ever expected to be taking financial advice from. In fact, about ten years ago, if anyone had asked me, I would have said that by this time you'd be as crazy as your father was!"

"What did you say?" Rupert asked, feeling as if an invisible hand had reached into his chest and grabbed his heart.

"Your father— Oh, dear boy, you look like you've seen a ghost. You do know about your father, don't you? I'd never say he was a nice man. . . ."

"Get to the damn point," Rupert muttered. The hand was off his heart now, and it was thudding sickeningly against his ribs.

"Your father was, to put it as politely as possible, a

535

madman, a raving, certified lunatic."

"Who told you this?"

Hugo took a quick step backwards, alarmed at the cold silver light in Rupert's eyes. "It's common knowledge, I'm afraid. Ask Henry, if you don't believe me."

"It doesn't matter," Rupert replied coldly, and then he stalked out of the room, feeling as though the red leather walls were closing in on him.

If I don't move, I'll collapse, he thought, and stifling the urge to dash out the door to the cold, deserted street, he climbed the stairs and made his way to the music room.

He sank into a corner of a pale blue silk-covered loveseat, hardly aware that at the other end of the room the musicians were tuning up. Somewhere a musical clock was chiming the hour.

Fifteen minutes ago I didn't know about any of this, he thought, the agony inside him growing. I can live with the blackmail because I have no other choice, but this.... Funny, I thought "Smyth" had to be lying. Hugo has no reason to lie—"Ask Henry"— What do I say—by the way, was my father ...? My father was a madman, a lunatic, certifiable, and everyone knows what they say about madness running in families ... straight through generations without a stop ... no escape for anyone ...

"Rupert, please, what is it?"

For a long minute, Rupert simply stared at Mallory, all ability to speak temporarily suspended.

A half-hour between the end of dinner and the start of the music, all the time it took to ruin my life, he thought, and it seemed as if all the light and happiness he'd found since August was now nothing more than a mass of shattered crystal.

Almost as if he were coming out of a dream, Rupert noticed that the music room was filling up with the other guests. The low hum of conversation and scraping of chairs and the rustling of expensive fabrics all seemed an unbearable calliope of sound. The Wedgwood blue walls were an assault on his senses, and the sound of the musicians tuning up were rubbing his shattered nerves raw.

"Rupert—" Mallory's voice was quiet but insistent. "Let me help you."

"We can't leave."

"I know, darling, I know. Just listen to the music, and then we'll go home and it will be all right."

The first selection was *The Magic Flute*, but tonight Mozart held no charms, no relief, and as the music scaled upwards, he held Mallory's hand, certain that nothing in his life was ever going to be good or right or happy again.

One Lexington Avenue

"What's this?" Rupert asked as they came into the living room at shortly after one in the morning and he saw a deep blue Brooks Brothers box propped up against the sofa closest to the bookcases. "I know Brooks Brothers likes to cater to their customers, but isn't this rather late for a delivery?"

"It's a present for you," Mallory said, trying desperately to keep her voice even, afraid that if she said one word too many she would start to cry and not be able to stop.

And what help is that going to be to Rupert? she asked herself as they went over to the sofa. I'm never going to be able to forget his face when I came into the music room. Earlier tonight, I thought the worst was over, and now I think it's only starting.

"What is all of this?" he asked, seeing not only the oversized box, but a neat stack of train schedules and hotel brochures and stationery with detailed notes made in Mallory's handwriting.

"I asked Dovedale to put all of this out after we left," Mallory said as she sat down. "I thought tonight would be a good time to discuss the final arrangements for our honeymoon trip, and you could open your present. It was going to be a surprise for you—" Mallory's voice ended on a ragged note, and Rupert knelt in front of her.

"It's a beautiful surprise for me, darling," he said, taking her in his arms. "You couldn't know in advance that my own personal problems, caused by my own stupidity, would—would—"

His own voice became too shaky to go on, and for a few minutes they held each other tightly, not daring to say a word until the worst of the moment was over.

There was nothing Mallory wouldn't do for Rupert, but as she held him, her face buried against his shoulder, she knew that whatever he had to tell her, however awful it was, would have to be reached at his own pace and in his own way.

"Tell me about your plans for us," he said at last in a muffled voice, sitting beside her on the sofa, an arm tight around her waist, holding on to her as if she were his last link to reality.

"I thought we could spend a few days in Chicago," Mallory responded in a voice that didn't sound particularly normal to her. This was silly, ridiculous, but if it were going to help Rupert talk, she was more than willing to discuss their travel plans. "We have tentative reservations at the Hotel LaSalle—we'll have to confirm our arrival date with them next week. I like the idea of a hotel where each floor has its own waiters and maids as well as a lady clerk," Mallory went on, aware that she was rambling, but more than willing to keep talking. "I want to go to the Art Institute and Marshall Field, and of course we have to have representatives from O'Connor and Goldberg pay a call."

"If you're so eager to buy shoes, we can go to their showroom in the Republic Building."

"But half the fun is that they have salespeople who'll bring the entire line for men and women to our suite."

"But you love to go shopping," Rupert protested with the faintest glimmer of amusement. "And you've never been one of those women who expects the stores to come to her."

"The joy of traveling, my darling, is doing all the things you don't do at home. And as long as we're on the subject of shopping, I decided I wanted to buy you something suitable for California. Mr. Webb was very helpful. Of course if you don't like it . . ." Mallory let her voice trail off as Rupert parted the snowy tissue paper and took out a polo coat of white wool trimmed with top stitching and mother-of-pearl buttons.

"It's perfect," he said, standing up and throwing it over his shoulders, and for a minute he looked like his old self, even to the extent of being able to wear an informal coat over white tie and tails and make it look right.

But it was all a facade he couldn't keep up.

"Please keep talking," Rupert said, sagging back against the bookcases.

Obligingly, her heart heavy with apprehension, Mallory outlined plans for San Francisco. "I was wondering," she went on, a shade too casually. "Do you think I should take some clothes from Lane Bryant with me? Once we can put aside all our precautions, I don't think we'll have too long to wait before we start a baby, and as long as I'm healthy there's no reason why we can't stay in California, and who knows what kind of maternity things I'll find out there? I don't see any reason why I shouldn't be prepared for all eventualities . . ."

"Mallie—" Rupert's voice was laced with pain. "There's something we have to discuss. Something I have to tell you."

It's going to be something awful, she thought with a rush of certainty that left her queasy with fright. It didn't have to do with them specifically. She'd bet every penny she had on it. It was some awful third thing that was threatening them, the same thing that had been eating at Rupert for the past weeks.

I have to help him and I have to be careful—very, very careful, she thought, and held out her hand to him.

"I'll listen to anything you have to tell me."

"Not here," he said quickly. "I don't want to spoil our home with what I'm going to tell you. Come downstairs with me."

"I'll get my coat," Mallory said instantly.

Upstairs in their bedroom, she knew that the evening wrap she'd worn to the de Veigas was too thin for prolonged exposure to the cold night air, and moving quickly she opened the closet and took out Rupert's birthday present to her, a full-length French seal coat with a long roll shawl collar, brocaded silk lining and three fur buttons. There was no time to change into a warmer dress, and she put the fur on over her evening gown, put the matching turban over her hair, found a pair of fine leather gloves lined in cashmere, and finally opened a Revillon Freres box. A few weeks ago on her birthday, Rupert had given her the coat and hat and two muffs, one of white ermine, the size of a snowball, and the other of black mink banded in brocaded silk Beauvais tapestry, and snatching up the latter from its tissue paper bed, Mallory ran for the stairs.

Rupert was waiting for her in the foyer, wearing the coat she'd just given him.

Without exchanging a word, they left the apartment for an equally silent trip down the elevator. As they approached the front door, Mallory tucked her right arm through Rupert's.

"Which way?" she asked, knowing instinctively that this was one of those times that required as few words as possible.

"Across the street."

At his equally brief words, Mallory's heart sank. Whatever Rupert was going to tell her had to be particularly awful, or else why would he select the private enclave of Gramercy Park?

History is a collection of agreed upon lies.

—Voltaire

Gramercy Park

New Yorkers like to point to Gramercy Park as their own little bit of London in Manhattan. Here—with the Third Avenue El only a block away—surrounded by distinctive town houses and new apartment buildings, is a private park, and entrance to the grounds is restricted to those fortunate residents who live facing its perfectly tended greenness. At almost all times of the day, the neighborhood was free of crowds, and now, at half-past one, there was no one around to watch in curiosity as a young man, dashing even at this odd hour in a white wool coat, and a young woman swathed in elegant furs, unlocked the high iron gate and entered the park, gently closing the swinging gate behind them.

For a few minutes, Mallory and Rupert walked along the silent paths before sitting down on a bench in the shadow of 34 Gramercy Park.

"I feel so stupid," Rupert said at last, closing his fingers around her wrists, just above where the muff ended. "When this began, I decided I could handle it all myself, that there was no reason to taint you with my problems."

Mallory was nonplussed. "*Taint*? You can share your problems, or you can even burden someone, but *taint* . . . ?"

545

"In my case, it happens to be very appropriate," Rupert said, tense and bitter. He had never planned to tell her any of what he was going through, but at the moment he should have used all his male strength and pride to keep her out of this sordid affair, his heart had taken command, and now it was too late for second thoughts. "I'd like to pretend that my life began in August 1903 when I got off the *Lucania*. I pretend a lot of other things, also," he went on in a voice that was too controlled. "I wasn't even fifteen when it happened the first time, but I loved it, loved all the rich, titled women who were getting back at my pious, self-absorbed mother by taking her son to their beds and teaching him about sex. I loved it all," he said as a cold wind swept through the leafless trees, and instinctively they moved even closer together. "Do you want me to tell you all about it?"

"If you want—if it will help," Mallory said, growing colder and colder in a way that had nothing to do with the weather. "You can tell me anything at all; I don't think I can say that enough. Have—have one of these women come back?"

"If I were a praying man, that would be what I would hope for. I could handle that happening. But this—"

The light from the closest street lamp made Rupert's face look oddly yellow, but the pain and distress on his face was no illusion.

"I'm being blackmailed," he told her at last, and the ugly word seemed to have a life of its own, hanging in the air long after he finished pronouncing it. "I'm being blackmailed," he repeated, feeling as if his chest were breaking open, "and I've just found out that by the time I'm forty-five, I'll be helplessly, hopelessly insane."

How long they sat together on the bench, Mallory

would never know. Somewhere, a very long way off it seemed, she could hear a car's engine as it turned down Irving Place, and the only indication that they were not alone were the lights switching on and off in various windows. The Third Avenue El had made its last run for the night over two hours before, and at this moment the wind sounded louder than Rupert's breathing. Even with her fur coat, she was rapidly chilling clear through, but as Rupert poured out the story of the past weeks, beginning with the letter and ending with Hugo's comments only a few hours before, nothing short of a blizzard would have made her move.

We have the ultimate privacy here, she thought as Rupert finished his tale. And where else to hear about a cruel, ugly, obscene action but in a place of beauty—the highest of all possible ironies.

"You're not insane now, and you're not ever going to be," Mallory said, speaking from her heart. "It's a lie what they told you, a cold, heartless lie told by one man for greed and by another out of jealousy!"

"No, it's a story told by two men who have nothing to do with each other. Hugo, no matter what his short-comings are, is not a blackmailer, or in league with one. On the other hand, my 'Mr. Smyth' has a great deal to gain—to the sum total of one hundred thousand dollars."

She was raised to money, never had to consider a price tag or worry about paying a bill, and yet the amount of money the blackmailer wanted as the price of his silence struck her with the force of a blow.

"I'm never going to miss the money," Rupert said as if he were reading her mind.

"I know that, but I can't stand the thought of your paying hush money, and just because your 'Mr. Smyth' has the voice and manners of an English gentleman, it doesn't make him any less of a bloodsucker!"

547

"Well, I've decided to let him take it all in one swoop—and I hope he chokes on it," he said in a savage voice. Now that it was finally out, now that he could finally tell Mallory, Rupert felt all his suppressed vitriol pour out. "This Friday, he gets it all. A proper day-after-Thanksgiving present as it were. I'm paying him off, and then I'm going."

A cold trickle of fear spread through Mallory. Nothing, she thought, could be more unbelievable than the last twenty minutes, and it isn't over yet. The only question I have now is if Rupert's including me in his plans or not.

"Can you be ready to leave town on Friday afternoon? If my Englishman has any questions for me, I'm really not interested in being here to answer them."

All the bright, wise, or otherwise witty remarks Mallory might have made, she bit back with an almost superhuman effort. Rupert was in no condition for a cross-country trip, but she couldn't tell him that. In his state, he didn't want reasonings, only an answer.

"You know I can be ready to leave on this afternoon's Century, if it comes to that. Do you think he's going to go back on his word and find a publisher?"

"That's what I've been afraid of all along."

"But couldn't you go to Henry or Cliff?"

"They wouldn't help me even if they wanted to. Don't you see," he went on in stark agony, "I'm all alone."

"You have me," Mallory said. "Why didn't you tell me this from the beginning? I'm not some helpless little girl you have to hide difficulties from!"

"I wasn't going to pay the blackmail." His voice was tired, hollow. "I was going to have it out with Dad—I knew he'd stand behind me and damn *Town Topics*. I was going to tell you at another time, but then Dad had his heart attack, and the only thing I could do was pay the bloody money and keep quiet about it. I can stand paying blackmail, but the idea that I'm going insane—"

"Stop that! You're no more crazy than I am!"

"Not right now, perhaps, but I will be. You know the rule about insanity running in families, passing from father to son," he responded bitterly.

"There's no such thing!" Mallory cried, wishing she could be entirely sure. "Insanity—genuine insanity—manifests itself in a lot of small ways over a period of years. If you were unbalanced in any sort of way, you'd never be able to accomplish what you have!"

"When I was seventeen, my father died in Switzerland in some exclusive sanitarium," Rupert went on dully as if he hadn't heard her. "I never even asked what he died of."

"Rupert, please, it's all right." Mallory knew her words were all but useless—comfort falling on ears that couldn't or wouldn't listen. "I'm here for you. I always have been and I always will be."

"Are you sure about that? What happens in ten or twelve years when I'm ready to be shipped off to a sanitarium?"

"You're not going anywhere except back to our apartment with me."

"I'm so tired," he said unexpectedly. "I don't feel as if I'm capable of doing the simplest thing. All I want to do is cry. Isn't it funny how all accepted ideas about masculine behavior seem to slip away when one's life crashes down in ruins?"

"I can see where a man really shouldn't cry during a board meeting or while he's on the floor of the Stock Exchange," Mallory said softly, reaching out to place her gloved fingers over the hot tears streaming down his face. "But no one ever said that crying in private is wrong, and Gramercy Park at two in the morning is as private as our own bedroom," she went on as she took Rupert into her arms.

The policeman whose beat included Gramercy Park

approached the park from the El side of Twentieth Street, and in the low glare of the street lamps he saw the couple huddled together on the bench. In any public park, his immediate reaction would have been to approach and ask them about their business, but Gramercy Park wasn't public property, and any questions that he had about the suitability of the couple, that somehow they might have broken through one of the gate's excellent locks, vanished as he came closer.

There wasn't the slightest doubt in his mind that they had a key, and huddling closer inside his uniform coat, he made it his business to walk as quietly as possible past the bench, where, on the other side of the gate, the young woman in the expensive fur coat held tightly to the young man in the white wool coat who was weeping with his face buried on her shoulder.

How seldom people find their happiness on a darkened stage; they must turn up all the limelights to find it.

—Daisy, Princess of Pless

Pier 52

Romney Sedgewick stood on the Cunard pier, watching as the longshoremen prepared the *Lusitania* for its berthing. A few more lines tied here and there and it would be time to set up the gangplanks. Only a few more minutes to wait, but it felt like hours.

Could anyone feel as happy as he did on this cloudy, cold Monday, shortly before noon? Romney seriously doubted that, but his spirit was so generous on this unappealing-looking day, he sincerely wished every lonely or misplaced person could one day feel the joy he was now experiencing.

Scarcely aware of the brisk, steady wind blowing off the North River, Romney anxiously scanned the deck of the luxury liner, looking for one very special face. No sign of her yet, but he could be patient. After all, what else had he been since the day they'd found they'd fallen in love but concluded marriage would have to be postponed? Her show and his book came first, they had reluctantly decided, and more than that, he wanted to have a home to bring her to when she came back from London, and no hotel suite, not even the grandest offered

551

by the St. Regis or the Plaza would do.

With a quiet smile, Romney recalled Tildy's flat at Cadogan Gate, and the time they'd spent there together when he'd been in London in early October. Of course he'd been properly registered at the Savoy, but that was purely for show, and except for the few hours each night, as well as Wednesday and Saturday afternoons when her presence was required on the stage of the Drury Lane Theatre in *Belinda of Bond Street*, they had been all but inseparable.

The first-class passengers were beginning to disembark now, and Romney turned his attention back to the present, his heart pounding with anticipation.

I feel like a schoolboy, he thought, and then realized he didn't care. Men and women with that tired, chilled look that comes from having to make a late November crossing, were passing him, but he only had eyes for the tall, slender woman in the full-length black carcaul coat with the rich opossum collar and cuffs, her blond hair hidden by a lavish hat the size of a tea tray.

"Romney—here I am. Oh, I thought we'd never finish docking!" Tildy exclaimed as she ran into his arms. "I've missed you so much, and during the trip I was so worried that you'd found someone else and wouldn't be here at all!"

"No, never that," he said, holding her close to him, not wanting to admit to himself how many things can go wrong at the last moment. He kissed her, not the kind of kiss he really wanted to share with Tildy, but better than none at all.

In short order, Tildy's luggage was cleared through Customs, and then they were free to leave the pier for the Cadillac waiting just outside the doors.

"What luxury," Tildy said as they settled against the

soft leather upholstery.

"It's just hired for the day, we'll see about a permanent car and driver later on," Romney said, noticing for the first time that she looked rather pale. "Are you all right, darling?"

"Oh, I'm perfectly healthy—more or less," Tildy replied a bit evasively. "I don't know how you're going to take this, I mean, we've never discussed this except in passing, but nothing works all the time and—"

Romney felt as if a shaft of sunlight was making its way into his body, illuminating all the dark corners and banishing all the ghosts.

"Tildy—"

"I may be pregnant. It's too soon to tell," she went on swiftly, her china blue eyes bright, "and I wasn't sure of your reaction . . ."

"How could I be anything but delighted?"

"Men have been known to have very funny reactions to this sort of news," Tildy remarked as their driver moved the car skillfully through the heavy pier-side traffic. "I—I didn't take any precautions while you were in London. I wanted this to happen."

"I think I wanted it also," Romney said delightedly, taking her into his arms. "We have a wonderful apartment waiting for us with an extra bedroom that'll make a perfect nursery."

Secure in his arms, Tildy began to laugh, all of her last-minute apprehensions gone. "Oh, I was hoping you'd say that. But Romney, I thought you told me our apartment was at One Lexington Avenue? We're going in the wrong direction!"

"Oh, no, we're not. I told the driver exactly where to take us, and as it turns out it's going to be a very appropriate place," Romney said, laughter evident in his voice. "In a few days, when you've recovered from the trip over, we can go south if you like, but as for right now— Darling, you've been away from New York for so long that you've forgotten that the license bureau is downtown. And all things considered, our going there right now is the best way for us to begin our life together!"

It is discouraging to reflect how needlessly unhappy people make themselves and each other.

—Noel Coward

One Lexington Avenue

George Kelly regarded the plates of cucumber sandwiches and frosted sponge drops with such delight that he completely forgot his stock of Shakespearean quotations.

"Now, Mrs. Randall, you didn't have to do this— particularly since you've asked me here to discuss business," he told Mallory as they sat on the sofa.

"There's no reason why we can't discuss this matter in comfort. It's such a nasty afternoon, I thought you'd like a nice fire and a cup of tea," Mallory pointed out as she reached for the tea things. "Lemon or sugar? You don't look like the sort of man who takes milk."

"And ruin this fine China tea?" he said, accepting a white Limoges cup and saucer with a wide gold band. "Clear will suit me very well, thank you, Mrs. Randall." In the past eight years, his career as a bodyguard and private detective had taken him inside the residences of those who were far wealthier than he, and he knew by heart the role he was expected to play. But this was one of the few homes he'd come to by appointment and had been given tea with the lady of the house.

"I hope you haven't had to drastically adjust your schedule to come here this afternoon," Mallory said, adding a small lump of sugar to her tea. "This is an

555

emergency, I'm afraid."

"I'll be glad to help you in any way I can."

"I hope so, George. My husband is being blackmailed."

For a countless minute, George could only stare at the young woman who sat beside him in a Cheruit dress of bottle-green broadcloth with a yoke and deep cuffs of Venice lace. For a split second, he wondered if she were joking, but one look at her face told him she was telling the truth.

"Has—has this something to do with another lady?" he questioned as discreetly as possible, and was thoroughly nonplussed when Mallory began to smile.

"Oh, George, it has to do with any number of women, all of whom my husband knew long before me," she said, and told George everything that Rupert had shared with her in the early hours of Sunday morning in Gramercy Park.

Even now, on late Monday afternoon, Mallory felt as if she'd fallen down a flight of stairs. Her body ached, her head seemed caught in a vise, and the only thing that kept her from going up to the bedroom and staying there was that Rupert was suffering far more than she ever would. He was too distraught to help himself, and it was up to her to make the first move toward straightening out this whole ugly mess.

As she sat in the warm living room, she suddenly felt as chilled as when they'd come back from their interlude in Gramercy Park. They had fallen exhausted into bed, but sleep had given them no relief, and as for love . . . Instead of his revelation making things easier between them, it had somehow made it more complicated, and the passion that had always flowed so easily between them was now a pale imitation of their previous splendor.

This morning, after Rupert had left for Wall Street, Mallory had examined the choices open to her. She could either go along with Rupert's wishes not to do anything, let him pay off the blackmailer in one fell swoop, and leave for California immediately afterwards; or she could go behind his back, to Henry for information, and to Cliff to obtain reassurance that the firm could withstand a certain amount of notoriety from *Town Topics*; or she could seek out a third party.

Three choices and there was only one right one to make, and as soon as she was dressed for the day, Mallory rang up George Kelly.

"That sounds a little, well, unusual for the sort of blackmail I'm generally used to hearing about," George said at last. "They seem to prefer something a bit more current, if you understand my drift."

"Exactly, but this isn't the entire tale." Mallory smiled grimly. "It's for a set sum of money to be paid every Friday, in cash, to a box at the General Post Office," she went on, giving him every detail.

"As I said before, very unusual," he remarked when she was finished. "Usually, a blackmailer likes to keep his victim on a string. It sounds as if the person Mr. Randall is dealing with is well aware that the information he has really isn't all that damaging, and he wants to milk it for all it's worth."

Suddenly, a single ray of hope pierced through Mallory's despair. "George, are you trying to tell me that the extortionist *knows* his information isn't all that horrible, but he's been able to convince my husband that it is?"

"Most times, the shock is so bad that no convincing is necessary. A normally intelligent man will fork over money to keep information out of the scandal sheets that the rags wouldn't be interested in in the first place! Take the money and run, as they say. And with Mr. Randall being so vulnerable following Mr. Seligman's heart attack. . . ."

Mallory closed her eyes for a moment. "But the

557

business about his father—"

"Well, that depends on whether or not it's true."

"The scandal sheets don't care about paltry things like the truth." She refilled their cups and put another sponge drop on George's plate. "To tell you the truth, I have no idea if it's a twisted man's fantasy supported by gossip, or an ugly fact that Rupert and I are going to have to face together. But that's not why I'm hiring you," Mallory added swiftly. "That is, if you want the job."

"How could I say no?" George looked amazed that she would even suggest such a thing. "Guarding ladies wearing diamond tiaras can't measure up to finding out a blackmailer. Besides, there's nothing interesting on my schedule until the opening night of that new opera, *The Girl of the Golden West*."

"I don't feel as if I can thank you enough. I'm finally feeling a little bit hopeful again. You can't imagine how the machinations of that ghastly man has been affecting us."

"People who make their livelihood by extorting money are an abomination, Mrs. Randall. But then, as the Bard of Avon said in *Othello*, 'there's many a beast then in a populous city, and many a civil monster.'"

There was no way around it, Mallory decided as she finished fastening her Callot Soeurs at-home dress of thin velvet in soft red trimmed with dull silver embroidery and selected a pair of silver slippers. Rupert was going to have to write the sanitarium in Switzerland where his father died and request information regarding the circumstances surrounding Leonard Randall's demise. It would be far easier for Rupert to take this situation up with Henry, but there was about as much chance of his doing that as there was in their spending a weekend in Paris, she told herself wryly, adding on a few more strategic dabs of *Narcisse Noir*. No, it was going to have to be handled through the mail. Two weeks at least, if he writes tonight, then we'll know one way or another, she thought, a cold fear passing through her at the realization that, no matter how much she reassured Rupert, it might all be true. . . .

Don't think about that until you have to, she warned herself. You know perfectly well that even if Rupert's father went insane, it doesn't necessarily mean it's an inherited condition. . . .

"Would you care to tell me what George Kelly was doing here? Not that I don't have a good idea!"

Startled, Mallory swung around to see Rupert standing in the doorway, and her heart lurched when she saw him. It wasn't his expression of barely controlled anger that frightened her, but the way he looked. Now, for the first time, the effect of the past weeks and last Saturday night were marking him, showing on his face. She could deal with his fury, but the dark circles under his eyes and his obvious loss of weight, all accentuating the heavy look of strain on his face, left her feeling raw and painful and close to tears. What she wanted to do was cross the space between them, take him in her arms and kiss away all his misery, but he was wrapped in a total coldness that prevented her from making the slightest move toward him.

"I asked a rather simple question," Rupert went on in a clipped voice that sounded more British than it had in years.

"George was here because I've just hired him to find your blackmailer."

Slowly, deliberately, and with exaggerated care, Rupert closed the bedroom door, and the sound of the latch clicking shut struck a far colder note in Mallory's heart than any amount of angry slamming could have.

"I don't recall asking you to do that," he said, a queer

559

light in his silver eyes as he advanced toward her.

Mallory stood her ground. "Of course you didn't ask. And please don't presume that both of us are at cross purposes about this matter. You want to know who's doing this to you!" she flashed at him.

"Did you ever consider that it's enough that I have to give this 'Mr. Smyth' one hundred thousand dollars of my own money without knowing his real identity? What good is it going to do? As far as I'm concerned, as soon as he collects the last eighty thousand dollars I owe him, that's the end of that!"

"*Owe him!*" Mallory exclaimed in disbelief. "What exactly do you think you owe this awful little man? Look what he's done to you," she said, putting her arms around his hard, unyielding frame. "How much longer can you go on pretending that there's nothing wrong? You look as if you're waiting for some terrible disaster to strike—"

"That's generally what going insane is—a disaster," Rupert said in a voice that went beyond pain. "Don't you understand that we're not going to have a normal life together, only a time bomb waiting to go off." He pulled away from her. "In twenty years, I'll be as insane as my father was!"

"You don't know that! You don't know if it's even true. *Please* talk to Henry."

"For what? To have the news confirmed and then spread around?"

"Henry wouldn't do that. But there is an alternative. Write to the sanitarium in Switzerland where—"

"No!" He pulled back from her, horror in his eyes. "I know the answer, and the confirmation—either from Henry or the doctor in Lausanne—will be just about the last thing I can take!" he told her passionately, and then, as if all his strength suddenly drained out, he sat down in the nearest chair. "If I'm going insane, that's just how it is. I can't fight any more. I can't even fight for our love."

"What!"

"I can't fight Romney Sedgewick for you."

"Me and Romney?" For a minute, Mallory couldn't breathe from the disbelief, and then rage exploded inside her. "I've been decorating his apartment, and if you think there has been anything else, you're not insane, you're crazy—crazy as in imagining things that aren't there!"

"That *is* insanity, in case you haven't heard!" Rupert shouted at her, his anger returning, displaying the resignation he was forcing himself to feel."I'm trying to be reasonable about this. I'm trying to tell you that I understand. It's a little unusual, most marital menages involve a younger man and an older husband, but I guess we'll blaze a new trail. Not that anyone will know, of course."

"Will you please stop rambling. If you're accusing me of something, of carrying on with Romney behind your back, say it outright."

This wasn't happening the way it was supposed to. Where was their calm discussion, their agreement to face their problem together? Her hiring George may have been a tactical mistake, but it was her one chance to make a move, and she wasn't about to back down from it.

Yes, you idiot, you made a move, and now what was only strained is actually falling apart right in front of you, she thought, desperately trying to sort out everything that had happened in the last twenty minutes. Right now, I can't decide if I want to kick Rupert for being so stubborn, or take him in my arms.

"The worst part of this," Rupert began in a detached voice before Mallory could speak, "is that we can't have a family together. But the Randall family insanity has to end with me," he said as he stood up. "I wish Romney and I looked more like each other, but—"

561

Rupert's plan for the future was abruptly cut off by Mallory's silver-backed hairbrush striking him squarely on the shoulder.

"What did you do that for?"

"You bastard! Just what do you think you're suggesting?" Mallory demanded as they faced each other down. There was no more time for gentle talk and understanding, she decided. The only thing left for them was to have it all out. If Rupert was too worn out to fight for their love, she wasn't, and whatever fantasies his exhausted mind was spinning out had to be smashed before they could take root and become a future source of contention between them. "Do you want me to sleep with Romney Sedgewick, or do you think I've done that already?"

Rupert stepped backward as Mallory advanced on him. "It isn't because he hasn't tried," he told her, a wave of jealousy passing through him. "He's made himself very clear on how taken he is by you, and how it's all he can do not to push me aside!"

Mallory didn't know what to say. Loyalty ran deep in her, and Romney had trusted her with a secret about his personal life. Even now, it was not her place to betray his confidence. When Rupert had walked in on them, that had been Romney's opportunity to tell Rupert that he was secretly engaged and explain why he had been spreading all those misleading compliments about her. But no clarification had been made, and now Mallory began to wonder if his ridiculous idea could have begun to form then.

"In case you've forgotten, I was the witness to a charming little scene between you and our favorite Foreign Office official," Rupert went on as Mallory remained silent. "You can't say that you aren't interested in him."

"Interested as a friend, not as a lover!"

"But one frequently turns into the other!"

"How can you even suggest such a thing?"

"You know why!"

"No, I'll never believe you're a madman waiting to happen unless it's confirmed by Henry, or by your father's doctor!" Mallory said, her eyes filling with tears. "For four years, I tried to get past us, to put our relationship behind me, until the day I realized that there wasn't another man for me but you. I kept my love for you, and in your own way, you held on to yours for me. We couldn't have come together the way we did unless both of us, in our own separate lives, nourished that flame until we were ready to come together again. I'd never debase what we have by taking a lover, any lover, just to have a child!"

The air between them was heavy with the sort of misery that comes only when a very special love has gone temporarily but nonetheless very, very wrong. They were at cross purposes, and neither could reach the other. Mallory felt her neck muscles tighten mercilessly, but Rupert looked as if he were about to faint, and she made one last attempt to reach out to him.

"Rupert, please, this isn't the time to discuss this—"

"Then when are we supposed to? When I'm ready to be carted off in a straitjacket to an insane asylum?"

"Will you stop this?" Mallory flung at him. "*It's not going to happen*! You're not insane and you're not going to be, but you are threatening our marriage!"

"I'm trying to save it!"

"By telling me to take Romney Sedgewick for my lover?" Mallory was incredulous. "No, thank you. I'd do anything *for* you, Rupert, but not *because* of you. I won't squander our love, or soil it, no matter what plans your tired, overworked mind is spinning out."

He grabbed her shoulders. "Why won't you *see*?"

"All I see is the man I love—"

"Going crazy."

"I'm the one who's going crazy—and I'm being driven there by you!"

"Then tell me, what do you want?"

"Right now, all I want is for you to leave me alone and not bother me again until you're ready to forget that you want me to have a lover, and that you're going to turn into someone fit only for a padded room!"

"Perhaps I'd better leave."

"And not come back until I ask for you." The horrible words slipped out before Mallory could stop them, and a second later she would have given anything to take her ultimatum back. "Rupert, I didn't mean—please, don't look like that—"

"I think you meant exactly what you said." Rupert's voice was quiet, with a note in it that was sadder than anything Mallory had ever heard, but the anger was still there, a smoldering mass of fury that couldn't explode. "And since I'm not a husband who doesn't pay attention to his wife's requests, I'm leaving. I've only been trying to do what's best for you, to protect you, to tell you that our life together can never be what we expected. When you're willing to listen to *me*, I'll be back," he said with a cold finality that left Mallory rooted to the spot as Rupert left the bedroom, and by the time she moved again, it was too late. As she reached the top of the stairs, all she heard was the unmistakable sound of the front door being slammed shut.

Rupert jabbed at the doorbell again and again, his carefully controlled anger growing as no one came to the door. Where was Romney? It was too early for him to be out for the evening, and too late to be anywhere else—unless he were seducing another man's wife. Somehow that thought gave him a fresh source of rage. If Romney

Sedgewick were that crazy (and *why* did he have to keep coming back to *that* word?) about Mallory, he could at least try and be faithful to her.

He was about to give up when he heard the lock being turned, and a moment later the door opened.

"What do *you* want? You look like a damn thundercloud," Romney remarked ungraciously.

"My, what a welcoming host you are," Rupert mocked, observing Romney's pajamas and dressing gown and slippers. "Are you ill?"

"Hardly. But that's none of your business, and I don't recall our having an appointment."

"We don't, but we have to talk."

"About what?"

"Whom. Mallory."

An expression of pure amazement spread over Romney's face, and he opened the door the rest of the way. "You may as well come in. I haven't the slightest idea of what you're talking about, but we're not going to say another word in the corridor. There's no need to entertain the neighbors."

Coming into Romney's apartment was like being with Mallory again, and sitting down in the living room was a physically painful act. Everywhere Rupert looked he could see Mallory's fine taste, her sense of proportion, her ability to create a room that didn't obscure the owner's personality. What he had to do was going to be worse than he ever imagined.

"I'm not offering you a drink since it looks like the last thing you need," Romney said bluntly as he sat down opposite Rupert. "Also, as much as I'd like to discuss Mallory, I really don't want to make this a long conversation."

"What I've come to discuss is your . . . well, feelings for my wife," Rupert said, oddly relieved to be able to jump into the middle of the subject without a lot of

565

useless, meaningless formalities. "I want to know what you plan to do about them. For reasons I don't care to go into, I won't stand in your way unless you make too many advances in public," Rupert went on quickly as Romney's mouth dropped open. His heart was pounding, and he was aware that the room was far too warm. "I don't dare have a child with Mallory, and since you've made your feelings about her well known—"

"You want to know if I'm interested in providing stud service," Romney interrupted, incredulous. "You were a rat eight years ago, Rupert, and I'm sorry to say that, appearances to the contrary, you're still a rat. And what does Mallory say to this? I assume you've brought the matter to her attention. What does she say?"

"She just threw me out of our apartment."

"A very smart lady. You must be making her life a hell."

Rupert flinched at Romney's appraisal. "I can't expect you to understand, but from what I've heard, you'll be very happy to ease her unhappiness."

"I most certainly am not!"

"You've been making your intentions quite clear. It's a little too late to back out now! You got here too late to marry Mallory yourself, but I'm offering you the next best thing."

"You've gone stark, raving crazy!"

"Then I'm way ahead of schedule," Rupert muttered.

"Listen to me, you stupid ass. I like Mallory, I always have, and I certainly admire her talents and abilities, but I do not love her, and have no plans to love her—in any sense of the word!"

Rupert felt a thick cloud of confusion close over him. "That isn't what you've been telling everyone."

For the first time, Romney looked upset. "There was a reason for my doing that, one that I'm not in any way proud of. If you'd wanted a complete and total explanation last week, I would have given you one. In any case—" Romney stood up. "Hello, darling, there's someone here I want you to meet," he said to one of the loveliest women Rupert had ever seen. As he rose to his feet, he couldn't place her exactly, but her face was familiar. "This is Rupert Randall."

"Of course, you're Mallory's husband," she said as they shook hands. "I love our apartment, and I can't wait to tell her that."

Rupert threw a questioning look to Romney, standing alongside the vision in a blue velvet tea gown from Lucile, a proud look on his face.

"Rupert, I'm very pleased to introduce you to the former Miss Matilda Barnett, recently of the Drury Lane Theatre, but as of early this afternoon, my wife."

"We've been secretly engaged for months now, and it doesn't seem quite possible that we're finally married."

"*This* is why I sometimes made inappropriate comments about Mallory. I couldn't let anyone know. Of course, both Tildy and Mallory have told me in no uncertain terms exactly what they thought of my actions, and I'm properly ashamed of myself. But you see, Rupert, these past months, it's been easier to pretend I had a special interest in your wife rather than having to play the available extra man or let anyone into my private life."

If she had ever tried to imagine a terrible night, a night that would never seem to end, nothing else would be able to measure up to the last eleven hours, Mallory decided as she sat on the window seat, watching the first approach of dawn, waiting for Rupert to call or come home, and having absolutely no idea of where he might be.

Taking a deep breath, Mallory uncurled herself from her perch and returned to bed. She was thoroughly chilled, and between too little sleep and being almost frantic with worry over Rupert, she felt as if all she held dear was crumbling around her.

I'm not going to do myself any good, and I'm certainly not going to help Rupert if I fall apart, Mallory told herself, her teeth chattering as she pulled the comforters closer around her. And don't even *think* about how much you miss not having Rupert alongside you when you wake up—and don't cry—it didn't do any good earlier, and it certainly isn't going to help now.

Somehow, for the first hour or so after Rupert walked out, Mallory had kept functioning. First, she had to face the Dovedales, and the apparently simple task of telling them that tonight there wouldn't be any need for dinner became an incredibly hard task. There was nothing else for her to do now but wait, and the last thing she expected was the telephone call from Romney and Tildy, telling her that Rupert had been in their apartment and had left, looking as though he were on the verge of collapsing.

Was there anything they could do? they wanted to know, and when Mallory told them as much as she could, discreetly and carefully, the Sedgewicks offered to come and wait with her.

"Not on your wedding night, I won't hear of it. It's going to be all right," she told them, wishing she could be as confident as she made herself sound. "Please have dinner and don't worry— You're sending to Sherry's? That'll take hours. Let me take care of that. The Dovedales will be down shortly—"

For the next fifteen minutes, she had something to take her mind off Rupert, as she told Hugh and Margaret Dovedale to take the dinner she and Rupert would have eaten to the Sedgewicks' apartment. As the couple transferred the tomato soup and squab with wild rice and the salad and the chocolate rum mousse from the stove and the icebox to serving dishes, Mallory busied herself selecting china and silver and crystal and a bottle of champagne. But as soon as the Dovedales wheeled the laden tea cart out the door, the faint sense of happiness at doing something for someone else faded swiftly and was replaced by a heart-pounding sense of foreboding and depression. And it was only the start of the long night she knew was streteching out ahead of her—a night in which there would be no word from Rupert.

When Mrs. Dovedale returned, she insisted on fixing a tray for Mallory, who ate everything as if it were made of cardboard and sawdust. She ate dinner because she had to—it was just another way to kill a bit more time.

Reading was another way—or so she always thought. Mallory had at least half a dozen books she wanted to read, but as she went from romance to whodunit to biography to social commentary, nothing held her interest. She tried to sleep, but any rest she got was shallow and rarely lasted more than an hour at a time, and by five she was wandering through the apartment, trying to think where Rupert might have gone, and what she could do now.

One thing she would definitely not do was tell George Kelly that she no longer needed him. All of this business about Rupert's father nonwithstanding, she did not want this blackmailer forever casting a shadow over his—their—life. What had seemed to be only one endeavor was now two and would have to be handled as such, she decided at shortly after five-thirty, climbing the stairs. Without thinking, she went into the second bedroom, and for a long minute after she switched on the lights, she just looked at the perfect, silent room.

Do you think there's some sort of message here for you? she asked herself, pulling her cream-colored cashmere robe closer around her for warmth. I know I'm not going to find Rupert here, but it does bring me a little closer to him. It isn't going to make Rupert walk through the front door on his own. Even if he wants to by now, his pride will keep him away. I know what I have to do as soon as it's a reasonable hour. . . .

Seven-fifteen, Mallory thought, looking at the clock on her beside table. I'd better make that call now, and I just hope I've made the right choice.

She put on her robe and tied the heavy silk cord as she walked across the floor to her writing table. Quickly shutting any last-minute doubts out of her mind, she gave the operator the number she wanted.

This number wasn't listed in either the telephone directory or the Social Register; it was strictly a private number given only to family members and very close friends and was reserved for the greatest of emergencies.

"And this is certainly one," Mallory murmured as her call went through. "Cliff," she said a moment later, "it's Mallory, and I have a problem."

"What did Rupert do, and where is he?"

"I can answer the first part of your question, but I'm afraid the second part of it is up to you—if you'll help me, that is."

"How could I say no? You sound worn out. You two must have really gone at each other. Now, start from the beginning—"

I am no longer what I was. I will remain what I have become.

—Chanel

Wall Street

Rupert opened his eyes and looked at the ceiling of his office, wondering why he was here, stretched out on the leather chesterfield, half-dressed with his overcoat thrown over him for warmth, instead of in his bed, with Mallory beside him. It took a full minute for his memory to come back, and as it did come he closed his eyes, a wave of shame sweeping over him. How could he have said all the horrible things he did to Mallory, how could he have stormed out on her, and now, most difficult of all, how could he ever face her again?

As far as his impromptu visit to Romney Sedgewick's apartment—

"Well, when you decide to ruin everything, why go by half?" he said out loud.

He pushed aside his coat, and swung his legs to the floor, but the next logical step, standing up, was too much of an effort. Every ugly detail was parading through his mind, and he tried to get some sort of grasp on reality, but whatever essential element it took to get him functioning again was missing, and he continued to sit motionless, all of the strain of the past weeks taking its revenge on his body and mind.

When he left Romney's apartment the night before, his rage at Mallory, who couldn't see that everything he was doing was just for her, had dissolved and was replaced by intense confusion. Romney's revelation that he had been engaged all along and had never had any designs on Mallory had left him with the feeling that nothing had gone the way it should.

As upset as he was, Rupert knew that he couldn't go back to their apartment, that the atmosphere between them was too raw to attempt to make any sort of amends just yet. There was no better way to put some time between his actions and having to explain them than by having dinner. On Gramercy Park, he hailed a passing taximeter motor cab, and fifteen minutes later was in Child's on lower Broadway, and ten minutes after that, after he had selected and paid for his meal, he was seated at a corner table looking at a tray of food, all of it fresh and well-prepared, for which he had no appetite.

Somehow he managed to eat everything without having his stomach turn, but by that time he had come to the unhappy conclusion that he was not a welcome sight at One Lexington Avenue, and it might be quite some time before he could talk to Mallory again—if he still had a marriage left.

Someplace to spend the night. That was next on his agenda. But where? Not to the home of anyone he knew. For no amount of money would he begin to explain what had happened earlier tonight. He had no luggage, so that left out the option of a hotel, and although Rupert knew he wouldn't be either the first or the last man to check into the Columbia University Club following a major disagreement with his wife, he didn't want an all male, clubby refuge. He wanted to be alone, and there was only one place for that.

At least he'd had the good sense to take his briefcase with him when he stormed out of the apartment, he thought with relief as the building's night watchman let him in. The man gave him a sympathetic look and said he shouldn't work so hard as he took him upstairs and unlocked the mahogany doors.

The strange, eerie mood of the large, deserted office had mirrored his own feelings exactly, but now, at half-past seven in the morning, it all seemed much more normal, and no matter how he felt, there was a full day of work ahead of him, and he forced himself to get to his feet and go into his private bathroom.

If he had to wear the same suit over again, at least he kept a fresh shirt and tie in the office to change into, Rupert thought some forty minutes later as he stood in the middle of the bathroom, working a cuff link into his shirt, reluctant to take the next step of knotting his tie since it would involve his looking into the mirror above the marble sink.

"You look like a ghoul," he told his reflection as he began knotting his tie. With his hair still slightly damp from the shower and the dark circles under his eyes and his face showing a definite weight loss, he might not look as though he stepped straight from a horror tale, but this was not the way his coworkers and clients expected him to look.

"I'll just have to do it and hope I don't frighten anyone," he remarked out loud. "But I wonder if this is what I'll look like when I go insane?"

"Oh, surely you can come up with something better than that!" a familiar, mocking voice said behind him, and Rupert swung around to find Cliff leaning against the open door. "Believe me, in New York, insanity isn't all that remarkable."

"Don't you knock?" Rupert asked, finishing up with his tie.

"After what you did last night, just be glad that I'm not going to put your head under the cold water tap and keep

it there until you get some sense into your thick skull!"
Cliff snapped. "I want to talk with you, and I'd really like
to sit down."

Cliff spun on his heel and walked off, leaving Rupert
hastily shrugging into his vest as he followed him to the
chesterfield.

"You had quite a night, didn't you?" Cliff asked,
dropping into a comfortable chair, dourly eying a low
table littered with wrappers from chocolate bars, empty-
looking cigarette boxes, and an ashtray overflowing with
ashes and butts. "You and Mallie must have had quite a
row if you've taken up smoking again." Cliff picked up
one of the packages of Pall Malls, found the lone
remaining cigarette, lit it and sat back to wait for Rupert
to sink down on the leather couch. "Care to talk about
it?"

"From the way you came in, I assume you know all the
ugly details already. Did Mallie ring you up?"

Cliff blew a smoke ring. "Yes, she used the private line
that goes to the breakfast room, and even though I didn't
finish my eggs, I got the chance to do a good deed *and*
test out how fast my new car can get from Fifth Avenue in
the Seventies to Wall Street. Cawley was in his element,"
he said, referring to his driver. "But on the other hand,
you don't look at all well. Wouldn't you rather go home
and forget about all of this?"

"At this point, I'm not quite sure I still have a home. I
said some very beastly things to Mallory. She told me to
leave her alone, and now I think that may just be the best
thing for me to do."

"Oh, don't be more of an idiot than you absolutely
have to! Mallory's wildly worried about you."

"It would be better for both of us if she never wanted
to see me again."

"Well, if I ever told my wife that she should have a

574

baby with another man, that's just what she would do. I thought that would get me your full attention," Cliff remarked with obvious satisfaction.

"Mallory told you that?" Rupert said, feeling oddly relieved that he wouldn't have to tell the whole sickening story all over again. True, he had a lot of explaining to do, and it didn't change the sad fact that he was probably going to end up like his father, but at least he no longer had to repeat last night's scenario.

"It was very brave of her, but she felt I really couldn't help you if I didn't know what had been going on in your lives in the past few weeks." Cliff smashed out his cigarette and looked straight at Rupert. "Why didn't you come to me when you got that first blackmail threat?"

"I wasn't going to pay him a cent," Rupert said dully, too tired to care who knew. "I was going to take it up with Dad. I was sure he'd stand behind me. Unfortunately, the letter came the night before his heart attack."

"And what about me?"

"I thought you'd throw me to the wolves. You've been waiting seven years to do it."

"Oh, Rupert," Cliff said, and Rupert thought it would be easier to bear Cliff's temper than his obvious sympathy.

"After what you said that morning—about my not having ruined anything and being glad I was part of the firm—I thought my fate was pretty well sealed." Rupert pressed his hands against his temples. "It was easier just to pay up and hope for the best."

"And that was a pretty poor choice. How much?"

"One hundred thousand dollars to be paid between the twenty-eighth of October and the fourth of March."

"Which means you've paid twenty-thousand so far—and that's your final payment. You're not to give that

575

extortionist another penny."

"It's too late."

"What do you mean?"

"I sent the last eighty thousand over to the post office yesterday along with a note telling 'Mr. Smyth' that here was all the money he wanted, and to do what he liked with the information he had, but not to bother me again."

"Do you mean that right now, in a box at the General Post Office, is eighty-thousand dollars in cold, hard American cash?" Cliff asked, his incredulity giving way to laughter. "Well, we won't have to worry about your not seeing that money again."

"How do you mean?"

"Did you forget about George Kelly?" Cliff looked as pleased as if he'd hired George himself. "When is the pickup day?"

"Friday."

"The day after Thanksgiving. Rather appropriate, don't you think? George is going to get your blackmailer *and* get your money back."

"Is that really going to stop him?"

"You don't know George very well," Cliff responded with a satisfied smile. "Besides, his file on you isn't all that damaging. Slightly embarrassing, yes, but nothing worth paying one hundred thousand dollars for. Think about it."

Rupert did, and felt his face flush. "I *am* an idiot," he said at last.

"Extenuating circumstances," Cliff allowed. "You should have listened to John when he told you not to work too hard."

"I don't have any secrets left, do I?"

"This isn't a day for secrets, and you can live much better without them. And as for your father— I think all of this business about inherited madness is pretty much a lot of bunk. Sorry, Rupert, you're not going to get off that easy. You have a lot of life ahead of you. Come on," he said in a voice that only his father and J. P. Morgan would have ignored, and Rupert rose to his feet.

"Where are you going?"

"I'm taking you home."

"But the work—"

"Can be handled by someone else. As of right now, you're on a very extended vacation and you're going to have the honeymoon trip you and Mallory should have started in October."

"What a mess I've made, and it all could have been avoided if only—"

"Forget it," Cliff interrupted. "You can't go back, and don't make things worse by trying to readjust your life. It doesn't work." Unexpectedly, Cliff put his arms around Rupert and embraced him. "Mallory's waiting for you, and you have your whole lives to live together." He put a hand on Rupert's forehead. "You're a bit feverish," he said with the expertise that only the father of three children could have.

"You don't have to sound so satisfied about it," Rupert shot back.

"You're the one who should be satisfied. You're going home for a nice rest, and if it all works out, you and Mallory can leave for California right on schedule. Now, get your belongings together and put on your jacket and coat while I make a quick call. When I get back, we'll leave."

Instinctively, without even having to ask, Rupert knew that Cliff was going to telephone Mallory.

"What are you going to say to anyone we run into? It's almost time to open."

"Simple. You have a touch of influenza, and it was

577

only after you got here that you realized you're too ill to work. And that's the story we'll stay with. I think you'll agree that it's close enough to the truth."

"How did you locate me?" Rupert asked some ten minutes later as they left the elevator and crossed the lobby, attracting nothing more than a few early morning nods.

"It was very easy. Once I called the Columbia University Club and found you hadn't checked in, I figured your most natural refuge was right here. Also," he continued with great amusement, "I was lucky enough to catch the night watchman before he went off duty. The first thing he told me was how hard you're working! Ah, here we are," he said, adroitly changing the subject as they went through the doors onto the cold, windy street. "My new chariot, and I expect Dad is going to have a thing or two to say about my not buying an American car."

"It'll be worth it," Rupert said, catching sight of the black, gleaming brilliance of the latest model Rolls Royce Silver Ghost, just delivered from England. "That is, when Julie and the kids let you use it!"

Once they were inside the soft, silent interior, and Cawley was guiding the Rolls through the heavy traffic, Rupert began to relax. The events of the past twelve hours, added on to everything else, was still too painful to investigate in any great detail, but he wasn't going to have to put up any longer with a crafty individual throwing mud at him.

"Cliff, I have one more question to ask you. Why?"

"Why what?"

"Why are you helping me? I didn't mean what I said earlier about your waiting to throw me to the wolves. I know that if I'd come to you at the beginning, you would have helped me. What I was afraid of is that you wouldn't let me forget it. But I'm not worried about that now; you won't throw it back at me. What made you come through like this for me?"

"Oh, hell," Cliff said as he flung a fur-lined lap robe over Rupert, looking every inch the man caught doing a very unexpected good deed. "What else are older brothers for?"

Love is not getting but giving. . . . If a man is worth loving at all, he is worth loving generously, even recklessly.

—Marie Dressler

One Lexington Avenue

Rupert was dreaming. It was his wedding night. Not the one he and Mallory had shared nine weeks earlier, but the one they would have had if they had gotten married in 1906.

With the strange comprehension that comes in dreams, he understood all of this. He knew they were in the St. Regis Hotel and he knew that something was very, very wrong—and it was all his fault.

He was drunk, a wild, uncontrollable sort of drunk that was frightening Mallory, and all his actions, instead of calming her, were only making matters worse. His hands were at his belt, and then they were on Mallory, pulling her close to him, attempting to unbutton the long row of tiny, tiny buttons that fastened her dress down the back. Her hands were on his chest, cool against his feverish skin, and she was calling his name over and over again. Rupert . . .

"Rupert . . ."

His eyes flew open, his dreams spinning backwards to the depths from where they were formed. He was in bed, with Mallory leaning over him, and her hands were on his chest. Her hair was falling around her face and her eyes were full of concern and love.

581

"I was dreaming," he said at last, his voice still thick with sleep. "Something about the wedding night we would have had four years ago. It wasn't very nice."

"It was just a dream," she said, kissing him on the forehead. "Do you think you can go back to sleep? It's only seven."

"In the morning?"

"I certainly hope so."

A dart of panic entered his heart. "What day is this? I've lost all track of time."

"Friday."

"My God. What happened to Thanksgiving?"

"That was yesterday."

Rupert ran his hands through his hair and pushed the pillows up behind him. "I've really lost a week, haven't I? It seems like a century since Tuesday morning."

"I know. And don't worry, everyone is very solicitous of your having the flu."

"I just bet they are," Rupert said with his first real smile in four days. "I feel like a pig," he said as Mallory kissed his beard-stubbled cheek. "I haven't shaved since Tuesday morning."

"I don't mind."

"And we haven't talked, either."

"We can do that now," Mallory pointed out, adjusting her pillows so they could lay facing each other. "It looks like it's going to be an awful day. We can just stay right here for awhile. John wants you to get as much rest as possible."

"When he saw me on Tuesday morning, there really wasn't much else left for me to do," he said, holding her hands against his heart. "I owe you so much right now—beginning with an apology for not telling you the truth when John said I was run down and needed a long rest."

"A proper honeymoon."

"Whatever. No, I needed you and a long, wonderful

582

time for us to begin our married life with no outside influences pressing in on us. But I got caught up in my own pride—the thought that I could carry off any responsibility without having to ask for help. I'd forgotten how to pace myself. If it hadn't been for the other things," he went on, "I might have pulled it all off, but I was too close to the edge, and the strain of being blackmailed and the news about my father sent me over it." His voice became bitter. "When 'Smyth' told me my father was insane, I thought he was making it up, but Hugo was coming from another corner entirely. He said he knew all the details. Or intimated that he did. At this point, I can't really tell."

"One thing at a time."

"Damn Hugo. I hope all the investment advice I gave him goes bad."

"That would be fitting punishment."

"If it hadn't been for him, I wouldn't know," Rupert said, his mind returning to the one subject that had been playing on his mind since the night of the de Veigas' party. "I swear, Hugo was worse to take than 'Smyth.' I wish I could say I hate Hugo, but I don't. He can't help the way he acts. It's part of his personality, if he just didn't find such *delight* in what he says and does."

"Do you really want to delve into what goes on behind that facade of his?"

"God, no. That's Edie's problem. Come here," he said, suddenly brightening. "I've just realized that after three days of not having very much contact with reality, I'd very much like to hold my wife."

Mallory felt as though she'd lived through twenty years since Monday evening. Even now, laying in Rupert's arms while he slept again, she could bring up the feeling of pure relief when Cliff had called her on

Tuesday morning to tell her that yes, just as he'd expected, he'd found Rupert in his office. Not even Cliff's advice that she call John and have him come over as soon as possible could dim her joy.

Twenty minutes later, he had come home, and while Cliff retreated gracefully to the dining room, she and Rupert had melted into each other's arms.

"It's my fault and I'm sorry," he said, his arms tight around her waist. "Everything just came down on me at once. I can even explain about Romney—"

"Later," she said, kissing him. "We'll talk about it after you've had a chance to rest. John is on his way over right now."

"Then I'd better tell you that he warned me this would happen." Pain flickered across his face. "I lied to you that day. I've been going on nerve alone for weeks."

"It's all right. The only important thing is that you go upstairs to bed."

Bed meant their bedroom, not the second bedroom where Rupert kept his clothes. Mallory wanted Rupert in a room that was light and airy and gave the impression of sun even when there wasn't any, a room where he wouldn't feel isolated and where he knew she was going to be near him.

John's diagnosis was what it had been in August: exhaustion brought on by overwork and worry. "He needs a lot of plain, old-fashioned rest," he told her when he came downstairs again and came into the dining room where Cliff was eating waffles while Mallory kept him company with a soothing cup of tea and cinnamon toast. Margaret Dovedale believed that there were few occasions that couldn't be helped by food. "Let him sleep, and when he wakes up only tea and fruit juice and soup for the next few days. I'll be back to check him again in a day or two. . . ."

That had been Tuesday, and now it was Friday—three

days gone, one of them a national holiday, and the only thing Mallory was certain of was that Rupert's badly frayed system was slowly beginning to knit itself back together.

And the rest of it is in George Kelly's hands, she thought. He'll do his best not to fail. But there is one thing that only I can do—

It was after eleven now, and an awful day, one to stay safe inside, a delight that Mallory knew she was going to have to give up until later in the afternoon. Careful not to disturb Rupert, she got out of bed. The weather nonwithstanding, she had an errand, and when she was dressed she placed her phone call from the other bedroom.

"Lord and Lady Tilmore's suite, please," she told the Plaza's operator, and a moment later, Farrell, Hugo's valet, picked up at the other end.

"I'm so sorry, Mrs. Randall," he said politely, "but his lordship and her ladyship are both out at the moment. They're lunching at Lord and Lady Thorpes'. Yes, I agree that you certainly know the address. . . ."

Rupert came awake again, this time easily and peacefully, to see Mallory leave her dressing table.

"Are you leaving me already?" he asked, eying her deceptively simple Cheruit frock of black velveteen with yoke and cuffs and belt and side panel of faded blue Persian cloth. "I hate to think that you're taking my stupid advice to heart."

"Oh, no such luck," Mallory smiled. "You're stuck with me for the next fifty years or so." She sat down on the edge of the bed. "I have to go out for a while."

Rupert glanced toward the window. "In this weather?"

"I won't melt, and I do have something to take care of. Don't worry, the doorman's getting a taxi for me. I don't trust myself to drive today."

"You do look rather like you're going to do battle."

"I may just have to." Mallory stood up. "If you're hungry, Mrs. Dovedale will make that Drogheda Irish Oatmeal you like, and I left over a few orange muffins from my breakfast."

"Thank you—I might," Rupert grinned. "You'll be back for tea?"

"A nice, big gooey one. I've already given Mrs. Dovedale instructions. And hopefully we'll have some answers to go along with our cake," Mallory said as she swirled out the door, leaving her scent lingering in the air behind her.

*To tell a lie in cowardice, to tell a lie for gain, or to avoid
deserved punishment—are all the blackest of black lies.*

—Emily Post, *Children Are People*

135 Central Park West

Sybil Fleming was very happy with her sublet apartment
at the Langham. Despite her mother's remarks to the
contrary, Sybil found that this twelve-story building that
occupied the entire blockfront from Seventy-third to
Seventy-fourth Streets was comfortable to the point of
luxury with its generously proportioned rooms and the
layout that limited to four the number of apartments on
each of the floors.

American apartment buildings are so up-to-date, she
thought with satisfaction as she surveyed the smallest of
the five bedrooms, now fully decorated as the new
nursery. True, it wouldn't be needed until March, but it
was far easier to have these things ready well in advance,
and Best and Company's Liliputian Bazaar had come
through admirably, and there were such lovely baby
things this year, the saleswoman had assured her, writing
salescheck after salescheck.

"I suppose she thinks Toronto is an absolute outpost
of civilization," she murmured aloud, checking over a set
of exquisite handmade bibs she had not been able to
resist, as well as all the other baby things that Alix and
her friends had thoughtfully passed on to her.

There had not been a day since the afternoon when

they'd first seen this apartment that Sybil had not been grateful to Alix for her friendship. If it hadn't been for her interest and support, Sybil was sure she simply would have folded up under the sheer force of her mother's personality. Instead, she had found the strength within herself to stand her ground and live her life free of her mother's.

Not that Evelyn seemed to care all that much, Sybil had to admit as she wandered over to the window seven floors above West Seventy-fourth Street. As Alix had predicted, the older woman had become totally absorbed in her own enterprises. But exactly *what* those enterprises were, Sybil had no idea, and it disturbed her endlessly.

Her mother now had money. More money than Sybil could ever remember seeing her handle. Piles of it, and in large bills. *Where* was it coming from? Not from any honest source, she reluctantly admitted to herself.

The first time she'd seen the money, in the library, spread out on the desk, her mother had taken full advantage of her shock at the sight of all the twenty and fifty and one hundred dollar bills, and in her sophisticated, blasé fashion had evaded the subject so that it was now too late to confront the matter.

Sybil hadn't seen any money since that day, but she knew her mother was still getting regular payments. But from whom, and because of what?

At least Mama isn't buying me things with her new-found wealth, Sybil thought, recalling her mother's purchases from the best New York stores. If I hadn't been such an idiot as a girl, I'd have a better idea how to handle things now. I wish Peter were here, but he can't solve my problem, only I can do that. But if Mama is really doing something illegal, do I want to know about it?

Resolutely, Sybil left the nursery and went down the corridor, past the other bedrooms, past the dining room where the maid was setting the table for lunch, past the quiet living room, and across the foyer toward the library where her mother had secreted herself with the announcement that she was going to be busy doing her "accounts."

"—and would you care to tell me *why* you haven't been able to contact Rupert Randall? God knows, it's simple enough to ring someone up in this city. The best people seem to take the most perverse pride in being listed in the telephone directory."

"That may very well be, but if I can't get him at the other end of the line, all the availability in the world isn't going to make any difference. He isn't at the ofice, and his butler says he can't come to the phone—something about influenza."

"Influenza, my foot!" Evelyn Weldon was having a bad morning. When one doesn't have enough money to live on in the proper style, not even the most enterprising sort of blackmail could smooth the way, she reflected, prowling around the library, two spots of color the exact shade of her red wool Worth dress appearing high on her cheekbones. Her fingers nervously plucked at her red and purple satin belt. "I should have known better than to trust this to you!"

"I'll thank you to remember that if it weren't for our precipitant meeting on the *Mauretania*, you wouldn't have the money you do now. The fact that you can't control your tendency to wager way above your means, plus your taste for only the most expensive and exclusive, is not my concern. I'm doing quite well with my modest part of our weekly receipt," Roland Gresham said with deliberate blandness.

"And we're not here to discuss the way we each spend our money. What we're here to discuss is how we can get more money from Rupert. Whoever would have thought that that little beast would turn out so well?" she fumed. "If only he'd carried on here the way he did in England. Still, what we do have on him caused him to meet our demand fast enough. And he'll gladly pay more with the threat of the scandal papers hanging over him."

"But we have a plan—" Gresham began. "We take the payments for the prearranged sum, and then, in March, we ask him for a larger sum—a farewell gift, so to speak."

"That's nearly four months off, and I don't intend to wait! Now, what has Henry been saying?"

"Precious little," he said as Evelyn joined him on the sofa. Instinctively distrustful of women, he now regretted ever getting involved with this woman and her schemes. Blackmail, extortion, taking money from a young man who had so much of it. At first it had been interesting, even amusing, particularly his meeting with Rupert in the bar at the Marie Antionette, but now her avarice was beginning to frighten him. "For a man who used to be amazingly casual on the phone, ever since Tuesday he's been very careful."

"That means something has changed. I wonder if Rupert has been in contact with him?"

"He might have been, if he thought I was going to Colonel Mann."

"Then let's just hope he doesn't figure out that all the stories you threatened him with would be of little or no interest to the scandal sheets. How fortunate for us that Mr. Seligman had his heart attack when he did." Evelyn smiled narrowly. There was always the chance that a selected victim might refuse to pay, or, after paying a certain amount decide he'd had enough and take his chances on exposure. Like Hugo Tilmore.

"Mr. Randall doesn't strike me as the sort of man who'll accept having to pay money week after week. His temperament is very poor."

"You're putting it mildly. That's why we need the most amount of money in the least amount of time." Suddenly, a terrible thought struck Evelyn. "Suppose he's left town?"

"Decamped? I never thought—"

"No, you wouldn't. But we've both forgotten that Rupert is basically a street rat, and he'll run at the first opportunity." The idea that at this very moment the box at the General Post Office might be empty became too horrible to bear. "What time is it?" she cried.

"Let me see," Roland replied, turning around to look at the clock. "Oh, my—"

Evelyn craned her neck to see what her companion was so upset about. The shock and dismay a normal woman might have felt at this moment were unknown emotions to her. Instead, it was anger and annoyance that flashed through her when she saw her daughter standing in the doorway.

"Well, what do you think you're doing?" Evelyn asked after Sybil continued to stand in the doorway, her face a blend of hurt and outrage. "Can't you think of something to say?"

"I might ask you the same question," Sybil replied quietly, advancing into the library, her simple blue dress of French serge trimmed with black soutache cut on graceful lines to make her look as if she weren't pregnant at all. "For months now, I've been wondering what you've been up to. Blackmail, as it turns out. Have you just developed this interest, Mama, or is there something you've never told me?"

"How dare you talk to me like this!" Evelyn gathered together all the righteous anger she'd always used on her daughter. "Go to your room!"

Sybil regarded her mother evenly, any remaining love that she had for this calculating, selfish woman fast disappearing. "In case you've forgotten, Mama, you're not paying the rent on this apartment, Peter is, and that makes this *my* home."

"How high and mighty we are! Well, my pretty one, how do you think I paid for all of those dresses for you when you were growing up, not to mention little things like a French governess and pocket money so that you could give proper tips when you were invited to weekend parties? All paid for out of the fortunes of wealthy men who couldn't keep their peccadillos under control. It was all for you—"

"Oh, don't say that! There was precious little for me, no matter what you say now, and suddenly I'm very glad of that!"

"It was all for you, and you betrayed me!" Evelyn was on her feet now, her eyes burning with a zealot's fire. "I wouldn't be here now if it weren't for your running off with Peter. You made a laughingstock of me with your 'romance'—"

"Why Rupert?" Sybil interjected, a wave of nausea that had nothing to do with her pregnancy coming over her. "He's never done you any harm. Is that why you came to New York?"

"To tell you the truth, I accepted your invitation because of Hugo Tilmore. It became necessary for me to leave England, and what could be better than coming to stay with my dear and loving daughter?"

Sybil flinched at the sarcasm, but stood her ground. "I expect you met your—accomplice on the *Mauretania*?"

592

she said with a sweeping look at Roland Gresham who was trying to inch his way toward the door. "Look at the sort of man you chose, Mama! He doesn't even have the nerve to turn his back and walk out like a man!"

"Oh, he is a worm," Evelyn agreed, her voice full of malice. "But a very useful worm with a very important contact—Henry Thorpe!"

"I remember you now—you're Henry's secretary! Alix always knew there was something fishy about you."

"Lady Thorpe and women of her sort are of very little interest to me," Roland replied, speaking for the first time since he'd seen Sybil standing in the doorway. Who would have thought that this quiet young woman had so much fire in her? Oh, but he wanted to get out of here! He'd even let Evelyn have all of this week's money just not to have to come here again. "We thought Lord Thorpe would make an excellent subject, but he has no secrets—"

"I'll tell this, if you please! With Roland in the flat all day to keep an eye on things, Henry would have been perfect, only the man's slate is clean. Fortunately, Rupert's isn't. Isn't it funny how sensitive men are about their pasts? And there was so much going on with the wedding—so much wonderful gossip. Old gossip, my dear, the very best kind. That poor idiot doesn't even realize that he's being taken—"

"Leave this house." Sybil's voice was cold, but not as cold as the feeling around her heart. "You awful, horrid woman. I'm tired of having to defend you, and I'm sick that you're my mother."

"You can't throw me out of here."

"Just watch, Mama, just watch. I want you to leave right now, before my children come back from the Norths'. You can send for your things later. And truthfully, I'll be very happy if you do go back to England on the next ship!"

"What an ungrateful little bitch you are!" Evelyn snarled. "I don't need your pathetic hospitality. I may not have as much money as I want from Rupert, but it's enough until the next time," she went on grandly, making her exit. "Come, Roland, we have some funds to collect!"

People are subject to moods, to temptations and fears, lethargy and aberration and ignorance, and the staunchest qualities shift under the stresses and strains of daily life. Like liberty, they are not secured for all time. They are not inevitable.

—Ilka Chase, *Free Admission*

The Dakota

Mallory tapped her foot on the floor of the Dakota's elevator, trying hard to hide her impatience from the operator. She knew it wasn't the woman's fault. The Dakota's elevators were notoriously slow, but the ascent to the sixth floor seemed longer than ever. Finally, they were there, and she thought she would scream until the car was made level with the floor and the door opened.

"Thank you, Sally," she told the black bombazine-clad operator. "Did you have a nice Thanksgiving?"

The fact that she was impatient, seething with anger, and wanting nothing more than to get into Henry and Alix's apartment had nothing to do with not being nice to the elevator operator she'd come to know over the years.

Wait until I get my hands on Hugo, was all she had thought in the taxi coming uptown, and even though she was now in far more control of her feelings in that she wasn't going to punch Hugo in the nose, there was something primitive in her that wanted this confrontation. There were times when all the logical discussions in the world got nothing and all that worked was a direct confrontation. Something, she hoped as she pressed the bell, that Hugo hadn't had too much experience with.

"Good afternoon, Miss Mallory—I mean, Mrs. Randall," Hodges said pleasantly as he opened the door for her. "How nice to see you again."

"Thank you, Hodges. Are Lord and Lady Tilmore still here?" she asked, stepping into the entry foyer and pulling off her gloves.

"Yes, madam, they're still at lunch. If you'll wait in the drawing room, I'll tell her ladyship that—"

"No, Hodges," Mallory interrupted skillfully, stepping around the butler. "I have to speak with Lord Tilmore, and there's no better time then when a man is having a superb lunch."

Hodges was so stunned by her behavior that by the time he realized that she was on her way to the drawing room, it was too late to do anything but follow in her perfumed wake.

Mallory reached the closed set of double doors, her heels sliding slightly on the highly polished floor, and with Hodges following her, mystification apparent on his usually reserved face. She could hear laughter coming through the heavy wood panels, and with one grand motion, she slid open the door and walked into the dining room.

For both couples at the table, enjoying the intimate day-after-Thanksgiving luncheon, their laughter ceased when they saw Mallory advancing on them. Only Alix, elegant in Poiret's Persian voile over pink and blue changeable taffeta, was undismayed by her cousin's swooping down on them. One look at Mallory's face beneath her black velvet Reboux hat, and she decided to sit back and enjoy the show until it was time to intervene.

Mallory had promised herself that she was going to keep her temper under control, but all it took was one look at Hugo, telling stories and trading *bon mots* and no doubt dropping other bits of interesting gossip, and her good intentions fell away. He smiled at her, and a red film seemed to settle over her vision.

"My dear Mallory! What an unexpected—" he began as she reached his side, and then a look of fright came into his eyes as she slammed her purse into the table with a force that made the stemmed glasses tremble. Her leather gloves hit the table next, landing on the linen tablecloth with the force of a whip.

"I have one question, Hugo. One simple question that really shouldn't be too difficult for you to answer," she said in a quiet voice that dripped ice, looking down at him. "Why did you tell Rupert that his father was a madman?"

The wave of shock that struck the table was almost visible, and Mallory watched as the color ebbed out of Hugo's face. For the first time, his witty repartee was rebounding on him, and it was abundantly clear that no one was going to help him out of his tight spot.

"Do you decide what you're going to say in advance, or is it more of a spur-of-the-moment decision?" Mallory pressed.

"I'm sorry, Mallory, truly I am," Hugo said in a strangled voice. "I never should have tried to turn the situation into a witty remark but, unfortunately, what I said *is* the truth."

"Mallory, Hugo, would you care to tell us what this is all about?" Henry asked in a reasonable voice from the other end of the oblong Chinese Chippendale table. This was not the luncheon party he and Alix had planned, but he had known Hugo and his well-thought-out attitude for far too long not to let him pay for his rapier tongue—just this once. "It's a little late to ask if you'd like a bit of privacy."

Mallory looked directly at Henry. "It's very simple, actually. At the de Veigas' dinner party, Hugo asked

Rupert for some financial advice, and after he had it, Lord Tilmore thanked my husband by telling him that he was sure by this time he'd be as insane as his father was!"

"Hugo, there are times your bad taste amazes me," Henry said distastefully, motioning for Hodges, who had been an unwilling participant in this little drama, to come in and take Mallory's fur.

Mallory handed over her seal coat, hat and accessories to the butler, and waited until he left before continuing. Her body was flooded with adrenalin, and she felt ready to take on anyone who dared spread slander about Rupert. But was this what she really wanted? To upset Hugo, to humiliate him in front of his wife and friends?

In an awful way, the answer was yes. Rupert had suffered enough from the blackmailer, and Hugo, unwitting as she was sure his role was, had delivered the coup de grace. Why should he walk away unscathed?

Mallory was startled out of her reverie by someone touching her shoulder, and she looked into Alix's sophisticated, concerned, and faintly amused face.

"Wouldn't you like to sit down?"

"I'd rather have an answer."

Alix nodded and looked down at Hugo. "Don't you have anything else to say?"

Hugo rose slowly to his feet. "Only that I wish I hadn't opened my mouth. This is a case of where the truth aids no one. All I can say in my defense is that I thought Rupert knew his father was—" He paused, utterly miserable. "Certified."

"That isn't true," Mallory challenged. "It can't be."

"There has to be an explanation for this," Edith said, her Lucile dress of date-colored taffeta rustling softly as she stood up and came to stand with her husband. She had always known that Hugo's wicked repartee would get him into trouble, but she never thought it would come about like this.

"There is an explanation, and since we're just about finished with lunch, I suggest we go into the drawing room," Henry said, standing up. "What Hugo said *is* true, but not the way he thinks, and the time has come to begin to set the record straight."

A half hour later, when Henry finished his story, Mallory was very grateful for the strong, hot café filtré that Alix served. The cold rain had turned to icy sleet, but now she felt warm and relieved and slightly tired.

"I'm sorry I jumped down your throat," she said to Hugo. "And I never thought you had anything to do with the blackmailer."

"But I have a relationship to Rupert's blackmailer," Hugo said, his face oddly serious. "You see, I was her victim as well."

"Her?" Mallory put down her cup. "Rupert was dealing with a man."

"Yes, a different method of operations devised for the colonies, no doubt. There are some similarities—" he began, but broke off when the sharp, loud ringing of a bell filled the drawing room. "My God, Alix, what is that?"

"Oh, that's the bell from the Roosevelt Hospital ambulance," Alix said, looking out the window. "It just turned into the park. Awful day for an accident. Yes, Hodges?"

"Excuse me, my lady, but it's Mrs. Fleming, and she's rather distraught. Shall I show her in?"

"Right away. Sybil, what is it?" she asked a moment later. "You look so ill."

"Oh, Alix, I hate to burden you, to interrupt your party."

"Oh, I did that about forty-five minutes ago," Mallory said from the corner of one of the sofas. "Don't worry about it."

"Come and sit with us," Edith offered, but Sybil hesitated.

"When I tell you, what I've come to say, you might not feel like that," she said. "This morning, I found out something awful about my mother. Ever since I was old enough to understand that we didn't have the sort of money that counted, I've been aware that my mother . . . did things to help makes ends meet. After I went to Canada with Peter, my mother felt she didn't have any reason to stay too respectable and—and—" Agonized, Sybil looked at Mallory, and then at Hugo. "I found out this morning that Mama has been blackmailing Rupert, and before that, Hugo." Quietly, she began to cry. "I can't tell you how this makes me feel. I cabled Peter to come to New York at once, and as soon as he gets here, we'll try to make restitution."

"In my case, at least, don't bother," Hugo told her gently. "It's far too much money, and I don't want to bankrupt you and Peter."

"And the same for me and Rupert," Mallory said, aware that only an hour before she would have seriously doubted that there was a single area in which she and Hugo could find common ground. "Besides, I hired a private detective to find out our blackmailer, and we'll get the rest of the money back this afternoon."

"Well, I hope your detective is prepared for battle," Sybil said a bit more calmly. "Mama is desperate for the money she's been . . . been . . ."

"Collecting?" Alix suggested with the sinking feeling that the events unfolding weren't even half over.

"She won't give the money up easily."

"Neither will George Kelly," Mallory responded. "But I want to know who your mother's accomplice is. Rupert told me that his blackmailer is a man."

"A bag man, as an old Tamany Hall friend of mine would say. That's the person who does the collecting of

600

extortion money for a small fee," Alix explained. "I can see where Evelyn wanted to remain anonymous here in New York. Sybil, is this the man your mother met on the *Mauretania*?"

"Yes, and this disclosure isn't going to be any better than the others," Sybil said, and told them about the conversation she'd overheard and the confrontation that followed. "Mama said that if it hadn't been for you, Hugo, she might not have had to blackmail Rupert."

All eyes turned automatically to Hugo, who sank back against the sofa pillows, his face pale again.

"Tell them, darling, it's all right," Edith urged.

"I won't bore you with all the sordid details, except that it all started in the usual way. I like to gamble, as does Evelyn, the only difference being that I can control myself at chemin-de-fer and tend to win quite a bit more often. That probably sparked your mother's interest, Sybil, and my other fall from grace made her decide that I was a proper subject for her.

"Last winter, Edie's mother was ill, and she was spending most of her time in the country with her. It was stupid of me, and now I actually think I might have been set up. There was a chorus girl at the Gaiety who was the favorite of another peer—" A flush spread across his cheeks, and Edith reached out and took his hands in hers. "Nothing too terrible happened, but Evelyn said that if word got around, I would definitely be compromised, but if I agreed to pay her a certain sum on a continuing basis, she'd make sure that the girl's protector, not to mention our friends, never found out—"

"I didn't want him to pay," Edith put in. "He was being used as a victim of circumstance. I said that I didn't think anyone would cut him because of it."

"Nonetheless, I paid—and paid. By July, I couldn't stand it any more, and I went to see an acquaintance of mine, a detective on the Metropolitan Police. He paid a visit on Evelyn—unofficial, of course—and the next thing I heard was that she'd left town."

"Hugo, I am sorry," Mallory said when he finished. "Did you lose a lot of money?"

"More than I'll ever tell anyone about. That's why I needed financial advice from Rupert—which started a whole other problem."

"I think we've forgotten something," Henry pointed out. "Who is Evelyn's special friend?"

Sybil looked directly at him. "It's Roland Gresham—your secretary."

"I knew it—I knew that man was up to no good!" Alix's voice was triumphant. "*Now* do you believe me?"

"This will teach me not to not listen to my wife," Henry said, very well aware that Alix now considered herself vindicated from the role of a complaining wife. "I'll fire him immediately, of course, and after what I've just heard— What is it, Hodges?" he asked as the butler once again appeared in the drawing room, his face wearing the expression of the definitely put-upon.

"Excuse me, my lord, but Mr. George Kelly is here, as are two police officers, and they want to see her ladyship. I've shown them into the living room."

"Are you sure they didn't ask to see me as well, Hodges?" Mallory asked, mystified at her exclusion.

"No, Mrs. Randall, just Lady Thorpe."

"When I left, I told Dovedale that if George Kelly wanted to reach me, I'd be here."

"Well, we'll find out in a few minutes," Alix said as she stood up.

"And this was supposed to be a quiet little luncheon party," Henry remarked wryly. "And whoever said that the day after Thanksgiving is supposed to be quiet, didn't know what they were talking about!"

For the next few minutes, they all tried to distract each other with conversation about Christmas shopping and

California—subjects that only served to kill time when their true attention was with Alix.

She was back within fifteen minutes, George Kelly trailing behind her. "Sybil, this is George Kelly, the private detective Mallory's hired. He's also an old friend of mine, so you don't have to be worried about talking to him."

A look of alarm formed on Sybil's face. "Something awful has happened, hasn't it, Alix?"

"Yes, dear, I'm afraid it has." Alix sat down beside Sybil and put an arm around her waist. "Your mother is dead, Sybil. She died in an accident in the park a little while ago. George will tell you what happened, and then I'll take you into the living room where a police officer and a detective are waiting. Can you go through with that?"

"Yes, of course I can. But my mother. Where—?"

"In the morgue at Roosevelt Hospital. I can make the identification, if you want. But first—" She turned to George, and indicated that he should sit down.

"Was my mother running away from the police, Mr. Kelly?" Sybil asked, putting her worst fear first.

"Not exactly, but I think George had better explain every detail," Alix said quietly.

"I already know about my mother's activities, Mr. Kelly," Sybil said, noticing that George looked as if he didn't know where to begin. "I also know why Mallory hired you."

"That does make my job easier, Mrs. Fleming," he said, relieved. There were very few things left in life to shock him with, but the events of the past few hours had left him startled and drained, and he was not used to having to give a report that was essentially a tale of avarice and tragedy in front of an audience. "Since all of you know the details, and since the police are waiting to speak with Mrs. Fleming, I'll make this as brief as possible," he went on, looking at Mallory, who nodded in agreement.

"As you know, Mr. Randall's agreement with Mr. Smyth—whom we all know now is Mr. Gresham—was that he was to leave five thousand dollars in cash in a rented box at the General Post Office every Friday until the sum of one hundred thousand dollars was reached. For whatever reason, Mr. Randall decided that today was the last day he was going to pay any extortion money, and he left a package containing eighty thousand dollars in the box. I've been at the post office since it opened this morning, watching the rented boxes, and about an hour ago, I saw Mr. Gresham take the package. I've been a private detective and a bodyguard for years. I know all about watching people without anyone being aware of it, and today I forgot all my own rules," George said bitterly. "I let my emotions get the better of me. The idea of that little man having such a hold over Mr. Randall's life. . . . Well, as soon as he took one step outside the building—it wouldn't be right to take any action on government property—I came up behind him, put a hand on his shoulder, and said I'd like to have a word with him concerning Mr. Rupert Randall."

"He ran away from you, George, didn't he?" Mallory asked.

"Like a shot. He isn't very big, and from the way he looked, I wasn't expecting any resistance. The element of surprise was on his side—that and the fact he had an automobile waiting. A Rover, not a new model, and off he went in the traffic, with me following in his own car. I wasn't trying to chase him down," he explained. "I had the make and the license number, and I could track him down by tonight."

"Was Evelyn Weldon with him?" Henry asked, as raptly interested in this tale as everyone else.

"That she was, Mr. Thorpe. She was in the passenger

seat. I remember thinking how odd she looked, such a grand lady in an expensive fur in the sort of car an office clerk saves up to buy."

"Gresham was always careful about his pennies," Henry remarked wryly. "Go on, please."

"Well, he isn't familiar with New York City traffic, that's for sure, and in the end it was his undoing. He went chugging up Sixth Avenue at such a speed that I thought any minute he'd run the machine into one of the El's posts."

"*That* certainly would have solved a few problems," Hugo muttered, his buried anger and resentment bubbling to the surface. "I'm sorry for you, Sybil, but—"

"Please don't explain, Hugo. I understand. It isn't as if my mother were some man's hapless dupe. She was the mastermind who made Mr. Gresham her pawn." Sybil felt calm, almost detached. Her mother was dead—why didn't she feel her loss? Why was there nothing except this faint feeling of relief that came from the knowledge that her mother's years of schemes and machinations were finally over? "Mr. Kelly, please go on."

"If you'll forgive me for saying so, Mrs. Fleming, I believe it was your mother egging him on. I was just going to follow at a safe distance, but he took off as if I had a warrant for his arrest. He tore up Sixth Avenue, but he made a wrong turn at Columbus Circle, and went into the park, and if he had trouble with the city streets, the park's paths were a complete puzzle to Gresham. I never saw anyone so lost, so frantic to get away in my life."

"That's because he's never had Evelyn Weldon in the seat beside him," Mallory whispered to Hugo, who gave her a smile of agreement.

"There was an accident in the park," George went on, treading gingerly as he approached the worst part. "I think he was trying to get back to Fifty-ninth Street, but he was going west on an eastbound path, and there was a collision with a taximeter cab. Gresham's little tin can didn't have a chance; I'm amazed that he's still alive."

"What!" Henry was disbelieving. "That man is still walking around?"

"Well, not quite. He does have several broken ribs and a good number of contusions."

"Wouldn't you know he'd get off lightly," Alix remarked. "What happened when you got to the scene of the wreck?"

"It's not a sight I'm ever going to forget, and not for the reasons you might think," George said, deciding that the more gory details were best left to the police; no need for Mrs. Fleming to hear all of it twice. "Inside the car, the package with the money had broken open, and the bills were all over. Eighty thousand dollars in one thousand and five hundred and one hundred dollar bills." He shook his head. "There was a note as well. The letter Mr. Randall wrote to Mr. Gresham alias Mr. Smyth, telling him that this was the last of the money, and if he wanted any more he could whistle."

"Or words to that effect," Alix commented. "Sybil, can you face the police now?"

"Yes, Alix. But I can't help thinking that if I'd come to you as soon as I told my mother she wasn't welcome in my home, instead of brooding about how this ghastly business ever started, we might have managed to avoid all of this," she told everyone sadly.

"We don't know that, Sybil," Alix said as she and Henry prepared to take her to meet the waiting police. "But one thing you can't do, *mustn't* do, is blame yourself. That isn't going to solve anything, or change circumstances. You have to think of yourself and your children and the baby you're having. I know how this sounds, but your mother didn't do those awful things for anyone but herself. You're not responsible for her actions, and all anyone expects you to do now is what's right—no less and certainly no more."

"Thank you," Mallory told George when they were alone with the Tilmores. "This isn't what I expected, but if it weren't for you, we'd all still be stumbling around in the dark, putting pieces together."

"And thank you from us also," Hugo put in. "And since I'm sure Henry and Alix will want to go with you to see Rupert, Edie and I will stay with Sybil. We owe her that at least."

"That would be so good of you," Mallory said sincerely. "I'm anxious to get downtown as soon as possible. I didn't tell Rupert where I was going. He's still so tired, and I didn't want to upset him."

"Well, by this time, he must be quite concerned," George said knowingly. "After all, as the Bard of Avon so aptly put it in *Henry VIII*, 'things done without example—in their issue are to be feared.' So I would imagine that by now he's quite apprehensive, and no one would blame him."

Life can only be understood backwards, but it must be lived forwards.

—Kierkegaard

One Lexington Avenue

"Well, I've been expecting you for some time, but I didn't think you'd bring a house party with you," Rupert said, coming into the foyer a moment after Mallory closed the door. "Welcome to our humble establishment," he told Henry and Alix, and then kissed Mallory. "George has already been here, and I hope this visit is going to be happier than the last one."

"So this is your simple honeymoon retreat," Henry said as they went into the living room. "What have you done with the Matisse?"

"Somehow I knew that was the first question you'd ask, Henry," Mallory said, and laughed. She was so delighted to find Rupert up and dressed and—except for the dark circles under his eyes—looking very, very handsome. At this moment, even the last few hours filled with startling events, were able to recede to some quiet backwater.

"Well, where is it?" Henry insisted, but his brown eyes were twinkling.

"In the dining room. Go ahead and have a look at it," Rupert said as they all sat down.

"Wouldn't you rather hear what we have to tell you first?"

The old look of wariness returned to his eyes. "Is it that bad?" he asked, and reached for Mallory's hand.

"There are two stories to tell you, and I think we'd better let George start."

When Henry spoke in that firm quiet voice, few people ever disagreed with him, and George was not going to be among that unfortunate minority.

Without embroidery, he retold the events of that day, except that this time he did not have to make evasions for delicacy's sake. As awful and gory as the scene in Central Park had been, he didn't have to worry that his descriptions were going to affect Rupert badly. From all Mr. Randall had been through, to tell him anything less than the total truth would not be treating his experience with the seriousness it deserved.

"Evelyn Weldon," was all Rupert could say when George finished. "Why couldn't I figure it out for myself? That scheming— No, I can't say that, can I?" he went on bitterly. "She would have bled me white, given half a chance, but now propriety intervenes. But what about Gresham? I can press charges, can't I?"

"Yes, that letter of yours is pretty clear. The police think that pretty much makes your case. Gresham is in Roosevelt Hospital right now, and he's certainly going to be brought up on charges of reckless endangerment," George supplied.

"But you may not want to do that," Henry put in before Rupert could answer. "I can understand how you would want revenge, and there's no doubt that you'd obtain it, but please ask yourself if that's the best thing."

"I never thought you'd be an advocate for a criminal escaping justice, Henry," Rupert said, a cold look on his face.

"I'm not—not really," Henry replied cautiously. "But if you do press charges, everything you wanted kept quiet will come out at the trial. You'll have to take the stand

and tell everything that happened, from the moment you opened that letter to this afternoon. And even after all of that, there's no guarantee of a conviction."

"So that old goat is going to get off," Rupert said, and they all knew what his actions would be. "No doubt he's already planning on how to entrap his next victim."

"I doubt that. Evelyn was probably his first and only fall from grace."

"How delightful," Rupert said coldly.

"I'm going to speak with a friend of mine at the State Department," Alix offered. "I'm fairly sure that he can arrange to have Roland Gresham deported as an undesirable alien as soon as he's well enough to leave the hospital. He'll never be allowed into the country again."

"And as soon as the police complete their investigation, you'll get your eighty thousand dollars back, plus whatever extra Gresham saved out of the pittance Evelyn gave him," Henry added. As for the rest of your funds—Sybil and Peter will probably offer to make up the difference."

"I won't take a penny from them. Sybil's had to suffer her mother all her life, and there's no reason to let that awful woman's schemes reach out past the grave. No, I'll take my loss and consider it a bad investment."

"And you won't press charges?"

"No, Henry, I won't," he said, and looked at Mallory, love and devotion in his silver eyes. "I have a lot of things I want to do with my life, and I won't spend time extending this experience—particularly since it'll give me the newspaper attention I didn't want in the first place. Cliff rang up a little while ago, and we had a long talk," Rupert went on. "At the end of it, we came to the conclusion that I should tell Dad everything in a nice, long letter. Cliff is going to ring him up at the Barauchs' first, to smooth the way. We decided that it wouldn't be a good idea to have any hidden secrets coming back when we least expect it."

At his last words, Henry and Alix exchanged significant looks, and George Kelly knew that the moment had come for him to remove himself from the scene.

"I think it's time for me to leave—" he began, but Mallory stopped him.

"I won't hear of it. I invited you for tea, and you're staying."

"Of course you are, George," Alix echoed. "But would you do us all a favor and tell Mrs. Dovedale that we'll be five for tea in about twenty minutes?"

When George had left on his tact-inspired mission, Rupert and Henry regarded each other, neither giving an inch.

"I think the moment has come to tell some rather old secrets," Rupert said evenly, his heart pounding irregularly. "Was my father insane?"

"Yes," Henry said, knowing that there was no other way to answer this question except directly. "But not in a way that is going to affect you."

"Why? Insane is insane—not to mention frequently inheritable."

"I hardly think so in your case. Not unless you have syphilis," Henry said, and felt his own heart lighten as he saw the beginning of comprehension dawn in Rupert's eyes. "This is a horrible thing to tell you, but since it's pretty much a day for bad news—" He paused for a moment, having to prepare himself as well as Rupert. "When your father died in Switzerland nine years ago, he was a syphilitic madman. You were young, Rupert, certainly not in terms of experience, but in terms of years. You were still at Harrow, and we wanted to protect you."

"People shouldn't try so hard to protect each other from things they eventually get hit with and then can't defend themselves because someone else wanted to keep them 'safe.'"

Henry acknowledged Rupert's bitterness. "In retrospect, you're entirely right, but as for the circumstances . . . Patrick and Isaac and I decided that you were better off left in the dark for the time being, and that we would tell you at a later date."

"And in the meantime, I went whoring my way through Oxford."

"That's what we were afraid of, that you would end up like your father, and we couldn't let that happen."

"Hence my year of scrubbing floors and washing windows at St. Desmond's."

"You brought that experience on yourself," Henry reminded him with a slight smile. "But then, after you came to New York, it didn't seem important to tell you, and I just let it slide. That was unforgivable of me. I really thought that it had all been forgotten."

"If you think that, just talk to Hugo."

"Yes, I know all about that," Henry said, and then told Rupert about Hugo's own involvement with Evelyn. "He was only repeating the gossip that went around London."

"You should have seen his face when Mallory burst into the dining room and faced him down," Alix related. "I think at that moment, he preferred blackmail."

Rupert gave Mallory a special look. "So that's where you ran off to this morning. I thought you were going to check up on George."

"I thought he had enough problems for one day, and I was so worried that if Hugo told you that he knew your father was insane, well, he'd tell anyone else who'd listen. I think I just wanted to frighten him into silence."

"I think you frightened about five years off him," Henry remarked. "And he's very anxious that you don't hold it against him."

"Oh, I won't, but I think I'll let Hugo wonder about that for awhile," Rupert said with a wicked smile, and pulled Mallory against him. "Are you hungry?" he demanded.

"Absolutely famished!" she said, laughing as Rupert pulled her across his lap. "We have guests," she reminded him, kissing him under one ear.

"Are you telling me to behave myself?"

"I wouldn't dream of it."

"I didn't think so. Do you suppose we'll be sent to our room?"

"And wouldn't you just love that!"

"That's enough," Henry said, laughing. "Alix and George and I will be on our way soon. Surely you can act like the proper host and hostess for another hour or so."

"We'll give it a good try. I just need a few minutes for unbounded joy before the reaction to all of this sets in. Probably, by the time we're alone together, all I'll want to do is have a long, serious discussion with Mallory. We have to talk about a great many things. Most likely, I won't smile again for days."

"And if you believe any of that," Mallory said as she heard the sound of the tea cart approaching, "there's an excellent chance of your being able to buy the Brooklyn Bridge at a fantastic price!"

When working for young people, one had to get used to certain things. After all, one did not want to be in the employ of a pair of stuffy prigs. Margaret Dovedale had repeated those words over and over again to her husband since they'd entered the Randalls' employ, whenever Hugh had to contend with a couple who unlocked the front door themselves and hung up their own coats and mixed their own drinks and any of a half-dozen small things that a butler-valet was supposed to do. She comforted her husband, and made him a pot of hot tea and told him it didn't really matter.

And it didn't, but now, late on Saturday morning, it was quite another thing to have Mrs. Randall, looking quite beautiful in a caftan of apricot brocade and her hair pinned loosely on the top of her head, come into the kitchen to help put the breakfast tray together.

"I can take care of that, madam," Margaret said as she took down the tin of Maillard's breakfast cocoa and began to measure out what she'd need. "Why don't you go back upstairs? This will all be ready in just a few minutes."

"I know you can see to everything, and it will be perfect, but this is a special morning." As she spoke, Mallory placed a crystal bud vase holding one perfect rose on a large, square silver tray already set for breakfast. "Aren't wedding presents wonderful, Mrs. Dovedale? You never run out of special things to have at the appropriate moments."

"Yes, madam, it's very nice," the older woman agreed. Moving quickly so that none of her other duties would be usurped, Margaret put cracked ice into stemmed goblets, added the new Dole's pineapple juice that everyone liked so much, and poured the hot chocolate into the cobalt-blue chocolate pot. With a deft movement, she took the small basket of croissants from the oven's warming tray and added it to the tray.

"All ready," Mallory announced, putting down a butterfly-shaped dish with strawberry conserves on one side and orange marmalade on the other. "Just put it on the dumbwaiter and I'll collect it upstairs," she told Mrs. Dovedale gaily, and bent over to whisper a comment to the cook just as her husband entered the kitchen.

"What did Mrs. Randall just tell you?" he inquired when they were alone. "You look rather . . . well . . ."

"Oh, don't be such a stuffed shirt, Hugh," she chided her husband as they set the tray in the dumbwaiter and sent it upstairs. "They've made it up, and that's all that matters. I wouldn't want them to go through Monday night again for all the tea in China, and you wouldn't either."

"No, I wouldn't," he admitted, "and Mrs. Randall was very brave this past week, what with Mr. Randall being so ill, and all that business about his being—"

"No," his wife interrupted, laying a hand on his black-sleeved arm, her merry blue eyes very serious. "We must never mention that again, not even to each other, what we've overheard. That's over, finished."

"You're right, of course, but *what* did Mrs. Randall tell you?"

"Oh, just that having a dumbwaiter almost makes up for not having a sunken tub in the bathroom!"

"Another feast from the kitchen of Mrs. Dovedale!" Rupert announced jauntily as Mallory placed the laden tray in the center of the bed, just as he came out of the bathroom, buttoning the jacket of a new pair of silk pajamas. "Did you harass her unmercifully?"

"Setting up our breakfast tray is not harassing the cook," Mallory informed him as they curled up on the bed and kissed each other over the tray before settling back against the pillows.

"The Dovedales are the sort of servants who entered our employ ready for a couple having major and minor disagreements, a not quite completely furnished apartment, not to mention the possibility of children and all the complications they cause. They'll take all of that with a smile and a good paycheck, but not the mistress of the house poking around in the kitchen!"

"Oh, shut up and drink your juice!" Mallory advised lovingly. "You don't really expect me to turn into a woman who scarcely knows where her kitchen is, and Mrs. Dovedale is just going to have to adjust!"

"Just don't try to attempt a dinner for twelve and I'm

sure she'll get used to your culinary interests." He parted the large napkin and regarded the fresh-baked croissants with the same awe that, Mallory decided, Joseph Duveen must display when finding a passed-over Old Master. "Do you think the butter will still melt on them?"

"You look pretty healthy to me," Mallory said, pouring out the hot chocolate. "Put on some butter and find out for yourself—and while you're at it, do a croissant for me with a touch of strawberry conserves."

"Anything for my wife," he said, and then his smile faded. "I mean that, Mallie. I know I let you down quite a bit in the last few weeks, but I won't do it again."

"Oh, Rupert, no. You didn't let me down, and I don't want you to think that," Mallory said passionately. "You're strong, Rupert, and you know the right thing to do, but you were under so much of a strain that *no* decision could look or be right."

"I suppose Romney thinks I'm the greatest idiot he's ever met."

"Of course not. He used to work for the Foreign Office, remember."

"Funny."

"No, the truth," she said as they began to eat. "Romney called earlier—I think Henry may have had a word with him—and he wants you to know that he doesn't hold any of what happened last Monday night against you. He said that if he had the same problems you were facing, he'd act exactly the same way. And he's also very embarrassed about behaving as if he had some great interest in me. Romney said that his behavior should cancel out yours, and that makes you both even."

"He's being very generous about it," Rupert allowed. "Still, I'm very happy that we don't have to see him again for a while."

"You're certainly better off than Hugo. He's going to have to face you every day while we're in Santa Barbara."

"That isn't going to bother him greatly," Rupert said as they shared the last croissant. "He'll feel rotten for the next seventy-two hours or so, and then it'll start wearing off. But I don't care. That's Hugo, and he wouldn't be fun any other way. Of course, if he feels constrained to pass any more comments about my stability, I'll take some other very definite action."

"I just bet you will."

"Just watch me," he promised with a teasing smile, and then looked down at the tray. "It appears that our breakfast didn't last long."

"Mrs. Dovedale will be thrilled," Mallory replied, standing up and taking the tray.

"I have a letter to write," Rupert reminded her a minute later.

"Really?" Mallory feigned disinterest. "I put the tray back on the dumbwaiter so that Dovedale won't be coming up here. Now, after doing that, do you really think I'm going to let you out of bed?" she went on, pulling her caftan over her head to reveal a clinging nightgown of pale apricot satin.

"Not anytime soon, I hope," Rupert said, holding out his arms to her.

"It seems like I've been waiting months for you instead of just a few days," Mallory whispered, curling up next to Rupert, her fingers undoing the buttons of his pajama jacket. "How could you ever think that I would want another man after I've had you?" She pulled the jacket off his shoulders and kissed the warm hollow at the base of his throat. "You really weren't going to be that generous, were you?"

"No," he whispered, taking the pins out of her hair. "Not even if the lie had been true. I can live without a child, but not without you."

"It took you long enough to say it," she said, waiting until Rupert removed his pajamas before pushing him

618

back against the mass of pillows. For a moment, she considered kissing him, and then, with great patience, beginning at his hairline, she started to draw an invisible line down the center of his body. She went down his forehead, between his eyebrows, along his nose, and over his mouth and chin.

When she paused for a moment to tickle him under the chin, Rupert began to laugh, but by the time her finger had traveled over his throat and down the center of his chest, he closed his eyes and abandoned himself to Mallory and to the warm and immediate reaction of his own body.

"Don't stop," he whispered thickly as her finger moved around the rim of his navel, making an outline before dipping in to twirl a fingertip against his sensitive skin.

He moaned softly as Mallory completed her exploration and moved lower still, moving down the center of his fast-rising flesh and not stopping until her hand came to rest between his thighs, stroking the firm flesh until he began to writhe under her motions.

Mallory allowed herself a moment to drink in Rupert's fully aroused body before placing herself over him. She wanted to make him happy, to give him the pleasure they'd lost in the past days that had contained only fear and pain and confusion and clarification that hurt even while it healed. This was the moment to start putting it all behind them, she thought, and pressed herself down on his vibrant flesh, the heat of their joining surprising her.

For a moment, they stayed locked together without moving.

"I—don't—believe—this," Rupert gasped thickly as he pulled the satin nightgown over Mallory's head. His eyes were fever-bright and tiny beads of perspiration formed on his temples and upper lip. This feeling of oneness, of each of them having found their missing half in the other, had never been so strong, almost as if the last weeks had been mere prelude to this moment. "Love me."

"Yes—yes." She kissed him and then moved her hips, straining for every last bit of pleasure available to them. Made for each other, was all she could think as she made love to him, their bodies ardent for all they had to discover, all they had to share. It was all going to be over too quickly, but as she placed her hands against Rupert's damp chest, her left hand over his racing, pounding heart, she closed her eyes and pressed against him again and again, her body reaching for its own pleasure, and nothing mattered but the swirling, spinning joy that overwhelmed them at the same moment.

A long, lovely time later, as they lay across the bed, Rupert propped himself up on one elbow.

"Have you seen anything you like?" Mallory asked, delighting in his artistlike scrutiny.

"Only every single inch of you."

"You always know what to say," Mallory said as he lay down alongside her again and they cuddled together. "Right now, I feel so loved, so wonderfully happy, that all we've been through in the past weeks is taking on a little perspective; it happened, but it's over and it can't come back again. We can go on together and rediscover what we almost lost."

"We almost lost it all twice," Rupert reminded her. "The first time because I was afraid of what I wanted, afraid that you could really make me so happy; and this time because of circumstances that came at us from the outside, but now—"

Mallory smiled slowly, and slid a hand provocatively down the long length of his back to span his tight buttocks.

"What about now?"

Rupert's eyes turned stormy with renewed passion. "Right now, I intend to make love to you for a very long time, and later on today, much later," he said, turning Mallory on her back and slipping a leg between hers. "I think we can have a nice, productive talk about our going to California next week."

From *Vogue*, December 15, 1910:

Randall.—Mr. and Mrs. Rupert Randall have gone to California. They will return late in the summer.

Life in Los Angeles is a tonic. Optimism, hopefulness and courage are in the air. As one comes downtown in the morning one feels ready for the day's battle, like a giant refreshed with new wine.

—The Los Angeles Times, 1906

Los Angeles

From the corner of Fifth and Spring Streets, where the elegant Alexandria Hotel welcomed the best of Los Angeles's visitors with a sixty-foot high lobby rich with marble columns and Turkish carpeting and gold-leaf decoration, as well as five hundred rooms and suites that were worth competition to those in the finest New York hotels, a brand-new 1911 Locomobile "30" limousine and an equally new Rolls Royce Silver Ghost following behind it, traveled through the finest of the city's many neighborhoods.

With a gentle crunch of gravel, the Locomobile turned into the driveway of a fine Tudor mansion on the six hundred block of West Adams, the most fashionable street in the two miles that stretched from South Figuero Street to Western Avenue. In this section of the city, handsome mansions lined West Adams Boulevard and Westmoreland Place, proving to all that Los Angeles was going to be more than just a looked-down-upon cousin of San Francisco—and a city that could offer a better climate, besides. . . . Not that Mallory and Rupert had complaints about the weather or anything else since they

623

arrived in California at the beginning of December, and found that they had truly reached the end of America's rainbow.

They had left a cold and cloudy New York on the last day of November for the frigid temperatures of Chicago, arriving on the Century, and spending the first two days of December and half of the third visiting the Art Institute and shopping at Marshall Field's before taking the Overland Limited to San Francisco.

This was Mallory's first trip across the country, the first time she'd ever been west of Chicago, and in the secluded luxury of the de Veigas' private railway car, she had been riveted by the beauty of the scenery of the western states.

Rupert had delighted in pointing out landmarks and areas of interest, and for both of them, San Francisco, even in current condition of still being rebuilt, was a city just made to be fascinated with. The mornings might be foggy and the nights cold enough for Mallory to need to wear her fur coat, but the days were perfect—like late September in New York, with the addition of palm trees.

Mallory and Rupert spent two weeks in San Francisco. Two weeks of seeing all the sights, of shopping at I. Magnin and the City of Paris, of having dinner with Mr. and Mrs. Thaler at Presido Terrace, and of going out to Hillsborough to visit with Nell Tierney who lived quite happily with her daughter in a splendid Italian Renaissance mansion, buying real estate and making business deals with great flair, happily reaping great financial benefits.

On December twentieth, they boarded the Lark for the overnight trip to Santa Barbara, and found that Southern California was an experience unlike any other. The beauty of the countryside, the perfection of the weather,

and the incredible feeling of *space*. And their conviction
that no matter how much expansion and development
took place, this part of the country could never be filled
up, caused their hosts no end of amusement.

"Why Santa Barbara's the sleepiest little town you
could imagine!" Regina told them, laughing gently at
their first impressions. "And since there's no harbor
here, and not likely to be one, it'll stay like that. Of
course, I wish they'd do a bit more paving than just State
Street and the main roads, but they will in time."

"Do you mean to say that in time we're going to stop
thinking in terms of what Southern California could be?"
Rupert inquired in mock horror their first night at dinner
in the MacIversons' handsome Spanish Mission-style
mansion with its outstanding view of the Santa Ynez
Mountains.

"I certainly hope not," Ian said as the chocolate
soufflé was served. "Development is very important to
this part of the country, but the right sort of development
in the right areas. We can talk about shipping lines and
citrus groves and vineyards to begin with—and who can
tell what this nickelodeon business is going to turn into."

"A lot," Regina said. "The countryside around here
can lend itself to any and all backgrounds. Three years
ago, they filmed the beach scenes for *The Count of Monte
Cristo* at Santa Monica, and that's only the beginning."

"And definitely worth keeping an eye on as to which
companies will thrive and which aren't going to last out
all the changes." Ian's voice was considering. "The one
thing I learned from all my years in India is that even if a
fortune is just waiting for you to pick it up, you have to
treat it with great respect and not force excess
development on an area where it wasn't meant to be."

"Well, we're not here to grab a million dollars out of

the ground," Mallory put in. "We may not be totally disinterested, but right now is for taking it easy with no rush, the way a honeymoon ought to be—and we've certainly earned ours."

"Of course you have," Ian said, not really understanding, but willing to give the benefit of the doubt. "Now, does anyone want more whipped cream with their soufflé? As soon as Hugo and Edith get back from dinner at Sin and Caro's, we'll trim the tree. But in the meantime," he went on expansively. "Rupert, would you care to tell me why my brother apparently wants to avoid you as much as possible?"

Christmas in California. A holiday season with no snow, but rich with palm trees and sunny skies and temperatures in the low sixties. But there was a Douglas fir hung with old family ornaments and plenty of presents to exchange and the usual round of parties, the grandest of which was Sinclair and Caroline Poole's New Year's Eve dinner-dance where fifty couples from all over the state gathered at the Mediterranean-style mansion near the ocean in the Santa Barbara suburb of Montecito to welcome 1911 in great style.

Mallory and Rupert had been hearing about the great potential of Southern California in general and Los Angeles in particular since the day they arrived in Santa Barbara, and the area's greatest boosters were Regina and Ian MacIverson and Caroline and Sinclair Poole. Now, in January, between long horseback rides and picnics and tennis games and exploring the missions and walking along the beach, there was plenty of time to discuss the future of shipping and railroads and manufacturing and orange groves and vineyards and whether or not anything would come of Biograph Studios having sent its own D. W. Griffith out to set up a studio behind a tavern

626

on the corner of Sunset Boulevard and Gower.

When they were in the privacy of their yellow and cream bedroom with the great white lacquer bed hung in great swags of old yellow silk, Mallory and Rupert discussed everything they heard regarding the potential of Southern California, and together they worked on the report he was preparing to send back to Cliff in New York.

"Where do you think this is all going to lead?" Mallory speculated as they walked their horses along the beach at the end of January, a week after the completed report was mailed to New York. "To tell you the truth, I didn't plan on our spending part of our honeymoon working on an analysis and prospectus of the development of the southern region of California!"

"You have a great hold of the lingo," Rupert complimented. "And if I were the intense, work-obsessed man you just described, that report could have been done in much less time than the month it took. I happened to enjoy prolonging our bedroom consultations."

"So that's what they were," Mallory teased. "And people have the nerve to say that financial men have no imagination," she went on as they stopped and she put her arms around his waist. "I love you, and it seems that ever since we got to California, it's all so much more *real*."

"I feel the same way," Rupert said as they looked out over the Pacific's endless blue expanse. "Back in November, New York seemed very unreal, very unfocused. Not us," he amended swiftly. "In those weeks while I was being blackmailed—and later when I couldn't stop thinking about going insane—you were the only real thing I had to hold on to."

"I hate to say this, but there are times when I think back on what you went through and I always get the same conclusion—that what you did was the only way it could

627

have been handled."

"I know what you're trying to say." His arms tightened around her. "But I'm still too close to all of it to be philosophical. And when you get right down to it, I'm not the sort."

"Neither am I."

"Right now, it's enough to know that it's over, and there are other things we have to do."

"Such as?"

"Do you know how beautiful you look in riding clothes? There's something very feminine about a woman in riding breeches."

"You've seen me in riding gear dozens of times."

"As you told me before, it's California, and everything looks better."

"I see. And what do you have in mind to do next on the list of things we have to do?"

"First, I think we should finish our ride, and then go back to Sin and Caro's for lunch."

"That sounds nice. But unless I miss my guess, there is an interlude between riding and eating—and I'm not referring to our changing clothes!"

"And neither am I. I've decided that if we time things properly, we can enjoy a lovely session of working on a new prospectus that involves just the two of us . . ."

That had been almost a month ago, and now it was Valentine's Day, and they were in Los Angeles to take the first steps in establishing the Seligmans' first office in Southern California.

"You and Sinclair had this all plotted out between you before we even got here, didn't you?" Rupert asked Ian as they got out of his Locomobile.

Ian feigned innocence as he looked at Regina. "Darling, do you think I did some extraneous planning and plotting in order to see to it that Mallory and Rupert stay on in California?"

"I really can't recall your being particularly Machiavellian," Regina said too blandly, an unmistakable gleam in her eyes. "That is, no more so than usual when you've decided something has to be done a certain way!"

"So much for wifely loyalty," Ian grumbled goodnaturedly while Regina and Mallory and Rupert laughed. He cast a considering eye at the Rolls pulling up behind his Locomobile. "Sin, do you have some sort of unhealthy interest in that Silver Ghost of yours?" he called out, and was rewarded by more laughter.

"Sour grapes," Sinclair Poole replied, removing his long, elegant body from the equally elegant automobile, followed by Caroline and Edith and Hugo. "You could have had your own Rolls, so don't begrudge me the joy of being the owner of this machine," he returned smartly, dark amber eyes sparkling. Ten years before in New York, Sinclair Poole had been considered notorious, but now, after eight years of marriage to Caroline Worth and eight years of a new life in Southern California, he was regarded by the community as merely a devoted husband and father and superb businessman. After his years of scandal, he did not make friends easily, and Ian MacIverson came closest to the top of the list of men he trusted.

"You boys can talk about your toys later," Caroline observed tartly. A tall and elegant thirty-five, Caro Poole was reaching the height of her beauty which she chose to set off with a Lucile dress of lapis blue Canton silk with a neck embroidered in red and green and gold silk and a black satin belt, finished off with a Tappe hat of fine cream-colored straw with a wide brim banded in black velvet shading her face. "We're here to make sure Mallory and Rupert really like our home enough to rent it."

"Right now, I don't think they're terribly interested in the finer points of real estate," Edith said with great amusement. On a day like today, the cold weather and England seemed very far away indeed. "They've gone ahead into the house."

"Well, that's what we gave them the key for," Caro laughed.

"Why don't we muddle around with the picnic things?" Hugo suggested wisely. "We can always catch up with them later. It's true that I haven't had much experience in exploring a new house, but right now I think Mallory and Rupert would much rather be left alone."

In the spacious dining room that had wall panels of old paper showing scenes of Venice, Rupert came up behind Mallory and put his arms around her waist, hugging her close to him. "Yes?"

"Yes to anything, if it concerns you," she said, turning in his embrace and putting her arms around his shoulders. "We seem to have successfully lost the others, so would you care to elaborate on your question?"

Rupert looked under the brim of her Jeanne Lanvin hat of black Milan straw faced with black maline and a taffeta crown covered by two straight ostrich quills. "Yes to this house?"

"Is there another answer possible? Since we're going to be in Los Angeles through the summer, at least, I like the idea of renting this house from Caro and Sin. Lucky for us, their new house on Chester Place is ready for them to move into, and this does seem to suit us."

"When we got married, I was thinking in terms of a nice apartment, not a twelve-room house."

"No New York-style apartment houses in Los Angeles,

630

but we do have certain advantages. No snow, for one."

"And a beautiful garden and a garage and a stable for our horses and beautiful room *and* the Dovedales—"

"They're coming? They agreed? Why didn't you tell me?" Mallory laughed in delight as Rupert picked her up and swung her around.

"I got their letter this morning and wanted to find an appropriate spot to tell you." Rupert looked around him as he set Mallory down. "The dining room seems to fit my requirements."

"I think it does. But we have to telegraph them back and say we won't need them for at least another month."

"That and not to worry about the possibility of an Indian attack on the Southern Pacific."

"You're impossible!"

"Well, they did ask."

Laughing, they left the dining room for the entry foyer.

"I never thought I could like English Tudor again," Rupert murmured.

Built in early 1906 when Sinclair Poole's business reached a point that it demanded he and Caroline spend part of the year in Los Angeles, they had engaged a fine San Francisco architect and given him explicit specifications which included inlaid parquet floors and substantial closet space and square, high-ceilinged rooms designed to show off their collection of Oriental arts and furniture from Caro's years in China and Sin's as a dealer in New York. Needless to say, a good portion of the furnishings would be moved over to their new house, a twenty-room adaptation and tribute to the chateaus of France's Normandy, that was located practically next door to the mansion of Edward Lawrence Doheney, the oil magnate who was Los Angeles's wealthiest citizen, but they had been very generous in what Mallory and Rupert could have.

"When we finish living here, Sinclair will probably be able to sell this house at a huge profit," Mallory said as she finished outlining her decorating plans to Rupert as they stood in the center of the drawing room, their feet sinking into the antique Chinese presentation rug with a background of antique ivory and a border of porcelain blue with figures and medallions of Gobelin blue and cloudy pinks and salmons and soft sage green and pure Chinese yellow that had once graced the drawing room of the Worth house in Peking a dozen years earlier. "And what I'm going to be able to do with this room, with the whole house! It was perfect for Sin and Caro, and now I'm going to make it perfect for us," she said, making a final, brief tour of the sunny room, her Poiret dress, a smart model of white rajah with a plain, straight skirt, diagonal closing of black buttons embroidered in red, and a red satin belt embroidered in heavy white silk floss shown off to its best advantage by the room's fine decor. "Also, what would you say to my doing some professional work while we're here in Los Angeles?"

"As long as you're referring to the same profession you left New York with."

"Funny," Mallory said, coming back to him and putting her arms around his tight waist. "Just remember who's doing your new office, or I'll turn you over to the nearest junk dealer!"

"Do you know how exciting you are when you threaten me?" Rupert teased.

"Excited enough so that you're ready to explore the bedrooms?" Mallory challenged, a delightful thrill running through her as Rupert led her to the drawing room's double doors.

"I'm ready to explore a bedroom with you at any time and in any mood," he said as they went up the curving staircase to the second floor. "Did you know this was here?" he demanded a minute later as they stood in the master bedroom with its graceful marble walls and floors, lapis lazuli fixtures, and dominated by a sunken Roman poolbath.

"Of course I did. In fact, Caro made it one of the major points in our renting the house. She said that I wasn't likely to find something like this in one of those bungalows that are being built on those new subdivisions over in Laurel Canyon. This makes moving day something to look forward to, doesn't it?" she said as they returned to the master bedroom where lacquer and cane bedroom furniture with pale blue and cream accents made residence an extremely pleasant contemplation.

"I think we can safely say we've found ourselves here," Rupert said several minutes later after they'd toured the remainder of the rooms and came back again to the main suite. "I don't think that I ever realized how nice it is to be out of New York in the cold weather—and I didn't quite appreciate the wonderful effect it was going to have on our honeymoon." He stretched out across the bed. "Or is this just being in love?"

Mallory took off her hat, tossed it on the dressing table, and joined Rupert on the bed. "Oh, I think it would be utter bliss with you in a cabin in the Canadian woods with a blizzard howling outside."

"Especially with a blizzard," Rupert said, turning on his side and pulling her close to him.

"I thought we'd find you like this," a voice said, and more than a bit surprised, they turned and saw Caro and Sin in the doorway. "Couldn't you two wait until we signed the rental agreement?" Sinclair asked.

"Oh, don't be a spoilsport, darling," Caro pointed out, amused. "Do you remember our first tour of our house in Montecito? I don't think the original owners have recovered to this day!"

To Mallory and Rupert's great delight, the worldly, sophisticated Sinclair Poole flushed a bright pink from his shirt collar up to his center-parted dark brown hair.

"Oh, all right. I'm caught. I admit it. But come on downstairs, you two. Our picnic is ready."

"Good timing—we're famished. We've been discussing our redecorating plans."

"Just remember that we're leaving our Ch'ing Dynasty porcelains in your care," Sinclair said.

"Yeah," Rupert said with a grin. "The new stuff."

"Blame me, Sin," Mallory offered, unable to smother her laughter. "I was the one who told Rupert that all of your blue and white porcelain was made between 1850 and 1875."

"So much for my attempt to point out all the wonderful extras that come with this house," Sinclair said with mock resignation.

"Don't worry, darling, a chicken leg or two and a few glasses of champagne will help you," Caro soothed. "And in case you haven't noticed yet, we're thrilled that you like our house," she continued. "And right now is the best time to be setting up shop in Los Angeles. We're almost at the point where our schedule between here and Montecito is determined by the school year. You don't have that complication."

"Yet," Sinclair added with amused significance. "And if you really do love our house, you'll show it by putting your own little occupant in the nursery down the hall. We'll leave you two to think about it. Come downstairs anytime you want as long as it's reasonable."

"What do you think about that?" Rupert asked a minute later when they were stretched out across the bed together.

"To having a baby? I thought that was going to be one of our most pleasurable activities while we're here in California."

"That may be longer than we originally planned. Tomorrow," he went on, brushing a tendril of her hair back, "we'll have the Alexandria put up a picnic basket for us and we'll borrow Ian's car and driver and go out to one of the piers—Huntington Beach or Seal Beach or Long Beach—and we'll walk out on the pier until we're well over the Pacific and we can look toward China, and then back to the beach where there are so few people it's almost as if we're all alone."

"That sounds like one of the loveliest, most romantic ideas."

"Only one of many. And isn't this the part where you're supposed to remind me that tomorrow I should be overseeing the transformation of the second-floor suite at the Alexandria into the Seligmans' first Los Angeles office, as well as making plans about whom to hire and all the rest?"

"If you think I'm going to do anything like that, then you're really married to the wrong person," she said, tracing half-circles under his eyes. "This is the first time in months that the smudges under your eyes are all gone, and you don't have to do any extra work until you have to. We have another week here in Los Angeles, then we go back to Santa Barbara for the rest of our honeymoon, and then we come back here to live at the end of March. No office hours until then."

"I like that. But to get back to having a baby—"

"I'd like that also."

"You might have to have it here. I know we're supposed to go home by summer, but I have an idea we'll be here until next Christmas."

"Do you suppose Emily and John would like a trip to California?"

"Do you suppose we'll like life in Los Angeles?"

Mallory's smile faded a bit. "For now, I want us to stay on in Los Angeles. I missed out on San Francisco with you four years ago, and this is our chance for an adventure together. But Ian told me something the other day, and he may have a point. He said that we really don't have the sort of personalities it takes to transport our entire lives to Southern California, and that eventually we'll have to go home because we really can't be happy unless we're in New York City."

"Ian's probably right," Rupert said wryly as they got off the bed and went over to the window and looked down at the rich green lawn and finely tended hedges and abundant rose bushes. "Would you like to know what Mrs. Farrell said about us?"

"The wife of the vineyard owner you had a dance with last night?"

"The very same. While we were dancing she told me that whenever she saw us together she was reminded of two ripe vines just waiting to be joined so they could have the very best of new fruit."

Mallory choked on her laughter. "I think that's one of the most erotic things I've ever heard of! Just imagining the process gives me all sorts of interesting new variations we can try together," she said, pressing closer against Rupert as his hands curved around her waist. "When we get back to the Alexandria, we'll have plenty of time before the Valentine Day's dance tonight to lock the door of our room and do a bit of grafting!"

Rupert roared with laughter. "Grafting? That is what you do with vines. We'll have to see how it works when you apply the theory to a man and a woman," he said, pulling her even closer for a kiss. "I love you."

"And I love you. And we have so much to do here. You have a California office to set up from scratch, just the way you want it."

"And you're going to search out all sorts of hidden antiques among the Pasadena set and the old Spanish land grant families to send back to Thea."

"And let's not forget about The Broadway and Bullocks. You can always tell how good a city is going to be by its department stores."

"And we have the Alexandria Hotel. You can also tell a lot about a city from its finest hotel and the quality of its dance band."

"And do you know what I think right now?" Mallory asked as they regarded each other in delight as they finished with their review of Los Angeles's good points. "I have a very strong feeling that we're on the verge of being very, very happy!"